Denis O. Smith's interests range from logic and the history of London to Victorian society and railways, all of which contribute to giving his stories a true flavour of the period. He lives in the heart of Norfolk, England, from where he makes occasional trips to London to explore some of the capital's more obscure corners.

Recent Mammoth titles

The Mammoth Book of Best New SF 25
The Mammoth Book of Jokes 2
The Mammoth Book of Horror 23
The Mammoth Book of Slasher Movies
The Mammoth Book of Street Art
The Mammoth Book of Ghost Stories by Women
The Mammoth Book of Best New Erotica 11
The Mammoth Book of Irish Humour
The Mammoth Book of Unexplained Phenomena
The Mammoth Book of Futuristic Romance
The Mammoth Book of Best British Crime 10
The Mammoth Book of Combat
The Mammoth Book of Quick & Dirty Erotica
The Mammoth Book of Dark Magic
The Mammoth Book of New Sudoku
The Mammoth Book of Zombies!
The Mammoth Book of Angels & Demons
The Mammoth Book of the Rolling Stones
The Mammoth Book of Westerns
The Mammoth Book of Prison Breaks
The Mammoth Book of Time Travel SF
The Mammoth Quiz Book
The Mammoth Book of Erotic Photography, Vol. 4
The Mammoth Book of ER Romance
The Mammoth Book of More Dirty, Sick, X-Rated and Politically Incorrect Jokes
The Mammoth Book of Best New SF 26
The Mammoth Book of Hollywood Scandals
The Mammoth Book of Best New Horror 24
The Mammoth Book of Shark Attacks
The Mammoth Book of Best New Erotica 12

THE MAMMOTH BOOK OF

THE LOST CHRONICLES OF SHERLOCK HOLMES

DENIS O. SMITH

ROBINSON

RUNNING PRESS
PHILADELPHIA · LONDON

Constable & Robinson Ltd.
55–56 Russell Square
London WC1B 4HP
www.constablerobinson.com

First published in the UK by Robinson,
an imprint of Constable & Robinson Ltd., 2014

Grateful acknowledgement to the Conan Doyle Estate Ltd. for permission to use
the Sherlock Holmes characters created by the late Sir Arthur Conan Doyle.

A copy of the British Library Cataloguing in Publication
Data is available from the British Library

UK ISBN: 978-1-47211-059-6 (paperback)
UK ISBN: 978-1-47211-073-2 (ebook)

1 3 5 7 9 10 8 6 4 2

First published in the United States in 2014 by Running Press Book Publishers,
A Member of the Perseus Books Group

US ISBN: 978-0-7624-5220-0
US Library of Congress Control Number: 2013946639

9 8 7 6 5 4 3 2 1
Digit on the right indicates the number of this printing

Running Press Book Publishers
2300 Chestnut Street
Philadelphia, PA 19103-4371

Visit us on the web!
www.runningpress.com

Printed and bound by CPI Group (UK) Ltd, Croydon, CR0 4YY

Contents

The Adventure of the Crimson Arrow	1
The Adventure of Kendal Terrace	21
A Hair's Breadth	73
The Adventure of the Smiling Face	90
The Adventure of the Fourth Glove	148
The Adventure of the Richmond Recluse	177
The Adventure of the English Scholar	211
The Adventure of the Amethyst Ring	258
The Adventure of the Willow Pool	278
The Adventure of Queen Hippolyta	386
The Adventure of Dedstone Mill	412
An Incident in Society	483

The Adventure of THE CRIMSON ARROW

BETWEEN THE YEARS 1881 AND 1890, I enjoyed the privilege of studying at first hand the methods of Mr Sherlock Holmes, the world's first consulting detective, and during this period kept detailed records of a great many of the cases in which he was involved. A large number of these concerned private family matters, the details of which never reached the public press, but in others we would find ourselves in the very midst of the leading news of the day, and I would know that the actions my friend took one day would dictate the newspaper headlines of the next. Such a case was the Buckler's Fold tragedy of '84.

Readers will no doubt recall that Buckler's Fold in Hampshire was the country estate of Sir George Kirkman, a man who had amassed great wealth from his interests in metalworking, mining and railway engineering. Beginning in a modest way, as the owner of a small chain-link forge in Birmingham, he had risen rapidly, both in wealth and eminence, until a fair slice of British industry lay under his command and he had received a knighthood for his achievements.

At the time of the tragedy that was to bring the name of Buckler's Fold to national prominence, Sir George had held the estate for some eight years. It was his custom, during the summer months of the year, to invite notable people of the day to spend the weekend there. It was said that he prided himself upon the happy blend of the celebrated who gathered at his dinner table upon these occasions, and it was certainly true that many of those renowned at the time in the worlds of arts, letters and public life had made at least one visit to Buckler's Fold.

Indeed, it was said in some circles that one could not truly be said to be established in one's chosen field until one had received an invitation to one of Sir George Kirkman's weekend parties.

One unusual feature of such gatherings was an archery contest for the gentlemen, which, by custom, took place on Sunday, upon the lower lawn behind the house. Sir George had in recent years developed an interest in the sport, at which he had achieved a certain proficiency, and was keen to introduce others to what he termed "the world of toxophily".

In the early part of May, 1884, the renowned African explorer, E. Woodforde Soames, had returned to England and become at once the most sought-after guest in London. He and his companion in adventure, Captain James Blake, had spent the previous six months exploring the upper reaches of the Zambezi River, and had several times come within an inch of their lives. Many stories of their adventures circulated at the time: of how their boat had sunk beneath them in a crocodile-infested river, of how a month's provisions had been washed away in a matter of minutes, and of how Captain Blake had saved Woodforde Soames from a giant python at Zumbo. News of the hair-raising entertainment provided by these stories soon reached the ear of Sir George Kirkman, and as he himself had played a part in organizing the finance for their expedition and, it was said, looked for some return for the time and effort he had invested, an invitation to the two men to spend the weekend at Buckler's Fold was duly dispatched. Among the other guests that weekend, as I learned from Friday's *Morning Post*, was the rising young artist Mr Neville Whiting, whose engagement to the daughter of the Commander of the Solent Squadron had recently been announced. At the time I read it, his name meant nothing to me, and I could not have imagined then how soon the name would be upon everyone's lips, nor what a significant part in his destiny would be played by my friend Sherlock Holmes.

The newspapers of Monday morning occasionally included a brief mention of the weekend's events at Buckler's Fold, and when the name caught my eye on that particular morning, I glanced idly at the accompanying report. In a moment, however, I had cried out in surprise.

Holmes turned from the window, where he was smoking his after-breakfast pipe and staring moodily into the sunny street below, and raised his eyebrow questioningly.

"'A tragic accident has occurred'," I read aloud, "'at Buckler's Fold, country home of Sir George Kirkman, in which one of his guests has been struck by an arrow and killed. An archery competition is a regular feature of parties at Buckler's Fold, and it is thought that the victim was struck by a stray shaft from this event while walking nearby. No further information is available at present.'"

"The longbow is a dangerous toy," remarked my companion. "Hazlitt declares in one of his essays that the bow has now ceased for ever to be a weapon of offence; but if so, it is a singular thing how frequently people still manage to inflict injury and death upon one another with it." With a shake of the head, he returned to his contemplation of the street below.

Holmes had been professionally engaged almost continuously throughout the preceding weeks, but upon that particular morning was free from any immediate calls upon his time. It was a pleasant spring day, and after some effort I managed to prevail upon him to take a stroll with me in the fresh air. Up to St John's Wood Church we walked, and across the northern part of Regent's Park to the zoo. It was a cheery sight, after the long cold months of the early spring, to see the blossom upon the trees and the spring flowers tossing their heads in such gay profusion in the park. As ever on such occasions, my friend's keen powers of observation ensured that even the tiniest detail of our surroundings seemed possessed of interest.

We were walking slowly home through the sunshine, our conversation as meandering as our stroll, when we passed a newspaper stand near Baker Street station. The early editions of the evening papers were on sale and, with great surprise, I read the following in large letters upon a placard: "Arrow Murder – Latest".

"Murder?" I cried.

"It can only refer to the death at Buckler's Fold," remarked Holmes, a note of heightened interest in his voice. Quickly he took up a copy of every paper available. "Listen to this, Watson," said he, reading from the first of his bundle as we walked along. "'The death of E. Woodforde Soames, shot in the back with an arrow at Buckler's Fold in Hampshire yesterday, and at first reported to be an accident, is now considered to be murder. The Hampshire Constabulary were notified soon after the death was discovered. Considering the circumstances to be of a suspicious nature, they at once requested a senior detective inspector from Scotland Yard. Arriving at Buckler's Fold at six o'clock, he had completed his preliminary investigation by seven, and proceeded to arrest one of the guests, Mr Neville Whiting, who was heard to protest his innocence in the strongest terms.' They must have considered it a very straightforward matter, if they were able to make an arrest so quickly," Holmes remarked as we walked down Baker Street, "although why anyone should wish to murder Woodforde Soames, probably the most popular man in England at the moment, must be regarded as something of a puzzle!"

When we reached the house, we were informed that a young lady, a Miss Audrey Greville, had called for Sherlock Holmes, and was awaiting his return. As we entered our little sitting room, a pretty, dark-haired young woman of about two-and-twenty stood up from the chair by the hearth, an expression of great agitation upon her pale features.

"Mr Holmes?" said she, looking from one to the other of us.

"Miss Greville," returned my friend, bowing. "Pray be seated. You are, I take it, the fiancée of Mr Neville Whiting, and have come here directly from Buckler's Fold."

"Yes," said she, her eyes opening wide in surprise. "Did someone tell you I was coming?"

Holmes shook his head. "You are clearly in some distress, and on the table by your gloves I see a copy of the *Pall Mall Gazette*, which is open at an account of the Buckler's Fold tragedy. Next to it is the return half of a railway ticket issued by the London and South Western, and upon your third finger is an attractive and new engagement ring. Now, what is the latest news of the matter, and how may we help you?"

"Neville – Mr Whiting – has been arrested," said she, and bit her lip hard as she began to sob. I passed her a handkerchief and she dabbed her eyes. "Forgive me," she continued after a moment, "but it has been such a great shock."

"That is hardly surprising," said Holmes in an encouraging tone. "What is the evidence against Mr Whiting?"

"We had had a quarrel, earlier in the day," the young lady replied. "He accused me of flirting with other gentlemen."

"With Woodforde Soames?"

"Yes."

"And were you?"

She bit her lip again. "He seemed such a grand figure," said she at length, "and has had such exciting adventures. Perhaps I *was* paying him an excessive amount of attention, but if I was, it was no more than that. Neville became so jealous and unreasonable. He said that Soames's opinion of himself was big enough already, without my making it even bigger."

"What happened later?"

"The archery contest took place early in the afternoon. I had persuaded Neville to take part, although he said he was not interested and had never fired a longbow in his life. It was foolish of me."

"He was not very successful?"

"He did not hit the target once. I did not think it would concern him, considering that he had said he was not interested, but perhaps I was wrong. There were seven or eight gentlemen taking part, and although one or two of the others did scarcely any better than Neville, that appeared to afford him little consolation. I think he felt humiliated. Mr Woodforde Soames was the eventual winner and, I must admit, I found myself cheering as he shot his last arrows. I looked round for Neville then, but found that he had already left the lawn. I asked if anyone had seen him, and was informed that he had gone off into the nearby woods and taken his bow and quiver with him."

"When did you next see him?"

"About an hour and a half later. My mother and I were taking tea on the terrace when he returned. He appeared in a better humour and apologized for his earlier temper. I asked him where he had been and he said he had taken a long walk through the orchards and the woods and loosed off a few practice arrows at the trees there."

"Was Woodforde Soames present when Mr Whiting returned?"

Miss Greville shook her head. "No," said she. "He had gone for a walk shortly after the archery contest ended, as had several of the others. All had returned within an hour or two, except Mr Soames. Then one of Sir George Kirkman's servants ran onto the terrace, his face as white as a sheet, and whispered something to Sir George, who then stood up and announced that one of his gamekeepers had found Mr Woodforde Soames dead in the woods. It appeared, he said, that he had been struck by an arrow. I don't think that anyone there could believe it. Mr Soames had had an air of indestructibility about him and had, moreover, just returned unscathed from six months in the most dangerous parts of the world. That he should shortly thereafter lose his life in a wood in Hampshire seemed simply too fantastic to be true."

"Much of life seems too fantastic to be true," remarked Holmes drily. "What action was taken?"

"Sir George sent one of his men to notify the local police authorities. They later sent for a detective from London, who arrived early in the evening and interviewed everyone there. In little over an hour he had arrested Neville."

"On what grounds?"

"The quarrel we had had earlier in the day had been witnessed by several people, who had overheard Neville's wild remarks concerning Mr Woodforde Soames."

"That is all?" said Holmes in surprise.

The young lady shook her head but did not reply immediately. "No," said she at length. "The arrow that killed Mr Soames was one of Neville's."

"How was that established?"

"The shafts of the arrows were stained in a variety of colours, and each man taking part in the archery contest was given a quiver containing a dozen arrows of the same colour. Neville's were crimson, and it was a crimson arrow that killed Mr Woodforde Soames. But, Mr Holmes," our visitor cried in an impassioned voice, "Neville could not have done it! It is simply inconceivable! No one who knows his gentle character could believe it for an instant!"

Holmes considered the matter for a while in silence. "What is the name of the detective inspector from London?" he asked at length.

"Mr Lestrade," replied Miss Greville.

"Ha! So Lestrade is on the trail! Is he still at Buckler's Fold?"

"Yes. He stayed in the area last night, and returned to the house this morning to take further statements from everyone. When it came to my turn to be interviewed, I asked him if there was any possibility that his conclusions might be mistaken. He shook his head briskly and declared that the circumstances admitted of no doubt whatever.

"But is it possible, in such a case," I persisted, "to seek a second opinion, as in medical matters, where one's general practitioner can call upon a consultant?"

"'There is Mr Sherlock Holmes of Baker Street,' said he after a moment, in a dubious tone. 'No doubt he would provide you with a second opinion, but I very much fear that it would differ little from mine. Still, I understand your relation to the accused and appreciate that you would wish to clutch at any straw.'"

"Why, the impudent scoundrel!" cried Holmes, rising to his feet. "I certainly shall give you a second opinion, Miss Greville. Would you care to accompany us, Watson?"

"Most certainly."

"Then get your hat, my boy! We leave for Hampshire at once!"

In thirty minutes we were in a fast train bound for the south coast, and two hours later, having changed at Basingstoke, we alighted at a small wayside halt, deep in the Hampshire countryside. I have remarked before on the singular ability of Sherlock Holmes to drive from his mind those things he did not for the moment wish to consider, and our journey that day provided a particularly striking illustration of this, for having spent the first part of the journey silently engrossed in his bundle of newspapers, he had then cast them aside, and passed the remainder of the time in cheery and incongruous conversation with Miss

Greville, for all the world as if he were bound for a carefree day at the coast. As we boarded the station fly, however, and set off upon the final part of our journey, a tension returned to his sharp, hawk-like features, and there was an air of concentration in his manner, like that of a hound keen to be upon the scent.

We had wired ahead from Waterloo, and upon our arrival at the house, as Miss Greville hurried off to find her mother, we were shown into a small study, where Inspector Lestrade was sitting at a desk, writing.

"Mr Holmes!" cried the policeman, turning as we entered. "I was surprised to receive your telegram – I had not expected to see you down here so quickly!"

"I felt obliged to match the speed with which you moved to an arrest," returned Holmes. "You are confident you have the right man?"

"There is no doubt of it."

"Then you will not mind if we conduct our own investigation of the matter."

"Not at all. Indeed, I will show you where the crime occurred, although, in truth, there is little enough to be seen there."

He led us along a corridor and out at a door which gave onto a paved terrace at the rear of the house. Several people were sitting there, taking tea. A large, clean-shaven, portly man stood up from a table as we passed, the rolls of fat about his jaw and throat wobbling as he did so.

"Who are these men, Inspector?" he demanded of Lestrade.

"Mr Sherlock Holmes and Dr Watson, Sir George," the policeman replied. "Miss Greville has engaged them to look into the matter on her behalf."

"You are wasting your time," Sir George Kirkman remarked in a blunt tone.

"A few hours spent in the pleasant Hampshire countryside is never a waste of time," Holmes responded placidly.

Sir George Kirkman snorted. "Still," he continued, "if the young lady insists, there is nothing to be done about it. And I suppose you would not wish to turn down an easy fee, if times are slack."

I saw a spark of anger spring up in Holmes's eye. "You must speak for yourself, Sir George," said he at length, "and I will answer for my own work. Come along, Lestrade, there are clouds in the sky, and I should not wish to be hampered by rain!"

"I'll come with you," said Kirkman. "It will be interesting to watch an expert at work."

We descended a steep flight of steps from the terrace to the lawn. There, Lestrade indicated a door immediately to the side of the steps, which gave access to a storeroom built under the terrace itself.

"The archery equipment is kept in here," said he, opening the door.

Inside, hanging up behind gardening tools and similar implements, were a dozen or more longbows and quivers.

Holmes took down one of the quivers and extracted an arrow. The shaft was stained dark green. For a moment he turned it over in his hands.

"The murder weapon was crimson, I understand," said he at length to Lestrade.

"That's right. From the quiver that Whiting had been using."

"It hardly proves that Whiting fired the shot," remarked Holmes. "Surely anyone could have used one of the crimson arrows?"

Lestrade shook his head. "Each of the quivers contains twelve arrows of a single colour, and all the quivers are different – blue, green, crimson, purple and so on. Whiting took his bow and quiver off with him into the woods – to practise, he said – and did not return until much later, so it would have been impossible for anyone else to have used his arrows."

"I understand, however," said Holmes, "that Whiting left early, before the competition was finished."

"That is so," said Lestrade, "but I cannot see that that makes any difference to the matter."

"Only this," said Holmes, "that if the competition was still in progress when he left, it would not have been possible for Whiting to retrieve the last arrows he shot, which I understand all missed the target, and would thus be lying on the ground. Once the contest was over, and the competitors had dispersed, anyone might have picked those arrows up from the ground and used them."

"It sounds a bit unlikely," said Sir George Kirkman. "Of course, I realize that in murder cases, those acting for the defence must always do their best to contrive an alternative explanation, however far-fetched, to try to cast doubt on their client's guilt."

"Unless it can be proved that the arrow which killed Woodforde Soames came from those still in the quiver, rather than those on the ground," continued Holmes, ignoring the interruption, "then the colour of the arrow shaft is, it seems to me, of no significance whatever. Where did Whiting leave his bow and quiver when he returned from his walk?"

"He dropped them on the ground near the targets," said Lestrade, "on the archery field, where all the other equipment had been left at the end of the contest."

"Were they still there when you arrived?"

"No. All the equipment had been collected up by Sir George's servants and put away in this storeroom. I did ask them if they had observed anything unusual about the equipment – if any of it had been left in an odd place, for instance – but they said not. Some of the arrows had been lying on the ground, they said, and some had been in the quivers, but they could not remember any details."

"In other words," said Holmes, "no one can say with any confidence where the fatal arrow came from, nor which bow fired it. It seems to me, then, Lestrade, that most of your case against Neville Whiting collapses. Did anyone other than Whiting leave the archery field before the end of the competition?"

Lestrade shook his head. "Everyone else stayed until the end. Sir George presented a little trophy to Woodforde Soames, who had won, and then they all drifted away, some to the house and some to take a walk over the estate."

Holmes nodded. "Has anyone left today?"

"Two Members of Parliament were obliged to return to London this morning."

"But everyone else who was present over the weekend is still here?"

"All except Sir George's secretary, Hepplethwaite," Lestrade returned. "He left yesterday afternoon to visit a sick relative."

"Have you verified the matter?" Holmes queried.

"I did not think it necessary," Lestrade returned in surprise.

"No? Surely it is something of an odd coincidence that this man Hepplethwaite should leave the house at the same time as Woodforde Soames is killed. I should certainly have felt obliged to satisfy myself as to the truth of the matter."

"No doubt," responded Lestrade in a tone of irritation, "and no doubt I would have done so, too, had there been the slightest possibility that Hepplethwaite had been involved in the crime in any way. But he left the house only a few minutes after the archery competition finished, at which time Woodforde Soames was still very much alive, for he sat over a cup of tea on the terrace for some five or ten minutes at about that time, talking to various people – including Miss Greville and her mother, as it happens – before going off for his walk. That's right, isn't it, Sir George?"

"Absolutely," responded Kirkman. "I had just returned to my study, shortly after presenting the archery trophy, and Woodforde Soames and the others were taking tea, as you say, when Hepplethwaite entered with a telegram he had received. It informed him that his father was ill. He asked if he might leave at once, and I agreed to the request. As far as I am aware, he left the house a few minutes later."

"I see," said Holmes. "Well, well. Let us now inspect the spot where Soames met his death."

Lestrade led us across the lawn and down another flight of stone steps to a lower lawn, surrounded on three sides by trees. Along the far side, a number of wooden chairs and benches were set out. It was evidently upon this lower lawn that the archery contest had taken place, for at the left-hand end stood two large targets. Behind them, a long canvas sheet had been hung from the trees to catch any arrows that missed the targets.

We crossed the lawn at an angle, and followed Lestrade through a gap in the trees, immediately to the right of the canvas sheeting, from where a narrow path curved away into the woods. After a short distance this path was joined by another, and we followed it to the left, crossing several other smaller paths, until we came presently to a wider, well-used path which ran at right-angles to our own. Lestrade turned right onto this path and we followed its winding course for some twenty or thirty yards. The trees in this part of the wood grew very close together, and there was an air of shaded gloom about the place. Coming at last round a sharp turn to the left, we arrived at a place where the path stretched dead straight for some twenty yards ahead of us. Lestrade stopped before a small cairn of pebbles which had been placed in the middle of the path.

"I have marked the spot," said he. "These paths wind about so much that one could easily become confused as to where one was in the wood."

"Very good," said Holmes in approval. Then he squatted down upon the ground and proceeded to examine with great care every square inch of the path for fifteen feet in either direction. Presently he rose to his feet, a look of dissatisfaction upon his face.

"Found what you were looking for?" asked Kirkman in an undisguised tone of mockery.

"The ground is very hard, so it is unlikely that there would be much to be seen in any case," replied Holmes in a placid tone, "but so many feet have passed this way in the last twenty-four hours that the little there may have been has been quite obliterated." He looked about him, peering into the dense undergrowth on either side, then walked up and down the path several times. "Soames was found face-down, stretched lengthways on the path, I take it," he remarked at last to Inspector Lestrade.

"That's correct, Mr Holmes," the policeman replied. "He had been shot in the back, as you're no doubt aware, an inch or two left of centre. The local doctor who examined the body said that the arrow had penetrated quite deeply, and he thought that death would probably have occurred within a few seconds."

He broke off as there came the sound of footsteps behind us. I turned as a stocky, middle-sized man appeared round the bend in the path. His sunburnt face was clean-shaven, save for a small dark moustache, and there was a military precision in his manner as he stepped forward briskly and introduced himself as Captain

Blake, the former companion in adventure of Woodforde Soames. He had, he said, just heard of our arrival, and asked, as we shook hands, if he might accompany us in our investigation.

"By all means," said Holmes. "In which direction was Soames facing when he was found?" he continued, addressing Lestrade.

"With his feet pointing back the way we have come, and his head towards the straight section of the path in front of us," Lestrade replied. "The path we are now on begins near the kitchen gardens, by the side of the house. It is evident, therefore, that he was coming from the house, or somewhere near it, and heading deeper into the woods."

Holmes stood a moment in silence, then he shook his head.

"I disagree," said he at length, in a considered tone.

"Why so?" asked Lestrade in surprise.

"The disposition of the body is, in this case, of less consequence than the disposition of the path," said Holmes.

"What on earth are you talking about?" demanded Kirkman.

"I think that when struck, Soames must have turned before he fell," Holmes continued. "The force of the blow, just below the left shoulder blade, would probably have been sufficient by itself to spin him round. But he may also have tried to turn as he fell, to see who it was that was attacking him."

Sir George snorted dismissively, but Lestrade considered the suggestion for a moment. "It is certainly possible," he conceded at length. "But what makes you think so, Mr Holmes?"

"See how thickly the trees are growing just here, and how dense and tall the undergrowth is. It is scarcely conceivable that anyone could have forced a passage through that, or could have had a clear sight of Woodforde Soames if he had done so. Therefore, whoever fired the shot must have been standing upon the path at the time."

"That seems certain," said Captain Blake, nodding his head in agreement.

"Now, behind us, in the direction of the house," Holmes continued, "the path is very winding, whereas ahead of us, away from the house, it is fairly straight for some considerable distance. Whoever fired the shot must have had a clear view of Woodforde Soames's back. From the direction of the house that is impossible. Immediately before this spot there is a right-angled bend in the path, and before that there are more twists and turns. From the other direction, however, the archer would have had a clear and uninterrupted view. Therefore, Woodforde Soames was shot when returning to the house from somewhere ahead of us. Where does this path lead to?"

"I do not know," Lestrade admitted. "I saw no reason to explore the path further, as I didn't believe that the murdered man had been any further along it than the spot we're now standing on."

"Does this path go anywhere in particular, Sir George?" queried Holmes.

"Not really," Kirkman replied. "It meanders on for a mile or so, and comes out by the water-meadows near the river."

"I understood that this was the way to the folly," Captain Blake interjected.

"Oh, that old thing!" said Kirkman in a dismissive tone. "It is meant to look like a Roman ruin, so they tell me, but it looks just like a pile of old bricks to me."

"Let us follow the path a little distance, anyway," said Holmes, "and see if we can turn up anything of interest."

"Oh, this is a complete waste of time!" cried Kirkman in an impatient voice. "I shall leave you to it," he continued, turning on his heel and walking rapidly back towards the house as we followed Holmes further along the path.

At the end of the long straight section, the path again turned sharply to the left, and there, just a few yards further on, on the right-hand side of the path, was the mouldering, ivy-covered ruin to which Kirkman had referred. It appeared little greater in size than a small shed, but it was so smothered in creepers and brambles that its shape was difficult to discern. It was clear, however, that there was a wide arched doorway at the front, and a dark, sepulchral chamber within.

Holmes frowned as we approached this singular structure.

"Halloa!" said he. "Someone has been in here very recently!"

"How can you tell?" asked Blake.

"The cobwebs across the doorway have been recently broken. Let us have a look inside."

He pushed aside the trailing fronds of ivy, which hung like a curtain across the entrance, and made his way into the gloom within. Captain Blake held the ivy aside, and we watched as Holmes struck a match and looked about him. Then he bent to the floor, where mounds of dead leaves and other vegetation had accumulated. A moment later, he looked round and gestured to us.

"I think you had best all see this," said he in a grave voice.

We squeezed past the tangle of ivy and dusty cobwebs as Holmes struck another match. There on the floor, partly hidden under the dead leaves and with a longbow lying beside him, was the body of a man.

"Who the devil is it?" cried Lestrade in astonishment.

"My God!" cried Blake. "I know that man! It is Hepplethwaite, Sir George Kirkman's secretary!"

We lifted the body from its dark resting place and laid it upon the path outside. A brief examination was enough to tell me that he had been killed by a severe blow to the back of the head, where the hair was thickly matted with blood.

"What can it mean?" said Lestrade in a tone of utter stupefaction. "When did he return from visiting his sick relative? What was he doing here in the woods? And why has he got a bow with him?"

"I should say he has been dead at least twenty-four hours," said I, looking up. "Where is Holmes?" I added in surprise, for he was nowhere to be seen. Even as I spoke, however, he emerged from a narrow gap in the vegetation at the side of the folly.

"There is a way through here to another path, which runs along behind this little building," said he, "and it is clear that someone has spent some time standing there fairly recently."

"What does it mean?" said Lestrade again.

"I rather fancy that Hepplethwaite's sick relative does not exist," returned Holmes.

"He lied about it?"

"No, not he; Sir George Kirkman."

"What!"

"I think I know what's happened here," said Captain Blake in a tone of sudden enlightenment. We turned as he continued.

"You have probably heard," said he, "that the Zambezi expedition nearly foundered when many of our stores were washed away by the flooding river. As far as it goes, that is true, but it is only half the story. There had never been sufficient provisions in the first place, and when we returned to our base camp the replacement stores that should have been awaiting us were not there. Although we eventually managed to reach the coast, it was a close-run thing, I can tell you.

"When we arrived back in England, Woodforde Soames at once made enquiries of all our suppliers, and it began to appear that money held by Sir George Kirkman which should have been used for the expedition had not been paid. Why this had happened, we could not discover – various rumours were circulating – so we came down here this weekend determined to get to the bottom of the business, and in no very good humour, as you will imagine. Sir George has been occupied with his guests, however, and it proved impossible to get him on his own to discuss the matter. Then, on Saturday evening, Soames took me to one side and told me that Kirkman's secretary – this poor devil here – had approached him in confidence, seeking advice. He had recently learned, he said, that money rightfully belonging to the African expedition had been improperly diverted elsewhere by Kirkman, and he was unsure what to do with this information. Torn between loyalty to his employer and his own sense of honesty, he had found his position intolerable, and the strain of it had nearly driven him mad, he said. Moreover, the money dishonestly taken from the expedition's fund was, he was convinced, but a small part of a very large scheme of fraud. This information certainly bore out the rumours we had heard in London, but had been scarcely able to credit, that Sir George Kirkman is as good as bankrupt and has been engaging in all kinds of financial chicanery to try to conceal the fact."

"Bankrupt!" cried Lestrade incredulously. "What about his mines?"

"The rumour is that they are all practically worked out."

"His iron foundries?"

"Running at a loss for several years."

"His engineering works, then?"

"No orders. Woodforde Soames had the impression, from what Hepplethwaite told him, that Kirkman has been engaged in one financial swindle after another for many years, and there seems a possibility that his entire fortune has been built on such foundations. Soames and Hepplethwaite did not have time to conclude their conversation on Saturday, but the secretary said he would try to speak to my friend again on the subject the next day. That, so far as I know, is how matters stood on Saturday night. It seems to me now that Soames's death on Sunday afternoon cannot simply be coincidence."

Holmes nodded. "It is probable, then, that Hepplethwaite arranged to meet Woodforde Soames here at the folly, once the archery competition was finished. But Kirkman must have suspected what was afoot, and followed his secretary, picking up a spare bow and arrow from the archery field on the way, as I suggested earlier. No doubt it was he who hid behind the folly, where he would have been able to overhear their conversation. I imagine that when they had finished speaking, Soames left first, and the secretary stayed behind a few moments so that no suspicion would be aroused by their being seen together. But Kirkman must have slipped through this gap in the undergrowth by the side of the folly, struck his secretary on the head with a stone, and then followed Soames down the path and fired the shot that killed him."

"No wonder he was so interested to see where your investigations would lead you!" I cried.

Holmes nodded. "And no wonder he left so abruptly when he did. He would know that if we examined the folly we were certain to find Hepplethwaite's body. Quickly! We must get our hands on him before he can work any further villainy!"

We ran back along the path at the top of our speed. Two men were working in the kitchen gardens, and Holmes instructed them to bring the body of the unfortunate secretary from the folly to the house. In a garden by the side of the house, we encountered Miss Greville and her mother, sitting on a bench.

"Oh, Mr Holmes!" cried Miss Greville earnestly, rising to her feet. "Do you see any hope for Mr Whiting?"

"Indeed I do, Miss Greville," returned Holmes briskly. "Have you seen anything of Sir George Kirkman recently?"

"Well, it really is most odd," returned Miss Greville's mother, "and I am not sure that I entirely believe it, but there is a wild rumour going round that he was seen driving himself off in a dogcart towards Winchester about fifteen minutes ago! They say he was lashing the horse as if his life depended on it! Absurd, isn't it?"

"He must have gone to catch the London express," said Lestrade, consulting his watch. "It leaves Winchester in about five minutes."

"How long will it take him to get to the station there?" Holmes queried.

"About a quarter of an hour. He will have reached it in time, but we cannot. He has escaped us."

"What of the halt where Watson and I alighted earlier? That is barely seven minutes' distance from here in a trap, and the London train must come this way and pass through there."

"That is true, Mr Holmes," Lestrade replied. "Unfortunately, however, the London express does not stop there, but steams straight through."

"It will stop if we tell it to!" cried Holmes. "There is, I observed, a signal-box at the halt. If we can get the signals set to danger, the train will have to stop!"

"By George! I think you have it!" cried Lestrade.

In a few moments the groom had put a horse in the shafts of a trap, and we were rattling at a furious rate down the winding country lanes. We clattered to a halt in a cloud of dust in the station yard, leapt down and ran onto the platform. In the distance, a plume of smoke indicated the rapid approach of the London express.

The signalman looked up in alarm as we sprang up the steps and burst into his little cabin. Quickly, Lestrade identified himself and instructed the man to alter the signals, but he hesitated.

"It is strictly against regulations," said he.

"Regulations be blowed!" cried Lestrade angrily as there came a sharp whistle from down the track and the distant beat of the engine came to our ears.

"It is almost upon us," said the signalman. "It is too late."

"There is a murderer on that train," said Holmes. "Let it pass and he will escape. Stop it and your name will be honoured for ever!"

"Here," said Captain Blake abruptly, stepping to the row of heavy levers. "Never mind this man. I'll do it myself! I learned about these things when I had a spell with the Royal Engineers."

At this, the signalman sprang forward. "Very well," said he. "Let me do it." He pulled two of the heavy levers towards him, as the bright green locomotive, wreathed in smoke, burst into view round the distant curve and thundered towards the little station. There came an ear-splitting din, as the driver saw the signal ahead of him and applied the brake, and the wheels skidded with a shriek along the shining steel track. Through the platforms the train roared and screeched, and past the signal cabin, which shook like a leaf in a storm as the heavy engine passed it, until finally, in a cloud of steam and smoke, it came to a halt some thirty yards further on.

Sherlock Holmes sprang down the steps, and I followed him along the track to the back of the train, and round to the other side. We heard Lestrade call out, as he caught sight of his quarry in one of the carriages, and at that moment a door on our side was flung open, and the portly figure of Sir George Kirkman sprang down and landed heavily on the ballast. We rushed forward as he rose to his feet and withdrew something from within his coat.

"Look out, Watson! He's got a gun!" cried Holmes, flinging himself upon the fugitive before he could raise his arm. The two of them struggled wildly for a moment, until Holmes managed at length to wrench the pistol from the other's grasp and send it spinning through the air and into the bushes beside the track. Then, as Kirkman seemed about to break away, Holmes caught him with a right hook to the jaw, and he fell heavily to the ground. In a moment Lestrade and Blake had joined us.

"Thought you'd make a fool of the law, did you?" cried Lestrade, as he clapped a pair of handcuffs on his prisoner. "We'll see about that!"

"Well, well," said Holmes to me, as he stood up and brushed the dust off his clothes with his hands. "That appears to be that! I don't know what your plans are, Watson, but I should very much prefer to be back in London this evening. So, what say you to taking this train which has so conveniently stopped for us?"

The Adventure of KENDAL TERRACE

AMONG THE MANY strange and puzzling problems presented to Mr Sherlock Holmes during the time we shared chambers together, the story which was told to us by Mr Henry Claydon holds a special place in my memory. To an outside observer, there were certainly aspects of the affair that appeared absurd and almost farcical; but for those intimately involved in the matter it must have seemed anything but humorous. What is undeniable is that it was a very perplexing business, and one, moreover, which, but for the intervention of Sherlock Holmes, would very likely never have been solved at all.

It was a pleasant evening, just a few days before midsummer. Our meal concluded and cleared away, we had fallen into a discussion of the latest scientific opinion on the nature of sunspots, and of the possible effects of these phenomena upon terrestrial events. From these rarefied heights, our conversation had drifted on by way of other natural phenomena that were not yet fully understood to a consideration of the more mundane but equally intriguing mysteries with which the history of human society abounds. I had often observed that despite Holmes's occasional pretence of ignorance of some field of human enquiry when he was not in the conversational vein, there was in reality scarcely any subject I could raise upon which he did not have an informed opinion. But upon the unsolved human mysteries of past centuries his knowledge was perfectly stupendous. Whether it was an inexplicable murder in the sixteenth century, a puzzling theft in the eighteenth, the baffling disappearance of some famous person or the mysterious publication of an anonymous manuscript, my friend appeared to have all the facts at his finger-tips, and he held me enthralled as he ranged widely over these fascinating, unsolved problems. Some of his conclusions were at once so surprising and so interesting that I may one day make them the subject of one of these short sketches. Some of them, indeed, seemed on first hearing simply too startling to be true, but as he explained to me how he had arrived at his conclusions, I was in almost every case convinced that he had indeed hit upon the truth.

"You appear to have made a close study of these ancient problems," I remarked.

"I have had little else to occupy my time recently," said he.

"You have no case in hand?"

My friend shook his head. "I have had three prospective clients call upon me this week. Two of the cases were entirely devoid of interest. In both of them I was able to make a few suggestions, which I trust will be useful, as I sat here in this room, but I did not propose to enter into either matter to any greater extent than that. In the third case, that of Mr Tanner of Norwood, as you may recollect, I accompanied that gentleman back home to investigate the curious incidents he had described to me, only to find when we reached Norwood that someone had reported the matter to Scotland Yard, and that, despite taking almost four hours to respond to the report and travel the short distance to Norwood, they had already made an arrest. Furthermore, I could not doubt, from the facts available to me, that they had the right man, for it was the very person to whom my own suspicions had been drawn by my client's account."

"I shall have to remind you of this," I remarked with a chuckle. "You have often said that the official force can scarcely ever be trusted to do the right thing, but it seems that in this case at least they were, by your own admission, entirely correct."

"Perhaps so," returned my friend, "but they had received some material assistance. The man they arrested had already made a full confession of his part in the affair before the police even arrived. It would therefore have been somewhat difficult for them not to have identified the villain. For all the intellect involved, Scotland Yard might as well have sent a pair of Trafalgar Square pigeons down to Norwood. They would probably have managed the matter just as successfully, and would certainly have arrived somewhat sooner. In short, Watson, I have had no worthwhile case all week, and time lies heavy upon my hands."

"It may be that your practice is following the pattern of most medical practices," I observed, laughing. "One old physician for whom I worked for a few months while a student never ceased to lament how the arrival of fine weather always brought a severe decrease in the numbers of his patients."

My friend nodded. "Perhaps it is. But sometimes it seems that the present age has abandoned altogether the production of interesting mysteries. I have therefore been occupying my all too abundant leisure time in working back through those of past centuries. At my present rate of progress, I should soon be on to the cave murders of the Stone Age."

I laughed. "Perhaps your missing clients will all turn up together one rainy day, as tends to happen in a doctor's practice."

"I rather doubt it," responded Holmes with a dry chuckle. "Anyhow, I have now abandoned all hope that any clients will appear this week, and can only hope that next week will show an increase in business!"

As it happened, however, my friend was on this occasion mistaken, and his despair premature. Scarcely five minutes after he had uttered these words our conversation was interrupted by the mad jangling of the front-door bell.

"What an impatient caller!" I remarked, as the wild ringing of the bell continued in an unbroken clamour.

"It is a client, or I am much mistaken!" cried Holmes in delight, springing to his feet and clapping his hands together. "I recognize the symptoms. Let us clear away this litter you have left, Watson," he continued, picking up the day's newspapers, which were scattered upon the floor beside his chair, and tossing them into a corner.

A moment later, our landlady appeared with a card upon a salver. "Mr Henry Claydon to see you, Mr Holmes," said she.

"Ask him to step up, Mrs Hudson," responded Holmes, but scarcely were the words out of his mouth when there came a rapid drumming of footsteps upon the stair. Moments later, a young man, breathless and frantic-looking, appeared behind the landlady and, without further ceremony, edged his way into the room. Though he was dressed in the smart clothes of a City man, they were dishevelled and grubby looking. He had a black eye, there was blood upon his face, and the bowler hat he carried in his hand was in a sorry, crumpled state.

"Pray excuse my abrupt entry," cried he, "but my situation is desperate." Behind him, Mrs Hudson closed the door quietly, an expression of disapproval upon her face. "Mr Holmes!" he continued with a cry, rushing suddenly forward and grasping my hand. "You cannot imagine the terrible thing that has happened!"

"I am sorry, but you are under a misapprehension," I interrupted, shaking my head. "I am not Sherlock Holmes."

"What!" cried he, springing back as if he had received an electric shock from touching my hand. "Oh, no!" he continued in a wailing tone, clutching the sides of his head, as if in great pain. "Don't say it is happening again!" With a vigour that was alarming to witness, he abruptly cast himself down to the floor with a cry of, "Madness! Madness! All is madness!"

"My dear sir," said Holmes in an anxious voice. "Pray be calmed. I am the man you seek. I am Sherlock Holmes."

"You are?" cried the other, abruptly ceasing his moaning and looking up. "You really are? Why, then, you at least are where you are supposed to be. The Lord be praised!"

"It is clear you have suffered some misfortune," said Holmes in a measured tone. "If you will take a seat and tell us about it, perhaps we can be of assistance."

"Misfortune?" cried our visitor, rising to his feet and dusting himself off. "Ha! What I have suffered, Mr Holmes, is a unique and terrible experience. Why, sir, it knocks all other mysteries of the world into a cocked hat."

"Pray, let us have the details."

"Certainly," returned the other, who appeared a little calmed by Holmes's soothing manner. "Some men, as you know, have their pockets picked in the street, and lose their watches. Other men have their houses broken into and lose the odd candlestick or two. I have lost to a thief something far greater in every sense than these trifles."

"Pray be precise."

"Gentlemen, while I was at work today, thieves have been busy in Kendal Terrace, North Clapham, where I have lived happily for six weeks. I returned home this evening to find that my house has been completely stolen away!"

"What!" cried Holmes and I as one.

"You see?" said our visitor, a note of satisfaction in his voice at our surprise. "It is enough to drive a man insane!"

"But surely," I suggested, "you have made a mistake? Surely, if your house does not appear to be there, you have simply turned inadvertently into the wrong street? Many suburban streets in London are of very similar appearance. Might you not simply have confused one street with another?"

"Certainly not!" retorted Claydon. "I think I know my own street well enough, thank you, though I have lived in it but a little while. Besides, I could see through the parlour window of the house that my furniture was still in place."

"Ah!" said Holmes. "I see. So the house itself has not disappeared? It is still there?"

"Certainly."

"But it is now occupied by someone else?"

"Precisely."

A look of intense disappointment came over Holmes's features at this mundane explanation of what had promised to be a more *outré* mystery. "Is it not possible," said he, "that there has merely been some sort of confusion over the letting arrangements? Perhaps, under the misapprehension that you have moved out, the agents have given a key of the house to someone else, so that they can look it over. I recommend that you speak to your landlord on the matter, Mr Claydon."

"No! No, no!" cried Claydon in protest, springing to his feet and shaking his head wildly. "You do not understand! The people in my house are not simply looking it over, they are living there as if they have always done so, and as if my own memory of living there is nothing but a pitiful delusion! And nor is the presence of these strangers in my house the only amazing thing: there is also the question of where my own household has vanished to. Where is my wife? Where are the servants?"

"What sort of people are these strangers?" asked Holmes after a moment. "Are they vagabonds, or otherwise disreputable?"

"Absolutely not," returned Claydon emphatically, resuming his seat. "On the contrary, they appeared highly respectable. That is what is so amazing! The lady of the house came to the door eventually, after I had been haggling for some time with a maid who would not let me in, and she was, I must say, very well spoken. She was highly indignant when I insisted that I lived there, and expressed herself most forcefully upon the point, but never ceased to be ladylike, if you know what I mean."

"Did you consider calling a policeman to assist you?"

"I had no need. The lady of the house – the lady of *my* house, I should say – called one herself, and he threatened to arrest me if I didn't clear off!"

"He took the lady's part rather than yours?"

"I should say!"

"What of your neighbours? Could you not have asked them to vouch for you?"

Claydon shook his head, a mournful expression upon his features. "I do not know any of them yet," he returned. "Since we moved to Kendal Terrace I have been very busy and preoccupied, so that I have been unable to pay any social calls. My wife has met one or two of the neighbours, but I have not. She says they are charming, which is as one would expect, for it is a very pleasant, somewhat select neighbourhood."

Our visitor broke off abruptly and sprang to his feet again, a wild expression on his face. "Why am I spouting this rubbish?" he cried. "Select neighbourhood, charming neighbours – what do these things matter when my house has been stolen and my wife has disappeared? Where is my Lucy? What has become of her?"

Again he broke off, a strange smile spread across his features, and he began to laugh in a harsh unpleasant way, which made my hair stand on end. All my medical instincts rebelled at that terrible sound.

"Stop it!" I cried, rising to my feet. "Get a grip on yourself, man!"

"Here's an odd thing," he continued, ignoring my words as if he were quite unaware of my presence and grinning from ear to ear as he spoke: "I spend some part of every working day considering the likelihood of events which people wish to insure themselves against, and here I am, a victim of an occurrence that lies quite beyond all calculation! What premium could I possibly recommend?"

His eyes wild and rolling, our visitor threw back his head and let forth a fresh gale of uncontrolled and cacophonous laughter. I stepped forward and struck him hard across the face with the flat of my hand, and in an instant the laughter ceased. He put his hand up to his cheek and eyed me with an expression of curiosity.

"Here," said Holmes, dashing brandy and water into a tumbler and handing it to me. "Give him this! If he doesn't recover himself quickly, we may lose him altogether!"

I pressed the tumbler into our visitor's hand, but it was only after considerable effort that I at length persuaded him to take a sip. Presently, however, when he had emptied the glass, he appeared to recover control over himself. He passed his hand across his face, as if in an effort to clear his head, and resumed his seat once more.

"I beg your pardon, gentlemen," said he after a moment, looking from one to the other of us. "You must forgive me if I have spoken a little wildly; but this business has quite unhinged my brain. It may be," he continued, running his hand through his hair, "that you will consider me a deranged fool and will decline to assist me, but if so I beg that you will reconsider. What I have told you is the literal truth."

"My dear Mr Claydon," interrupted Holmes in a firm but soothing voice. "It is evident that you have had a most disturbing experience, one that is quite beyond the experience of most men. How impudent it would be, therefore, for anyone more fortunate in his experiences to presume to judge you. I, for one, should certainly not dream of doing so. As to begging, sir, it is quite unnecessary. I sit here, waiting only for your statement of the case in order to take it up. And once having taken it up, I promise you that I shall not put it down again until it is resolved. If, furthermore, we are unable to resolve the matter this evening, you need not fear that you will lack shelter and somewhere to rest your head tonight: you may consider the couch over there to be entirely at your disposal!"

"Oh, thank you, sir!" cried Claydon, clasping his hands together in joy. "You perceive the fears within my soul before I have even voiced them."

"Very well," said Holmes with a chuckle. "Let us waste no more time, then. The sooner you begin your account, the sooner we can begin to help you. Have you ever before been the victim of strange or unexplained events?"

"Never."

"Pray, explain to us briefly, then, how and when you came to reside in Kendal Terrace, and then describe to us the events of this evening."

"Certainly. My wife and I, who are both from Northampton, have lived in the house only six weeks. Five years ago, I secured a position in the Northampton branch office of the Commercial Fire and Accident Assurance Company, for whom I have worked ever since. Twelve weeks ago I was offered the opportunity of advancing myself in the company by moving to London and taking up a more senior post. Accordingly, I arrived here ten weeks ago to begin my duties. For two weeks I lodged with a family at Mildmay Park, then my wife joined me and we moved to a small hotel just north of St Paul's. There we stayed for a further two weeks while we looked for a house to rent. Having inspected several properties, we at length settled on Fourteen, Kendal Terrace as the most satisfactory, and moved in there six weeks ago tomorrow. It is very conveniently situated, only a short distance from Clapham Junction, from where trains run directly to London Bridge.

"Since that time, my new responsibilities at work have kept me very busy, and I have frequently been late getting home in the evening. This has meant, as I remarked, that I have not yet had the opportunity of making the acquaintance of our new neighbours.

"On Monday, Mr Stutchbury, who is my superior, informed me that it would be necessary for someone from the London office to travel to our northern office in Manchester at the end of the week, in order to apprise the manager there of certain decisions which have recently been made. He asked me if I would like to perform this duty and, of course, I was thrilled and honoured to be entrusted with such a task, and at once agreed. It was arranged that I should leave work a little earlier today, and take the afternoon train from Euston to Manchester, where I would be met by Mr Glossop, who is the manager of our northern office. All week I have been looking forward to it. Imagine my dismay, then, when at three o'clock this afternoon a telegram was received, informing us that Mr Glossop and half his staff had gone down with measles, and that he would not, after all, be able to meet me. There was nothing for it but to cancel my journey to the north. I therefore left work at the usual time and, feeling somewhat disappointed, caught the usual train home."

"One moment," interrupted Holmes. "Had you notified your wife that you would, after all, be returning home this evening?"

Claydon shook his head. "There did not seem much point in sending a message to say that I was coming when I should shortly be arriving home in person. I realized, of course, that my wife would be surprised to see me, but the surprise would at least, I hoped, be a pleasant one. On the train home I fell into conversation with a man called Biggins, whose acquaintance I have made over the last six weeks as he also travels between Clapham and London Bridge every day. He was telling me what had befallen a friend of his who kept pullets in his back garden, and as he had not finished the story when we alighted, he invited me to join him at the local hostelry to hear the end of his account. It is not the sort of thing I should normally have done, but I had been feeling somewhat down in the dumps since the cancellation of my trip to Manchester, and, besides, his story was an interesting one – somewhat far-fetched, but fascinating, nonetheless – so I agreed. You will see the relevance of this in a moment.

"My acquaintance took me to a public house not far from Clapham Junction. We were standing near the bar and he had just handed me a glass of beer, when a large man to the side of me had some kind of spasm and fell heavily into me. In his efforts to maintain his balance, he flung out his arm, which knocked the glass from my hand, and spilled the contents all over my clothes. Not only that, but the back of his hand struck me hard on the nose, making my eyes water, and his fingernail scratched my cheek. Still, he was in a worse state than myself, I thought, for he had fallen to the floor in a heap, so I bent down to help him to his feet. Unfortunately, as I did so he abruptly raised his arm, and his elbow caught me a very painful blow in the eye. I stepped back sharply, pressing my hand to my eye, which felt as if it had been dislodged from its socket, and my hat fell off my head. The man on the floor was still trying to rise to his feet, so I stepped back again to get out of his way, and as I did so, I trod on my hat and squashed it flat. At that moment, my nose began to bleed copiously.

"'Oh, bad luck!' cried Biggins in a cheery tone. 'Don't worry about the beer, Claydon – I'll buy you another!' Perhaps understandably, I had quite lost my taste for the whole enterprise, but in order not to appear rude, I acquiesced and stayed just long enough to hear the end of the story, then left the pub and set off for home. It was only a short distance to Kendal Terrace, and as I turned into the street I hoped fervently that none of my neighbours would catch sight of me, for I knew that in my dishevelled state I must present a very unattractive appearance. Fortunately, there were few people about, but I made sure that I had my latch-key ready and in my hand some time before I reached the house, for I wanted to slip in through the front door as quickly as possible. When I put the key in the lock, however, I found to my great surprise that it would not turn. I took it out and examined it, to make sure it was the correct key, then tried it again. Still it would not turn. I banged hard on the door knocker, and as I did so I glanced round. Some people on the other side of the street were staring at me and I began to feel distinctly uncomfortable.

"The door was opened after what seemed an age by a girl I had never seen before in my life, dressed neatly in a maid's uniform. She had evidently put the chain on the door before she opened it, for it only opened a few inches. Upon her face was an odd, sullen sort of expression.

"'What!' I cried in surprise. 'Who are you?'

"'Pardon me,' she returned in an impudent tone, 'but who are *you*?'

"'What do you mean?' I demanded. 'And why is the chain on the door?'

"'To keep out prying busybodies like you!'

"'How dare you!' I cried. 'This is my house!'

"'Oh yes?' said she. 'And I'm the Empress of Japan! Be off with you, and stop being a nuisance to honest folk!'

"For a moment then, as I stood there, my mind seemed to reel in complete confusion, and I could not form a single logical thought, far less utter any aloud. So great was the shock of seeing this perfect stranger in my house that I was utterly dumb-struck. One can respond, adequately or otherwise, to all sorts of strange and surprising situations in which one occasionally finds oneself, but this was literally beyond the bounds of comprehension.

"The silence was broken by a second voice, from within the house.

"'What is it? What *is* going on there?' asked a woman's voice, which sounded older and more cultured than the maid's.

"'There's a dirty-looking rascal at the door, madam,' replied the girl. 'He's trying to force his way into the house.'

"In a moment a second face had appeared above that of the maid, in the narrow gap between the door and the frame. She was a strong-featured woman, about five and thirty years of age. Although she was as much a stranger to me as the maid, there was something vaguely familiar about her appearance, and I wondered if I had seen her about somewhere.

"'Well?' demanded she. 'What is it you want?'

"'Want?' I repeated. 'I want to come in. This is *my* house, and I insist on knowing what you are doing in it!'

"'Don't be absurd!' she returned sharply. 'I've never heard anything so ridiculous in all my life! If you don't stop pestering us this minute, I shall call the police! Yes,' she continued, looking past me and across the road, 'there's a policeman now. Constable!' she called.

"I turned to see a large, formidable figure crossing the road towards us. He came up very close behind me, looming over me as it were, and addressed the woman.

"'Yes, madam?' said he. 'What appears to be the trouble?'

"'This man is making a nuisance of himself,' said she. 'He has tried to force his way into the house, he has frightened my maid, and he will not leave us alone!'

"'Here, you!' said the policeman to me. 'You scoundrel! What's your game?'

"Before I could reply, the woman spoke again. 'He's been drinking,' said she. 'He reeks of alcohol. And he appears to have been in a fight.'

"This is where my mishap in the public house played so unfortunate a part in the matter. Had my appearance been as normal, I might have had a slim chance of persuading the policeman to listen to my side of the matter. But my appearance told against me.

"'Yes, madam,' returned he, in answer to the woman's observations. 'I had noted the gentleman's appearance. You, sir,' he continued, addressing me, 'are you not ashamed of yourself, getting into such a state?'

"'I am not *in* a state,' I retorted with some warmth, but the policeman did not seem to hear.

"'I can assure you, sir, that had you been a common ruffian I should have run you in as soon as look at you. It is evident, however, from your dress' – here he looked me up and down appraisingly – 'that you were once a gentleman. But look at you now! Your hat is ruined, your shirt and waistcoat are stained with beer, your suit is sodden and crumpled. Just think what your poor mother would say if she could see you now!'

"'My mother?' I cried in surprise. 'What the deuce has my mother got to do with it?'

"The policeman held up his hand and frowned, as if admonishing me for speaking so sharply. 'A word of advice, sir: never turn your back on your mother. If you do, you will be turning your back on the truest friend you ever had and will regret it to your dying day.'

"'I am *not* turning my back on my mother,' I cried in exasperation. 'But my mother is irrelevant to the situation. In any case, I am a married man!'

"'Very well, then, sir, consider the feelings of your poor dear wife, waiting at home alone while you stagger about the streets in this intoxicated fashion. Take my advice, sir, go home now, sleep it off, and vow that tomorrow you will make a fresh start!'

"'I am trying to go home!' I protested. '*This* is my home!'

"'What nonsense!' cried the woman. 'Why, I have never seen this man before in my life!'

"The policeman nodded. 'And you, sir?' he asked, turning to me. 'Have you ever seen this lady before?'

"'No, I certainly have not,' I replied vehemently.

"'Well, then? Don't you think you ought to run along and stop making a nuisance of yourself?'

"I hesitated. So monstrously unfair did all this seem that I was quite at a loss for words. Then my eye lit on the sign beside the door. It is a small oblong piece of wood, bearing the name 'Worthing Villa'. I made it myself and put it up just three weeks ago, after I had read an article in a magazine that described how to inscribe lettering on wood with a red-hot poker. My wife and I wished to commemorate the very happy holiday we spent last summer in Worthing.

"'I can prove to you that this is my house,' said I to the policeman. 'You see that sign?'

"'Yes, sir,' he replied cautiously.

"'I made it.'

"The policeman turned his gaze from the sign to me, and I could see at once, from the expression on his face, that I had made a mistake. For although my statement was perfectly true, it must have seemed just the sort of stupid and unbelievable thing that a real liar would have said. So far from establishing the truth of my story, therefore, it merely served to confirm my mendacity in the policeman's eyes.

"'I shall give you one last chance,' said he. 'If you clear off in the next ten seconds, I shall let you go. If you are still here in ten seconds' time, I shall march you straight round to Brixton Police Station, where you will be charged with causing a breach of the peace, and will spend the night in the cells.'

"I could see that he was in earnest. This left me little choice. I hesitated but two seconds of the allotted ten, then turned, ran off down the road, and did not stop running until I had put some distance between me and Kendal Terrace. I felt in a state of complete despair. What had happened to the world? Where was my wife? Where were my own servants?

"I stopped, in a daze, by some shops and looked about me. I was hot and my head was beginning to ache, so I loosened my collar and tie. As I did so, I saw that the nearby butcher's shop, George Lubbock and Son, was still open, although most of the other shops were now closed. This was undoubtedly the shop from which my wife purchased our meat. Perhaps if I explained the situation to the butcher, he could vouch for me and help me to prove that it was not me but the woman in the house that was lying. I put my head in at the shop doorway. There was a man there, scrubbing the chopping block. I coughed to attract his attention and he looked round.

"'I'm closing up,' said he, 'so you'll have to be quick! What do you want?'

"'Are you Mr Lubbock?' I asked.

"'Yes, I'm Lubbock. Why do you want to know?'

"'You don't know me,' I began.

"'That's true,' replied he in a curt fashion, and returned to his scrubbing.

"'No, I mean, we haven't been introduced, but I believe you know my wife. She trades here.'

"The butcher paused in his scrubbing and eyed me curiously. 'Oh?' said he after a moment. 'Where does she live?'

"'Kendal Terrace.'

"'A tall woman, with spectacles?'

"'No.'

"'Well, then, a small woman, with ginger hair?'

"'No, medium-sized, with medium-brown hair.'

"Again the butcher looked at me for a moment.

"'I know your game,' said he at last. 'If you think you're going to walk out of here with a pair of lamb chops unpaid for on the strength of your supposed connection with a woman I've never seen, then you've got another think coming!'

"'No, no,' I said quickly, seeing the way his mind was working. 'I don't want to buy anything.'

"'I'm sure you don't,' said he. 'You're one of those types that always wants something for nothing.'

"'No, you misunderstand me,' I persisted. 'I don't require meat at all.'

"'Oh, don't you? Well, you can clear off, then! Or perhaps you didn't notice that this is a butcher's shop.'

"'If you will just allow me to explain myself,' said I, raising my voice in desperation. 'I would like you to help me establish my identity.'

"'I'll help you establish a thick ear!' returned he in a menacing tone, making his way round the counter, his large scrubbing brush in his hand. I waited no longer to discover what his intentions might be, but admitted defeat, turned and ran once more. No one, it seemed, had any interest in my sad plight.

"Thus I found myself wandering the streets alone, friendless and unrecognized, in what had, but a few hours previously, been my home. Slowly, I made my way back to the centre of town, unable to think what I could do in these changed circumstances. I called in at the offices of the Commercial Fire and Accident, on the off-chance that there might be someone there that knew me, but, as I had expected, the building was all closed up for the night and everyone had gone home. Onward then I wandered, aimless and hopeless, until, as I passed along the Strand, I saw a group of cabbies standing in conversation by a water-trough. On a sudden whim I stopped and asked them if they knew of any private detective who might be able to help an innocent man cast down by mysterious circumstances. After a brief consultation, their collective opinion was that you, Mr Holmes, were the man I should seek out."

"I am glad they reached that conclusion," responded Holmes after a moment. "Your story interests me greatly, Mr Claydon."

"You do believe, then, that what I have told you is true?" asked Claydon in an imploring tone.

"I do not doubt it for an instant."

"Thank the Lord for that! What has happened to me is so strange and terrible that I had begun to doubt that I could ever persuade anyone to believe it! The circumstances must surely be unique!"

Holmes shook his head. "There you are mistaken," said he. "There was an almost identical case reported from Brussels only last year, and something very similar in Copenhagen the year before that."

"Oh?" said Claydon in surprise. "What was the outcome in those cases?"

"As to the Copenhagen case, I am not certain," returned Holmes, "but I believe the house burned down."

"Good Lord!"

"In the Brussels case, however, the rightful occupant of the house, having been denied access at the front door, succeeded in forcing his way into the house through a rear window."

"Good for him!"

"Yes, he displayed a certain enterprise. Unfortunately, having succeeded in entering the house, he was then set upon by the villains within and badly beaten."

"Lord preserve us!"

"Sometimes, as it is said, discretion is indeed the better part of valour. You have taken the wisest course, Mr Claydon, in seeking me out. I, in turn, shall waste no time in enlisting the help of the official force."

"What! The police? Judging by the specimen I encountered, they will not be very interested."

Holmes shook his head. "All the cards were against you earlier," said he, ticking the points off on his fingers. "In the first place, the woman was in possession of the house while you were out on the street. In the second, she was no doubt neatly attired while you were in a state of unaccustomed disarray. And in the third, she spoke with a firmness and authority which you, shocked as you were by these unprecedented events, could not match."

"I'll say," agreed Claydon ruefully.

"I am known to some of the senior men at Brixton Police Station," continued Holmes, "and I am confident they will listen to what I have to say. If we run down there now and give them a sober account of what has happened, I have no doubt that someone will accompany us to Kendal Terrace and help to see that justice is done. Our most immediate need, you see, is not for analytical subtlety, but simply to gain entry to your house, and in such circumstances the presence of a couple of burly policemen must add immeasurably to our side of the argument."

"I understand, sir, and I must say you fill me with hope!" cried Claydon, his eyes shining. "Words cannot express the relief I feel at having unburdened myself of the matter to you. Are you confident of getting to the bottom of it?"

"We shall do our best," replied Holmes with a friendly smile. "Now, if you would care to wash the blood and grime from your face, and to neaten yourself up a little before we set off, Dr Watson would, I am sure, be delighted to show you where you could do it!"

When I returned to the sitting room, Holmes was still seated where I had left him, staring moodily into the hearth.

"What is it?" I asked.

"I am concerned about Claydon's wife," replied my friend.

"You think she may be in danger?"

"That is certainly a possibility, but it is not my chief concern. More likely, I fear, is that she is implicated in the matter in some way. If so, Claydon's day of unpleasant surprises may not yet have run its course."

"Do the other cases you mentioned suggest as much?"

"The testimony of the other cases is inconclusive on the point. In one, the wife did indeed turn out to have been behind the whole business. In the other, she was perfectly innocent of any involvement, but the outcome was still not entirely satisfactory."

"What do you mean?"

"The wife was murdered."

"Good God!"

"You will appreciate why I did not wish to expound on those cases in the presence of my client. However, to return to the present business: the crucial point, it seems to me, is that Mr Claydon was not expected to return home this evening. According to his own testimony, today was to have been the first time in six weeks that he would be absent from the house. It is also the day when strangers appear to have taken over the house. If these two events were purely coincidental the odds against their joint occurrence would be fairly long. It therefore seems likely that they are not simply coincidental, but are linked in some way."

"That is surely almost certain," I agreed.

"And the link between the two events seems most likely to be the wife. She believes that her husband will not be returning for another twenty-four hours, she is in complete control of the house in his absence: surely it must be she who has arranged for these strangers and their servants to be there."

"Perhaps so; but for what purpose? It seems such a very strange and inexplicable thing to have happened that I am not really surprised that Mr Claydon felt he was going mad. What can any of those involved hope to achieve?"

Holmes shook his head. "We are certainly in the dark at present," said he, "and there is little point in speculating. However, I am hopeful that we shall understand the matter a little better before the evening is done. In the meantime we must endeavour to keep my client's spirits buoyed up. I am concerned that his grip on his mental faculties may still be but fragile, and that further shocks may loosen it again. But here is Mr Claydon now, as neat as a new pin, and with an appearance of resolve upon his features that suggests he is ready to step once more into the fray! Your hat, Watson! We leave at once!"

In a minute the three of us were in a growler, and making our way across the centre of town in the evening sunshine.

"Pray, tell me something of your family," said Holmes to his client as we rattled along. "Do they all still reside in Northampton?"

"Yes. My mother and father still live in the house in which I grew up. I have one brother, who is a commercial traveller in the shoe trade. He and his wife live just five minutes' walk from my parents' house, near where I lived when I was first married."

"How long have you been married?"

"Two years this month."

"And your wife, I believe you said, is also from Northampton?"

Claydon nodded. "It is there that we were married."

"Had you known her for very long before your marriage?"

"Several years."

"You will be familiar, then, with her family?"

"Indeed I am. I know them almost as well as I know my own family. Her father has a position of some importance with one of the shoe manufacturers in the town. She also has a brother and sister. The sister, Joan, is several years younger, and is away at boarding school. The brother, Leonard, is just a couple of years younger than Lucy. Eighteen months ago he took himself off to America, rather against his parents' wishes, I might say. We did not hear anything from him for a long time after that and feared that he had come to grief, but he appears to be established now, for the last we heard of him, he was living in New York, and studying law."

"I see," said Holmes, nodding his head. "I think that that gives us a clear enough picture of your immediate relations. Your domestic staff, now: what servants do you keep at Kendal Terrace?"

"Just two. We have an excellent cook, Rosemary Quinn, who also acts as housekeeper and helps my wife with sundry matters. She is very experienced and a particularly good pastry cook. Our only other servant is a young girl, Susan Townley. She is a local girl – her parents live at Battersea – and it is her first position. Susan is in many ways the opposite of Rosemary: she is very inexperienced and sometimes seems to know nothing about anything, but she is a sweet-natured girl and very willing to learn, so we are quite satisfied with her."

We had crossed Westminster Bridge while they had been speaking and passed down the Kennington Road towards Brixton. The traffic in the streets had thinned a little as we left the centre of town behind, but the fine weather seemed to have encouraged half of London to leave their houses and take the air, for the pavements were crowded with all manner of folk, strolling along arm in arm in the evening sunshine, or standing in small groups at street corners, gossiping. There was evidently some sporting event taking place at the Oval, for a sizeable crowd was milling about there, spilling from the pavements onto the road. Past this crowd we rattled, and on down the Brixton Road, and I found myself thinking how incongruous it was that on this beautiful evening, we should be journeying to investigate such a strange and mysterious business.

We soon reached Brixton Police Station, where Claydon and I remained in the cab while Holmes went inside. In less than five minutes he was back out again, accompanied by a large, broad-chested man in a braided uniform.

"This is Inspector Spencer, Mr Claydon," said Holmes. "He and two of his men will follow us in their own vehicle. I have given him an outline of the matter, and am confident that with his help it will soon be resolved."

As he spoke, a police van drawn by two black horses emerged with a clatter from a yard to the side of the police station.

"Right-ho, Mr Holmes," said the inspector. "Lead on and we shall follow!"

When we turned into Kendal Terrace a few minutes later, the evening sun was slanting into the street from the far end, casting a golden glow upon the houses. There was no one about save a small group of men at the corner, standing in idle conversation. They glanced at us with little curiosity as we passed, but looked round with somewhat keener interest at the police van that followed us into the street.

Kendal Terrace consisted of two identical rows of flat-fronted, pleasantly proportioned houses, which faced each other across the dusty street. We pulled up before a house about halfway along on the right-hand side. A short flight of steps led up to the front door, and affixed to the wall immediately to the right of the door was the small wooden sign that identified it as Worthing Villa. Claydon waited until our party was assembled on the pavement, then led the way up the steps. Having reached the front door, however, he seemed hesitant of proceeding.

"Try your key in the lock," prompted Holmes in an encouraging tone.

"It did not work last time," returned Claydon dubiously, fishing the key from his pocket, and slipping it into the lock. Next moment, however, the key had turned and the door had opened without difficulty. With an expression of surprise upon his face, Claydon led the way into the hall. "Everything appears in order," said he, looking about him. For a moment, he stood at the foot of the stairs and called, "Hello!" very loudly, but no answer came and the house had that air of complete silence, which unoccupied buildings always possess.

"I am a busy man," declared Inspector Spencer in a loud voice, standing in the hall and peering up the stairs. "I must say I have never known you to waste police time before, Mr Holmes, but it is clear that nothing is amiss here. Perhaps your client has been suffering from a mental delusion of some kind."

"One moment, Spencer," returned Holmes. "Let us take a quick look about, before we reach any conclusions!" He pushed open a door on the right of the hall and we entered a neat and pleasant sitting room. Through the window, which overlooked the street outside, I could see that the crowd of loafers had followed us along the street and were now standing outside the window, staring in at us. I glanced about. The room was well furnished, with comfortable-looking sofas and chairs. Against the wall opposite the window was a piano, on the top of which was a photograph of a child in a silver frame. On a small table beside one of the chairs a tray had been set with tea things. There was a teapot on the tray and two cups, which were both half full of tea. Beside the tray on the table was a large glass vase containing some pink flowers. In the alcove to the right of the fireplace was a highly polished tallboy, and in the alcove on the left was a bureau, above which, on a shelf, was a pretty little brass clock. There was another, larger clock made of some dark wood on the mantelpiece. Beside this clock were numerous small ornaments, and above it, on the chimney breast, hung a large framed print of a church.

My survey of the room was interrupted by a sharp cry from beside me.

"That picture!" cried Claydon, pointing at the picture of the church above the mantelpiece. "What is it doing there?"

"Is it not usually there?" asked Holmes, looking up from something he was examining closely on the floor.

Claydon shook his head. "It is not usually anywhere," he returned with emphasis. "I have never seen it before in my life!"

Holmes stood up, lifted the picture carefully from the wall and turned it over. On the back was a small label on which was printed "St Paul's".

"It doesn't look much like St Paul's to me," remarked Inspector Spencer with a snort.

"I think we may take it that it is a different St Paul's from the one you are familiar with, Spencer," said Holmes. "Do you recognize the church, Mr Claydon?"

"No. I have never seen it before," returned the other. "And who on earth is this?" he cried, picking up the framed photograph of a child from the top of the piano.

"It is not anyone you know?" queried Holmes.

"Certainly not."

"It could not perhaps be an old photograph of someone you know only as an adult – your wife, for instance?"

"No. This child looks quite different from anyone I have ever seen." He held the photograph out for us to see. In it, a little girl, perhaps six or seven years of age, was standing against a painted backdrop of trees, holding a doll. Between the photograph and the frame was a cream-coloured mount, and across the bottom of this, in pencil, had been inscribed "Victoria, O Victoria".

"How very curious," remarked Holmes, but he was interrupted by another sharp cry from Claydon.

"My flowers!" cried he all at once, picking up the glass vase from the table. "Someone has removed all the roses and left only the other flowers!"

"Perhaps they were past their best and were thrown out," suggested Inspector Spencer without much interest.

"No, no!" insisted Claydon. "I bought them only yesterday, at a stall near London Bridge station, on my way home from work. They were very fresh and bright. Someone has taken them!"

"Why should anyone take a bunch of flowers?" asked the policeman.

"Let us look in the other rooms before we begin to formulate any theories," said Holmes, leading the way back into the hall. To the left of the sitting-room door was another, similar door, which Claydon informed us was that of the dining room. He pushed this door open, but stopped abruptly in the doorway with a strangled cry.

"What is it?" asked Holmes, and on receiving no reply, squeezed past the young man into the room. "Here's something more serious for you to consider, Inspector," said he as we followed him in.

In the centre of the floor, to the side of the dining table, a man in a dark suit lay on his back on the carpet. His arms were folded across his breast, and upon them lay a bunch of red roses.

"Stand back, everyone," cried the policeman. "It's clear there's been some mischief here."

"I am a doctor," I said. "May I examine him?"

"Why certainly," returned Spencer. "I was not aware we had a medical man with us."

I crouched down and examined the still figure for any sign of life, but there was none.

"He has been dead a little while," I said, as I concluded my examination, "perhaps for two or three hours, but not longer than four or five, I should say."

"Do you see any indication of the cause of death?" asked Holmes.

I shook my head. "There are no obvious signs, and certainly no signs of violence."

"Could he have been poisoned?" asked Spencer.

"I can't be certain," I replied, "but I don't think so. A more thorough examination may, of course, turn something up. At a guess, though, I'd say he had had some kind of heart seizure."

"Are these your missing flowers?" Holmes asked Claydon. "Then that is one little mystery solved, anyhow," he continued, as the young man nodded his head. "Do you recognize this unfortunate fellow?"

Claydon shook his head vigorously. "I have never seen him before in my life," said he.

"Hum! I see that the cover of his watch is open and the glass is broken," remarked Holmes as he examined the lifeless figure. "That suggests the possibility that he fell to the floor and crushed the watch as he did so, which would tend to support your view of a sudden seizure, Watson. There are no shards of glass in the waistcoat pocket, however, so the watch was clearly out of the pocket when he fell. Either he was consulting it at the time, or it slipped out as he fell. But the watch-pocket is a tight one," he continued, feeling in the pocket with his fingers, and trying the watch in it. "Therefore it could not have slipped out, and therefore he was consulting it at the time."

"What does that prove?" asked Spencer in a dismissive tone.

"It helps us to build up an accurate picture of what occurred in the house earlier," returned Holmes, who was examining the watch very closely, through his magnifying lens.

"My theory," said the policeman in a sarcastic tone, "is that he was consulting his watch because he wanted to know what the time was. I do not see the point as being of any importance whatever," he continued, bending down and feeling in the dead man's pockets. "Ah! This is what I am after!" he remarked, as he withdrew a leather pocket book. "This should tell us something a little more interesting about this unfortunate gentleman than whether he looked at his watch or not before he died, such as what his name is."

For several minutes, the policeman leafed through the contents of the pocket book, turning out tickets, receipts and the like, but evidently, as I judged from his silence, no indication of their owner's name.

"His cufflinks bear the initials P. S.," remarked Holmes at length, as he continued to examine the body closely.

What on earth was this man doing here, in the house of a total stranger, I wondered, as I went over and over the matter in my head, trying to make sense of it. My thoughts were interrupted, however, as another cry came from Claydon, who had been standing in stupefied silence for some time. I looked up and saw that he was staring out of the window, which overlooked a narrow back garden.

"There's another one!" cried he. "Out in the garden!"

I stepped quickly to the window. In the middle of the garden was a scrubby patch of lawn, and in the very centre of this was the still figure of a man in a brown suit, lying upon his back, his face staring up at the sky.

"Saints preserve us!" cried Inspector Spencer. "This place is like a charnel house! It is clear that there's more to this business than meets the eye! Are you sure you know nothing about it?" he abruptly demanded of Claydon in an aggressive tone.

"I assure you I know no more than you do, Inspector," the young man replied, an expression of bewilderment upon his features.

"Come along!" said Holmes. "Let's take a look at the fellow outside!"

We passed through the hall and into a small back room, where a door gave onto a short flight of steps to the garden. We had just reached the lawn, Claydon and Spencer close behind us, when, to my very great surprise, the figure on the lawn abruptly sat up and looked at us. Claydon let out a cry of alarm, and the policeman muttered some oath under his breath. The man before us, who appeared about thirty years of age, yawned, stretched and rubbed his eyes in a casual and unconcerned sort of way. A moment later, he stood up and brushed himself down.

"Hello there," he began in a friendly tone. "Who might you gentlemen be?" Then, as if he had all at once recalled something, he glanced about him, an expression of puzzlement upon his features. "Where am I?" he asked of no one in particular. "And what am I doing here?"

"That is what *we* should very much like to know," returned the policeman in a stern tone. "Who *are* you?"

"Me?" returned the other in surprise. "You must excuse me," he added, rubbing his eyes again. "I have been asleep." He pulled a small card from his breast pocket and handed it to the policeman. "Falk of the *Standard*," said he.

"Well, Mr Linton Falk," said Inspector Spencer, reading from the card, "just what are you doing here?"

Again the other man looked about him. "I can't tell you what I'm doing here," he returned at last, "for, to be honest, I don't know where I am. But I can tell you what I was doing earlier."

"We are all ears," said the policeman, whereupon Falk explained that he had received a letter that morning at the newspaper office. This had informed him that if he wanted to learn something of very great public interest, he should come to 14, Kendal Terrace, North Clapham, at five o'clock in the afternoon.

"Who sent the letter?" interrupted Holmes.

"A woman calling herself 'Mrs Robson', although she admitted that that was not her real name."

"Do you get many such letters?"

"A few. It is usually fairly easy to detect if the writer is simply a crank, with nothing of interest to say. This letter was different, and I thought it might be worth looking into, as did my chief."

"Do you have the letter with you?"

"I should have," replied the newspaperman, feeling in his pockets, "but it's gone. Someone must have taken it."

"Very well. Pray, continue with your account."

"I arrived at the address given a little after the time stated, and was admitted into the parlour by a maid. Several minutes passed before the lady of the house entered the room. She was a tall woman, with strong features. She seemed very agitated, and was breathing very heavily, but I put this down to nervousness. She identified herself as the 'Mrs Robson' who had written to me, and said that another guest she had been expecting had been delayed and would not be arriving for a further ten minutes. She would rather not go into the matter until this other person arrived, she said, at which point I privately began to wonder if she was not perhaps, after all, a deranged crank with no information of interest. However, there was something in her manner and speech, some refinement or education, which persuaded me to at least wait until this other person arrived before making a decision as to whether to leave or not. In my profession, one encounters a large number of strangers, and one learns instinctively to assess them and to assess the information they might possess. In this case, I was convinced that

'Mrs Robson', as she continued to call herself, was sincere, and that her intentions were considered and serious.

"A few moments after 'Mrs Robson' had entered the parlour, the maid returned with a tea tray, which she set down on a little table. She poured out the tea and handed me a cup, as 'Mrs Robson' began to ask me about parliamentary reporting in general, and whether I had ever found that the private lives of Members of Parliament impinged upon their public duties."

The newspaperman paused. "Do you know," he said after a moment: "I can't remember anything I said to her. It has all quite gone from my head. All I remember is hearing her voice, going on at some length, although I cannot recall what she was saying, either. I do remember her taking the teacup and saucer from my hand, but after that, all is a blank, until your arrival just now woke me up. I can only suppose that I fell asleep as she was speaking to me, incredible though that seems. I feel rested enough now, anyhow," he continued in a more vigorous tone, rubbing his hands together, "and ready for anything! But you haven't told me who you are, nor what you are doing here. I can see that this gentleman is a policeman, but what is happening? And where are we?"

"One moment," said Holmes. "Did you find that the tea you were given was somewhat bitter?"

"Why, yes, it was," returned Falk in surprise. "She explained that the maid had made it a little too strong, and offered me more sugar, which I took. Even then it was not the best cup of tea I have ever had, but I drank it out of politeness."

"I think it likely that a few drops of chloral, or something similar, had been added to your cup before it was brought into the room. Would you agree, Watson?"

"Definitely," I replied. "Just a few drops of chloral are generally sufficient to induce a deep, refreshing sleep, and it does have a decidedly bitter taste. A chemical analysis of the remains in the teacup will no doubt confirm the matter if necessary."

"Quite so," said Holmes. "As to where we are," he continued, turning to Falk, "we are in the garden of the house you called at earlier, 14, Kendal Terrace. This gentleman is Mr Claydon, whose house it is. He arrived home from work today to find that his wife and servants had disappeared and strangers had taken over the house. No doubt the woman you saw, who called herself 'Mrs Robson', was one of them. We have only recently arrived and have found a dead man in one of the downstairs rooms."

"What!" cried Falk.

"What do you know of the matter?" demanded the policeman fiercely.

"Nothing whatever, I assure you. My whole connection with the place is as I described to you. During the short time that I was in the house, I never saw any man, just the lady and her maid."

"Come and take a look at him," said Holmes, "and you can tell us if it is anyone you know."

"Certainly," returned Falk, "although I should think it highly unlikely."

Claydon went to make a quick survey of the rest of the house as we followed Holmes back into the dining room. The newspaperman leaned down and scrutinized the dead man's face for a moment, then I saw his mouth fall open with surprise.

"Do you recognize him?" asked Holmes.

"I cannot be certain," returned Falk, frowning, "but I think it may well be Percival Slattery, Member of Parliament for New Bromwich in the Midlands."

"You must be right," said Holmes, nodding his head, "for the initials P. S. are on his cufflinks."

"Good Lord!" I cried. "What on earth is a Member of Parliament doing here?"

"You know something of him?" Holmes asked Linton Falk.

"A little. We have never been personally introduced, but I have heard him deliver a speech or two. As you may know, he has a reputation for being extremely radical. When he was first elected, he announced that he would be 'the New Broom from New Bromwich', and declared that it was his intention to sweep away 'the cobwebs of history which the centuries have bequeathed us'. He has made a great show of supporting those whom he considers to be downtrodden or oppressed, which is no doubt admirable, but there has always lurked the suspicion that he has done so more with a view to drawing public attention to himself than in order to actually alleviate anyone else's hardship. His speeches have always been very flowery and have certainly roused his audiences, but their content has often been slight, so that his opponents generally refer to him as 'the New Bombast from New Bromwich'."

Claydon returned from his survey of the house as Falk finished speaking. He shook his head when Holmes asked if he had found anything more amiss. "Everything seems in order upstairs," said he, "but of my wife and servants there is no sign."

"Did you notice if the woman who denied you entry earlier had a Midlands accent?" Holmes asked him.

"I do not think so," replied Claydon with a shake of the head. "I am familiar with most Midlands accents, and hers was quite different. I could not quite place it."

"I would agree with that," interjected Falk. "The woman I saw – if it was the same woman – certainly did not have a Midlands accent. Besides, if you are thinking of a possible connection with Slattery's Midlands constituency, you are barking up the wrong tree, for he himself does not come from those parts, and had probably never been there before he became MP for New Bromwich. As far as I remember, he was born and bred in Australia."

"This is getting us nowhere," interrupted Inspector Spencer in an impatient tone. "I shall have to make arrangements to have the body removed at once. And then you, Mr Linton Falk, must accompany me to the police station, to answer further questions."

"Me?" cried the newspaperman. "But I have told you all I know. I have nothing more to add."

"We shall see about that. If you will not come willingly, I shall arrest you, and you will be taken there under guard."

"Arrest me?" repeated Falk. "On what grounds, pray?"

"On the grounds that you were found to be present on premises where a suspicious death has occurred, and that you are obstructing the police in the execution of their duties."

The newspaperman began to protest in the strongest terms at this, and the exchange between the two of them quickly became heated. Holmes, meanwhile, after standing a moment in thoughtful silence, had slipped from the dining-room, and into the sitting-room. Two minutes later, when I was just about to see where he had got to, he returned, a glint of triumph in his eye.

"What is it, Mr Holmes?" asked Inspector Spencer, breaking off from his dispute with Falk. "You look pleased about something."

"The situation has become clearer to me."

"Oh? Have I missed some clue, then?"

"That is not for me to say."

"Well, then, what do you consider the most significant clue?"

"The matter of the clocks."

"What 'matter'?"

"As you have probably observed, there is no clock here in the dining room, but there are two in the sitting room, both showing the correct time."

"What of it?"

"That is it. You asked what I had found the most significant clue, and I have now told you. It is undoubtedly the business of the clocks – in conjunction, of course, with the watch and the slivers of glass on the sitting-room carpet. What? You did not observe them? They are there, I can assure you, near the little table on which the tea things are laid."

"All this seems nonsense to me," snorted the policeman. "We have a dead man on the floor in here and a suspicious character found in the garden" – at this Falk began to protest again, but Spencer ignored him – "and the fact that someone has broken a glass in another room seems neither here nor there to me!"

"I think, Inspector," began Holmes, but he stopped as there came a sudden sharp rat-a-tat-tat at the front door. The inspector hurried to open it, and found one of his constables there.

"I've got two women here, sir," said he to his superior, "who claim that they live in this house."

Before Spencer could reply, a young woman in a grey costume and bonnet pushed past the constable and in at the front door. Her small, pretty face, framed by tightly curled brown hair, bore an expression that spoke both of fatigue and determination. "Henry!" she called out loudly as she reached the hall. "What on earth is going on?"

"Lucy!" cried Claydon, a note of overwhelming relief in his voice, as he ran forward to greet her. "Where in Heaven's name have you been? I have been so worried."

"I have had a terrible, exhausting day," replied the woman. She turned and waved to another woman, who was struggling to get past the constable on the doorstep. "Come along, Rosemary!" she called.

"This is my wife," said Claydon to us, "and here," he added as the other woman, taller and more angular than the first, pushed past the constable, "is Rosemary, our housekeeper."

Mrs Claydon looked from one to the other of us, an expression of puzzlement upon her features. "Who are all these men, Henry? What are they doing here? Why are there policemen outside? Why are you not in Manchester?"

"I, too, have had a terrible experience," returned her husband. "I should not go in there," he added quickly as she made to push open the dining-room door, but he was too late to stop her. She marched into the room and the next moment the air was rent by a piercing scream, which faded away abruptly and ended with a dull thud.

"What is it, madam?" cried the housekeeper, rushing forward impulsively into the room. "Oh, my goodness!" she cried in a wailing tone. "There is a strange man in here, and Mrs Claydon has fainted!"

I hurried after them and found Rosemary bending over her mistress, who lay insensible on the floor, beside the body of the dead man. "Have you any *sal volatile* in the house?" I called to Claydon. "Then fetch it at once, and some brandy, too!"

The next quarter of an hour was a period of some confusion, but there were some positive achievements. Mrs Claydon was eventually restored to her senses, and gradually recovered her composure, and Inspector Spencer directed the removal of the body, which was taken away in the police van. Outside in the street, meanwhile, a large crowd had now gathered, pressing forward to peer in through the sitting-room window, and through the front door each time it was opened, perfectly heedless of the exhortations of the single constable who remained on duty there that there was nothing to be seen and that they should all move along at once.

At length, perhaps half an hour after Claydon's wife had arrived, we were all gathered in the sitting room, Holmes and I, Claydon and his wife, Inspector Spencer, Linton Falk, and the housekeeper, Rosemary Quinn.

"Let us all share whatever information we possess," said Holmes, who had taken charge of the situation, "and see if we cannot shed some light on what has happened here today! I shall begin by recounting what befell your husband," he continued, addressing Mrs Claydon, "and no doubt he will correct me if I go astray.

"His arrangement to travel to Manchester was cancelled at the last minute, owing to ill-health in the northern office. This occurred just before he was leaving work, so he thought it unnecessary to notify you of the change as he would be home himself shortly. On the way home, however, he had a mishap which resulted in a glass of beer being spilt all over him, and during which he also received a series of accidental blows to the face – he can give you the details later – the upshot of which was that his appearance slipped somewhat below his usual standard. When he arrived home, he found that his key would not turn in the lock. As it has since worked perfectly well, it is probable that someone had simply engaged the safety catch inside the door, but he had no way of knowing that at the time. When he knocked at the door, it was answered by a parlour maid he had never seen before, who was shortly joined on the threshold by her mistress, a woman who was likewise unknown to him. They refused to admit him to the house, which they claimed was their abode, and dismissed his own claim upon the house as a lie. A passing policeman was summoned to aid them in getting rid of him, who, seeing the respectable appearance of those in the house and the somewhat less respectable appearance of Mr Claydon, incorrectly, but perhaps understandably, took the part of the former against the latter, and threatened Mr Claydon with arrest if he did not absent himself promptly. Realizing that further protest was useless, he did as the policeman requested, arriving to consult me some time later in a state of bewilderment and shock.

"Mr Falk, meanwhile, who is employed by the *Standard* as a parliamentary and general reporter, received a letter this morning, signed by someone calling herself Mrs Robson, which informed him that if he wished to learn something of great public interest, he should call at this house at five o'clock in the afternoon. When he arrived, he was shown into this room and offered a cup of tea. Some narcotic had evidently been added to his cup, however, for he quickly fell into a deep sleep, from which he did not awaken for several hours, at which time he found himself lying on the lawn in the garden.

"When Dr Watson and I arrived here, with Mr Claydon and Inspector Spencer from Brixton Police Station, we found the body of a man upon the dining-room floor, who was subsequently identified as Percival Slattery, the well-known radical Member of Parliament for New Bromwich. There was no clear indication of how he had met his death. In this room, a strange, unknown picture had been hung upon the wall above the fireplace, and a framed photograph placed upon the piano. Some flowers had also been removed from a vase and placed upon the breast of the dead man in the other room, as a mark, no doubt, of respect. Nothing else in the house appears to have been touched.

"Now, Mrs Claydon," Holmes continued after a moment. "Pray, give us a brief account of your day."

"Very well," said she. "At about ten o'clock this morning, I received a telegram from my brother, Lenny. It had been sent from Portsmouth."

"But that cannot be!" interrupted Claydon. "Lenny is in New York, studying law!"

"I know that as well as you do," returned his wife in a pathetic tone, "but I thought that perhaps some sudden misfortune had befallen him and driven him back home. The telegram asked me to come at once to Portsmouth, where he would meet me at the railway station and explain to me then how matters stood. Concerned that he might be in some terrible difficulties, I set off within the quarter-hour and reached

Portsmouth in the early afternoon. There was no sign of Lenny there, and after waiting fretfully on a bench on the platform for nearly forty minutes, I gave my name to an official, and asked if any message had been left there for me. After hunting about the office for a while and consulting with his colleagues, he at length was able to show me a note which had been handed in late that morning, addressed to 'Mrs Claydon, passenger – care of the station master'. I opened it and found it was from Lenny. He expressed regret for the trouble he was causing me, but said that he had been obliged to go on to Southampton, and asked that I join him there, when he would explain what was afoot. I did as he asked, reaching Southampton about tea-time. There I waited for a further hour and a half, but there was no sign of my brother, nor any message left for me. Eventually, I gave up all hope of seeing him, and caught a train back to London. When I reached Waterloo station, I met Rosemary, who had recently arrived there herself, and we came home here together."

"Do you have the telegram your brother sent?" asked Holmes.

Mrs Claydon shook her head. "The last time I can recall seeing it was when I was waiting at Portsmouth, so I think I must have left it there."

"No matter," said Holmes. "Do you have the note he left for you at Portsmouth?"

"Yes, I have that," said she. "Here it is."

She handed a folded sheet of paper to Holmes, who glanced at it for a moment and then held it up so we could all see it. It was a very brief missive, containing the message she had described to us and no more.

"Is this definitely your brother's hand?" asked Holmes, examining the script closely.

"I believe so," replied Mrs Claydon. "Are you suggesting that it might be a forgery?"

"Well, it is possible, is it not, that the sole purpose of the telegram and note was to get you out of the house and keep you away from London for as long as possible? Do you have a recent letter of your brother's from America, so that we could compare the handwriting?"

Mrs Claydon opened the top of the bureau, extracted a long white envelope, and passed it to Holmes. He took out the letter and held it up beside the note.

"It is close enough," said he, "although it would not be too difficult to counterfeit your brother's hand in so short a note. However, the issue is not a crucial one: if you hear nothing further from your brother, as I suspect, we may take it that, however cleverly done, this note is indeed a forgery. Let us move on now to our last witness, Miss Rosemary Quinn."

"My account will not take long, sir," began the housekeeper. "About three hours after Mrs Claydon had left, a telegram arrived here, addressed to me. It was, I found, from Mrs Claydon herself, and had been sent from Portsmouth railway station. It instructed me to take five pounds from the tobacco jar on the mantelpiece and bring it at once to Portsmouth. I packed the maid, Susan, off to her parents' house at Battersea – she is a mere slip of a girl, and I could not leave her here alone all day – and set off at once. I caught the first train I could, but when I reached Portsmouth, there was no sign of Mrs Claydon. I waited for nearly an hour by the station entrance, then I enquired at the booking office if they knew anything of the matter. Eventually someone there remembered that a woman of that name had waited there for some time about lunch time, but had eventually left for Southampton. I asked if she had left any message for me, but was informed that she had not. I could not think what to do for the best then. I waited a little longer, but eventually decided I would have to give up and return home. It seemed pointless to follow Mrs Claydon to Southampton, for I did not know whereabouts she might be there, and I thought it very unlikely that I would find her. When I got back to Waterloo, I saw that a train was due from Southampton shortly, so I decided to wait and see if Mrs Claydon was on it. To my relief, she was, but I could see at once that her day had been even more tiring and fruitless than my own."

"Presumably," said Holmes, addressing Mrs Claydon, "you sent no telegram from Portsmouth."

"No, I did not," returned she with emphasis.

"Do you have the telegram?" Holmes asked Miss Quinn.

The housekeeper shook her head, an expression of regret upon her face. "I took it with me," said she, "but I think I must have left it on the train, for now I can't find it anywhere."

"Well, well, it is not important," said Holmes. "Does anyone else have anything to add?"

There was a general murmuring of voices. The housekeeper went to make a pot of tea, as a discussion of the day's happenings began.

"If you ask me," remarked Claydon at length, "the whole business is sheer lunacy! These strange people come in here, take over my house for a while, and then leave again. What could be more pointless and insane than that?"

"They didn't all leave again," interjected Inspector Spencer. "One of them was still here when we arrived, if you recall, lying on the dining-room floor."

"That's horrible!" cried Mrs Claydon.

"Horrible or not, madam, it is true, nevertheless. It may be that while they were here, these people fell out for some reason, there was violence, and the man, Slattery – if it is indeed he – was murdered."

"But there were no signs of violence on him," observed Claydon.

"Well, perhaps they poisoned him," returned the policeman in a vague tone. "After all, poisoning was rather in their line, seeing as how they slipped something unpleasant into Mr Falk's drink – or so he says."

"That's what puzzles me," said Falk, "why they should summon me here, only to give me some kind of sleeping-draught almost as soon as I arrived, and then dump me unceremoniously in the back garden!"

"That's part of the lunacy of it all," agreed Claydon, nodding his head. "None of it makes any sense!"

"Anyhow, I'd best be off, if no one objects," said Falk, rising to his feet and looking enquiringly at the policeman. "I'll have to write a report on Percy Slattery's death pretty quickly, otherwise I'll not get it into the morning edition. What is it, Mr Holmes?"

My friend had held his hand up as the housekeeper entered the room with a large tray containing two teapots and a pile of cups and saucers.

"Stay a moment," said Holmes, "and take tea with us."

"I don't know," replied Falk in a dubious tone. "The last time I had tea here, it didn't entirely agree with me."

"I think the experience this time will be somewhat more stimulating," said Holmes with a chuckle.

I had observed that while the others had been discussing the day's events, Holmes had remained in silent thought, as if weighing the matter up. Now, as was clear to me who knew his habits well, it was as if he had reached a decision. What he was about to do or say, I had no idea at all, but that the next few minutes would be highly interesting, I could not doubt.

I watched as the housekeeper poured out the tea and passed round the cups. She had also brought in a plate of small cakes, which she placed on the little table by my chair. For some moments Holmes regarded these cakes, a thoughtful expression upon his face.

"Surely you have made a mistake," said he abruptly to the housekeeper, as she made to withdraw from the room.

"Sir?" responded she in a puzzled tone, looking from Holmes to the plate of cakes.

"No, not in the confectionery," said he, shaking his head. "They appear excellent, and I am sure they are, for I understand that you are a first-rate pastry cook."

"Thank you, sir."

"But in your account of the telegram you received."

"Sir?"

"You mentioned that the telegram instructed you to remove a sum of money from the tobacco jar on the mantelpiece and take it to Portsmouth. Is that correct?"

"Yes, sir."

"Is that the jar in question?" asked Holmes, indicating a small barrel-shaped jar made of two different types of wood, which stood on the corner of the mantelpiece.

"Yes, sir."

"Now, the instruction about the tobacco jar might seem reasonable if the telegram in question had in fact been sent by Mrs Claydon, but we know that it was not. It was therefore sent by a stranger, intent, presumably, on luring everyone away from the house. But how could this stranger know that Mrs Claydon kept a reserve of money in the tobacco jar on the mantelpiece? It is hardly a general rule in every household in the land."

"No, sir. I don't know, sir," responded the housekeeper, glancing at her employer.

"It's no good anyone looking at me," remarked Mrs Claydon. "I can't shed any light on it, for I didn't send the telegram."

"Have you told anyone about the money in the tobacco jar?" asked Holmes.

"Certainly not," replied Mrs Claydon.

"Then how could anyone know about it?" Holmes asked the housekeeper again.

"I don't know, sir."

"Is it possible, do you think, that you have misremembered the matter, and that the telegram did not actually mention the tobacco jar at all?" queried Holmes. "Perhaps it merely instructed you to bring some money, without specifically mentioning where the money was to be found. Could that have been the case?"

I saw the housekeeper hesitate and frown, but I could not tell what was passing in her mind.

"Perhaps, sir," said she at length.

"But you are not certain upon the point?"

"No, sir, I *am* certain. I remember now: it did *not* mention the tobacco jar, but of course I knew that was where Mrs Claydon kept the money."

"I see. Some people might think it surprising that in a communication which was doubtless less than a dozen words, you should have been unsure as to whether the words 'tobacco jar' occurred or not, but I pass over that. The message instructed you to take five pounds from the jar. Is that correct?"

"Yes, sir."

"And was that amount in the jar?"

"Yes, sir."

"In sovereigns?"

"Yes, sir."

"Here is another mystery, then: how could a stranger to the household have known that such a sum would be available?

There cannot be many households in which a sum as large as five pounds is left in an unlocked jar on a mantelpiece."

"No, sir; it is a lot of money. I was anxious all the time I had it with me, in case I lost any of it, and gave it over to Mrs Claydon as soon as we met, at Waterloo station. I took very great care of it, sir."

"I do not doubt it, but that is not the point at issue, which is, rather, how anyone outside of this household could have known of the money. Of course, if such a telegram had in fact been sent by Mrs Claydon, the question would not arise, as she must be presumed to know how much money is in her own house, but Mrs Claydon did not send the telegram. You see the problem?"

"Yes, sir," responded the housekeeper, nodding her head.

"Fortunately, I have a solution."

"Sir?"

"Yes. What I suggest is that the telegram stipulated neither the tobacco jar nor the sum of five pounds, nor, for that matter, Portsmouth, nor anything else that you mentioned, for the simple reason that the telegram never existed. It is a figment of your imagination, designed to explain your own apparent absence from the house this afternoon."

"No, sir!" cried the housekeeper in protest, taking a step backwards.

"I imagine that you waited until the maid, Susan, was busy elsewhere in the house, then you opened the front door and rattled the knocker yourself. Moments later, you informed her that a telegram had arrived for you, necessitating a journey to Portsmouth, and that she would therefore have to return home for the day. She is very young, I understand, and would accept what you told her without query. Once she was out of the way, your plan could proceed."

"No, sir! It's not true!" cried the housekeeper.

"I further suggest that you did not travel to Portsmouth at all, but were busy in London all afternoon. Later you went down to Waterloo station specifically to intercept Mrs Claydon, which you thought would help to confirm your make-believe story."

"Madam!" cried the housekeeper, turning to her employer in entreaty. "This is unjust! Why is this gentleman accusing me?"

"You have a sister, I believe?" continued Holmes, ignoring the woman's protest.

At this she hesitated. Her mouth opened, but she did not speak.

"Come, come," said Holmes in a genial tone. "It is no crime in this country to have a sister. You need not fear arrest on the grounds of having a sister. You have a sister?"

"Yes, sir," responded the housekeeper at length, in a reluctant tone.

"Her name, I believe, is Violet," continued Holmes.

The housekeeper's jaw dropped, her eyes opened wide with surprise and fear and she flung her hands up to her face.

"How can you know that?" asked she in a strained, cracked voice.

"It is my business to know things," responded Holmes calmly, regarding her face very closely. "They are pretty names, Violet and Rosemary. Your parents must have been very fond of wild flowers. Your sister, Violet, was, I believe, married to Percival Slattery in 1870, that is to say, seventeen years ago. He later deserted her and treated her very shamefully."

For a moment, the housekeeper seemed to sway unsteadily on her feet, then she fell to her knees on the floor, clutched her head in her hands and burst into a storm of sobbing.

"Is this true, Rosemary?" asked Henry Claydon after a moment.

She tried to answer, but was sobbing so heavily and loudly that she was unable to form the words. Instead, she nodded her head vigorously.

"Perhaps you could describe to us exactly what occurred today," suggested Holmes in a soft, kindly tone, "and then we might understand it a little better."

Again the housekeeper nodded her head, but it was several minutes before she had composed herself sufficiently to begin her account. Then, seated on a chair that Claydon had brought in for her from the dining room, she made the following statement:

"My sister, Violet, is two years older than me. She and I were born and raised here in London, the only children of Patrick and Mary Quinn. When she was fourteen and I was twelve, the family moved to Melbourne, Australia, where my father had hopes of good employment in the gold fields. I became a kitchen maid, then later cook, in the household of Colonel Hayward, who was posted out there at the time. When he and his family returned to England, he asked me to accompany them, which I agreed to do. My sister, meanwhile, had married Percival Slattery at St Paul's Church in Melbourne when she was twenty-one. Percy was a fine figure of a man, I must say, and I could not fault her decision in that respect. But although fine to look at, and a grand talker, he never achieved anything. He was always speaking of great schemes, and making glorious predictions for their future, but nothing ever seemed to come of any of it. Then, when they had been married a little over two years, he took himself off to some newly discovered gold fields, hundreds of miles from Melbourne, declaring that he would return home a wealthy man. Alas, he never returned at all, and my sister heard a year later that he had been killed in an avalanche. By that time she had a baby girl, for she had been with child when he left her. Her life in Melbourne, where she worked as a nurse, was not an easy one, as I learned from her letters.

"Many years passed. My employer, Colonel Hayward, died, but I was by then very experienced and had no difficulty in finding fresh employment, first with a family at Greenwich, and later with Lord Elvington, who kept a very grand establishment in the West End. His connections with the very highest level of society were extensive, and many great and noble guests would grace his table of an evening. Sometimes I would hear the gentlemen discussing politics, and although I cannot claim that I really understood all that they were saying, I was fascinated by their manner of discourse, and by the weighty matters under discussion. One evening, I heard a visitor mention the name of Percy Slattery, and comment upon something he had said in a recent speech. The name struck my ear with a particular resonance, as you will imagine, but I could not really believe that the man referred to was the same as I had known all those years ago.

"A few days later, however, Lord Elvington gave a dinner for a large number of parliamentarians, and among the names on the guest list was that of Percival Slattery. Impelled by curiosity, I contrived to get a view of this man without being seen myself, and almost fainted with shock when I did. He was somewhat more stolid in appearance now than when I had known him as a young man, but there could be no doubt in my mind that this was indeed my sister's husband, long presumed dead. It seemed clear what had happened: he had failed in his search for fortune in the gold fields and, no doubt unable to bear the shame, as he saw it, of returning home empty-handed, had taken himself halfway round the world to seek anew for fame and fortune in England. That his personal pride at failing in the gold fields should have been a weightier consideration for him than any bond, either of duty or of affection, for his wife, was entirely consistent with what I knew of his character.

"I hesitated for several weeks before informing my sister of this discovery, for I knew how deeply it would shock and grieve her to think that her husband, and the father of her daughter, was living comfortably in England without a thought for her, while she endured a hard, struggling existence in Australia. Eventually, however, I decided that the truth must be told. What my sister's feelings were upon learning this news, I will not burden you with. Suffice it to say that she poured out her heart to me in many, many letters. From that day forward, she was determined that she would one day come to England, and confront her faithless spouse.

"More time passed, then, six months ago, having saved up sufficient money to pay for the passage of herself and her daughter, Victoria, my sister arrived in England. After some time spent fruitlessly seeking employment in Southampton, her experience as a nurse eventually helped her secure a position at a doctor's dispensary in Portsmouth. At the same time, she succeeded in placing her daughter as a tweeny in the household of a retired admiral there. Since then, we have met and discussed the question of her husband several times. The chief difficulty in approaching him lay in what we knew of his character. He has always had such grand social aspirations, such a keen nose for sniffing out the wealthy and titled, among whom he had always desired to move, that to approach him with an appearance of beggary would, as likely as not, elicit only scorn, if not contempt. But if Violet could present herself as comfortably off, then she would, she felt, possess a greater influence over him.

"My employment with Lord Elvington ended, as he took up a post as governor of one of the Indian provinces, and I did not wish to leave England. Mr and Mrs Claydon very kindly offered me employment here, and it was then that Violet and I had the idea that if, on some occasion when my employers were away, Violet could invite Percy here and pretend that it was her own residence, it would exactly suit her purpose. Of course, having devised this scheme, we were impatient to put it into practice. Then, when I learned that Mr Claydon would be absent from home this evening, it seemed the very chance we had been waiting for. If it could be arranged that my mistress, too, was absent for a few hours, then Violet would have the perfect opportunity to meet her husband here.

"I had heard Mrs Claydon speak often, with some concern, of her brother, Leonard, in America, and knew that she would respond readily to any communication from him. My sister therefore sent the telegram this morning from Portsmouth as if from Leonard. Before catching the train to London, she also handed in at the station the brief letter that Mrs Claydon was later given there. I had previously written this myself, copying his hand as well as I could from his letters, which are in the bureau, and sent it down to my sister. She, meanwhile, had composed a letter to her husband, which she sent to me here, so that I could post it at the local post office.

"It was still possible, we thought, that Percival would treat my sister in a high-handed and scornful manner, would adopt a brazen attitude and simply dare her to make any accusation against him. But if he had cause to fear that the whole story of his desertion would inevitably become public knowledge, then he might act differently. To this end, I wrote a letter to Mr Falk, inviting him to come here today, a little after the time set for Percy's appointment. I had seen Mr Falk's name in the newspaper, and knew he was a parliamentary reporter, for Mr Claydon generally takes the *Standard*, and I have sometimes glanced through it when he has finished with it, looking for any mention of my sister's husband. Mr Falk's presence here would, I felt, force Percy to act more decently than he otherwise might."

At this point, Miss Quinn abruptly stopped and burst once more into a torrent of sobbing.

"I am sorry," she cried at length in a heartfelt tone, her eyes brimming with tears. "I am sorry for all the trouble and anxiety I have caused to everyone. Would that I had never heard the name of Percival Slattery! Would that my sister had never clapped eyes on him again after he had left for the gold fields!"

"Your scheme did not go quite as planned," remarked Holmes after a moment, as the housekeeper sobbed quietly before us.

"That is correct, sir," responded she after a moment. "Percival Slattery arrived on time, I stayed out of sight and Violet received him in this room. She had brought with her the old picture of the church, which you see on the wall there. It is the church in Melbourne where they were married. She had hoped that such a reminder of the vows he had made might stir some embers of decency in his soul, but I think that the hope was a vain one. Then she reminded him of the presents they had given each other when they became engaged to be married, and she showed him the little jewelled brooch that she still wore, and asked him if he still had the watch she had given him. Reluctantly, he pulled his watch from his waistcoat pocket and she saw that it was indeed the very one she had given him, inscribed with their names, all those years ago. At that point, Violet's daughter, dressed in her maid's uniform, brought in a tray of tea for them.

"'There is something that you don't know,' said Violet to her husband then.

"'Oh?' replied he in an unconcerned manner. 'And what might that be, pray?'

"'You have a daughter,' said she.

"At first he dismissed what she said and would not believe her, but as she gave him the details of the matter, he fell silent, and it was evident that he accepted she was speaking the truth. After a moment, she spoke again:

"'It is she who just served you with your tea.'

"'No!' cried he. 'That was your maid.'

"'That is she,' said Violet, and called Victoria back into the room. 'Percival, meet your daughter! Victoria, meet your father!'

"At this, he sprang to his feet, but the shock of the occasion proved too much for him. He coughed and spluttered and began to weep, but then all at once clutched his chest and cried out in pain. A moment later he had fallen to the ground in a heap.

"I dashed into the room as Violet cried out in alarm, but it was clear at once that there was nothing we could do for him. He had stopped breathing, his eyes were wide and staring, and he was stone dead.

"At that very moment there came a sharp knock at the front door. 'It must be Mr Falk, the newspaperman,' said Violet in alarm. 'Quickly! Help me get Percy into the back room!'

"We dragged him through there as quickly as we could, then Victoria went to admit the visitor. Violet had brought with her from the dispensary at Portsmouth a small bottle of chloral, in case of emergencies, and she decided at once that she would put some into Mr Falk's tea. 'It will not hurt him,' said she. 'It will just put him to sleep for a little while.'

"A minute or two later, she joined Mr Falk in the sitting room, and shortly afterwards Victoria took in the tea, with a few drops of chloral already in one of the cups. Within a few moments, Mr Falk had fallen into a deep sleep, and we were just carrying him out into the garden when there came another sharp rap at the front door. Victoria ran to answer it as we laid Mr Falk out on the lawn, then Violet joined her daughter at the front door, and found to her horror that the caller was the rightful occupier of the house, Mr Claydon, who had come home after all. Not only that, but she saw that a policeman was at that moment passing down the street. She decided, on the spur of the moment – Lord forgive her for her lies! – to brazen it out. Well, as you know, she succeeded and Mr Claydon departed. Then the three of us, Violet, Victoria and myself, left by the back door, through the garden and out into the back lane behind the house. So hurried was our departure that we forgot to remove the pictures Violet had brought with her, as you will have noticed. I travelled with Violet and her daughter as far as Waterloo, and saw them onto the train there. Then, seeing that a train from Southampton was due within the hour, I waited there until it arrived, when I met up with Mrs Claydon."

"What did you intend to do about the body of Mr Slattery?" asked Holmes.

"I thought that Mrs Claydon and I could find it when we got back here, and then notify the authorities," replied Miss Quinn. "As everything that could have gone wrong with our scheme seemed to have done so, I did not think that anything further could go amiss, until we reached Kendal Terrace and saw a police van waiting there and a huge crowd of people in the street."

"This is a very grave business," said Inspector Spencer, rising to his feet. "I must ask you to accompany me to the station and make a full statement there," he continued, addressing Miss Quinn. "Failure to notify the authorities of a death is a very serious offence."

"I was going to do so," returned the housekeeper.

"So you say. But so everyone says who is arrested for not doing so. Then there is the question of the wilful assault on the person of Mr Falk by the administration of a dangerous drug, not to mention a possible charge of blackmail, extortion or demanding money with menaces from the deceased."

"The woman was his wife, Spencer," interjected Holmes, "and as such was surely entitled to some claim for financial support from him."

"Perhaps so – if she really was his wife," returned the policeman in his most official tone, "but that will be for others to consider. I will make my report and pass it to my superiors and they will decide what action should be taken."

"Well, I'm off, anyhow," said Linton Falk, springing to his feet. "What a story! I am obliged to you, Mr Holmes, for suggesting that I delay my departure. I thought I had a story then, but I have an even better one now!"

"You just make sure you stick to the facts, young man!" said Spencer in a stern tone, as the newspaperman made to leave the room. "You reporters are all the same: give you one fact and you make up three!"

A minute later, Holmes and I had left the house that had been the scene of such mysterious and surprising events, and were walking up the main road in the twilight.

"You can hardly maintain, after the events of this evening," I remarked, "that the present age has ceased to produce interesting mysteries."

"That is true," conceded my companion. "And yet, after all, it was a simple affair."

"I confess it did not strike me in that way," I returned with a chuckle.

"Well, of course, it possessed a certain superficial complexity, but beneath the surface it was simple enough."

"What do you think will become of Miss Quinn?"

"It is hard to say. Claydon strikes me as a decent and forgiving soul, so I don't imagine he will press charges of any kind; but I doubt he will keep her on, for the bond of trust, which is essential between those sharing a household, has been broken. Besides, he has his wife's opinion to accommodate, and she is, I perceive, made of somewhat sterner metal than her husband."

"You are probably right," I concurred. "What led you to suspect that the housekeeper was at the bottom of it all? And how on earth did you know she had a sister called Violet, and all the rest of it?"

"Ah! There you touch on the one really interesting point in the whole business," replied my friend with enthusiasm. "Should you ever include an account of this case in that chronicle of my professional life which you have threatened for so long, Watson, you must ensure that you stress the importance of the slivers of glass on the sitting-room carpet, and the fact that there were two clocks in the room. These things constitute a perfect example – a text-book illustration, one might say – of the maxim that the solution of a problem is generally to be found by a close examination of its details.

"You see," he continued, "when we entered the sitting room for the first time, upon our arrival at the house, Claydon remarked almost at once upon the unknown picture on the wall, the photograph upon the piano and the missing roses. But the first thing that caught my own eye was a reflected glint of light from something upon the floor. When I examined it, I found that it was a tiny sliver of glass. Then I saw a second, and a third, nearby, beneath one of the chairs. The glass was thin, but seemed fairly strong, and each of the slivers had a slight curve to it. It struck me that they might be from a broken wine glass, but I kept an open mind on the matter.

"When we discovered Slattery's body, a quick investigation revealed that the glass on the face of his watch was broken. As I examined what remained of it, I could not doubt that the particles of glass in the sitting room were from the same source. Clearly the damage to the watch had occurred in the other room. I tried to close the cover of the watch, which was open, and found that I could not do so, as it had been twisted slightly on its hinges. This would have required some force, and I conjectured that the damage to the watch had been caused when its owner had fallen unconscious to the floor. I tried the watch in the waistcoat pocket. It was a tight fit and would not have slipped out as he fell. Therefore he had had it in his hand at the time he fell. This was suggested also by the damage to the hinge, which must have occurred while the lid was open.

"The shards of glass informed me that it was in the sitting room that Slattery had fallen. But why did he have his watch in his hand in the sitting room? For in the sitting room there is not one clock, but two, both working and both showing the correct time."

"He might have taken it from his pocket by sheer force of habit," I suggested, "oblivious to the presence of other timepieces in the room."

"Yes, that is possible. It is also possible that he had taken it from his pocket not to see the time but to make a gesture, to indicate, say, that he was a busy man, whose time was of some value. But what seemed equally possible was that he had been consulting the watch for some other purpose altogether."

"I cannot imagine what that could have been."

"No more could I. But one must always allow in one's calculations not merely for the unknown, but for the unimagined. I inspected the watch closely, with the aid of a lens. Upon the underside of the lid, rubbed almost to invisibility, was an inscription. At the top were two large letters, 'P' and 'S', twined together in a monogram. These initials, of course, matched those I had already observed on the dead man's cuff-links. Below the monogram was a date, 1870, and, below that, two lines of writing, which I deciphered only with considerable difficulty. The first said 'fond affection', and the second 'Violet Q'. Of course, the initial 'Q' at once suggested the surname 'Quinn', and the fact that 'Violet' and 'Rosemary' are both flower-names seemed too much of a coincidence to be the result of mere chance. I therefore conjectured that the woman, Violet, who had evidently given the watch to the dead man, was the sister of Rosemary Quinn, the Claydons' housekeeper. There was one other possibility, I considered, which was that these two were one and the same person, namely Violet Rosemary Quinn, who had perhaps been known as 'Violet' when she was younger, but chose now to be known as 'Rosemary'. But considering that there was definitely another woman involved in the matter – the woman whom Claydon had found to be in possession of his house when he returned from work – I discounted this possibility. The suggestion that that woman was indeed the sister of Claydon's housekeeper was given added support by his observation that her appearance struck him as vaguely familiar. So already, you see, I had established a probable link between one of the usual members of the household and the apparent strangers who had taken possession of the house this afternoon."

"Your reasoning seems very sound," I remarked. "I am fascinated!"

"Thank you," said Holmes. "Now, when Falk came to examine the body, and identified it as that of Percival Slattery, he informed us that Slattery had been born and bred in Australia. This instantly strengthened my theory, for Claydon had remarked that the woman who met him at his front door, although well spoken, had had an accent that he had been unable to place. Perhaps, I conjectured, her accent was an Australian one, and perhaps she had known Slattery when they both lived there. If so, she had probably given the watch to him then. As I considered this, the meaning of the photograph of the child on the piano became all at once very clear to me. There was, if you recall, a pencilled inscription on the mount of the photograph, which read 'Victoria, O Victoria'. This appeared to be an ejaculation or lament of some kind, although the significance was not clear. But what if the 'O' in the inscription was not an ejaculatory 'O', as it appeared to be, but had been intended as an abbreviation of the word 'Of'? I examined the photograph closely through my lens and, sure enough, immediately after the 'O' was the very faintest of pencil marks, a mere tick, but one which had clearly been intended as an apostrophe. The child's name was therefore Victoria, and, evidently in a moment of whimsy, someone, probably the child's mother, had inscribed the photograph 'Victoria of Victoria', Victoria being, of course, one of the colonies of Australia. That, therefore, was where the child had been living at the time the photograph was taken.

"But the presence of this mysterious and previously unseen photograph in the room where Slattery was met by Rosemary Quinn's sister could, realistically, mean only one thing: that the child was his. The presence, furthermore, of the old picture of a church suggested that something to do with a wedding was the issue between them. Either he had married her and then deserted her, or he had perhaps jilted her at the altar rail. In either event, the whole case seemed now as clear as crystal, and I was able to conjecture – accurately as it turned out – the reason Falk had been invited there, and what it was that had caused Slattery to have a seizure. The only task that remained was to unsettle the housekeeper's composure, so that when I mentioned her sister she would already be in a nervous state, be unable to conceal her surprise, and would very likely give herself away. She herself had presented me with the opportunity to ask unsettling questions by her somewhat vague description of the telegram she claimed to have received, and its unlikely contents.

"Of course, logically speaking, if the telegram really had included a reference to the tobacco jar on the mantelpiece, it would, although surprising, not necessarily have proved anything one way or the other against the woman. But I perceived as soon as I questioned her on the point that she herself could see that it sounded distinctly unlikely. At that moment, her edifice of untruth began to collapse about her, and the rest you know."

I stopped, turned to my companion and held out my hand. "Congratulations!" said I warmly.

"What is this?" returned he with a puzzled smile, shaking my hand.

"Your conduct of the case was exemplary," I explained. "I have known you some years now, Holmes, and have seen you solve a good many cases – many, no doubt, of greater difficulty than this one. But I don't know that I have ever seen a more accomplished and workmanlike demonstration of the art of detection!"

"Well, thank you, Watson," said my friend, and I could see that he was quite affected by my sincere approbation. "It is kind of you to say so. Now, here is something else for you to consider," he continued in a lighter tone, "as we traverse these seemingly endless streets of south London. Many of them are not entirely unattractive – indeed, Kendal Terrace itself is only wanting a tree or two to make it a very pleasant little thoroughfare – but they are, in the main, somewhat banal and unromantic. That can scarcely be denied. Is it not strange, then, that in such unpromising terrain should bloom such brilliant and fascinating flowers as these cases, which it is my delight to investigate, and yours to record? For it cannot be denied that the dull grey streets of London present the finest field there is for those who take pleasure in such things. It is as if Nature must always find a way of compensating, just as, in the densest of tropical jungles, so I am informed, where the trees grow so closely together that the ground is in constant shade, there flourish the brightest and most spectacular blooms that nature can show."

"It seems a somewhat fanciful notion," I remarked. "What about sparrows? The sparrow is undoubtedly the most common bird in cities and towns, and should, therefore, on your theory, be surpassingly beautiful. But whatever other good points it may have, the sparrow is undoubtedly the dullest-looking bird imaginable."

Holmes laughed, in that strange, silent way that was peculiar to him.

"You are a good fellow, Watson," said he at length. "You anchor me to reality when my flights of fancy threaten, like a runaway balloon, to carry me off to the dangerous reaches of the upper atmosphere! But here is a cab, trundling empty back to town!" he continued, stepping to the edge of the pavement and holding up his hand. "Let us take a ride to the Strand. I understand that a new restaurant has recently opened there, of which very favourable reports have been given!"

A HAIR'S BREADTH

THE WEEKS that immediately succeeded my marriage were a hectic time for me. As every married man will know from his own experience, so much that is new must be attended to then, and all the careful planning and preparation one has done beforehand inevitably turns out to have been either inadequate or misguided. For some weeks, therefore, I had seen nothing whatever of my friends. Indeed, so dramatically did the free time at my disposal seem to have shrunk since my bachelor days, when I had shared rooms with Sherlock Holmes in Baker Street, that I had scarcely had a moment to consider anything beyond the immediate concerns of my new household. I certainly did not expect to see Holmes for some time, and was surprised, therefore, as I stood one afternoon upon the kerb in Holborn, to hear through the noise and bustle about me that familiar, somewhat strident voice calling my name. It was a cold and wintry day, with a strong wind blowing, and I had been preoccupied with finding a cab. Now I turned to see Holmes standing at my elbow.

"My dear Watson!" said he, clapping me upon the shoulder. "It is good to see you looking so well. Your recent translation from solitary bachelorhood to the joys of married life has clearly been a success! You have the air of one happy with his lot!"

"And you, Holmes," I returned with a smile, "you, too, appear in good spirits."

"Well, well! I, too, have my little triumphs and pleasures! Just three weeks ago I was pleased to drink a toast in your honour, Watson, and to congratulate you upon your happiness. Now it is for you to congratulate me!"

"My dear fellow! I had no idea!"

"We have been regrettably out of touch lately," said he with a shake of the head. "But it is true. Congratulations are in order! I have solved the Yelverton murder case!"

"What!" I cried.

"I can see that I have surprised you!"

I laughed. "You amaze me, Holmes! But I had no idea you were involved."

"I was consulted at a late stage, at the express request of Lady Yelverton's nephew, when it was apparent that the police were making no progress whatever. I take it you have followed the case?"

"I could hardly have failed to do so. It has been impossible to pick up a newspaper in the last week without reading something of the matter. It is undoubtedly the most sensational crime of the year!"

"Certainly, in terms of the publicity it has received, although in itself it is really a very trifling affair."

"And you have found the murderer, you say?"

My companion nodded. "Indeed. I am hoping to pay a call on him later this afternoon, at his lodgings."

"He is not yet in custody, then?" I asked in surprise.

"No."

"But you know his whereabouts?"

"Precisely."

"You have informed the police, no doubt?"

Holmes shook his head.

"Why ever not?" I cried in surprise. "Surely you must act quickly, before he has a chance to make his escape once more."

"It is not quite so straightforward as you seem to imagine, Watson. I do not yet have all the evidence in my hands."

"Evidence? But the case is as plain as a pikestaff! The man was practically seen to commit the crime!"

"Come, come," said my companion, chuckling. "It is too cold a day to stand debating the matter on the pavement like this. You are having a busy day, I perceive."

"That is true, but how—?"

"No matter. You know my methods, Watson! You have had one appointment already, this morning, and you have another one this afternoon. Can you break it?"

I shook my head. "I have to see a solicitor in Cheapside in ten minutes," I replied, glancing at my watch.

"But no doubt you could make the appointment a brief one?"

"If necessary."

"Good. I am meeting Inspector Lanner in Brown's Coffee Shop on Ludgate Hill, at three o'clock. If you could be there by that time, Watson, you might find it an interesting experience!"

I drove to Cheapside with a thrill of excitement rising in my breast. The Yelverton case had been the single topic of conversation on everyone's lips for the past week. That I might be able to play a part in the matter, if only as a spectator, sent the blood coursing through my veins. The meeting with Mr Scrimgeour, the solicitor, which had been dominating my thoughts for days, now struck me as a mundane matter indeed, and little more than an irksome distraction. I was determined to get it over with as quickly as possible, in order to get to the meeting place by three o'clock.

In the cab, as it made its slow way through the dense traffic along Holborn, and in the solicitor's anteroom, I turned over and over in my mind all that I had read of the Yelverton case. The chief difficulty in the matter, as I understood it, was not so much in discovering who had committed the terrible crime, as in tracking down the culprit, for he had so far defeated all attempts to find him.

The facts of the matter were simple enough. Lady Yelverton had been a delicate old lady of seventy-odd, living alone quietly in the house in South Audley Street in which she had lived for more than fifty years, with a large staff of servants, some of whom were almost as old as their mistress. She had been widowed for nearly twenty years and had suffered ill-health for almost as long. Two years previously she had been very ill, and for several months her life had been despaired of, but much to everyone's surprise, she had at length recovered. It was said that the gratitude she felt to her physician, one Dr Illingworth, was so great that she had subsequently included a substantial bequest to him in her will. But though her health had recovered, her illness had left her somewhat debilitated, with both her hearing and her eyesight, which had in any case been failing for years, severely weakened. As a consequence of this decline in her faculties, she rarely went out, but was always pleased to receive visitors, and offered a warm and hospitable welcome to everyone. Her visitors were not numerous, however, for many of her old friends had died, or were, like Lady Yelverton herself, somewhat frail, and she had but one surviving near relation, Mr Basil Thorne, a gentleman of about forty, the only son of her late husband's younger brother. A man well known in London society, he would occasionally call by at his aunt's house to bring her the latest news and gossip of London life, which she was always pleased to hear.

In recent years, she had taken a particular interest in charitable causes, and acted as honorary patron for several of them. Though debarred by her frailty from taking an active part in charitable work, her financial donations were said to be munificent. This, then, was the quiet household into which brutal violence had erupted in such a startling manner.

About three months previously, an elderly gentleman by the name of Quinlivan, with an untidy mane of white hair and a beard to match, had paid his first call upon Lady Yelverton. Her servants, noting the sheaf of pamphlets in his grasp, and his odd, jerky way of talking, had marked him down as some kind of eccentric, and had been disinclined to admit him to the house. Upon receiving his card, however, which indicated that his interests were charitable and religious in character, she had asked for him to be shown into her drawing room. There he had stayed for an hour, in deep discussion with Lady Yelverton, and it was evident that he had made a favourable impression upon her, for she had informed the servants afterwards that he would be returning at the same time the following week, and was to be admitted without demur.

After four weeks, the frequency of his visits increased occasionally to twice a week. None of the servants was ever present during these interviews, but it was clear from the sound of Quinlivan's raised voice that he was a voluble and impassioned speaker. After each visit he would leave behind him a fresh religious tract, but although the language and sentiments contained in these were sometimes excessively vehement, they appeared unexceptionable. Nevertheless, Lady Yelverton's old housekeeper, Mrs Edwards, became worried that her mistress was falling too much under Quinlivan's influence, for Lady Yelverton had begun to lose interest in her other visitors. She therefore raised the matter in confidence with Basil Thorne, when next he called. He had previously been unaware of Quinlivan's visits, for his aunt had mentioned the man but once, and then only in a passing remark which Thorne had not followed up. He was both surprised and concerned, therefore, to learn from Mrs Edwards that his aunt had lately become more withdrawn and silent, and generally less interested in the world about her. As delicately as he could, he raised the matter with his aunt at the first opportunity, but she brushed his remarks aside. The second time he mentioned the subject, a week later, she became, he said, quite angry, and forbade him from ever raising the matter again.

Having failed in this direction, then, and becoming increasingly concerned at the influence that this stranger appeared to be gaining over his aunt, Thorne determined to speak directly to the man upon his next visit, in order to form his own opinion of him. He therefore waited in a carriage in South Audley Street at the hour that Lady Yelverton's servants believed Quinlivan would call, but his vigil proved fruitless, for the man never came at all that day. Twice this occurred, which made Thorne suspect that it was the presence of the carriage in the street which had deterred him, or that he had been forewarned in some other way. In either event, the implication as to his character was hardly reassuring, and Thorne therefore set about trying to discover anything he could of the man's antecedents. Despite making enquiries, however, he had, at the time of the tragedy, made no progress in this direction either.

At about this time, Lady Yelverton's domestic staff noted with alarm that the vehemence of Quinlivan's manner was increasing with each visit. Lady Yelverton's footman, Alfred King, a young relative of the housekeeper's, who had twice lost positions through insolence, took it upon himself to speak to the man one day as he was leaving, informing him in no uncertain terms that he did not think it right that he should "go about shouting and agitating everyone". Quinlivan responded in what was later described as an offensive and aggressive manner, whereupon the footman, well known for his short temper, struck the older man and knocked him to the floor. What might have happened next could only be conjectured, for at that moment Lady Yelverton herself appeared in the hallway. Informed of what had occurred, she at once gave the footman notice. He left the house the next day, words of bitter recrimination upon his lips.

One week after this incident came the dreadful event that so shocked all who read of it, and brought the name of Lady Yelverton and her quiet house in South Audley Street to national attention. It was a cold Tuesday afternoon, and Quinlivan had called and been shown directly into the drawing room, as usual. No sooner had the door closed behind him than his raised voice was heard, although no words could be discerned. After perhaps a minute, a complete silence descended, then the door of the room was opened abruptly and Quinlivan ran out, shouting angrily and incoherently at a maid, Susan Moore, who was in the hallway outside. She ran to the kitchen in terror, informing the other staff that Mr Quinlivan looked fit to kill someone. Anxious for the safety of her mistress, Mrs Edwards ascended at once to the drawing room. Receiving no answer to her knock, she opened the door and saw to her horror that her mistress lay slumped in her chair, her head and face a mass of blood. Of Quinlivan there was no sign, and it was clear that he had let himself out of the front door, for it stood open onto the street. Dr Illingworth was quickly summoned, and arrived within minutes, but pronounced Lady Yelverton dead almost at once.

This, then, was the crime that had taken place in South Audley Street, as horrific and brutal a murder as could be imagined, made yet more monstrous by the frailty and kindliness of the victim. The cause of death was given as repeated blows from a blunt instrument, possibly a life preserver, and a warrant was at once issued for Quinlivan's arrest. So universal were the shock and horror with which the crime was regarded that it was thought inconceivable that anyone would shield the criminal, and without such help, it was believed, a man of such distinctive appearance could not evade discovery for long. But the police were soon to learn that Quinlivan's arrest and prosecution were not to be as straightforward as they had supposed, for several days' enquiries produced no result, and he appeared to have vanished without trace.

I opened the *Standard* one morning to read that, acting on information they had received, the police had moved their search from London to Leicester. It was soon evident that their quarry had once again escaped the net, however, for I later read that the search had moved on to other places. Such was the state of the matter, so far as I and other newspaper readers were aware, on the day I ran across Sherlock Holmes in Holborn. It will be appreciated, then, how eager I was not to miss the appointment with Holmes and the police inspector. But Mr Scrimgeour, a slow and careful solicitor of the old school, unaware of the thoughts that were now uppermost in my mind, discoursed in his measured and guarded manner like a lumbering, low-geared piece of machinery, so that an interview of less than an hour seemed to my impatient mind practically interminable.

A church clock was striking three when I at last found myself on the pavement of Cheapside once more. As fast as I could, I hurried past St Paul's churchyard and round into Ludgate Hill. When I reached the coffee shop, I was relieved to see that Inspector Lanner, whom I knew well, was still there, sitting at a table near the window. Of Holmes, however, there was no sign. In a moment I had joined the policeman, and he was acquainting me with the latest facts in the case.

"Early last Friday morning," he began, "a Mrs Unwin, who runs a small boarding house near the Midland station in Leicester, reported to the police that one of her temporary lodgers, a man calling himself Varney, seemed to her very like the description of Quinlivan she had read in her newspaper. She had not yet seen him that morning and believed that he was still in bed. The police quickly went round there, but found that his room was empty. Clearly he had left before Mrs Unwin herself had risen. He had spoken the evening before, she said, of taking a train to Hull, so the police at once notified their colleagues there to be on the alert. What they did not know at the time was that on that same morning we had received a letter in London from Quinlivan himself, posted in Leicester on Thursday afternoon. Most of the letter was taken up with protestations of his innocence. But he was convinced, he said, that if he gave himself up he would never receive a fair hearing."

"I cannot see how he can possibly be innocent," I remarked. "The matter could scarcely be clearer!"

"His claim," Lanner explained, "is that someone must have been in the house before him, for he says he found Lady Yelverton dead when he entered her drawing room. It was this, he says, that made him cry out in anguish as he entered, making him appear deranged to the maid."

"Could it be true?"

Lanner shook his head dubiously. "A window at the back of the drawing room was found to be open," he replied, "despite the fact that the day was a cold one. It is just possible that someone could have climbed out from there into the back yard, and escaped that way."

For some minutes I sat pondering the matter in silence.

"What does Holmes make of it all?" I asked at length. "When I saw him earlier, he said that the case was as good as closed, and that he knew Quinlivan's whereabouts."

Inspector Lanner appeared surprised at this information.

"All he has said to me," he replied, "is that we are dealing with a very cunning and resourceful villain."

"He has certainly managed to give you the slip so far," I remarked. "Were any further clues found in Leicester?"

The policeman nodded. "Mr Holmes and I travelled down to Leicester on Saturday," said he. "We examined the room at Unwin's boarding house, which the man calling himself Varney had occupied, and made one or two discoveries. He had spoken on Thursday evening of taking a train to Hull the next day, but when I examined his room I found a pocket railway timetable under the bed, which had been folded back at the page showing the Glasgow trains. It might have been there a little while, of course, and been missed by the maid who cleaned the room after the previous occupant, but it did make me wonder if the mention of Hull had been a blind, to throw us off the scent if we ever managed to trace him as far as Leicester. We had had no word back from Hull, anyhow, so I at once alerted the Glasgow police. That this man, Varney, was in reality Quinlivan was confirmed, incidentally, by a letter I found in the room, on the floor beneath a chest of drawers, where it had probably slipped down as he was packing. It was a single folded sheet of paper, without an envelope. The writer had not put his address, and the message was a brief one: 'Dear Matthew,' it said, 'you must give yourself up to the police at once. It is the only thing to do. We are convinced of your innocence, but if you remain in hiding, no one will believe you. Heed my advice. Your true friend, Rev B. Arnold.'"

"That certainly sounds as if it were sent to the man you are seeking." I remarked. "Has anything come of these enquiries?"

"Well, we have not yet got the man, but a discovery was made yesterday which proves that his talk of Hull was indeed a blind. A sorter at the General Post Office in Glasgow noticed a letter addressed to Mr M. Quinlivan and marked 'to be called for'. A warrant was at once obtained and the letter opened. It proved to be similar to the one I had found in Leicester: 'You must give yourself up. Do not despair' – that sort of thing. It was signed by the same person, the Reverend B. Arnold. There was again no address at the top of the letter, but the envelope was postmarked 'London East'."

"Have you been able to trace this man, Arnold?"

"Not so far. He calls himself Reverend, but we can find no clergyman of that name in London."

"Perhaps he belongs to some small and obscure non-conformist Church."

"That must be so. But all our resources have so far failed to find him."

"You are not aware of any other discovery that Holmes has made?"

The policeman hesitated a moment before replying.

"Just one, that I know of, Dr Watson, and between ourselves, it seemed more to indicate that his mind was losing its grip than anything else. It was as we were examining the bedroom at Unwin's boarding house. Mr Holmes had picked up a white hair from the hearth and fallen silent. I spoke to him but he did not answer. He just stared at the hair, examined it with his lens, stared at it again, and did not open his mouth for thirty minutes or more. On the train back to London, I could see that he was excited about something, but he said little, except that the murderer had made a slip, 'a tiny, tiny slip', he said. 'He has been very clever, and has come within a hair's breadth of getting clean away,' said he, 'but he will not evade us for much longer now.' Then he laughed, in that odd, silent way of his. Quite frankly, Dr Watson, had it been anyone but Mr Holmes, I should have found myself another compartment to sit in at the first opportunity. One gets accustomed to Mr Holmes's odd ways, but confined for a hundred miles or more with someone laughing to himself the whole way is almost too much for anyone to stand."

At that moment, the shop door opened and Holmes himself appeared before us, an expression of urgency upon his features.

"Pray forgive the delay," said he in a brisk manner. "If you will come now, I have a cab waiting outside."

"Where are we going?" asked Lanner in surprise.

"To arrest Mr Quinlivan," said Holmes.

There were two four-wheelers standing in the street outside. Holmes opened the door of the first one, and I was surprised to see that it already had one occupant, a thin, reserved-looking man, with short dark hair and a small beard.

"This is Mr Woodward," said Holmes as we climbed in. "He is to assist us. Our first port of call will be Gordon Square," he continued as the cab rattled off, "home of Mr Basil Thorne, nephew of the murdered woman. He asked me to notify him at once when I had some positive news, and I think he should be present when his aunt's murderer is arrested."

"You believe Quinlivan has returned to London, then?" I queried.

"I am absolutely certain of it, Watson. Has Inspector Lanner brought you up to date with the case?"

"Indeed. He informs me that you attach great significance to a hair."

My friend chuckled to himself. "It may appear a somewhat slender thread on which to hang a case," said he at length, "but it has proved sturdy enough for the task. It is, after all, a horse's hair."

"A horse's hair!"

"Indeed. And it has led me at a merry gallop, from a small boarding house in Leicester to the present whereabouts of the most sought-after villain in England! He is a very cunning man, Watson, and if we had not found him now, I think it likely he would never have been found at all!"

No more would he say, and we travelled on in silence. As we turned into Russell Square, I observed that another four-wheeler, which had been behind us in Southampton Row, turned the same way.

"That cab appears to be following us," I remarked. "I am certain I saw the same one in Ludgate Hill, as we left Brown's Coffee Shop."

"So it does," said Holmes with a chuckle. It was clear from his tone that he knew something we did not, and Lanner glanced behind us with a frown on his face.

"I wish I knew what was afoot," said he.

"All will be revealed shortly," cried Holmes gaily. "Trust me, Lanner, and you could yet gain the divisional superintendent's position you aspire to!"

With a sigh, the policeman sat back in his seat. "Very well," said he. "We are in your hands, Mr Holmes."

Arriving at Basil Thorne's house in Gordon Square, Holmes, Lanner and I were shown into a richly decorated chamber, used as a study. A tall, broad-shouldered, handsome man, with firm features and a small dark moustache, Thorne listened with an expression of intense interest as Holmes quickly explained to him what had been discovered in Leicester and Glasgow.

"But what makes you think that Quinlivan is in London again?" he asked in a puzzled voice as Holmes finished. "Do you believe he's staying with the man whose letters you found?"

Holmes nodded his head. “Yes,” said he, “the two of them are together. But I had quite forgotten Mr Woodward!” he cried abruptly, springing from his chair. “Perhaps his testimony will make matters clearer.” He hurried from the room and returned a moment later with the thin man who had travelled with us in the cab. “This is Mr George Woodward,” said he, “who has some very important information.”

For a moment the newcomer glanced about the study, as if somewhat abashed by the opulence of his surroundings. Then, at a nod from Holmes, he raised his hand and spoke with an abruptness that set my hair on end.

“That is the man,” said he, pointing at Thorne.

For a moment there was silence, then Holmes spoke.

“I should perhaps explain,” said he in an urbane voice, “that Mr Woodward is a clerk at the left-luggage office at Leicester railway station. He was on duty there on Friday morning when you deposited a bag, Mr Thorne, before catching the early train back to London.”

“He must be mistaken,” said Thorne in a tone of puzzlement. “I have never been to Leicester in my life.”

“Matthew Quinlivan was there.”

“So I understand, from what you have told me, but I fail to see the relevance of that to myself.”

“You are Matthew Quinlivan.”

“What!” we all cried as one.

“It was a very clever scheme,” said Holmes calmly, addressing Thorne, who had taken a step backwards in alarm. “You have been living above your income for some years. Two years ago, you expected your aunt to die and you ran up very large debts in anticipation of your imminent inheritance. Inconveniently for you, she did not die, and you therefore determined to take matters into your own hands. It was vital, of course, that in the event of her death no suspicion should ever attach to you, and to that end, you conceived the idea of establishing the existence of a fictitious character – Quinlivan – who would commit the crime in as obvious a manner as possible, so that there could be no doubt as to who had done it, and then vanish without trace. Knowing your aunt’s weakness for charitable causes, especially those with a religious connection, you could be reasonably confident that 'Quinlivan' would gain access to her, and confident also that, because of her very poor eyesight and hearing, she would not detect the imposture."

"Nonsense!" Thorne interrupted with a cry, his voice dry and hoarse. "What of the letters Quinlivan received from the clergyman you mentioned?"

"You wrote them yourself, Thorne, to add to the air of verisimilitude surrounding the murderer's flight."

"It is nonsense, I say!" Thorne cried again. "You seem to forget, Mr Holmes, that it was I who called you in to the case in the first place!"

"No, I have not forgotten that. It was your first mistake. You were confident that your deception would never be uncovered, and considered that it could only add to your appearance of innocence if you feigned impatience with the police and consulted me. But the truth is now known. The bag in which you secreted the clothes, wig and false beard, which you had worn when playing the part of 'Quinlivan', is now in the hands of the railway police."

"You devil!" cried Thorne in a voice suffused with hatred. "You clever, clever devil!" He made a sudden dive for the desk that stood behind him, yanked open a drawer and drew out a heavy-looking pistol.

In half a second Holmes was across the room and had flung himself on the other man. For a moment they wrestled for the gun, then, with a deafening crash, it went off and a shower of glass fell to the floor as the bullet struck a picture on the wall. Lanner and I sprang forward and attempted to bring Thorne down but, with a hoarse cry of effort, he gave up his struggle for the gun, thrust us aside and raced for the door. In an instant, Holmes had a whistle at his lips and had blown a shrill blast. There followed the sound of a great commotion in the street outside, and we hurried to the front door. Upon the pavement before the house, his face contorted with rage, lay Basil Thorne, held securely in the grip of three uniformed policemen.

* * *

"As I have had occasion to remark in the past," said Holmes as we discussed the case over a whisky and soda in his rooms that evening, "all evidence – even, sometimes, that of eye witnesses – is like a crooked signpost on a winding woodland path. The direction in which it is pointing is never entirely clear, and is apt to change as one changes one's own position.

"The evidence found in Leicester appeared to indicate that Quinlivan had gone on to Hull, or possibly, as Lanner conjectured, Glasgow. But I was not convinced: if a man is cunning enough to present his pursuers with one false scent, might he not as easily present them with two? It struck me as unlikely, under the circumstances, that both the letter and the timetable should have been left behind as they were. It was almost as if he wished his pursuers to know who he was and where he had gone. There was no envelope with the letter, so we could not say where he had been staying when he received it, and no address upon the letter itself, so we were also unable to find the whereabouts of his one supposed connection, the man who signed himself 'Reverend Arnold'. There seemed something excessively coincidental about this, and I began to feel the presence of a calculating, guiding hand behind it all, attempting to lead us carefully away upon a path of his choosing. At first glance it appeared we had made discoveries, but in truth we had learnt nothing whatever. Underlying this exercise in futility I seemed to dimly perceive a pattern unfolding; but to what end? This was the question that vexed me, Watson. And then I found the hair, and my perspective on the case altered completely.

"It was a white hair, and seemed likely, therefore, to have come from the head of the man we sought. But it was coarse to the touch, and I quickly realized it was not a human hair at all, but that of a horse. Now, it was not impossible that an ordinary horse's hair might have been carried into the house on someone's clothing, but the fact that it was the same shade as the hair of the man who had stayed in the room most recently seemed an odd chance. A closer examination with the aid of a lens revealed that one end of it had been neatly cut, almost certainly with a pair of scissors, while the other end had traces of glue adhering to it. I could not doubt then that it had come from a manufactured article, and it required no great leap of imagination to conjecture that the article in question had been a wig, worn by the room's last occupant.

"But what did this mean? Why should anyone pretend to be Quinlivan? There seemed no point to it. Unless, I thought, as the idea struck me like a bolt of lightning, the same person pretending to be Quinlivan in Leicester had pretended to be Quinlivan all along! That there was, in other words, no such person, and never had been! That would make sense of the false trails he was strewing before us, for it would clearly have been in his interests to make his assumed character as solid and real as possible for a little while. Then, in a trice, he would take off his disguise and 'Quinlivan' would vanish utterly from the face of the earth. But if this were true, then all that had happened must have been planned well in advance, for the fictitious Mr Quinlivan had been flourishing for three months or more. There seemed only one conceivable purpose for such an elaborate plan, and that purpose was the deliberate murder of Lady Yelverton."

Holmes paused and took a sip from the glass at his elbow.

"You see, Watson, how the discovery of a single hair transformed my view of the case? One moment I was helping Lanner to trace a violent eccentric who appeared to have killed Lady Yelverton in hot-blooded anger, the next I saw unfolding before me a carefully constructed, cold-blooded plot to murder a defenceless old lady. But if 'Quinlivan' did not really exist, who was it that had played the part so convincingly for the past three months? I at once thought of Thorne, who had never been seen at the same time as 'Quinlivan', who would know of his aunt's susceptibility to charitable callers and who stood to gain substantially from her death. The case seemed clear.

"Our enquiries at the railway station in Leicester quickly established that no one who had been on duty there on Friday morning could remember seeing a man matching Quinlivan's description. This puzzled the police, who believed he had purchased a ticket there for Hull or Glasgow; but I took it as a further confirmation of my theory: Lady Yelverton's murderer had removed his disguise and entered the station inconspicuously as himself, probably, I conjectured, to return to London. If this were so, it was possible he had deposited his disguise somewhere safe, to be collected later, when the hue and cry had died down. I gave Thorne's description to the clerk who had been on duty at the left-luggage office on Friday, and was gratified to learn that a man exactly answering to it had deposited a leather bag there early in the morning.

"When we returned to London, I made discreet enquiries into the state of Thorne's affairs, and was soon able to learn that he is very heavily in debt and that his creditors are pressing for their money. Yesterday I travelled down to Leicester again with a recent photograph of Thorne cut from one of the society papers. This was recognized by three separate railway officials who had been on duty the previous Friday: the left-luggage clerk, the ticket clerk and a porter who had been on the platform when the Sheffield to London Express had pulled in.

"I then explained the whole matter to the superintendent of the railway police there, and he ordered Thorne's bag to be opened at once. Inside we found a white wig and a false beard, together with various items of clothing which Quinlivan had been wearing when last seen. My conjectures were thus precisely confirmed. The superintendent naturally wished to announce the discovery at once, but I managed to persuade him that the better course of action was to say nothing until we had the villain in our grasp. He and two of his men brought Thorne's bag with them when they came up to town this afternoon with the left-luggage clerk, whose testimony provided us with the dramatic *denouement* that such a case demands. You know my taste in these things, Watson: the dramatic touch, the rapier-thrust of truth. Life without such moments would be flat indeed!"

"It really is a sensational success for you," said I in unfeigned admiration. "Without your intervention, Holmes, the case would probably never have been solved! Tomorrow morning, and for weeks, your name will be blazoned in every newspaper in the land!"

"I very much hope not," said he, a note of alarm in his voice. "It might make my life here somewhat unendurable. I have told Lanner that he is at liberty to take as much credit as he pleases from the case, but he is an honest man, so I suppose I may receive a brief mention at the foot of a column on the back page!"

I laughed as I rose to my feet and put on my coat. "I had best be off," I said. "I have a number of things to do. No doubt you will be taking a well-earned rest over the next few days!"

"On the contrary," said he, "the Yelverton case has whetted my appetite for something a little more challenging! When I have finished this whisky and soda, I must turn my attention at once to those papers by your chair. They contain details of some bizarre and threatening letters received recently by the Earl of Redcastle, which promise to furnish me with a very pretty little problem!"

The Adventure of THE SMILING FACE

THE NOTEBOOKS AND JOURNALS in which I recorded so many of the cases of my friend Sherlock Holmes hold much that is strange and dramatic and very little that is merely commonplace. For Holmes was generally recognized not only as the final court of appeal in cases which others had given up as unsolvable, but also as the first port of call for those who were sorely troubled but who had little in the way of facts or evidence with which they might enlist the sympathy and aid of the authorities. Among these latter cases, those that spring readily to mind include the strange tale of the hidden garden of Balethorpe House and the surprising nature of what was discovered there, the enigma of the thirteen steps at Hardshaw Hall, and the mystery surrounding the eminent archaeologist, Professor Palfreyman, and the old cottage in Stagg's Lane. It is this last case which I now propose to relate.

It was a cold and foggy day in November, 1884, when Miss Georgina Calloway called at our chambers in Baker Street, shortly after nine o'clock in the morning, as I was glancing over the papers. She was a very handsome young lady, no more than four and twenty at the outside, I judged, with delicate, intelligent features and curly, gingery hair. Holmes showed her to a chair by our blazing fire, where she removed her gloves and held her hands out to the flames appreciatively.

"It is a cold morning," said she, with a shiver.

"At least you have not had far to come," remarked Holmes.

"That is true," she returned, then paused, a look of surprise on her face. "How do you know how far I have travelled?" she asked.

"You have brought with you on your instep a little of that distinctive North Kent clay," replied Holmes. "It is quite unmistakable. You have come up from some rural corner of Beckenham, I should say."

"You are quite right," said she. "Our cottage lies in an old country lane, about twenty minutes' walk from Beckenham railway station. It is a very remote spot, considering how close it is to London. I used to think it simply quaint and peaceful, but now . . ."

"Now?"

"Now I find the isolation disturbing. Recently, I have been anxious and on edge all the time, as if waiting for something dreadful to happen. I shall speak honestly to you, so you will understand, even if you think me absurd. Some days recently, when the daylight has faded and the fog is creeping through the woods, I have not simply been anxious, I have been terrified."

Our visitor's face as she spoke these words seemed to lose all colour and become so white that I thought she would faint, but she bit her lip and turned to the fire for warmth.

"It is clear you are very upset," said Holmes in a sympathetic tone. "Watson, please be so good as to ring for a pot of tea. I think we could all do with a cup! Now," he continued after a moment, addressing Miss Calloway once more, "pray let us have some details, so that we may understand your circumstances better. Have you always lived where you live now?"

"No, for less than a year."

"Do you live alone there?"

"No, with a distant relative, Professor James Palfreyman."

"Is that the archaeologist?"

"Yes, that is he. I act as his housekeeper, and also as his secretary and assistant."

"Is there anyone else in the house?"

"Mrs Wheeler, our cook, who is a widow. When I was first there, Mrs Wheeler's daughter, Beryl, acted as housemaid, but in the summer she ran off with an Italian waiter who was staying at Penge. This was no great loss from the point of view of the household, as she had had a somewhat cavalier attitude to her work. Now Mrs Wheeler and I share the household duties between us. It is not very onerous, as Professor Palfreyman is not a great one for dusting and cleaning, so I just do what strikes me as absolutely necessary and leave the rest."

"That sounds agreeable enough," remarked Holmes with a chuckle. "I take it that your residence there did not initially cause you any anxiety."

"No," replied his visitor. "When I was first there everything seemed fine."

"In that case," said Holmes, "tell us how you came to be in such a rural spot, and what has happened since." As he spoke, he leaned back in his chair, and closed his eyes. For a moment, Miss Calloway appeared surprised, but then she began the following account.

"My connection with Beckenham, and with Professor Palfreyman, dates only from the time of my mother's funeral," she began. "My father had died some years previously, when I was away at boarding school in Sussex. My chief interest at school had been botany, at which I was said to show promise, and I was hopeful that I might be able to continue my studies in that field, either at London University or the Botanical Institute at Kew. Shortly before I was due to leave school, however, my mother's health began to decline, and I was obliged to abandon my plans and return home to look after her. We lived quite comfortably in Peckham, for my father had left her fairly well provided for, but to be honest I found it a somewhat dull existence. Then, in early December last year, my mother's health suddenly declined markedly, and inside a week she had died.

"It had all happened so quickly and with so little warning that I was in a state of shock for several days. I was also thrown into turmoil by the immediate uncertainty of my financial situation. The income my mother and I were living on came mainly from an insurance policy my father had taken out many years previously. This provided for my mother while she was alive, but ceased absolutely upon her death. Apart from that income, we had very little, and I was flung into wild despair as to what I could possibly do. A quarter's rent would shortly fall due, and I could not afford to pay it, let alone pay for the other necessities of life. This is the state I was in on the day of my mother's funeral: great sadness at her departure and utter despair at my own future.

"It was a cold day in December, with a few flakes of snow blowing in the air. There had been hardly anyone at the funeral, save myself and an elderly neighbour, and I was leaving the cemetery alone, deep in thought, when, to my surprise, a distinguished-looking elderly man approached and spoke to me. I had seen him standing a little way off, but as it was no one I knew, I had paid him no attention. Now he introduced himself as Professor Palfreyman, a distant cousin of my mother's. He had seen a notice of her funeral in the local paper, he said, and although she and he had not met in the last ten years, he had wished to pay his last respects. I must have cut a sorry picture, for after a few moments he offered to buy me lunch at a nearby hotel, an offer I accepted.

"Over lunch, he explained to me that although he and my mother had seen little of each other in the last thirty years, they had always stayed in touch, if only by one letter a year, as she was, so far as he was aware, his only relative, and he hers. We chatted a little about family matters, and I must say I found him a very pleasant and thoughtful gentleman. Of course, I had no desire to bore him with the details of my own miserable financial situation, but somehow it came out, at which he looked most concerned.

"'If you wish, Miss Calloway,' said he, 'you can stay with me for a few weeks, until you get on your feet again.'

"Of course, I responded that I could not possibly impose myself upon him, but he insisted that it would be no trouble to put me up, and that it was the least he could do for my mother's memory. In the end, common sense won the day over pride and politeness, and I moved into his house, Bluebell Cottage, in Stagg's Lane, near Beckenham, two days before Christmas last year.

"It is an interesting old house, somewhat larger than the name 'cottage' would suggest, and full of odd corners, narrow corridors and crooked stairways. It has a small garden at the front, and a much larger one at the back, which extends some way into a dense wood, where Professor Palfreyman sometimes likes to walk, or sit and smoke his pipe. He had been Professor of Classical Archaeology at London University, and when he retired he had chosen Bluebell Cottage because of its remote, secluded situation, so that he could work on a number of books he had planned to write without being disturbed. Stagg's Lane itself is little more than a cart track, a byway off another byway called Aylmer's Lane.

"Remote and secluded it may generally have been, but it could also, on occasion, be very lively, for Professor Palfreyman's former colleagues would sometimes call in to see him to discuss academic matters, and I must say I found their visits immensely stimulating. Among these visitors was Professor Ainscow, who had succeeded Professor Palfreyman to the chair of Classical Archaeology. He is a large, jovial man, whose habitually dishevelled appearance belies a keen intellect and ready sense of humour. Not all the visitors were quite so entertaining, however. Dr Webb, who had once been a rival of Professor Palfreyman's for the chair, is somewhat irritable and short in manner, and tends to stick tightly to his subject and avoid all other matters. I have had the impression once or twice that despite the evident respect he has for Professor Palfreyman's professional opinions, he still bears his old rival a grudge for having beaten him to the chair many years ago. Dr Webb was accompanied on one or two occasions by his son, Paul, who is, if anything, even less agreeable than his father. While Dr Webb was in discussion with Professor Palfreyman, his son appeared to think that my presence in the house was entirely for his benefit, both mentally and physically, and he was unpleasantly overfamiliar in his manner. Mercifully, I have seen nothing of him in the last few months.

"One Saturday in the spring, Professor Ainscow arrived for lunch with a young man by the name of Timothy Martin, whom he introduced with a chuckle as his 'latest recruit'. Mr Martin, he explained, had come down from Oxford the previous summer, having studied Classics and the History of Art, and was now doing research for his thesis in the department of Classical Archaeology."

There was some slight alteration in the tone of Miss Calloway's voice as she mentioned this young man, and Holmes evidently noticed it, too, for he opened his eyes for a moment.

"This young man is more agreeable than the other one you mentioned?" said he.

"I suppose he is," returned Miss Calloway, looking slightly flustered. "Anyway, to return to my account: the first few weeks at Bluebell Cottage seemed to pass very quickly, and all my efforts to obtain a suitable position of employment for myself came to nought, as did my attempts to resume my studies. By then, the little money I'd had left after I had sorted out my mother's affairs had dwindled practically to nothing. I think that Professor Palfreyman had guessed this, for one evening after supper he asked me if I would be interested in acting as housekeeper for him for the time being, for which he would pay me a small salary. To be honest, I think that in his kindness he would willingly have given me a little money for doing nothing, and that the suggestion of acting as his housekeeper was made more as a sop to my pride than out of any real need. Anyway, after I had protested, as before, at his unwonted kindness, I accepted his proposal. I saw no other option for myself.

"The work was not difficult, and I had, as I mentioned, Mrs Wheeler and her daughter to help me. Soon, when I had become accustomed to the weekly routine, I found myself with a lot of time on my hands. I flatter myself that the professor had realized by then that I was capable of somewhat more than simply ordering the groceries and parcelling up the laundry once a week, and when he asked if I would like to assist him in tidying some of his professional papers, I readily agreed. From that moment on – a month or two after I had first arrived at Bluebell Cottage – I became the professor's unofficial assistant and secretary, and he increased my salary accordingly. This work I found very interesting, and I have learnt a lot about archaeology, about which I previously knew very little, and also about ancient Greece and Rome, which are the professor's special field of expertise.

"Sometimes, of an evening, we would sit by the fire with our cocoa and he would tell me the most fascinating anecdotes of his explorations in the wildest parts of the world, and of the great advance in knowledge which the discovery of an insignificant-looking piece of pottery might represent. I think he was pleased that I took such an interest in his work, and he began to show me some of his own collection of artefacts and works of art, which is extensive but utterly disorganized. Most of these things are from the Classical period, as you would expect, but there are also items dating from the Middle Ages and the period of the Renaissance. Professor Palfreyman was in Italy at the time of that terrible earthquake in Rienzi, about twenty years ago, when the church there was practically destroyed, and he played a major part in saving much of value from the rubble, and in subsequently excavating the ruins. As a mark of their gratitude, the regional authorities presented him with an enormous bundle of old documents and similar things, much of which he himself had rescued from the church crypt. Most of this material languishes still in a dusty old tin box, as Professor Palfreyman has never found the time to sort it all out. I suggested that I might make a start in trying to catalogue it for him, to which suggestion he readily agreed. You will appreciate, then, how, as the months passed, I was kept very busy.

"A few weeks after he had first visited Bluebell Cottage, Tim – Mr Martin – began to call more frequently, which also made my life there more interesting. Professor Ainscow and the other members of the department began to use Mr Martin as a willing messenger, to convey sundry books and documents between the university and Professor Palfreyman. He also called sometimes on his own initiative, and although I am not so conceited as to suppose that it was to see me that he called, rather than to consult Professor Palfreyman, it is certainly true that we saw a great deal of each other. During the university's spring vacation, he came down to see us several times a week, and helped me get the professor's papers and other documents into some kind of order. This period was one of the happiest of my life.

"But if most of my daily life at Bluebell Cottage was interesting and enjoyable, there were other aspects of it which were more than a little odd. Not long after I had first moved in there, I was passing the professor's study one morning when I heard voices. Thinking that he must have a visitor whom I hadn't seen arrive, I knocked on the door and put my head in, to enquire if they would like a pot of tea. Imagine my surprise, then, when I found that there was no one in the room but Professor Palfreyman.

"'I thought I heard you speaking to someone,' I said.

"He looked a little embarrassed. 'I sometimes speak aloud when I am thinking about something,' said he.

"Later, I asked Mrs Wheeler if she had ever heard the professor speaking to himself.

"'Bless you, my dear!' was her response. 'The professor is always talking to himself. It'd be a rare day if he wasn't!'

"'But he sounded so agitated,' I persisted, 'as if he were quarrelling with someone.'

"'Ah,' said she. 'But you see, Miss Calloway, when he is discussing things with himself, sometimes he agrees with himself, and sometimes he doesn't.'

"This sounded nonsensical to me, but I did not pursue the matter further. After that, I frequently heard the professor speaking to himself, and occasionally calling out loudly, as if in a heated discussion. The most common phrases I heard him repeat were 'I'm sorry' and 'I don't know'. The former varied in tone from a muttered, subdued utterance, as if he were accepting the blame for something, to a louder, more defiant statement, as if his apology were not quite genuine and he felt he was being accused of something that was not entirely his fault. The latter – 'I don't know' – was generally spoken with great emphasis, as if to deny an accusation of knowledge upon which he perhaps should have acted but had not."

"As the months passed, I became more accustomed to Professor Palfreyman's eccentric ways, although I never really got used to his talking to himself. Sometimes at night, I would hear him talking to himself in his bedroom, and I was never quite sure whether he was asleep or awake. One night, however, I had confirmation that the professor's troubled mind was not confined to the hours of wakefulness. It came at the end of what had been an odd day, which had begun with a most curious incident. It may be of no significance – I cannot judge – but it sometimes seems to me that a slight decline in Professor Palfreyman's competence and health dates from about that time. He and I were seated together at breakfast, one morning in the spring, when the maid brought in the post, which had just been delivered. There were a couple of tradesmen's accounts and one expensive-looking long envelope.

"'I wonder what this can be?' said the professor as he opened it and drew out the letter from within. Next moment, he let out a little cry of surprise. He held up the sheet and turned it over, and to my great surprise I saw that it was perfectly blank.

"I laughed. 'Someone has made a rather silly mistake,' I said.

"The professor did not reply, but looked again intently at the outside of the envelope.

"'Do you recognize the handwriting?' I asked, as I saw his face assume a thoughtful expression. He did not respond to my question, but after a moment asked me if I knew what the date was.

"I glanced at the calendar on the wall. 'It is May the fourteenth,' I said. At this an odd look came over his face, which contained something, I thought, of fear, and he sat without speaking for several minutes. 'Perhaps there is a secret message on the sheet,' I ventured at length in a jocular tone, as much to break the silence as because I thought it at all likely.

"'What do you mean?' he asked.

"'I remember seeing in an *Adventure Book for Girls* which I read at school that spies and people of that sort send messages to each other in invisible ink.' Afterwards, I regretted saying this, but what is done cannot be undone, and I wasn't to know the effect it would have upon the professor. I had simply been trying to lighten the mood a little.

"'How could we read it if it's invisible?' the professor asked.

"'I understand that if you heat it the writing becomes visible,' I said. I picked up the blank sheet, and, using the fire tongs from the coal scuttle, held it just in front of the blazing fire. At first nothing happened, then slowly something began to appear on the sheet. It wasn't a message, however, but a drawing, a sketch of a human face. It was fairly crude, but I could see it was the face of a woman, with long hair and a broad smile. A strangled cry from behind me made me turn. The professor's eyes were wide with fear.

"'What do you know of this?' he demanded sharply.

"'Why, nothing,' I cried in alarm. 'What do you mean?'

"A moment later, the spark of anger in his eyes had vanished. He sunk his head in his hands and remained motionless for several minutes. I turned back to the fire, to see that the flames had caught the bottom edge of the paper, and it was beginning to burn. Quickly, I tossed it onto the fire, and watched as the flames consumed that strange smiling face. Then I turned once more as I heard the professor stand up from the table.

"'Forgive me, Georgina, for speaking to you in that way,' said he in a gentle tone. 'I didn't know what I was saying. Either someone has made a silly mistake, as you say, or someone is deliberately playing a trick upon me. In either case, let us say no more about it.' He picked up the envelope from the table, tore it into several small pieces and threw them onto the fire, where they blazed up in an instant. He then began to speak to me about the architecture of ancient Sicily, which was something I had asked him about the previous day, and the incident of the letter was not mentioned again.

"That night was very dark and overcast. I had been fast asleep, when I was abruptly awakened by a terrible cry. Scarcely knowing what I was doing, I struck a match and lit the candle beside my bed. It was, as I saw from my bedside clock, about quarter to four. The next moment came that terrible cry again, a cry of utter terror, and I knew then for certain that it was Professor Palfreyman. His bedroom is next to mine and the walls are not particularly thick. It was evident that he was having some kind of awful nightmare, and I sat up in bed, unsure what to do. Then I heard him cry again, 'No!' Then, after a slight pause, 'Don't look at it! For God's sake, don't look at the face!' This was followed by a series of bangs and crashes, and I wondered if the professor had fallen out of bed. I flung on my dressing gown, picked up my candle and went to see what had happened.

"My knock at his bedroom door brought no response, so I pushed the door open. Professor Palfreyman was sitting on the side of the bed in his night clothes, looking somewhat dazed, as if he were not fully awake. Before I could speak, he looked up and stared at my face with very great intensity, then emitted the most dreadful cry of fear that I have ever heard in my life, and put his hands up to cover his eyes.

"'Professor!' I cried, taking a step forward. 'Professor! It is I, Georgina! There is nothing to fear!' I lowered my candle, so that it was not casting my face in a strange light, which I thought might have frightened him in his half-awake state. As I did so, he looked up and lowered his hands.

"'Georgina,' he said. 'Is it really you?'

"I assured him that it was, at which a look of indescribable relief came over him. 'I heard you cry out,' I said. 'Did you fall out of bed?'

"'I suppose I must have done,' he replied. 'I can't really remember anything about it.'

"I could see that he was embarrassed and ashamed of the whole episode, so I did not ask him any more about it. 'I think,' I said, 'that you must have had a nightmare.'

"He nodded his head, but insisted that, after a sip of water, he would be all right. I therefore returned to my own room, after lighting his candle from my own. Whether or not he managed to get back to sleep, I do not know, but I heard nothing further that night. I don't know if Mrs Wheeler had heard much of this night-time commotion – she sleeps in the attic and is, besides, somewhat deaf – but her daughter, Beryl, certainly had. The next day I chanced to overhear her speaking to her mother about it and referring to the professor as 'a madman'. I told her that she shouldn't speak that way about Professor Palfreyman. 'He has had rather a lot on his mind recently,' I said, 'and he simply had a bad nightmare, that is all. It could happen to anyone.' She didn't say much to this, but I think she resented being scolded by me, and it was not long after this that she ran off, as I mentioned earlier.

"A few days later, when I was taking some books back to the university library for Professor Palfreyman, I mentioned his nightmare to Mr Martin, who was in the library, working on his thesis. I didn't want to appear a gossipmonger, but I felt the need to speak to an educated person about it. I think I had thought that Tim might laugh it off and thus cheer me, but his response was surprisingly grave.

"'I am not sure it is entirely wise for you to stay with the old fellow any longer,' said he, shaking his head.

"'Why, whatever do you mean, Tim?' I returned. 'Professor Palfreyman has been very kind and considerate to me. I could not simply walk out and leave him just because he had a bad nightmare!'

"'Of course, I understand that,' said Mr Martin, 'and I understand the gratitude you feel towards him. But,' he added after a moment, 'I still find it a little worrying, Georgina. You must know that when people start to lose their grip on reality it can be a very steep downward slope.'

"I was shocked that he should say such a thing and protested vigorously. 'You sound just like our housemaid,' I said, and told him what Beryl had said.

"He laughed. 'I'm sorry if I've offended you, Georgina,' said he, 'but I'm just speaking my mind. How would I feel, do you imagine, if I simply said something to soothe your nerves and told you that there was nothing to worry about, and then heard later that something terrible had happened and you were hurt? I should never forgive myself! It is always better to err on the side of caution, Georgina, even if it means offending someone.'

"'You don't know the professor at all if you think he might do anything which would hurt me!' I retorted, annoyed by his response. 'Why, the professor is the very last person on earth who would ever do anything of the sort! He is the kindest, gentlest man I have ever known, and is, I fear, much more likely to cause harm to himself than to another!'

"'No doubt. But I am only thinking of you, Georgina. You cannot always be taking on other people's problems; sometimes you have to think of yourself. And don't forget that most people who have ended up being described as "mad" didn't start off that way. Rather, they slipped by tiny, imperceptible steps away from normality. So, for all we know, may it be with Professor Palfreyman. He has been a very great scholar in his day and everyone has admired him. He has also been very kind to you. But that does not mean that there cannot ever be anything wrong with him. Come away from there, Georgina, if not for my sake, then for your own safety and peace of mind. Leave Bluebell Cottage.'

"By this time, I was so annoyed that I flatly refused to listen to any more such remarks, and we left it at that. As I travelled home on the train later that afternoon, however, Mr Martin's words came back to me, rattling around in my head, and I found that I could not dismiss them so easily then as I had done earlier in the day. What the future might bring, I could not say, but I determined there and then that I would try my best to remain hopeful and cheery, and that if anyone were gloomy or downcast, it would not be because of me."

Miss Calloway paused and sipped her tea in silence for a few moments, a thoughtful expression on her face.

"Some weeks passed, the bright spring turned into a fine summer, and our existence at Bluebell Cottage settled down once more into a peaceful and placid routine. Professor Palfreyman worked on his manuscripts most days and, once I had attended to the routine work of the household, I assisted him in keeping his papers in order, and also proceeded slowly in identifying and cataloguing his archaeological and artistic specimens. I was also able to indulge my own interest in botany by making sketches of the many wild flowers that grow in the woods behind the house. Sometimes the professor accompanied me and made sketches of his own. He is quite an accomplished artist. One of the books he is working on is an account for younger readers of daily life in Ancient Greece, which he hopes to illustrate with simple drawings of his own. He asked me if I would mind posing with a small amphora on my shoulder, so that he could make a naturalistic sketch of it, which of course I didn't, and he subsequently made numerous other drawings of me in a variety of interesting poses, so one day I may be immortalized in an illustrated book!

"During this period, the professor's academic colleagues continued to drop in to see us from time to time, and in August we had Professor Schultz of Berlin University to stay for two weeks. During the summer vacation, Mr Martin came more frequently, too. Sometimes he would help me in attempting to bring order to the chaos of the professor's possessions, and sometimes, if the weather was fine, we would go for walks through the nearby countryside. Of course, throughout this period, Professor Palfreyman continued to talk to himself, but in a subdued, amiably eccentric sort of way, and I never once heard him sound alarmed or angry. Sometimes, too, I heard him talking in his sleep, but there was no repeat of what had occurred that night in the spring, and if he suffered any nightmares, he kept the fact to himself. A new problem now arose, however, concerning the professor's memory, which had become a little unreliable. Sometimes, he would put something down somewhere and then forget where he had put it, and I would have to search round the house to find it for him. Generally, I was successful, but on one particular occasion I was not, although my failure led to the professor's making an interestingly philosophical admission. The object in question was an ancient Phoenician terracotta oil lamp, which had in the past stood on a low shelf at the side of the study, although it had often been buried under mounds of loose papers and other things. On the day the professor happened to miss it, I searched high and low for it, but in vain. Eventually, although I was reluctant to blame Beryl as she was no longer there to defend herself, I suggested that she had perhaps knocked it off the shelf and broken it some weeks previously, while dusting, and, afraid of admitting what she had done, had simply hidden the pieces somewhere. Professor Palfreyman did not seem very convinced by this explanation at first, but at length he conceded that it might be correct.

"'Although Mrs Wheeler is a charming and warm-hearted lady,' said he in a low voice, closing the study door so that we should not be overheard, 'her children, I regret to say, do not take after her, but rather follow her late husband, who was something of a bad lot.'

"'Children?' I repeated. 'Do you mean to say there are more than just Beryl?'

"The professor nodded his head. 'Mrs Wheeler also has a son, Sidney. His father was often in trouble with the police, and Sidney has followed his father closely in that respect, causing his mother considerable anxiety and unhappiness. He came to visit her here once, and although I tried to be welcoming, I found him rude, charmless and unpleasant. It turned out, anyway, that the only reason he had come here was to try to get some money from his mother, to help him escape from the police, who had a warrant out for his arrest. Where he is now and what he is doing, I have no idea. Anyway,' he continued with a shake of the head, 'with regard to the Phoenician lamp, I felt sure I had seen it since Beryl left us, but I suppose I must now accept that my memory is not as good as it used to be. Ah, well!' he added in a philosophical tone. 'Perhaps it will turn up again, some time in the future. Then again, perhaps it won't! Life is too short, Georgina, to waste it in fretting about inanimate objects, however much one might feel attached to them!' This remark, I felt, rather typified the professor's new attitude: a reluctant acceptance of his slightly declining powers, and a sort of resolute determination to make the most of what remained. All in all, then, I think I could be forgiven for believing that the troubled times were behind us and that our future prospects were in the main only happy ones. Alas! Our troubles, like some foul beast of mythology, were not dead, but simply sleeping, and about to burst upon us anew.

"The summer had passed and autumn was well advanced when, one day, the morning post brought a small package for Professor Palfreyman as we were seated at the breakfast table. This was just two or three weeks ago, in the middle of October.

"'It is probably one of those Etruscan specimens I have been after for a while,' said he in an enthusiastic tone as he cut the string and unwrapped the parcel. 'Let us see!'

"Within the brown paper was a stout cardboard box, and within the box was loose straw and similar packaging material. Professor Palfreyman thrust his hand into this and withdrew a wide, flat object, wrapped in tissue paper, which I thought might be a tile of some kind. He laid it on the table, and I stood up and came round behind his chair to get a better look at it. As he unwrapped the tissue paper, I saw that it was indeed a glazed tile, about four or five inches square. In colour, it was a creamy-white, and on it, in shallow relief, was depicted a most beautiful smiling female face.

"'Oh, how lovely!' I cried aloud, but even as I did so, I knew that something was wrong. With a strange, inarticulate cry, Professor Palfreyman pushed his chair back from the table and staggered to his feet. For a moment he stood there, swaying unsteadily, his eyes staring wildly, his mouth agape, then, abruptly, he pitched forward senseless upon the breakfast table. I called Mrs Wheeler, and between us we managed to lay the professor on the hearthrug, with a blanket over him and a cushion under his head. Mrs Wheeler brought in some fresh strong coffee a few minutes later, and when he stirred, I got him to take a sip. Presently he sat up, but as he did so, he groaned and clutched his head.

"'Oh, my head!' said he. 'What happened?'

"Then, as he remembered, a grim expression came over his face. He stood up unsteadily, then, without another word, picked the tile up from the table and walked out of the house with it. A few moments later, I heard a noise outside, and when I looked out I saw that he had taken a hammer from the tool shed and, with a series of violent blows, was smashing the tile up on the ground. He then picked up all the broken pieces, placed them in a small pail, and carried them off down the back garden and into the woods. When he returned to the house ten minutes later, he made no reference to what had happened. He simply asked me if I would be so good as to clear the debris from the breakfast table, then disappeared into his study to work on his manuscript."

"One moment," said Holmes, holding his hand up to interrupt Miss Calloway's narrative. "When you cleared away the wrapping paper and other materials that had enclosed the tile, did you observe where it had come from, or where it had been posted?"

Miss Calloway shook her head. "It was the first thing that occurred to me," she replied, "but there was no label or other identifying mark anywhere on the package. The postmark was smudged, and all I could see of that was that it had been posted somewhere in London. I also went most carefully through the packing materials, to see if there was a note anywhere in it that we had missed, but there was not."

"What became of this material?"

"I burnt it all in the incinerator in the garden."

"Very well. Pray continue with your account."

"The professor has never referred to this incident since, and there is something in his manner that has prevented my asking him about it. Of course, I have often thought about it and wondered what it might mean, but could make nothing of it. But that it had had a profound effect upon the professor I could not doubt. The following day, I carried some papers into his study and found that he was not at his desk as usual, but had pulled out an old tin trunk from under a chest of drawers and was rooting around in it. Presently, he found what he was looking for and held it up, and I saw that it was a very small revolver. I was aware that he possessed such a weapon, for he had often told me how some of his archaeological expeditions in years gone by had taken him into wild and dangerous places, in which possession of a pistol might be the difference between life and death, but I had never seen it before. He then spent the next hour cleaning and oiling this revolver and, having found an old box of cartridges, spent half the afternoon in target practice at the bottom of the garden. When I went out to ask him what he was doing, he answered me in a grave tone.

"'There are circumstances, Georgina – and one must recognize them when they arise – in which one must be on one's guard at all times.' He then offered to teach me how to use the little pistol effectively, but I declined the offer.

"A few days after this, I had been up to town on various errands, and returned by the late afternoon train. It was a cold, foggy day, and the light had almost gone by the time the train reached Beckenham. There were few people about as I left the station, and by the time I had been walking for two minutes, I was all alone on the road. This did not particularly concern me: I had walked alone down that quiet and remote road so many times in the last year that I felt I could have done it with my eyes closed; but as the grey, drifting fog closed in around me, it did feel uncommonly cold and lonely. I could see only a few feet in front of me, and practically nothing on either side. I had been walking for perhaps ten or twelve minutes, and had turned down the long narrow lane that leads towards Bluebell Cottage, when I had the distinct impression that there was someone else on the road, somewhere behind me. Of course, the fog creates strange echoes of one's own footsteps, in addition to the constant dripping noises among the trees, but on this occasion the impression was so strong that I stopped and turned. There was nothing to be seen there but a white wall of fog, and the other footsteps I'd thought I had heard had stopped when my own did. I turned again and resumed my progress through the fog, but this time at a brisker rate. Then I had the impression that someone or something was in the wood at the side of the road, keeping step with me, and I hurried forward. But the other steps, and the rustling in the trees, at once increased in pace, too, and I began to run as fast as I could. By the time I reached the garden gate of Bluebell Cottage and could make out the hall light shining through the fanlight over the door, I was almost completely out of breath. However, relieved though I was, I did not pause, but pushed open the gate, ran up the short path and hurried in at the front door.

"As I took my coat off, I put my head into Professor Palfreyman's study to tell him I was home, but saw to my surprise that he was not there. I then went through to the kitchen, where Mrs Wheeler was making pastry, and asked her if she knew where the professor was. She said that she thought she had heard him go out to the garden half an hour previously and had not seen him since.

"'But it's quite dark now,' I protested. 'What is he doing in the garden in the dark?'

"Before she could answer, we heard the front door open and, looking out of the kitchen, I saw it was the professor, looking grim-faced. As he came in, I saw that he slipped his little pistol into his jacket pocket.

"'I thought I heard someone moving about out there,' said he in answer to my query. I suggested that it was perhaps me he had heard, as I had only recently arrived, and asked if he had been up the road at all, but he shook his head. I then ventured to suggest that we had perhaps both been mistaken, but this suggestion seemed to irritate him intensely, and I wished I had not made it. Then, as we stood there in the hall, we both heard the unmistakeable sound of footsteps on the garden path. A moment later, there came a loud rat-a-tat-tat at the doorknocker. Professor Palfreyman yanked the door open and there, blinking in the light of the hall, stood Professor Ainscow.

"He looked from one of us to the other, an expression of curiosity on his features. 'I'm sorry to barge in on you without warning, Palfreyman,' he said at last. 'You appear a little preoccupied. But I wanted to discuss the exhibition at the British Museum with you.'

"'That's perfectly all right, Ainscow,' returned the professor in an affable tone. 'We were just discussing something. It's nothing, really. We thought we heard someone out in the garden, that's all. Do come in, old man. Will you stay for supper?'

"'If it's not too much of an imposition.'

"So Professor Ainscow dined with us that evening, and I must say I was glad he did, for his presence lightened the mood considerably. The two men continued their discussion for some time after supper, then Professor Palfreyman accompanied his colleague to the railway station. I was unsure whether this was out of courtesy to his guest, or because he wished to see if there was anyone loitering outside in the lane. When he returned, he looked a little agitated again, but this might simply have been the result of coming into the bright house from the dark lane outside.

"'Did Professor Ainscow catch his train?' I enquired.

"'Yes, yes, he did,' Professor Palfreyman replied, but in an abstracted tone, as if his mind were on something else. 'Georgina,' said he after a moment, 'there is something I wish to tell you. However,' he added, 'I think I will wait until tomorrow. Thank you, by the way, for being such very good company at the supper table this evening. I am sure Ainscow was very glad he came. I probably shouldn't tell you this, but he paid you a great compliment as we walked up the road. He said he thought you must be the prettiest assistant that any archaeologist had ever had, and if I ever felt that I no longer required your services, he would take you on like a shot.'

"I laughed heartily at this, as much from embarrassment as

humour, but the laughter died on my lips as I saw the professor's grave face. 'For my own shortcomings and failings, Georgina,' he said, 'I am very sorry. I sometimes think I may have outlived my usefulness in this world.'

"'What nonsense!' I cried, patting his arm. 'Don't say such things, Professor! Don't even think them! What you need is a good night's rest, and then I'm sure everything will seem better!'

"Alas! He might have needed a good night's rest, but I don't think he got one. I heard him talking to himself in his sleep in the small hours of the night, and it was clear he was experiencing a terrible nightmare, for his voice gradually grew louder and more agitated, though whether from fear or anger, I could not quite decide. Some of the phrases I heard him use were such as I had heard before: 'Don't look at it! For God's sake, don't look at the face!' and similar exhortations.

"The following morning, the professor's features bore a haggard look, but after a solid breakfast – which we ate largely in silence – and several cups of coffee, he seemed restored to his usual affable and urbane self. It was as I was about to leave the breakfast table that he spoke to me.

"'Georgina,' said he, in a kindly, thoughtful voice, 'I will tell you now what has been weighing on my mind lately, and what I am going to do about it. I feel it is only fair to you. You have had to put up with a lot lately.'

"'Not at all,' I began, but he waved my protests aside.

"'There are things in my past of which I am not especially proud,' he continued after a moment, 'and one thing in particular. This is not entirely a secret: most of the facts have always been known to my colleagues, to the relevant authorities and to anyone else who cared to enquire about the matter, but my thoughts – the thoughts I had at the time and have had since – are known to no one but me. They relate to some of the disturbances you have had to endure recently, Georgina. What I am therefore going to do is to write out a full, honest and accurate account of what happened, so that if – when – I die, you will be able to read it, and then you will understand everything.'

"'Don't talk like that, Professor!' I interrupted. 'I'm sure you have many good years ahead of you! You'd better have, for you haven't yet finished even one of those three books you intended to write!'

"Professor Palfreyman smiled at me. 'It is good of you to be so encouraging, Georgina! But I do sometimes wonder if I shouldn't perhaps think of making way for the younger generation. I'm not sure I deserve to live any longer.'

"'Nonsense!'

"'This brings me to the other thing I wished to say to you. I know, from conversations we have had, that although of course you wished to care for your dear mother as well as you could, you nevertheless felt somewhat imprisoned in the house while you were doing so. You found life there very dull and tedious. You should know, then, that the very last thing I should ever wish upon you is that you should feel imprisoned in this house, Georgina. Much as I enjoy your presence here, you should not feel you have any duty to remain if you don't wish to.'

"'It is quite unnecessary for you to say these things,' I responded. 'I can assure you that the last year has been the happiest year of my life. If the remainder of my life were just half as happy, I should be more than satisfied.'

"'It is kind of you to say so,' said he, 'but the fact remains that you are young, and may meet someone of your own age with whom you wish to spend the remainder of your life. In which case, I should not wish you to feel in any way restricted by the fact that I have found you such a pleasant companion here. I am not so selfish as that, and I do not wish you to think that I am.'

"'If you are referring to Mr Martin,' said I, 'then I should tell you that he is simply a friend to me, and I certainly have no plans for our relations to be other than that. Besides, he himself has proposed nothing to me of the sort you suggest.'

"'Perhaps not, and I express no judgement as to whether Mr Martin would or would not be a suitable candidate for you, Georgina, but I know that it is in his mind to make such a proposal to you. One man generally knows what another man is thinking so far as these matters are concerned.'

"'Should he, or anyone else, ever make such a proposal to me, then I will let you know what my response is,' I said. 'Until then, I should prefer to drop the subject.'

"Professor Palfreyman laughed. 'Very well!' said he, 'At least I have aired what I wished to air. Now let us be about our work!'

"That was last Thursday, and since then Professor Palfreyman has been scribbling away on his foolscap most of the time and has scarcely spoken to me except at mealtimes. He did go up to town on Friday morning on some errand or other, but I don't know what for, as he didn't tell me. It has been a strange few days. Dr Webb called in on Monday afternoon, and was very rude. When I happened to mention that Professor Palfreyman had been very busy lately, he retorted, 'He's not too busy to see me,' which was not at all what I had meant, and when I took a cup of tea into the study for him, he completely ignored me. When he left, he did not say a word to me, despite the fact that I was standing in the garden when he walked down the path.

"Yesterday morning, Professor Palfreyman had another of those letters, containing a blank sheet of paper. This time I made no suggestion about invisible writing, or anything of the sort, and he simply tore it up and threw it on the fire. In the afternoon, I took some papers up to town for him, and as the train passed Herne Hill I happened to think of Mrs Walsh, an old acquaintance of my mother's who used to live there. Then an occasion when she visited us came into my mind, when she had spoken in glowing terms of you, Mr Holmes. She said you had helped a neighbour of hers, Mrs Trubshaw, who had been receiving unpleasant anonymous letters."

"Ah, yes!" said Holmes. "Edith Trubshaw! I remember the case well! As I recall, I was able to sort the matter out to her satisfaction."

"So Mrs Walsh said. As soon as I remembered that, I at once wondered if you could perhaps sort my troubles out, too. There and then, I resolved to consult you as soon as possible. At the university archaeology department I met Mr Martin and mentioned my idea to him. To be honest, he was a bit dubious at first; he was unsure what you would be able to achieve, but as we discussed it, he became more enthusiastic. 'If Mr Holmes could somehow discover what it is that lies behind all this,' said he, 'and what the secret is that Professor Palfreyman is keeping to himself, then perhaps it would be better for everyone. On the other hand,' he added, 'if the professor wants to keep his own secrets, that is his right, and we can hardly go prying into his private affairs. It cannot be denied that he sometimes seems rather delicately balanced, and we would not want our interference to make him worse.'

"'No, of course not. But I shall put the matter in the hands of Mr Sherlock Holmes first thing tomorrow morning and see what he has to say about it. It will be a great relief to me to know that someone else is discreetly looking into the matter.'

"'I agree,' said Tim. 'Do you know, Georgina, I think I shall call in at Bluebell Cottage later tomorrow, so you can tell me all about it!'

"I had several jobs to do in town before I could catch the train back to Beckenham. After my experience the previous week, I wanted to make sure this time that I didn't leave it too late, so that it would still be light by the time I reached my destination. Unfortunately, however, I just missed the train I had intended to catch, and the one I did get was held up for nearly half an hour at Herne Hill, and then stuck in Penge tunnel for a further twenty minutes, so that by the time I reached Beckenham the light had gone completely. I considered taking a cab, but there were none there, so I set out to walk home as usual. This time, at least, I thought, I was mentally prepared and should not be so nervous on the quiet lanes to Bluebell Cottage. By the time I turned off the main road, however, there was absolutely no one about, and nothing to be heard but the drip, drip, drip among the trees on either side. The trees themselves, even those nearest to the lane, were but dark, shadowy shapes to me, and I began to wish I had waited for a cab after all. Forcing myself to look straight ahead and ignore the shifting fog among the trees, I pressed on. It was extremely cold and my cheeks felt as if they were touched by icy fingers.

"Then, when I knew I must be approaching Stagg's Lane – although so thick was the fog that even the familiar little roadside landmarks were quite hidden from me – I heard, above the constant dripping of the trees, what sounded like someone moving through the wood to the left of the lane. I increased my speed slightly, but the movement at the side seemed to stay with me, then, out of the corner of my eye, I thought I saw a shadowy shape slip from one tree to the next. Without turning my head to the side, I picked up my skirts and broke into a run, breathing heavily. On down that lonely, muddy lane I ran, madly, frantically, as if running for my life. For an instant, I had the impression of something in the air to my left, then something struck me hard on the side of the head, and with a scream I tumbled forward into the mud.

"What happened next, I don't know. As I tried to push myself up from the muddy ground, I heard muffled footsteps rapidly approaching. I think I may have screamed again, and then I passed out.

"When I came to, I was lying on the couch in the sitting room at Bluebell Cottage, with a fire blazing in the grate and a plaid blanket laid over me. Professor Palfreyman and Mrs Wheeler were standing there, speaking quietly, and they turned to me as I opened my eyes.

"'There, there,' said Mrs Wheeler. 'How are you, my dear?'

"'I feel a bit sick,' I said. 'What happened?'

"'You've had a fall, my dear. Professor Palfreyman found you lying in the lane, in the mud, and carried you in. Here,' she continued, picking up a cup and saucer from a side table, 'have a sip of this. It'll make you feel better!'

"'Would you like something stronger?' the professor asked as I sipped the tea, but I shook my head.

"'I shall be all right in a minute,' I said. I sat up, swung my feet to the floor and tried to stand up, but I staggered slightly and nearly fell over.

"'Don't try to stand,' said the professor, rearranging the rug over my knees. 'We must keep you warm,' he added, pushing the couch a little nearer to the fire.

"'What *has* happened to me?' I repeated, feeling a little dizzy.

"'I don't know,' said the professor, shaking his head. 'Luckily, I happened to be out in the garden, and heard you cry out. You had fallen just near the corner of the lane. Did you trip?'

"'No,' I said. 'Something struck me on the side of the head.'

"The professor leaned over and examined the side of my head. 'There is a muddy mark there,' said he, 'but the skin is not broken. I wonder what it could have been?'

"'I believe there was someone out there,' I said, 'who flung something at me. If it hasn't cut me, then perhaps it was not a stone but a bit of stick. It certainly hurt, anyway.'

"'How dreadful!' said Mrs Wheeler.

"The professor shook his head in puzzlement. 'It will be too dark out there to see anything now, but I'll have a look first thing in the morning and see if I can find anything.'

"Later, Mrs Wheeler recommended a hot bath as being the best cure for a fall, as she referred to it, so I followed her suggestion. Afterwards I came downstairs in my dressing gown and sat for some time in the kitchen, watching her prepare some buttered toast and cocoa for me.

"'What was Professor Palfreyman doing out in the garden in the dark?' I asked her.

"She hesitated for a moment. 'It was because of you, miss,' she replied at length. 'He didn't want me to tell you, but he's been worried about you all week. He came in the kitchen earlier, saying, "Isn't that girl back yet?" and when I said, "No," he said, "I'm worried about her, Mrs Wheeler. I think I'll go out, walk up the lane a bit and see if I meet her!" The next thing I knew, he was coming in at the front door, carrying you in his arms and telling me to put the kettle on.'

"I retired to bed early last night, as you will imagine. Perhaps because of that, I woke in the middle of the night. I lit my candle and saw that it was half past three. As I did so, I heard the professor's voice from the room next door. 'No!' he cried, 'I don't know!' Then something about 'danger!' Then, after a long silence, 'Don't look at it!' This was followed by a dull thud, and I guessed that he had knocked something over, or even fallen out of bed again. But this time, I stayed where I was. I felt too worn out and shaken up myself to minister to him. After a time, all was silent, and eventually I fell asleep once more. This morning I felt for the first time that I could no longer go on in this way, so as soon as we had had breakfast, I put my coat on and came away. There you are, Mr Holmes. Now you know everything, and here I am!"

Sherlock Holmes opened his eyes, but did not respond at once. Instead, he stared into the fire for some time, as if he might see a solution to this strange mystery in the flickering flames.

"Do you know," he asked Miss Calloway at length, "if Professor Palfreyman has made any enquiries into where these strange, anonymous letters might have come from?"

"I don't believe so," she replied. "If he has, he has said nothing about it to me and, as I mentioned, he threw them both in the fire almost as soon as he had received them."

"And the tile with the smiling face on it?"

"He has never mentioned it again since the day it arrived, when, as I described, he smashed it into pieces."

"Do you know what he did with the pieces?"

"I think he may have buried them in the wood at the bottom of the garden. There is a glade in the wood, which is a favourite spot of his, where he sometimes sits on a log and smokes his pipe when he has some knotty problem to resolve. Perhaps he buried the broken tile there."

Holmes glanced at the clock. "It is certainly an interesting case you have brought us, Miss Calloway, but one that is beset with difficulties. There are, so far as I can see, seven possible explanations for all that has occurred in and around Bluebell Cottage in the last year, although some of them are fairly unlikely. The two likeliest explanations . . ."

"Yes?"

". . . are what I intend to concentrate on. Tell me, Miss Calloway, have you heard, from Professor Palfreyman himself, or from Mrs Wheeler or her daughter, whether there were any mysterious occurrences in previous years, before you joined the household?"

Our visitor shook her head. "Not as far as I am aware," said she. "Mrs Wheeler had often heard the professor muttering to himself when concentrating on his work, but that is all."

"Well," said Holmes in a thoughtful tone. "That is suggestive, is it not?"

Miss Calloway's features expressed surprise. "I don't know what you mean," she said. "I have had nothing to do with what has occurred."

Holmes leaned over and patted her gently on the arm. "No, no, of course not," said he. "That was not my meaning." He lapsed into silence and remained unmoving for several minutes, a look of intense concentration upon his face, then, abruptly, he sprang to his feet. "There are some features of this case that cause me particular anxiety," said he, "and I don't think we should waste any time in getting down to Beckenham. The quickest way from here will be by the direct line from Victoria, I imagine."

"Undoubtedly," concurred Miss Calloway.

"Then that is the way we shall go. Will you come, Watson?"

"If I can be of any help to you."

"Most certainly! Your presence may be invaluable."

Less than thirty minutes later, we were seated in a first-class carriage as our train rumbled out of the station, across the Thames and down through the southern suburbs. Although I tried to apply my mind to the mystery Miss Calloway had brought us, I could make little of it, and could not imagine what we would do when we reached Bluebell Cottage. It was clear that Professor Palfreyman was sorely troubled by something in his past, but whether the guilt or remorse he felt was justified or not, we could not say. It was also clear that he suffered a certain degree of mental instability, but this seemed to vary considerably from one day to another, and sometimes even within the same day, and what could Sherlock Holmes, or anyone else, hope to do about that?

As we were leaving Beckenham station, a stout gentleman was approaching, who greeted Miss Calloway warmly. She introduced him to us as Professor Ainscow, introducing us simply as friends of hers.

"I'm not having the best of luck today," he said. "I'd arranged to meet Dr Webb at Ludgate Hill station to travel down here, but although I waited an hour, he never showed up, so I came on alone. Then I walked all the way down to Bluebell Cottage, only to find that there was no one at home!" He turned as a train approached the station. "My train, I think!" he called as he hurried off. "I've left a large envelope for Professor Palfreyman on the front doorstep. You can't miss it!"

There were no cabs about in the station yard, so we set off on foot at a brisk pace.

"Why is your cook, Mrs Wheeler, not at home?" Holmes asked Miss Calloway, as we walked along. "Will she have gone into Beckenham, to the shops?"

"No. She goes to visit her sister in Norwood every Wednesday morning. After getting the kitchen fire going, she left early, before breakfast, as she always does."

"So Professor Palfreyman has been left by himself all morning?"

"Yes," said Miss Calloway, sounding slightly amused, "but I'm sure he can cope!"

After a few minutes we turned south off the main road, down a narrow and muddy country lane, which Miss Calloway informed us was Aylmer's Lane. A little further on, we passed two farm-worker's cottages on our right, and then the lane entered a wood, the trees a dense screen on either side. The day had seemed only moderately foggy in the centre of Beckenham, but now, as we made our way deeper into the damp countryside, the wisps of grey mist thickened among the trees, seeming to move like wraiths as we passed by.

"Are these the woods in which you believe someone was lurking last night?" asked Holmes.

"Yes," replied Miss Calloway, "only a little further on."

The lane twisted and turned as it passed through the woods, until, ahead of us, we saw another lane branching off to the left.

"That is Stagg's lane," said Miss Calloway. "Bluebell Cottage lies about thirty yards along there on the left. And here," she added, as we approached the corner, "is the spot where someone threw something at me."

We turned into Stagg's Lane, and in a few moments had reached the garden gate of the cottage. A rustic-looking man in leather gaiters was in the garden, trimming the hedge with a pair of shears.

"Hello, Perkins," said Miss Calloway. "Have you been here long?"

"No, miss, about five minutes. There didn't seem to be anybody at home, so I thought I'd just do what we agreed last week."

"Very good," said she. "I'll speak to you again in a few minutes."

"Did you see anyone on the road as you came down here?" Holmes asked the gardener.

"No, sir, not a soul."

Leaning against the front door was a large manila envelope, which Miss Calloway picked up, then she unlocked the door and we followed her into the house. We waited in the hall while she went looking for the professor, but she was back in a few moments, declaring that he was nowhere about.

"Perhaps he has gone for a walk," said she. "I have a little desk at the side of the dining room, where I deal with some of the professor's papers," she added, "and sometimes, when we have missed each other, he leaves a little note there for me, to tell me where he has gone. I'll see if there's any message today." We followed her into the dining room, which was at the rear of the house. It was a neat little room, with a view over a long back garden. "Yes," said Miss Calloway after a moment. "Here we are!" She picked up a folded slip of paper from the top of the desk, opened it out and read it.

"Does it say where the professor has gone?" asked Holmes.

Miss Calloway shook her head. "No," she replied and passed the note to us.

It contained a brief message, which ran as follows:

My dear Georgina,

I have mentioned to you recently that I was writing an account of a passage in my earlier life, which I would leave for you to read when I am gone. Having finally completed it, however, I now feel that there is little point in postponing the matter, and you may as well read it now. I think you deserve an explanation for all the upsets and disturbances you have had to endure in the last year, and I hope you find the explanation satisfactory. For myself, I must say that having set it all down on paper, I feel as if a great weight has been lifted from my shoulders. Should I not be here when you wish to read it, you will find the papers in the Chinese box.

Ever yours,
James Palfreyman

"What is this Chinese box he refers to?" asked Holmes.

"It is a small chest in the professor's study, in which he keeps his private papers. When Beryl was here, she would sometimes muddle up his papers when supposedly 'tidying', and he found it useful to have somewhere to keep his most important papers where Beryl could not interfere with them. The chest cannot be opened unless one knows the secret."

"Can you open it?"

"Yes. The professor showed me how. Save only what happened to him many years ago, I don't believe there are any secrets between us."

We followed Miss Calloway into the professor's study, which was very untidy, with little piles of paper on every surface, some of which had slipped to the floor. Upon a side table by the wall stood a black lacquered chest, about eighteen inches wide and twelve inches deep, its surface adorned with yellow and pink flowers, painted in a characteristically Chinese style. "As you see," said our guide, "some of these flowers are slightly embossed. The secret is to press this yellow one firmly, and then slide this pink one sideways." She did as she described, and we saw a narrow gap appear between the chest and the lid, into which she inserted the tip of her finger, and thus lifted up the lid. Within the chest was a disordered litter of envelopes and loose papers, but upon the very top of the pile was a long cream envelope, addressed in a neat hand to "Miss Georgina Calloway". She picked it up, opened it and took from within it several sheets of folded foolscap.

"I certainly think you ought to read it now," said Holmes, "but the question is whether you or Professor Palfreyman would object to our hearing it, too."

"This account is addressed to me," replied Miss Calloway after a moment's thought, "and is therefore mine to do with as I think fit. My opinion is that you should hear it, too, gentlemen; for the more information you have, the more chance you have of successfully helping both the professor and me. If you would read it aloud, then we can all hear it at the same time."

Holmes took the papers and passed them to me. "I think Dr Watson's sonorous tones will be best-suited to the task of narrator," said he with a chuckle. We therefore returned to the dining room and seated ourselves round the table, where I began the following account:

> You should know first, Georgina, that in those relatively far-off days – over thirty years ago – the head of our archaeological faculty was Professor Ormiston, an elderly man who was approaching retirement, with no obvious successor. Of the younger men who hoped to succeed Ormiston, there were three with a realistic chance of doing so: David Webb, John Strange and myself. Although we were therefore in this respect rivals, we were friendly rivals, and there was no acrimony between us – at least, so far as I was aware. Of the three of us, the strongest candidate – especially in his own opinion – was Strange. He was undoubtedly brilliant, but his brilliance was somewhat flashy and superficial, and was, moreover, marred by an arrogance and conceit that prevented his ever forming any real friendships among his fellow researchers. I mention these facts not because they had any direct bearing on what I am about to relate, but simply so you will understand the general background.
>
> It was during a warm period in May that Strange and I were on an expedition in a mountainous and barren region of Western Macedonia. This is sometimes referred to as Pelagonia, although, more accurately, it was a border region between the old kingdoms of Orestis and Lynchestia. It was a wild and arid region, and, outside of a handful of small villages, was inhabited mainly – save for a few wandering shepherds and their flocks – by bears, wolves and lynx. You will understand, then, why I always travelled with a pistol in my pocket. Nor were the dangers confined only to the wild animals I mentioned. It was then only a few years after the

conclusion of the Crimean War, during which time the region had seen several uprisings against the Turkish authorities. These uprisings had been suppressed, but the grievances of the people remained, and they were likely at the slightest provocation to vent their feelings not only on any figures of authority, but also upon outsiders of any sort who ventured into their territory.

What had brought us to this inhospitable corner of Europe were persistent reports we had found among ancient records that the tomb of the mysterious and largely forgotten King Pellas II was located there, somewhere in these barren, rocky hills. Pellas had ruled for a very short time during the fourth century BC – less than a year – and many histories of the period do not even mention him. It had therefore become something of a challenge to us to find out all we could about this shadowy and largely unknown figure. Where had he come from? Why was his reign so short? How did he die, and where was he buried? It was this last question to which we thought we might have a clue. In an old monastery in the Pindus Mountains, we had been shown a cache of ancient manuscripts, many of them much older than the monastery itself. My knowledge of ancient Greek was good, as was that of Strange, but many of these documents were in a variety of Greek that we could scarcely recognize, let alone understand, and translating them was very difficult. Eventually, however, we understood enough to be confident that some of the very oldest documents referred to Pellas II, the elusive figure we sought.

As far as I could make out, Pellas's final resting place was in a cave high in the mountains, where it was said to be protected by the goddess Thesprotia. This name I recognized as one of the most ancient deities of the region, venerated in other places under a variety of different names, and whose name has been used for a small settlement by the coast, many miles away over the mountains. As we studied these ancient texts, endeavouring to work out the precise location of the cave that held the mortal remains of Pellas II, we came across a curious instruction or warning, concerning Thesprotia.

"There is danger," it said, "for he who regards the face of the goddess"; and in another place it repeated this warning: "Do not gaze upon the face of Thesprotia." What this might mean, we had no idea. Strange dismissed it as what he described as the usual ancient superstitions, but I was not so sure: such repeated warnings were unusual, and I wondered if the meaning might become clearer should we ever find Pellas's final resting place.

The Turkish authorities had not been particularly helpful to us, but they had provided us with a guide who was also an interpreter. Unfortunately, the man was not much use in either role, and it soon became clear to us that his chief function in our party was to act as a spy, watching everything we did and reporting it all back to the authorities. However, he did do us one very great service. We had been camped in a particularly inhospitable spot in the mountains for three days without making any significant discoveries when, on the afternoon of the fourteenth of May, our guide returned from a long ramble round the area. He was in a state of high excitement and insisted we come with him at once. What he showed us, about a mile from the camp, was a carefully executed carving on a low outcrop of rock, which had been almost hidden beneath a thick little thorn bush. This carving was of a sixteen-pointed sun, which we realized at once was of immense significance.

The sixteen-pointed sun is a symbol unique to that part of the world, although its use has varied greatly over the centuries. Sometimes it seems to have represented the royal line of Macedonia, sometimes the leader of some lesser mountain tribe, and sometimes its use is obscure and seems to refer back to yet more ancient times and the worship of the sun as a deity, in the mist-shrouded days of pre-history. Whatever its meaning might be in this case, I reasoned, the fact that someone had gone to the great trouble of carving it so carefully into this very hard rock must be of significance.

The topmost point of the carving was a little longer than the others and, as one faced the symbol, seemed to indicate some spot higher up the mountain. I suggested to Strange that we mount an expedition in that direction at first light the following morning, but he, headstrong and impulsive as always, wanted to set off at once. I was against this, for the afternoon was well advanced and I knew, from rambles in the Pennines as a boy, that, in hilly country, somewhere that appears relatively close at hand can take you three hours to reach. Strange, however, would not be dissuaded – I had never once known him take anyone else's advice, though he was always quick enough to give his own – so, reluctantly, I agreed to go with him. Our guide returned to the camp and Strange and I set off together.

For several hours, and with some difficulty, we ascended the hill before us. The higher we went, the poorer the footing became and the sparser the vegetation among the loose, broken rocks. Eventually, almost exhausted, we sat down to rest for a few minutes on a broad flat ledge. Even as we did so, we both noticed, on a boulder at the back of the ledge, another sixteen-pointed sun carved into the face of the rock. This clearly indicated that we were on the right track, and after a brief rest, we continued our ascent of the mountain. By this time, we were so high that there were no signs that even the mountain sheep or goats ever ventured up there. At last, as the daylight was beginning to fade, we surmounted a narrow ridge and came upon another small plateau. At the back of this plateau, and perfectly invisible from lower down the mountain, was a cluster of stunted thorn bushes, and behind them, quite visible now, the dark, gaping mouth of a large cave. There could be little doubt that this was the place to which the sun symbols had directed us.

After another short rest to catch our breath, we lit the lanterns we had brought with us, and made our way into the cave.

"Be careful, Strange!" I cautioned.

"Don't be so timid, Palfreyman! There's no point in hanging back!" he returned in characteristic fashion. Strange was one of those people who seemed unable to converse without insulting the person he was speaking to. I was not especially timid, and nor was I "hanging back", as he put it. On the contrary, he had brusquely pushed in front of me as we made our way into the cave, as if to ensure that he was the first to enter. I don't think that in all the years I had known him, I had ever once seen him enter a room behind someone else. He really was, in many ways, the most dislikeable person I had ever known.

Slowly, holding up our lanterns to light the way, we made our way deeper into that very dark cave. The floor beneath our feet was surprisingly damp and smooth in places, as if sculpted by a considerable flow of water at some time in the distant past, and by the occasional flow even now, perhaps after one of the violent storms that are a feature of some months in those parts. Then, all at once, I descried another carving of the sixteen-pointed sun, quite small, on a projecting rock at the side of the cave, and called my companion back to see it.

"We are definitely going the right way," said he, and set off forwards once more.

The floor of the cave had been sloping down for some time, quite steeply in places, but presently it levelled off again, and was covered in sand and other small debris. We had progressed some way – perhaps twenty yards – along this easier terrain, when something caught our eyes on the right-hand wall of the cave. I was about three or four yards behind Strange, but I think we saw it at the same moment.

"What on earth is that?" said I.

"It's a tile of some sort," Strange murmured, as much to himself as to me, and as I approached a little closer I could see that he was right.

It was a large tile, some seven or eight inches square, which seemed to have been set into a carved recess in the wall of the cave and affixed with mortar, some of which was visible round the edges. The tile itself, although a little dusty, was clearly creamy white in colour and highly glazed, showing in relief the face of a woman. It was a beautiful face, smiling in an angelic manner. At a glance, I could see that in its general style and craftsmanship it was from a later era than the time of Pellas II – at least late Greek, and possibly even Roman. This suggested that the tomb of Pellas II – if it were indeed in this cave – had been venerated centuries after his death. But as these thoughts flitted through my mind, I also recollected the warnings we had read in those ancient manuscripts.

"Thesprotia!" I cried. "Strange, it's Thesprotia! Be careful! Remember the warnings!"

"Don't be absurd, Palfreyman!" came Strange's reply, although he did not turn to me, but kept his eyes fixed upon that smiling face, almost as if he were physically unable to remove his gaze from it. "Don't be superstitious!" It was then that a bitter thought flashed through my brain. I did not put it into words, not even in my own head, but, had I done so, it would have been something like, All right, Strange, you conceited fool! Be it on your own head! Die, if that is what you wish! A moment later, I had suppressed this thought, and cried aloud again.

"Strange!" I cried as he leaned forward to brush the dust from the tile with his hand. "Don't look at it! Don't look at the face!" Then some slight noise or sixth sense made me look down at his feet. There was something wrong there, I felt sure, although I could see nothing. I lowered my lantern to get a better look. "Strange!" I began. "The floor!"

"The flaw is in your reasoning, Palfreyman," he returned in that lazily arrogant manner of his, but the words died abruptly on his lips and, as there came a sudden sound of cracking and crumbling, he let out the most dreadful, deafening scream of fear. There was a puff of dust, and in a fraction of a second, my companion had vanished utterly from my sight. Clouds of dust had been stirred up and swirled about me, and for the best part of a minute I could see nothing at all. Then, as the dust cleared, I saw that where my colleague had been standing, in front of the tile on the wall, was a large gaping hole. It was clearly a classic Macedonian death trap, of which I had heard vague stories – a pit for the unwary, covered with sticks, dust and other debris, designed to protect the tomb of Pellas, and precisely what those ancient manuscripts had warned against. I ran to the edge of the hole, lay on the floor and peered down, but it was pitch black and I could see nothing. Evidently, Strange's lantern had been extinguished as he fell. I held my own lantern as far down in the hole as I could, but it did not help. The pit was evidently very deep.

"Strange!" I called, again and again, but received no answer. In other circumstances, I might have lit a bundle of dry brushwood and tossed it down the hole to illuminate the bottom of the pit, but of course I could not do that while Strange was lying down there. Nor could I lower my lantern down on a rope, for we had brought no rope with us. I cursed myself for this, although, in truth, it was not my fault but Strange's. If he had not been so impatient and determined to set off at once to look for Pellas's tomb, we might have equipped ourselves properly for such an expedition.

Eventually I gave up calling down that dark pit, from which the only response was the echo of my own voice. I could do nothing further by myself; I would have to go and get help. I made my way to the mouth of the cave, where I found to my dismay that night had fallen, and the world outside the cave was as pitch black as that within. There was no moon that night, and save only the faint, cold light of the stars above me, there was not a light to be seen anywhere, from one horizon to the other.

I set off, picking my way carefully down the hill, but if the climb up had been difficult, the descent in the dark was almost impossible. I slipped, I stumbled, I fell. I picked myself up and carried on, but almost at once slipped again on the loose stones with which this part of the mountain was littered. It was almost hopeless, but I could achieve nothing by staying where I was, so I pressed on, testing every foothold before I put my weight on it. Then, perhaps inevitably, one small ledge, which had seemed firm when I tested it, abruptly collapsed when I put my whole weight on it, and in an instant I was plunging down the hill, head over heels, bringing down an avalanche of small rocks and stones with me, and with no idea whatever of where I was falling to. At some point in the fall, I cracked my head on a rock and knocked myself senseless, and that was the last thing I knew.

When I came to my senses, it was broad daylight and two of our porters were bending over me. My clothes were torn, my head ached furiously and I was covered in cuts and bruises. They helped me to my feet, but I could not walk unaided. Mercifully, I had no broken bones, but both my ankles were badly sprained. I explained to the men what had happened the previous evening, and an expedition was mounted to find and rescue my lost companion. The porters had brought a coil of rope with them, and we lowered a lantern into that dreadful pit into which Strange had fallen. It was very deep – at least twenty-five feet down – and we could see by the light of the lantern that Strange lay unmoving at the bottom. One of the porters volunteered to be lowered down, and he reported that, as we feared, Strange was dead. With some difficulty, we eventually got his body out of the pit, and it was dreadful to see the broken remains of what had been a strong and forceful man.

This, then, Georgina, is a true account of what occurred in the wilds of Western Macedonia all those years ago. I recovered soon enough from my injuries, and was feted as the discoverer of the lost tomb of Pellas II, although I always made sure I gave full credit to the part that Strange had played in its discovery. His death at our moment of triumph was sad, but perhaps the most melancholy aspect of it was that no one seemed to mourn him. He was unmarried and had no close family, and when I at last succeeded in discovering some distant relatives of his, and informed them of his death, it was clear from their response that the matter was of no consequence to them. The strangely ironic conclusion of it all, then, was that I, who had disliked the man so intensely in life, was the only one saddened and affected by his death.

Later, when Professor Ormiston retired, I became the new head of the archaeological department, and I suppose I should be happy that my subsequent career was a reasonably distinguished one. But I have always been haunted by what happened that evening in Macedonia. That brief fraction of a second, when Strange screamed and vanished from my sight in a cloud of dust, is the worst moment of my life, and I cannot shake my brain free of it. Could I have done more to save him? Could my warning about the ground beneath his feet have been given more quickly, or in a louder tone? Could I have been more insistent in my warnings about Thesprotia? Were my actions – or lack of them – influenced in any way by my personal dislike of the man? I do not know the answers to any of these questions, but they will not leave me alone. They plague my thoughts during the day, and haunt my dreams at night. For all my professional success, and respected position in society, I have never in my life known untroubled happiness. At risk of embarrassing you, Georgina, I will say that the closest I have ever come to true happiness is in the last year, since you have moved into Bluebell Cottage. I am sorry that in return for the happiness your presence has brought me, I have been the cause of such alarms and upsets for you. It really is not fair on you, and I am not so selfish as to think it is. Sometimes I think that this state of affairs cannot, or should not, continue.

That, I believe, is everything, Georgina, and I hope you will think none the worse of me for it. In conclusion, I should like to offer you three observations, which the above experience and other episodes in my life have taught me. First, that no man, however clever he may think himself, ever really knows what will happen next. Second, that you should always be on your guard, for although first, superficial impressions can sometimes be surprisingly accurate, occasionally they are not, but are, on the contrary, quite misleading. Third, that there is nothing more terrible in all the world than a smile on the face of evil. Remember these things.

Your good friend, James Palfreyman

We sat in silence for some time when I had finished reading the professor's account.

"Well, well," said Holmes at last. "It is a singular document indeed, which explains what has been weighing so heavily on the professor's mind. As he mentioned to you last week, however, Miss Calloway, most of the facts connected with the matter are already widely known – if not to you – so the only really new information concerns his very honest depiction of the strong antipathy he felt for this man Strange. Moreover, he makes no mention of the tile or the anonymous letters he has recently received through the post. I should very much like to know what his private thoughts are on those things. In his absence, however, we must do the best we can, and it is certainly upon the tile that we must now concentrate all our energies."

"What could the tile possibly tell us?" asked Miss Calloway.

"Someone deliberately sent that tile to the professor," replied Holmes, "and no doubt the same person also sent the anonymous letters. The aim seems clear enough – to torment him, and upset his equilibrium – and if so, it has certainly been successful: the professor's worst moments, as you have recounted them to us, have generally followed the receipt of these unwelcome items of post. That is where we must therefore focus our attention, and as the letters have been destroyed, we are left only with the tile."

"But the professor has buried it somewhere!"

"Then we must dig it up."

"But it is smashed!"

"Then we must get hold of some strong glue, and try to put it together again. We may then be able to tell where the tile came from, whether it was purchased somewhere, or made individually by the person that sent it."

"But who would do such a thing?"

"That is what we must discover."

"There is something that troubles me," I interrupted. "We have intruded upon Professor Palfreyman's privacy so far as to read this account, which he wrote specifically for Miss Calloway, but to dig up without his permission something which he himself has buried seems to me a yet deeper invasion of his privacy."

"I can understand your misgivings, Watson," returned Holmes, "but I do not share them. I am acting for Miss Calloway, and she has been in danger, as that bruise on the side of her head bears testimony. Her well-being is my first consideration. Compared with that, Professor Palfreyman's privacy seems to me a secondary matter, and I feel sure that, if it were put to him in those terms, the professor himself could not but agree with me. Now, let us be off to the woods, and Miss Calloway can show us where the professor may have buried the broken tile!"

We passed through the kitchen, where Miss Calloway noted with surprise that the back door from the kitchen to the garden was not locked.

"I have never known the professor to go out and leave the house unlocked before," said she.

"Then that is certainly curious," responded Holmes, "but perhaps the reason will become clear to us shortly."

We followed Miss Calloway down the long back garden, Holmes pausing to pick up a trowel and small pail which were lying on the ground beside a garden shed, until we reached a small wicket gate. "This is the way into the woods," said our guide as she pushed open the gate and led the way through it, into the wood beyond. It was a dense wood, where the trees grew close together and brambles and other undergrowth filled much of the space between them. Most of the trees had lost their leaves now, and stood bare and damp-looking, but it was still not possible to see very far through the wood, for the cold grey fog had thickened in the last hour, and all but the nearest trees were little more than shapeless blurs.

All at once, Holmes stopped and let out a little cry of surprise. "Halloa! Someone has passed this way today," said he, indicating clear footprints on the soft earth of the path.

"It was probably the professor," said Miss Calloway. "Perhaps we shall find him in the woodland glade, smoking his pipe and ruminating."

"I'm not sure about that," said Holmes, speaking to himself as much as to our companion. "There is something decidedly odd about these tracks. Please keep as much to the side of the path as you can."

From that moment on, Holmes led the way, his keen eyes following the footprints in the soft earth beneath us, and occasionally stopping to examine some mark at the side of the path that had caught his eye. Presently we came to a steep incline, where the ground ahead of us rose up ten feet or more.

"Professor Palfreyman believes these tall ridges which run through the wood are evidence of pre-historic agricultural practices," remarked Miss Calloway, "and have been here since long before the trees. He has often said he will investigate them more thoroughly when he has the time."

We had been climbing this steep little hill as she had been speaking. Now we reached the top and stood a moment on the narrow ridge. Immediately below us, the ground dropped down once more to a narrow gully, perhaps six feet wide, then rose up again to another ridge, similar to the one on which we were standing. It was not the ground that seized our attention, however, but something else, which had just become visible to us. On the second ridge, or just beyond it, stood a large, spreading tree, and from a low, horizontal branch of this tree, silhouetted against the grey mist, hung a rope, looped in the form of a noose.

"What in heaven's name is that thing?" cried Miss Calloway in alarm.

"It is a hangman's noose," said Holmes. "What devilry is this?" He dashed down the slope and up the other side of the gully, Miss Calloway and I following close behind him. Again, we paused at the top of the ridge, and with a thrill of horror I surveyed the scene before us. Immediately ahead of us now was a small, open glade, perhaps twenty feet in each direction, and hemmed in on all sides by the dense wood. Upon the damp, leaf-strewn turf of this glade, stretched out on their backs about a dozen feet apart, were the motionless figures of two men, their sightless eyes staring up at the clouds above.

Miss Calloway began to scream, but the scream died on her lips, and she collapsed and would have tumbled back into the gully had I not caught hold of her. Holmes sprang down into the glade and bent to examine the two figures on the ground. The first was an elderly man with grey hair and moustache.

"Dead," said Holmes after a brief examination. "Head stove in at the back."

Then he turned his attention to the other figure, a younger man.

"Also dead," said Holmes. "Shot through the heart."

Miss Calloway showed some signs of returning consciousness, and Holmes helped me get her off the ridge and into the glade, where I sat her on a large fallen log and put my arm round her, as much to physically support her as to comfort her.

"Who are these people?" Holmes asked her as she looked about her in bewilderment.

"That is Professor Palfreyman," she replied, indicating the grey-haired man, "and the other is Tim – Mr Martin. Are they both dead?"

Holmes nodded. "We can do nothing for them now. Watson, please take Miss Calloway back to the house and give her something suitable to drink, and send that gardener for the police. You'd better write a note for him to take. Stress that the matter is of the utmost urgency. Don't bother with any details; just state that two men have been found dead, and that they may need to call in someone from Scotland Yard."

The hardest part of what Holmes had asked me to do was getting Miss Calloway back to the house. She was, understandably, in a state of extreme nervous collapse, and almost fainted twice more before we reached the kitchen door. In between times, she kept bursting into tears and weeping copiously, and I had to keep stopping to comfort her.

"The two people I have been closest to in the last year!" she cried in anguish, clinging on to me for support. "Both dead! Who could have done such a terrible thing?"

"Have no doubts," I replied, "Mr Holmes will find out. He always does. Justice will prevail, Miss Calloway, and the guilty shall not escape!"

Once in the kitchen, I settled her in a chair, found some brandy in a cupboard and poured out a tot for her and one for myself. I am not ashamed to say that my nerves, too, seemed shot to pieces. It had been a tremendous shock to suddenly come upon those lifeless bodies lying in that peaceful woodland glade, and I could scarcely comprehend the matter any more than my distraught companion could. I found a piece of paper in the professor's study, wrote a brief note, in which I mentioned Holmes's name, and gave it to the gardener, then returned to the kitchen. The fire there had all but gone out, so I set about rekindling it with paper and sticks, so that I could boil a kettle. While I was doing this, and Miss Calloway sat watching me in a sort of numb silence, the cook, Mrs Wheeler, returned. I explained to her briefly what had happened and, after coping with her momentary hysterics, left Miss Calloway in her care and hurried down the garden again to see what Sherlock Holmes was doing.

When I surmounted the ridge immediately before the woodland glade, I saw that Holmes was down on his hands and knees at the far side of the clearing, inspecting something on the ground. For some time he moved about in this fashion, like a hound following a scent, then he eventually stood up and turned to me, a slight frown on his face. "I have made a broad sweep round the whole area," said he, "to verify one or two points." I told him that Mrs Wheeler had returned and was looking after his client, and he nodded his head. "I am glad you have come back, Watson. You can hold the fort here, if you wouldn't mind, as I wish to look at something in the house. I shouldn't be more than five minutes."

It gave me a strange, eerie feeling, to be left alone in that silent, fog-shrouded glade, with two men lying dead on the grass at my feet. Why had these two – an old man and a young man – been killed in this strange, unforeseen way? What was the meaning of that sinister hangman's noose that hung, like a symbol of death and retribution, over this terrible scene? Backwards and forwards I paced round the edge of the clearing, unable to rest, either mentally or physically. What, I wondered, did Sherlock Holmes make of it all? What could anyone make of it? Would this be the one occasion when even Holmes was lost for an answer, when the mystery was too dark even for his great analytical skills to unravel?

My friend was away a little longer than he had predicted, but when he returned the frown had gone from his face and he seemed almost relaxed. "I have found what I was looking for," said he in answer to my query. "My case is complete."

"What do you mean by 'complete'?" I asked in amazement.

"Simply that I believe I now know all that there is to know about the matter."

"What! You know who killed Professor Palfreyman?"

"Yes."

"And Martin?"

"Yes."

"And why they were killed in different ways?"

"Yes."

"And the meaning of that hangman's noose?"

"Yes."

"What do we do next, then?"

"We sit on that log and smoke our pipes, Watson! We can do nothing further until the police arrive, and must hope that they send someone with more than just sawdust in his head! There is nothing I find so wearying and tiresome as having to explain everything ten times over before I am understood!"

"I will not ask you any more questions, then, until the police arrive," I said.

"Good man!" cried my friend, filling his pipe with tobacco and putting a match to it. "That is considerate of you!" I lit my own pipe, and we sat smoking in silence for some time.

"It seems so unfair," I said at length, "that Miss Calloway should be involved in this dreadful business when it is really nothing whatever to do with her."

"Ah!" said Holmes. "The fair Georgina! I rather fancied that that was the way your thoughts were tending, old boy. But as a matter of fact she is not quite as irrelevant to the case as you perhaps suppose."

"Whatever do you mean?"

"I'll tell you in a moment. I think I hear the heavy tread of regulation police boots!" He knocked out his pipe and sprang to his feet. "I must warn them to avoid obliterating the footprints on the path," he called over his shoulder as he hurried off to meet them.

A few moments later, he reappeared in the company of four uniformed policemen and a tall, flaxen-haired man whom I recognized at once as our old friend Inspector Gregson, the Scotland Yard detective. He greeted me amiably and we shook hands. "You have arrived very promptly," I remarked. "Were you already at Beckenham?"

"No, Penge. But I got a message that something was afoot down here, and when I heard that Mr Holmes was involved, thought it would be worth my while to take a look. I'm now officially in charge of the case." The policeman surveyed the scene for a moment, then he bent down and examined each of the bodies in turn. "This older man seems to have had his skull crushed in at the back," said he. "This large stone near his head has blood on it, so that appears to be what killed him. This younger man – why, bless my soul! – he's been shot through the heart!" He stood up and shook his head. "It looks as if there is some kind of homicidal maniac on the loose!"

"I think not," said Holmes. "Things are not quite as they appear."

"You don't think the murderer is likely to strike again?"

"No."

"You sound very sure."

"I am. Incidentally, Gregson, the revolver that fired the shot that killed the younger man is over there on the ground, near the edge of the clearing. I have not moved anything, but left it all for you to see."

The policeman walked over, picked up the pistol and examined it for a moment. "Only one shot discharged," he said aloud. "I wonder why the murderer left it here for us to find?" He turned to Holmes, with a frown of puzzlement on his features. "What on earth has been happening here, Mr Holmes?" he asked. "Who are these men? What are they doing here, lying dead in the middle of this wood? Who killed them? And what the devil is that noose doing there?"

"I will tell you," said Sherlock Holmes, "but it will take me a few minutes, so you must be patient."

Gregson nodded. He dismissed the four constables, instructing two of them to guard the front gate of the cottage and not let anyone in or out, and the other two to perform a similar duty at the gate leading from the back garden to the wood. "And don't trample down any of those footprints on the path!" he added with a glance at Holmes. "Now, Mr Holmes," he said, "I am all ears."

Briefly, then, Holmes described for the policeman Professor Palfreyman's career, his colleagues at the university and the enduring, if unjustified, guilt the professor had felt for the death of his colleague, John Strange, thirty-odd years previously, which had caused him such mental anguish. He then explained Georgina Calloway's connection with the professor, how she had come to move into Bluebell Cottage the year before, and the chief incidents during the year, including the arrival in the post of the anonymous letters and the tile. Finally, he mentioned the account that the professor had written for Miss Calloway of what had occurred in Western Macedonia.

"I see," said Gregson, taking off his hat and scratching his head. "In the light of all that, things are beginning to look a little different. If we try to reconstruct what has happened here, then, it seems that after writing his account for Miss Calloway to read after his death, the professor changed his mind and left it for her to read now. That suggests to me the possibility that he felt he had had enough of life, and had decided to end it. He therefore came here, to what you tell me was his favourite spot in the woods, and rigged up that noose with the intention of hanging himself. It's a sad business, but not so unusual, if truth be told. A lot of the bodies fished out of the Thames each year are of those who felt they had had enough of life, and had deliberately flung themselves into the river."

"No doubt. But in this case, of course, the professor did not in fact hang himself, so the analogy with bodies in the Thames does not really apply. What do you make of the presence of the younger man, Timothy Martin?"

"I'm not sure. Do you know anything about the gun that killed him?"

"Not specifically. But Miss Calloway mentioned to us that Professor Palfreyman had a small pocket pistol, which is what that is, so I take it that that is the professor's."

"I see. Although, of course, just because the gun is his, it doesn't prove that he fired it."

"No," said Holmes, "but other evidence strongly suggests it. If you examine the professor's right hand, with your nose as well as your eye, you will detect a strong smell of gunpowder. It is an old gun, and he was using old cartridges, and the powder has leaked backwards out of the chamber. There is a slight burn on his index finger, near where it meets the thumb."

Inspector Gregson did as Holmes suggested, and after a moment nodded his head. "You are quite right, Mr Holmes. I agree completely. There is a singe mark in the crook of the thumb. Therefore Professor Palfreyman fired the shot that killed Mr Martin. I think we must conclude then," he continued after a moment, resuming his seat on the log, "that, as Professor Palfreyman was about to hang himself, Martin arrived and tried to dissuade him. But by then, I suppose, the professor was so determined to do away with himself that he resented the other man's interference, drew his gun and threatened him with it. Martin probably persisted – as anyone would in the circumstances – and the professor lost his temper and shot him. These would-be suicides can be uncommonly determined, you know. Then I think what must have happened is that the burn on the professor's hand caused him to fling the gun away – which is why it was lying several yards over there – as well as causing him to stagger backwards, trip over and crack his skull on that little rock. Do you agree with that analysis?"

"No. The only part I agree with is that the burn on his hand caused him to drop the gun, and that the burn and slight recoil of the gun may have contributed to his falling backwards. But why did he not break his fall with his hand or his elbow? And although his head undoubtedly struck that stone – the fresh blood on it declares as much – such a blow would not, in my opinion, have caused such a terrible wound as the back of his head displays. But let us leave that for a moment, and consider something else. How was it, do you suppose, that Martin arrived here just as Professor Palfreyman was about to hang himself?"

"I don't see that as a very important point," Gregson replied in surprise. "No doubt he called at the house, and someone there told him the professor had taken a walk into the woods, so he followed him and found him about to hang himself."

"But there was no one in the house then, Gregson. Miss Calloway was in Baker Street, consulting me, and the cook was away visiting her sister in Norwood. The house was empty."

"Then perhaps seeing that the professor was not at home, Martin guessed where he might have gone to, and came this way."

"But as I showed you earlier, there was only one set of footprints on the muddy path before we arrived here."

"Then one of the two men must have come by a different route from the house."

"There is no other route. There is a fence at the bottom of the garden, and anyone wishing to pass from the garden to the wood must pass through the wicket gate in that fence."

"Then one of them – Martin, I suppose – must have come not from the house at all, but directly through the woods from the road."

"Why should he do that?"

"Because he heard something from the woods, or saw something."

"The wood is very dense between here and the road. It is not possible to see this spot from the road, and although the road is not far away, it is too far, in my opinion, for any but the loudest of sounds to be heard there. Besides, this speculation is superfluous, for I have made a very wide sweep of the whole area around this glade, and there is not a single footprint anywhere about, not one. Believe me, Gregson, when I say I would stake my reputation – my entire life's work – on it!"

"If you say so, Mr Holmes," said Gregson after a moment, "then that is good enough for me. But do you realize where your argument leads? We have two men murdered in this isolated spot, and yet we have, according to you, not three sets of footprints leading here, as I had first expected to find, being those of Palfreyman, Martin and their murderer, nor yet two sets of prints, which according to my later theory would be those of Palfreyman and Martin, but only one set of prints. It is completely impossible! Indeed, it is not only impossible, it is absurd!"

"Yes," said Holmes, in a dry tone. "It does appear on the face of it to be impossible. You're a good man, Gregson, one of the best, and I have gone carefully through all the evidence, so that when I tell you what really happened here, you will understand

and believe me. With a lesser man, I probably shouldn't have bothered."

Inspector Gregson took a small cigar from his waistcoat pocket, struck a match and lit it. "Go on," he said. "I am still all ears."

"Very well," said Holmes. "What we have here is a clear case of murder."

"Well, yes, of course," returned Gregson. "We know that Professor Palfreyman murdered young Martin. As you yourself agreed, the professor shot him with his pistol."

Holmes shook his head. "No," said he, "you have it the wrong way about. Palfreyman did not murder Martin. On the contrary, Martin murdered Palfreyman."

"What!"

"It is one of the most callous, calculated, cold-blooded murders I have ever encountered. What you see here before you is, apart, of course, from his own death, the culmination of Martin's scheme for murder which I believe he planned many months ago."

"You amaze me, Holmes!" I cried. "I cannot believe what you are saying! How on earth do you arrive at that conclusion?"

"I will tell you my reasoning, Watson, and you can see if you can find any flaw in it. First, let us return to the matter of the footprints. As you remarked, Gregson, the fact that there appeared to be but one set of footprints leading here seemed an impossibility. There is, however, one way in which it could have come about, and that is if one of the two men was in fact carrying the other. Now, in what circumstances might that occur? Surely only if one of them was incapacitated, probably by being unconscious.

"I had noted the single set of footprints earlier, when the three of us first came along the path, but gave it little thought at first. I assumed the footprints were those of the professor, and the fact that there were prints leading into the wood, but none coming back, suggested that – unless he had gone further afield – we might find him sitting smoking his pipe in the woods, as Miss Calloway had told us he often did. Then, however, I noticed an odd thing: the footprints in question were unusually deep – much deeper than either Dr Watson's or my own – with the heels especially marked. This suggested that the man that made them was carrying an exceptionally heavy burden of some sort. My attention having been drawn to this curious feature, I then observed that although, to judge by his shoe size, the man was of roughly average stature, the footprints were often much closer together than one would expect, which also suggested that he was struggling with a heavy burden.

"When we reached this clearing, and found the two dead men, I examined their shoes and established that the footprints on the path had been made by Martin. There were no other footprints anywhere about in the woods surrounding the clearing, so it was evident that, as I suspected by then, Martin had carried the professor here. The more I considered the matter, the more it seemed crystal clear that Martin had intended to murder the professor by hanging, to make it appear to have been a case of suicide. Martin had often visited Bluebell Cottage, and would be familiar with the routine of the household, so he would know that the cook always went over to Norwood to see her sister on Wednesday morning. When Miss Calloway told him that she was going to consult me this morning, he would have realized that there would be no one but the professor in the house, and he would thus have the opportunity he needed to put his evil scheme into effect. He must therefore have called in at the cottage on some pretext or other, and been let in by the professor himself. But how did he manage to subdue the professor in order to get him out here? Clearly, by striking him on the back of the head, probably as the professor sat at his desk. This is what would have caused that very severe wound to the professor's head, which simply falling over and banging his head on that stone over there could never have done.

"What I think must have happened when they reached the clearing here is that Martin dropped the professor to the ground while he rigged up that noose on the branch of the tree. But the professor, who was, in a sense, dying at that moment, and would probably not have lived another ten minutes under any circumstances, must have regained consciousness sufficiently to see what Martin was doing. When Martin turned back to him, the professor had drawn his pistol – it is very small and weighs little, which would explain why Martin failed to notice that it was in the professor's jacket pocket – and shot his assailant with it at point-blank range. The recoil and the burn on his hand made him fling the gun to one side and stagger backwards, where he fell to the ground and struck his head on that stone, which finished him off. It is because he was so severely injured, and probably scarcely conscious, that he was unable to break his fall. He may even have been dead before his body struck the ground. Therefore, to sum up: Martin murdered Palfreyman, and although Palfreyman undoubtedly shot and killed Martin, that was not, legally speaking, an act of murder, as he was acting in self-defence. That, I believe, is what happened."

We sat in silence for some time after Holmes had finished speaking. If his analysis was correct, what had happened here in this quiet woodland glade seemed both too terrible and too fantastic to contemplate, yet I felt sure that, on the evidence, he must be right.

"If you require any further proof of the truth of my view," said Holmes after a few moments, "then you could look in Martin's jacket pocket. He trimmed the rope with which he made the noose, and there is a small length of the rope in his pocket, along with a sharp jack-knife. There is also a mark of blood on the back of his jacket, near the shoulder, which must have come from the professor's wound when he was being carried out here. I also took a look in the professor's study, to see if there was any evidence there to support my theory that it was there that Martin had attacked the professor, and found among the disorder that the poker in the hearth is smeared with blood and hair. That is clearly the murder weapon. I have left it where it was, in the hearth, for you to see, Gregson. No doubt Martin left the kitchen door unlocked because he intended to return to the house to tidy up the study and conceal what had happened there."

"But surely," said Gregson, "if Martin's scheme had succeeded, and we had found the professor hanged here in the woods, our suspicions as to what had really happened would have been instantly aroused by that savage wound on the back of his head. Martin could not have supposed that we would not notice that!"

Holmes nodded. "I doubt that he originally intended to strike the professor quite so violently. Having done so, he would probably wait until he was sure his victim was dead by hanging, and then contrive to make it look as if the noose had slipped from the tree, and the professor had fallen and struck his head on a stone."

"Had you any suspicions of Martin before we arrived here and found them both dead?" I asked my friend.

"I had noted that Professor Palfreyman's really tangible troubles – the arrival of the anonymous, blank letters, and the tile – only began after Martin started calling at the house. Of course, that might have been mere chance – after all, the same observation could be applied to Miss Calloway herself. But it was also notable from Miss Calloway's account that Martin seemed to take every opportunity he could to try to persuade her that Professor Palfreyman was dangerously insane, and that she should leave Bluebell Cottage. There was, moreover, one particular incident that I thought especially odd: when Miss Calloway mentioned her intention to consult me, Martin at first dismissed the idea as pointless, but when he changed his mind he said that perhaps I could somehow discover what lay behind the professor's troubles. But there was no mystery there to be uncovered, nor had there ever been. Apart from the professor's private feelings of guilt, what had happened in Macedonia all those years ago was a matter of general knowledge to all of Palfreyman's colleagues, and thus, probably, to Martin, too.

"No one, as far as we know, seemed to attach any blame to Palfreyman over the matter: the guilt he felt about it was simply his conscience prodding him with the thought that he could perhaps have acted differently. This feeling of personal guilt was, of course, exacerbated by the fact that – as he willingly admitted himself – he disliked Strange intensely. In other words, the trouble, up until this year, was really all in Professor Palfreyman's head, and there was nothing there that a detective could 'discover'. The arrival of the letter and the tile, however, were quite different. They were not simply in the professor's head, but definite, provocative acts, which any detective worth his salt would see as the starting point of his investigation."

"I quite agree," said Gregson. "When you were describing the matter to me earlier, I at once thought that those things were the most important part of the case."

Holmes nodded. "And yet, Martin, a supposedly highly intelligent, and certainly highly educated young man, did not mention them to Miss Calloway at all, but referred simply to what had occurred many years ago. It seemed to me almost as if he was deliberately trying to deflect her attention from what was obviously the central part of the whole case – as indeed he probably was. It seems certain now that it was Martin himself who sent those things to Professor Palfreyman."

"But why?" I asked. "What could his aim have been?"

"He knew, as did everyone, that the professor was troubled in his mind – that he suffered from nightmares and so on – and considered, I imagine, that by persecuting him he might be able to drive him mad and suicidal. And if he couldn't succeed in making the professor kill himself, then he would contrive to make it appear that he had – which is what this hideous and evil tableau was about. In fact, of course, the professor was nowhere near as unhinged as Martin seemed to think: guilt-ridden certainly, a little unbalanced perhaps, but otherwise, he was, for most of the time, as sane as anyone else.

"When he dug out his little pistol from the old tin trunk in which it had lain for twenty-odd years it was not to use it on himself, but to protect himself against the threat he recognized was closing in upon him. I even wonder if he suspected that the threat might come from Martin. His questions to Miss Calloway concerning her future, and her feelings for Martin, were somewhat ambiguous, and it may be that he was in fact 'fishing' for information as to what she really thought about the young man."

"What of the person loitering in the woods?" asked Gregson. "Do you reckon that was Martin, too?"

"It must have been. He would know when Miss Calloway was likely to catch her train home, and it would have been easy for him to take an earlier train and get down here before she did. His intention was no doubt to frighten her into leaving Bluebell

Cottage altogether, as this would make it easier for him to pursue his scheme against the professor, and would allow him to portray himself as Miss Calloway's 'protector', and thus advance his matrimonial prospects. In addition, if Miss Calloway was unsure of Professor Palfreyman's whereabouts at the time of these frightening episodes, she might begin to suspect that the professor himself was responsible, which thought, to judge from her account, had already crossed her mind, and which was all to the good for Martin's evil scheme to make the professor appear insane."

"But why?" I repeated. "I understand all that you are saying about Martin trying to make Professor Palfreyman appear insane, but what could he possibly hope to gain by murdering the man or driving him to suicide? Was it simply some form of vengeance for the death of Strange?"

Holmes shook his head. "I very much doubt it," said he. "According to Professor Palfreyman's account, no one really mourned Strange's passing, let alone harboured any grievance about it. The professor wrote his account for Miss Calloway about thirty years after the events he described in it, and it is evident that in those thirty years he had not encountered any ill feeling over the matter, so I think we may take it that there is none. It seems apparent, then, that Martin was using the Macedonian business – 'the Smiling Face' – simply as a means of achieving his aim, and that his true motives lay elsewhere."

"But what on earth could those motives be?" I asked in some puzzlement.

"There are certain facts you may be overlooking," responded Holmes after a moment. "In the first place, Georgina Calloway is the professor's only known relative, and as such would, upon his death, inherit anything he possessed."

"I admit that that hadn't occurred to me," I said.

"In the second place," Holmes continued, "you must remember that although Martin was working on his thesis under the guidance of the archaeology department, that had not previously been his principal field of study. He had studied art and history of art, and was no doubt something of an expert in that field. Perhaps, I speculated, while helping Miss

Calloway to sort and catalogue the professor's random heaps of paintings, sculptures and drawings, as she described to us, Martin had come across something which he, and he alone, recognized as being of immense value. If so, that might have provided the motive for his wicked plan. He would have realized that he could not hope to get away with simply stealing what he wanted, but if he could get rid of the older man and persuade Miss Calloway to marry him, then he could get his hands on a possible fortune."

"It is certainly an interesting notion, and it would make sense," said Gregson. "There is usually avarice at the bottom of this sort of crime. Do you have any evidence for it, Mr Holmes, or is it just speculation?"

"I had a quick look through some of the things in one of the professor's old tin trunks when I was examining the study earlier," replied Holmes. "I am no expert on art, but there were a large number of sheets there which looked to me suspiciously like pages from a notebook of Leonardo da Vinci's. He generally wrote backwards, you know, Gregson. I think he referred to it as 'mirror writing'. It is quite distinctive. On another large, folded sheet there is what looks to me like a series of preliminary sketches for his celebrated painting, *The Virgin of the Rocks*."

"Great Heavens!" I cried. "That is incredible!"

"Indeed," said Holmes. "There are things in the professor's battered old trunk that would probably fetch more at auction than we three could earn in a lifetime!"

"Good Lord!" said Gregson. "That is, I suppose, enough to tempt some men to any sort of wickedness. But Martin was an intelligent, educated man," he added with a shake of his head, "a young gentleman and graduate of Oxford University! You would have thought he would be above that sort of temptation."

"Perhaps there are things about his character that we don't yet know," said Holmes. "Now," he continued, rising to his feet, "our investigation is completed, and we come to the most difficult part of the business."

"What do you mean?" I asked.

"I must explain the true facts of the case to Miss Calloway, Watson. It is undoubtedly my responsibility to do so, but it is not a responsibility I particularly welcome. You will come with me, old man?"

"Of course."

"As to Martin," Holmes continued, addressing Inspector Gregson, "I recommend a thorough investigation into his antecedents. There may be dark secrets there, unknown to anyone. But the terrible, simple truth is that once evil enters into the heart of a man, it cannot easily be eradicated, but will drive all else out, and poison every fibre of his being."

Sherlock Holmes's speculations as to Martin's character and antecedents were very soon borne out. Two days after the events recorded above, a firm of solicitors in the Temple handed in to Scotland Yard a sealed letter, which had been left with them the previous Friday by Professor Palfreyman, with the instruction that, in the event of his sudden death, it should be handed at once to the authorities. In this letter the professor mentioned that one of his valuable artefacts, a primitive oil lamp of Phoenician origin, was missing from the house, and although he had no proof, he could not see how anyone but Timothy Martin could have taken it. He also mentioned that he had seen Martin, believing himself to be unobserved, looking through other things in the house in what the professor described as "a sly and furtive manner". The professor had therefore come to have strong suspicions about the man and his motives, but had felt unable, without further proof, to voice them, for fear of alienating the affections of Miss Calloway, who, he believed, had developed a liking for Martin, and whose affections he had come to value above all else.

The suspicions the professor had harboured about Martin had led him to speculate that it was Martin who had sent him the tile and the letter with the face on it. Indeed, he was, he said, "practically certain" that the handwriting on the envelope of the first letter, although disguised, was Martin's. As to why Martin should have sent these things to him, the professor admitted he had no idea. This had led him to speculate further that Martin was perhaps simply, as he put it, "one of those strange people one encounters occasionally, who have a warped and vicious cast of mind, who smile a lot, but seem devoid of all real human emotion, and who lie almost every time they open their mouths. "If so," the professor concluded, "he keeps his true nature well hidden, especially from Miss Calloway."

Subsequently, when the police made a thorough examination of Martin's lodgings in Bloomsbury, they found Professor Palfreyman's Phoenician oil lamp there and, among numerous other things, a small early sketch by Poussin, later identified as having also been taken from Bluebell Cottage. Another surprising find was a small oval framed portrait by Nicholas Hilliard of the Earl of Essex, dating from around 1590, which was at length identified as having been stolen from St Aidan's College, Oxford, three years previously, at the time Martin had been an undergraduate there. In the course of that robbery – which had remained a perfect mystery until this discovery – one of the college servants had been so severely beaten about the head that he had been unable to work again for nearly a year.

Of Georgina Calloway, I am pleased to say, I have happier information to record. She eventually recovered from the shock and horror of what had taken place at Bluebell Cottage, and was offered a position with Professor Ainscow similar to the one she had held with Professor Palfreyman, which she accepted. She remained in that position for nearly three years, while at the same time pursuing her studies in botany. During this period we kept in touch, she dined with us a number of times, and I had the privilege of escorting her to the theatre on two or three occasions. Then, with the kind assistance of Professor Ainscow, she at last succeeded in gaining a position at the Royal Botanical Institute at Kew, where to the best of my knowledge she remains to this day.

The Adventure of THE FOURTH GLOVE

THE LATCHMERE DIAMOND is without doubt one of the most celebrated gems ever to have found its way to England. Unearthed in some remote corner of India, it is first recorded in Golconda, from where it passed to the trading post at Madras. There it was purchased, in 1783, by Samuel Tollington, later the third Viscount Latchmere, who had been travelling in the Far East with his uncle, Sir George Tollington, the well-known diplomat. Its arrival in England later that year created a sensation, for it was the largest diamond ever seen, and everyone, from the King downwards, wished to behold this prodigy. However, within six months of its arrival, the first of many attempts to steal it had been made. A second attempt was made in 1792, which cost the viscount his life, and a third in 1799, during which two of the robbers were killed. The tumultuous period of the Napoleonic Wars proved a relatively quiet time for the Latchmere Diamond, but in 1819 another attempt was made to steal it, and in 1834 yet another, which again cost the robbers their lives.

In 1842, the fifth viscount had the diamond re-cut and mounted as a pendant, to be worn by each future viscountess on her wedding day, but this change in the diamond's appearance brought no change in its violent history, for within six months it was stolen, and was not recovered for three years. In 1865, a further attempt was made upon the diamond, in which two of the robbers and one of Viscount Latchmere's servants were killed. Throughout this history of violence, the diamond was also gaining the reputation of being an unlucky possession for the Tollington family. Indeed, the first tragedy had struck before the diamond even reached these shores, when Sir George Tollington was lost at sea in a terrible storm off the coast of Madagascar when returning from India, and, in addition to the viscount who was murdered in 1792, two more to bear that title also met an untimely end, one in a riding accident and one who was drowned while sailing on the Solent.

Like most people, I imagine, I had read the history of this fabulous stone with mere idle curiosity, never thinking for a moment that I should ever have any personal connection with it. Yet, surprisingly, in early October 1885, that was precisely what happened, as a result of my sharing chambers with the renowned detective Mr Sherlock Holmes.

We were seated at breakfast, on a fine, crisp autumn morning. The dawn mist had already cleared, and the bright sun gave promise of a fine day. But this attractive prospect outside our sitting-room window aroused mixed feelings in my own breast. The wound in my leg, which I had brought back with me as an unwanted memento of my service in Afghanistan, had begun to throb painfully in recent days and became worse whenever I tried to walk. I was thus condemned, on what promised to be the loveliest day of the autumn, to a day spent in a chair by the fire with my left leg raised up on a cushion. It will be readily imagined what a thoroughly depressing prospect this was, and why I applied myself with unusual zeal to the morning papers, in an effort to distract my mind.

"It says here," I remarked to my companion as a small paragraph caught my eye, "that the Latchmere Pendant has disappeared and is believed stolen."

Holmes looked up from the papers he was studying and raised his eyebrow. "Surely not again?" said he in a languid tone. "Was anyone injured?"

"It doesn't say so. It is thought that the pendant was taken during Saturday night from Lady Latchmere's private dressing room."

"That is one blessing, anyhow! So great has been the violence done for the sake of that ill-starred lump of crystal that I have sometimes thought it should be mounted not in gold but in blood! Are there any details?"

"Nothing of interest. It says that the viscount and viscountess were entertaining a small weekend party at Latchmere Hall in Hertfordshire, their guests being the Rajah of Banniphur, the Honourable Miss Arabella Norman, Mr Peter Brocklehurst and Miss Matilda Wiltshire – whoever they may be."

There had been a ring at the doorbell as I had been reading, and a moment later the maid entered with a telegram for Holmes. He tore it open and read the contents, then, with a chuckle, tossed it over to me as he scribbled a reply. I read the following:

PENDANT MISSING. COME AT
ONCE. LATCHMERE.

"Will you go?" I asked.

Holmes nodded. "Certainly. I just have time to do justice to these splendid-looking kippers," he continued with a glance at the clock, "and then I can catch a fast train from King's Cross and be there in half an hour!"

The morning crept by at a snail's pace, my own mood alternating between boredom and irritation, both at my own physical weakness and at the dull, predictable content of the newspapers. So devoid of interest were they that I spent most of the morning reading a long article from the previous month's *British Medical Journal* on the suggested treatment for some obscure tropical disease which I had never even heard of before and in which I could raise little interest. It was not until the afternoon was well advanced that I heard my friend's characteristically rapid footsteps on the stair, and looked forward eagerly to hearing how his investigations had gone.

"It was a somewhat mixed morning's work," he replied in answer to my questions, as he helped himself to bread and cheese from the sideboard.

"Has the Latchmere Pendant indeed been stolen?"

"So it would appear."

"And have your investigations turned up any clues?"

"There are a number of suggestive indications. The difficulty is, they point in contradictory directions."

"You intrigue me."

"It is a singularly intriguing business!" my friend responded with a chuckle. "I will tell you how matters unfolded, Watson, and you can see what you make of it!"

He settled himself in his chair by the fire and began his account:

"You may perhaps have seen a picture of Latchmere Hall at some time, Watson. It lies about five miles north of Hatfield and is a very handsome old place – early Jacobean, with turrets and chimneys at every corner, and with its ancient walls half hidden under a thick growth of ivy. Inside, everything is very old, dark and highly polished. I doubt there is a single item of furniture there that is less than a hundred and fifty years old, and some of it is much older than that. The present family acquired the property in 1730, so I understand, and have held it ever since.

"When I reached the Hall, I was at once shown by the butler, Yardley, into Viscount Latchmere's private study, where he was seated at his desk.

"'I am told you have a familiarity with the criminal classes in London,' said he without preliminary, looking up with an irritable expression from a litter of papers before him. 'The policeman informed me that this theft might be the work of the Foulger gang, who, he says, are operating in this district, or of some villain by the name of John Clay. Look, I don't care how you do it, Holmes, but you must get the pendant back. Do you understand? You won't be aware, but I have posted a two thousand pound reward for its return. So if you succeed in getting it back, the reward is yours, on top of anything else we may owe you.'

"I nodded and explained that I would wish to begin by examining the scene of the crime, and then interviewing briefly anyone in the house who might have seen or heard anything during Saturday night.

"He shook his head dismissively. 'The police have already done all that,' he said, 'so there's no point your doing it all again.'

"I explained that I could not realistically offer much hope of success unless I were allowed to conduct the investigation in the way I thought best. I also pointed out that the police were not infallible, and had often been known to overlook or misunderstand evidence in the past, a point the viscount grudgingly conceded. What might have happened next, I cannot say, for at that moment the door was opened abruptly and a very handsome young lady entered the room. She was slim, of medium height, about two-and-twenty years old, with a very fine head of chestnut-coloured hair. It was evident that this was Viscount Latchmere's wife. She began to speak, but stopped when she saw me.

"'What is it now, Philippa?' her husband asked, in a preoccupied tone.

"'Who is this gentleman?' she asked in response.

"'He is a detective I have hired to find and recover the pendant. As you're here, you can tell him what you told the police inspector yesterday, and then he can get about his business.'

"She turned to me and, for a moment, I could see her eyes looking me up and down, as if appraising me. 'There is little enough to tell,' said she at last. 'I went to my room just after half past ten on Saturday evening. My maid assisted me for a little while, then left me, and I retired to bed. That was at about eleven o'clock.'

"'And the pendant?'

"'Was in my jewel case, which was in the dressing room that adjoins my bedroom.'

"'Was the case locked?'

"'Yes.'

"'But the key was left in the lock,' her husband interjected. 'I have said so many times that you should put the key somewhere safe.'

"'I usually do,' his wife retorted, 'but on Saturday night I forgot. I could hardly have expected that someone would climb into the room while I was there asleep.'

"'Was the bedroom door locked?' I asked.

"'Yes, I always lock my door, and there is no other way into the dressing room except through my bedroom – apart from through the window, of course.'

"'Was the window open?'

"'The window in my bedroom was closed, that in the dressing room was ajar.'

"'And the pendant was definitely in the jewel case when you retired for the night?'

"'Yes. I had just removed it and placed it in there myself.'

"'When was the loss discovered?'

"'Yesterday morning. I opened the case to get a pair of earrings, and at once saw that the pendant was missing.'

"'And – forgive me, Lady Latchmere, but I must ask you this – do you believe you can trust your personal maid?'

"'Why, most certainly,' replied Lady Latchmere quickly and with great emphasis. 'She has been in my service for several years. I would trust her not merely with my jewellery, but with my life! If you knew her at all, you would understand the absurdity of your question!'

"'Thank you, Lady Latchmere,' I said, bowing my head. There was a tension in her manner and she appeared to be breathing heavily. She had tried to sound indignant, but the dominant note in her voice, I thought, had been one of relief, as if she had feared what I had been about to ask her. I wondered if her husband had observed this. It might, of course, mean nothing; she might simply be a nervous sort of young woman – she was, after all, relatively young, at least ten years younger than her husband – but it was nonetheless something I noted.

"'Was there anything else?' she enquired, but before I could reply, her husband spoke in a voice full of irritation.

"'The ring,' he prompted. 'You have not told him about the missing ring. A yellow topaz ring that belonged to my mother has also been taken,' he added, turning to me.

"'I have explained that already,' she responded. 'As I said to you before, I believe I misplaced the topaz ring some time during the last week. Do not worry, Edward, I will have just put it down somewhere, that is all. It will turn up.'

"'That is nonsense!' retorted her husband. 'It was in the top tray of your jewel case on Friday evening. I saw it there myself when we were having that discussion in your dressing room, if you recall.'

"Lady Latchmere's cheek burned red. 'Oh,' said she. 'Then perhaps it was on Saturday afternoon that I saw it was missing. I distinctly remember noticing some time that it was not in its usual place.'

"Viscount Latchmere's expression indicated that he was dissatisfied by this suggestion, and he was about to speak again when the door opened once more and the butler entered to announce that Inspector Sturridge of the Hertfordshire Constabulary had arrived.

"'Inform him that I am engaged at present and cannot see him,' said Viscount Latchmere in an irritable tone. 'And take this man with you. He can get on with his work now. Show him whatever he wants to see.'

"He spoke not another word to me, Watson. Indeed, he did not even glance in my direction as I followed the butler from the room. I thought him unconscionably rude, not only to me but, even more so, to his wife – to speak to her in that fashion in front of a perfect stranger – but I had no desire to make an issue of it and was simply relieved to make my exit from what had been a most uncomfortable scene."

"I can see it must have been dreadfully embarrassing for you to be present when husband and wife were quarrelling like that!" I said. "Viscount Latchmere sounds something of a Tartar!"

"That is certainly one way of describing him!" said Holmes with a chuckle. "He is of the type I generally classify as a gentleman by birth but not by nature. I must admit that I was sorely tempted to leave Latchmere Hall there and then, and leave its unattractive occupants to recover their precious pendant themselves, but the case had begun to intrigue me. It was possible, I thought, that there was more to it than was at first apparent, so, simply for my own professional satisfaction, I decided to prolong my visit and look a little further into the matter.

"At my request, the butler showed me the spot in the garden that lies below Lady Latchmere's dressing-room window. Then, while he went off to find the policeman, I devoted myself to a close examination of the ivy and other plants on the wall of the house, and of the lawns that surrounded it. You know my methods, Watson; they are founded upon the observation of detail, for it is generally among the smallest details of a case that the truth is to be found. But in this case, I was obliged to admit, after the most careful scrutiny, that I could detect not a single sign anywhere of Saturday night's thief. Indeed, I began to wonder if I was not, perhaps, on a perfect fool's errand, looking for something that simply did not exist.

"The butler reappeared after ten minutes, and I asked him to conduct me up to Lady Latchmere's bedroom, which was on the first floor. I will describe to you the disposition of the rooms, Watson, to try to make it clear to you. At the top of the main staircase, corridors go off to left and right. Along the left-hand corridor lies Lord Latchmere's own bedroom, and some other rooms which are not in use at present. In the right-hand corridor lies Lady Latchmere's bedroom, and also the rooms occupied by Lord Latchmere's guests. On the left-hand side of this corridor, the rooms are, in this order, first, that of Lady Latchmere herself; second, an empty room, which suffers from damp and is not in use at present, and third, the room occupied by Lady Latchmere's cousin, Miss Matilda Wiltshire. On the right-hand side, the rooms are first, that occupied by the Honourable Miss Arabella Norman; second, that occupied by the Rajah of Banniphur, and third, that occupied by Mr Peter Brocklehurst. A little further beyond these rooms, the corridor leads to another staircase, by which one may descend to the ground floor, or ascend to the floor above.

"Lady Latchmere's own chamber is a fairly large one. As you enter the room, the bed is over against the right-hand wall, and there are the usual items of furniture – tallboys, chests and so on – against the other walls. Immediately on your left is another door, which gives on to the much smaller dressing room, which contains a dressing table, a tallboy and a small side table. The window in there, like most of the windows in the house, is of the casement type. If it had been left ajar, it would have been very easy for someone to pull it fully open from outside and clamber in. On the side table was what was evidently the jewel case, which was locked, the key being nowhere to be seen. The case was a large, square one, covered in yellow leather, rather like a small chest with a flat top. Lying next to the jewel case was a pair of ladies' gloves, made out of some soft, grey material, with a little coloured embroidery on the back. I mention these gloves to you, Watson, not because I thought them of any significance at the time, but because of something I was to learn subsequently.

"As I concluded my examination of the dressing room – which I confess had turned up precisely nothing – I asked Yardley if the police had discovered anything there. He shook his head, and said he thought not. I then questioned him about the domestic staff of the household. I will spare you the details, which were not of any great interest, and simply give you a summary of what I learned. There are in total seventeen servants in the house, of the usual varieties. The outdoor staff – gardeners, grooms and so on – of course lodge elsewhere on the estate. With the exception of two of the youngest maids, they have all been there for several years. Having discussed them in some detail with the butler, including questions as to where they sleep, whether the floorboards and stairs creak, and so on, I am satisfied that none of them could have had anything to do with the disappearance of Lady Latchmere's jewellery. I may, of course, be wrong, but that is certainly my conviction at the moment. Speaking of creaking boards, I should perhaps mention to you that the corridor on which Lady Latchmere's and the other bedrooms lie creaks alarmingly, especially in the middle, in between the unused room and that occupied by the rajah. It is practically impossible to avoid the creaking parts of the floor altogether, as I discovered by stepping all over it for several minutes.

"I then returned downstairs to interview Viscount Latchmere's guests, who were all staying to take luncheon there, but were leaving immediately afterwards to take the train back to London. As we descended the stairs, I asked Yardley if there had been any other visitors recently, and he informed me that a Mr James Ellison, who farms a few miles to the north of the Latchmere estate, had called by on Saturday afternoon to discuss some business with Viscount Latchmere. His business concluded, he had stayed to take tea with the family and guests, which, the day being a pleasantly mild one, they had taken out of doors, on the small terrace at the side of the house. I asked the butler if Mr Ellison was a frequent visitor.

"'Indeed he is, sir,' said he, 'in recent months, at least. I believe he is a very humorous gentleman. Whenever he is here, there always seems to be a lot of laughter among Viscount Latchmere's guests, especially the ladies.'

"Viscount Latchmere's present guests were in a somewhat more subdued mood, understandably, perhaps, under the circumstances. The Rajah of Banniphur and Mr Peter Brocklehurst were in the morning room, both reading in silence, and Miss Matilda Wiltshire and the Honourable Miss Arabella Norman were seated on the terrace outside in the sunshine, each apparently lost in her own thoughts.

"The rajah is an interesting character, Watson, and probably not your first idea of an Indian nobleman. He was dressed in a tweed suit, looking every inch an English country gentleman. Apparently he was sent to England as a boy, to attend school here at Eton, which is where he first met Viscount Latchmere, twenty-odd years ago. His great interest now is the education of his fellow countrymen. He is keen to found a school along the lines of Eton in his native province, and it is this that has brought him to England on this occasion. As to the events of Saturday night, he was unable to tell me anything that might have been helpful. He retired to bed just before eleven o'clock, fell asleep almost immediately and heard nothing until a maid woke him with a cup of tea the following morning. His manner was very pleasant and open, but I got the distinct impression as we were talking that he was picking his words with care, as if there were something in his thoughts that he did not wish to put into words.

"Peter Brocklehurst is a distant cousin of Viscount Latchmere's. Since coming down from Oxford last year, he informed me, he has been casting about for something to do, without, as yet, finding anything suitable. On Saturday evening, he informed me, he retired to bed shortly after eleven. He admits he had had rather too much to drink during the evening, and says he fell into a very deep sleep, after which he heard nothing until the next morning, when he awoke to learn that the Latchmere

Pendant had been stolen. As we spoke, I sensed that he had something on his mind other than the subject of our discussion. What this might be, I could not tell, but to judge from the frequency with which he glanced out through the French window to the terrace outside, it may have had something to do with Miss Matilda Wiltshire.

"Miss Wiltshire herself is a pretty young thing, if not, perhaps, the most profound thinker. She is a first cousin to, and just a couple of years younger than, Lady Latchmere herself. They have, apparently, been friends since childhood, and she is a fairly frequent visitor to Latchmere Hall. Her father is a solicitor, with chambers in Gray's Inn. I think she found Saturday evening dreadfully dull, as Viscount Latchmere and the rajah were, she said, discussing schools and methods of education interminably. The only thing she seemed to take away from the conversation was that the rajah prefers to be addressed by his friends as Saju. She ended the evening tired, she said, and with a slight headache, so having ascended to the upper floor in the company of Lady Latchmere, she repaired straight to her room, and five minutes later was in bed, endeavouring to get to sleep. However, possibly because of the headache, sleep would not come, and she lay awake for some time. She says she heard others come to bed, and then, a little later, heard the rajah snoring loudly, which kept her awake for a further ten minutes or so, until she eventually dropped off. She heard nothing further.

"The Honourable Miss Arabella Norman, who is a distant cousin of Viscount Latchmere's, is an elderly lady and describes herself as 'a relic'. She was also disturbed by the rajah's snores on Saturday night – he was in the room immediately next to hers – which she says kept her awake 'for hours', although she concedes that that may be an exaggeration. She admits that as she has got older, she has become a very light sleeper and has found it increasingly difficult to sleep anywhere but in her own bed at home. She therefore makes social visits much less frequently than she did when younger. I was, in a sense, somewhat disappointed by my conversation with Miss Norman: sometimes, elderly ladies are very keen observers of all that is happening about them; but if Miss Norman had observed anything, she was keeping it to herself. She went to bed about ten minutes after the younger women, she informed me, and, apart from the rajah's snoring, heard nothing more all night.

"As I was speaking to Miss Norman on the terrace, I saw a man in the distance, examining the ground by the side of the house. Thinking that this might be Inspector Sturridge, I took myself over there and introduced myself. My conjecture proved correct, but the welcome he afforded me was not a friendly one. Indeed, he appeared determined to take offence at my presence.

"'I was wondering when someone of your type would show up,' said he in a disagreeable tone, 'now that a reward has been offered.'

"I assured him that my presence there had been specifically requested by Viscount Latchmere himself, and that I had been perfectly unaware that a reward had been offered until within the last hour. This seemed to satisfy him and, from that point on, he became decidedly more genial. He is, in fact, a very genial man, but an absolute dunderhead as a detective. He described to me what he had discovered so far, which was, in truth, practically nothing.

"'As Lady Latchmere's bedroom door was locked,' he said, as we walked round the outside of the house, 'and as the little dressing room that adjoins it can only be entered from that bedroom, it is clear that the thief must have climbed in through the open dressing-room window. It would not be very difficult for an intruder to climb up there: this part of the house is covered with ivy and other climbing plants, as you can see.'

"'Have you found any signs of such an intruder?' I asked as we stopped below the window in question.

"'I cannot say in all honesty that I have,' he replied. 'It is this that makes me think it must be the work of some highly professional criminal gang; but the creepers are so intertwined and tangled just here that any such signs would be difficult to make out, in any case.'

"'Any footprints?' I asked, as I surveyed a strip of bare earth by the house wall.

"Inspector Sturridge shook his head. 'As you can see, the ground is dry and hard just here. I had a good look round, but didn't find anything – apart from the glove, of course.'

"'What glove is that?' I asked in surprise.

"'Have they not told you? It is not of any significance, I am afraid, Mr Holmes. It is just one of Lady Latchmere's own gloves. I found it on the ground, just here where we're standing. The thief must have accidentally got it caught up in his clothing, I imagine, and dragged it out of the window as he was making his escape. The only other explanation I could think of for its presence here was that the thief had used it to signal to a confederate who was standing out here on the lawn, but that seems unlikely, for several reasons.'

"'Not the least of which is that it would have been pitch black at that time of night.'

"'Precisely. So, as I say, it is probably of no significance. The glove is lying on the chest in the entrance hall. They left it there in case I wished to see it again, but I don't.'

"Inspector Sturridge returned to the house then, to try once more to gain an audience with Viscount Latchmere, while I, thinking that I might have missed something during my first examination, applied myself again to the search for evidence that an intruder had been there on Saturday night. Fifteen minutes later I was obliged to conclude, as I had earlier, that there was not the slightest trace on the outside of Latchmere Hall that any intruders had been there at all, let alone that one of them had climbed up the wall below Lady Latchmere's dressing-room window. Of course, I could be wrong – I occasionally am – but I have handled perhaps seventy-odd cases in which shrubberies or creepers on the wall of a house have played some part in the matter, and I cannot recall a single one in which I have been so completely unable to detect any sign of human presence. I even attempted to climb the wall of Latchmere Hall myself, and although I am reasonably agile, and certainly not heavy, I at once broke several small stems on the creeper – damage which, if anyone else had caused it, I could not possibly have failed to observe.

"I then returned to the house. In the hallway, I examined the glove that Inspector Sturridge had mentioned. It was a woman's right-hand glove, of a soft light-grey fabric, with small embroidered flowers on the back, very similar to the gloves I had seen upstairs in Lady Latchmere's dressing room, except that the embroidery on those had included two little pink flowers, whereas the embroidery on this one contained two little blue flowers. There was nothing at all unusual about it, and no sign that it had been used for anything out of the ordinary. This glove intrigued me, Watson. The whole business was admittedly impenetrable, but over all the other mystifying points in the case, this glove reigned supreme. I could not agree with Inspector Sturridge that it had fallen or been dragged from the window accidentally. It had, I felt sure, been cast out deliberately.

"Then it struck me that there was something which I had overlooked, namely the other glove of the pair. In Lady Latchmere's dressing room I had seen a pair of grey gloves, a left hand and a right; here was a third glove, but where, then, was the fourth? I could not recall seeing it anywhere. I asked Yardley, who had been hovering about all this time, to conduct me once more to Lady Latchmere's chamber, and I took the odd glove with me. There, I proceeded to make a thorough search for the fourth glove. It was nowhere near the other pair, nor, indeed, anywhere in the dressing room, but I did find it eventually. In the bedroom, immediately to the side of the doorway into the dressing room, stood an upright wooden chair, on the seat of which lay a large-brimmed straw hat. Beneath this hat lay the fourth glove. I asked the butler if the room had been cleaned or tidied since the robbery, and he shook his head.

"'Viscount Latchmere gave strict instructions that it should remain untouched until the police had completed their examination of it,' he said, 'and no instructions to the contrary have yet been received.' Clearly, then, the glove I had found under the hat had been there since Saturday.

"And that, Watson, is that!" said Holmes, leaning back in his chair. "I believe I have given you a reasonably accurate account of my morning's work, if in a somewhat condensed form. It illustrates well," he continued as he took up his pipe and began to fill it with tobacco from the old Persian slipper, "what should be the fundamental tenet of any detective's work, that one should never make assumptions before beginning an investigation, but should follow with an open mind wherever the evidence leads. That genial dunderhead, Inspector Sturridge, having assumed at the outset that there were intruders at Latchmere Hall on Saturday night, is obliged to make more and more assumptions – as to the almost supernatural cleverness of these intruders, for instance – when the evidence fails to confirm his initial assumption. I, on the other hand, made no such assumption, and the evidence has led me to a quite different conclusion."

"What, then?" I asked in surprise.

"There were no intruders at Latchmere Hall on Saturday night, Watson. The pendant was taken by someone staying in the house, someone who deliberately threw that glove out of the window to lead us astray."

I confess I was astonished at this suggestion. "But they are all highly respectable people, Holmes," I protested.

"Highly respectable they may be, Watson, but I am convinced that one of them is a thief. Incidentally, all those concerned are now in London. I have their addresses here," he continued, taking his notebook from his pocket: "The Rajah of Banniphur is staying at Claridge's Hotel, Miss Norman has an apartment in Ladbroke Gardens, Mr Brocklehurst is at an address in Curzon Street and Miss Wiltshire is at her parents' house in Doughty Street. Lady Latchmere herself is also in town, staying at their house in Belgrave Square for a few days. I could, of course, go to see any of them in pursuit of my enquiries, but I do not think it will be necessary. They were not able to speak freely at Latchmere Hall – that much was clear – and may wish to amplify their answers to my questions in circumstances of greater privacy. I have given each of them my card, and strongly suspect that one or two of them will come to see me before the day is out."

I watched as he lit a spill in the fire and applied it to the bowl of his pipe, then leaned back once more in his chair, puffing away contentedly.

"But we have heard that Lady Latchmere's bedroom door was locked on Saturday night," I said after a moment, "and there is no way into her dressing room save through that bedroom. So how could anyone in the house have got in there to take the pendant?"

"Quite so. The evidence as we have it has brought us to an *impasse*. It makes it equally impossible that the pendant was taken either by someone outside the house or by someone inside the house. And yet it was certainly taken by someone, Watson, as it is no longer in the jewel case. I believe I know the answer to this conundrum, an answer I have been led to by the evidence of the fourth glove. This not only suggests to me who has taken the pendant, but suggests also that at least two people – possibly more – have lied to me."

My friend fell silent then, and sat for several minutes with his eyes tightly closed and his brow furrowed with concentration. I knew better than to question him further. It was evident he was re-weighing all the evidence in his mind and verifying his conclusions to his own satisfaction. He would enlighten me when he felt ready to do so. As to my own thoughts on the matter, for some time I went over and over all that my friend had told me, but, despite my best efforts, reached no sensible conclusion.

All at once, the silence in our room was broken by a sharp pull at the front-door bell. A moment later, the maid entered to announce that Mr Peter Brocklehurst had called for Sherlock Holmes, and a tall, angular, dark-haired young man was shown into the room. Holmes waved him to a chair, but for a moment he hesitated and glanced in my direction.

"There is something I thought you ought to know," he began, addressing Holmes. "I mean no offence to your colleague, but I would rather speak to you alone."

"Whatever you wish to say you may say as well before Dr Watson as before me. He is the very soul of discretion."

"I do not doubt it, but it is a very delicate, private matter, and I must insist that you do not repeat to a soul what I tell you."

"You have our word on that."

"Very well," said the young man. "The fact is," he continued, taking the chair that Holmes offered him, "that something rather odd occurred at Latchmere Hall on Saturday evening, which may perhaps have a bearing on your attempt to recover the pendant. Whether it does or not, I don't know, but I didn't want you to waste your time on a wild-goose chase. It is not really any concern of mine, and under other circumstances I should not have dreamt of interfering, nor of retailing unpleasant gossip. Nor should I have said anything – whatever the circumstances – if I had thought that you were one of those common enquiry agents who will snoop and spy on anyone for a few shillings. But I could see when we spoke earlier that you are a gentleman, Mr Holmes, and it is in that belief that I will entrust to you what may be extremely delicate information."

"I will endeavour to justify your trust in me."

"Then I will come straight to the point. I did not enjoy the dinner at Latchmere Hall on Saturday. The trouble was that I couldn't think of a single thing to say to anyone. At Oxford I was considered something of a wit, but at Latchmere on Saturday I was like a block of wood. The conversation was dominated partly by matters to do with the Latchmere estate, and partly by the subject of education, and, to speak frankly, I was bored. I attempted to have a sort of side-conversation with Miss Wiltshire, but that was not successful. I also attempted to intervene in the main conversation with some humorous remarks, which I thought might draw Miss Wiltshire in – for she was almost as silent as I was – but my remarks fell flat, and that, too, proved a failure.

"As a result of all this, I drank rather a lot of wine – there didn't seem much else to do – and as I became more intoxicated, my attempts to join in the conversation became wilder and – I must be honest – more stupid. Matilda – Miss Wiltshire – whom I admit I had hoped to impress in the course of the evening, became even less interested in me than she had been earlier, if that is possible, and I saw a look of disdain written plainly enough on her face.

"When the meal was finished and we had passed through the usual tedious and boring rituals, the three women took themselves off to their beds. This was some time between half past ten and a quarter to eleven. About fifteen minutes later, the viscount and the rajah did the same, leaving me mercifully to my own devices. I said I would find myself a book in the library, but when I got there, the room, which was in darkness save for the low glow from the fire, seemed warm and cosy, and I sat down in the big winged armchair by the hearth. I don't know which made me feel worse, the large quantity of wine I had imbibed or the fact that I had made a fool of myself in front of Miss Wiltshire. Anyway, for one reason or another, I fell into a brown study and, not long after, fell fast asleep.

"I was awakened some time later by the sound of the door being opened and quietly closed, which was followed by the rustle of a woman's skirts and soft, rapid footsteps across the library floor behind my chair. Even though I was still half asleep, I knew at once, without really thinking about it, that it must be either Philippa – Lady Latchmere – or Matilda. Uppermost in my mind was the thought that she – whoever it was – might be badly startled to suddenly find me there when she had been in the room for some time, so I made to stand up at once and declare my presence. Before I could do so, however, there came the sound of a curtain being drawn back and a window being quietly opened. This was followed moments later by hushed voices, a man's and a woman's, too low for me to make out what was being said.

"Of course, I had no idea what this was all about, but it was clear it was something secret and furtive. I at once saw what a dreadful position I was in. If my presence were discovered, the situation would be unendurably embarrassing for all concerned. These people – whoever they were – might even believe that I was deliberately spying on them. I could not think what to do. Carefully, I turned my head, and peered round the side of the chair, but could see nothing: the woman was on the other side of the curtain. I considered slowly rising to my feet, and tiptoeing to the door; but then I remembered how much the floor by the fireside chair had creaked earlier, and I decided against it. I should just have to stay in the chair and hope she didn't see me. If she did, I would pretend to be asleep, and thus to have seen and heard nothing. I tried to make myself as inconspicuous as I could and waited. How long they continued speaking, I don't know: probably not much more than five minutes, although it seemed like half an hour to me. Eventually, I heard the window being quietly closed, a movement of the curtain, then soft footsteps once more across the library floor. The door was opened and closed, and the room returned once more to silence. I was all alone! I cannot tell you what relief swept over me at that moment! I waited five or ten minutes, then made my way up to my room, remembering to go by way of the side staircase, to avoid the creaking floorboards on the landing outside the bedrooms. I looked at my watch when I got to my room, and it was then five minutes to midnight."

"Could you see if there was a lamp still lit in any of the bedrooms?" asked Holmes.

"No, all were in darkness. I climbed into bed and went to sleep, and heard nothing further. I believe the rajah was snoring, but it didn't bother me."

"Thank you for this information," said Holmes after a moment. "I appreciate how uncomfortable the situation must have been for you, and how difficult to tell me. Whether it will have any bearing on my own investigation, I cannot say, but you need have no anxiety about such a delicate confidence: neither Dr Watson nor I shall ever repeat what you have told us."

Holmes's manner was one of polite if subdued interest in Brocklehurst's story, but when the young man had shaken hands and left us, looking greatly relieved at having unburdened himself of his secret knowledge, Holmes's manner changed completely. He sprang to his feet and paced about the floor in silence for several minutes.

"Was it Lady Latchmere or Miss Wiltshire?" I asked at length.

"It was Lady Latchmere, Watson. It must be."

"Does this new information change your view of the case?"

My friend shook his head vehemently. "On the contrary," said he, "it confirms precisely what I had already deduced. I doubt Mr Brocklehurst appreciates the significance of what he has told me." Then he resumed his silent pacing about, and would say no more. At length he sat down at his desk with a frown, and took up a sheet of notepaper and a pen.

"How best to proceed?" said he aloud, speaking as much to himself as to me. "If I go there, I at once place myself at a disadvantage, and everything I say is simply denied. If on the other hand, I send a summons to come to this address, then the recipient suffers all the anxiety of wondering what it is that I know, and how to respond."

He scribbled a few lines on his notepaper. "There," said he after a moment: "'If you bring the pendant, I may be able to save you from disgrace. If you do not, then the truth must come out, and you will be ruined.' That should do it!"

When he had sealed and addressed his letter, he rang for the maid and instructed her to send it at once by special messenger, then he curled up in his chair by the fire and closed his eyes, as if exhausted. An hour and a half later, the maid brought in a letter that had just been delivered. Holmes roused himself, tore open the envelope and scanned the contents, then tossed it over to me without comment. The note was a brief one, and ran as follows:

> Dear Mr Holmes – Propose to call on you this evening at nine o'clock.
>
> Banniphur

At a quarter past eight there came a ring at the front-door bell. A few moments later, the maid announced the Honourable Miss Arabella Norman. She was a small, somewhat frail-looking elderly lady, with grey hair and a slight stoop. Holmes waved her to his chair by the hearth and brought up another chair for himself. For several minutes she sat there in silence, warming her hands at the fire, then Holmes spoke:

"You have something to tell us, I believe," said he, "concerning the events of Saturday night."

She turned to him, but did not respond.

"You wish to tell us," Holmes continued, "that on Saturday night you could not sleep and, as you lay awake, you heard Lady Latchmere's bedroom door open and her footsteps on the landing. You opened your door a crack and saw that, clad in a dressing gown over her nightclothes, she was going downstairs. On an impulse, you crossed the landing and entered her bedroom, where you unlocked her jewel case – the key was in the lock – and removed the Latchmere Pendant. To make it appear the work of an intruder, you took a glove, from a pair that lay under a straw hat on a chair, and threw it from the window to the lawn below, where you knew it would be found the following morning. You then returned to your own room, and hid the pendant in your luggage."

Miss Norman did not reply, and after a few moments, during which I could see that he was observing her features keenly, Holmes continued:

"Now you have returned home with your booty, and have realized that your momentary impulse has placed you in a difficult – even possibly disastrous – situation. You do not really want the pendant: you cannot wear it, and nor can you possibly sell such a well-known piece of jewellery. What is to be done? And then you received my letter, offering a way – perhaps the only way – out of your difficulty."

"If you were right," Miss Norman interrupted, "and I did in fact have the pendant, would you be able to return it to Viscount Latchmere without mentioning my name in any way?"

"Yes. That is my intention. Nothing would be gained, and much lost, by dragging your name through the mud."

"Very well," said she in a tone of resignation. She unfastened the capacious bag that lay in her lap and took from it a small bundle, wrapped in an embroidered handkerchief. This she unfolded, and held it out for us to see. Upon the handkerchief, in an elaborate gold setting, lay the largest gemstone I have ever seen in my life. The flickering light from our fire caught the facets of this remarkable stone, which flashed and sparkled with every slight movement of Miss Norman's hand. "Here is my 'booty', as you call it," said she. "That is all that I took. I know nothing about the missing ring."

Holmes took the pendant from her hand and held it up by the chain, so that it flashed as it twisted. "There you are, Watson!" said he. "This little object – this little lump of compressed carbon, as a chemist would describe it to us – has been a focus for men's greed and violence for more than a century! What a record of bloodletting and hatred it has carved for itself in that time! Here," he continued, leaning across and placing the pendant in my hand. "You realize, of course, my dear fellow, that you are now, technically speaking, a handler of stolen goods! Miss Norman," he continued, turning to our visitor, "you are an intelligent woman. What can have possessed you to commit such a bizarre and uncharacteristic crime?"

"I will tell you," she responded. "There are facts of which you are unaware, Mr Holmes. But first, would you please indulge me by telling me how you knew that it was I that had taken the pendant? You are evidently a better detective than Inspector Sturridge, who seemed content simply to make our blood run cold with a list of gangs – Foulgers, Clays, and I don't know who else – who were likely to climb in at our bedroom windows any night of the year. Or did you just guess?"

"I never guess," returned Holmes firmly. "It is destructive of the logical faculty. Occasionally one must balance probabilities in order to proceed, but in this case that was scarcely necessary: the indications were clear enough." He described to Miss Norman his thoughts on the glove found on the lawn, and the absence of any trace of an intruder. "It seemed to me then that the glove had been tossed on the lawn deliberately to throw us off the scent. What could this mean but that the pendant had in fact been taken by someone in the house? As I had, to my own satisfaction, eliminated the household staff from any suspicion, that left only Viscount Latchmere's four guests and the viscountess herself. Unlikely as it may seem, the possibility that Lady Latchmere had herself had a hand in the disappearance of the pendant could not be dismissed. Her manner was certainly odd, and I was convinced she was keeping a secret of some kind, although whether that related to the missing pendant or not, I could not say.

"However, when I found the fourth glove, it clarified my view of the matter. Presumably the glove found on the lawn had been with the other one of the pair, under the straw hat. But why, then, had that particular glove been chosen to act as a blind, rather than one of the other pair which lay on the table in the dressing room? The only conclusion I could reach was that whoever threw the glove from the window wished it to be found the following morning, when, of course, the loss of the pendant would also be discovered, but did not wish its absence to be noted that evening, so that the precise time of the theft would not be known, and the notion of an intruder would therefore be plausible. But the only person who could have noticed that evening that a glove had disappeared was Lady Latchmere herself. Obviously, it is absurd to suppose that she would take such a precaution against herself, and therefore the glove was not taken by her, but by someone else.

"I was thus faced with something of a dilemma: if Lady Latchmere's account were true, that she had retired for the night and locked her door immediately her maid had left her, then no one but she herself could have taken the pendant. On the other hand, the evidence of the fourth glove was that some-one other than Lady Latchmere had moved the glove and taken the pendant. If that were true, then Lady Latchmere was not being entirely truthful and must have left her bedroom, if only for a few moments. How to resolve this conundrum? On balance, I felt more certainty in the mute testimony of the gloves than the testimony of Lady Latchmere, and therefore decided that the pendant had been taken by one of the guests, and that Lady Latchmere had indeed left her room, despite what she had told me. I dismissed the rajah as a possibility. Everyone seems to have heard him snoring, and although one can feign snoring for a few moments, it is not possible to keep it up for any length of time without bringing on a state of physical collapse. Neither Mr Brocklehurst nor Miss Wiltshire could have reached Lady Latchmere's bedroom without treading on the creaking floor-boards on the landing, and as you stated that you slept very badly away from home, and lay awake for a long time on Satur-day night, you would have heard this noise, but you did not. This, I regret to say, left only yourself, Miss Norman."

"It all sounds so obvious now you have explained it," remarked our visitor, "that I am surprised I wasn't arrested first thing on Sunday morning."

"Now you must answer my question," said Holmes with a chuckle. "Why did you steal the pendant?"

"I have been a visitor at Latchmere Hall for forty years or more," replied Miss Norman after a moment. "As an unmarried female relative, I was aware that I was, generally speaking, noth-ing but a nuisance to the family, but I did have one specific merit: being single, I was always useful as a simple way of balancing the numbers and the sexes at dinner parties. The present viscount's father always included me in any gatherings he had arranged. I think he hoped to marry me off to one of his single male guests – then he would have satisfied his family duty and could forget about me with a clear conscience – but for various reasons it never happened. So as the years rolled by, I continued my respectable but penurious existence in a small apartment to the north of Notting Hill, answering the summons to Latchmere Hall at regular intervals – the previous viscount always sent me the train fare – to solve the dinner-setting problems of my wealthy relations, and gradually becoming transformed, in the eyes of the world, from young and marriageable, if a little too independent-minded, to elderly and eccentric."

"How is your family related to that of the viscount?"

"My father was a distant cousin, on the poverty-stricken side of the family. He succeeded to the Barony of Patrington as a young man, but it was not a title that brought any tangible benefit and he hardly ever used it. For many years, he farmed in the East Riding of Yorkshire, which is where I was raised, but he could never entirely break free from debt, and at the time of his death the farm was heavily mortgaged. My brother, Thomas, had been an officer in the Indian Army, but had lost his life during the Mutiny, and my mother had been dead some years, so, upon my father's death, I was thrown very much on my own resources. I scraped together what money I could, from the sale of the farm and a few other odds and ends, and moved to London, where I had a few friends and where I could supplement my meagre savings with a little teaching work.

"I used to enjoy my periodic visits to Latchmere Hall – at least I knew I would get a square meal there, and would occasionally meet some interesting people – but my enjoyment has faded a little with each passing year. Of course, the estate is beautiful at this time of the year, clothed in the colours of autumn, but I can get a similar pleasure by taking a walk in Hyde Park. My main reason for continuing to go is so that they don't forget I exist and will continue to invite me down for Christmas. The main problem is that I don't care very much for the present viscount. Still, I didn't mean to bore you with my personal concerns. I don't expect you to understand, and I know it is no justification for my moment of madness, but I have come to resent the viscount's wealth and my own poverty. It would not matter if they were not so mean. I know there was a time when my father approached the old viscount for a loan, which could have saved him from great difficulty, and which the viscount could easily have afforded, but he turned him down. I mentioned to you that the old viscount used to send me my train fare for visits to Latchmere, but I should add that when I had bought a return ticket from King's Cross to Hatfield, there was usually not a penny left over. The present viscount is, if anything, even meaner than his father was, and when I had to sit and listen to him on Saturday evening, describing at length how his income from the estate – which I happen to know is huge beyond the dreams of avarice – had declined slightly this year, I'm afraid it made my blood boil. And the irony is that that precious stone, of which Viscount Latchmere and his predecessors have made such a show over the years, does not even really belong to them."

"What do you mean?" asked Holmes.

"There is a persistent story in the family that Samuel Tollington, who later became the third Viscount Latchmere and was the one that brought the diamond back from India, had in fact murdered his uncle, Sir George Tollington, in order to get his hands on it."

"Is there any evidence for that?"

"Not directly, but there is an affidavit, sworn in 1803 by one James Forrest, a former officer of the East India Company, that the diamond was purchased at Fort St George, Madras, not by Samuel Tollington, but by his uncle, who disappeared overboard in mysterious circumstances during the voyage back to England. The Tollington family tree is a complex one, and I will not trouble you with the details, but suffice it to say that I am a direct descendant of Sir George Tollington."

"Has this document ever been made public?"

"No. My Grandfather apparently considered doing so, but was advised by a legal expert that in the absence of any other corroborative evidence, it would carry no weight, and would simply be denounced by the viscount as a pack of lies."

"That is probably true," said Holmes. "I can understand your feeling somewhat bitter at the whole business, Miss Norman, but there is more to life than diamonds. Besides, possession of the pendant does not seem to have brought the viscounts much good fortune or happiness." He appeared about to say more when there came a ring at the doorbell. A moment later Mrs Hudson announced that the Rajah of Banniphur had arrived. Holmes made a quick gesture to me and, perceiving his meaning, I at once stuffed the pendant into my pocket.

The man who entered our room was somewhat below medium height, with a trim athletic appearance. His dark skin and very black hair made a striking contrast with the landlady's pale face and hair. He stopped when he saw Miss Norman, an expression of surprise and confusion on his keen, intelligent features.

"Excuse me, but have I arrived at an inconvenient moment?" he asked. "I was not aware that you had another visitor."

"Not at all," returned Holmes in a cheery tone. "We were just discussing the case and related matters. Pray, take a seat, my dear sir!"

I offered him my chair by the fire, which he took, and brought up another chair for myself.

"One moment," said Holmes. "This gathering calls for a pot of tea! I'll just catch Mrs Hudson!"

"It is indeed a fortunate coincidence that we should meet in this way!" said the rajah to Miss Norman as we waited for Holmes to return. "I had been very much hoping to speak to you again, but did not know how best to approach you. I was very struck by some of the suggestions you made on Saturday evening. I have an appointment with the Prime Minister on the ninth, and would very much like to discuss your ideas further before seeing him. You seem to have a better understanding of the needs of education than anyone else I have spoken to."

"You flatter me, Rajah!"

"Not at all, madam! And, please, call me Saju! I wonder, would you do me the honour of taking luncheon with me at

Claridge's tomorrow, when we can discuss these matters further?"

"I should be delighted," replied Miss Norman.

"Now!" said Holmes, hurrying back into the room and rubbing his hands together. "The tea will be here in a minute!"

"Have you been able to make any progress in the case?" the rajah asked him.

"Indeed I have!"

"Thank Heavens for that! I rather feared it might prove a more complicated or delicate matter than it at first appeared. That is why I have come to see you."

"What did you have in mind?" asked Holmes, a note of curiosity in his voice.

"May I speak frankly? Yes? Very well, then – but you must not repeat what I say." He shot a nervous glance at Miss Norman. "Excuse my speaking so boldly of your relatives, madam, but there seems to me something seriously amiss at Latchmere Hall. Viscount Latchmere is not the boy I remembered from school, and – to speak frankly – I do not imagine I will visit him again. The household is not a very happy one. The viscountess acts strangely and is clearly unhappy. I did wonder if she herself had not perhaps done something with the pendant, Mr Holmes."

Holmes chuckled. "That was also one of my first thoughts," said he. "However, I am glad to say it is not the case."

"You know where the pendant is?"

"Yes, it is at this moment in the possession of a handler of stolen goods."

"You are certain?"

"Yes. I know he has it, and he knows that I know. I am confident of recovering it and returning it to Viscount Latchmere tomorrow."

"Thank Heavens! Then we no longer need worry about it. And the topaz ring?"

"Ah!" said Holmes. "That is a rather different matter. It was not taken with the pendant. In fact, I don't believe it was stolen at all."

"I think that Lady Latchmere believes she has simply misplaced it," interjected Miss Norman.

An odd silence fell on the room then, and the rajah shuffled his feet uncomfortably.

"You think," said Holmes at length, addressing the Rajah of Banniphur, "that Lady Latchmere has given the topaz ring to someone, but you do not wish to be disloyal to your old school friend by spreading unpleasant gossip."

"You are reading my mind precisely," responded the rajah.

"Do you know why Mr James Ellison called at Latchmere Hall on Saturday?" asked Holmes after a moment.

"I may be mistaken, as he was very guarded in his remarks," said the rajah, "but my impression was that Mr Ellison had wished to borrow some money from Viscount Latchmere, but the latter had refused."

"You believe, then," said Holmes, "that Viscountess Latchmere, unbeknown to her husband, has lent Mr Ellison the ring to use as security in arranging a loan elsewhere?"

The rajah hesitated. "Yes, I do," he said at length. "Lady Latchmere was – how shall I put it – very taken with Mr Ellison. That was clear for anyone to see."

"I had the same thought," said Miss Norman. "She took him to see the autumn flowers at the other end of the garden, and they were out of earshot for a very long time. I did wonder what they were finding to talk about for so long."

"He is a very engaging man," said the rajah, "but—" He broke off, as if ordering his thoughts. "There is an old saying, where I come from," he continued at length: "'The bee makes honey for himself'. The meaning is that however much we may enjoy his honey, this is of no interest or importance to the bee. He makes the honey not for our benefit, but for his own."

"I did not have the pleasure of meeting Mr Ellison," said Holmes, "but I am prepared to accept your perception on the point, for your conclusions are broadly in agreement with my own. I have some experience of that type myself: the most charming man I ever met ended up destroying the lives of almost everyone who had ever had any dealings with him. Let us hope it is not so at Latchmere Hall, although the signs are not propitious."

Mrs Hudson brought in a tray of tea and biscuits then, and our conversation moved on to other topics. When our visitors had left, I took the Latchmere Pendant from my pocket and held it up by the chain. As it revolved slowly, flashing and glinting as it caught the light from our lamps, I pondered how such a small thing could have been the cause of so much trouble over the years. Holmes refilled his pipe, and sat for a long time by the fire, staring into the flickering flames with a thoughtful expression on his face.

"It is a complex world we live in, Watson," said he at length, "in which causes and effects are often interwoven, like a tapestry, and cannot very easily be unpicked. Miss Norman would never have taken the pendant had Lady Latchmere not left her room in the way that she did. Lady Latchmere would not have left her room and gone to her secret meeting with Mr Ellison at the library window had she not already felt estranged to some degree from her husband. So it could be argued that the theft of the pendant is a direct consequence of the state of the viscount's marriage."

"What will you tell him?"

"About the pendant, nothing. About the ring, only that I have been unable to locate it, and believe that, as his wife stated, she has put it somewhere. I am retained only to find and recover that object you have in your hand, not to furnish any explanations. The fundamental cause of this whole business, Watson, lies in the relations between Viscount Latchmere and his wife, and that is a problem they must solve for themselves."

The Adventure of
THE RICHMOND RECLUSE

PART ONE: A NIGHT AT HILL HOUSE

IN PUBLISHING THIS SERIES OF MEMOIRS, my constant aim, however imperfectly realized, has been to illustrate the remarkable mental qualities of my friend, Mr Sherlock Holmes. In most of the cases he took up, his involvement was decisive: without it, it is likely that the problems would have remained unsolved, and the truth for ever unknown. In a few cases, however, the part he played was less pronounced, and it is possible that the truth would eventually have come to light without his intervention. In the main I have passed over these cases when selecting those which were to be published. Yet among this group are some in which the facts of the matter are in themselves of sufficient interest to warrant publication, despite offering my friend few opportunities for the exercise of those gifts of observation and deduction that he possessed in so high a degree. Especially memorable among cases of this kind were the affair of the Purple Hand, and the Boldero Mystery. It is the latter case I now propose to recount. Regular readers of the *Surrey County Observer* will need little reminding of what that newspaper termed "The Richmond Horror". But the press accounts of the time were all very brief, and concentrated solely on the dramatic conclusion of the matter, to the exclusion of what had gone before, so that even those who are familiar with the case are unlikely to be aware of what lay behind those shocking events.

Our introduction to the matter came on a pleasant afternoon in the early spring of '84. Sherlock Holmes had received a letter from Farrow and Redfearn of Lincoln's Inn, the well-known firm of solicitors. He glanced over it, tossed it across to me and returned to the papers he had been studying before the letter's arrival had distracted him. I read the following:

> Sir,
>
> We beg to advise you as follows: that our client, Mr David Boldero, is desirous of learning the whereabouts of his elder brother, Mr Simon Boldero; that the whereabouts of the latter having been unknown for some three months and the circumstances being unusual, we have recommended that our client consult you, which he proposes to do at four o'clock this afternoon, when he will be able to apprise you of the details of the matter.
>
> We remain, sir, your obedient servants,
>
> Farrow and Redfearn

"They have put a number of choice cases my way in the past," remarked Holmes as I finished reading. "Let us hope that it is not too troublesome a matter. I am somewhat preoccupied at present with this business of Archduke Dmitri's diamonds."

"It does not sound a very desperate affair," I remarked, aware of my friend's oft-stated rule that one case should not be allowed to intrude upon another. This was not from any fear that his mental capacities might be over-stretched, for in truth there was little doubt that, like a chess master giving an exhibition, he might successfully have handled half a dozen separate cases at once had he so wished. It was rather that his neat and logical mind preferred above all things an orderly, concentrated mode of thought. Yet it was also true of him that he rarely declined a case that had succeeded in capturing his interest, so that, despite his preference, this, of all his personal rules of work, was the one he most frequently set aside. As I waited for Holmes's client to arrive, I speculated idly as to the nature of his case, and wondered if it would provide any of those touches of the *outré* that so delighted my friend's intellect. The dry communication he had received from the solicitor did not appear to presage a case of any very great interest, I judged. But in this opinion, as it turned out, I was quite mistaken.

Mr David Boldero arrived on the dot of four. He was a tall, broad-shouldered and strongly built young man, of about seven-and-twenty, with wavy black hair and a determined set to his strong, clean-shaven features.

"I see you are smokers," said he, observing the wreaths of blue smoke that spiralled in the air above my companion's head. "I will venture to fill my own pipe, then, if I may."

"By all means," responded Holmes, waving our visitor to a chair. "Pray make yourself comfortable and let us know how we can help you. It is always a pleasure," he added after a moment, "to greet a member of the diplomatic corps, newly returned from overseas."

Boldero looked up in surprise as he lit his pipe. "Now, how on earth do you know that?" said he. "I can hardly suppose that my return to England warranted a paragraph in the morning papers!"

"Your suit, Mr Boldero, while of excellent quality, is of a distinctively continental cut. The top button is a touch higher than English tailors are wont to place it. You have evidently bought the suit abroad. The same, I might add, applies to your boots. Nor has your period abroad been merely a brief excursion, for your tobacco, too, is very characteristic of continental mixtures. Most English travellers, in my experience, take with them sufficient home-produced tobacco to see out their journey. You have clearly been abroad long enough to acquire a taste for the native variety. It is not Dutch and it is not French, but could possibly be Danish. You do not have the cut of a man of commerce, and the pallor of your skin precludes any prolonged exposure to the Mediterranean sun. I am therefore inclined to place you as an *attaché* at one of our embassies in the north of Europe."

"Well I never!" cried our visitor, leaning back in his chair.

"To be precise," said Holmes, "you have been at the British Embassy in Stockholm for over two years."

Boldero's mouth fell open in astonishment.

"You have a small medallion on your watch chain," explained Holmes, "which I observed as you sat back. It is a decoration

– the Order of St Margaret, I believe – which is conferred by the Court of Scandinavia on all foreign diplomats who have served there for a period of at least two years."

"That is amazing!" cried Boldero.

"On the contrary, it is perfectly elementary," said Holmes. "Now, if we might hear the details of your problem? I know only that you wish to discover the whereabouts of your brother."

"He has disappeared without trace in the most mysterious circumstances," returned our visitor, his features assuming a grave look. "But there is more to the matter than that, Mr Holmes. Last night, so I believe, an attempt was made upon my life."

"How very interesting! Pray, let us have the details!"

"My brother and I have seen little of each other in recent years. Circumstances have obliged each of us to pursue his own individual course through life. We were left very poorly off when our father died. There is great wealth elsewhere in the Boldero family, but little of it came our way. I was fortunate enough to secure a post in the diplomatic service some four years ago, but it has meant that I have spent much of that time abroad, after my posting to Stockholm. My brother, meanwhile, has been pursuing a career with a firm of solicitors. I last saw him three months ago, in January, on the occasion of my engagement. He attended the little celebration we had, and seemed at that time to be in excellent spirits."

"He had no pressing financial concerns?"

"He has never been very well off, if that is what you mean. Neither of us has. But it did not appear to be causing him any particular anxiety. On the contrary, he seemed more cheery than I had seen him before."

"His health?"

"First rate."

"He is not married?"

Our visitor shook his head. "He lives alone in a little house just off Camberwell High Street. It was to there I went to look him up when I returned to England last week. We have never corresponded with any great regularity, but during the last three months he has not replied to any of my letters, and I wished to know why. If he was in difficulty of some kind, I wished to help him if I could. I have a key to the front door of his house, so I was able to let myself in. Inside, the apartment resembled the *Marie Celeste*: everything was in perfect order, the table in the dining room neatly laid for a meal, but of my brother there was no sign. The only circumstance that gave indication that Simon had not simply stepped out of the house five minutes before my arrival was the large number of letters lying in a disordered heap upon the doormat. All the letters I had sent in the previous three months were there, together with dozens of others. I quickly sifted through them and established that Simon had not been in the house since the third week in January."

"Your brother kept no domestic staff?"

"He lived very simply. A local woman came in once a day to attend to cleaning and similar duties."

"Did she have her own key?"

"No. My brother always admitted her himself in the morning before he left for town, and when she had finished her work she would lock the door with a spare key, which she then posted through the letter-box. I found that key on the doormat."

"No doubt you have interviewed her?"

"I have tried to, but without success. It appears she left the area some time in February, and no one there could tell me her present address. They did tell me, however, that she had been more annoyed than puzzled by my brother's disappearance. She presumed that he had simply gone away on business and forgotten to inform her of the fact, and he had left owing her a little money, according to the local sources."

"You say you found the table laid for a meal," interrupted Holmes. "Could you tell, from the disposition of the cutlery and so on, what sort of meal this was likely to be?"

"I am afraid I did not notice," returned Boldero, his features expressing surprise at the question.

"That is a pity," remarked Holmes, shaking his head.

"I cannot see that the point is of any significance."

"Nevertheless, it is. It might, for instance, have indicated whether your brother's housekeeper had expected him to return that day, or to stay away for the night. Were you able to establish more precisely the date of his disappearance?"

Boldero nodded. "In his study was a copy of the *Daily Telegraph*, dated Thursday, 17 January, which had clearly been read; and on his desk was a note he had written to remind himself to do certain jobs on Friday, 18 January. Simon often left himself such *aides-memoires*. When he had done the jobs in question, he would cross off the items on the list. None of the items on the note I found had been crossed off. I take it, then, that he was last in the house on the seventeenth."

"Excellent!" cried Holmes. "Your observation is commendable! Were everyone so thorough in their attention to detail I should soon find myself without work!"

"I have the note here," said Boldero, producing a folded sheet of paper from his pocket. He passed it across to Holmes, who studied it for a few moments, then handed it to me. The items listed were all of a domestic nature and unexceptional: "Baker – see again. Pay wine merchant – enquire about sherry. Settle butcher's bill for the month".

"I have spoken to all the tradesmen mentioned in the note," Boldero continued. "None of them could recall seeing Simon on the day in question, which confirms what I thought."

"That may be interesting," remarked Holmes in a thoughtful voice.

"I should hardly have called it 'interesting'," responded Boldero in a tone of surprise, "except that it indicates that my brother had the same mundane concerns as everyone else at the time of his disappearance."

"That was not my meaning," said Holmes. "Pray continue. You have made enquiries, I take it, at your brother's professional chambers?"

"Indeed. There I learned that he had informed his colleagues he would be taking two weeks' leave of absence from 14 January. He did not say why he required this, but they understood that he was engaged upon some legal research. They could shed no light whatever on his prolonged disappearance, and had all the time been expecting to hear from him with an explanation. I subsequently made thorough enquiries at the police station and at all the hospitals, in case Simon had met with an accident, but learned nothing. It appeared that my brother had simply disappeared off the face of the earth. Then Beatrice – that is to say, Miss Underwood, my fiancée – suggested that I try my cousin Silas, to see if he had any information on the matter. I thought it unlikely, as Silas is practically a recluse, going out very little and receiving visitors even less, and I was not aware that my brother had had anything to do with him for years; but in the absence of any other direction for my enquiries, I agreed to take myself off to Hill House, at Richmond upon Thames, which is where Silas lives.

"I perhaps ought to tell you a little about Cousin Silas, and about the family in general, so you will understand the situation. You may have heard of my great-grandfather, Samuel Boldero. He was one of the last of the great eighteenth-century merchants, and made a fortune in trade. Indeed, he was reputed at the time to be the second wealthiest commoner in the country. At his death, all his wealth passed equally to his two surviving sons, Daniel and Jonathan. Each of these two had, in turn, one son, Enoch and Silas respectively. Enoch Boldero was my father.

"Unfortunately, my father and grandfather quarrelled and became estranged, and when my grandfather died, when I was an infant, it was found that he had virtually cut my father out of his will altogether, and had left almost all he possessed to his nephew – his late brother's only son, and thus my father's cousin, Silas.

"Cousin Silas, as you will therefore appreciate, is very wealthy, having inherited the entire Boldero fortune, half from his own father and half from his uncle, my grandfather. My brother and I hoped, without being at all avaricious, that a little, at least, of this enormous wealth might perhaps find its way to us, especially after my father's sadly premature death, which left us in some difficulty. By the time we had established my mother and my sister, Rachel, in a small house at Tunbridge Wells, near to my mother's relations, we were left with practically nothing. Simon was endeavouring to pursue a career in law, and was attached to Nethercott and Cropley, a firm of solicitors in Holborn, but he was finding his lack of money a distinct handicap. Recalling that Silas had himself followed a similar career for a time in his younger years, Simon thought that his cousin might feel some sympathy for his position. He therefore appealed to Cousin Silas's generosity. Unfortunately, Silas does not have any. Every excuse one could conceive was brought in to explain why he was unable to help. The best he felt able to offer my brother was a small, inadequate loan, offered for an inadequate period of time and at such an extortionate rate of interest that one could easily arrange a more favourable loan any day of the week in the City. Needless to say, Simon did not take up the offer. That was about four years ago, since which time, so far as I am aware, there has been no communication between them. I have myself seen Silas but once in that period. Last August I took Miss Underwood and her mother boating on the Thames, and knowing that our way would take us past Richmond, I proposed to Silas that we pay him a call. He received us into his house for an hour, but I cannot honestly say that he made us welcome. Miss Underwood formed a very poor impression of him, and the whole episode was an acute embarrassment to me. I had wanted her to meet Silas, as he is the senior member of the Boldero family, but my chief concern afterwards was whether, having seen what my relations were like, Miss Underwood would be permanently prejudiced against me."

"Does your cousin have any family of his own?" Holmes interrupted.

Boldero shook his head. "He never married," he replied. "He has always led a completely solitary life, and for the last twenty years has lived in almost total seclusion. As far as I am aware, his last appearance in public was about fifteen years ago, when he read his monograph on 'The Dragon Lizards of China' to the Society for Snakes and Reptiles – or whatever the body is called. This society was formerly his chief interest in life, but about ten years ago, so I understand, there was a disagreement between Silas and the other members. He could not get his way over some matter and resigned."

"As I understand your account, then," said Holmes, "you and your brother are Silas's only kin, and will inherit whatever he has to leave when he dies."

"That is correct, but our inheritance is by no means assured. Cousin Silas is quite likely to will all his money away, if not to the Society for Snakes and Reptiles, then to some similar body. I have certainly never founded my plans on any bounty I might receive from that direction!"

"From what you have told me, you are probably wise not to do so. Pray continue with your narrative."

"I went down to Richmond yesterday afternoon, having notified Silas that I was coming for the night. Hill House is a strange, rambling old place, near the top of Richmond Hill. It is a dark and unattractive building, and has been made more so by the various additions and extensions that have been made to it over the years. It stands in its own very large grounds, which are entirely surrounded by a massive eight-foot-high brick wall. From the stout wooden gate, a gravel path runs dead straight for thirty yards or so to the front porch of the house, and this path is entirely enclosed, both above and at the sides, by a curious glass structure, something like a narrow, elongated greenhouse. This is not, as you might suppose, to protect visitors from the weather, but rather to prevent the denizens of Silas's garden from escaping, for his grounds are alive with all sorts of odd and unattractive creatures, which he has imported from the tropics: lizards, snakes, anteaters and other things even less appealing. I have used the word 'garden', but that is perhaps misleading. The grounds of Hill House are a complete wilderness, and must be the nearest thing to a jungle outside of the tropics. I shouldn't think that they have benefited from any human attention in forty years. I was taken there once as a small boy, by my father, and I can still recall the horrified fascination with which I regarded that tangle of luxuriant weeds and brambles, and the slimy creatures that slithered and crept about in the darkness beneath them. Now the place is even more overgrown than it was in those days, and the glass veranda over the path is covered with green mould and slime, so that practically nothing can be discerned through its murky panes.

"The daylight was beginning to fade as I arrived at the gate. I pushed it open, and was surprised to see a shabbily dressed woman coming along the path under the gloomy, shadowed glass tunnel. She was short and frail-looking, her garments were frayed and dirty, and she had a black shawl pulled tightly round her shoulders. Her head was down and she did not see me until she was almost upon me. When she did, she started as if terrified, and the eyes she turned up to me had a disturbing look of fear in them. We passed in silence, but as we did so she suddenly shot out an arm from beneath her shawl and plucked the sleeve of my coat. Startled, I stopped and turned to her.

"'Yes?' said I.

"'Don't go through that door,' said she after a moment in a low, cracked voice, nodding her head very slightly in the direction of the house.

"'Why, whatever do you mean?' I asked in surprise.

"For a moment she hesitated, then, mumbling something in which I caught only the word 'regret', she pushed past me and hurried on to the gate. It was an unpleasant and unsettling incident, but I concluded that the poor woman was half-witted, and dismissed it from my mind.

"As I approached the front door of the house, I saw that it was slightly ajar. The hall within was in deep shadow, with no sign of anyone there. I knocked and, pushing the door further open, stepped into the hall, calling out a greeting as I did so.

"The silent house returned no answer, but at that moment the front door behind me creaked slightly on its hinges. I turned to find Cousin Silas in the act of closing it. He had evidently been standing in the shadows behind the door as I entered. Aware of his eccentric ways, I made no comment. I don't know if you are familiar with William Blake's somewhat whimsical painting of 'the flea', but it has always seemed to me that anyone seeing Cousin Silas might well imagine that he had been the model for the picture. There is something shifty, stooping and watchful in his manner, which could not be described as attractive. His facial expression habitually hovers somewhere between a sneer and a calculating smile, without quite being either; for in truth it appears scarcely like a human expression at all, resembling more that unpleasant reptilian grin you see on the faces of those creatures in whose company Silas has spent so much of his time. Were he not so bent and stooping, it may be that he would be quite tall. He certainly has broad shoulders and a powerful chest, and there must have been a time, in his youth, when his appearance was not unattractive. Now, however, both his appearance and his manner border on the repulsive, and as I watched him close the front door I could well understand the effect he had had upon my fiancée. I waited, and he advanced towards me in his queer shuffling way, never quite lifting his feet fully from the ground. Then he gripped my arm and thrust his face close to my own.

"'Well, my boy,' said he in a thin, reedy voice, 'I don't have many visitors here. It's put me out a little, if I am to speak frankly, but I think you'll find I'm ready for you.'

"'It is good of you to put me up at such short notice,' I responded and made to move away, but he held me back.

"'That person you met on the path is my charwoman,' said he in a low voice, breathing in my face. 'She's quite mad, you know. It's difficult to get servants out here.'

"'Is it?' I asked in surprise.

"'Yes, it is,' said he sharply. 'She said something to you, I believe, as you passed. What was it, eh?'

"'Nothing intelligible.'

"'But you replied to her. I saw you speak.'

"'I tell you, I couldn't understand what she was talking about.'

"'Not at all?' persisted Silas in a tone of disbelief.

"'I think she wondered if I had come to the right address.'

"'Bah!' said he, stamping his foot on the floor in anger. 'Interfering nuisance! I'll teach her to meddle in my affairs, you see if I don't! Still, that is something for me to consider later.'

"'I take it you received my letter,' said I, endeavouring to change the subject.

"For a long moment he did not reply, his hooded eyes flickering from side to side, as if he were considering whether he could deny having received the letter and if he would gain anything thereby.

"'What if I did?' said he at length in an unpleasant, argumentative tone.

"'I am anxious to discover Simon's whereabouts.'

"'What is that to me, eh?'

"'I thought, as I mentioned in my letter, that he had perhaps written to you, or even visited you, before his disappearance.'

"'Why should he do that?' retorted Silas quickly in a suspicious tone.

"'I cannot imagine. But I can find no trace of him elsewhere.'

"'Well, he didn't. I haven't seen him for years! Still,' he continued in an unpleasantly unctuous tone, evidently fearing he had spoken too sharply, 'we can consider the matter over dinner.'

"He led me through the darkened house to the dining room, where two places were laid for dinner. A single small candle in the centre of the table provided the only illumination. Silas must have sensed the despondency with which I viewed this dismal scene, for he chuckled.

"'No sense in wasting money on light we don't need,' said he, laughing unpleasantly.

"There followed what I can only describe as the most wretched meal of my life, the central features of which were a miserable-looking joint of tough and highly salted bacon, and a bottle of wine that tasted like vinegar, of which, Silas informed me with great self-satisfaction, he had been fortunate enough to purchase a whole case at 'a quite remarkably low price'. It quickly became clear that I should learn nothing from him concerning my brother, and I began to regret that I had ever gone to Hill House at all. His only suggestion was that Simon might have gone to Italy, but when I enquired why he should think so, he replied only that 'people do go there sometimes, you know' and laughed unpleasantly at this feeble and inappropriate jest. As soon as the meal was ended, therefore, I began yawning ostentatiously. Silas reacted with alacrity to this cue and offered to show me to my room. Taking the candle from the table, he led the way up the dirty, uncarpeted staircase and along a dusty, crooked corridor. Everywhere the smell of damp and rot rose from the bare floorboards. Presently he stopped and opened a door.

"'This is your room,' said he, ushering me through the doorway.

"He lit the stump of a candle, which stood on a small table beside the bed, and turned to go. As he was closing the door, however, he put his head back in.

"'There's water in the jug,' said he, indicating a large, dirty-looking ewer which stood on a lop-sided washstand at the side of the room. 'If there's not enough, you'll find more through there,' he added, nodding at a door in the shadows at the far side of the room.

"It was a dark and grim chamber in which to pass the night. Apart from the bed, table and washstand, the only furniture was a stained and rotten-looking chest of drawers. The stench of damp seemed even stronger in the bedroom than elsewhere in the house, and the wallpaper was hanging from the walls in sheets, yellowed and dirty and dotted all over with the black marks of mould. I was glad to climb into bed and pull the covers over my head. For a while I lay awake, listening to the sounds of small creatures scurrying about beneath the floor, but at length I fell asleep. Before I did so, I vowed to myself that I would never spend another night in that wretched house.

"Some hours later, I awoke suddenly. A pounding headache seemed to split my head asunder, my throat was hot and parched, and I felt desperately thirsty. I struck a match and lit the candle, surprising a dozen large spiders on the wall above my head. Whether my thirst was the result of the salty meat I had eaten, the foul wine, or something else, I had no idea. I knew only that I must have a drink of water. I climbed wearily from my bed, but found that, despite what Silas had told me, the jug was empty. Feeling a little annoyed at this, I took the candle across to the door he had indicated and attempted to open it. I had presumed it would open inwards, as the other door did, but as I turned the doorknob it swung away from me and, still half asleep, I stepped forward into the blackness beyond. Never in my life have such terror and confusion gripped my heart as at that moment. For in stepping from the rough wood of the bedroom floor, my bare foot found nothing whatever, but trod on empty air. I think I must have cried out, but I cannot be certain, for my memory of that terrible moment is exceedingly confused. The step I had taken had created a forward momentum I could not stop, and in a split second I was plunging into the black void and had dropped the candle, which blew out almost at once. Scarcely conscious of my own actions, I somehow twisted round as I fell, stretching my arms out blindly and desperately. Abruptly, my right arm hit the door frame, then the edge of the bedroom floor, which I gripped with all my might. I realize now that all this must have occupied the merest fraction of a second, but as I relive it now it draws out to great, horrific length.

"For a moment my fall was arrested, but it was only for the very briefest of moments, for the edge of the floor at the doorway was wet and slimy, and my fingers, which did not have a proper grip on anything, were slipping rapidly towards the edge. With a great effort I lunged upwards and forwards with my left hand, even as my right completely lost its grip. This time I was more successful. I had reached further into the room, past the slimy doorway, and my fingertips had found a narrow crack between two floorboards. I doubt it was a quarter of an inch wide, but it saved my life. Using this tiny finger-hold as a base, I managed to reach further with my right hand until that, too, had found a secure grip, and so, by slow degrees, I hauled myself to safety.

"For some time I lay on the floor of the bedroom, almost delirious, but presently I came to myself once more and determined to see the nature of the dark pit into which I had so nearly plummeted. I crept carefully to the edge once more and peered over, but could make out nothing whatever in the darkness. As I crouched there, eyes straining, I became conscious of a foul, mephitic vapour that seemed to rise from the pit before me, smothering and choking me with its stench. I was turning my head away in disgust, when a slight noise from below made me stop. It was a soft noise, like the lapping of water, but with an odd and unpleasant heaviness about it. There followed a splashing sound, then what I can only describe as scratching noises, which were quite horrible to hear. For a moment my heart seemed to stop beating and the blood ran cold in my veins. There was something in the pit below me, something which was moving quietly about in the darkness.

"Scarcely daring to breathe, I drew back from the edge of that foul hole, dressed as quickly as I could in the darkness and sat on the side of the bed to gather my thoughts. Then a slight noise set my jangled nerves on edge once more, and I quickly struck a match, but there was nothing to be seen save the dark open doorway, through which, I was convinced, Silas had intended that I should fall to my death. I could not rest while the door stood open like that, so, striking match after match to light my way, I leaned out into the void, managed to grip the panelling of the door, and pulled it shut.

"My supply of matches was by now almost exhausted. I had opened the curtains, but gained no more light, for the night was a dark one. Then it occurred to me that there might be a spare candle in the chest of drawers. I pulled each drawer out in turn, examining them by the light of the matches, but they were all quite empty. The top drawer was a very shallow one, and as I was pushing it back in, I could feel that there was something hampering it. I pulled it right out again and examined the recess behind it by the light of another match. It appeared there was some woollen article there. I reached in, freed it from the nail on which it was snagged and pulled it out. To my utter amazement, I recognized it at once. It was a striped woollen muffler, belonging to my brother, Simon. I knew I could not be mistaken, for my sister, Rachel, had knitted it for him herself and given it to him at Christmas. I had seen him wearing it in January, at the time of our engagement party. Clearly he had been at Hill House some time shortly after that, despite Silas's claim that he had not seen him for years, and had stayed in the very room in which I now stood.

"As you will imagine, I was already extremely agitated and excited by my experiences, but this latest discovery almost drove reason from my mind. I threw my few belongings into my bag, together with Simon's muffler, and crept from the house as quietly as I could, letting myself out of the front door. The first pale light of dawn was showing over the hill as I reached the road. Without pausing, or even considering what I was doing, I walked quickly down into Richmond and on to the railway station, caught an early train, and was back in town by seven o'clock. At nine I was at the door of Farrow and Redfearn's office, seeking their advice, and they, as you see, have sent me on to you."

Sherlock Holmes had sat in silence, his eyes closed in concentration, throughout this strange narrative, and he remained so for several minutes longer.

"It is certainly a singular story that you tell," said he at length, opening his eyes and reaching for his old clay pipe. "It interests me greatly. Although one or two small points are not yet entirely clear to me, it seems undoubtedly a bad business."

"I am convinced that Cousin Silas knows what has become of Simon," cried Boldero. "Otherwise, why should he lie about having seen him in January?"

"Why indeed?" said Holmes. "You have not reported the matter to the police?"

"It was in my mind to do so as I walked through Richmond this morning, but there are difficulties."

"The chief one being that you have no real evidence to substantiate your suspicions."

"Precisely, Mr Holmes. I cannot prove that any of my story is true, not even, now that I have removed it, that Simon's muffler was ever at Hill House. Mr Farrow was of the opinion that the police would do nothing unless I could produce more telling evidence. He recommended that I seek your help at once."

"I am honoured by his recommendation. What do you propose?"

"That you accompany me to Richmond, as my witness, and that we confront Silas with our suspicions. Beneath his shiftiness, he is mean-spirited and cowardly. I do not think he would dare lie so brazenly if you were there."

Holmes did not reply at once, but sat for some time in silence, evidently considering the matter in all its aspects.

"I will certainly accompany you," he responded at length, "and Dr Watson, too, if he will be so good. But it is necessary for us to prepare the ground a little before we confront your cousin, Mr Boldero. We must be armed with as much information as possible. I shall therefore spend the next twenty-four hours doing a little research into the matter. Be at the bookstall at Waterloo station at three o'clock tomorrow afternoon, and we can travel down to Richmond together!"

* * *

"What a very odd affair!" I remarked when our visitor had left us.

"It is certainly somewhat *recherché*," agreed Holmes. "The curious arrangement of the door in the bedroom, which leads only to a bottomless pit, is quite unique in my experience. As a way of ridding oneself of unwanted guests it may have its merits, but it is hardly a feature the builders of modern villas are likely to include in their brochures!"

"Can it all be true?" I wondered aloud. "The black void into which he so nearly tumbled, the horrible noises he heard; they sound like the stuff of a disordered and terrifying nightmare!"

"Boldero himself is sufficiently convinced of their veracity to seek our advice on the matter," responded my companion. "We must see if we can bring a little light into the darkness tomorrow. You will accompany us?"

"I should certainly wish to," I returned, "if my presence would be of any use to you. The matter is so grotesque and puzzling that it seems to me quite beyond conjecture. The only hope of an explanation must be down there at Richmond, at Hill House."

"And yet," said Holmes after a moment, "even there we may have difficulty in arriving at the truth. If, as appears to be the case, Silas Boldero has indeed murdered his cousin, Simon, and intended last night to take the brother's life also, we come up against the question of motive. What possible reason could Silas have for murdering his cousins in this way? He is, after all, the one with all the money. It would make more sense the other way round: if it had been Simon Boldero who had tried to murder Silas, in order to bring forward his inheritance a little."

"Perhaps that is indeed what happened," I suggested. "David Boldero appears a pleasant and honest man, but we know nothing, really, of his brother. Perhaps Simon did try to murder Silas, and Silas killed him in self-defence. Then Silas, frightened, perhaps, that he would be accused of murder, hid the body and decided to pretend that Simon had never been to see him at all."

"It is possible," conceded Holmes, "but it seems unlikely. You must remember that Silas had already made plans to murder his cousin, David, last night – the highly salted meat, the jug with no water in it, the suggestion that more water could be found through the side door – before David Boldero had expressed any suspicions at all. Why could he not simply deny having seen Simon and leave it at that? He could not have known that David Boldero would find his brother's muffler, which is the only real evidence that Simon was ever at Hill House. Indeed, the muffler would probably not have been found at all had our client's rest not been disturbed so alarmingly. I sense, Watson, that we may be fishing in deeper waters than was at first apparent."

PART TWO: A RAINY AFTERNOON

When I descended to breakfast the following morning, I found that Holmes had already gone out, without leaving any message. I took it that he was pursuing his research into the Boldero case, although where he might begin such an investigation, I could not imagine. Unable to make any sense of the matter, I endeavoured to dismiss it from my mind, but the story of David Boldero's terrifying night at Hill House had gripped my imagination and returned unbidden to my thoughts throughout the morning.

Just after one o'clock, a telegram arrived for me, which had been sent from Richmond. I tore it open and read the following: "DELAYED. MEET RICHMOND STATION 3.45. S. H". Evidently, Holmes's enquiries had taken him down to Richmond already. Knowing my friend's amazing resources, I could not doubt that he had made progress, and I looked forward eagerly to hearing the results.

I met David Boldero at Waterloo station as we had arranged, and we travelled down to Richmond together. It wanted ten minutes to the time Holmes had mentioned as our train pulled into the station, but there was no sign of him there, so we waited by the main entrance. It was a pleasant, sunny afternoon, with a light breeze blowing. Fresh green leaves adorned the branches of the trees, and in the air was the smell of spring.

After a few minutes, I observed a thin, disreputable-looking man approaching slowly along the road. He was dressed in a tweed suit with a bright red cravat round his neck, and he carried a rolled-up newspaper under his arm. Even from a distance I could see that he was unshaven and that his face was red and blotchy. I observed him particularly because he was, so it seemed to me, keeping his gaze fixed steadily upon us.

"That man appears to want something of us," remarked Boldero to me as the stranger drew near. I was about to reply when the man approached us and spoke.

"You are a little early, gentlemen," came a clear and well-known voice.

"Holmes!" I cried. "I had no idea—"

"I judged it best to adopt this little disguise for my local research," said he. "I am sorry if I startled you, Watson. You were regarding me so keenly as I approached that I was convinced you had recognized me. Now," he continued in a brisker tone, "let us be down to business. There is a hotel across the street where you can order a pot of tea while I bid *adieu* to Albert Taylor, footman out of position, and *bienvenue* once more to Sherlock Holmes, consulting detective!"

In ten minutes my friend had discarded his disguise and joined us in the parlour of the hotel, his appearance as neat and clean as ever.

"I have had enough indifferent tea already this afternoon," said he with a shake of the head as I made to pass him a cup. "As Albert Taylor, I have made the acquaintance of Miss Mary Ingram, known locally as 'Mad Mary', who is the woman Mr Boldero spoke to on his cousin's path yesterday afternoon. I have consumed large quantities of tea with her and, I believe, gained her confidence. She is a little unhinged, it is true, but not quite so much as is generally believed. She witnessed Simon Boldero's arrival at Hill House one afternoon in January, but never saw him leave, although she was at the house early the following morning. She had been told by Silas to make a bed up for the visitor, but when she saw it the following day, it appeared not to have been slept in, and she assumed that Simon had simply decided against spending the night there."

"But his muffler was in the bedroom," said Boldero.

"Precisely," said Holmes in a grave tone.

David Boldero put his head in his hands and groaned. Holmes reached out and put his hand on his shoulder.

"Have courage," said he. "I think we must accept that your brother is dead, and that his death occurred at the hand of your cousin, Silas. It is our duty now to ensure that that unpleasant old man is brought to justice!"

"I shall wring the truth from him with my own hands!" cried Boldero in a suddenly impassioned voice, his eyes flashing with emotion.

"That may not be necessary," responded Holmes calmly. "There is now sufficient *prima facie* evidence, I believe, to lay the matter before the police. A slight snag is that Miss Ingram's somewhat eccentric manner is likely to mean that her testimony is given less credence by the authorities than it merits. Fortunately, my enquiries have brought to light one or two other points of interest."

"I still wish to confront Silas myself," said Boldero in a determined voice.

Holmes glanced at his watch. "Come, then," said he. "Let us be off to Hill House. I can give you the details of my discoveries as we go."

The breeze had freshened and the clouds were piling up ominously as we left the hotel and made our way through the little town.

"There is a newsagent's shop on the way to Hill House," said Holmes as we walked along, "the window of which contains several interesting advertisements. Two of them, yellowing and faded, offer positions for hardworking servants in the establishment of Mr S. Boldero, one for a maid, the other for a male servant, duties unspecified. I enquired the details of the newsagent, representing myself as a footman seeking a post, and remarked that the advertisements appeared to have been in his window for some time. He acknowledged the truth of this observation.

"'Old Boldero's establishment is not such as appeals overmuch to the average domestic,' said he, sucking on his pipe. 'His advertisements have brought few enough replies, fewer still have ever taken up a position there, and none of them has ever stayed long enough to make it worth Boldero's while to remove the notices from my window. He's reduced now to relying on the services of "Mad Mary", a local woman. She goes in to the house most days, but she won't stay there. She could tell you a thing or two about Hill House, I'd wager!'

"I took this as my cue, and enquired Mary's address, saying I should like to learn a little about Hill House before I applied for the position offered there. Thus it was that I came to make the acquaintance of that unusual lady, with the results I mentioned earlier. Here is the newsagent's," he continued as we approached a row of small shops.

We stopped by the window, and Holmes pointed out to us the advertisements he had mentioned.

"There is also this," said he, directing our attention to a large piece of card towards the bottom of the window. The announcement on it ran as follows:

> MISSING: THOMAS EVANS, sometime footman to the Marquess of Glastonbury, butler to E. J. Archbould Esq. of Chelsea, and latterly butler to Mr S. Boldero of Hill House, Richmond Hill. Last seen on the morning of 14 November 1883, leaving his employment at Hill House. Will anyone having information as to the whereabouts of the said Thomas Evans please communicate with his sister, Miss Violet Evans, of Ferrier Street, Wandsworth.

"Who can say whether Mr Evans ever really left Hill House?" remarked Holmes in a thoughtful tone as I looked up from the notice. "If Cousin Silas is the source of the information, I think we are justified in being sceptical of its accuracy."

"The more we learn of it, the worse the matter becomes!" I cried.

Sherlock Holmes nodded his head gravely. "The sooner Silas Boldero and the Old Bailey make acquaintance with each other, the better for all concerned!" said he. "Come, let us make haste to Hill House!"

"But we still cannot say," remarked David Boldero in a puzzled voice as we walked briskly up the hill, "why Silas should wish to take Simon's life, and attempt to take my own; nor, for that matter, why Simon went to visit him in the first place."

"I am now able to shed a little light on those questions," responded Holmes. "You recall the *aide-memoire* that your brother had written for himself, and which you showed us yesterday?"

"What of it?"

"One of the items on his list was 'Baker – see again', in which the word 'Baker' was begun with a capital letter. This might, of course, have been of no importance: the word 'Baker' was the first word on the list, and there might have been no more significance to its capitalization than that, but it did at least make it possible that the 'Baker' referred to was not the man who supplied your brother's bread, but someone bearing the surname 'Baker'. Who this man might be, however – if he existed at all – there was no way of telling."

"It all sounds a little unlikely to me," remarked Boldero in a dubious tone.

"No doubt, but you must remember that 'the unlikely' falls, by its very definition, within the bounds of the possible."

"But even if your supposition were correct, it seems a very trifling matter."

"My work is built upon the observation of trifles," said Holmes. "Now, I had pondered last night what might have been your brother's purpose in calling upon your cousin, an unfriendly and miserly man, whom he had no reason to regard with affection and every reason to detest. The only significant connection between the two men was their shared ancestry. Perhaps, then, I speculated, it was some family matter that brought Simon down here to Richmond. This suggested to me your father and grandfather, which in turn suggested to me your grandfather's will, and I decided to see this document for myself. I therefore took myself down this morning to the Registry of Wills, and examined the copy of your grandfather's will, which is deposited there."

"I have seen it myself," Boldero interrupted. "It is very straightforward. Save that it gives away my family's inheritance to our odious cousin, it is of little interest."

"That rather depends on what one is looking for," said Holmes. "The will, I saw, had been drawn up by the firm of Valentine, Zelley and Knight, of Butler's Court, Cheapside, and witnessed by two of their clerks there. The appointed executor of the will was a junior partner in the firm. What do you suppose his name was?"

"I really have not the remotest idea," replied Boldero.

"Baker!" I cried.

"Very good, Watson!" said my friend, smiling. "You have the advantage, of course, of having witnessed 'the unlikely' occur with surprising frequency in the course of my work! Yes, the executor was a Mr R. S. Baker! You will imagine the satisfaction this discovery afforded me. But why, then, should Simon Boldero wish to see the executor of his grandfather's will more than twenty years after that will was proved? It appeared from Simon's *aide-memoire* that he had seen Baker at least once already, and intended to see him again on the Friday, having, as I believe, visited his cousin Silas on the Thursday evening. Two such surprising appointments in the space of twenty-four hours must surely be related, I argued, and there must, therefore, be some connection between Baker and Silas Boldero. Upon consulting the Law Society records, I discovered that your cousin's own career as a solicitor, which he abandoned many years ago, as you mentioned last night, was spent entirely with this same firm, Valentine, Zelley and Knight, and that he and this man Baker had been contemporaries."

"That is so, I believe," remarked Boldero, "but Silas cannot have interfered with my grandfather's will in any way, if that is the conclusion to which your argument is leading, for he had already left the firm a year or two before my grandfather died."

"Quite so," responded Holmes, "as I confirmed for myself from the records. He could not, therefore, have interfered personally with your grandfather's will. But he could, of course, have bribed another to do so, especially if that other was someone he had known well for nearly twenty years."

Boldero stopped abruptly and turned to Holmes.

"Is such a thing conceivable?" said he.

"Betrayal of his client's implicit trust is the very worst crime a lawyer can commit," said Holmes. "Regrettably, however, it is not unknown. But come, we must make haste, for it looks as if we are in for a heavy downpour!"

I glanced up at the sky as we hurried on. The clouds had built up into a single, dark grey mass, and the wind was colder than before. After a moment, Holmes continued his account:

"I was quickly able to establish that Baker was still in practice, and with the same firm, so I called round at their chambers late this morning. Baker is an elderly man, grey, wrinkled and distinguished in appearance, and his manner towards me was at first extremely supercilious.

"'I understand from this note on your card that you consider your business to be both urgent and personal,' said he in a peevish tone, 'but I do not know you.'

"'You know, at least, the man I represent,' I returned: 'Mr Simon Boldero.'

"At the mention of this name, the old man's face lost what little colour it possessed, his jaw sagged and he appeared in an instant to have aged ten years.

"'I have been expecting him for some time,' said he eventually in a weak voice. 'Has something prevented his coming in person?'

"'Indeed,' said I, 'but I am acting for him in the matter.'

"'I have had a long and honourable career,' said he in a broken, defeated voice, 'and had every hope of a respected retirement, but Mr Boldero found evidence of the one moral lapse of my life.'

"'The business of his grandfather's will is a very serious matter indeed,' said I in a grave voice. Of course, I knew practically nothing of the matter, but if you have ever played cards, you will know that it is sometimes possible to give the impression that your hand is stronger than it really is.

"Baker nodded his head sorrowfully. 'And now what is to be done about it?' said he. 'As you are probably aware, the will I executed after old Daniel Boldero's death was one he made in a moment of stubborn anger, following a quarrel with his son, Enoch, who was Simon's father. He soon repented of it, however, and before a month had passed he made a fresh, more equitable will, by which all his property passed to Enoch, as he had originally intended.'

"'That was the will that Silas Boldero bribed you to destroy,' I ventured.

"Again he nodded. 'I was not a wealthy man, and he offered me a thousand pounds if I would do it. Many men would have been tempted.'

"'And many men would have resisted that temptation. So you destroyed the will.'

"'No, no!' he cried in surprise, eyeing me with suspicion. 'Was that not made clear to you? I could not do it! All my professional training – everything I held dear – rebelled at the thought of destroying a legal document! Instead, I concealed it where no one might find it, and after Daniel Boldero's death, so far as the world knew, it had never existed. Of course, I have often regretted it bitterly, but what could I do?'

"'You could have told the truth.' At this he fell silent, his head in his hands. 'You must do exactly what Mr Simon Boldero proposed,' I continued, feeling that my position was now a strong one. 'It is your only chance.'

"'Mr Boldero was, I must say, surprisingly magnanimous considering the circumstances,' Baker remarked after a moment. 'He said – bless his kindness! – that he would rather there was no scandal, for the sake of the family. I gave him the will, and he said he would confront Silas with it and try to come to some arrangement with him. If Silas was amenable, then the whole matter could be dealt with privately and the world need never know of it, but if Silas refused to meet Simon's terms, he would, he said, lay the matter before the authorities. This would, I need hardly add, mean ruin and disgrace for me. When Mr Boldero did not keep the appointment he had made with me, I feared the worst. But it seems, now that you are here, that everything will be all right.'

"'I am afraid not,' said I. 'It has now become a capital matter. Simon Boldero has disappeared, and all the evidence suggests that he has been done to death by Silas.' At this, the old man's lips turned white and I feared he would have a seizure. I waited a moment before continuing. 'As a party to the original conspiracy, and having seen Boldero recently and perhaps, for all anyone knows to the contrary, having deliberately sent him to his death at his cousin's house, you will of course be charged as an accomplice to this murder—'

"'No, no!' he cried feebly. 'I knew nothing of this, as Heaven is my witness! Is there no way I can convince you?'

"'Unfortunately,' said I, 'if, as seems likely, Simon Boldero took the will to Richmond with him, Silas will have destroyed it by now. There is therefore no evidence remaining that you had repented your earlier crime and were assisting Simon.'

"'Wait!' cried Baker, springing from his seat with an energy that surprised me. 'At the time the original will was made, a copy was prepared, to be deposited at the Registrar's office, but of course I never sent it. It is still here now, in a trunk of my private papers in the lumber room upstairs. It will take me some time to find it, I am afraid, but if you would not mind waiting . . .'

"'I have more important business to attend to,' said I. 'You have my card. If that document does not reach the address upon the card by four o'clock tomorrow afternoon, then I can protect you no longer from the full force of the criminal law!'

"Baker seemed to visibly shrink as I spoke those last words. I declined the hand he held out to me, took my hat and left the chambers, feeling that I had done a good morning's work."

"And so you have!" cried David Boldero in amazed admiration. "I can scarcely believe what you have discovered! I shall for ever bless the day that Farrow and Redfearn sent me to consult you!"

"Well, well," said Holmes, clearly moved by his client's gratitude, "it is largely a matter of experience, and I am a specialist. Once you have examined two hundred little problems, the two hundred and first does not present quite the same difficulties to your brain as the first one. But I have timed my account well! Here is Hill House, and we must deal now with Cousin Silas!"

"And here comes the rain," said I, as the first icy drops fell upon us.

Boldero's face had set in a rigid mask of determination as we approached the house, and he made no remark as we pushed open the heavy wooden gate and entered the grounds. As we did so, the rain began to fall more heavily, making a soft drumming noise on the roof of the glass structure under which we made our way along the path. A movement off to the right caught my eye, and I peered through a murky pane of glass just in time to see some small dark creature slip swiftly beneath a bush.

For several minutes, our knocking at the front door produced no response, and as we waited on the step I caught the distant sound of raised voices from deep within the house. At length, someone approached the door, and there came a voice, thin and querulous, from the other side.

"Who is it and what do you want?"

"It is your cousin, David," Boldero called back, "and I wish to speak to you again about Simon."

"I've already told you I know nothing about him. Why can't you leave me in peace?"

"I know that Simon was here in January."

"No, he wasn't!"

"I found his muffler in the room I slept in."

"If there was any muffler there, you put it there yourself!"

How long this exchange might have continued, it is hard to say, but Holmes had clearly heard enough.

"If you do not open this door at once," said he in a masterful tone, "we shall put the matter in the hands of the police immediately."

For a moment there was silence, then we heard the sound of a bolt being drawn and the door was opened. The man who stood back to let us enter was one of the oddest human beings I have ever seen. He was somewhat over middle height, but strangely hunched about the shoulders, so that his neck and head protruded forward like that of a tortoise. His chest and shoulders were very stocky, but the rest of him seemed to taper away almost to nothing, ending with a pair of very small feet.

"Come in, then, if you must," said he in an impatient tone, waving his arms at us. As we did so, there came a terrific racket from somewhere upstairs, a woman's voice, shouting raucously, and a violent banging noise, as if someone were kicking at a door. "It's only the maid," said Silas irritably. "She's probably got herself locked in the broom cupboard again. I'll deal with it in a minute." He closed the front door behind us, and as he did so the noise upstairs subsided. "Thank goodness for that," said he in an unpleasant tone.

"Now," he continued, addressing David Boldero, his head protruding forward as he did so. "You wish to speak to me of your brother. It is true, I admit, that I saw him in January, but I had good reason for denying it, as you will understand shortly. The matter is more complex than you perhaps suppose. You had best all come this way, and I will explain everything."

He opened a door at the right-hand side of the hall and led us into a dusty, unfurnished room. A penetrating smell of damp filled the air, and plaster had fallen from the walls in chunks and lay in crumbling heaps upon the bare boards of the floor. As I closed the door behind us, I thought I heard the woman shouting again upstairs.

"You will excuse the slight disarray," Silas remarked over his shoulder, as he led the way to a door at the far side of the room. "This room is in need of a little redecoration. This will be the quickest way," he continued, throwing open the door and passing through it.

We followed him along a narrow flagged corridor, which ran along the right-hand side of the house and appeared to have been added as a way of getting from the front of the building to the back without passing through the inside of the house. A row of dirty, smeared windows on our right looked out over the gardens, which were as Boldero had described them: a confused mass of overgrown shrubs and tangled creepers, upon which the rain now fell steadily.

At the end of the corridor was another door, with a small rectangular pane of glass set in it near the top. Silas Boldero glanced through this, then drew back a bolt and pulled the door open.

"Come on, come on!" he said impatiently. "Let's get out of the cold!"

We filed through the narrow doorway after him into a long, high-roofed conservatory, built on to the back of the house. The air in here was much warmer, very moist, and had an odd, unpleasant smell to it. I was the last to enter, and as I did so it was clear that our host was becoming very irritable.

"Hurry up!" he cried, putting his hand on my shoulder as I passed him at the doorway. "Let's get this door closed!"

"Look out!" cried Holmes, but his warning came a fraction of a second too late, for at that instant I received a violent push in the middle of the back, lost my balance and stumbled into the others. In that moment of confusion, Silas Boldero slipped back through the doorway, slammed the door shut behind him, and shot the bolt home. A moment later we heard his rapid footsteps ringing on the flagstones of the corridor. Above us the rain drummed heavily on the glass roof of the conservatory, so that we had to shout to make ourselves heard.

"What the devil is going on!" cried Boldero in an angry tone.

"We have been tricked," said Holmes, his keen eyes darting round the strange structure in which we found ourselves. It had been built against the wall of the house, so that on our left was a tall blank wall of brick. Incongruously placed high up in this wall, directly above where we stood, but with no way of reaching it, was an ordinary-looking door.

"That must be the door through which I fell last night," said Boldero, following my gaze. From the house wall, the roof of the conservatory sloped down steeply to a lower wall, on our right, which was composed entirely of glass panels. At the near end of this wall was a pair of doors of similar construction, which gave onto the garden. A quick examination showed that these doors were locked.

But though I quickly took in all these features of the building, it was the floor that arrested my attention. Where we stood it was composed of large square flagstones, moss-covered and slimy, which extended for about twenty feet. Beyond that, the floor sloped gently downwards, into what appeared to be a deep bathing pool, which extended for a further thirty or forty feet, to the far end of the building. The surface of the water was green-skimmed and unhealthy-looking, and covered with drifting vegetation and other debris. Even as I looked, however, I saw something moving there, a purposeful dark shape beneath the water.

"Holmes!" I cried, but he had already seen it and his keen face was rigid with tension. Whatever it was, it was moving up the pool towards us, its swift, gliding motion sending little ripples out as it approached. Then, above the slime on the surface of the water, I saw the front of its snout, two large nostrils dilated to suck in air, and, some way behind, two large, evil eyes, fixed steadily upon us.

"My God!" cried Boldero in terror. "What in Heaven's name is it?"

"It appears to be an African crocodile," responded Holmes quietly in a voice that was icy cold. "The largest and most deadly reptile on earth. It is a monster of the species, too: it looks a good eighteen feet in length."

As we watched, the creature slowed and then stopped altogether, lying still in the water barely ten feet from the edge of the pool, its unblinking eyes watching our every movement. Whether this quiet observation represented mere curiosity or was the prelude to a sudden assault, it was impossible to tell.

Without turning his head, or taking his eyes from this awesome vision, Holmes reached into his pocket and drew out a pistol, which he passed to me, pressing it firmly into my hand. "It may be utterly useless against such a beast, but we have nothing else," said he softly. "If it moves any closer, Watson, shoot to kill! Now, quickly, Boldero, help me! We must try to break down the doors!"

Behind us, on the flagstones, stood a low wooden bench. Holmes seized hold of one end, but Boldero had been struck rigid with fear at the sight of the terrible creature and did not move.

"Boldero!" cried Holmes again in an urgent tone. "For your life, man!"

At that moment there came a crash above us, as that singular door high up in the wall was flung open. Framed in the doorway stood Silas Boldero, and from his hand hung a large canvas sack. For a moment he looked down upon us in silence, a horrible sneering smile upon his face, then he laughed harshly and drew from the sack what appeared to be a large piece of raw meat. With a careless movement of his arm, he flung it out into the air, and it fell with a splash in the shallow edge of the pool. The creature in the water made no discernible movement, and yet I had the disturbing impression that it had drifted very slightly nearer to where I stood.

The sudden appearance of his cousin at least had the effect of breaking the spell of fear that had held David Boldero motionless. Now he quickly bent his strength to the wooden bench that Holmes was lifting, and the two of them charged with it at the garden doors of the conservatory. With a terrific crash of breaking glass and a splintering of wood, the lock gave way, the doors flew open and the colder air of the garden rushed into the building. For a split second, as the doors were burst open, I had taken my eyes off the monster in the water, but now I saw, to my horror, that it was moving smoothly and swiftly forward, its long scaly tail thrashing the water behind it.

I raised the pistol, aimed between the creature's eyes and fired. The bullet must have struck the top of its head and bounced harmlessly off the thick, armoured scales there, for it struck the brick wall with a ringing crack farther along the building.

"Watson!" came a shout from outside the shattered doors. "Leave it! Fly for your life!" But I could not. The creature was too close. In a moment it would be on top of me. Like something from an evil nightmare, it rose up out of the water before me, its huge red and grey mouth gaping open viciously, ready to crush me between its rows of colossal pointed teeth. I let off three shots in rapid succession as I backed away towards the door, at least two of which struck it in the throat. With a mighty splash, sending fountains of water up to the roof, it crashed down into the pool, but its wicked eyes were still fixed upon me as I backed out into the garden and turned to run.

Even as I did so, there came a cry of anger and a string of foul oaths from Silas Boldero. Glancing up, I saw that his face was contorted with rage, and he was stamping his foot in the doorway and shaking his fist at me, like a spoiled child whose plans have been thwarted. Behind him, in the gloom of the bedroom, there seemed some slight movement, and I thought I descried another, slighter figure, a woman clad in black; but I paid little heed, for I saw, too, that the crocodile was stirring once more.

Clearly hurt by my shots, but not fatally so, it was beginning to rise out of the water once more.

I turned away, but I had not taken two paces when the shouting and foul language gave way all at once to a long shriek of terror. I turned quickly to see Silas Boldero tumbling headlong into the conservatory, his arms waving wildly and uselessly in the air. He hit the hard floor with a heavy thud, and lay perfectly still. Up above, in the open doorway, the woman in black looked down. Whether he had simply lost his footing in his agitation and slipped on the slimy edge of the doorway, or whether she had startled him, struck him, or even pushed him from the ledge deliberately, it was impossible to say. I had little time to consider the matter, however, for my attention at that moment was entirely directed at the crocodile. It was now out of the water, revealing its full gigantic length for the first time, and making its way towards the still figure of the recluse.

Holmes and Boldero were some way ahead of me, but had seen what had happened and ran back to join me outside the conservatory. It was clear, even at that distance, that Silas Boldero's head and neck hung at a strange, unnatural angle, and that his eyes were wide open and unblinking.

"He's dead," cried Boldero. "We can do nothing for him now."

Abruptly the crocodile lunged forward, its hideous mouth agape, seized hold of the crumpled body on the floor and made to drag it back into the water.

"Have you a round left, Watson?" said Holmes tersely.

I stepped forward and, from just outside the conservatory doorway, took careful aim and fired. The shot hit the monster in the side of the mouth and it stopped and loosed its grip on its terrible bundle. Then slowly, but with infinite menace, it turned its baleful eyes upon me.

"Quickly, Watson!" cried Holmes, tugging at my sleeve. "We can do no more here!"

We turned and ran, and as we did so there came a terrific crashing noise from behind us. I looked back in trepidation to see that the awesome creature was smashing its way through the remains of the conservatory doors as if they had been made of paper and card, and lumbering after us at a pace that both surprised and terrified me. Through the bushes we plunged, taking any route that seemed to offer a clear run, and dreading above all else running into a blind alley of vegetation, from which there would be no escape. Behind us, without pause, came the heavy padding of the monster, the constant crack and crash of broken branches as it forced its way through the undergrowth informing us that it was still upon our trail. All the time the rain lashed down remorselessly.

We must have run halfway round the grounds, in the direction of the road, when I saw Holmes stop a little way ahead of me and look in alarm at the path and the glass structure that covered it. We could neither pass it nor penetrate it, and could not, therefore, reach the gate.

"The wall!" he cried abruptly, and set off towards a section of the high wall that appeared to have lost much of its mortar, and which might thus offer the possibility of hand-holds. Then, just in front of me, Boldero put his foot into some small creature's burrow and fell to the ground, crying out with pain. In a second, Holmes was back and had hold of his left arm. I took his right, and together we managed to get him to the foot of the wall. We could hear the crocodile close behind us now, smashing its way through the tangle of brambles near the wall.

In a trice, Holmes had shinned up the wall and was reaching down for Boldero's hand, while I stayed at the bottom to help him up. I was still standing flat-footed on the ground as Boldero dragged himself onto the top of the wall when, with a deafening crash, the monster burst through the last of the undergrowth and thundered towards me.

"Your hand!" cried Holmes.

I thrust my arm up blindly, he seized it, and with quite extraordinary strength dragged me bodily up the wall. I swung my legs up onto the top just as the creature charged, its colossal, dripping mouth mere inches from my feet.

"You have saved my life!" I cried, panting with exhaustion.

"We have saved your foot, at any rate," returned my friend in his customary dry manner.

"God's mercy!" cried Boldero suddenly, in a voice suffused with terror. "It is climbing the wall!"

Indeed, incredible to see, it was raising itself up and clawing at the wall with its front feet, its fearsome snout almost reaching the top of the wall, where we stood. As one, the three of us sprang down into the road, Boldero crying out in pain as he landed on his twisted ankle.

"It will not get over that," said Holmes, eyeing the wall as he dusted off the knees of his trousers. "Now we must make haste to notify the authorities of all that has occurred here."

"The woman—" I began.

"Oh, 'Mad Mary' will be safe enough," returned my friend. "When she leaves the house she will do so by the covered pathway from the front door, where the creature cannot get at her."

After a moment to recover our breath, we set off at a brisk walk down the hill, through the pouring rain, and half an hour later, having described our experiences to an amazed and incredulous police inspector, we were sitting with a glass of brandy by the fire in the hotel. I was soaked to the skin and my clothes had been torn in several places during our flight through the garden, but the closeness of our escape from death had made me almost light-headed, so that such trivial matters seemed of no consequence. I believe the others were affected in the same way, for when Holmes spoke, there was a note of elation in his voice.

"Let me be the first to congratulate you upon at last coming into your inheritance!" said he, addressing David Boldero, who answered the remark with a rueful smile. "The circumstances may not have been ideal, I grant you, but they have a certain memorable quality! I am sure that Miss Underwood will be interested to hear of your adventures!"

"Beatrice!" cried Boldero abruptly, clutching his head. "I had quite forgotten! I am supposed to be dining with Beatrice and her parents this evening! I shall have to send a note to say I cannot come."

"No, no! You must go!" insisted Holmes, laughing. "This may be the one evening in your life when your late arrival for dinner will earn no disapproval! After all, it is not every prospective son-in-law who can honestly inform his fiancée's parents that he was delayed by an enraged crocodile!"

The Adventure of THE ENGLISH SCHOLAR

CONSIDERED SIMPLY as someone with whom to share chambers, my friend Sherlock Holmes could never have been described as ideal. An enthusiasm for conducting malodorous chemical experiments at all hours of the day and night is not, after all, the first quality one looks for in a fellow lodger. When not occupied in this or similarly unsavoury activities, he would often sit for hours in silent reflection, during which time he would do little save smoke enormous quantities of the strongest shag tobacco. Not infrequently, I would retire to my bed at night, leaving him busy with his chemical researches or simply engrossed in his own thoughts, only to find upon rising the following morning that he was in precisely the same position as I had left him the night before, the only difference being that the atmosphere of the room had deteriorated somewhat in the meantime. This was not, on the whole, conducive to a pleasant start to the day. No matter how good one's breakfast may be, it is difficult to derive full pleasure from it when the air in the room is scarcely breathable.

Then there was his untidiness. In the early days of our shared tenancy in Baker Street, our chambers remained neat and uncluttered, and I could not have imagined then into what depths of disorder they would later descend, as towering piles of papers and documents accumulated in every corner of the room. It surprised me at first that a man so trim in his personal appearance and habits could allow his surroundings to degenerate in this way, but I soon came to understand the problem. When Holmes was engaged upon a case, his energies were devoted exclusively to its solution, and all other considerations were set aside. At the conclusion of a case he would fall at once into an exhausted lethargy, which might last for several days, during which time he would do nothing whatever, save move from one easy chair to another. Then, not infrequently, just as I had detected signs that his energies and spirits were recovering, and hope stirred within me that if I could dissuade him for a moment from his chemical researches he might at last address the confusion in our rooms, a new case would be brought to his attention and all other matters would once again be set aside. As his practice increased, and the time at his disposal between cases shrank accordingly, so did the condition of our rooms gradually deteriorate. But understanding the problem did not make it any the less bothersome. Once or twice I had offered to help put his papers in order, but he always rebuffed my offers, declaring that only he could arrange the papers how he wished them to be arranged.

In addition to these minor inconveniences, there was the less frequent, but more disturbing matter of the danger which my fellow lodger seemed to draw to himself like a magnet, and which was likely to fall, also, upon anyone who spent any time in his company. Though Holmes himself was among the most cultured and reasonable of men, his work brought him into contact with many who lacked his refinement, who cared little for the subtleties of argument, and whose first resort if thwarted was to violence. I could not begin to enumerate the many occasions upon which our prosaic little sitting room was the scene of heated quarrels, fisticuffs, violent assaults and, on at least two occasions, attempted murder.

These, then, were some of the chief disadvantages of sharing chambers with Sherlock Holmes. Hardly suitable lodgings, it might be supposed, for a retired Army officer on a wound pension, with generally uncertain health and few social contacts. And yet, for all that, I cannot in all honesty say that I would have wished to reside anywhere else. I could certainly have enjoyed a quieter existence elsewhere, but what a world of experience I should thereby have missed! Where else might I have descended to breakfast to find a baffling cryptogram propped up against the cruet stand, or a mysterious chart fastened to the corner of the mantelpiece with a thumbtack? Where else could I have learned all the details of the most intriguing crimes and mysteries of the day from the one man in the country who truly understood them? What other circumstances could possibly have provided such a thrill as when I was privileged to be present as Holmes's clients told of the often strange, sometimes terrible events that had brought them to seek the help of the famous detective? Such intellectual pleasures were more than sufficient compensation for the practical inconveniences of life at 221B, Baker Street.

As to Holmes himself, he was a man of many parts and many moods. He could on occasion be taciturn and uncommunicative for days on end, but he could also, when he chose, be the most stimulating company imaginable. And although his sense of humour sometimes seemed a queer one, and could occasionally be caustic and harsh, he was nevertheless quite the sharpest, wittiest man I have ever known.

As the months of our shared residence in Baker Street passed, and we perhaps got the measure of each other more precisely, he began to speak to me more frequently of his work, occasionally recounting in detail some episode in which he considered that his theories as to the art of detection had been particularly well vindicated. On one occasion I ventured to suggest that if one or two of his more interesting cases were to be written up in a form designed to appeal to the general reader, it might make his views more widely understood.

"An excellent suggestion," was his affable reply, "provided, of course, that appropriate emphasis is laid upon the methods by which the solution was reached. But if it is to be done, then it is you that must do it, Watson, for I certainly cannot spare the time."

I said that I would make an attempt at the job, and would endeavour to do justice to his theories, and there, for the moment, the matter rested. But from that day forward, as if recognizing that I could perhaps perform a service for which he himself had neither the time nor the inclination, he began to involve me more intimately in his investigations, and even occasionally specifically requested my presence. It was then that I realized fully for the first time how frequently in the course of his work he placed himself in physical danger. Nor, as I soon discovered, was it ever possible to predict with any accuracy which of his cases might have such an outcome, for upon countless occasions an investigation which had appeared at first to be but a trifling matter would lead us ultimately into a situation of mortal peril. A case that illustrated this well was that which concerned Mr Rhodes Harte of Ipswich and the mystery of Owl's Hill, and it is this that I shall now recount.

It was a pleasant morning in that period of late spring when the flowerbeds in the parks and gardens of London are full of colour and all but the tardiest of the trees have opened their buds and are covered with bright green leaves.

A telegram had arrived for Sherlock Holmes as we awaited breakfast. He had scribbled a brief reply, but passed no remark. After breakfast, however, after leafing through the newspaper in a desultory fashion for a while, he tossed it aside and asked me if I knew where Little Gissingham was.

"I have never heard of it," I returned. "Why do you ask?"

"It was from the railway station there that the wire came this morning. A gentleman there, a Mr Rhodes Harte, wishes to consult me. He is arriving by the late morning train."

"Does he give any indication as to the nature of the matter?"

"Only that it is 'a perplexing problem'. But let us see where he is journeying from!"

He took down a gazetteer and atlas from his shelf of reference works, and turned the pages over for a few moments in that rapid, almost birdlike manner with which I was familiar. "Here we are," said he at length. "It is in the county of Suffolk, Watson; very close to the border with Essex. 'Little Gissingham'," he continued, reading from the gazetteer. "'A pretty little village. Parts of the church are Anglo-Saxon, and the porch is Norman. There are several fine half-timbered houses, and one inn, the Fox and Goose.' That is the extent of our information."

"It sounds something of a rural backwater," I remarked.

"Indeed. And the impression is confirmed by the evidence of the map. There are a number of such small villages in that part of the country, nestling in the river valleys that wind between the hills near the Essex border, but even in such quiet, secluded company, Little Gissingham appears relatively insignificant."

"It has a railway station, at least," I observed.

"That is true, although I doubt that that bespeaks any importance in the place itself. It appears from the map that it simply happens to lie on the route of a railway line between other, more notable, places. In any case, the line in question is not an important one, but a mere side shoot from the Cambridge line, which meanders in a leisurely manner across the countryside until it meets up with the coastal line near Colchester. Hum! Let us hope that Mr Harte does not have to wait too long for a connecting train, and that he arrives here soon to enlighten us as to his problem!"

It was almost lunchtime before our visitor arrived. He was a man of about five and forty years of age, of middle height, erect in his bearing, and with a lively and intelligent face. He was dressed in the dark frock coat and pearl-grey trousers of a professional man, and under his arm he carried a large brown-paper package tied up with string, which he placed upon the table as I took his hat.

"I see you have been looking up Little Gissingham," he remarked, eyeing the map book, which lay open upon the table.

"I find it as well to furnish myself with the fullest knowledge of any matter I am asked to look into," returned Holmes, shaking his visitor's hand and ushering him into a chair. "It generally saves time in the end."

"I couldn't agree more," said the other in an appreciative tone. "My professional experience has been precisely the same. As to Little Gissingham, it appears a very quiet little place, but the events of last night prove that, even in such a sequestered spot, the strangest of things can occur."

"You arouse my curiosity," said Holmes, rubbing his hands together in delight. "Am I to understand that you had never visited Little Gissingham before yesterday?"

"Never. I had passed through the railway station there once or twice, but had never paid it any attention."

"Was it your work as a solicitor which took you there yesterday?"

"Not really. But how do you know my business? Do you know of my connection with Mr Halesworth?"

Holmes shook his head. "The seals upon your watch chain appear to be those of a solicitor," said he. "But if it was not professional work that took you to Little Gissingham, Mr Harte, perhaps it was something to do with that bulky package you have brought with you. Whatever the reason," he continued as his visitor nodded his head, "it is apparent that you intended to remain there for only a short time, and then to return home before nightfall. Evidently something occurred to delay you. You missed the last train, I imagine, and were obliged to put up at the Fox and Goose."

"That is correct in every detail," exclaimed Harte in surprise. "But how do you know all this?"

"Forgive me for mentioning it – I have no desire to embarrass you," responded Holmes after a moment, "but there are certain features of your appearance which suggest that you were unable to devote as much care to your toilet this morning as you might have wished. This in turn suggests that you did not have with you those necessities with which a man would equip himself if he knew he would be staying away from home for the night. The conclusion is clear: that your sojourn at the Fox and Goose – the only inn in Little Gissingham, according to my gazetteer – was unpremeditated."

"That is so, Mr Holmes. I slept last night in my shirt and passed the most uncomfortable night of my adult life. This morning I endeavoured to make the best of myself, but lacked a razor, a clean collar and everything else one takes for granted at home. Dear, oh dear!" he murmured, shaking his head. "I had no idea that my appearance fell so short of a desirable standard!"

"Be assured, sir, it does not. But it is my business to observe such trifles. I am sure that no one else would have noticed anything amiss with your appearance. Let us see! Did anything of the sort strike you, Watson?" he asked, turning to me.

"Certainly not!" I returned.

"You see?" said Holmes to his visitor. "You have no cause for anxiety!"

"Thank goodness for that!" cried the other in evident relief.

"Now," said Holmes, "if we may proceed with the matter? It was not legal business, you say, that took you to Little Gissingham?"

Rhodes Harte shook his head. "Only very indirectly," he replied. "I am, as you conjectured, a solicitor, and have been in partnership with Mr Halesworth in Ipswich for many years. About six weeks ago I had occasion to travel across the county to visit an old client of ours, Mr Packham. He lived formerly in Ipswich, but when he retired he moved to Saffron Walden, about forty-odd miles away on the other side of Essex. He is an elderly gentleman and has difficulty getting about, and as he seemed very keen to consult me, I agreed to go and see him. It was a delightful spring day, and although the journey involved changing trains a couple of times, and was thus quite a long one, it nevertheless made a pleasant break from routine to be away from my chambers for a while.

"On the way home, I was obliged to wait for some time at a rural railway junction. It was a sunny afternoon, and I was enjoying sitting on the bench on the platform, listening to songbirds in the nearby trees. There was another man sitting there, reading a book, a scholarly-looking, elderly man with a high domed forehead and mane of white hair, and after a while we fell into conversation. I had observed that the book he was reading was *David Copperfield*, and I passed some remark as to its being a very entertaining book.

"'It is more than entertaining, sir!' returned he, closing the book up and giving me a piercing glance. 'It is extremely stimulating to the intellect!'

"'Oh, quite so,' I agreed. 'I meant merely that it contains some very amusing characters and situations.'

"'That can scarcely be denied,' conceded the scholarly gentleman in a somewhat grudging tone, 'and yet those characters and situations for which the book seems to be most renowned are, in my opinion, among its least interesting features. The characters of Mr Micawber and Uriah Heep, for instance, are certainly entertaining enough, but it is arguable whether they shed much light upon human beings in general. Some of the other characters, however, and the relations between them, are drawn with very great subtlety and profundity, and it is there, I would argue, that the book's true merit lies. It is certainly a good book. That is generally agreed. Unfortunately, it is, for this reason, not infrequently given to young people of fourteen and fifteen years of age, as a school prize or birthday present. You are wondering, no doubt, why this is unfortunate. Because, sir, although such young people, whose intellects are just beginning to mature from childhood to adulthood, will no doubt derive some pleasure from the book, they are unlikely to really appreciate – or even fully understand – its subtleties. And having read it once, most of them will never read it again, and thus will be denied the opportunity to appraise the book with a mind fully matured by experience of life.'

"With that he put the book down altogether, stowing it away in a leather satchel at his feet, and asked my opinion of the matter. I made some response, and soon we were deep into a broad and fascinating discussion upon literature in general, English literature especially, and Charles Dickens in particular, and I must say that it was quite the most stimulating conversation I have had on any subject in the last twelve months. My companion's views, which he delivered with great eloquence, were highly original and fascinating, and I should have been perfectly content simply to sit there and listen to him until the train arrived, but he was very keen, also, to elicit my opinions, as if to weigh them against his own, and to every word I uttered he gave the most careful and courteous consideration. He was, in short, not simply a very learned scholar, but a true gentleman. He introduced himself as Dr Kennett, and informed me that he was returning from a public lecture he had attended that day in Cambridge. I was a little surprised at this, for it seemed to me that it might have been more profitable for all concerned if a man of such erudition, and with such a passion for his subject, had been employed in delivering a lecture rather than in listening to one. Nor was his enthusiasm for learning confined to literature. He mentioned in the course of our conversation that he had alighted at that little rural station on the merest whim, having been attracted by the appearance of some woods that bordered the railway line. On the spur of the moment, he explained, he had decided to break his journey there and explore the area, which was unknown to him. I asked him if his exploration had been interesting.

"'Very much so,' said he. 'The wild flowers in the woods are fascinating at this time of the year. I tramped about there for quite some time, and when I was satisfied that I had seen all that there was to see, I refreshed myself at a nearby inn, and am now ready to resume my journey.'

"Our train arrived shortly after that and we took a compartment together, continuing our most interesting conversation, as the train made its way along a peaceful river valley, and through a succession of little village stations. By the time we reached the station at Little Gissingham, our literary discussion had, I recall, moved on to Shakespeare, and my companion was expatiating on what he saw as similarities of theme in *Hamlet* and Dickens's *Great Expectations*, when all at once he broke off and sprang to his feet with a cry.

"'Do excuse me, but this is my station,' said he. 'I was enjoying our discussion so much that I quite forgot to take any heed of where we were!' In great haste, he opened the carriage door and sprang onto the platform. 'I do hope we meet again, Mr Harte!' cried he as he slammed the door. At that moment, the guard blew his whistle, and a moment later the train moved off and began to pick up speed. My carriage was scarcely clear of the platform, however, when I noticed that my companion's leather satchel was lying on the floor at my feet. In his haste to leave the train, he had clearly forgotten all about it. I quickly opened the window and leaned out, but he had already left the platform. A moment later, the train passed round a curve, and the little station had vanished from my sight. There was nothing more that I could do.

"When I reached Colchester, I handed the satchel in at the lost property office. 'The owner's name is Kennett,' I said, as the official wrote out a receipt for me. 'To the best of my knowledge he lives at Little Gissingham. It might be worthwhile to notify the station master there that the satchel has been found, in case the gentleman makes enquiries about it.'

"The official said he would do as I suggested, and there I left the matter. Not knowing my new acquaintance's address, I could not think that there was any more that I could do. And that, gentlemen," said Harte, breaking off from his narrative and pausing a moment, "marks the end of the first part of my story. An unexceptional little episode, you might think. However, I'll warrant you will think otherwise about the second part, all of which took place just yesterday."

"We are keen to hear the sequel," returned Holmes. "I take it from your manner that events have taken a somewhat surprising turn."

"Indeed, several. Do you mind if I smoke?" continued Harte, taking a cigar case from his pocket. "I find a cigar is soothing. My nerves are all shot to pieces by this business!"

"Not at all," cried Holmes with a chuckle, tossing across a box of matches to his visitor. "We would not want your nerves to prevent your continuing your account!"

For some time the solicitor sat puffing at his cigar in silence while we waited for him to continue.

"Yesterday," said he at length, "I was obliged again to travel across the county to see old Mr Packham at Saffron Walden. I took the train down from Ipswich to Colchester, as before, and finding that I had a little time to wait for my connection, thought I would enquire if Dr Kennett had retrieved his satchel from the lost property office there. Our delightful discussion on literature had returned to my mind several times during the intervening six weeks, and I had often wondered how the splendid old fellow was getting along. To my surprise, I was informed that the satchel was still lying on a shelf in the lost property office, and that no one had ever been in to claim it.

"'Was the station master at Little Gissingham informed that it was here?' I asked.

"'Yes, sir,' the official replied, consulting a label that was attached to the satchel. 'As a matter of fact, I reminded him of it myself, just a week ago, and he sent word back that no enquiries had been made to him about any satchel.'

"This struck me as very odd, but I thought it possible that Dr Kennett was somewhat absent-minded and, perhaps unable to recall when he had last had his satchel, could not think where to begin to look for it. Personally, I should have thought that the very first place one would enquire for something mislaid on the day one had undertaken a railway journey would have been the lost property office at the station, but as my legal work has taught me, one can never assume that anyone else's thought processes will be the same as one's own. At first I was inclined simply to dismiss the matter from my mind. It was, after all, not really any business of mine. But then, just as my train rolled into the station, I decided on a sudden impulse that I would return Dr Kennett's satchel to him myself. If he had no idea where he had lost it, I was sure he would be overjoyed to see it once again, and besides, it would provide me with an excuse to renew our acquaintance, something I was keen to do. I showed the railway official the receipt I had been given for the satchel, and he handed it over to me, declaring that I could do with it as I pleased, as no one else appeared to want it. Clutching it tightly, and with a thrill of anticipation in my breast at the prospect of calling upon my unusual railway acquaintance, I sprang aboard the train just as it moved off.

"I took the satchel with me to Saffron Walden, where I bought some brown paper and string from a hardware shop and wrapped it up. How surprised Dr Kennett would be to see me, I thought, and how surprised to see what I had in my parcel!

"On the way back from Saffron Walden, I alighted at Little Gissingham station with a sensation of pleasurable excitement. At my time of life, one doesn't experience many novelties or adventures, and I was thoroughly enjoying this unusual expedition. When I enquired of the station master if he knew where Dr Kennett lived, however, my expedition received its first setback.

"'Never heard of him,' said the official, a note of finality in his voice.

"'An elderly, white-haired gentleman,' I persisted, giving as full a description of Dr Kennett as I could.

"'Oh, *that* gentleman!' said the official at length, evidently recognizing the description better than the name. 'There's a gentleman much as you describe, sir, lives at Owl's Hill.'

"'Where might that be?'

"'Go right through the village, past the inn, and about a mile further on you'll see a house all on its own, on the right beyond the forest. You can't miss it.'

"I thanked him for the directions and set off with a spring in my step, looking forward to meeting up once more with my scholarly acquaintance. Little Gissingham is a pretty little place, I must say. It has a broad village green, on one side of which is a stream, and on the other a row of very old half-timbered houses. Beyond the green is a low, spreading inn, the Fox and Goose, which is a very ancient-looking building. I should imagine that it has stood in that spot since before the Tudors ascended the throne of England. I admired it as I passed, little thinking as I did so that I should later be obliged to seek shelter for the night within those antique walls. Down the road I walked, past the last few outlying cottages of the village, and into the rolling, thickly wooded country beyond. It was a pleasant day, and I was enjoying being out in the fresh spring air. I knew that I had a good couple of hours at my disposal, before the time of the last train.

"I had been walking for about twenty-five minutes when I began to suspect that I might be going in the wrong direction. There had been no sign of any house such as the station master had described to me, on either side of the road, and it appeared that I was approaching the outskirts of another settlement altogether. With a sigh, I stopped and turned, and began to retrace my steps.

"In twenty minutes, I was back in Little Gissingham. At once I saw how I had fallen into error. Just beyond the Fox and Goose was a fork in the road. I had taken the left-hand road without really giving the matter any consideration, as the road on the right had appeared to be little more than a lane, leading only to a row of cottages. But now, as I surveyed it with somewhat greater care, I could see that it continued beyond the cottages. I therefore turned my steps in that direction, confident that I was now on the right road. I had lost about fifty minutes by my mistake, but judged that I still had plenty of time left.

"Once past the cottages, the road broadened out a little as it skirted the garden of an ancient farmhouse, the roof of which was crowned with tall Tudor chimney pots, then passed a pleasant-looking meadow in which cows were peacefully grazing. Beyond that, it rose, fell and rose again, and passed between dense woods. Presently, after a long, gentle climb, I reached the brow of a hill, beyond which the road dropped away into the distance. About a hundred yards further on, down the hill, there came a break in the woods on the right, and there, behind a trim hedge and surrounded by neat and attractive gardens, was a substantial brick house. It was a fairly modern house – not more than forty or fifty years old at the most – but if it lacked the venerable charm that age confers upon a property, it nevertheless had a very solid, reassuring air. On the gatepost was a plate bearing the name 'Owl's Hill'.

"I had my hand on the gate when two people appeared from round the side of the house. The first was a tall, erect, middle-aged lady, with grey hair done up in a bun. Something in her manner, or her carriage, impressed upon me that this was a woman of forceful character. The second was a workman of some kind, clad in a worn-looking jacket and leather gaiters, and with a small sack over his shoulder. They were speaking, and the lady was pointing to various parts of the garden, and I judged that the man was a gardener or odd-job man, receiving his instructions for the following day. I pushed open the gate and entered the garden as the man raised his cap to the woman in a farewell salute and turned in my direction. At that moment, the woman caught sight of me for the first time, and her features assumed an expression of surprise. She remained without moving on the flagged path, and waited as I approached.

"'Yes?' said she.

"I doffed my hat and introduced myself. 'I am looking for Dr Kennett,' said I. 'Six weeks ago, we shared a railway carriage. He left his satchel behind when he alighted, and I have come to return it to him.'

"A frown of puzzlement seemed to pass across her face.

"'I don't believe I know anyone by the name of Kennett,' she responded after a moment. 'Do you know his address?'

"'As a matter of fact, I thought he lived here. Does he not?'

"'Certainly not,' said she. 'You are quite mistaken.'

"'This house is Owl's Hill?'

"'Yes, as it says on the gatepost.'

"'I was informed that that was the name of Dr Kennett's house.'

"'Then you were badly misinformed.'

"I quickly described my literary acquaintance, as I had done earlier for the station master, in the hope that she might recognize the description. To my disappointment, however, her face seemed to set more firmly than ever.

"'I have never seen such a person in these parts,' said she.

"'But when I gave that description to the man at the railway station,' I persisted, 'he at once directed me down here.'

"'I cannot imagine why,' said she in an indignant tone. 'But wait,' she added after a moment's pause. 'Now I come to think of it, I do believe that the man who lived in this house before we moved here was somewhat as you describe. That must be the man the station master was thinking of.'

"'When did you move here?' I asked.

"'Why do you want to know?' the woman demanded. 'What is that to you?'

"'I simply wondered if it was very recently,' I replied, taken aback by the sharpness with which she had spoken.

"'No, it was not very recently. Does that satisfy your curiosity? I am sorry I cannot help you further. Good day!'

"With that she turned on her heel and walked quickly towards the front door of the house. But as I passed through the gate, I glanced back and saw that she was still standing upon the front step, watching me. Somewhat dejected by my failure to find Dr Kennett, and by this odd woman's unfriendly manner, I set off up the road. As I did so, I heard the front door of the house slam shut. I can scarcely describe to you how utterly disappointed and dispirited I felt then. All my fond hopes for a pleasant reunion with my fascinating acquaintance had been dashed, and I was overcome all at once with a feeling of hopelessness and fatigue, and wished I had never come.

"Some distance ahead of me, almost at the brow of the hill, I could see the old gardener, slowly plodding his way homeward towards the village. Even as I looked, he reached the brow of the hill, and in a moment had vanished from my sight. I stopped then and considered the matter. There was something in the woman's manner that troubled me. Why had she been so determinedly hostile and unhelpful to me? After all, I was confident that my appearance was not in the least offensive or threatening in any way. Now, my experience as a solicitor has taught me that when people bluster or speak aggressively, it is very often an indication that they are not telling the truth. As I stood there in that lonely country lane, I became convinced that such was the case now. The woman had lied to me, I felt certain of it. But why?

"The sky had clouded over now, and the light was beginning to fade. I glanced at my watch. It still wanted three-quarters of an hour until the time of the last train. I peered through a narrow gap in the hedge. There was no one in the garden. It was as deserted as the road on which I stood. I was all alone, in that shady, isolated spot. No one could possibly see what I was doing. There and then, I determined to take a closer look at Owl's Hill and see if I could not learn something of its occupants.

"I had observed earlier, as I approached the house, that at the side of the garden, and separating it from the dense woods through which the road had passed, lay a narrow cart track. Now, as I reached the corner of the garden hedge, I examined this track more closely. It passed along the side of the garden and appeared to lead to a field which lay behind the house. Taking a quick look about me, I turned up the track and made my way cautiously along the side of the garden hedge.

"After the first few yards, the hedge was not continuous. Instead, the boundary between Owl's Hill and the cart track was marked by a narrow thicket of bushes and trees. I was easily able to slip in between the bushes, and press forward until I had a clear view of the side of the house. Facing me, on the ground floor, were French windows, in front of which was a small, flagged terrace. At the side of this terrace was a broad flowering bush, which partly obscured my view of the window, but I could see enough to tell me that the room within was a drawing room. A couple of high-backed armchairs were visible. One of these was empty, but the other, the back of which was to the window, was occupied by someone reading a book. I could see the book and what appeared to be the sleeve of a man's jacket, resting on the arm of the chair. Just then, a door was opened into the room, directly opposite the window, and the woman I had spoken to in the garden entered the room, crossed to the French windows and looked out.

"I quickly drew myself back into the shelter of the bushes and crouched down. For several seconds, she stared in my direction and I held myself perfectly still. I was filled with dread at the thought of being seen. I felt uneasy and shameful as it was, spying into someone else's house, which was not something I had ever done before in all my life. The thought that I might actually be discovered in such a low act made my cheeks burn. I was on the point of giving up the whole absurd and dishonourable enterprise and withdrawing from the garden at once, but at that moment I saw the woman begin to speak, addressing the occupant of the armchair near the window. My resolve to withdraw evaporated in an instant as I became consumed with curiosity as to who it might be that was sitting in that chair.

"The woman rapidly became very animated, gesticulating wildly with her hands. It appeared that she was speaking in a raised, angry voice, but the sound did not carry and I could hear nothing. For several minutes I watched this strange dumb show, then the woman's tirade appeared to draw a response from the occupant of the chair, for she paused for a moment, her mouth open, and I saw the chair's occupant close the book and extend his arm, as if gesturing as he spoke. If only I could get a clearer view into the room. I glanced up. Immediately above my head was a spreading tree of some kind. Perhaps from a branch of the tree I should have a better angle of vision, and my view of the drawing room and its occupants would be unimpeded!

"I slipped out backwards from my hiding place, pushed my brown-paper parcel under a bush, and surveyed the trunk of the tree. I suppose the last time I climbed a tree was thirty-odd years ago, but there were plenty of little side branches, and it did not appear too difficult a prospect. The daylight had almost gone now, and the garden was in deep shadow, so I thought it unlikely that I would be seen. Quietly, and with an ease that surprised me, I shinned up the tree, until I was upon a stout branch almost directly above where I had been crouching. My view into the drawing room was now as clear as could be, and as my own position was shielded by a screen of leaves, I was confident that I would not be seen. I watched as the woman in the drawing room lit a lamp, and then another, and the room became ablaze with light. Then, for the first time, I had the impression that there was a third person in the room, for the woman paused, half-turned, and appeared to be listening to someone who was out of my sight, to the right. All at once, the occupant of the armchair near the window stood up and appeared to be speaking rapidly. I had a very clear view of him. There was not a shadow of a doubt: the man I was looking at was Dr Kennett, my literary acquaintance of six weeks ago. Hardly had I absorbed this fact, however, when, to my very great surprise, the woman raised her hands and, with an expression of anger upon her face, pushed him roughly back down into his chair. For a moment, then, she disappeared from my sight, to the right-hand side of the room. When she reappeared she was holding in her hand a large stick or cudgel of some kind, which she brandished menacingly in Dr Kennett's face.

"You will appreciate how astonished and distressed I was by what I was witnessing. But I had little time to dwell upon it, for just then a very strange and disturbing thing occurred. I had heard a rustling sound on the ground beneath the tree, and I glanced down, thinking it might be a cat or a hedgehog, or even possibly a fox. Imagine my shock and horror when I saw beneath me a man, crouching in the very position in which I had been but a short time earlier. It was now so dark that I could make out practically nothing of him, other than that he had on his head a wide-brimmed, low-crowned sort of hat. For several minutes I held myself absolutely motionless, scarcely even daring to breathe, my gaze alternating between the bright rectangle of the drawing-room window with its strange dumb show, and the dark, shadowed figure beneath my feet."

Mr Rhodes Harte paused, cleared his throat and asked if he could have a glass of water.

"Your story is a singular one," remarked Holmes, as I poured out some water from a carafe. "It is quite the most intriguing little problem to come my way for some time."

"There is yet more," returned the solicitor, sipping the water.

"Excellent! Pray, continue then!"

"You have perhaps experienced that awful physical sensation of nausea which can suddenly sweep over one in certain illnesses. Now, in my precarious perch in the tree, I was assailed by a sort of mental nausea, which overwhelmed my brain like a wave, so that I feared for a moment that I would pass out. There was I, at forty-three years of age, a respected solicitor of twenty-odd years' standing, halfway up a tree like a schoolboy, in the dark, in a stranger's private garden, with some other stranger skulking about in the shrubbery beneath my feet. What had I been thinking of to get myself into such a dreadful predicament? What would my friends and neighbours at home think of me, were they to learn what I had been doing? I should be ruined, both professionally and privately, and should be obliged to leave the district in disgrace! Such thoughts flooded my brain as I clung on desperately to the gently swaying branches, closed my eyes and prayed that I would not fall.

"When I opened my eyes again, the grey-haired woman was standing by the French windows, staring out into the garden with a rigid expression upon her face. Abruptly, she drew the curtains across the window. From beneath me in the darkness came the sound of movement, and as I strained my eyes to pierce the black void below, I heard the mysterious figure push his way through the bushes, back towards the cart track outside the garden, then I heard his rapid footsteps on the track as he made his way down to the road. A dizzying wave of relief passed over me. Now I, too, would be able to get away from this terrible, alarming place. I would wait for two minutes to ensure that the other man was well out of the way, and then climb down and make my way back to the village. I did not know what the time was, but thought that if I hurried I might still be able to catch the last train.

"I had waited a little while, and was about to feel my way down to a lower branch when I heard a sound that brought my heart into my mouth. The front door of the house had been opened. I pressed myself to the trunk of the tree, as someone stepped out into the garden carrying a lantern, and made his way across the lawn towards me. I could not think what to do. Like a little creature fascinated into immobility by the eye of a snake, I stared with a perfectly blank and useless mind at that little swinging light as it approached ever closer to the tree in which I was hiding. But whatever those in the house thought they had seen or heard outside, it was not me. The figure holding the lantern passed slowly along the edge of the shrubbery. It sounded as if he was poking about carefully in the bushes with a stick, but he never, so far as I could tell, looked up into the tree. As to who it was, I had no idea. I had the impression that it was a man rather than a woman, but more than that I could not say. Presently, he gave up his search, and the light of the lantern moved slowly away again, across the lawn towards the front door of the house. I waited in an agony of tension – I had scarcely moved an inch in five minutes – until I saw the light vanish and heard the front door bang shut, then I lowered myself as carefully as I could down through the branches of the tree to the ground.

"As I was scrabbling about in the darkness beneath a bush, groping blindly for my parcel, I thought I heard a slight noise, like a furtive footstep, from over near the front door of the house. The hairs rose on the back of my neck as it struck me with the force of a thunderbolt that if the man with the lantern had suspected there was someone hiding in the garden, he might have only feigned to enter the house. For all I could tell to the contrary, he might have opened the front door, put the lantern inside and extinguished the flame, then closed the front door with a bang while remaining outside upon the step. He might even now be standing there in the darkness, listening as I searched for the parcel. For a second I remained perfectly still. I could hear nothing, but I knew from earlier that footsteps upon the lawn would make very little sound. Then my fingers touched the parcel, and in a wild panic I seized it in my hand, pushed my way between two prickly bushes and set off down the cart track.

"The clouds were low and heavy, and the night was now a very black one, so that I could scarcely see where I was going, but frankly, I did not care where I went, so long as I could get away without delay from that dreadful place. At the foot of the track I turned into the road and hurried onwards through the darkness.

"I had almost reached the brow of the hill when I thought I heard footsteps behind me. I increased my pace, but the other footsteps seemed at once to become more rapid, too. Then, as they appeared to be gaining on me, I stopped, and with a great effort of will turned round. All about me was dead silence. Had I imagined those dreadful footsteps following me remorselessly along the road? Was it simply some kind of echo from the woods of my own rapid steps? Then, as I stood there in the pitch-black silence, I heard them again, and the blood seemed to turn to ice in my veins: footsteps, soft and furtive now, but rapidly getting closer to where I stood. Panic gripped my heart then and I turned and ran for my life. Uphill and downhill I ran, along that winding road, never once pausing for breath, until a faint light ahead of me indicated that I was approaching the village. Even then, there was little enough illumination, but it sufficed to guide me through the village and down the track to the railway station, which I reached in a panting, breathless state. There, as I feared, I learnt that the last train had already gone; but the station master was still about, and I was able to send a telegram to my wife, explaining that I had been delayed and should return the next day. The station master suggested I enquire at the Fox and Goose, being the only place which might offer a bed for the night, so there I betook myself. As I passed again through the dark and silent village, I looked keenly about me, but as far as I could discern, not a soul was abroad save me. As you will imagine, the evening's events had left me in a highly nervous state, and I was much relieved when I reached the safety of the inn.

"It seemed very bright and cosy in the Fox and Goose, and the landlord greeted me in a friendly fashion. In answer to my request for a room for the night, he conducted me to a little bedroom situated over the front door. It had a musty, damp smell, but I was in no position to be particular about such things, and thanked him warmly for accommodating me. He had another gentleman staying that night, he informed me, a Mr Bradbury, who was a commercial traveller for a firm of farm equipment manufacturers. When we returned to the parlour, downstairs, he introduced me to that gentleman, and then went to prepare us some food.

"The relief that washed over me as I sat before the blazing fire in the parlour of the inn, chatting with Mr Bradbury and smoking a cigar, can scarcely be described. Of course, I did not mention, either to him or to any of the other men there, the circumstances in which I had passed the last couple of hours. I appeared a big enough fool already in my own eyes, and I had no wish to announce my foolishness to the whole world. Instead, I told them that I had inadvertently alighted from the train at the wrong station and knew no one in the area, which was why I had been obliged to seek shelter for the night at the inn, and lacked the luggage that a traveller would normally have with him. If this story made me appear foolish in the eyes of my audience, it was, I felt, a lesser species of foolishness than the truth would have revealed. As it happened, I need not have been so anxious, as they did not appear to think too badly of me for my folly. In any case, Mr Bradbury was in a similar situation. He had come down that morning from London, expressly to meet one of the largest of the local landed proprietors, to discuss the latest farm machinery, but had received word upon his arrival that he could not be seen until the next day. He had therefore been kicking his heels in idleness all day, as he put it. Like me, he was looking forward to a good night's sleep, and to making a fresh start on his business in the morning.

"The landlord provided us with an excellent supper, and after that, and a little liquid refreshment, I felt quite restored. My situation did not now seem to me so bad. Presently, I announced that I would retire for the night, and bade the landlord and the other occupants of the parlour good night.

"The staircase of the inn was an ancient, narrow, winding affair, and as I was mounting the stair, a red-haired young man I had not seen before came hurrying down. I stood aside to let him pass, but he did not acknowledge this courtesy. In fact, he did not speak at all, but pushed past me in brusque silence. This struck me as exceedingly rude, but I doubt if I should have considered the matter further but for what I found when I reached the top of the stair. There, the door of my little bedroom stood wide open, and I saw at once that the room had been ransacked. The drawers of a little dressing table hung open, and the mattress and bedclothes had been tipped onto the floor. I heard a door bang downstairs, and at once stepped to the window. Outside, as I could see by the dim illumination of the lamp that hung by the door of the inn, the rude young man I had encountered on the stair was hurrying away. Pulled down tight on his head was a low-crowned soft hat. I could not doubt that it was the same man I had seen crouching below me in the bushes when I had been up in the tree at Owl's Hill, and a thrill of horror passed through me at the thought. Next moment, he had vanished from my sight into the darkness.

"I hurried downstairs and told the landlord that someone had been in my room and turned it upside down. He and a couple of the other men in the parlour accompanied me back upstairs to see for themselves what had happened. Upon seeing the chaotic state of my bedroom they said nothing, however, merely looking from the room to me and back at the room again, as if struck dumb by the unprecedented nature of the business. Then Mr Bradbury pushed open the door of his bedroom, which was next to mine, and we saw that it was in the same sort of disorder. Drawers had been pulled out, cupboards opened, and his bedding tipped onto the floor.

"Some of the men there, I suspect, had wondered for a moment if I was deranged, and had, in my insanity, upset my bedroom myself. But the disorder in the other gentleman's bedroom lifted this suspicion from me, for it was obvious that I would not have had time since leaving the parlour to cause such havoc in both bedrooms. I told them then about the man who had pushed past me on the stair.

"'Have you ever seen him before?' the landlord asked me.

"'Never,' I replied. Of course, I could not tell them that I had seen him in the garden of Owl's Hill, as I should then have to explain what I had been doing there myself.

"'Well, I don't know, I'm sure,' said the landlord, scratching his head. 'This has never happened before! We have a constable in these parts,' he added, addressing me. 'He's not much use for anything, but I'll have a word with him tomorrow, and tell him what's happened.'

"We straightened the rooms then, and shortly afterwards I retired to bed. Sleep eluded me, however, and I lay awake half the night, starting at every creak of a floorboard. I could not get the events of the evening out of my head, and over and over again I considered the matter from every angle. By the morning I had resolved that I simply could not return to my chambers and resume my routine legal work as if none of these strange events had occurred. Mr Holmes, I must learn what lies behind it all! Why did the woman tell me that Dr Kennett does not live at Owl's Hill? Why is he so ill-treated there? Is he held in that lonely spot against his will? He certainly appeared to be at liberty on the day I met him on the train. But if he is at liberty, why does he stay there? Who is the man who was hiding in the bushes, and what was his purpose in being there? Why were the rooms at the inn ransacked? I know I shall never rest easy until I know the answers to all these questions! I remembered that my partner, Mr Halesworth, spoke of you in glowing terms about a year ago, Mr Holmes, and I thought you sounded the very man to help me discover the truth. So here I am, that is my story, and if there is anything more you wish to know, please ask."

"Thank you," responded Holmes after a moment. "Your account has been a very clear one, Mr Harte. I shall do what I can to assuage your anxieties on the matter. It is certainly a singular little mystery! You have been lied to, your room at the inn has been rifled, and you have every right, it seems to me, to know what lies at the bottom of it all. Before we proceed any further, however, could you clear up one point?"

"Certainly."

"Did the mysterious intruder at the Fox and Goose take anything from either of the bedrooms?"

"I do not think so. A few loose items of Mr Bradbury's had been scattered around, but he said that as far as he could see there was nothing missing. He also had a locked trunk, which was pushed under his bed, but that did not appear to have been touched. I, of course, had no luggage of any kind, except for the wretched brown-paper parcel that I had been lugging around fruitlessly all day, so I had nothing to lose."

"The parcel was still there?"

"Yes."

"Where?"

"On top of the wardrobe, where I had flung it earlier."

"Very well. And that is the parcel in question, I take it," said Holmes, indicating the brown-paper bundle that Mr Harte had placed upon the table. "May I see the contents?"

"By all means," returned his visitor. He unfastened the parcel on the hearthrug, and produced from within it a stout-looking leather satchel with a shoulder strap. This he passed to Holmes, who examined it closely for several minutes, turning it over and over. At length, evidently satisfied, he stood it on the rug, unfastened the two buckles at the front, opened it up and took out the contents. These consisted of two thick volumes, one of which appeared very new, a few loose foolscap sheets and some folded brown paper, a small square bottle of black ink, two pens, a pencil and a short length of string. Each of these items Holmes examined carefully, then placed upon the rug. He then turned his attention to the interior of the satchel. On the underside of the lid were two lines of faded lettering, and after squinting at these for a moment, Holmes took his magnifying lens from the mantelpiece and carried the satchel over to the window, where he examined the lettering very closely for several minutes.

Presently, he handed the lens and satchel to me without saying a word, then sat back down in his chair again, his eyes closed and his brow furrowed with intense concentration. I examined the satchel. The leather on the inside was an untreated, dull grey colour, lighter in some places than others. The lettering inside the flap was faded and faint, and very difficult to make out. It appeared to have been worn away by years of rubbing against books and documents. The first letter in the line was almost certainly a capital "A", and the second might have been a small "d", but there then followed several letters which were impossible to decipher. After a gap came what might have been a capital "K", followed by more indecipherable smaller letters, the last of which appeared, when I examined it through the lens, to be a small "s". Below these letters, in small capitals, was the name "KARL", followed by a full stop, then the numbers "3" and "8".

Holmes had risen from his chair and was standing by his shelf of reference works, thumbing through a thick red-backed volume. Finding the page he was looking for, he carried the book to the window and stood reading it in silence for several minutes.

I picked up the books and papers from the hearthrug. The copy of *David Copperfield* was bound in dark blue morocco, moderately worn and rubbed at the corners. On the fly leaf, in ink, were the initials "A. K.". A thin piece of blank card was inserted between the pages as a bookmark, near the middle of the book. The other volume was *The Story of English Literature, from the Earliest Times to the Present*, by Professor Walters of Trinity College, Cambridge. This was bound in dark green cloth, and appeared to be new. On the fly leaf was an inscription written in ink, in a florid hand, which read as follows: "A. K. Kindest Regards. Your friend, D. W.". The loose sheets of paper had very little written upon them. There were the titles and authors of what appeared to be three works of literary criticism, and five or six lines of notes, little more than odd words, such as might be jotted down by someone listening to a lecture.

Holmes had put down the red-backed book he had been reading and extracted a volume of his encyclopedia from the shelf, turning over the pages rapidly until he had found the entry he was seeking. For a minute he stood reading, with a frown upon his face, then he shut the book with a bang and began pacing the floor in silence, his chin in his hand.

"What is it?" asked Harte after a moment, appearing slightly anxious at the intensity of Holmes's manner. "It is certainly a perplexing business, is it not?" he continued when Holmes did not reply.

"Not at all," responded Holmes abruptly, ceasing his pacing about. "It is crystal clear."

"What!" cried Harte. "Are you saying that you have fathomed the mystery already?"

"Precisely."

"But how is that possible? How can you pretend to understand what is happening at Owl's Hill simply by sitting here in this room?"

"By using my brain," responded Holmes testily.

"I thought that, having heard my story, you would wish to make a few enquiries and perhaps travel down to Little Gissingham yourself."

"That is the question."

"What is?" asked Harte in a tone of puzzlement.

"Whether to travel down to Suffolk now, or – but, no, I must go! The alternative is impossible! I could make enquiries in London to confirm matters, but that would take a day, perhaps two. I could consult Superintendent Richards at Scotland Yard, who may know something, but that would waste another day, and besides, that part of rural Suffolk is probably beyond his jurisdiction. No, we must go down there now!" He pulled open the top drawer of his desk. "Will you come with us, Watson?"

"Certainly."

"Then look up the trains in Bradshaw, will you?" he continued, as he took out his revolver and a box of cartridges. "Is your own pistol ready for service?"

"I believe so," I replied in surprise as I picked up the railway timetable. "Do you expect that it will be necessary?"

"Very likely. Unless, of course, the murder has already been committed before we get there! Let us hope that we are not too late!"

"What is all this talk of firearms and murder?" cried Harte in alarm. "Surely you exaggerate? I did not expect such a response when I decided to consult you."

"My response is to the facts," returned Holmes in a preoccupied tone as he loaded his pistol.

"But what *are* the facts?" demanded Harte.

"That cold-blooded murder is planned. I shall give you the details on the way down. Have you found the train times yet, Watson?"

"We have just missed one," I replied. "There is a train at eighteen minutes past four, which would enable us to reach Little Gissingham not much after half past six."

"That will have to do, then. The sun does not set until about half past seven, so there should be sufficient daylight for our purposes. Will we be able to get away from Little Gissingham again tonight?"

"The last train, the one Mr Harte missed yesterday, leaves at about quarter past eight."

"Excellent! I shall just write out a couple of telegrams, and then I think we should make our way to Liverpool Street station straight away! However bad the traffic is now, it will be worse later in the afternoon. There is an excellent and economical restaurant, which serves luncheons all afternoon, just round the corner from the station in Bishopsgate. We can get a meal there and ensure that we are at the station in good time. Whatever happens, we must not, under any circumstances, miss that train!"

Thus it was that at four-eighteen, the three of us were in a first-class smoking compartment as our train puffed its way noisily beneath blackened girders up the steep incline from Liverpool Street towards the higher ground of Essex.

"Mr Harte's satchel and its contents are singularly suggestive, are they not?" said Holmes to me. "They help one to form a clear picture of the man to whom the satchel belongs. I take it you drew the same inferences from these materials as I did."

"There are certainly some indications," I returned cautiously. "It is evident, for instance, that the owner of the satchel is an enthusiast for English literature."

"But not one of very long standing."

"Why so?"

"The book describing the history of English literature, worthy volume though it is, is introductory in nature and written for a general audience. The fact that it is clearly new, and evidently recently purchased, suggests that its owner, however enthusiastic he might be, is not yet in an advanced stage of literary scholarship."

"That may be so," I returned, "but the book is inscribed, and thus may be a present from a friend. In which case, of course, you cannot so reliably judge the owner's level of sophistication and scholarship from it."

"Generally speaking," said Holmes, "that would be a sound observation. Your attention to detail does you credit."

"Thank you."

"In this particular case, however, your reasoning is erroneous."

"Why?"

"There are two distinct parts to the inscription. The first part, at the top, consists of the initials 'A. K.', the second part is the remainder, 'Kindest regards. Your friend, D. W.', if I recall it aright."

"These two parts, as you call them, seemed all one to me."

"Not at all. Not only are the initials 'A. K.' in a different hand, they are written with a different pen."

"Let us see," said Harte, unfastening the satchel and taking out the book.

"You may be correct," I conceded as I examined the inscription.

"I am certain of it," said Holmes. "The 'K' in 'A. K.' is formed quite differently from the 'K' in 'Kindest regards'. Now, this suggests that the owner of the book, whom we must presume is this 'A. K.' – for the book is undoubtedly a new one and has not been owned by anyone before – bought the book himself and wrote his initials in it, and only subsequently asked his friend to inscribe it. You will note that the inscription says neither 'To A. K.' nor 'From D. W.' but simply 'Kindest regards, your friend, D. W.'"

"But why should he ask his friend to write in his book if his friend did not buy the book for him?" asked Harte in a tone of puzzlement.

"The friend may not have bought the book," returned Holmes, "but it appears likely that he has played a significant part in the business."

"What do you mean?"

"Simply that the friend – 'D. W.' – is almost certainly the author of the book."

I glanced at the book's title page. "Of course, you must be right!" I cried as I read the name of Professor David Walters of Trinity College, Cambridge.

"It seems likely, then, that 'A. K.' – the man you met on the train, Mr Harte – had bought himself this book while in Cambridge to attend a lecture. There is a little gummed label on the inside of the back cover, giving the name of the bookshop. No doubt the brown paper and string in the satchel came from that shop, too. We do not know whether the lecture that 'A. K.' attended was given by Professor Walters, but whether it was or not, 'A. K.' must have approached Professor Walters at some time during the day and asked him to inscribe this book for him. If the two men were strangers, Professor Walters would surely have satisfied the request by writing 'Best wishes', or something of the sort. But he has specifically called himself 'Your friend, D. W.', so we must suppose that the two men are well acquainted. Professor Walters is an eminent figure in the world of scholars, and it is a fair assumption that many of his acquaintances are from that same class of society, including, perhaps, the man calling himself Dr Kennett. We are, you see, slowly but surely building up a picture of that gentleman."

"It is not conclusive," I observed.

"No, it is not, I agree, but the balance of probability surely lies upon that side. Dr Kennett is certainly highly intelligent and highly educated, as Mr Harte's testimony of their lengthy literary discussion attests. In any investigation, it is of course preferable if one can deduce one fact from another, and then a third from the second, and so on. Sometimes, however, the data are so meagre that it is not possible to make such deductions with any certainty. In that case, one must construct a tentative hypothesis, and be prepared to alter it at any time, if new facts come to light. The process is somewhat akin to the erection of his wigwam by a Red Indian. None of the poles he uses, taken alone, can possibly support the wigwam, but when he has several poles leaning together, each providing mutual support for the others, the structure can stand. Thus it is in this case: none of the deductions we can make from the satchel or its contents are certain. Taken all together, however, they lend fairly sturdy support to the wigwam of our hypothesis, and we can thus feel a reasonable degree of confidence in our conclusions. If we turn now to the other volume in the satchel, Dickens's

David Copperfield: this appears to have been read before, but not more than once, I should say. It is not by any means what might be described as 'a well-thumbed copy', and in fact appears to be a fairly recent edition."

"That is true," I agreed.

"Now, while it is possible that Dr Kennett had already read *David Copperfield* in a different edition when he was younger, it seems most likely, taking the condition of this volume together with his remarks about the book, that it is a novel he has come to for the first time only recently, in maturity."

"That had not struck me before," said Harte in a considered tone, "but now that I recall again his conversation, I am inclined to think that what you suggest is correct."

"But as Kennett himself observed, *David Copperfield* is commonly given to children of fourteen and fifteen years of age. How is it, then, that such an intelligent and cultured man as Kennett should never have read the book before?"

"Perhaps because all his intellectual energies have been applied to other subjects," I suggested.

"It is possible," said Holmes. "Perhaps, like John Stuart Mill, he had an education which was rigorously devoted to scientific and technical subjects, to the exclusion of the more artistic aspects of human life. Mill writes somewhere that because of the intense educational process to which he was subjected, which had been devised by his father, he heard scarcely a note of music or a word of poetry until he was an adult. But in this case, other, simpler, explanations are possible."

"What do you have in mind?" asked Harte.

"That the man calling himself Dr Kennett is not in fact English. If that were so, he might, of course, be highly educated, and perhaps familiar with the literature of his own country, but not with that of England."

"He certainly sounded English," observed Harte. "He had no particular accent that I could discern."

"Well it is, of course, possible that although foreign, he has been a fluent English-speaker for many years. Some foreign English-speakers – those from France and the other Latin countries, for instance – never really lose their original accents, no matter how long they live in England, but for others – some Germans and Scandinavians, for instance – the speaking of English seems to come more naturally, and after living here for a few years many of them could pass for natives. Perhaps it is so with Kennett. The conjecture that he is a foreigner is, of course, but one of half a dozen different possible explanations, but I will not trouble you with the others, all of which I was able to eliminate in light of the data presented to us by the satchel. May I now draw your attention to the inscription on the inside of the satchel?"

"It is scarcely decipherable," I remarked, as Harte turned back the flap so we could see. "The lettering has been almost completely worn away."

Holmes shook his head. "Not worn away," said he, "but deliberately scratched away, probably with a small penknife. The general hue of the inside of the satchel is a somewhat grubby grey; but you can see that where the letters have been obliterated, the colour is slightly lighter, indicating that the obliteration of the name has been done relatively recently, perhaps within the last year or two. For some reason, the owner of this satchel has wished to conceal his identity."

"Perhaps it belonged previously to someone else," I suggested, "and the new owner simply wished to remove the previous owner's name."

"I think not, Watson. For it is evident that although he has deliberately scratched away most of the name, he has left the initial letters untouched. They are, as you see, 'A. K.', the same initials as in the books. Clearly, he does not care if the initials are seen – he can, after all, make up a new name to match them – but it is vitally important to him that his true name is never seen. This suggests, although not conclusively, that he has reason to suppose that his true name is one that would be recognized. There is corroboration in the satchel, incidentally, that whatever the English scholar's true name is, it is not Kennett; for the space taken up by the second name in the satchel is definitely too short to accommodate 'Kennett', and, in any case, so far as I could determine with the aid of a lens, it ends with an 's'."

I nodded my agreement on the point.

"May I further draw your attention to the smaller letters and figures below the excised name?" Holmes continued.

"I noticed them earlier," I remarked. "There is the name 'KARL', followed by a three and an eight. What the name 'KARL' might signify, I cannot imagine, although as it is a Germanic name, it lends support to your hypothesis that the satchel's owner is not a native Englishman. As to the numbers, perhaps they constitute some sort of code, inscribed by the manufacturer of the satchel, or by the shop from which it was purchased."

"And yet," remarked Holmes, "the numbers have been inscribed with the same pen and ink as the rest of the lettering."

"Why, so they have!" cried Harte.

"This suggests that they are figures of significance for the owner of the satchel. As to 'KARL', that may not be a personal name at all. The obliterated letters above, following the initials 'A. K.', must surely be the owner's name, so why would a second name be inscribed in the satchel? Now 'KARL' has a full stop after it, which suggests it may be an abbreviation. It is therefore at least possible, it seems to me, that it is an abbreviation for the German name of what we know as Charles University in Prague, the oldest university in Central Europe. If that is so, the figures may well be the date – 1838 – when the satchel was purchased by A. K. as a young student. That would suggest that he was born about 1820, which would make him about sixty-one or sixty-two now. Did the man on the train appear to be of that age, Mr Harte?"

"Almost exactly, I should say."

"Very well, then. The supposition is confirmed, not conclusively, but very strongly. That the satchel has been owned by A. K. for many years is indicated also by the numerous repairs which have been made to it, some of which appear to have been made many years ago. The shoulder strap, for instance, is clearly a replacement for an earlier one – the colour and texture of the leather are slightly different from the rest of the satchel – but such a strap might well be expected to last for twenty years or more, and the present one has the appearance of having been in place for a good ten years."

"Where does this bring us to?" enquired Harte after a moment.

"It brings us to the true identity of the satchel's owner," returned Holmes, taking his pipe from his pocket and beginning to fill it. "It has taken me some time to explain to you my reasoning from the clues which the satchel and its contents presented. It is always far more laborious and time-consuming to explain such reasoning than it is to perform it. Sophocles, in one of his plays, describes man's thought as 'wind-swift', and that is an accurate observation. But a perception that occupies one for less than a second is likely to take several minutes to explain. Dr Watson has sometimes considered that my occasional neglect to explain to him my reasoning springs from some perverse urge to secrecy; but generally it is that I simply do not have the time for explanations. My perceptions may be so swift as to seem like instantaneous intuitions, but the explanation of them is always likely to prove a somewhat lengthy monologue.

"To return now to specifics, and to the true identity of the English scholar," continued Holmes after a moment, putting a match to his pipe, "we conjecture from the indications available to us that he is intelligent and cultured. He is possibly a foreigner, although he speaks English like a native. He is probably about sixty-two years of age, and may be a graduate of Prague University. He is a personal acquaintance of the eminent Professor Walters of Cambridge, and although something of a novice in the field of English literature, he is probably eminent in some field himself, for he has made great efforts to conceal his identity. Though his name is not Kennett, his initials are 'A. K.' and his second name ends with an 's'. In short, Mr Harte, the man you conversed with so amicably on the train can be none other than Adolf Kraus."

The solicitor shook his head in evident puzzlement. "The name sounds vaguely familiar," said he, "but I cannot quite place it."

"Surely," I interjected, "you do not mean the former Prime Minister of Bohemia?"

"Precisely, Watson. He is, according to my reference book, sixty-two years of age. He first attended Prague University in 1838, and continued his studies subsequently at Vienna, and at

Cambridge, here in England. He later returned to teach at Prague, where he became Professor of Cultural History in 1861. During his stay in England, incidentally, he met and subsequently married Constance Dowling, daughter of the professor of moral philosophy, a circumstance which would, of course, have served to improve his English accent."

"But what on earth is he doing here, sequestered in one of the most rural corners of England?" I asked in astonishment.

"Leading as quiet a life as possible, I imagine."

"But why?"

"Do you not recall the troubles in Bohemia, a few years ago, which reached a climax with riots in the streets of Prague?"

"I heard something of the matter at the time," I replied, "though I cannot claim a very thorough understanding of what lay behind it all. As far as I recall, it blew over fairly quickly."

Holmes shook his head. "I rather suspect that for some it did not blow over at all," said he. "Lives were lost, and no doubt grudges were borne, when the authorities used force to put down the riots. Adolf Kraus was prime minister at the time, and was blamed by some elements for what had happened. To what extent that censure was justified, I do not know, but I do know that two separate attempts were later made upon his life, and that he and his family were hounded out of the country."

Harte's features expressed incredulity. "I cannot believe that the gentleman I met on the train could be guilty of any dishonourable act," said he.

"From my own information, I should be inclined to agree with you," responded Holmes, "but, of course, it matters little what you or I believe."

"I understand," said Harte, nodding his head. "It is your opinion, then, that Kraus is in hiding from his enemies?"

"That is what we must assume. It would explain why he and his family have chosen to live in what sounds from your account to be one of the most isolated houses in southern England. But I fear that his enemies have once more caught up with him, and that his life is once more in peril. The man you saw hiding in the bushes at Owl's Hill must have been an advance scout for the assassins. Now that they have found their quarry, they will waste no time in exacting their revenge. Adolf Kraus's life hangs by a thread at the moment, and with each hour that passes his peril increases. Now, Mr Harte, perhaps you will understand the sense of urgency that overwhelmed me in Baker Street, and understand, too, why arms may be necessary. We must at all costs prevent the terrible crime that is in prospect!"

"I am dumbfounded!" cried Harte after a moment. "I can scarcely credit that it is true! I simply wished to return the old gentleman's satchel to him, but it seems I have become embroiled in a deadly conspiracy! It is clear now why the woman at Owl's Hill lied to me. She must be Kraus's wife, and she probably feared that I had some connection with the people pursuing her husband. No doubt when I saw her expressing anger towards him, she was berating him for his carelessness in losing his satchel, and thus, as she saw it, placing his life in danger."

"It must be so. Now we must warn them of the real danger that threatens."

"Surely we should notify the authorities at once?"

"I wired the Chief Constable of Suffolk from London," returned Holmes. "But our first priority must be to warn Kraus himself of the grave peril in which he stands. If we had delayed our journey in order to discuss the matter with the authorities, it is likely that before they could act, Kraus would be dead. There are occasions when, for better or worse, a man must act upon his own judgement, or know that the issue is lost. I sent a wire also to Owl's Hill, but it was, of necessity, a mere brief warning. It may serve, at least, to put them on their guard. But only in person can we explain to them the nature of the danger, how we know of it, and what our interest in the matter is."

"You have acted very promptly," I remarked. "I cannot think that there is anything more you could have done."

My friend nodded his head. "Thank you, Watson," said he. "It is good of you to say so. Now the matter lies somewhat precariously in the lap of the gods."

Our train reached Little Gissingham station a little after twenty to seven. It was a fine evening, and though the sun was far in the west, the air was still warm and only the lightest of breezes stirred the blossom on the trees by the station master's house. As that official examined our tickets, Holmes asked him if many visitors had alighted at the station that day. He shook his head and declared that there had been few travellers and all of them had been local folk.

"That is good news, at least," remarked Harte, as we made our way up the short track towards the village. "For it means we have arrived before Herr Kraus's enemies."

"Unfortunately, we cannot be sure of that," returned Holmes with a shake of the head. "They may have alighted at one of the other stations on the line – the last one we passed was only about two miles back – in order to avoid arousing comment here. It would not take them very long to make their way here across country. We must make all haste!"

Harte led us through the picturesque little village, past the green on which two children were playing with a little dog, past the ancient-looking inn, and along the road that led to Owl's Hill. For some time, the road passed through dense woods, which threw long shadows across the road, and here, unseen among the shaded trees, the birds were chirruping their evensong. Presently, when we had been walking for about a quarter of an hour, we reached a crest, and saw the road winding down the hill ahead of us. A hundred yards further on, there was a gap in the woods on the right, and I descried a trim garden hedge. Behind this hedge, set a dozen yards back from the road, was a solid-looking red-brick house. "That is Owl's Hill," said our guide.

As we turned in at the garden gate, the house presented a silent and deserted appearance, and but for a thin wisp of smoke which rose from one of the chimneys, I might have imagined it unoccupied. Our ring at the bell was answered by a young girl in a parlour maid's uniform. Holmes asked her if her mistress was at home, and intimated that we would wait at the door for a reply.

In a moment she had returned, and with her was a tall, middle-aged woman of striking appearance. Though her hair was grey and her face showed that the cares of life had not passed her by, there was yet a fineness and delicacy about her features, and a vividness about her grey eyes, which spoke of a nobility of spirit and a firmness of resolution.

"Yes?" she demanded in a peremptory tone. Then, as her eyes alighted on Holmes's client, she started slightly. "Oh, it's you again, is it?" said she sharply. She half turned and called loudly into the recesses of the house. "Joseph! Joseph! Come here at once!"

"It's all right, Mother; I'm here already," came a low, firm voice from behind us.

I turned quickly. Behind us in the garden stood a tall, lean young man with dark red hair. In his hand was a revolver, pointed at us. Clearly he had slipped out of a back door and approached silently round the side of the house. "If any of you makes an untoward movement," said he in a cold voice, "I am quite prepared to use this pistol."

"This is the man that rifled my room at the inn last night," cried Harte in a tone of fear.

"He was looking for the satchel," said Holmes. "He ransacked both rooms, because he did not know which one was yours."

"You seem to know a lot!" cried the young man.

"I know everything," returned Holmes in a calm voice. "I understand your caution," he added, eyeing the pistol. "In this case, however, it is misplaced. We have come expressly to warn you that your father's life is in great danger."

"What do you know of my father?" demanded the young man in an angry voice. "You are armed!" he cried all at once. "You have a pistol in your pocket!"

"Yes, I am armed," returned Holmes, "and so is my colleague here," he added, indicating me. "We came prepared to defend your father, if necessary."

"Why should we believe you?" demanded the young man. "Who are you?"

"My name is Sherlock Holmes. Did you not get my wire?"

"Your name means nothing to me," retorted the young man.

"Nor to me," said the woman.

"I am a consulting detective, madam," said Holmes, turning to the woman. "This gentleman, Mr Harte, came to see me this morning, as a result of certain unpleasant and puzzling events which occurred yesterday evening. His only wish had been to return your husband's satchel, which had been left on a train, and he was convinced that you had lied to him when you said that the gentleman in question no longer lived here."

I read hesitation in the woman's face.

"If the satchel is ours, I will accept it," said she at last, holding out her hand. "Then Mr Harte's wishes will be satisfied, and you must go and trouble us no more!"

"No, madam," said Holmes in a firm voice as Harte handed her the satchel. "You must believe me when I tell you that your husband is in mortal danger. Yesterday evening, after you had spoken to Mr Harte, he saw a man hiding among the bushes at the side of the garden, spying on the house."

"I knew it!" cried the young man to his mother. "I told you that I had heard someone moving about out there. Was this man aware that you had seen him?" he demanded of Harte.

"No."

"Why not?"

"Because I, too, hid and kept very still."

"What makes you think my husband's life is in danger?" the woman asked. "The man Mr Harte saw in the garden may have been some local simpleton playing a game."

"Your husband is in deadly peril, madam," returned Holmes, "because he is Adolf Kraus, late Prime Minister of Bohemia."

"No!" cried she, a terrible note of anguish in her voice.

"Yes!" returned Holmes in a firm voice. "His initials are in the satchel, and from that and other indications, we were able to work out a solution to these puzzling events."

The woman clutched her head in both her hands and appeared in a terrible state of indecision and fear. But at that moment a door opened in the hall behind her, and a tall, broad-chested elderly man with a mane of white hair stepped forward into the light. He put his arm round his wife's shoulders, and she turned and buried her head in his chest, sobbing loudly.

"I am indeed Adolf Kraus," said the man in a measured tone. "Mr Rhodes Harte," he continued, "I have been listening to everything which has been said. It is a pleasure to see you again, sir! Do you vouch for these other two gentlemen?"

"Certainly I do," replied Harte promptly. "This is Mr Sherlock Holmes, the leading criminal investigator, and this is his colleague John Watson, who is a medical man."

"Then come inside," said Kraus. "Put up your pistol, Joseph. If Mr Harte vouches for these gentlemen, that is good enough for me. Mr Harte is an honourable man, or I am no judge of character!"

He led us through the hallway into a large drawing room. Then, having seated his wife in a chair by the hearth, he turned and addressed us. His features appeared careworn and tired, and in his voice was a note of resignation.

"You say, gentlemen, that my life is in danger. You tell me that you have seen men hiding in the bushes. I do not doubt that you are right. I have seen such things before. But what can I do, save sit here all night with a pistol in my lap?"

"You must get away from here immediately," replied Holmes in an urgent tone.

"I am weary of flight. Besides, where can I go?"

"Perhaps Professor Walters could put you up for a few days."

"What do you know of Professor Walters?" asked Kraus in surprise.

"His name was in one of your books, in the satchel. Would he do it?"

"Yes," said Kraus, appearing roused from his apathy by the suggestion. "Yes, he might. He did say that I should not hesitate to approach him, should I ever need help."

"Then pack a travelling bag at once," said Holmes. "You must catch the last train; time is running out!"

"Yes! I will do it now," cried Kraus's wife, springing from her chair with renewed spirit. "Come and help me, Joseph. We can do it in three minutes! Tell Emily Jane to throw a jug of water onto the kitchen fire, then gather her things together and be ready to leave the house in five minutes!"

"Is it your intention to take the girl with you?" Holmes enquired of Kraus, as his wife and son hurried from the room.

"Certainly," returned Kraus. "We have grown very fond of her and could scarcely imagine life without her. Besides, she is an orphan and has nowhere else to go."

"Are there any other servants in the house?"

Kraus shook his head. "We have a cook, but she is away at present, visiting her sister. Mr Harte," he continued, turning to the solicitor, "I must thank you for returning my satchel. It is very kind of you. I could not think where I had lost it. I had not even mentioned the loss to my wife, for I knew that she would be angry at my carelessness. When she informed me yesterday that you had called with it, I wanted to go after you, to speak to you, but she would not hear of it, and said I should be putting myself in danger unnecessarily. And whenever I went out in future, she insisted, I should take a cudgel with me, in case I was attacked. Then Joseph said he would walk to the village and take a look in the inn, to see if he could find the satchel. His search was not successful, and we concluded that you had left the district and gone home. He informed me, however, that he had heard a man on the road ahead of him in the dark, but he had not been able to see who it was."

"I was that man," said Harte. "I thought he was pursuing me."

"Dear, dear!" exclaimed Kraus. "I am very sorry if you were alarmed, my dear Mr Harte. I know only too well how dreadful it is to be pursued! Do you know, gentlemen," he continued after a moment, "why it is that I have been pursued so relentlessly?"

"Because you were head of the government in Bohemia at the time of the Prague riots," replied Holmes. "Lives were lost and, rightly or wrongly, you were blamed."

Kraus nodded his head slowly. "That is indeed the immediate explanation of the matter," said he, "but there is a larger, more abstract reason. Everything bad that has happened to me in my life has happened because I was persuaded against my better judgement to enter the world of politics. It was not a world for which I was suited, either by nature or by education. I was naive and gullible and believed what I was told. This fact was my undoing.

"As you may be aware, I taught for many years at the Charles University in Prague. In that relatively modest capacity I was content to serve, and had no desire to make any greater mark upon the pages of history. Some years ago, however, when certain issues concerned with both the history and the future of Bohemia were the subject of intense public debate, I wrote several letters to the Press, in order to correct what I saw as misapprehensions which were prevalent at the time. My letters were responded to, I wrote more, and soon, to my surprise, I found that my opinion was being constantly sought by influential parties on every side of the debate. I was, with some reluctance, persuaded to address public meetings. Then the regional government itself requested my advice, and later appointed me to lead a committee of enquiry into the governance of Bohemia. I flattered myself at the time that the merits of my views had been recognized. The truth, of course, was somewhat different. As I learned later, express orders had been received from Vienna that I be appointed to the committee of enquiry in order that my hands should thereby be tied and my tongue stilled.

"After a time, my committee presented its report, and shortly afterwards I was asked to join the government itself. I had never for one moment sought such a position, but the circumstances were such that it was practically impossible for me to turn down the request. It seemed to be as it says in the book of Ecclesiastes: 'The race is not to the swift, nor the battle to the strong; but time and chance happen to them all'. Time and chance certainly appeared to be happening to me. I had been in the government for but a few months when a singular series of events took away my senior colleagues one by one – one man was implicated in a financial scandal and resigned his post, another man resigned for family reasons, a third fell ill and retired – and I found myself elevated to the position of prime minister almost by default. I thus found myself, a man who had never sought any role in public life, at the very pinnacle of the Bohemian regional government. What I did not appreciate then, however, was that my colleagues, more experienced in the subtle twists and turns of politics than I could ever be, had already foreseen the troubles which were fast approaching, and were taking steps to remove themselves from the arena, leaving me alone to bear the assault. Needless to say, most of them miraculously overcame their personal difficulties and returned to public life once the troubles had passed and I had fallen from grace. Still, I knew none of this at the time, and saw only that I had arrived at a surprising and unlooked-for position of eminence. I was determined not to stay in that position for very long, but to do as much good as I could while I was there. As you will imagine, the first of these two aspirations was satisfied somewhat more fully than the second.

"You may have surmised from my name that I am of the German race, and you may be aware that the population of Bohemia is part German and part Czech, the latter being the more numerous. I determined to do what I could to address various grievances, which were causing ill-feeling among the Czechs, and believed that I was making some progress in this respect, when certain repressive laws and regulations came into force by order of the Imperial Government in Vienna. These led to great resentment and public unrest. Although I bore no responsibility for these laws, as the head of the regional government I was blamed for them, and became the focus of popular hatred. This was grossly unfair, but what was worse was that I was hated most bitterly by those I had striven so diligently to help. Still, that distinction scarcely matters, as I was hated by all parties alike. I was hated by the Germans of Bohemia because they considered that I had betrayed their interests and favoured the Czechs, and I was hated by the Czechs simply because I was a German. I struggled to restore public order once more, but at last I was forced to admit failure and composed my letter of resignation. Alas, before it could be announced, heavily armed troops were sent from Vienna to put down the riots in Prague. I tried to prevent the troops from entering the city, but I was overruled. There was great violence, and many of the rioters were killed. Within days it became clear to me that I was held responsible for this tragedy, even though I of all men had done my utmost to prevent it. I resigned then, but unfortunately this only confirmed the popular belief that I admitted responsibility for what had occurred. Shortly afterwards, two attempts were made upon my life, and I realized that we could no longer live safely in Bohemia. We moved to Berlin, but had been there scarcely six months when every window in our house was broken one night, and I received a death-threat through the mail. Once again we were obliged to move, and this time we came to England. We stayed for a time in London, but I was recognized in the street one day and decided that it would be safer to move to the countryside, where no one would know me.

"We chose this house as it was the most isolated place we could find, and here we have lived peacefully for several years. Now, it seems, we must move again, for there are men in the shrubbery with murder in their hearts. Are they Czech? Are they German? Are they even Austrian, perhaps? Who can say? It makes no difference: they all hate me, and for things I did not even do."

As Kraus finished speaking, he shook his head in a gesture of weary resignation, and at that moment his wife and son returned.

"Do not be downcast, Adolf!" cried his wife, as she saw his forlorn countenance. "Do not despair! Have strength once again and we shall make a new home somewhere else, even better than this one. Consider also your work," she continued, as he showed no sign of responding to her encouragement. "The research in which you are engaged cannot be done so well by any other man in Europe. You must not yield to these murderers."

"If you are all ready," said Holmes, consulting his watch, "we had best be off. You do not keep a pony and trap?"

Frau Kraus shook her head. "We have had no need of one," said she. "It takes only twelve minutes to walk to the village, and fifteen to the railway station. If you gentlemen will help us with our bags, we shall manage perfectly well."

In a minute we were in the road, and Kraus and his family had turned their backs on the house that had been their home. The little serving girl, Emily Jane, was in a state of great agitation and fear. Although she did not fully understand what was afoot, she understood enough to know that danger was pressing. I took her bag and spoke a few words of encouragement to her. I hoped that I sounded calm, but in truth any calmness I displayed was almost entirely an act. Within, my heart beat with just the same agitation as hers, I am sure, for I knew only too well the peril of our situation.

We made a strange, and oddly assorted party upon that quiet country road that evening: the striking, almost comic figure of Herr Kraus, his top hat wedged crookedly upon his unruly mane of snow-white hair; his wife beside him, tall and queenly in her poise; Harte and I following behind, two vaguely professional-looking gentlemen, quite out of place on that dusty country road, and the pretty little servant girl, Emily Jane, her eyes wide with fear, keeping close to my side; beside us, guarding the right and left flank respectively, Holmes and Kraus's son, the latter lean and tense as a coiled spring, his sharp eyes darting this way and that in constant vigilance. What might a chance onlooker have made of this singular group? Could anyone possibly have divined the strange and fearful business that was taking us along that deserted road on that pleasant spring evening?

Above us, the pale blue sky was streaked with bands of red. The sun had been sinking below the horizon just as we left the house. Now, the deepening shadows within the woods and the purplish light upon the tree tops spoke eloquently of the fleeting time that is twilight. A few unseen birds still twittered fitfully among the trees as they settled down to roost for the night, but save only these soft sounds, the countryside had already slipped into the deep silence of evening.

As we approached the brow of the hill, a pony and trap came over the crest, appearing as a black silhouette against the pale sky behind. Down the hill towards us it came, at a slow, unhurried trot, and we moved in slightly to the side of the road to let it pass. Two men were on the seat, I observed, clad in overcoats and soft hats.

"Why it's my acquaintance, Mr Bradbury, the farm-machinery man from the Fox and Goose," cried Harte. He raised his arm and called a greeting as the trap drew level with us.

There are moments in a man's life that stay for ever in his memory, good moments and bad moments, and moments which seemed at the time neither conspicuously good or bad, but which are still lodged firmly in one's mind. Good, bad or indifferent, all can be brought into one's conscious thoughts at any moment, at the very slightest of bidding. You glance for a moment at the fire, and you are once again the five-year-old boy, gazing into the nursery fire and wondering what causes the little spurts of flame upon the sides of the black coals; you see a woman riding in the park and you are translated at once to a chilly schoolroom of long ago, where a nursery-rhyme illustration hangs on the wall, of "a fine lady upon a white horse".

There are other moments, too, dark, terrible moments, which need no bidding to emerge from the mysterious shaded recesses of memory, but which appear periodically of their own volition, for no apparent reason, often in the long drowsy watches of the night. The result is always the same: a sickening, jarring sensation, a frightening jolt to the mind, and in an instant one is fully awake and living again through that dreadful moment, the blood throbbing in one's veins, the beads of perspiration breaking out upon one's brow. It was a moment of this latter type that followed Mr Harte's friendly wave to the men on the trap. I cannot count the many times the scene has been replayed upon the stage of my memory, where each second of time occupies a minute, and each minute seems an eternity.

The echo of Mr Harte's greeting still hung in the air as the driver of the trap reined in his horse and drew it to a halt just in front of us. The man to the right of the driver seemed to grunt a response to the greeting and, as he did so, he drew back with his left hand the front of his overcoat, which was unfastened, and with his right brought out a heavy shotgun, which had been concealed beneath the coat, and began to raise it towards us. Mesmerized though I was by the strange, silent elevation of the deadly muzzle, I was conscious too of other movement, from Holmes on my right and Kraus's son on my left. Then, as the shotgun reached the horizontal and pointed straight at us, my eyes for an instant met those of the man holding it, and I read there his evil, remorseless intent, even as his finger tightened on the trigger. The girl beside me was gripping my right arm so tightly that I could not move it. Then came a flash of fire from either side of me, and the simultaneous reports of two pistols. The man holding the shotgun let out a blood-curdling cry as the two shots struck home, I saw blood spring from his breast as he reeled over backwards, and as he did so, the gun in his hand discharged with a flash like lightning and a roar like thunder, and the deadly shot passed mere inches above our heads. Frau Kraus screamed, the horse in the shafts reared up in terror, and the young girl beside me slumped senseless upon my arm. Even as all these things were happening, the driver of the trap had dropped the reins and pulled out a large revolver from within his coat. Again, two shots rang out in unison from beside me, and the man on the trap pitched sideways from his seat and fell in a heap to the ground.

Holmes stepped forward quickly and seized the reins, as the horse whinnied and made to bolt, his eyes bulging with fear. I carried the young girl to the side of the road and laid her down on a grassy bank, then quickly examined the two strangers who had come with such murderous intent into our lives. They were both dead.

I looked round. The sound of the explosions was still ringing in my ears, and the air was thick with smoke and the smell of gunpowder. Rhodes Harte was standing in perfect stillness in the middle of the road, as if stunned into senselessness by the terrible rapidity of the events. "But, Mr Bradbury . . ." he began in a tone of stupefaction. "I thought . . ."

"It was almost certainly he you saw hiding in the garden of Owl's Hill yesterday," said Holmes. "He was no machinery salesman, but must in reality have been the advance scout for the assassination party. No doubt he wired his confederates with the information this morning. They would have killed us all without a thought, Mr Harte. Here," he continued, thrusting his pistol back into his pocket, "help me turn the trap round and get the other man aboard. We have no time to lose!"

We passed no one on the road through the village, and reached the railway station with just a few minutes to spare. There, Kraus was momentarily nonplussed when he learnt that the last train was headed east, towards the Colchester line, and he would not be able to reach Cambridge that night.

"We can get from Colchester up to Ipswich, at least," cried Harte. "You must come with me and stay the night at my house,

Herr Kraus. You can make your way over to Cambridge on the other line, via Bury St Edmunds, tomorrow morning."

Kraus seemed reluctant to impose upon the solicitor's generosity, but his wife assured him that it was the only sensible thing to do, and he at length agreed. Harte then quickly sent a wire to his wife, instructing her to expect visitors, and as he rejoined us on the platform, the last train of the day drew noisily into the station of Little Gissingham.

Herr Kraus, his wife and son, Rhodes Harte and Emily Jane were quickly aboard, and the doors were slammed shut. Then, with a roar of steam and smoke, the train pulled away, quickly picked up speed and vanished into the darkness. For a few moments, Holmes and I stood there in silence, watching the red lamp on the last carriage until it had vanished round the curve, then we made our way out to the station yard.

"It is a terrible business," remarked my friend, shaking his head as he regarded the two lifeless figures lying in the back of the trap. "Our only consolation can be that were it not they lying there, Watson, then it would be you and I. Come! Let us find the local constable and see if we can begin to explain how it is that two professional gentlemen from London are wandering the countryside with a cart containing dead men. It may prove somewhat difficult, especially as we have quite improperly permitted most of the witnesses to depart the scene, but we must do our best."

The inquest upon the two dead men was held ten days later, at which, after much testimony had been heard, the verdict was recorded that they had been killed in self-defence. As to Herr Kraus and his family, I understand that they stayed only a short time in Cambridge, before moving once more, but I have little further information. I do recall that it was five years after the events I have described above that Adolf Kraus's famous book, *The Spirit of Man in World Literature*, was published to great acclaim, but where he and his family were living then I cannot say, for they had by that time passed quite beyond my knowledge.

The Adventure of THE AMETHYST RING

SHERLOCK HOLMES had called at my house in Paddington on a cold and foggy day in January, just as I was finishing my morning surgery. Now, my last patient having departed, he handed me a visiting card he had received in the post that morning. It had scalloped edges, tinted a pale coral-pink, and the brief message upon it stated that Mr and Mrs A. Carter-Smythe would be giving an informal supper party on the evening of the twenty-fifth, to which Holmes was invited.

"I have not heard you mention these people before," I remarked, looking up from the card.

"That is scarcely surprising," returned my friend, "considering that I was perfectly unaware of their existence until that card arrived this morning. They have evidently heard or seen my name somewhere, and consider that my presence at their gathering would provide an amusing diversion for their other guests."

"Will you go?" I asked.

"It is not my taste to act as an adornment at someone else's supper table," said he with a shake of the head. "I may say, Watson," he continued in a tone of reproach, "that there has been a distinct increase in the number of such unwelcome social summonses since the publication of your *Study in Scarlet* brought my name before the public."

"I regret any inconvenience I may have caused you," I responded somewhat tartly. "My intention was simply to gain for you the credit I felt you deserved in the matter."

"No doubt," said he. "No doubt also," he continued after a moment, "Mr and Mrs A. Carter-Smythe would be surprised if they knew where I have spent the last twenty-four hours. They might be somewhat less keen to welcome me to their supper party if they were aware of the company I have been keeping. I have been down in Rotherhithe," he continued in answer to my query, "by the docks. I have been looking into the disappearance of one Jack Prentice, landlord of The Seven Stars, an old riverside inn there."

"That does not sound much of a case for you, professionally speaking," I remarked with a chuckle. "Why, the number of men who supposedly 'disappear' in London each year is perfectly phenomenal! I read an article on the subject in one of the monthly magazines not long ago. The author was a retired police officer, who stated that of the many hundreds of people reported as 'missing' each year, a sizeable number simply disappear of their own volition, to escape from pressing debts, unbearable spouses and the like."

Holmes nodded. "I am aware of those facts," said he, "but there is something about this case that intrigues me, Watson. It possesses certain features that are decidedly uncommon. In contrast to the examples you quote, for instance, it seems that Prentice has managed his life in a very orderly manner in recent years and does not owe anyone a penny; furthermore, his marriage is, by all accounts, an unusually happy one. Everyone I have spoken to avers that he would do anything rather than cause his wife distress. But why, then, did he leave his house in the middle of a rainy night, without a word to his wife? Where did he go to? Why did he take a candlestick with him? And what is the meaning of the mysterious sheet of symbols he left behind? I can give you the details if you wish. As a matter of fact, it is this case that has brought me to see you. I was rather hoping that you might be able to accompany me to Rotherhithe. There is something I wish to investigate further there, and your presence would be of great assistance to me."

I glanced at the clock on the wall. "Some of the shops have announced end-of-season sales this week," I said, "and I did promise my wife that I would take her today."

"Oh, well," said my friend in a tone of disappointment. "If you can't come with me, I shall just have to manage alone."

"Wait one moment," I said as he made to stand up. I ran upstairs to speak to my wife, but was back again in a couple of minutes. "It is all arranged," I said. "She will go with Dora, my neighbour's wife, instead. To be honest," I continued as I put on my hat and coat, "I think she would prefer to go with Dora. It may sound highly companionable to attend such events with one's spouse, but it is probably a more enjoyable experience if one's companion fully shares one's enthusiasm for it. Speaking personally, I am somewhat more interested in learning about the disappearance of Jack Prentice!"

"I can give you all the details as we travel," said Holmes. "It won't take us long to get to Rotherhithe. We can get a Metropolitan train here at Paddington, which will take us all the way there. If only all my clients were so conveniently situated!"

Ten minutes later, we were seated in the corner of a first-class carriage, rattling along beneath the Marylebone Road, and my friend was explaining to me what it was about this unpromising-sounding case that he had found so intriguing.

"I might mention," said he, "that the authorities are taking more than simply a passing interest in the matter. This is chiefly on account of the missing man's former activities; for in years gone by he was frequently suspected of being involved in the disposal of stolen goods. Indeed, he served a sentence of two years in Pentonville Prison for such a crime, in the mid-'70s, although his conduct since then has been exemplary. But," he continued, taking a small notebook from his pocket, "I shall give you the facts in order:

"Prentice was born in Rotherhithe in 1843," he continued after a moment, turning the pages of his notebook, "so he's in his mid-forties now. As a young man, he took to the sea, and spent some years sailing between England and Australia. After a while, however, he tired of these long voyages and transferred his services as a crewman to the countless number of smaller vessels plying between England and the Continent. This decision was perhaps influenced by the fact that he had, in 1866, married a local girl, Ann Cooke. For the next eight years or so he worked on these relatively short voyages to all the many ports of the European mainland. During this period, two children were born to the Prentices, a boy, William, in '67, and a girl, Lily, in '68.

"On the surface, then, Jack Prentice's life appeared straightforward, law-abiding and above board. However, the police authorities in Rotherhithe began to suspect that there was a little more to it than there appeared to be. There had at that time been a spate of burglaries in the West End, and the police were concerned that very few of the stolen items – jewellery and so on – were turning up again. Although the police were not, it must be said, very successful at solving any of these crimes, their record of eventually recovering the stolen property was reasonably good, thanks mainly to a network of paid informers, but also to their own dogged persistence. Now, however, they were finding that the proportion of stolen goods that they were able to recover was much lower than it had been previously. Rumours reached them that much of this plunder was being smuggled abroad, where it would, of course, be much easier to dispose of. A sort of indirect confirmation of this theory was received when some jewellery turned up in London which subsequent investigation showed had been stolen in Paris two months earlier.

"Having had their attention drawn to this illicit cross-Channel trade, the police soon found their suspicions converging upon some of the criminal elements in Rotherhithe and, in particular, upon a notorious villain by the name of Elias Dack, who ran an old inn there called The Cocked Hat. Have you ever heard anything of Dack, Watson?"

"Never."

"Well, that is perhaps not so surprising, for he has little to do with honest citizens. But in that part of south-east London where his gang holds sway, his name is a byword for cruelty and violence, and strikes instant fear into the breast of anyone that hears it. From his lair at The Cocked Hat – a plague-spot on the face of London – he exercises ruthless control over the district and none dare cross him. Yet, despite his notoriety, the police have never been able to bring any serious charge against him. In the early '70s, the police were convinced that Dack was the guiding brain behind the crimes they were investigating, yet they could not get near him. Instead, therefore, they began to pick off the outliers of his criminal pack, particularly those who connected Dack with the cross-Channel trade. One of these was Jack Prentice, who was arrested early in '74, in possession of stolen goods, for which he was convicted and sentenced to two years' imprisonment. Prentice's wife informs me that she was shocked by this, as she had no idea that he had been engaged in anything underhand, and I believe her. She seems a decent sort, Watson, and deserves our help.

"Upon Prentice's release from Pentonville in 1876, his wife made him vow to give up his criminal ways, and abjure all his former associates, especially Dack, whom she says she has always detested. No doubt chastened by his time in prison, Prentice agreed to do as she said. Shortly afterwards, he also turned his back on the sea, became the landlord of The Seven Stars and settled down. There, for the last dozen years or so, he has remained. It is an interesting old inn, Watson, which has stood on that spot since before the time of Shakespeare and Marlowe. Much of it is little changed from those days, although part of the panelling in the tap room is said to be from an eighteenth century man o' war, and a fine painting of the ship in question hangs on the wall there.

"The Prentices' children, who are, of course, now grown up, helped them in the house for a time, but they have now both left. The son, William, married a girl from Deptford by the name of Daisy Weekes, and works in a local timber yard. There seems to be some slight ill-feeling between him and his parents, and he hasn't been in The Seven Stars for several months. The daughter, Lily, married one Teddy Bates, a sail-maker, and Mrs Prentice says she usually sees her at least once every week. The place in the household left vacant by the children's departure has been filled, partly at least, by the arrival of Maria, a young girl of about eighteen, from Corunna in northern Spain. She apparently arrived in Rotherhithe last summer, in the company of an English sailor who had promised to marry her when they reached London, but who, upon their arrival here, promptly deserted her and set sail for the Far East, leaving her destitute and homeless. Mrs Prentice saw her in the street one day, took pity on her and took her into her own home, where she helps with the cooking, cleaning and other household tasks. Other than this girl, there are no servants in the house. This, then, is the peaceful and settled household from which Jack Prentice has so mysteriously disappeared.

"To come now to recent events: Mrs Prentice informs me that she noted with displeasure that Elias Dack and two of his cronies called in at The Seven Stars one night last week and engaged her husband in conversation. After they had left, she asked him what Dack had wanted.

"'Nothing special,' said Prentice, 'just gossip.' She did not believe him but, as it was clear he did not wish to discuss the matter further, she did not press the point. A couple of days later, however, on the tenth, there was another unwelcome visitor in the pub, a man of the vilest antecedents, who glories in the name of 'One-eye' Vokes. Notorious in the district for his violence and criminality, he is known by everyone to be a sort of vicious emissary for Elias Dack. The ocular shortcoming that has given him his name is the result of a bar-room brawl several years ago, when he was hit in the face with a beer bottle, by one 'Spider' Wilkins. Wilkins himself was later found dead in mysterious circumstances, but evidence was lacking, and although the police strongly suspected that Vokes was responsible, no one was ever charged with the murder. After the visit of 'One-eye' Vokes to The Seven Stars last week, Mrs Prentice confronted her husband, warning him that if she ever found out that he had taken up his old criminal ways again she would leave him forthwith. Prentice protested his innocence and assured her he had told Vokes he did not want anything to do with him or Dack.

"The following evening, Mrs Prentice went to bed before her husband, but could not sleep. As she lay awake, worrying what he was up to, she heard a tap at the front door and, putting her head out of the bedroom window, she saw that 'One-eye' Vokes was standing there. Then her husband came to the door, and spoke to Vokes for some time, but she could not hear any of their conversation. Eventually, Vokes turned away and walked off up the street. When her husband came upstairs shortly afterwards, she asked him what Vokes had wanted.

"'They wanted me to do something for them,' he replied, 'but I told them I'm not interested.'

"On Monday evening of this week, Prentice again loitered downstairs after his wife had gone to bed, and again she did not fall asleep straight away. After a while she heard someone moving about downstairs, and thought she heard voices, so she put on her dressing gown and went to see what was happening. She found her husband alone in the tap room, sitting at a table, writing something on a sheet of paper. On the table next to the paper was an ornate gold ring containing a large purplish stone. As his wife entered the room, Prentice quickly picked up the ring and slipped it into his waistcoat pocket.

"'What's that ring?' she asked sharply.

"'It's an amethyst,' he replied.

"'I mean,' she persisted, 'what are *you* doing with it?'

"'Nothing. Someone asked me to tell them what it's worth, that's all.'

"'Give it back, Jack. Don't get involved.'

"'I'm not involved in anything,' he protested. 'I'll give it back, Annie, don't you worry.'

"Something in his tone reassured her, and although she was still anxious, she went back to bed and fell fast asleep. In the morning, when she woke, she saw to her surprise that her husband was not in bed, and when she went downstairs she found that he was nowhere about and the front door had been unlocked. There are two keys for the front door. One of them is usually left in the lock, and the other, the spare one, is kept on a hook behind the bar. Both keys were in their usual places that morning. All that day, Mrs Prentice waited for her husband to return from wherever he had gone, but he never came. This, she says, is very unlike him. For the last dozen years – ever since his spell in prison, in fact – he has been diligent and hard-working and always attentive to his wife's concerns. He has never before taken himself off Without telling her where he was going.

"By the late afternoon she was very anxious at his continued absence and went along to the local police station, which is not far away, to enquire if they had heard anything. They were unable to shed any light on the matter, but took down all the details she gave them and recorded her husband as a 'missing person'. When she got home, however, and gave it all more thought, she decided she was not satisfied with the police response. She suspected that, because of her husband's criminal record, they would do nothing, but simply wait for him to turn up. She therefore determined to take the matter into her own hands. No doubt, like the Carter-Smythes, she had heard my name mentioned somewhere, so she left Maria in charge of the pub and came to consult me.

"It was too late that evening for me to do anything much, but I made a note of the main facts, and the following morning – that is, yesterday – I went down to Rotherhithe to look into the matter. As you will imagine, I questioned Mrs Prentice closely on any aspect of her husband's affairs that might prove relevant, and stressed to her that she must answer me truthfully.

"'Do you believe that Elias Dack and his cronies have been trying to get your husband to help them dispose of stolen goods?' I asked her.

"She nodded her head. 'It must be that,' said she. 'You see,' she explained, 'although Jack himself hasn't been to sea for a dozen years or more, he knows an awful lot of men as do make their living that way. It's not just the men he knew when he was a sailor himself, neither. We gets all sorts coming in The Seven Stars, and Jack's a good landlord and often stands talking to them in the tap room for hours on end. I doubt there's anyone who knows more seafarers – both straight and crooked – than Jack, and I'm sure there's plenty as would do a job for him for a small consideration, no questions asked.'

"'Have you come across that amethyst ring anywhere?' I asked.

"'No, I haven't,' she replied, 'and I've had a good look round. Jack must have taken it with him. To tell the truth, I hope he has taken it and given it back. But I'm worried that if he's told them he doesn't want anything to do with them, there might have been violence done and Jack might be hurt. I wouldn't put anything past Dack, or that evil devil, Vokes.'

"'Did you see what Jack was writing on that paper on Monday night?' I asked her.

"'Not at the time I didn't; but I found it the next morning, where he'd left it in the tap room. I can't make any sense of it, though,' she added, as she handed me the sheet of paper. 'As you see, Mr Holmes, it's just ticks and odd letters.'

"This is the paper, Watson," said Holmes, taking a folded sheet from between the pages of his notebook and passing it to me. "It is a singular document, is it not?"

I unfolded the sheet upon my knee and studied it for a few moments. There were five rows of symbols, as follows:

VIIIIII – BCO
VIIIII – MNAB
VIIII – HBL
VIII – ARHAR
VII – OLGM

"I can't think what it might mean," I said at last.

"I think we may safely dismiss Prentice's claim that he was estimating the value of the ring," said Holmes. "That was, I take it, the merest humbug, something he made up on the spur of the moment for his wife's benefit. Yet it is evident he was working something out."

"The marks at the beginning of each line look rather like Roman numerals," I suggested, "in which case the first group would represent eleven, the second, ten, and so on."

"I agree," said Holmes, "although, of course, as 'eleven' is usually represented by an 'X' followed by an 'I', and 'ten' simply by an 'X', his use of the numerals must be non-standard in some way. What do you make of the other letters, Watson?"

"They may be the initials of something, or of someone, I suppose," I responded. "Perhaps if – despite what he told his wife – Prentice was considering helping Dack to smuggle stolen goods abroad, he was listing the initial letters of ships that he knew would be setting sail shortly. In which case," I added, "the figures at the beginnings of the lines may represent dates – the seventh, eighth, ninth, tenth and eleventh of next month."

Holmes nodded. "It is possible," said he, "although I doubt whether even Prentice – however well informed he may be about sailors and ships – would know the departure dates of so many different vessels several weeks hence."

"What then?" I asked. "Do you regard this paper as of any significance to the case?"

"Yes, I do, Watson. It was, after all, the last thing Mrs Prentice saw her husband attending to before his mysterious disappearance. I have a hypothesis, but it is somewhat tentative at present, and it is this I am hoping to either confirm or reject today. But, to continue my account, Mrs Prentice showed me a brass candlestick which stood on a shelf above the fireplace in the tap room.

"'There should be two of these here,' she said, 'but when Jack went off, he took the other one with him.'

"I picked it up and examined it. The base was hollow, and I wondered for a moment if Prentice might have hidden something in the base of the missing one – something, perhaps, which he did not wish his wife to see. But, of course, that would not explain why he had needed to take the candlestick with him; he could simply have removed whatever he had hidden there, and put it in his pocket, before leaving the house.

"I then took myself along to the local police station, where I am fairly well known, especially after the help I was able to give Inspector Quirke in a forgery case last year in Lavender Yard. Quirke was on duty, and when I mentioned Prentice's disappearance to him, he admitted to me that they were taking an interest in the matter, although he said they knew no more about it than they had heard from Prentice's wife. However, information they have received in recent weeks has led them to believe that Rotherhithe is once more becoming a major staging post in the disposal of stolen goods, and he suggested to me that Prentice's disappearance might be connected with that in some way. Although our conversation was an affable one, I sensed as we spoke that the inspector was holding something back, and I strongly suspect that the police have some plans afoot, which he did not feel able to confide in me. What they might be, I do not know. Anyway, having exhausted that source of information, I spent the rest of the day making general enquiries in the district, and interviewing people whose names Mrs Prentice had given me, without advancing my knowledge to any significant degree. It was only when I was on my way home, and was able to consider the whole business afresh in a detached manner, that I began to see my way to forming a hypothesis. It is this that I shall shortly put to the test, for we are nearly there." As he spoke, our train plunged into a long dark tunnel, where the thud and clank of the engine boomed around the close brick walls. "This is the Thames tunnel," said he. "We shall be at Rotherhithe in a minute."

As we left the station and turned east, the fog seemed even thicker and dirtier than at Paddington, and with a shiver I turned my coat collar up and followed my companion through the greasy, swirling coils, which drifted like a sea about us. We had gone perhaps a quarter of a mile at a fairly brisk pace when Holmes indicated a narrow side street on the right. "The Cocked Hat is along that way," said he. A little further on, we turned off left, down a lane that led to the river, where the dank, pungent smell of the waterside competed with the stench of the fog. Immediately ahead of us, revealed through brief rifts in the filthy veil, lay the great heaving breadth of the Thames. Close by the riverside, Holmes stopped before a low grey building on the right. Above the heavy oak door hung a grimy, weather-worn wooden sign, on which I could just make out seven faded yellow stars. Holmes pushed open the door and I followed him inside, glad to be out of the fog.

Inside The Seven Stars, several lamps were lit, and the brightness seemed at first almost dazzling after the gloomy murk outside, but even in here the reek of the foggy river seemed to fill one's nostrils. A cheery fire was blazing away in a very large old fireplace, however, and we stood for a moment warming our hands before it. As we did so, two women emerged from a doorway behind the bar. The first was a broad, comfortable-looking middle-aged woman whom Holmes addressed as Mrs Prentice, and behind her was a slightly shorter young female of perhaps seventeen or eighteen. She was dark-featured and raven-haired, and was evidently the Spanish girl, Maria, of whom Holmes had spoken. They were wearing their hats and coats, and carrying baskets, and Mrs Prentice explained that they were on their way out to the market. Holmes introduced me as a professional colleague with whom he wished to discuss the case, which seemed to satisfy her, and it was evident from her manner that my companion had made a very favourable impression upon her the previous day, although her face fell when he informed her that he had as yet no news of her husband.

"We'll get off now," she said, peering out of the window at the murk outside. "It's not going to get any better. We'll not be more than forty minutes, Mr Holmes. I'll lock the door so you won't be bothered by customers while we're out. If you do need to go out, you can use the spare key on the hook behind the bar." A moment later, the two women had gone and we were alone.

"Having the place to ourselves makes things somewhat easier," said Holmes in a brisk tone, as he took off his coat, then reached up and took down a brass candlestick from the mantelpiece. "This is the partner of the one that has disappeared," said he. He lit a spill in the fire, then lit the candle with it. "I'm going to take a look downstairs in the cellar, to test the hypothesis I mentioned to you," he continued. "You had best wait here, Watson, in case the women come back."

I sat down on a chair by the fire, wondering what was in my friend's mind. Perhaps, I conjectured, he considered it possible that the first candlestick had been used to illuminate something in the cellar, and had then been left down there. That certainly seemed more likely than that it had been used as a hiding place for something. I had very little time for reflection on the matter, however, for in less than two minutes Holmes had returned.

"It is as I thought," said he. "The hypothesis is confirmed. Now," he continued, as he snuffed out the candle and replaced it on the mantelpiece, "I have another task for you, Watson, if you would be so good. I shall look after things here, if you would kindly run along to the police station. Ask for Inspector Quirke, or whoever is in charge today, and give him my card, with the message that the matter is most urgent." He took a visiting card from his pocket and scribbled something on the back, then handed it to me. A moment later, after he had given me directions, I was hurrying along the road, back the way we had come.

The fog seemed particularly cold and unpleasant after the friendly warmth of the fireside, and I drew my muffler up over my nose and mouth. As I passed a brightly lit shop window, I turned Holmes's card over, to see what he had written on the back, and read "New development in Prentice case. Come at once. S. H."

At the police station, I handed the card to the officer on duty, who disappeared through a doorway with it, but returned a moment later and conducted me to Inspector Quirke's room at the back of the building. There, a large uniformed police inspector was seated behind a desk; but it was the other occupant of the room who caught my attention, for, with a start of surprise, I recognized our old friend Inspector Athelney Jones of the detective division of Scotland Yard.

"Dr Watson!" said he, rising to his feet and shaking my hand. "I did not know you were still hunting with Mr Holmes! We heard that you had thrown yourself entirely into medical matters since your marriage."

"So I have," I returned, "but Holmes needed a companion today, and I was glad to be of assistance. I am to tell you that the matter is very urgent," I added, sensing that Jones was about to enter upon a leisurely general discussion of life.

"I don't doubt that," interrupted Inspector Quirke, tapping Holmes's card on the edge of his desk. "I must say, I have never once known Mr Holmes to waste anyone's time. The difficulty, however, is that we have something of our own planned for this afternoon, and that, too, is very urgent. I wouldn't want this Prentice business to interfere with the other. What do you think, Mr Jones?"

Jones considered the matter for a moment. "You understand exactly what you are to do this afternoon?" he asked his colleague at length.

"Perfectly."

"Very well, then. What I propose is this: I shall go with Dr Watson and leave everything else to you. I should like to take one of your men – Constable Griffin, if you can spare him – but I think I shall ask him to follow us at a distance so as not to excite curiosity in the street. No doubt I shall get the matter sorted out in a few minutes and be back here before you leave, but if I am not, you go ahead as we agreed, and I shall see you later."

A minute later, Inspector Jones and I were making our way through the fog to The Seven Stars, with a very large constable following some distance behind us, his footsteps a dull, muffled echo of our own. As we walked along, I told Jones all I knew of the matter, which was not very much, and he nodded his head sagely. "They believe hereabouts," he remarked, "that Prentice has been on the straight and narrow for the last dozen years or more, but perhaps it's not so. Perhaps he's been deceiving them all along."

Our knock at the pub door was answered by Holmes. He then lit the candle once more, and the three of us descended to the cellar. Even halfway down the cellar steps, it was much colder than upstairs, and in the cellar itself the icy cold seemed to rise up from the old flagstones and penetrate to one's very bones. Holmes led us to a dark corner behind two very large barrels, where he lifted a tarpaulin sheet to reveal what he had discovered. With a thrill of horror, I saw it was the body of a man.

"Is it Prentice?" asked Jones, rubbing his chin.

"Yes," said Holmes, "and here, I think, is the weapon that struck him down – which solves another little mystery." He picked something up from the floor beside the body, and I saw it was the second brass candlestick. As he held it up, I could see that it was bent slightly out of shape and smeared with what looked like blood. "How long would you say he has been dead, Watson?"

"This is certainly the cause of death," I said as I examined a savage wound on the side of his head, where the hair was darkly matted with blood. "His skull has been fractured. As to the time of death, I am no expert, but it is evident that *rigor mortis* has already begun to dissipate, so he must have been dead at least forty-eight hours, I should say, and probably longer, as the cold air in this cellar will have slowed the whole process down."

"My conclusions precisely," said Holmes. "Let us get the body upstairs now, before the women return."

Between us, we carried the body of poor Jack Prentice upstairs and laid him out on the tap-room floor, covered in an old dust sheet we found in a cupboard.

"What made you suspect that Prentice's body might be down in the cellar?" I asked Holmes.

"The door to the street, Watson. Mrs Prentice found it unlocked on Tuesday morning, and it was supposed that Prentice had risen and gone out early. But at the time he was supposed to have left, the night would still have been pitch black. I could not believe that he would have left the door to the street unlocked when it was dark and the other occupants of the house were still asleep in bed upstairs. He would instead have locked the door on the outside and taken the key with him, knowing that there was a spare key behind the bar which his wife could use. It was possible, of course, that Prentice had been taken from the house by force, but it was equally possible that he had never left the building at all, and that the door was unlocked simply because he had never got round to locking it the night before. And if – dead or alive – he was still here, the cellar seemed the likeliest place to find him. That was the hypothesis I wished to test."

At that moment, there came the sound of a key being inserted in the lock, and a moment later we were joined by Mrs Prentice and Maria. There was a moment of dreadful silence, as they saw the shrouded figure on the floor, and the blood seemed to drain from their faces.

Holmes took a step forward and addressed Mrs Prentice. "I am afraid you must prepare yourself for bad news," said he, at which Mrs Prentice put down her shopping basket and began sobbing, leaning for support on the younger woman, who put her arm round her. Then, after a moment, she gathered herself together and stepped forward to identify the dead man. Inspector Jones lifted the shroud, at which she nodded her head and began to weep copiously. I brought forward a chair and sat her down on it, then went behind the bar to find some brandy.

"Who could have done such a thing?" the poor woman wailed, "and why?"

"Have no fear, madam," said Jones in a reassuring tone. "We shall catch whoever committed this terrible crime. He shall not escape us!"

"The 'why'," said Holmes in a grim voice, "is because of this list that Jack was writing the last time you saw him alive." He took the sheet of paper from his pocket and unfolded it. "He was certainly trying to work something out, but it was not the value of the ring that you saw. He was using Roman numerals so that you would not guess what he was writing, for it was something he was ashamed of, and he did not want to lose your trust, which I believe he valued above all else."

"But what was it he was working out?" asked Mrs Prentice in a puzzled tone as I handed her a tot of brandy.

"I believe he was calculating dates," said Holmes. "When I got home last night and examined this sheet anew, it seemed to me then that there was perhaps a slightly wider space after the third numeral on each line, and I conjectured that what he was writing in this deliberately cryptic fashion was perhaps a seven, followed by different numbers of single strokes, indicating 'seventy-four', 'seventy-three', 'seventy-two' and so on. This in turn suggests the years known by those abbreviations. If this is so, then the other letters must surely be the initials of the European ports that he remembered visiting in those years – Amsterdam, Hamburg, Oporto, Lisbon and so on. That is the only explanation that makes sense."

"But why should he be trying to remember what he was doing all that time ago?" asked Mrs Prentice. "Those days were before he served his time in Pentonville; and after he came out, he gave up the sea completely. That's all just ancient history now."

"It might not be simply ancient history to everyone," returned Holmes.

"What do you mean?"

"To someone who was born then, for instance, one of those years would undeniably be a significant date. Someone such as Maria, perhaps." He turned to the Spanish girl as he spoke, and she took a step backwards, a look of alarm on her face.

"I do not understand!" she cried.

"I think you do," returned Holmes. "I think you showed Jack Prentice that amethyst ring – a ring he had perhaps given to some woman he met in Corunna at a time when he was feeling fairly well-off from his ill-gotten gains – and you accused him of being your father. That is why I believe he was so concerned to recall everywhere he had been in those years of the early '70s."

"You lie!" cried Maria.

"I think not," said Holmes. "You are the one that lied. There is no 'C' on Jack Prentice's list – 'C' for Corunna – until '74, which is much too late for him to have been your father. I believe you were down here in hiding, late on Monday evening, when Mrs Prentice came downstairs to see what was happening. After she had gone back upstairs, Prentice, who had satisfied himself that he could not possibly be your father, confronted you and demanded to know, I imagine, what sort of a trick you were trying to play on him. In the ensuing quarrel, you seized the candlestick from the mantelpiece and struck him with it. You may not have intended to kill him, but that was the result. You then dragged his body down the cellar steps, and across the cellar floor. Your footsteps were quite clear in the dust down there."

"Lies! All lies!" cried the girl.

"If I am right," continued Holmes, turning to Inspector Jones, "she's probably got the ring on her. It's certainly not in any of Prentice's pockets. I suggest she be searched."

"I have no ring!" the girl protested. "I never have ring!"

"That's not true, Maria," said Mrs Prentice in a quiet tone. "I saw you fiddling with a ring one day last week, but I never saw what it was."

"All right," said Maria. "I have ring. I find it on floor."

"Let us see it, then," said Jones.

She stepped forward in a reluctant fashion and put her hand in her coat pocket. The next moment a dreadful thing happened. She took her hand from her pocket, but in it was not the ring we were all expecting to see, but a wicked-looking little dagger with a narrow, pointed blade. In that same instant, with a loud howl of rage, she flung herself forward at Sherlock Holmes, the dagger aimed for his breast. But quick though she was, Holmes was quicker. His hand shot out like lightning, seized her wrist and held it tightly, then he pressed her arm down and forced her to drop the knife. At that point she let out an ear-piercing scream and began to kick him violently on the shins, at the same time lunging forward to try to bite him. Jones and I sprang forward and pulled her away, and in a moment the policeman had clapped a pair of handcuffs on her. At that moment the door opened and Constable Griffin put his head in to enquire if everything was all right.

"There's a young woman outside, sir," he added, "who wants to come in – name of Lily Bates."

"That's my daughter," cried Mrs Prentice, rising to her feet. A moment later, a sandy-haired young woman pushed her way past the police constable and into the room. "Lily!" cried Mrs Prentice in a voice full of emotion. "Your father is dead!" The two women embraced, and in a few words Mrs Prentice gave her daughter a brief account of what had happened.

The younger woman's eyes flashed fire. "I knew it!" she cried, looking with anger at the Spanish girl. "I always thought she was a scheming little minx! You do know, Ma, that she's the reason William stopped coming round here. He didn't trust her. He always said she was no good and was up to something!"

"Here's a ring!" said Jones, who had been feeling in the Spanish girl's coat pockets. "Would you say that that is an amethyst, Mr Holmes?" he asked, holding up the ring, which contained a single large purplish stone. Holmes nodded his head, and Mrs Prentice confirmed that it was the ring she had seen her husband slip into his waistcoat pocket on Monday evening.

"That rather settles the matter," said Holmes. "I don't know what this girl was doing before she came here, Jones, but it wouldn't surprise me if she was put up to this scheme by 'One-eye' Vokes or Elias Dack."

"Elias Dack?" cried Maria abruptly in a voice suffused with contempt. "I spit on Elias Dack!"

"Well, at least that shows you know who he is," remarked Holmes in a dry tone. "As I was saying, Jones, I can't believe that having made her way all the way from Corunna to England, whether alone, or in the company of an English sailor, as she claimed, she just happened by sheer chance to land up in the household of the man she was later to accuse of being her father. What is more likely, I think, is that she had already fallen in with Elias Dack, or some member of his gang, and he saw the possibilities in the situation: that he could use this girl to blackmail Prentice into throwing in his lot with them in their dishonest activities, as he used to do in the days before his prison sentence. It is likely, I think, that Prentice himself had mentioned to Dack, many years ago, that he had given this ring to a young woman he had met in Corunna. Dack would know that the very last thing that Prentice would want would be a serious falling-out with his wife, and he could use this fact as a sort of evil leverage against him."

"It may well be so," agreed Jones. "And we may learn more about it later. Between you and me, gentlemen," he continued, taking us to one side and lowering his voice, "the important business that Inspector Quirke and his men are undertaking today is a raid on The Cocked Hat. We have had reliable information that the loot from most of those West End robberies is being stored there at the moment. A search warrant has been issued, and the raid should be starting any time now. With a little luck we should get our hands on both the stolen goods and Dack and his gang!"

As Holmes and I walked along to the railway station, I reflected on the whole sorry business.

"I was thinking," I remarked, "that Elias Dack, despite supposedly being an old friend of Prentice's – in days gone by, at least – was perfectly prepared to destroy Prentice's marriage just to get him to help them."

"That should not surprise you, Watson," returned Holmes with a harsh laugh. "Despite the efforts of some writers to romanticize criminals, in tales of highwaymen and other such villains, there is, in truth, as the old saying has it, no honour among thieves. These sort of people would sell their own sisters into slavery if it happened to suit their immediate purposes. People like Dack have no real friends."

I was to remember my friend's cynical words later, when I read a report in the newspaper of the police raid on The Cocked

Hat. For during the chaos and violence that followed the arrival of the police, Dack evidently scented treachery, and formed the opinion – rightly or wrongly – that the information the police had received had been given to them by his lieutenant, "One-eye" Vokes. Seizing a moment when no one was looking, therefore, he attacked Vokes with a knife he had concealed in his sock, and, before anyone could stop him, had plunged it into the other man's breast, killing him on the spot. That raid, and the trials that followed, marked the eradication of what Holmes had described as a "plague-spot" in south-east London, leaving the honest inhabitants of that district to thenceforth go about their business in peace. The part I had played in the matter was, of course, a very slight and peripheral one, and yet I do not mind admitting that it gives me a feeling of both pride and satisfaction to know that I played any part in it at all.

The Adventure of THE WILLOW POOL

I: CAPTAIN JOHN REID

MR SHERLOCK HOLMES was always of the opinion that no record of his varied professional career would be complete without an account of the singular case of Captain John Reid of Topley Cross, late of the West Sussex Infantry. It was without question an unusual case, and I should certainly have placed the facts on record long ago, were it not that those intimately concerned in the matter had expressed a specific wish that I not do so. That prohibition having recently been withdrawn, I lay the following narrative before my readers, to remedy the omission. The events I describe occurred in the autumn of the very first year in which I shared chambers with Sherlock Holmes following my return to England from Afghanistan, and just a few weeks after an Army Medical Board had finally determined that I was unlikely ever again to be fit enough to serve my country, and had therefore discharged me from further duty.

The Second Afghan War has already taken its place in the pages of modern history. Drawn unwillingly into a violent fraternal quarrel, in which a simple overture from one side justified one's slaughter in the eyes of the other, the British Army endured great suffering and reversals of fortune before its final triumph settled the matter and restored peace. I have little doubt that many years hence, when the history of the time is written from a longer perspective, the whole campaign will command but a paragraph or two in an account of the period. A vicious conflict, which no one had desired, marked by treachery and double-dealing, in a barren and inhospitable land in which no one had ever wished to set foot, it can scarcely be expected to excite that interest in future generations which other, more glorious, episodes in our military history might command. Yet the very misfortune and hardship that bedevilled the campaign brought forth courage and endurance in our forces such as has never been surpassed, and those who were in Afghanistan during this fateful period are unlikely ever to forget it.

Having been severely wounded at the Battle of Maiwand, where our forces had been outnumbered by ten to one, I was among the first to be sent home to England; but it was not very long before most of my compatriots had followed me, and by the end of April 1881, Afghanistan had been effectively evacuated. It may be imagined with what relief the returning troops set foot once more upon their native turf, with what hopes for rest and the sight of a friendly face they turned their steps towards the towns and villages of their youth. But for one man, at least, that relief proved short-lived and those hopes remained unfulfilled, for when Captain John Reid returned home to the scenes of his childhood, he encountered a hostility there which was, in its way, as implacable and incomprehensible as any he had endured with his companions abroad.

It was a dull, foggy day in October, and I had not ventured out of doors all day. Now, as the afternoon drew on, I stood for a minute at the window and surveyed the dismal scene outside. Like a dull brown sea, the fog swirled slowly about the street and lapped silently at our windowpanes, where it condensed in filthy, oily drops.

With a sigh I returned to the bright fireside and picked up the tedious yellow-backed novel I had been attempting to read before the ache from my old wound had driven me from my chair. Sherlock Holmes was engaged at his chemical bench, in some malodorous experiment that involved the rapid boiling of benzine in a flask, and neither looked up nor spoke as I passed. He had his watch on the table before him, and was clearly timing the process precisely. I watched as he took a pipette and extracted a little of the bubbling liquid. Evidently satisfied, he added a small amount of chemicals to the flask and watched as the liquid became suffused with a vivid violet tint. Smiling to himself, he came to the fireside and took his old brier pipe from the mantelshelf.

"Is your experiment of importance?" I asked.

"Professionally speaking, not at all," returned my companion with a shake of the head. "But it is not one I have performed before, and it is always worthwhile, I find, to verify for oneself the bland pronouncements of textbooks." He took a handful of tobacco from the pewter jar on the shelf, and regarded me for a moment over his pipe. "It is a great pity, Watson," said he at length, "that you and I cannot somehow combine our energies and our work. Between us we might just make one moderately useful citizen."

"Whatever do you mean?" I asked in surprise.

"You are not yourself," said he, "that is plain to see."

"I sometimes fear I never shall be again," I returned with feeling.

"Tut! Tut!" cried Holmes in a tone of admonishment. "You must not speak so! Time and rest will heal, Watson; I am sure of it! But it is clear that at present you are not in the best of health. You lack energy. On the desk I see a pile of foolscap, an atlas and your other books of reference. You desire, as I know, to pen a personal memoir of your time in India, and of the Afghan campaign especially; your work lies waiting for you to begin it, but at the present you simply do not have the energy to make a start. I, on the other hand, am blessed with excellent health and with energy sufficient for two men. But where is my work? Where is that for which I have trained myself for so long?"

"You have had no case lately?" I queried.

"Not a thing," he returned in an emphatic tone. "No case, no clients, no crimes, no puzzles to unravel. As you see, I am reduced to working out a few elementary experiments in chemistry, simply to occupy my mind. When I have finished one, I move on to another."

"In that case, I shall leave you to it," I remarked with a chuckle, rising to my feet. "Your experiments may serve to occupy your mind, Holmes, but they do tend also to occupy one's nose somewhat."

"My dear fellow!" cried he in an apologetic voice, his features expressing dismay. "Do not say I am driving you from the room!"

"Not at all," I returned, smiling at his expression. "You are not to blame for my feeling like a limp rag! I shall put my feet up for half an hour and then I shall be fine." I left him busying himself once more with his test tubes and retorts, and ascended wearily to my bedroom.

The next thing I recall is being shaken by the shoulder. I opened my eyes to find Holmes standing by my bedside, a look of concern upon his face. The room was warm and stuffy, for the window was closed, and a fire was burning in the grate. I had fallen asleep fully clothed, and now, as I awoke, my brow was wet with perspiration.

"I am sorry to disturb you, Watson," said he as I sat up, "but there is a brother officer of yours downstairs."

"What! A friend of mine?"

Holmes shook his head. "He has come to consult me professionally, but he, like you, has lately returned from Afghanistan, and your presence at the interview might prove of assistance."

"Is he ill?" I enquired.

"He is not, perhaps, in the pink of health, but his troubles, I fancy, are more spiritual than physical. He is finding it difficult to describe his circumstances to me. The presence of a brother officer, someone whose experiences are similar to his own, might set him at his ease. But do not feel obliged to come if you do not feel up to it."

"I shall be all right when I have splashed my face with water," I returned, setting my feet upon the floor. "Give me a minute and I shall be with you."

I was intrigued by this invitation. During the year we had shared lodgings together, I had taken a great interest in my companion's work. Indeed, without this interest, my life would have been a solitary and empty one, for I knew very few people in London, and my poor state of health frequently prevented my leaving the house for days on end. But, save in one or two exceptional cases, I had followed Holmes's work only at second hand, and generally knew nothing of a case until it was completed, when he would entertain me by giving me a lively account of it, and of how he had worked his way to its solution. Whenever one of his clients called, my habit, generally speaking, was to absent myself from our shared sitting room. That he should have specifically requested my presence in this instance therefore greatly aroused my curiosity. In a few moments, I had neatened myself up and joined them in the sitting room.

"Captain John Reid, of the West Sussex Infantry," said Holmes, introducing his visitor as I entered.

The man who rose to greet me was of about my own age, tall and spare, with sun-bleached, wavy brown hair and a clean-shaven, weather-beaten face. There was, I thought, something stiff and laboured in his manner, as if he was struggling to master his emotions.

"You have been in Afghanistan, I believe," I remarked as we shook hands.

"Indeed," he replied. Then he turned to my friend. "I do not recall giving you the name of my regiment, Mr Holmes," said he, an expression of curiosity upon his features.

"You did not," returned Holmes, "but your tiepin proclaims as much."

"How very observant of you!" declared our visitor.

"A trifle," returned Holmes. "But, to pass from mere observation to deduction, I perceive that though your regiment is based in Sussex, you have not come up from the country today. I take it you stayed in town last night."

"That is so, but how . . . ?"

"Tut! Tut! Your boots, Captain Reid! Their highly polished condition tells me that you have undertaken no lengthy journey today."

"Indeed not. I stayed last night at my club, the United Infantry in St James's Place. It was there, as I was talking to a Captain Meadowes of the Buffs, that I first heard your name, Mr Holmes. Captain Meadowes informs me that you can solve any problem presented to you."

"Captain Meadowes exaggerates. But, come, let us have the facts of the matter, and we shall see what we can make of them."

"I scarcely know where to begin."

"Is your service in India of any relevance?"

"Possibly," replied our visitor in a hesitant tone.

"Then begin with that. I am sure that Dr Watson, especially, would be most interested to hear it."

"Very well," said Reid. His manner as he began to speak was oddly uncertain and nervous, like that of a man who has lost all confidence in his own judgement; but gradually, as he described his time in Afghanistan and heard a little of mine, a strength and vigour returned to his voice.

"I sailed with the first contingent of my regiment aboard the *Jumna* on the last day of August, 1878," he began. "The remainder followed two weeks later on the *Euphrates*, along with a large number of Northumberland Fusiliers and several companies of Gloucesters. After a week in Bombay we all moved up north, to Peshawur. Things were quiet enough at first, but late in the year there were some heavy engagements, in the Khyber Pass, and at Jelalabad. After that it was calmer for a time, but there was a tension in the air, and we were all aware that trouble might flare up again at any moment. That moment came when Sir Louis Cavagnari was murdered at Cabul in September '79, and all hell broke loose. We were at once placed under the command of Sir Frederick Roberts, who led us at Charasiab, and in the engagements that followed around Cabul. The fighting was severe, and it was many months before things quietened down again and we had full control of the area.

"When news reached us the following August of fighting in the south of the country, and of the dreadful massacre at Maiwand, where I understand you were with the Berkshires, Dr Watson, we set off at once and marched down from Cabul to Candahar to relieve the siege there. As you will know, there was again very heavy fighting before the southern countryside could be considered safe. The West Sussex men did not leave the country until the spring of this year, and my own was practically the last company to do so. Since then we have been on easier duties, around Bombay."

"You have certainly seen your share of action," I remarked.

Our visitor nodded his head in a thoughtful way. "There were moments," said he, "when I think I sincerely believed that Afghanistan was the true location of Hell. And yet," he continued after a moment, "to be hated and attacked by strangers when you at least have your loyal companions about you is not, perhaps, the worst thing that can happen to a man." He paused, but neither Holmes nor I spoke, and after a minute's reflection he continued in a voice which trembled with emotion. "To be hated and abused by those from whom you had expected friendship and affection, and to bear this assault alone, is perhaps the hardest suffering to endure."

"Pray give us the details," said Holmes after a moment, "however painful it may be to do so, and then perhaps we can begin to shed some light on your troubles."

"My family has lived in Sussex for many generations," continued Reid after a moment. "My great-grandfather bought Oakbrook Hall and its estate at the beginning of the century, during the Napoleonic Wars, and there the family has lived ever since. The estate lies just outside Topley Cross, in the west of the county, near Petworth. My father was colonel of the West Sussex Infantry before his retirement, and had, I think, only two further aims in life: to marry off his only daughter, Louisa, successfully, and to see his only son follow him into the local regiment. The former was achieved five years ago, when Louisa married a solicitor from Cornwall, where she now lives, the latter not long afterwards. I joined the regiment four and a half years ago, at the same time as Arthur Ranworth, an old friend from my schooldays in Canterbury, whose home is at Broome Green, near Rye, at the other end of the county.

"In the summer of '78 we were posted to India, as I have described. Before we left, Ranworth frequently came to stay with us at Topley Cross, along with Major French and Major Bastable, friends of ours from the regiment. We always had a splendid time when we were all together, and it was evident to me that my father was as proud of me as any father might be. He has an old friend and neighbour, Admiral Blythe-Headley, who is the largest landed proprietor in the district, and whose property adjoins our own. They are great rivals whenever the respective merits of the Army and Navy are being debated, and I know that my father was particularly proud when he was able to inform his friend that I had followed him into the West Sussex. The situation is a little difficult, as our neighbour's own son, Anthony, who is a couple of years younger than me, seems only to cause distress to his father. At school he was regarded as an outstanding pupil, and showed every promise of a brilliant future. But he took up with a dissolute group of friends at university, and has since wasted his time in idle and frivolous pursuits. It is certainly not for me to judge him, but I know that he and his father have frequently quarrelled violently in recent years, not least when he forged his father's signature against a gambling debt, a matter that nearly came to court.

"Admiral Blythe-Headley, who is a widower, also has a daughter, Mary, who is about my own age, and is, I might say, the local beauty. When I was younger I spent many happy days at Topley Grange, the Blythe-Headley's home, and I remember with fondness the long hours spent playing rounders and other such games with Mary and her cousins. I had always hoped that one day she might join her future to mine, and a few words she spoke to me before I sailed for India led me to believe that my hopes in this regard might not be entirely unjustified. I am mentioning all these things to you so that you will understand that before I went away, everything was as right as could be. My mother, it is true, did not enjoy the best of health, but this had been the case for some years, so that although it was always a source of concern to me, it was not especially so at this time.

"There is splendid fishing in the district, and what with that, turning out for the village cricket team, lending a hand with the harvest, and a hundred and one other things, the summer before I left passed all too quickly. I was obliged to spend some time at regimental headquarters, near Horsham, but Topley Cross being at no great distance from Horsham, I was often able to get away at the end of the week, and I came and went regularly, as did Captain Ranworth. Occasionally, I was obliged to leave Ranworth to find his own amusement, when I was occupied with farming business or in helping my father, but this presented no difficulty for him, for he is almost as familiar with the people and places of the district as I am myself, having been a regular visitor there since our early schooldays. Earlier that year, my father had begun work on a history of the West Sussex Regiment, and had had one of the bedrooms upstairs turned into a study especially for the purpose. He had also engaged a secretary, William Northcote, a scholarly young man recently down from Oxford, to assist him. My father had underestimated the work involved, however, and even with Northcote's help would have found it altogether too much had I not been there to lend a hand. By the time the day of our embarkation arrived, however, he and his secretary had got into a routine and were making good progress. I know my father greatly appreciated the help I had been able to give him. In a letter I received from home a few weeks after my arrival in India, he described how well he and Northcote were now getting on with the work, and how invaluable my assistance had been.

"Half of this letter was written to me by my mother. Alas, it was the last communication I was ever to receive from her! I received two further letters from my father before the end of the year, but then heard nothing more – despite writing several letters myself – until some seven or eight months later. Then I received a brief note from my father, in the form almost of an official notification, to inform me that my mother's illness had at last overcome her and that she had died in the spring. This news saddened me greatly, although it was not, in truth, entirely unexpected. My mother had been in poor health for some years, and I had always feared that she might die while I was abroad. The news was made especially distressing to me, however, by the curt, impersonal character of the note that conveyed it. I replied at once, expressing my sorrow, but received no further communication from home whatever.

"I have given you a sketch of the part I played in the Afghan campaign, so I will not weary you with further details, except to say that no group of men could have acted with more resolution and dedication to duty than did the men of the West Sussex. You may have observed on my tiepin the regimental motto, *Fidus et Audax*. Believe me when I tell you that no men could have been more 'faithful and bold'. Some of my colleagues lost their lives in the campaign, and will not be forgotten; but every man that survived left that accursed country with his honour enhanced, and there is not one among them that does not deserve a decoration. For myself I make no claim to heroic status, but I did believe, as I returned to England, that I would be greeted as one, at least, who had fulfilled his duty to his native land to the fullest extent of his physical and mental capacities. I could not have imagined, on the long voyage home, that I would be met, instead, with cold indifference and contempt. What has happened in recent days has quite turned my brain, so that I feel I am losing my grip upon sanity, and can no longer trust my own thoughts or actions."

Sherlock Holmes frowned. "Pray, continue," said he in a soft voice as his visitor paused. "It is evident that something very strange must have occurred to disturb you in this way."

"The West Sussex Infantry returned to England towards the end of last month," continued Captain Reid after a moment. "I wired home as soon as I landed at Portsmouth, to say that I had arrived back safely and should be home in a few days. To this message I received no reply. I wired again from the regimental headquarters at Horsham on the morning I was leaving, with my time of arrival at the local railway station. When my train pulled in there, however, I saw, to my surprise, that there was no one there to meet me. Fortunately, the station fly was there, and was, I observed, still driven by the same fellow, Isaac Barham, who had often jested with me and teased me in my youth. I greeted him cordially, expecting some rustic witticism in response, or at the very least a smile of recognition. To my utter astonishment, a shudder of distaste seemed to pass across his features as he saw me. In a moment it was gone, and his face was once more impassive, but I knew that I could not have been mistaken.

"'What is it?' said I. 'You look as if you have seen a ghost!'

"He mumbled something in response, which I did not catch, threw my bag aboard and we set off, rattling along the narrow, hilly lanes. Not once did he open his mouth, although once or twice I caught him stealing a glance at me. We passed by fields and hedgerows and wooded dells, all alive with the scents of late summer, and an uprush of joy filled my heart to be home in this beautiful countryside once more.

"'It is good to be back in England,' said I aloud at length, unable to contain my thoughts any longer.

"'Is it?' was his mumbled response.

"'There were times in India when I feared I might never return,' I remarked, ignoring his surly, unfriendly manner.

"'It'd be better if you never had,' said he under his breath.

"'What did you say!' I cried, although I had heard it clear enough, but he just grunted and averted his eyes.

"This greeting, from the first person I had met who knew me was both remarkable and unpleasant, but I thought that Barham had perhaps suffered some personal tragedy recently, which had affected his brain, and I determined not to let it lower my spirits. Our way took us presently through the village of Topley Cross, and as we passed through the market place I saw several people I knew. I raised my arm to wave a greeting as we passed, but they turned away hurriedly, as if in a pretence of not having seen me, although it was perfectly plain that they had. I could conceive of no explanation for this, at least as pertaining to myself, and I wondered if it were Isaac Barham they were shunning. Perhaps, I speculated, my driver's morose and unfriendly manner was the result of some general falling-out between him and the rest of the district.

"Presently, we turned in at the gate of Oakbrook Hall, and as the drive passed between the gnarled old oaks, the tall elms and beeches, all clothed in the colours of autumn, I almost cried aloud, so joyful was I to be home. When we drew up before the Hall, I sprang down from the trap, paid off my surly companion with a sense of relief and hurried indoors.

"There was a stillness and silence about the house that seemed strange to me and was not how I remembered it. For a moment, I stood in the hallway and called, but this elicited no response. I glanced into the library, which is also my father's old study, but there was no one there. At length, I tugged the bell rope in the hall, and Bunning, my father's butler, appeared presently from the back of the house; but when he saw who it was that had summoned him he stopped dead in his tracks and clutched his chest. I thought at first that he was suffering some kind of heart seizure, but when he spoke it was clear to me that it was simply my presence there that troubled him.

"'Master John!' said he in a breathless tone.

"'None other,' said I. 'This is a fine welcome, Bunning, I must say! Is my father not at home?'

"'Colonel Reid is in the upstairs study, sir,' replied he. 'He is engaged upon his manuscript.'

"'I see. Well, kindly inform him, if he can spare a moment, that his son is home from India.' With that I returned to the library in no very good humour. But the library of Oakbrook Hall has always had a soothing effect upon me. There is a serenity there, in the smell of old leather and polish, and on that day these scents were mingled with those of late summer flowers, for the French windows stood open to the garden. I poured myself a glass of sherry from a decanter and emptied my mind of every thought save that of the pleasure I felt just to be there, at home at Oakbrook once more.

"A few minutes later I heard footsteps in the passage. It was not my father who entered the library, however, but his secretary, Northcote. He blinked at me from behind his spectacles, and informed me in his customary nervous, embarrassed manner that my father was indisposed. He had retired to his room, having left strict instructions that he was not to be disturbed, and would see me that evening at dinner.

"It seemed a strange, cold homecoming for one who had travelled so far, and for so long, in the hope of seeing once more his familiar house and home, but there was nothing I could do about it. I occupied myself as best I could for the remainder of the day and, in truth, the exhaustion that I had resisted during my long journey finally swept over me like a wave upon a beach, and I spent long periods of the day asleep on my bed.

"At dinner that night, my father greeted me with a cool formality. He had never been a very expressive man, and it was clear that my mother's death had affected him deeply, and I explained his lack of warmth on those grounds. Also, Northcote was dining with us, which perhaps placed a further constraint upon the conversation. Physically my father seemed much as ever, although his hair had turned white while I had been away, but mentally and spiritually he seemed to have aged by more than the three years I had spent in India. When I ventured to allude to my mother, he brushed aside my remarks and indicated quite clearly that he did not wish the subject to be raised. I told him, then, something of my exploits in Afghanistan, and was rewarded by a spark of interest in his eyes. But soon this spark had faded again, and when I paused for a moment in my account, he did not ask me to continue, but excused himself from the table and left the room.

"This left me alone with Northcote, and I endeavoured to learn from him what had wrought this change in my father's manner.

"'Did you not receive the letter that Colonel Reid sent you at Horsham?' said he.

"I shook my head.

"'No matter,' said he. 'Your father has had many worries, Captain Reid. Your mother's death was a blow from which he has never fully recovered.'

"I would have asked him more about all that had happened in my absence, but at that moment my father returned and summoned his secretary away, saying that he had some work he wished him to do, in connection with tenancy leases on the estate which were up for renewal. As Northcote followed my father from the room, he shot a glance my way, his features expressing confusion and apology. I shook my head slightly to convey to him that I understood the awkward position in which he was placed and would hold nothing against him on account of it. Indeed, I had the distinct impression that my father's true purpose in calling his secretary away was simply to prevent the two of us talking any further. Whatever the reason, I was thus left utterly alone in the silent dining room, upon the day of my return from the Afghan War.

"The following morning I had a letter from Horsham, which I opened while I was waiting, alone, for breakfast. It was from the regimental post office, and merely contained the letter from my father, which had arrived there the previous day, just after I had left. Intrigued, I opened this second envelope. Inside was a brief note above my father's signature. There was no word of greeting and just two lines of writing: 'It is better that you do not come home. Kindly make other arrangements. I have let it be thought in the district that you are dead.'

"For a long moment, I stared in stupefied disbelief at this message. Then I read those two lines over and over and over again as I paced the floor of the dining room, unable to believe that I had understood them correctly. What on earth could it mean? Why should my father, so proud when I sailed for India with the regiment, now think so little of me as to prefer that his neighbours think me dead? He wrote as if he were deeply ashamed of me, but there was no conceivable reason why he should be. I had certainly not given either him or the regiment any cause to regard me with shame. Could it be that there was something dishonourable I had done which had entirely passed from my memory? That was surely inconceivable. Or had I done something the significance of which I had not realized? I racked my brains until my mind reeled with the effort, but could think of nothing that might explain the matter.

"I determined there and then to have it out with my father, but my purpose was thwarted, as he kept to his own room and sent word that he was indisposed. I then remembered that my friend, Captain Ranworth, was arriving for a visit by the late morning train, as we had earlier arranged, and I hastened to the railway station to meet him. When I described to him the difficult situation at home, he was all for cancelling the visit altogether, but I insisted he stay for one night at least. As I drove the trap back through Topley Cross, it seemed to me that the eyes of the villagers bored into my back as we passed. Ranworth, too, could sense that something was wrong, but could suggest no explanation. After lunch, which we ate alone, Ranworth took himself off for a walk over the neighbouring countryside. It was clear he felt uncomfortable at the odd situation in which he found himself, and did not wish by his presence to add to my difficulties. For a while I sat alone, but eventually I could bear the silence no longer, and made up my mind that I would walk over to Topley Grange, the home of our friends, the Blythe-Headleys.

"It was a beautiful autumn afternoon as I stepped out across the fields, and I was glad to be out of doors and away from the house. The sun was shining brightly in a sky of blue, bathing the countryside in its warm golden light, and all along the hedgerows of the bare ploughed fields the hips and haws glowed a vivid red. But this beauty, which would on another day have thrilled my very soul, now served only to make my predicament seem yet stranger and more disturbing. What place had I in all this beauty, a man whom others would prefer were dead?

"About a mile north of Oakbrook Hall, at the boundary with the Topley Grange estate, there is a narrow, steep-sided little valley in which lies a small spinney known as Jenkin's Clump. A public footpath runs up the valley, from the Topley Cross road, over the hill to Belham Green, and in my younger days Jenkin's Clump had always been a popular spot with the local boys. I myself passed many a long summer's day there as a boy, in climbing trees, pretending to track wild animals like a Red Indian and suchlike games. Down through this wooded valley meanders a stream, and in the very centre of the spinney lies a long, narrow rushy pool, overhung for about half its circumference by graceful weeping willows, and known, in consequence, as the Willow Pool.

"My childhood memories of the place are of the woods ringing with boyish laughter; but now, as I began to make my way down the steeply sloping path through the trees towards the pool, I was conscious only of a great silence and stillness about me, so that my own footsteps upon the woodland floor and through the fallen leaves seemed an almost impertinent intrusion. No doubt my mood suggested strange fancies to my mind, but it seemed to me then that the stillness was like the stillness of death, the silence the silence of the grave. All at once, however, my solitary brooding thoughts were interrupted by a sudden rustling sound ahead of me, and a young man stepped out from behind a clump of bushes, down near the bottom of the path. He was not looking in my direction, but I recognized him at once as Noah Blogg, a slow-witted youth who lives with his family in Topley Cross. I know the family well, for his father, old Jack Blogg, has been the best bat in the village cricket team for nearly thirty years. It is Noah's habit to wander here and there without apparent purpose, and to appear without forewarning wherever he is least expected. He endures some gentle teasing from the local men, but this is unfair of them, for though a simpleton, he is a good-hearted lad and quite harmless. I called to him and he turned. I was perfectly prepared for his not recognizing me after my three years' absence, but what I could not have expected was the awful look of fear, which came like a spasm upon his face as he saw me. His eyes opened wide and his mouth fell open, as if I were a demon from the underworld, then with a shriek he turned and ran, his footsteps crashing away through the undergrowth.

"I quickened my pace and hurried down the hill. When I reached the bottom of the dell, where the public footpath runs alongside the stream, I peered to left and right, but there was no sign of Noah anywhere. My spirits had scarcely been improved by this strange encounter, as you will imagine, but I tried to put it from my mind as I continued my walk across the stream, up the hill on the other side, and so on to the Topley Grange estate. As I emerged from the woods, I descried a figure in the distance, on the brow of a hill, and thought at first that it was Noah Blogg, but saw in a moment that it was in fact my friend, Captain Ranworth, striding out vigorously. I called to him, but he was too far away and did not hear.

"The way from Jenkin's Clump towards Topley Grange passes over steeply undulating terrain, and as I surmounted a ridge a little further on, I could see the house in the distance, somewhat below me. To the side of the house, surrounded by a high brick wall, is the Topley Grange rosary, which is famous for its collection of old roses. There, in an alley between the rose bushes, I espied a young lady in a white dress, with a wide-brimmed straw bonnet upon her head. My heart leapt at the sight, for I knew that it must be Mary Blythe-Headley, and I pressed on with increased speed. Even as I saw her she seemed to turn and look in my direction, but I was still a long way off, and I could not say whether she had seen me or not. The path I was following descended steeply after that, and for a time Topley Grange passed from my view. When next I had a clear sight of it, neither the young lady in the white dress, nor anyone else, was anywhere to be seen.

"When I reached the house, I was shown into the drawing room, where I waited for some time. Presently the servant who had admitted me returned with the information that Miss Blythe-Headley was not at home. I was struck speechless by this, for I felt certain it was quite untrue. My mind reeled. What was the meaning of it? Why should she avoid me in this way? I had waited so many years to see her again, and invested so much hope in our reunion, that this conclusion rendered me almost senseless. For several minutes I stood in the drawing room in silence, quite unable to think what to say or do, then the servant asked if he might show me out, and I followed him meekly, in silence, to the door. It was then, for the first time, that I began to doubt my own sanity. Had I really seen Mary in the garden, or had the whole scene been merely a product of my own fevered imagination? Were any of these strange events really happening as I believed, or were they all but episodes in a chaotic and evil dream? I no longer felt confident in my ability to distinguish between reality and fantasy.

"Scarcely aware of what I was doing, I walked slowly round to the side of the house and into the rosary. There, on a low wooden stool between two rows of bushes, was a shallow basket containing gardening scissors, a pair of stout gloves and half a dozen cut blooms. Someone had certainly been there recently, cutting flowers. But I was unsure, quite frankly, whether that made my situation better or worse. Then a gardener appeared round the end of the row of bushes and, seeing me, hurried away with a look of concern upon his face. Whether he intended to inform his master that a stranger was loitering in his garden, or was merely frightened at the very sight of me, I did not know, but I did not linger to discover the answer. I made my way out of the garden through a gateway in the wall, and round to a little summer house that stands outside the garden wall, at the top of a long gentle slope, from which there is a wonderful view across the countryside to the Downs. Inside this pretty little structure, about which roses climb and ramble, there is a wooden bench upon which I had often sat with Mary and our other friends in sunny summers past. Now I sat there all alone, at my wits' end and feeling more forlorn than I had ever felt in my life before. What was happening to me seemed utter madness. I could hardly suppose, however, that all others in the parish had lost their wits at the very same moment, and could only conclude, therefore, that it was I who had slipped into insanity. But if this were so, why did no one tell me?

"Of course, such thoughts reached no sensible conclusion, but followed each other round in an endless spiral. Presently, I heard someone approaching, and then the sound of voices from the garden, over the wall behind the summer house, so I thought I had best be off. When I had gone some distance down the hill, I glanced back and saw that my progress was being observed by two men standing in the gateway of the rosary, but I was too far off by then to make out who they were.

"That evening at dinner, my father questioned Captain Ranworth about his Indian experiences, but it was clear that it cost him some effort to do so, and he soon made an excuse and left the table, requesting that Northcote accompany him to his study. When they had left us I described to Ranworth my experiences at Topley Grange. He was as amazed as I was by the strange reception I had been afforded there.

"'That is really too bad,' said he. 'Whatever can they mean by such behaviour? I am sure you are correct, Reid, by the way, and that both Miss Blythe-Headley and her father were at home this afternoon, for I believe I saw them in the gardens there while I was on my walk.'

"I made up my mind then. I would leave with Ranworth in the morning, travel up to London and stay a few nights at my club. Incredible though it seemed to be leaving so quickly the home to which I had yearned for so long to return, I could think of no other recourse. It was evident that for reasons I could not begin to imagine I was not welcome there, nor, it appeared, anywhere else in the district.

"The following morning at breakfast, a long buff envelope lay beside my plate. I picked it up full of curiosity, for I observed from the postmark that it had been posted locally the day before, and I did not recognize the hand that had addressed it. Before I could open it, however, there came a terrible cry from my father as he opened a letter of his own. He stood up from the table, his face grey and drawn, and I sprang up in alarm and approached him, for he appeared in the grip of a seizure; but with a feeble gesture of his arm he waved me away.

"'Leave me!' cried he in a frail, hoarse voice. 'You have dishonoured your home; you have disgraced the name and reputation of your family; you have broken your mother's heart and driven her to an early grave; you have estranged me from all my friends in the district, and still you are not satisfied!' I opened my mouth to speak, but he threw down the letter he had received onto the table, turned his back on me and walked from the room in silence.

"I glanced across at Ranworth, whose face was horror-struck at the scene he had witnessed. 'I must apologize profoundly for intruding upon your family troubles,' said he in a strained voice.

"'Not at all, Ranworth,' said I in as careless a manner as I could muster. 'It is I who should beg your forgiveness for inflicting such a business upon you.' I picked up from the table the letter my father had cast down. It was from his old friend Admiral Blythe-Headley, and was in the form of an account. 'To repair of wooden seat in garden pavilion, deliberately damaged by your son,' I read, 'including timber etc: seven shillings and sixpence.'

"I passed the letter to Ranworth and his mouth fell open in surprise.

"'What on earth does it mean?' cried he.

"'I have no idea,' said I. 'I have damaged nothing.'

"'I am sure you would not do such a thing deliberately, Reid,' said he, after a moment's thought, 'but is it possible that you could have accidentally damaged the seat and not realized what you had done?'

"'That is impossible,' I replied, 'unless I have become unaware of my own actions, which I take it you are not suggesting.' As I spoke, I opened the envelope that had been addressed to me. Inside was a single, folded sheet of coarse paper. This was blank, save for two large, printed letters: 'S. D.' Folded within the sheet, however, was— "

Captain Reid broke off abruptly, reached into his inside pocket and drew out an envelope. "Here," said he. "You may as well see it for yourselves."

He passed the envelope to Sherlock Holmes, who examined it for a moment.

"The address is in a somewhat uncultured hand," said he, then let out a cry of surprise as he took out the sheet from within and unfolded it, for upon it lay a pure white feather, which slipped from the paper and floated to the floor.

"A white feather," said Reid in a weak, broken voice, as I picked it up: "the worst insult a man can receive: the symbol of cowardice."

"It has certainly been used for that purpose on occasion," remarked Holmes in a matter-of-fact voice as he examined the sheet of paper that had enclosed the feather. "It does not always bear such a meaning, however, but is used sometimes to indicate other personal failings. Do the initials S. D. mean anything to you, Captain Reid?"

"Nothing whatever."

"They are not the initials of any man known to you in your regiment?"

"No."

"Nor anyone at Topley Cross?"

"Not that I can recall."

Holmes nodded his head, then sat for some time in silence, his brow drawn into a frown of concentration.

"The incident of the feather completes your account, I take it," said he at length. "Very good," he continued, as his visitor nodded his head. "Let us now review one or two points. First of all, are you absolutely certain, Captain Reid, that nothing occurred during your time in India that might, however unjustly, reflect badly upon you? I need hardly say that you must speak with the utmost candour and completeness if we are to help you. You need not fear that anything you say will pass beyond this room."

"I quite understand. But I can assure you that it occasions no difficulty for me to speak frankly of my period of military service. The events are as I detailed to your friend earlier. I would add, only as you have asked me to be complete, that I was mentioned by name in dispatches several times, was promoted, recommended for decoration more than any other man in the regiment, and have heard in confidence from Colonel Finch that I am to be breveted Major before our next overseas posting."

"Splendid!" said Holmes. "I am very glad to hear it! Now, if you will cast your mind back once more to the time immediately preceding your departure for India. Is there any incident you can recall that occurred then, however trivial, which struck you as odd, or unusual, or unexplained?"

Our visitor did not reply at once, but remained for some time with his eyes closed and his brow furrowed in thought. At length he opened his eyes and shook his head.

"I can recall nothing of the sort," said he.

"Has there ever before been any animosity shown to you or to your family, by anyone in the district?"

"I do not believe so. Topley Cross is generally a peaceful, harmonious little parish. I have never found there to be any significant ill-feeling there, directed either at us or at anyone else. We did have a windowpane broken one evening at Oakbrook Hall, just the week before I sailed, but I don't believe that any ill-feeling lay behind it."

"How did it occur?"

Reid shook his head. "I cannot be certain. Someone threw a stone through the window of the upstairs study. Who it was, we never discovered. One of the gardeners had reported seeing some of the village boys loitering in the orchard, earlier in the evening. He had told them to help themselves to a windfall apiece and then clear off. No doubt they returned later, when the gardener had gone, and were throwing stones, as boys do. I doubt very much that the breakage was deliberate, though. They are not bad lads, on the whole. Anyway, my father did not pursue the matter."

"Was the window that was broken situated on the same side of the house as the orchard?" asked Holmes.

"No. The orchard lies to the north of the house; my father's upstairs study is on the south side."

"Was there anyone in the room at the time?"

"No. We were all down at dinner."

Holmes nodded. "Admiral Blythe-Headley's garden seat, now," he continued after a moment, "do you know in what way it was damaged?"

Again our visitor shook his head.

"I have no idea. His note did not specify."

"Do you believe that the seat was in good order when you were in the summer house, earlier that day?"

"I am sure that it was."

"So whatever the damage was, it was done after you had been there. That would have been at about three o'clock, I take it."

"That is correct."

"But the damage must have been done before the evening, as there was evidently sufficient time after its discovery for Admiral Blythe-Headley to write the note to your father which was delivered at Oakbrook Hall the following morning. Why do you suppose they believed you responsible for the damage?"

"I really have not the faintest notion," said Reid.

"Well, well. Perhaps it was simply that you had been seen there and no one else had. No doubt that seemed clear enough evidence from their point of view. Hum! It is certainly a tangled skein that you have presented us with, Captain Reid!"

"The whole business does indeed seem utterly incredible and inexplicable as I sit here speaking of it," remarked our visitor with a puzzled shake of the head. "I could not be more dumbfounded if I had returned from India to find that the man in the moon had lately arrived in England and been proclaimed king. The behaviour of my family and friends towards me seems to admit of only one conclusion: either they are insane, or I am."

"Tut! Tut!" said Holmes quickly in remonstrance. "Do not entertain such debilitating thoughts, Captain Reid. If the problem is to be solved, we must assume as a premise in our little chain of logical reasoning that all parties concerned are acting rationally, as they see the situation. Let us turn now to the letters you received from home when you were overseas. You cannot recall anything there that might shed light on the matter?"

Captain Reid shook his head. "As a matter of fact, I received very few letters during my time abroad. I received one from my mother and father fairly soon after I arrived in India, as I mentioned before, a second and third a little later from my father, and then heard nothing more from home until the brief note informing me of my mother's death, after which I again heard no more. I received a single letter from Miss Blythe-Headley soon after my arrival. I replied to it promptly, but had no further communication from her. I also received three letters from my sister, Louisa, at very long intervals. Her letters were the only ones I received during my final two years in India."

"And you are certain that none of these letters contained any information which might have a bearing on your present situation?"

"No. They were all friendly and consisted almost entirely of quite trivial news."

"I see. Well, whatever the quality of the letters you received, which is, of course, a matter of which only you can judge, their quantity would, I feel, strike even the most casual observer as somewhat on the meagre side, considering the length of time you were away. Did this infrequency of communication cause you any surprise, Captain Reid?"

"Not with regard to my sister, Louisa, for she has always been a notoriously poor correspondent; but with regard to the others it certainly did. I am sure that there was scarcely another man in the regiment who received so few letters. Each time there was a delivery, I would enquire if there was anything for me, and generally I would be disappointed. My friend Ranworth was given charge of postal matters for our battalion, following an injury to Major Bastable, and I fear that he eventually became quite disconcerted by my constant queries. It embarrasses me now to recall the many times I obliged him to shake his head apologetically, as I enquired yet again if any letter had arrived for me."

"India is, of course, a vast place," remarked Holmes, "and with the troops being so widely scattered, especially during the Afghan campaign, I suppose it is possible that letters might sometimes go astray?"

"No doubt it happens occasionally, but the Army postal service is remarkably efficient, all things considered. I am sure I should eventually have received any letter which had been sent to me."

"No doubt. You have not seen your sister since your return?"

"No. I had been looking forward with pleasure to visiting Louisa and her family in Truro, but under the present circumstances I have decided to postpone it. I should not wish to inflict these difficulties upon them."

"Quite so. Do you know if your sister paid any visits to Oakbrook Hall while you were in India?"

"She returned very briefly for our mother's funeral, which she subsequently described to me. Apart from that occasion, she has not left Cornwall in the last three years, so far as I am aware."

"I see," said Holmes, nodding his head in a thoughtful manner. "Now," he continued after a moment, "how do you propose to spend the next few days, Captain Reid?"

"I shall be at my club for two more nights. On the thirteenth I am going down to stay with Captain Ranworth at Broome Green, and may be there a week."

"His address, if you please," said Holmes, opening his notebook. "I may need to write to you there."

"You will take the case, then?"

"Certainly."

"It is, as you will understand, a very delicate affair."

"Most are which are brought to my attention."

"It is such a personal, family matter that I should never have given details of it to a stranger were it not that I am utterly at my wits' end."

"I understand that perfectly," said Holmes. "You have acted wisely. I shall go down to West Sussex tomorrow and make a few discreet enquiries."

Captain Reid shook his head, an expression of perplexity upon his features. "I cannot think that there is anything you can learn which would explain the nightmare in which I have dwelt in recent days. The circumstances must surely be unique."

"They are certainly unusual," remarked Holmes, "but not, I think, unique. There is little in this world that is truly unique, I find. I shall communicate with you in a few days' time, Captain Reid. Until then, remember your regimental motto, *Fidus et Audax*, and do not despair."

When our visitor had left us, Holmes lit his pipe, and sat for some time in silence, then he turned to me with a smile.

"A very pretty little puzzle, Watson, would you not agree?" said he in the tones of a connoisseur, his eyes sparkling. "What would you say to a few days in the pleasant Sussex countryside?"

"Why, there is nothing I should like better than to exchange the London reek for the fresh air of the Downs," I returned, more than a little surprised at the question. "But would my presence there not hamper your investigation, Holmes?"

"On the contrary," said he. "It would be a great convenience to me to have a companion upon whom I can rely as events unfold, as I am certain they will. I have no doubt that Captain Reid will be more than willing to defray your expenses as well as mine if it means his problem is the more speedily solved."

"Then I accept your invitation with pleasure," said I.

II: IN QUEST OF A SOLUTION

In the morning a fresh breeze was blowing. A few wraiths of fog still hung about the streets as we made our way to the railway station, but by the time our train had passed Croydon and was through the North Downs the mist had cleared from the fields and the sun was shining. Wrapped in a long grey cloak, and with a close-fitting cloth cap upon his head, my companion appeared the very picture of the rural traveller, which was a strange sight to one who had only ever seen him upon the bustling pavements of London. He had scarcely spoken since we left Victoria, but stared silently from the window, completely absorbed in his own thoughts.

"I cannot imagine how you intend to proceed in the case, Holmes," I remarked at length, breaking the silence in the compartment. "The mystery surrounding Captain Reid appears utterly inexplicable."

"There are one or two indications," responded my friend, turning from the window and beginning to fill his pipe.

"If there are, then I confess I have missed them."

"You have no doubt been pondering the matter overnight," said he.

"I have certainly given it some thought," I returned, "but can make nothing of it. It seems to me to be perfectly impenetrable!"

"Let us apply a little logical analysis, then," said my friend as he lit his pipe, "and let our starting point be the one thing we know for certain: that the entire parish of Topley Cross appears, for some reason, to have turned against our client. We do not yet know what this reason might be, so let us, in the manner of mathematicians, call it 'x', the unknown, and see if we cannot, by reasoning around it, succeed in defining it a little more precisely. In the first place, whatever it is that has caused all these people to alter their opinions of Captain Reid must be considered by them a most serious matter. For surely only an occurrence of the utmost seriousness could have led them all – including, of course, Reid's own father – to act in the way that they have done."

"Well, that is fairly obvious," I agreed.

"Yet Reid himself disclaims all knowledge of such an occurrence. Now, if the matter in question pertained to his military career, he would surely have heard something of it from his fellow officers in the regiment. We are therefore led to the conclusion that our unknown 'x' occurred in West Sussex, in the parish of Topley Cross. This is also indicated by the fact that whereas letters to Captain Reid from Topley Cross practically ceased after a short time, those from his sister in Cornwall did not. We must take it that she knows no more of the matter than her brother, and that during her stay at Oakbrook Hall at the time of her mother's funeral, it – whatever it is – was not mentioned in her presence. As to 'x' itself, we must suppose that the facts of the matter are very clear, with evidence which appears to implicate Captain Reid directly, for we cannot think that his friends and family would turn against him on account, merely, of casual hearsay or local gossip."

"That seems indisputable."

"But here we encounter a difficulty. For it seems that when Captain Reid departed the area for India, his reputation was unblemished, his character unstained."

"Whatever occurred, then," I suggested, "must have occurred after he had left."

"But how, then, can it reflect badly on Captain Reid? You see the difficulty, Watson? Clearly, it is not the date of the incident itself which is important, but the date when the facts came to light. Something occurred while Reid was still in England – otherwise he could not possibly be blamed for it – but did not become public knowledge until after he had departed, otherwise he would have become aware of it before ever he left the country. We can, I feel, date these events quite precisely. He received a friendly letter from Miss Blythe-Headley soon after his arrival in India. This must have been written within a week or so of his leaving. He replied, but heard nothing more. Some matter therefore came to public attention in Topley Cross approximately two weeks after his departure. We have thus narrowed down the place and the time quite precisely."

"I cannot see that that helps us very much."

"On the contrary, it helps us a great deal. To have established the place and time so closely will save us wasting our energies in irrelevant enquiry, and will undoubtedly help us to reach the truth much more speedily than would otherwise have been the case. Now we must address the nature of the problem itself."

"There, I fear, we have nothing whatever to help us," I observed. "Captain Reid has no idea what it is he is supposed to have done, and as no one, it seems, is prepared to tell him, we have nowhere to begin."

"Come, come," said my companion, smiling, "the matter is not quite so featureless as you suggest. In the first place, it cannot be that our client is believed guilty of an act that is criminal, or otherwise illegal, for we may suppose that if that were so, he would have long since been made aware of the fact by the authorities. Nor, on the other hand, can the matter be a trivial one, which might be soon forgiven and forgotten, since he remains subject to obloquy three years after the supposed date of the incident. Clearly, the censure to which he is subject is moral censure. We must therefore seek an act or series of acts which are generally held to be morally reprehensible – and seriously so – but which are not criminal in the strict legal sense of that term."

"That leaves rather a wide field," I remarked with a chuckle. "Most people's idea of morality covers a very broad sweep of miscellaneous virtues and vices, great and small, but save for its sound provisions against murder and theft, the law of England chooses to concern itself with very few of them."

"A wide field it may be," returned Holmes, "but it is also an interesting field for speculation. We have also, let us not forget, the mysterious initials S. D. to help us in our enquiry. But, come! This next station is Pulborough, where we must take the branch-line train."

The countryside through which the branch railway passed was a delight to the eye. On either side lay a multi-coloured patchwork of fields, and between them the bright autumnal hues of the hedgerows and spinneys. As if he had said all that he wished to say of his case for the moment, my companion began then to discuss the farming methods of the land's first settlers, drawing numerous interesting observations to support his thesis from the landscape through which we were passing. He spoke almost as if he had made a special study of the subject, which surprised me very greatly, for I had never before heard him speak of anything save the ways of the denizens of London, and I had come to believe that his brain contained only such knowledge as was directly useful to his work, and which had its application strictly within a dozen miles of Charing Cross.

Presently, as our train pulled into a little rural station, its platforms brightened by tubs of flowers, Holmes sprang to his feet.

"Here I must leave you," said he abruptly, much to my surprise. "The station for Topley Cross is the next but one, Watson. Take care of the bags, if you would, old fellow, and see if you can secure a couple of acceptable rooms at the best-looking inn you can find. I shall join you there later this afternoon."

With no further word of explanation my companion was gone; the carriage door slammed behind him, and I was left to continue the journey alone. I did as he asked and took two rooms at the White Hart, a large, handsome old inn, which stood in the marketplace of Topley Cross. Then, I regret to record, although it was a beautiful autumn day, and I longed to walk to the end of the village and explore the countryside there, my illness overcame me. Tired by the journey from London, I lay exhausted upon my bed and soon fell into a deep sleep.

I was awakened by a tugging at my shoulder. Holmes was standing by my bed.

"I have made progress," said he. "I have ordered a pot of tea, if you would care to come downstairs and hear the details."

In a minute I was in the private sitting room of the inn and Holmes was giving me a sketch of what he had discovered.

"I have spent some time in the office of the local weekly newspaper," said he, "where I was able to study the editions of three years ago. My hope was that I might uncover some suggestive fact there, some clue, however slight, to Captain Reid's problem. I was prepared for a long and possibly fruitless search, and certainly could not have expected that success would be so swift. So narrowly, however, had we managed to define the time of that which has caused our client so much difficulty – our unknown 'x' – that in a matter of but a few minutes I was satisfied I had identified it beyond all possible doubt." He took a long folded sheet of paper from his pocket and spread it out on the table before him, before continuing: "Upon Tuesday, 10 September 1878 – that is less than two weeks after Captain Reid sailed for India – a local girl, twenty years of age and well-known in Topley Cross, where she lived with her parents, was found dead. She had drowned in a pond about a mile from the village. Her name, Watson, was Sarah Dickens."

"S. D.!" I cried. "Those were the initials in the letter Reid received!"

"Precisely. The stretch of water in which she drowned, incidentally, was the 'Willow Pool', to which Reid referred yesterday. Her body was discovered by two local youths, who were passing along the footpath that skirts the pool. So far as I can make out from the newspaper reports, the girl was from traditional yeoman stock. She was not especially beautiful, nor especially intellectual, but had a simple charm that endeared her to all who knew her. The reports describe her as friendly, good-hearted and very popular in the district. Now, at the inquest, which was held a few days later in Topley Cross, the verdict recorded was that of accidental death. There was no mark upon the body, save a small bruise to the side of the head, and it was suggested that the girl had slipped from the bank while picking blackberries – her purpose, apparently, in being at that spot – had fallen into the water, and had struck her head on a submerged stone. However, to judge from the tone of some of the newspaper reports, it was widely suspected in the district that the girl had in fact taken her own life while in a state of extreme distress. As you are no doubt aware, Watson, coroners' juries are notoriously reluctant to bring in a verdict of suicide, save in those cases where the evidence admits of no other conclusion. This is especially so in rural areas, when the deceased is often someone well known to the jurors."

"Was there any specific evidence that might have suggested the girl had deliberately taken her own life?"

"Her family deposed that she had not seemed quite herself for a week or two, and had taken to wandering off alone, as she had done on the day she died. When questioned during the inquest, they stated that she had been in somewhat better spirits on the day of her death, but this was not confirmed by other witnesses, and it seems likely that the observation was made chiefly to influence the jury against a verdict of suicide.

"It seems there was a man in the case somewhere – the old story, by the sound of it – but he is not named in any of the newspaper reports, and it is not clear from the reports if his identity was known to anyone. A note was found, which the girl had apparently written shortly before her death, in which she had expressed her anguish at being cast aside by this man. Her family confirmed that she had been seeing someone during the summer, but stated that they did not know who it was."

"Is the man not named in the note she left?" I asked.

"It would appear not. The tone of the note, to judge from the newspaper report, was one of melancholy distress, and it seems that the man she had been seeing had thrown her over. But the court was clearly of the opinion that the note was by way of being an epistle to herself, a record on paper of her own thoughts, and did not constitute a suicide note of any kind, otherwise the verdict would undoubtedly have been different."

"It appears the very epitome of a rural tragedy," I observed with a sigh. "One cannot doubt that it is, as you say, the old story: young, simple, innocent country girl, her affections captured by the attentions of a man, perhaps older and more sophisticated than herself, who later drops her without a care."

My friend nodded. "In which case, although not guilty of any crime in the eyes of the law, strictly speaking, the man in question would be widely held to bear some responsibility for the girl's death, whether she took her own life or lost it accidentally while in a state of distress. He would thus be subject to the very severest moral condemnation from all who knew of the case. There is little doubt in my mind, Watson, that this is the dishonourable act of which our client stands condemned in the eyes of the district. They will see in the dashing young officer and simple peasant girl the very type of one of the oldest tales known to man. He has sailed away to foreign lands, leaving her desolate, and, in her own eyes at least, ruined. And yet . . ."

Holmes broke off and stared for a moment at his untouched tea.

"And yet," he continued at length, "Captain Reid expresses astonishment at the reception he has been afforded upon his return and can make nothing of it. He is an intelligent man, and could not have failed to realize the meaning of it were he really guilty of this moral lapse."

"He did not recognize the initials S. D. in the letter he received," I observed.

"Indeed. He may know something of the girl, however, as she lived locally, without, perhaps, recalling her name. I have wired to him at his club on the matter, in the hope that seeing her name will stir his memory. I hope to receive a reply shortly."

Holmes had not long to wait, for within the hour a messenger arrived with a telegram for him. Eagerly, he tore open the envelope and scanned the contents, then passed it to me.

"Name you mention that of local girl," I read. "Bade good morning. Carried basket once or twice. Not seen since return. Ask Yarrow."

"It appears he is unaware of the girl's death," I observed.

"So it would seem. I wonder—" He broke off as the innkeeper entered the room. "Could you tell me, landlord," he asked, "who Mr Yarrow might be?"

"Why, sir, that's the vicar," returned the man in surprise.

"Oh, of course," said Holmes, smiling. "How foolish of me. I think I shall go to see him now, Doctor, while it is still light!" With that he stood up, put on his hat and was gone.

"Is your friend interested in the Roman remains?" asked the innkeeper of me when Holmes had left us.

"Among other things," I replied, judging it best not to reveal our true purpose in being there. "Why do you ask?"

"The last gentlemen down here from London were from the British Museum, come to study the remains," he explained. "The Reverend Yarrow is the local expert."

He produced a small pamphlet on the subject, which Mr Yarrow had written. It was certainly a very thorough account. But fascinating though the subject was, I found my mind wandering constantly from its explication of ancient mysteries to the more pressing mystery which had brought us to Sussex, so that I was still only upon the second page of the pamphlet when Holmes returned, just as the daylight was fading. He ordered two glasses of beer and lit his pipe before he described to me what he had managed to learn from the vicar.

"I found Mr Henry Yarrow a very pleasant, middle-aged man," he began. "He received me with every courtesy, and appears to have as good a grasp of all that occurs in the parish as anyone could have. He is highly intelligent and well-educated, Watson, and I should say a little out of place in such a rural backwater as Topley Cross. Such free time as he has he fills with intellectual pursuits, and he is a great pamphleteer: he has produced numerous monographs on such subjects as local antiquities, the flora and fauna of the district, and the parish church, which, he informs me, is one of the oldest in the county. At present, he is labouring on a history of the sheep breeds of West Sussex. However, to return to more pertinent matters: he knows Captain Reid very well, and it is clear that he holds him in the very highest regard. Indeed, so sincere were his expressions of affection for our client that I ventured to lay before him the whole matter, in the hope that he could shed some light upon it. You have often seen me work out a case, Watson, from such things as the measurement of footprints, or the traces of mud upon a man's trouser knee, but I am not averse to taking a more direct route when it offers itself. In this case, my confidence was rewarded. The vicar shook his head in sympathy when I described to him all that had befallen Captain Reid since his return from India.

"'If only he had come to me last week,' said he. 'I could at least have explained to him the likely source of his troubles, if not their solution.'

"He confirmed what we had surmised, that rumours have circulated ever since the death of Sarah Dickens that Reid was the cause of her sorrow and despair. He assured me that he gave no credit to these rumours himself, but having had no countervailing information, had been unable to combat the prevalent belief. 'I have always found,' said he with feeling, 'that an evil rumour is quite the most difficult of opponents to destroy: like the hydra of classical mythology it is a many-headed beast: cut off one head and another seven will spring up in its place.' I concurred with this opinion, and asked if he knew anything of the rumour's origins.

"'I cannot be certain,' said he, 'but the dead girl's brother, John, has undoubtedly played some part in it. If he did not originate the rumour, he has at least contributed to it, and to no small extent.' This brother, Yarrow informed me, had been extremely distressed by his sister's death, and treasures the note that the girl left, both as a memento of his sister and as an indictment against the man he believes treated her so ill. I asked the vicar then if he had any knowledge of the content of the note.

"'Indeed,' said he, 'for it was I that found it.'

"This was news indeed, Watson, for I had assumed from the reports in the newspaper that the note had been found among the dead girl's belongings at her home, probably by one of the family. I asked the vicar how he had come upon it.

"'It was on the day following the girl's death,' he explained. 'Her mother expressed a wish to visit the place at which the girl's body had been found, and asked me if I would accompany her. I of course agreed to this request, and the two of us walked up to that fateful spot at the Willow Pool. It was while we were there that I chanced to observe a crumpled sheet of paper lying among the brambles by the water's edge and, with some difficulty, managed to retrieve it. We had missed it the previous evening, which is not surprising. The light had almost faded by the time we eventually recovered the girl's body from the water.'

"'Did the finding of the note at the scene of her death not tend to confirm the suspicion that the girl had taken her own life?' I asked him, but he shook his head.

"'It was not a suicide note,' said he with emphasis. 'I should be more inclined to describe it as a rhetorical address to the man that had wronged her. The general opinion, with which I agreed, was that the poor girl had probably been reading the note to herself and reflecting upon it when she lost her footing and slipped into the water. As to the note itself,' he continued, 'I can recall its contents clearly, even though it is three years since last I saw it. The phrases it contained were just such as one might imagine a young country girl to use: "I trusted you and you betrayed me. I loved you and you used me". Need I say more, Mr Holmes?'

"I shook my head, for I could see that it caused him some pain to recall this distressing matter. 'Why do you suppose that everyone believed Captain Reid to be the man who broke this young girl's heart?' I asked him after a moment.

"'I cannot say for certain,' he returned. 'It may be that something the girl had previously said to her family suggested it to them. It cannot have been any more than a suggestion, however, for I know that they had no more definite knowledge as to the man's identity than anyone else. Reid had certainly spoken to the girl on many occasions. He is an exceptionally affable young man and was on conversational terms with almost everyone in the parish, irrespective of their rank or station. He also played regularly in the village cricket matches before his overseas posting, and as Sarah Dickens often helped with the refreshments on those occasions, no doubt the two of them came into contact then.'

"'He also mentioned carrying her basket for her once or twice.'

"'Ah, yes,' responded Yarrow. 'He may have done so many times, for all I can say, but on the occasion I recall, which occurred in the summer before he left for India, he and I were walking down the road from Oakbrook Hall to the village when we overtook Sarah Dickens, heavily laden with large baskets of fruit – plums, as I recall – which she had picked at one of the outlying farms. We naturally each took a basket to relieve her of some of her burden. At the church I left them, and the two walked on into the village together. I do recall now hearing that the girl had endured some light-hearted teasing on account of this incident. You can probably imagine the form that this took: "Now you have got the young gentleman to carry your basket for you, how much longer will it be before he is carrying you over the threshold?" It was, as I say, all light-hearted. Indeed, I believe it was Reid himself who mentioned it to me, in some amusement, the next time we spoke. But recalling this incident reminds me of another, which occurred at about the same time, just a few weeks before Reid left. In common with many of the young people in the village, Sarah Dickens was employed at Oakbrook during the apple-picking season. One day, during a period of exceptionally hot weather, she fainted with the heat and fell to the ground. With the help of one of the gardening staff, Captain Reid, who was nearby at the time, carried her to the house, where she remained, attended by the housekeeper, until she recovered. I suppose that that may have given rise to some talk, but if so it was absurd, for Reid would have done the same for anyone under the circumstances.'

"'I believe I understand the situation,' said I. 'But if Sarah Dickens was indeed seeing a young man during the summer of '78, and if that man was not Reid, who might it have been?'

"'There, Mr Holmes, I fear I cannot help you. Of course, I have often pondered that very question. But the ways of young people have become something of a mystery to me in recent years, I regret to say, and even to speculate upon the matter would take me quite beyond my province.'

"There I left it, Watson – a sad business for all concerned, but a particular misfortune for Captain Reid to be condemned for something of which he is perfectly innocent. What a great pity it is that he should have left the district at just the moment he did, and thus presented the rumour-mongers with a defenceless quarry, unable to respond to their foul accusations!"

"If any accusations were being made," I interjected, "it seems surprising that Reid's father did not take some steps to rebut them. He might, for instance, have placed the details of the rumours before his son in a letter and sought his response."

"Indeed," concurred Holmes. "The father's actions in this matter have caused me some puzzlement."

"Unless," I added, "the rumours and accusations appeared so overwhelming by the time they reached his ears that he felt unable to doubt their veracity. He is an old soldier and, from what we have heard of him, no doubt a man of unimpeachable integrity and honour. It is possible, also, that his wife's health was causing him anxiety at the time. Perhaps, then, he was simply so shocked and appalled by his son's alleged conduct that he could not bring himself to speak of it."

"It is possible," returned Holmes in a dubious tone, "but I would still regard the father's conduct as astonishing. I should hope that if ever I had a son, and that son was faced with serious accusations, I should not see fit to condemn him without a fair hearing. Still, I long ago learned that one cannot hope to solve these little mysteries of human life by dwelling on how people might have acted, but only by studying how they in fact did act, however surprising or disagreeable their actions might seem.

"Now," he continued in a brisker tone as he refilled his pipe and put a match to it. "If we review the case so far, Watson, I think we may say that we have made some definite progress. We have learned beyond doubt why it is that Captain Reid is shunned and condemned throughout the district. That seems to me a fair day's work. Our task now must be to do our utmost to clear him of the charges laid against him."

"That may prove considerably more difficult," I observed. "Rumours are such nebulous, elusive things. It is almost impossible to get a firm grasp upon them; and that which cannot be firmly grasped cannot easily be cast down and beaten. You have also, it seems to me, the difficult problem of trying to prove a negative, that is, that Reid had no close connection with the dead girl, and I cannot see how you can possibly prove such a general notion, especially now that three years have passed since the time in question."

"You undoubtedly state the matter fairly," returned Holmes after a moment. "But to have explained the nature of Captain Reid's troubles leaves our commission but half finished, Watson. We must do all we can to disprove these foul accusations which are laid against him. If we fail, then we fail, but at least we shall know that we have done all that we could. After all, what is the alternative? That Captain Reid leave his house and home for ever? For it would surely be intolerable to him to remain here in the present circumstances. But if he leaves his home now, he leaves it with this foul stain still upon his character. That alternative is surely unthinkable. Besides, bad as his situation is, it could yet become worse. So far, the rumours that besmirch his name are confined to this parish alone. But rumours, as you know, are like rank weeds and apt to spread wherever they can. It is possible that unless we destroy this particular specimen root and branch, it will spread further afield, perhaps to the West Sussex Regiment, or even as far as London Society."

"What you say is true," I concurred, "but I fear the case is quite hopeless, Holmes. There seems to me no way in which Reid's innocence can be proved."

"It may be that the only way to prove our client's innocence is to prove the guilt of another," responded my friend after a moment in a considered tone. "Now, as you will appreciate, Watson, I have no desire to expose the moral lapses of another man to public view, but if it is the only way to clear the name of an innocent man, then I believe I have no choice in the matter. Besides, it must be remembered that this man, whoever he is, has been content to allow our client to suffer quite unmerited condemnation for the past three years."

"But what can you possibly hope to discover after so much time has elapsed?" I protested. "What conceivable evidence could remain?"

"Let us not prejudge the matter," returned my friend with a shake of the head. "We shall proceed in an orderly, scientific manner and see what we turn up. Tomorrow morning I intend to look over the pond where the girl was drowned. Mr Yarrow has very kindly agreed to meet me there at two o'clock, to act as my guide and to furnish me with a few more details of the matter. He is taking lunch with Captain Reid's father at Oakbrook Hall tomorrow, as he has an appointment to see him about some business concerning the church roof, and he will come directly to the pool from there. Let us hope that this fine weather continues for a little longer, and then we shall see if we cannot make some further progress!"

III: THE WILLOW POOL

The following day dawned bright and clear. My bedroom at the White Hart overlooked a garden at the rear, and as I dressed I could see from the bedraggled state of the vegetation there that it had rained during the night. Already, however, the bright sunshine was warming the ground and raising a thin haze among the trees, and it showed every promise of a fine day ahead.

When I descended to the dining room, I was informed that Holmes had risen early and had already gone out. He returned as I awaited breakfast with a large-scale map of the district, which he had purchased at the local post office.

"The village high street appears to lie on the line of a Roman road," said he, spreading out his map in front of him. "See how it runs in a perfectly straight line from south to north. The White Hart stands here in the market place, at the south end of the high street," he continued, indicating the place on the map. "At the north end, as you see, just above the crossroads, stands the church. There the road takes a sweeping curve to the west round the churchyard, before resuming its course due north again. A mile or so further on, on the west side of the road, lies the entrance to the Oakbrook estate. A little way beyond that, the road crosses a small stream. On the west side of the road at that point is a small spinney, marked as Jenkin's Clump. The stretch of water indicated within it must therefore be the Willow Pool. Another half a mile or so further north up the road lies the entrance to Topley Grange. The sky promises fair weather, Watson, and I have arranged with Mr Coleman, our landlord, to furnish us with a flask of ginger beer and a little bread and cheese for our lunch, so when you are ready, our expedition can begin!"

The sun was warm on our backs as we made our way up the village street and past the long, curving wall of the churchyard. To the side of the church stood the vicarage. Beyond that, open farmland stretched as far as the eye could see, and the road dipped slightly, then began a long, gentle climb to the higher, rolling country to the north. On either side of the road, the hedgerows were ablaze with colour, the foliage a vivid mixture of greens, yellows and reds, among which shone the bright red berries of the hawthorn and the stout hips of the wild roses. Off to our right, where a ploughing team was at work in a field, flocks of lapwings and rooks circled noisily overhead, and all about us the air was full of the rich, mature scents of autumn.

We had been following this pleasant road for about ten minutes when the hedge on our left gave way to a high brick wall. A little way along this was a wide gateway, flanked with old, lichen-blotched stone pillars. A sign on one of these indicated that this was the entrance to Oakbrook Hall, and through the gateway I could see a long shaded avenue of oaks and elms, curving away to the left. A little further on, the wall gave way once more to a hawthorn hedge, punctuated at intervals by spreading oak trees, and the road dropped into a small vale. At the bottom of the vale was a stone bridge, spanning a stream. As we approached this, a gentleman on horseback came trotting down the road towards us, on the far side of the stream. He crossed the bridge, then slowed his horse to a walk as he approached us. He was, I observed, a young man of perhaps five-and-twenty, and he was dressed in a very smart riding costume.

"The remains of the Roman villa are the other way," he called out in a peremptory fashion.

"I am obliged to you," returned Holmes in an affable tone, "but we are not looking for the villa."

"You'll not find anything up this way," persisted the other, drawing his horse to a halt.

"Well, we shall find that footpath, at least," said Holmes, pointing to a gap in the vegetation a little way ahead of us, just before the bridge, which indicated the entrance to the path up to the Willow Pool.

"What on earth do you want to go up there for?" exclaimed the young man in a tone of surprise and disdain. "There's nothing of interest up there."

"Well, well. No doubt the exercise will be beneficial, anyhow!"

The young man snorted. "You're down here from London, aren't you?" he continued after a moment.

"That is so. And you, if I might venture to speculate, are a resident of these parts."

The young man did not reply, but flicked his horse forward. "Please yourself," he called over his shoulder in an unpleasant tone, "but you're wasting your time."

"We shall see about that," said Holmes to me as we resumed our walk. "It may be, Watson," he added, "that that egregiously rude young man is Admiral Blythe-Headley's son, Anthony, to whom Reid referred the other day."

I glanced back as we reached the entrance to the footpath. The rider had turned in the saddle and was staring back at us. "We seem to have aroused his curiosity," I remarked.

"Indeed," returned Holmes. "He appeared uncommonly keen to send us off in another direction, although whether he had any purpose in so doing, or is simply ill-mannered, we can only speculate."

The pathway through the woods rose gently at first, then levelled off, meandering among the thickly growing bushes and trees, but never far from the gurgling stream on our right. The canopy of foliage overhead was in some places very dense and cast the wood into gloomy shade, but elsewhere the sunshine pierced the gloom and sent shafts of light down to the woodland floor. Presently, a side path branched off to the right, and passing by stepping stones across the stream, vanished among the undergrowth beyond.

"That must be the path to the Topley Grange Estate," remarked Holmes.

Ahead of us, to the right, I spied the shimmer of water through the trees, and a moment later we came upon the boggy, reed-girt margin of the pool. In shape it was long and narrow, being scarcely more than twenty-five feet across, but a good sixty or seventy in length. At the other end, the pool was fringed by willow trees, their slender branches dipping into the water, but at the lower end, on the side where we stood, was a flat open area of damp, mossy turf, and on the other side a tangle of brambles and briars. Just by the patch of turf, another side path went off to the left and climbed steeply up the wooded valley side.

"This is evidently the way from Oakbrook Hall," said Holmes, looking up the steeply sloping path. At the top of the hill, which marked the limit of the wood, a bright rectangle of sunlight indicated where the path emerged from the shade of the trees into open country.

"It does not appear a very well-used path," I remarked.

"Why so?"

"The space where the grass is worn away on that path is considerably narrower than on this one," I replied. "The obvious conclusion is that fewer feet have passed upon that one than upon this."

"There, I regret, you fall into a popular error," observed my friend. "In fact, it makes little difference to the width of a path whether it is lightly or heavily used."

"You speak as if you have made a special study of the matter," said I with a chuckle.

"As a matter of fact I have," said he, to my very great surprise.

"You are surely in jest!"

"Not at all. During my second year at college, I became interested in this very question, as a result of certain observations I had made of the pathways that were most frequented by the undergraduates. It is one of those many matters to which the answer has always been assumed without verification and, as it turns out, assumed quite erroneously. The history of human knowledge is littered with such false assumptions. You will no doubt recall, for instance, that before Galileo, it was universally believed that if two objects identical in all respects save their weight are dropped from a height, the heavier of the two will strike the ground first. That esteemed gentleman alone considered the matter worth verifying. He therefore performed the experiment and discovered that the universal belief was quite mistaken: the two objects strike the ground at precisely the same moment. It is, as I remarked the other day, always worthwhile verifying universally held opinions for oneself. My interest in footpaths having been aroused, I made many score of measurements and calculations, and reached certain very definite conclusions. Among the chief of these is that the amount of human traffic on a footpath has no significant effect on the width of that path, and that a footpath's width is in fact almost entirely dependent upon the moisture of the ground. To put it simply, if the ground is wet, the path will become muddy, and in stepping to the side to avoid the mud, those who use it will widen it accordingly. The wetter the ground, the wider the path, even if it is used by only a few people each day. It is the same with pathways used by animals: I have seen sheep tracks in dry heathland, which were rutted almost a foot deep by constant use, but were scarcely three or four inches in width. The average width of the paths in the university grounds, incidentally, was exactly nine and five-eighths inches."

"I cannot but admire your thoroughness and precision," I remarked with a chuckle. "How was your research received?"

"Alas! I regret to say that my treatise, *Upon the Properties of Footpaths Occurring Naturally in Various Terrain, with some notes upon the effects of seasonal variation*, failed to arouse any great enthusiasm among the college tutors."

"Perhaps," I ventured, "they considered that however intellectually sound the research, it nevertheless constituted somewhat superfluous knowledge."

"If so, they were in error, and seriously so. We can never tell what use the future will make of our present research. Very often, it is the work that is highly praised upon publication and which satisfies current expectations that ultimately proves of no worth. The work that is done for its own sake, on the other hand, without any consideration of the prevailing fashion, and without, perhaps, any immediately obvious application, generally proves in the end to be of most benefit to mankind. Should anyone wish to avail themselves of the fruit of my labours, they will find it handsomely bound in black buckram in the college library – row 'J', as I recall."

All the time he had been speaking, he had been pacing up and down the margin of the pool, peering this way and that, as if his aim was to view the scene of the old tragedy from every possible angle. Then, breaking off a long stick from a fallen tree, he took himself across the stepping stones and through a tangle of brambles and briars to the other side of the pool. There the brambles were growing close to the water's edge, their branches trailing into the pool in several places, and I watched as he pushed his way through this undergrowth and made his way along the bank, poking with his stick into the depths of the water as he went. After a while he paused, broke off a small piece from the end of his stick and tossed it into the pool, then watched closely as it drifted slowly upon the surface of the water. He repeated this experiment several times, with increasingly larger pieces of wood, throwing them further out into the centre of the pool each time. At length, evidently satisfied with these experiments, he returned to where I was sitting on the fallen tree.

"There are no brambles on this side of the water, and nor does it appear that there ever have been," said he. "The ground here is probably too wet for them. Therefore, anyone collecting blackberries would have to do so on the far side, where the ground is firmer and the bushes are growing thickly. The brambles are very close to the water's edge there, however, leaving little space for anyone to stand, but of course they may not have been quite so close three years ago."

"Perhaps the narrowness of the gap between the brambles and the water is what caused the girl to slip," I suggested.

"Perhaps so," said he in an abstracted tone. For some time he stood in silence, his chin in his hand and his brow drawn down in a frown of concentration as he stared across the water at the tangled undergrowth on the far side, as if he would penetrate the veil of time and see for himself exactly what had occurred in that fateful spot three years ago.

The wood was very quiet, the only sound the constant soft splash of the water as it left the pool and spilled over the stones in the stream below. All at once, however, there came the robust voice of a man singing, somewhere higher up the wood. There was a curious, nasal quality to the voice, and its accent was undoubtedly a rustic one. As its owner approached, I caught some of the words of the song, the subject of which appeared to be "going to the fair". Holmes looked round in surprise as a large, powerfully built man came into view higher up the path, at the far end of the pool, clapping his hands as he walked along. He was a young man, little more than two-and-twenty at the outside, I judged, and he was clad in a coarse, loose-fitting shirt, knee breeches and leather gaiters. His face was ruddy and shining, and upon it was an expression of openness and good-natured simplicity.

"Good day!" cried Holmes as the newcomer approached.

"Good day to you, sir!" returned the other in a broad rural accent, giving a little salute. "Are you lost, sir?"

Holmes shook his head with a smile. "My friend and I are taking the air," said he.

The young man's mouth fell open a little and his features assumed a look of puzzlement and alarm. "Taking the air, sir?" he queried in an anxious tone.

"No, no," said Holmes quickly, chuckling to himself. "I mean, my friend and I are enjoying the fine fresh air of this beautiful countryside. You live locally, I take it. If so, you are indeed fortunate!"

"Yes, sir. Fortunately, I live at the hardware shop!"

"Ah, yes. I saw it as we walked up the high street: 'J. Blogg, Hardware'. You are, perhaps, Noah Blogg?"

"Yes, sir. Noah Blogg," returned the other, appearing pleased to hear his own name spoken.

"My name is Sherlock Holmes," said my colleague, extending his hand to the young man, who took it and shook it vigorously, "and this is my friend Dr Watson."

"Pleased," declared Noah Blogg with a broad smile, repeating his energetic performance with my own hand.

"This is an interesting spot," said Holmes, indicating the pool and its surroundings. "Do you come here often?"

"Often," repeated the young man.

"You like it here?"

The young man hesitated and appeared unsure.

"Sometimes," he responded at length.

"And sometimes not, eh?" said Holmes, regarding the young man keenly. "When do you not like it?"

The young man again looked unsure. His mouth opened, but he did not answer.

"Do you remember Sarah Dickens?" asked Holmes.

"My friend," was the simple reply.

"I am sure she was," said Holmes in a kindly voice. "It was sad that she was drowned here, was it not?"

"Don't know," the young man replied, appearing confused. His previously cheery face had assumed a sombre look, and his eyes moved to a spot at the edge of the water, close to where we were standing.

Holmes followed his gaze. "Is that where she was drowned?" he asked.

The young man did not reply. A variety of emotions passed across his features in rapid succession, and his lips moved without producing a sound. Then, with a suddenness that made my hair stand on end, he blurted out, "Don't know nothing," turned on his heel and ran very swiftly back along the path by which he had come.

"It appears that your questions have awoken painful memories for him," I remarked as the sound of Noah Blogg's heavy footsteps faded. "You were perhaps a trifle blunt."

Holmes nodded. "If so, I am sorry. I had no wish to cause him distress, but I could not neglect a possible source of information."

"Of course, it is arguable whether any information he provided would really be of much value," I remarked, but Holmes shook his head.

"Do not be too quick to dismiss it," said he. "If he was on friendly terms with the dead girl he may perhaps have been privy to her secrets. One can never tell in such a case who might hold the key that will unlock the problem."

For some time then, Holmes resumed his pacing about and his probing of the water, examining the area from every possible angle and muttering to himself constantly as he did so. Then he seated himself upon the fallen tree and slowly began to fill his pipe, a thoughtful look on his face.

"There is something in the air here," said he at last, looking about him. "Do you not feel it, Watson? Perhaps I am permitting myself to indulge in fancies, but many places have their *genius loci*, and the spirit of the Willow Pool is, I think, one of tragedy and misfortune."

"I have known cheerier spots," I remarked.

My friend chuckled. "Let us walk on a little way, then," he suggested, rising to his feet. "Mr Yarrow will not be here for a while, so we have plenty of time to follow this path out beyond the wood and take our lunch upon the hillside above."

Following the way, therefore, by which Noah Blogg had made his abrupt departure, we passed along the length of the pool and on through the wood, our path rising as it followed the course of the stream, until we emerged at last upon a sunlit upland. Of Noah Blogg there was no sign.

"Has your examination of the pool furthered your thoughts in any way?" I asked my companion as we sat on the springy turf, smoking our pipes after our humble lunch.

"Indeed. It has enabled me to see for myself the location of the event which is at the root of Captain Reid's problems," he returned, "and has provided further material for judicious speculation."

"Perhaps so," said I, "but I cannot see how anything you discover here can really make much difference to your client's lamentable position. The girl in question is dead. Nothing you discover, as to the precise circumstances of her death, can alter that fact, nor alter the generally held opinion that Reid was the cause of her sorrow."

"You enunciate one particular point of view very clearly, Watson," returned Holmes, "but as it is a view that would foreclose most possibilities before they have been examined, it is not a view I favour. I have undertaken sufficient investigations to know that new facts can emerge from the unlikeliest of quarters. There is an unresolved question about the girl's death: some in the district think it was an accident, others, despite the verdict of the coroner's court, believe that it was suicide. I am confident of discovering the truth of the matter, to my own satisfaction at least. Once I have established in my own mind precisely what occurred here three years ago, I can then address the remainder of the problem. I am hopeful that when Mr Yarrow arrives he will be able to furnish us with a little more information. Ah, there he is now!"

I followed my companion's gaze and saw that some distance off to our right, a dark-clad figure was making his way along the edge of a ploughed field towards Jenkin's Clump. In a few minutes we had retraced our steps and were once more within the shaded spinney, by the margin of the pool. A moment later there came a man's voice, calling to us from the path from Oakbrook Hall, and looking up the hill I saw a figure framed for a moment in the bright sunlit rectangle where the path through the wood met the open fields beyond. Holmes had been once more examining closely the ground at the edge of the pool, but he looked up as the vicar called to us, and there was a sudden stillness in his manner. I turned and saw that his face was rigid and tense, like a keen hound that has got the scent of game in his nostrils, and in his eyes was a steely glitter. What had wrought this abrupt change I could not imagine. In a moment his features had relaxed again, as the vicar joined us by the pool and we all shook hands. Mr Yarrow was a broad-faced, learned-looking man, with a shining bald head fringed with grizzled grey hair. He declared himself ready to answer any questions that we might have.

"I should be very obliged," said Sherlock Holmes, "if you would repeat the main points of the account you gave me yesterday evening. Dr Watson would no doubt appreciate hearing the details from your lips, and I wish to ensure that I have not overlooked any fact of significance."

"By all means," responded the vicar in an agreeable tone. "Let me see now. First of all, you should know that Sarah

Dickens lived with her parents and her brother, who was two years older than her, on the outskirts of the village. Her father farms there in a small way, on land rented from Admiral Blythe-Headley, the smallholding being known as 'Hawthorn Farm'. It is probably true enough to say that Sarah came from typical rural stock, but I do not mean by this that she was in any way a simpleton. She had learned her lessons at the village school very well and was a great reader. She had something of a taste for poetry, and had herself composed many little poems, the best of which she wrote up neatly in an exercise book that she had bought for the purpose. She had showed me one or two of these poems on occasion, and I had encouraged her to write more. She also went into the school fairly often, at the request of Miss Mead, the teacher, to help the little ones learn their letters, and I know that Miss Mead found her a great help.

"She was, I should say, plain and straightforward in all respects, both in appearance and manner. She was certainly not the sort of girl to turn the head of every man in the village, or anything of the sort, but she was not unattractive, in a rustic sort of way. She was a good-hearted girl, honest and hard-working, and the general opinion before her death had been that she would make someone a good wife. At the time of her death, she was, as far as one could ascertain, 'unattached', as they say in these parts; but since her death there have been persistent rumours that she had been seeing someone secretly, as you are only too aware.

"On that fateful day, that is, 10 September 1978, after occupying herself in the morning with various tasks about the house and farmyard, Sarah announced that after lunch she intended to pick blackberries up by the Willow Pool. Her brother had also been at home that morning, working on the family farm, but was employed that afternoon, as he often was, on the Topley Grange estate. He therefore said that he would accompany her up the road as far as Jenkin's Clump, and the two of them set off, she with her basket on her arm, at about a quarter to one. They walked together until they reached the entrance to this wood, just by the humpbacked bridge, as you probably observed, where they parted. Sarah's last words to her brother were that she would bake a blackberry and apple pie for his tea. That was the last time that she was ever seen alive.

"When she did not return that afternoon, her family were mildly concerned, but not greatly so, for she had of late taken to wandering off alone for hours on end in a brooding sort of manner, which was quite unlike the character she had displayed when younger. Later, in the early evening, two youths were passing along this path through the woods and saw her apparently lifeless body floating in the water. They were too frightened to approach it, and ran down to the village to get help."

"Do you recall the names of these youths?" asked Holmes.

"Yes. One was Noah Blogg, youngest son of Jack Blogg, who has the hardware shop in the village. He is a bit of a simpleton, I am afraid, but good-natured and harmless."

"Ah, yes. We met him earlier, just at this spot. Of course, we did not know then that he had been one of those who discovered the girl's body."

"It doesn't surprise me that you saw him here," Yarrow remarked. "He spends a lot of time up here. The pool appears to possess a morbid fascination for him, and I don't think he can quite get the girl's death out of his simple mind. Indeed, it seems to me sometimes that he returns here again and again in the hope of one day seeing her alive once more." He shook his head and sighed. "The other lad's name was Harry Cork. He joined the Navy a couple of years ago, and I have not seen him since. I don't think he has been back to Topley Cross in the last two years.

"When these boys reached the village, the vicarage was, of course, the first house they came to. I was in the garden at the time, for it was a fine evening, and they quickly described to me what they had seen. I instructed them to notify Sarah's father, and at once set off for this spot in the company of George Childers, the local jobbing gardener, who had been doing some work in my garden when the boys arrived. We got here in a little over ten minutes, I suppose, waded into the water and brought the girl's body ashore. It was at once clear that she was dead, and had been so for some time."

"One moment," interrupted Holmes. "You say that you waded into the water to reach the girl's body. I take it, then, that it was not far from the bank, for the middle of the pool is too deep for wading, as I ascertained earlier."

"That is correct. In the middle, the water is a good seven or eight feet deep, but it is quite shallow at the sides. The girl's body was only a few feet from the bank, and we were easily able to reach it."

"Which side?" queried Holmes. "This side or the other?"

"The far side, a little higher up the pool than where we are now standing."

"So – I am sorry to labour the point, Mr Yarrow, but I wish to be quite clear on the matter – you and the gardener went round by the stepping stones to the other side of the pool and approached the body that way?"

"That is correct. The brambles were growing very thickly there, but we were just able to reach the spot. Had she been any higher up the pool I don't know how we would have reached her, for the brambles were quite impassable further along the bank, and hung right down into the water. As a matter of fact, the poor girl's hair was caught on these brambles, and Childers and I had the distressing task of trying to disentangle it. Eventually we got her free, lifted the body onto the bank, then carried it round to this side and laid her on the turf here. By this time, several others had arrived. The light was then fading – it was very gloomy in these woods, as you can imagine – and there was nothing to be done for the girl, so between us we carried her lifeless body down to the village."

"And her basket?"

"Her basket?" repeated the vicar in surprise. "What of it?"

"Someone carried that down to the village, too?"

"I suppose so. Yes, I recall now that someone had it on his arm. I cannot see that it is of any importance."

"It was not you or Childers that retrieved it?"

"No. Our minds were on somewhat more important matters, Mr Holmes. Someone picked it up. It was just here, on the ground. I really cannot see the point of your interest in the basket."

"I am a great one for detail, Mr Yarrow. Sometimes, perhaps, I make a vice out of what should be a virtue. Do you recall if there were any blackberries in the basket?"

"No, there were not."

"Very good. The next day, I understand, you returned here with the dead girl's mother?"

"Yes, as I described to you last night. The two of us walked up here after lunch. She was in an extremely distressed state. It was then that I saw the slip of paper, down among the brambles by the water's edge, on the far side."

"Near where you found the girl's body?"

"Yes, a foot or two further into the tangle of brambles than the place from which we had entered the water. Just over there." He pointed across the water to a spot on the far side, a few yards higher up the pool than where we stood.

"It was not in the water?" asked Holmes.

"No. If it had been in the water it would probably have been unreadable. It was a foot or so back from the bank."

"I see," said Holmes. "I should very much like to see the note, to complete my mental picture of the matter. Do you think that would be possible? I understand that the girl's brother keeps it."

"That is so. I doubt he would take very kindly to exhibiting it, as it were, to strangers, especially if he thought those strangers were acting on behalf of Captain Reid, but perhaps I could persuade him to let us all have a look at it together." Yarrow glanced at his watch. "I happen to know that he will be at home this afternoon, so if you wish we could go along there now."

"Capital!" cried Holmes. "I shall be greatly indebted to you, Mr Yarrow!"

The day seemed very bright as we emerged from the shade of the woods, and the sun was surprisingly warm for so late in the year. It was pleasant indeed to walk down that rolling country road in such balmy weather, and to see the hedgerows ablaze with berries, and the clear blue sky alive with birds. When I reflected on our day's employment, however, I could not but think that we might as well have remained sitting in the parlour of the inn all day, for all the good our expedition had achieved. We had seen for ourselves the place where Sarah Dickens had died, and Holmes had drawn from our companion the details of the matter, but of what use was this to his client, Captain Reid? Whether the girl's death had been an accident or a deliberate act of suicide could make little difference now, I reflected, and would make no difference whatever to Reid's predicament. However she had died, he would still stand condemned in the eyes of the parish for having used her so ill, and having brought sorrow and anguish into her happy young life. I was curious to know what Holmes would do next, but could not but feel that so far his energies had been largely wasted.

In ten minutes we had reached the village. Our guide led us on, past the vicarage and the curving wall of the churchyard, and down the high street a little way to the crossroads. Here he turned left and, passing a few outlying cottages, we found ourselves in a pleasant lane, lined on either side with hawthorn hedges and large, spreading trees. Presently, when we had gone perhaps half a mile, we came to a small thatched cottage, behind which was a jumble of farm buildings.

"This is the place," said Yarrow, pushing open a small wicket gate and leading us along a path, which passed by the side of the cottage and brought us, through another gate, into a yard at the back. "Old Dickens has something of a reputation for keeping an untidy farm," murmured the vicar under his breath, and as I glanced about the yard I could not but think the reputation was well earned. Ducks, geese and hens milled about in apparent confusion around crates, sacks, mounds of straw and pieces of old machinery. In one muddy corner, a stout pig with a chain around its neck was rooting about in the earth, and in another corner, tethered to a post, a goat was chewing on a dirty-looking pile of hay, and eyeing us with no very friendly expression.

The vicar's knock at the door was answered by a robust woman in an apron, whom he greeted as Mrs Dickens. She invited us in, but he declined the offer, saying he would not trouble them, but wished to speak to her son, John, for a few moments. She disappeared from the doorway, and a moment later a short, powerfully built young man of perhaps four-and-twenty appeared. His manner was friendly enough, until Yarrow explained to him our purpose in calling there, whereupon he assumed a look of stubborn intransigence.

"No offence intended to you, Vicar," said he in a resolute voice, "but I should like to know why I should oblige John Reid or his friends."

"It is not a question of your obliging them, but only of obliging me," the vicar returned.

Several minutes of such debate ensued, the upshot being that Dickens grudgingly agreed to let us see his sister's final note. "You can hold it, Mr Yarrow," said he, "but I don't want these gentlemen touching it."

He disappeared into the shaded interior of the house and returned a moment later with a slip of white paper in his hand, which he passed to the vicar.

"I'll just take it out of the shadow of the house, if I may," said Yarrow, taking a few steps into the middle of the yard. "Here, gentlemen," he continued, holding it out so we could see.

It was an unexceptional little sheet of white notepaper, which showed evidence of having been folded and refolded many times. Upon it, written in pencil, in a copybook script, were the following lines:

> My heart is broken, for you have cast me away and do not care for me any more. You have gone away and left me, all alone in my sorrow. Now what can I do? I trusted you and you betrayed me. I loved you and you used me. How could you use a poor girl so?

It was a touching little epistle, moving in its simplicity, and I read it through several times. Holmes, too, read it over and over, his brows drawn into a frown of concentration. Then he took from his pocket a small lens and, craning forward until his nose almost touched the paper, examined it with the minutest attention.

"Here! What's your game?" came a cry from behind us. I turned as John Dickens advanced towards us, a look of anger upon his face. "I said you wasn't to touch it!" said he, taking the sheet from Yarrow's hand.

"No more they have," responded the vicar.

"Thank you for letting us see this note," said Holmes to Dickens in a pleasant, measured tone. "It has been most helpful."

The young farmer regarded him with a sullen expression, clearly indicating that he had not the slightest desire to be helpful.

"I understand," Holmes continued, "that your sister composed poetry, which she kept in a special exercise book."

"What of it?" demanded Dickens gruffly.

"I wonder if it would be possible for us to see it, just for a moment?"

"No, it would not," retorted the other. "You've got a nerve," he added in an angry tone. The set of the young farmer's face was one of resolute defiance, and there appeared little prospect of his agreeing to my companion's request. But Mr Yarrow intervened once more and, after considerable entreaty and persuasion, Dickens disappeared into the house again, with a great show of reluctance, and emerged a minute later with a slim, blue-covered exercise book in his hand.

"I'll hold it and turn the pages," said he in a tone that precluded debate upon the issue.

"By all means," responded Holmes affably.

On the first page of the book was inscribed a poem entitled "The Storm", which began with the words "The seagulls cry; the clouds race by" and described very well, I thought, the gathering gloom that precedes such an event. The poem on the second page was entitled "The Robin", and captured nicely the character of that friendly little bird. Thus the poems continued, painting a charming picture of everyday country life in that secluded corner of rural England.

"These really are very good," said the vicar after a moment in a quiet voice, to which I murmured my assent. Holmes, however, said nothing, but craned his head forward like some strange bird of prey inspecting its quarry. His face was tense and still, his every feature displaying his intense concentration. Only his eyes moved, darting about the pages swiftly as Dickens slowly turned them over for us, as if determined to absorb every square inch of their surface.

The poems came to an end just a few pages short of the middle of the book. The remainder of the leaves were blank. I could not wonder at Dickens regarding the book with some reverence; it was perhaps the most personal memento anyone could possibly have of the girl, displaying as it did so clearly the author's simple and unaffected character.

"Thank you," said Holmes again as Dickens closed the book at last. He extended his hand but the young man declined to take it.

"We shall speak again," said Holmes.

"I think not," returned the other.

"Perhaps not, but we shall nevertheless. I intend to get to the bottom of this matter."

With that, Holmes turned on his heel, and Yarrow and I followed him out of the farmyard. I glanced back as I closed the gate, and saw that John Dickens was still standing by the back door of the cottage, observing our departure. There was an odd expression upon his features, which had something of defiance about it, certainly, but something also, I thought, of grudging respect, and even perhaps of apprehension.

We parted from the vicar in the village high street, Holmes thanking him warmly for his kind assistance, and made our way back to the White Hart.

"The girl's exercise book yielded several points of interest, did it not?" remarked Holmes as we walked along together. "You observed, I take it, that two pages had been removed?"

"I saw that one leaf had been torn out near the middle of the book," I responded. "As it came after the last poem, I assumed that it was a blank sheet."

Holmes nodded. "Yes, that was of interest, although it was no more than we might have expected, of course. But the second missing leaf is certainly of very great significance."

"I did not observe any other."

"Really? It was near the beginning of the book, between the poem about the robin and the one about the daffodils – which, incidentally, I thought somewhat superior to Wordsworth's effort on a similar theme. It had been removed very neatly, with a small pair of nail scissors."

"But surely these things are of no great importance?" I protested.

"On the contrary," returned my friend in a tone of surprise, "they are very significant links in the chain of events that stretches unbroken from the summer of '78 to the present time."

"You will not, I hope, take it amiss," I ventured after a moment, "if I express my opinion on the whole matter?"

"Not at all," returned my companion, raising his eyebrow slightly. "Indeed, I should welcome your observations."

"Then I must, in all honesty, declare that I see little point in much of what we have done today, Holmes. A few details of the matter may perhaps have been elucidated – the circumstances surrounding the girl's death, for instance – but aside from that, which, in any case, scarcely seems pertinent to your client's predicament, our day's work has surely been essentially profitless."

"There, my dear fellow," returned Holmes, "I must beg leave to differ. You clearly believe that we have wasted our energies today. That is a suggestion with which I must disagree most strongly."

"Why so?" I asked, surprised at the vehemence with which he spoke.

"Because," said he, "I have solved the case."

IV: AT THE WHITE HART

When the mood was upon him, my friend Sherlock Holmes was undoubtedly the most maddeningly uncommunicative person I have ever known. Upon our return from Hawthorn Farm he had called in at the post office and sent a wire to Captain Reid, but had then fallen into a moody silence, and all my efforts to engage him in conversation had been answered only by preoccupied grunts, when they had been answered at all. At length I had admitted defeat and abandoned my attempts altogether. By dinner time that evening, however, he had evidently resolved whatever it was that had been exercising his mind, for he seemed more at ease as we ate, and spoke freely of many matters, although not of the case.

After dinner we repaired to the private sitting room of the inn, which was on the first floor, overlooking the market square. There, over a cup of coffee and a pipe, my friend's thoughts at last turned once more to the business that had brought us down to Sussex.

"I have a case here, Watson, which will ring about the country!" said he in a tone of suppressed excitement. "If this case does not make my name, then no case ever will! I have the whole matter here," he continued, holding out his hand with his fingers extended, "in the very palm of my hand!"

"You astound me, Holmes," I cried. "You spoke earlier of having solved the case, and I confess I was never so surprised in all my life! Surely you cannot be in earnest?"

"Perfectly so."

"But how can it be?" I protested. "For save only the information you gained from the newspaper office, which has been confirmed and amplified a little by Mr Yarrow, I cannot see that the case has advanced to any significant extent since we left Baker Street. You have certainly amassed a considerable amount of detail concerning the death of Sarah Dickens; you have established beyond all reasonable doubt that it is ill-use of that girl that is alleged against Captain Reid; but much of this must be common knowledge in these parts, so how can it go any way to proving Reid's innocence, or the guilt of another?"

"Is it possible that you do not yet perceive the truth of the matter?" said my friend. "Why, Watson, you have seen all I have seen, and have heard all I have heard! Like archaeologists sifting through the remains of some ancient Greek city, we have been delving into the past. The separate facts we have unearthed are like the shattered fragments of a decorated amphora, found scattered in the dust. Each fragment, considered in isolation, conveys very little to us, but we know that once, when joined together, the fragments bore a clear picture. Can you not put all the fragments of this puzzle together to reveal that picture?"

I shook my head. "It does seem that Sarah Dickens was seeing someone," I responded, "and if it was not Reid, then it was someone else. But there seem too many possibilities for us to be able to form a clear picture of the events, too many questions to which we are unlikely ever to find the answers."

"When we began our enquiries," said Holmes in a measured tone, after a moment, "there were indeed a number of possible explanations of the affair. But each little item of knowledge that we have collected has served to narrow down the field, until now only one remains. It is, as you know, an axiom of mine that when you have eliminated the impossible, whatever remains, however unlikely, must be the truth."

"I should very much like to hear your view of the matter," I remarked. "You stated earlier this afternoon that you regarded it as important to establish, in your own mind at least, the precise circumstances of the girl's death. I cannot see that this issue is of the first importance, but if you regard it as such, I am willing to allow it, for the sake of the argument. I take it that you are now satisfied that you know the truth of that matter?"

"I am."

"What then, Holmes, is your opinion?"

"I shall give you my opinion," responded my companion after a moment, "and then, I think, you will appreciate, Watson, why the issue is such an important one. But, wait! What is that?"

There had come the sound of footsteps on the stair and voices outside our room. A moment later there was a knock at the door, and Mr Coleman put his head into the room.

"Two gentlemen to see you," said he, opening the door a little wider to admit a broad-chested elderly man, with grizzled grey hair and beard, who carried a heavy, bulbous-headed stick. Accompanying him was a thin, dark-haired, pale-faced young man whom I recognized as the man on horseback to whom we had spoken near Jenkin's Clump earlier in the day. "Admiral Blythe-Headley and Mr Anthony Blythe-Headley," announced the landlord as he withdrew.

Holmes waved the two men to a seat and regarded them with an expression of curiosity. "To what do we owe this pleasure?" he asked at length.

Admiral Blythe-Headley thumped his stick upon the floor with a snort.

"It is no pleasure for us, sir!" said he in an angry tone. "It is no pleasure to be obliged to leave one's hearth and home in the evening to pay a visit to vermin!"

"Well, pleasure or not, I did not compel you to come," returned Holmes in an affable tone.

"Have a care, sir!" said the younger man sharply.

"You are come down here from London, I understand," continued the admiral in a loud voice.

"That is true," returned Holmes.

"You are acting on behalf of Colonel Reid's son."

"That is also true."

"You young men from London!" said the admiral in a tone of distaste. "You think you are so clever, in proving once a season that black is white and white is black."

Holmes's eyebrows went up in surprise, but he did not respond.

"Well, you had better understand this, young man," the other continued: "we do not care for your sort in these parts, and the sooner you are gone the better."

"We shall be leaving just as soon as we have righted the wrong that has been done to John Reid."

"Pah!" cried the old man. "In my day, any young man found guilty of such disgraceful behaviour as his would have lost his place in society for ever."

"Those who would take away a man's place in society would do well to be sure of their facts."

"Facts? Pah!" cried the admiral angrily, banging his stick on the floor once more. "For your information, Reid's conduct is common knowledge in these parts. Is the blackguard ashamed of himself? Does he seek to hide his face? Not a bit of it! The first thing he does upon his return is to call upon us as if nothing had happened, to pay court to my daughter! The brazen impudence of the fellow! The arrogant presumption that my daughter would want anything to do with such a vile scoundrel! He ought to be horsewhipped, and drummed out of the county! And as for your leaving, young man, you can pack your bags this evening, for you are leaving in the morning!"

"We shall leave when we are ready."

"You will leave in the morning. I own this inn, young man, and I do not care to have its name sullied by connection with Reid or any of his verminous associates. Anthony!" he continued, rising to his feet. "Let us be gone!"

"Well!" said Holmes, when our visitors had left. "Admiral Blythe-Headley is certainly a man of fierce disposition!"

"I should certainly not have cared to be under his command in the Navy," I concurred.

Holmes flung himself back into his chair and burst out laughing. For several minutes he was so convulsed with laughter that I thought he would choke.

"So," said he at length, "he fears that our presence will sully the name of his inn! Perhaps he fears we shall use our London cleverness to prove that the White Hart is really the Black Hart! Vermin, indeed! Why, there are enough mice in this inn to pull Cinderella's carriage ten times over!"

"He does seem mightily aroused by the business," I remarked.

"Indeed. When one considers how many soldiers have toyed with the affections of how many country maids over the last five hundred years, his uncontrollable wrath at Reid's supposed conduct appears almost excessive, especially as, on the face of it at least, the matter does not concern him. But no doubt his daughter plays a part in the calculation somewhere. It was ever thus, Watson: no prospective son-in-law is ever quite good enough for the girl's father! My advice to you, my boy, should you ever contemplate matrimony, is to ensure that the young lady that captures your heart is an orphan. It will save you an uncommon lot of trouble!"

"I shall remember the advice," I returned with a chuckle. "But what will you do now, Holmes? Does the admiral's intervention affect your plans?"

My friend shook his head. "I shall bring the case to a conclusion tomorrow, just as I intended. Whether I shall accept the apology that Admiral Blythe-Headley will then offer me, I have not yet decided. Halloa! More visitors?"

He sprang from his chair and pulled open the door, whence had come a gentle, almost timid knock. There, framed in the doorway, was a young lady, wrapped in a dark cloak. My first impression was one of almost radiant loveliness. Her hair was of a rich dark brown, and thickly waved, her complexion milky-white, with a roseate blush upon her bonny cheeks.

"Pray, come in!" said Holmes, smiling at this vision of loveliness as she held back in the doorway. "Come in and take a seat!"

"My name is Mary Blythe-Headley," the young lady began in a hesitant tone as she seated herself on the edge of the sofa.

"Your father and brother have left only a few minutes ago," said Holmes.

"I know," said she. "I have been waiting for them to leave, in the alley beside the inn. My father has forbidden me to leave the house, and the first opportunity I have had was when he himself left to come here. You are, I understand, acting on behalf of John Reid?"

"That is correct, Miss Blythe-Headley."

"He has been shunned by the whole district, and my father forbade me to see him when he paid us a visit last week."

"So I understand. Did he also forbid you to write to Captain Reid when he was abroad?"

She nodded her head sorrowfully. "At first I needed no forbidding, for I was angry at what they said John had done. But later I thought I could perhaps forgive him if he were truly remorseful. I wished to write to him on the point, but my father forbade it. The last three years have been very miserable ones for me, as they have for many in the parish. But during the last year I have begun to wonder if John is really guilty of using that girl in the way everyone says. It seems so unlike all else that I know of his character."

"Miss Blythe-Headley," interrupted Holmes, "be reassured of one thing at least: Captain Reid is utterly innocent of what is alleged against him. The truth is that he scarcely knew this girl. He had once or twice performed little kindnesses for her, had carried her basket and so forth, purely out of gentlemanly courtesy, and these actions, following her death, were grossly misinterpreted."

"I knew it," cried our visitor, her eyes shining with tears. "I knew the stories could not be true!" She clutched her hands together. "It was some other man that treated the girl so badly, and drove her to her sorrowful death."

"You may find the matter a little more complex than you suppose," said Holmes. "However, I shall present my findings later. First, I should like to take the opportunity of your presence here to satisfy myself on a point on which I am in ignorance."

"Certainly," said the young lady in surprise. "What is it you wish to know?"

"I understand that on the day that Captain Reid visited Topley Grange last week, a bench in the summer house was found to be damaged. Could you describe to me the nature of that damage?"

Mary Blythe-Headley blushed to the roots of her hair.

"Was something written upon the bench?" asked Holmes, eyeing her closely.

She nodded her head. "It was silly, really," she answered at length. "My father described it as vulgarity, but I thought it simply stupid. Someone had carved a few letters into the wood with a knife."

"Which said?"

"My own initials, 'M. B. H.', followed by the word 'PIG'."

Sherlock Holmes fell back into his chair and shook with silent laughter, and I confess that I, too, could scarcely suppress a chuckle. Mary Blythe-Headley bit her lip as a smile spread across her face.

"Yes," said she, "it is ridiculous, is it not?"

"It is somewhat puerile," said Holmes, endeavouring to stifle his laughter.

"I do not mind your laughing," said she. "I would have laughed at it myself, in other circumstances. But my father took it so seriously. He had no doubt that John was responsible, but I was convinced that could not be – unless John had become quite mentally deranged while in India. I became determined to find a way to speak to him, but before I could do so he had left the district again. Then, when I heard of your presence here, and learnt that my father intended to see you this evening, I made a plan to follow him as soon as he had left the house."

"I am very glad that you have come," said Holmes warmly. "This meeting has been of benefit to us both. Have no fear,

Miss Blythe-Headley. By tomorrow afternoon, if all goes well, I intend that the truth of this matter should be known once and for all. The shadow that has lain so unfairly across Captain Reid's character will be removed."

"Oh, can it be?" cried she, clasping her hands together once more.

Holmes nodded his head. "I must now ask something of you," said he. "Tomorrow I shall send your father and brother a summons to come to Oakbrook Hall. When it arrives, pray do all in your power to ensure that they attend as I request."

"I will," said she.

"Until that time, you must not under any circumstances speak of this meeting, nor of anything which has passed between us this evening. Do you understand?"

"I do," said she. "You can depend upon me."

At that moment, there came the sound of a carriage in the street outside the inn.

"Oh, Heavens! It is my father returned!" cried Miss Blythe-Headley, clutching her throat in alarm. "What am I to do?"

Holmes stepped swiftly to the window and pulled back the curtain. "I cannot see who it is," said he, "but they have entered the inn and may be coming up here. Quickly! This way!"

He flung back the door and ushered the young lady into the corridor outside.

"There is an alcove along here," said he. "You can hide in there and slip away when they have passed."

A moment later he was back in the room and seated in his armchair.

"I really cannot tell you how pleased I am that you are here, Watson," said he in a tone of great amusement, as he filled his pipe and put a match to it. "These little excursions and adventures would not be half so enjoyable were I alone."

"I am very glad to share them with you," I returned, filling my own pipe. "Perhaps when we get a moment free from interruption you could give me your analysis of the case. I am certainly looking forward to hearing it!"

"By all means," returned my friend, leaning back in his chair and crossing his legs over the chair-arm. "I am certain you will find it compelling, my dear fellow! But I fear that the pleasure for both of us must be postponed a little longer!"

At that moment had come another knock at our door. I had been expecting it, for I had heard, as had my companion, the sound of more footsteps on the stair. The landlord's face appeared round the edge of the door once more.

"Two more gentlemen to see you," said he: "Colonel Reid and Mr William Northcote."

Colonel Reid was a tall, spare man, with a lined, weather-beaten face and snowy white hair. I judged from his lean, athletic build that his usual posture was erect and upright, but now he was bent and leaned heavily on his walking stick and was clearly not in the best of health. Northcote was a thin, nervous-looking young man of about six-and-twenty. His spectacles and anxious manner gave him a scholarly, bookish appearance. The two of them sat down on the sofa.

"Good evening, Colonel, Mr Northcote," said Holmes in a pleasant voice.

"You are Sherlock Holmes?" the elderly man enquired in a thin, reedy voice.

"I am," returned Holmes, "and this is my colleague, Dr Watson."

Colonel Reid nodded to me in a weary way, as if even that small action cost him great effort.

"Your presence here has come to my attention," said he, then broke off as there came a slight sound from the corridor outside the door, and then on the stair. "What was that?" he asked.

"Mice," said Holmes quickly. "Or perhaps a rat. This inn is full of vermin."

The colonel gave him an odd look, as if he thought him a little mad, then shook his head slightly.

"I have come here tonight to ask you to desist from whatever it is you are doing, and to leave the district forthwith."

Holmes did not reply, and after a moment the colonel continued:

"Your presence here can do no good. This parish has suffered enough, and anything you do here can only serve to reopen old wounds. Three years ago, a tragedy befell the parish. I do not pretend that there was anything unique about it. These things happen, have always happened and probably will always happen. Nevertheless, it was distressing. When the facts came out, it seemed that my son held some responsibility for what occurred. I was, as you will imagine, devastated by this information."

"You call it information," interrupted Holmes, "but it was, in reality, merely rumour. Rumours may be right and they may be wrong. In this case, they were wrong."

"No!" cried the old man. "Would that it were so! Do you not think, Mr Holmes, that I wished it otherwise, wished it otherwise every morning I awoke? But there could be no doubt. The two of them, my son and that girl, had been seen together on numerous occasions. And they had evidently been together on other occasions when they had not been seen, for it was said that she oft-times slipped away from her home without telling anyone where she was going, and these unexplained absences of hers often coincided, as it turned out, with times when my son, too, was absent from home without adequate explanation."

"That seems slim evidence," began Holmes, but the old man cut him short.

"Hear me out," said he. "The note the girl left referred to someone that had gone away and left her. No one else in the parish had gone away at that time but my son. The reference could be to no one but he. Furthermore, in a pocket of her dress when she was found was a gilt cufflink, marked with the crest of the West Sussex Regiment."

Holmes nodded his head slightly, but did not respond, and after a moment, Colonel Reid continued: "Now, rather than admit his responsibility in the matter, he acts as if he has done nothing wrong, and recruits a hired-by-the-day detective in London, in an attempt to twist the facts and thus prove his innocence! I mean you no offence, Mr Holmes – every man must make his living as he sees fit, and if a man chooses to earn his keep by poking his nose into other people's business, then it is for him to answer for it – but I tell you again, you can do no good in this case; you can only make matters worse. Leave now, I beg of you."

"I will leave tomorrow," said Holmes after a moment, in a measured tone, "but on one condition only."

"Which is?"

"That you grant me a brief audience at three o'clock tomorrow afternoon, before I depart."

Colonel Reid looked surprised. "What possible good can that do?"

"I wish to speak to you about this matter in general, and about your son in particular."

"It is utterly pointless, Mr Holmes. There is no more to be said on the matter. Whatever you have in mind will be a waste both of your time and mine."

"Nevertheless, that is my condition."

The old man sighed. "And you will then leave, return to London, and drop this matter altogether?"

"I will."

"Very well, then. I shall expect you at three o'clock. Come along, Northcote!"

The secretary helped the old man to his feet, I opened the door for them, and the two made their way slowly down the stairs. As I was closing the door, I observed that Northcote's stick was lying on the floor, half under the sofa upon which our visitors had been seated.

"Northcote has forgotten his stick," said I, bending to pick it up, but Holmes put his hand on my arm.

"Leave it," said he.

I looked round in surprise. "If I hurry I may catch them before they leave," said I.

"He will return for it," said Holmes. "He left it here deliberately. Indeed, I should not be surprised if— "

He broke off as there came a knock at the door. I opened it and there stood Northcote.

"I have mislaid my stick," said he. "Thank you, Dr Watson," he continued as I handed it to him. "As a matter of fact, I left it here on purpose, as I wished to see you alone, gentlemen." He put his hand inside his coat and withdrew a long white envelope. "Things have been very difficult lately, and my own position has become almost unbearable," he continued. "I have written a letter to Captain Reid, in which – well, read it for yourselves and see. I should be obliged if you would pass it on to Reid, but as you are acting for him, it would probably be best if you read it yourselves, too, so please feel free to open it. Now I must go, or Colonel Reid will wonder where I have got to."

The secretary gave a little bow, blinked his eyes at us from behind his spectacles, and was gone. Holmes looked after him for a moment with a thoughtful expression on his face, then slit open the envelope and extracted a foolscap sheet, which he held out for me to see. Upon it, I read the following:

Dear Reid,

You will, I hope, forgive my writing to you in this way, and not think me impertinent for making reference to matters that are none of my business. But the difficulties which have arisen at Oakbrook recently have made me painfully aware that my presence there represents an unfortunate, and certainly unlooked-for, intrusion into the privacy of your family.

You should know, as I am sure you already confidently believe, that your father, Colonel Reid, does not discuss family matters with me, nor in my presence, and I should certainly never encourage him to do so. Nevertheless, my situation is an uncomfortable, and at times difficult one. In the last few days I have come to feel that my presence may be a hindrance to the restitution of harmony within the family, as it may act as a bar to free and frank conversation between family members.

I therefore propose to give notice to Colonel Reid at the end of this week that I should wish to be relieved of my duties and end my employment with him, for the time being at least, as soon as he feels able to dispense with my services.

I trust that this proposal meets with your approval, and hope that if I do not see you before I leave, we may meet again in more propitious circumstances.

Yours sincerely,

W. N. Northcote

"I suppose it is well intentioned," I remarked as I finished reading, "but the estrangement between father and son appears so complete at present that I doubt Northcote's presence or absence will make much difference."

My friend nodded his head. "In any case," said he, "if things work out tomorrow as I hope, then such a gesture will not be necessary."

"You have spoken of your plans for tomorrow to both Miss Blythe-Headley and Colonel Reid," I remarked. "You appear confident but, to be frank, I cannot imagine what you intend to do."

"I may need a dash of good fortune in the case of certain details – there are one or two matters I am hoping to finalize in the morning – but in the main I am confident that my analysis of the case is correct."

"I should be pleased to hear it," said I. "I confess that I am still very much in the dark. I seem to remember," I added with a chuckle, "although it seems a very long time ago now, before the deluge of visitors, that you were about to give me your opinion as to the precise details of the death of Sarah Dickens. The inquest, as we know, reached a verdict of 'accidental death', but some think otherwise, and believe that the girl deliberately took her own life. What is you opinion, Holmes?"

"My opinion is that the inquest was very seriously at fault. The girl's death was not an accident."

"You agree, then, with those who believe the girl took her own life?"

"No."

"What!"

"I agree with no one, Watson. They are all wrong. Sarah Dickens was murdered."

"What!" I cried again. I confess that I was almost dumbfounded by my companion's calm pronouncement. He stated as a fact a possibility that I had never, even in my wildest speculations, considered. "How can you know?" I cried after a moment.

"How can I know?" returned he. "How could I not know? Why, the matter is as plain as a pikestaff. The evidence admits of only one conclusion. No other is possible."

"But the coroner's court—"

"The problem at the coroner's court, I take it, was that even before the inquest began each man there had determined in his own heart that Sarah Dickens had in fact taken her own life, but was equally determined that, for the sake of the girl's memory and for the feelings of her family, that should not be recorded as the verdict of the court. This issue therefore dominated the thoughts of everyone there, including, from the reports I read, those of the coroner himself. Certain questions that were crying out to be asked were not even considered. No one wished to question the circumstances of the girl's death too closely – so, at least, it seems to me – just in case the answers to the questions made a verdict of suicide unavoidable. In its well-intentioned desire to spare the feelings of the girl's family, the court thus failed in its one bounden duty, that is, to uncover the truth. In this case, attempted kindness has led the court to inadvertently collude in the concealment of a most monstrous crime."

"You are convinced of this?"

"I am. This case exemplifies very clearly why truth and justice must always precede mercy. The time for mercy is when the truth is established beyond all reasonable doubt, and justice has apportioned each man's responsibility. To give premature consideration to mercy before truth and justice are satisfied will almost inevitably lead to the truth never being known, and justice never being satisfied. In this case the girl lies dead in the churchyard at the top of the road and her murderer walks free to this day. Every ounce of duty in my body compels me, Watson, to apply all my powers in this case; to bring justice, not only to John Reid, whose predicament, as you put it, is what has brought us into this case, but also to Sarah Dickens, whose foul murder cries out for justice!"

My companion thumped his fist into his hand as he spoke, and it was evident that he was very angry at what he saw as a serious miscarriage of justice. To one who had previously seen him only as the cool reasoner of Baker Street, and who had come to think of him as an isolated phenomenon of intellect, a brain without a heart, such a display of anger came as a surprise.

I confess I found it difficult to believe that he alone could be right, and all others who had considered the matter wrong, but I kept my doubts to myself. In later years I was to learn, as I came to know my friend better and studied his methods more closely, that such a state of affairs, in which he was right and everyone else wrong, was almost commonplace.

"What will you do?" I asked.

"First," said he, "I shall call a fresh inquest."

"I am no expert on such matters," said I, "but I do not believe that is possible."

"In this room, old fellow," said Holmes, shaking his head, "for I perceive that you harbour some doubts as to the truth of my conclusions. I shall be the coroner, and you, if you are agreeable, shall be the people of the parish, and act as both witness and jury."

"Certainly."

"Are you prepared to consider all the evidence fairly and impartially?"

"I am."

"Very well. Then let the inquest begin into the death of Sarah Dickens, who was found drowned upon 10 September 1878. Where was her body discovered?"

"At the Willow Pool, in Jenkin's Clump."

"Why had she gone there?"

"To pick blackberries."

"How do you know that?"

"Because she herself gave that as her intention to her family that morning. Also, she took with her a basket in which to collect the blackberries."

"Were there in fact any blackberries in the basket when it was found?"

"No."

"Did you observe any brambles on or near the road between Topley Cross and Jenkin's Clump?"

"I did. There are a great many."

"How would you describe the berries they bore, making allowance for the fact that it is now October and the fruit is past its best?"

"They were luxuriant. Even now, although I understand the fruit is not worth picking after the end of September, the bushes are laden with berries."

"And did you observe the brambles by the Willow Pool in Jenkin's Clump?"

"I did."

"How would you describe them in comparison to the others of which you have spoken?"

"They were relatively spindly and stunted. The fruit upon them was sparse, small and ill-formed."

"Can you suggest any reason for this?"

"Possibly the lack of sunlight in the wood. Brambles grow best in open country, when they are not overhung by trees."

"Do you think, Watson, that if you were a resident of Topley Cross you would choose to pick blackberries by the Willow Pool?"

"No."

"Can you believe that Sarah Dickens herself chose to pick them there?"

"No."

"In the light of that answer, would you like to reconsider your answer to the earlier question as to why Sarah Dickens went up to the Willow Pool on 10 September 1878? In particular, do you still believe that her chief or only purpose in going there was to pick blackberries?"

"No. She must have gone there for some other reason."

"Thank you. The point about the fruit is a perfectly straightforward one, you see. It must have been obvious to many people, including, no doubt, the girl's own mother, who had probably picked blackberries with her daughter in years gone by, but no one raised the matter. The reason they did not raise it, Watson, is that they feared to give support to the theory that the girl had deliberately taken her own life. The people of this parish, I am sure, are on the whole good and charitable people, but on this occasion their inclination to charity has led them astray. Now, if the girl did not go to Jenkin's Clump to pick blackberries there, then she went for some other reason. Can we say what that other reason might have been?"

I considered the matter for some time before replying. "Not with any confidence," I answered at length, "unless it was, as people have suspected, to take her own life."

"Is there no other reason that someone might go to a quiet, secluded spot, but to commit suicide?" queried my friend in a sceptical tone.

"To enjoy the peace of the countryside," I suggested, without any great conviction. "To reflect upon one's life, perhaps."

"Perhaps. But there are other, more commonplace reasons, which you seem determined to overlook. Do you recall the lunchtime of last Friday?"

"Certainly," I replied in surprise.

"You paid a visit then to the Criterion Bar. Why was that?"

"I had arranged to meet someone there."

"Precisely! Is it not at least possible, Watson, that Sarah Dickens went to the Willow Pool on the day of her death because she, too, had arranged to meet someone there?"

"Yes, I suppose it is."

"Thank you. Turning now from Sarah Dickens's purpose in going to Jenkin's Clump that day to the situation of her lifeless body when discovered, can you recall where it is said her body was found?"

"In the water, near the bank, on the far side from the footpath; that is, the northern bank, where the brambles grow thickly."

"Very well. From which part of the bank, then, do you think she entered the water?"

"The north side, surely, close to where her body was found."

"Why do you think she had gone round to that side of the pool?"

I hesitated. "It was thought that she had gone round to that side in order to pick blackberries," I replied after a moment, "but that does not now appear so likely."

"Quite so, especially when you consider that she had left her basket behind, on the south side of the pool. And nor had she returned to the north side to retrieve something she had dropped when picking blackberries earlier, for she had picked no blackberries earlier – the basket was empty. Nor can it be suggested with any plausibility that she took herself round to the north side of the water in order to stand and read her note there: it is a difficult, prickly spot, and there is barely space between the brambles and the water for anyone to stand. No one would choose to go there except to pick blackberries, and that, as we have seen, Sarah Dickens was not doing."

"Perhaps," I suggested, "her reason for going to the Willow Pool was to retrieve the note, which she realized she had dropped there on a previous visit. She may have seen it in the brambles from across the pool, left her basket by the footpath on the south side of the pool, and made her way round to the north side to try to reach the note."

"Ingenious, Watson!" cried Holmes with a chuckle. "That is, indeed, on the face of it, a possibility. Let us continue the hypothesis a little longer, then. What do you suggest happened next?"

"The most likely sequence of events is this," I began when I had considered the matter for a moment: "that she was stretching to try to reach the note, when she lost her balance, and perhaps her footing, too, and fell into the water. There she hit her head upon a submerged stone, as was suggested at the original inquest, lost consciousness and drowned."

"Capital!" cried my friend, clapping his hands together.

"You think there is some truth in that suggestion, then?" I asked, pleased that my hypothesis appeared to meet with his approval.

"No. None whatever."

"What!"

"I simply meant that you have presented your hypothesis cogently. It illustrates very clearly how convincing a hypothesis can be, even though quite fallacious, when it is derived from only a selection of the evidence, rather than from all of it."

"Pray, let us hear your own view, then," I retorted – irritated, I admit, by his tone of superiority.

"First of all," he replied, "on your hypothesis – and that which is implicit in the verdict of the original inquest – the girl would not have drowned had she not lost consciousness, and she would not have lost consciousness had she not struck her head upon a stone."

"That is so," I concurred. "Indeed, that seems an obvious inference."

"Well," said he, "it might well have been an obvious inference had there been any stones in the water. But there are none there, Watson, as I ascertained this afternoon. I am, I take it, the first person who has troubled himself to verify the assumption."

"Perhaps, then, she struck her head on the bottom of the pool," I suggested, "or on the bank as she slipped into the water."

"The bottom of the pool is soft and sandy, the bank grassy. Neither would have produced the bruise described by the local medical officer at the inquest."

"What then?"

"Well, it is your theory, old fellow. How do you account for the girl's drowning, if she did not knock herself unconscious?"

"We know from Mr Yarrow," I replied after a moment, "that her hair was tangled in the brambles that drooped into the water. Perhaps, then, after she fell in she became hopelessly entangled, with her head under the water and drowned in that way."

"The water is no more than three feet deep in that part of the pool," returned Holmes. "She could easily have stood up, out of the water."

"But if her hair was entangled?"

"Brambles are undoubtedly tough and troublesome," said Holmes, "but not so tough that a normal adult cannot overcome then. Besides, if the girl had struggled to free herself from prickly brambles, her hands would have been covered with scratches, and her scalp and face, too; yet the medical officer's report, read out at the inquest, specifically stated that there were no marks upon the body whatever, other than the bruise on the side of the head."

"Very well," said I. "I concede that you have disproved the view that Sarah Dickens's death was the result of mischance. The verdict of the inquest was wrong. But what of the possibility that she took her own life?"

"How might she have done that, do you suppose?" asked Holmes.

"I cannot pretend to be an expert in such matters, but I suppose she would have walked into the water until she was out of her depth, swallowed water and thus drowned."

"And then?"

"I am not sure what you mean. Presumably her body would have remained floating in the water until it was discovered."

"If we accept this hypothesis for a moment," said Holmes, "where, then, must the girl have entered the water?"

"There are only two places, realistically speaking," I returned. "Most of the circumference of the pool is thickly overgrown with brambles, briars, nettles and so on, and can thus be discounted. The two possible places are the flat, open area on the south bank, where we sat on the fallen tree, and the narrow strip by the brambles on the north bank, which we have spoken of already. Of the two, the former is by far the more likely. If the girl did not go round to the north bank in order to pick blackberries, or to retrieve that piece of paper, then there was no reason for her to go round there at all. It would be much easier, as well as more direct, for her to enter the water from the south bank."

"Very good. And do you recall the position of the body when found, according to the testimony of Mr Yarrow?"

"He said that it was a couple of feet from the bank on the north side, a little higher up the pool than the spot where one could pick blackberries."

"Did you observe the current in the pool?"

"I did. I observed your experiments with the sticks this morning. It runs, of course, from west to east, the direction of the stream that feeds and drains the pool."

"How do you suggest, then, that the body of Sarah Dickens was found on the other side of the pool, and upstream of the spot from where she must have entered the water?"

I considered the matter for a moment. The point had not, I confess, occurred to me before.

"Perhaps," I suggested at length, "the girl had waded up the pool a little way before she drowned."

"You say you observed my experiments with the sticks. Do you recall then, the fate of those sticks, large and small, which I threw into the centre of the pool?"

"Not specifically."

"Then I shall remind you. The current is much stronger and swifter in the centre of the pool, as one would expect, and anything floating there is swiftly borne to the extreme east end of the pool, where the stream leaves it."

"But if her hair had become entangled in the overhanging brambles?"

"It could only have become so entangled if her body had been carried by the current into that side of the pool. My experiments this morning established beyond doubt that the current in the pool has no tendency to do that."

"Then she must, after all, have entered the water from the far side."

"But the brambles there would have prevented her getting any higher up the pool unless she waded further out into the centre, and the current in the centre would then have carried her away from the bank, not towards it."

"Then it is impossible!" said I.

"Thank you," said Holmes in a magisterial tone. "This inquest has therefore determined that it is practically impossible that the girl's death was a mere mischance. It has also determined that it is practically impossible that the girl took her own life. What, then, is your final verdict?"

"I do not know," I responded with some hesitation. "Your analysis seems to make everything impossible!"

"Not quite everything," said he. "I refer you once more to the axiom that when you have eliminated the impossible, whatever remains, however improbable, must be the truth. I believe you see the truth, Watson, but are reluctant to voice it."

"I can still scarcely believe what you are suggesting," said I.

"It is not a question of what I am suggesting," returned my companion, "but of the verdict of this little inquest of ours. We have established beyond all reasonable doubt that the girl's death was due neither to suicide nor to accident. What then remains?"

"Murder," said I at last.

"Precisely, Watson. The verdict of the original inquest was 'accidental death'; the opinion of many in the parish is clearly that the girl's death was suicide; but they are all wrong. Sarah Dickens was murdered. She did not take her own life for love of Captain Reid, nor for love of anyone else, she did not accidentally lose her life while in a distracted state from love of Captain Reid or of anyone else; her life was cruelly taken from her in the most deliberate and cold-blooded manner. While all these people have been busying themselves in ostracizing poor Reid – who is, of course, perfectly innocent of all that he is charged with – the murderer of Sarah Dickens has been walking free, without a shadow of suspicion upon his name!"

"It is a terrible thought," said I, "and one that almost defies belief! Can it really be so? Can your theory really explain satisfactorily all the difficulties you have raised with regard to the other views of the matter?"

"Certainly it can," returned my friend in an assured tone. He refilled his pipe and put a match to it. "But you are right to ask the question, Watson. We shall make a detective of you yet, my dear fellow! One must, of course, always subject all theories to equally stringent analysis!"

"Well, then," I continued, "what of the bruise to the side of the girl's head, and the position of the body in the water, upstream of any place where she could have entered the pool?"

"Sarah Dickens was struck on the side of the head by the murderer," responded Holmes, "probably with a heavy stick, as there are no loose stones in the vicinity of the Willow Pool. The blow would have rendered her unconscious. The murderer must then have held her head under the water until she drowned, then propelled her lifeless body across the pool with some force, so that it reached the other side, a little way up the pool, where her hair became entangled in the brambles."

"Why should he push her body across the pool?"

"To delay its discovery. The footpath runs along the south bank of the pool, and an unobservant passer-by might well miss the body if it lay among the overhanging brambles by the north bank. So the murderer probably judged, anyway. He would wish to ensure that he was far from the scene before the body was discovered."

"But who, then, can the murderer be?" I asked after a moment. "What a great misfortune it is that so much time has passed since Sarah Dickens's death! There cannot possibly be any clue remaining now, after three years, which might guide us to her murderer!"

"On the contrary," returned my friend. "There are a number of indications. However," he continued, with a glance at the clock on the mantelpiece, "it is getting late, and as I must make an early start in the morning, I do not propose to stay up much longer. What I suggest," he continued, giving a pull on the bell-rope, which hung beside the fireplace, "is that we order a hot toddy and smoke a last pipe together, and then I really must turn in."

V: OAKBROOK HALL

I took my breakfast alone the following morning, for Sherlock Holmes had risen early and gone out before I was awake. He had been in a great hurry, so Mr Coleman informed me, and had declined the offer of breakfast.

"I understand you are leaving today, sir," the landlord added after a moment in a slightly hesitant tone.

"I cannot be certain yet as to our plans," I returned. "Did Mr Holmes inform you that we were leaving?"

The landlord shook his head. "No, sir. Admiral Blythe-Headley."

"I see. Well, he may be right, but I cannot yet say for certain."

"Admiral Blythe-Headley seemed very certain on the point," muttered Coleman to himself with a shake of the head as he left the room.

The morning passed very slowly. I understood the account of the case that Holmes had given me the previous evening, but the account had not been complete and I did not know what it was that he intended to do that day. I thus had no idea how long it might be until he returned. In vain I attempted to distract myself with one of the vicar's pamphlets on the prehistoric pathways of the South Downs, but the subject matter merely recalled to me the observations my friend had made on the subject of footpaths, at the Willow Pool, and brought my mind back once more to the strange business that had brought us down to this rural corner of England. I was aware from remarks

Holmes had made that he had tasks to perform that morning which he regarded as very important, and it was thus extremely frustrating for me to be sitting idly in the White Hart all morning, with no idea of how his plans were proceeding. Eventually, impatient to be doing something, whatever it was, I took my hat and stick and set off to walk the length of the high street, up to the churchyard.

It was another balmy autumn day, and the street was bathed in sunlight, but there were few people about and the village seemed very quiet. As I passed the hardware shop, I paused to examine the quite amazing variety of merchandise which was displayed in piles and stacks on the pavement outside. The door of the shop stood open, and I had lingered there a moment, when all at once, to my very great surprise, I heard the voice of Sherlock Holmes from within. I could not catch what he was saying, but his clear, slightly strident tone was unmistakable. I glanced in through the doorway, but could see no one there. Evidently, Holmes was in some back room, but what he was doing there, I could not imagine. Puzzled, I continued my walk.

In the churchyard, I rambled for some time among the gravestones, until at length, in the remotest corner, I found myself by chance before the gravestone of Sarah Dickens. For a long while I stared at it, reading over and over the inscription it bore, as I fell into a brown study. Here rested the mortal remains of a young girl who had supposedly met her death as the result of a tragic accident. Many people no doubt believed that to be the case. But it was evident that many others were equally convinced that she had deliberately taken her own life. Holmes alone dissented from both these opinions. In his view, the girl had been murdered. As I stood there in silent contemplation in that quiet country churchyard, the dappled sunlight playing upon the old stones, this struck me afresh as so shocking and horrible that I was once more assailed with doubt. Surely, it was too strange and terrible to be believed? Was it really possible that my friend, clever and perceptive though I knew him to be, could be right in this matter and everyone else entirely wrong? In a state of some doubt and puzzlement, I retraced my steps down the road to the White Hart.

As I approached the wide front door of the inn, a dog cart drew up in front of it. Two men were on the box, one of whom immediately sprang down with an appearance of great haste. I recognized him at once as Captain Reid. The other man I had not seen before. He was tall and lithe, with a sallow complexion and a thin moustache. I quickened my pace, followed Reid in through the inn door and caught him up in the hall, where we shook hands. I explained that Holmes had been absent all morning, but might have returned, and led him upstairs to the residents' sitting room. There, in a chair beside the fireplace, Holmes was sitting smoking his pipe, the blue smoke curling in lazy spirals above his head. He appeared deep in thought as we entered, but sprang to his feet in a moment.

"Captain Reid!" said he, shaking his client by the hand. "I am glad you have been able to return so promptly. I have much news to impart. And Watson! I was wondering where you had got to, old fellow!"

"Ranworth and I came as quickly as we could," responded Reid. "We caught the very first train from Rye this morning, but the connections were a little difficult. I am keen to hear your news, Mr Holmes, for I understand from your wire that you have discovered something that sheds light on the troubles I have had."

Much to my surprise, Holmes shook his head. "No," said he, "I have not discovered something, Captain Reid; I have discovered everything. I am now in a position to offer an explanation of every little incident that has puzzled you and caused you distress, from the broken window at Oakbrook Hall shortly before you left for India, to the white feather you received last week."

"I am amazed and thrilled to hear it," returned Reid. "But there is one thing, at least, that you cannot know."

"What is that, pray?"

"That another window has been broken at Oakbrook, in mysterious circumstances."

"What!" cried Holmes in surprise. "When did this occur?"

"Last night, apparently. Ranworth and I went straight to Oakbrook from the railway station this morning, and have just come from there now. The window that was broken is in a small dressing room that adjoins my bedroom. It must have occurred very late in the night, for no one heard it. Northcote was up late, working in the upstairs study, but that is at the other side of the house, and he says he heard nothing. The sound would have been slight in any case, for the panes of glass in that window are small ones, and whoever was responsible had smeared treacle on the glass and covered it with scraps of cloth, to muffle the noise and hold the pane together when it broke."

Holmes's keen, hawk-like features assumed a look of the most intense concentration, and it was clear that this news had surprised him. Then, with a groan, he slapped his hand to his forehead. "Of course!" cried he. "What a fool I have been! I should have expected such a development. An intruder has been in your dressing room, Captain Reid."

"That is evident," returned the other. "My travelling-trunk, which was in there, has been rifled."

"Is there any evidence of how the intruder might have gained access to the window? Is there a ladder anywhere about?"

Reid shook his head. "That would not have been necessary. Just below the window is the low roof of a pantry, from which it is very easy to climb through the window. I have climbed in there myself many times, as a boy."

"I see. Has anything been taken?"

"A small leather satchel containing my most private papers – diaries I kept while on active service, letters, copies of official dispatches and a few pencil sketches I made of the terrain around Candahar."

Holmes nodded. "When was the theft discovered?"

"Not until Ranworth and I reached Oakbrook a short while ago. I was attempting to speak to my father – with no great success, I am afraid – and Ranworth had gone up to my bedroom to look for a book of his, which I had borrowed from him the last time he was here and had left in my room. The door to the dressing room was open, and he at once observed the broken glass on the floor and the rifled trunk. The break-in could not have occurred earlier than last night, incidentally, for the maid was in my room yesterday, dusting the furniture, and she says she saw nothing amiss then. Do you believe this incident has any connection with any of the other matters that have occurred, Mr Holmes?"

"Indeed it has, Captain Reid. It follows with iron logic from all that has gone before," returned Holmes. "Where is Captain Ranworth now?"

"He is waiting for me in the trap, outside."

"Very good. We shall not keep him long. Now, if you will be seated here, I shall give you a sketch of what I have been able to discover – I shall provide a more detailed account later this afternoon – and then I shall explain to you a specific task, which I should like you to perform later this afternoon. First, however, there is a small point I wish to clear up. Do you recall losing a cufflink, some time during the summer of '78?"

"Why, yes, I do," returned Reid. "Of course, it seems such a long time ago now. I remember wondering if Major French or Captain Ranworth, who were staying here then, had taken it by mistake, as they both had similar cufflinks, but they said they had not. In the end I decided I must have dropped it in the orchard somewhere. We were helping with the apple-picking at the time, and I had rolled my shirt sleeves up and slipped the cufflinks into my waistcoat pocket. I suppose it must have fallen out as I was bending down. How on earth did you hear about it, Mr Holmes? Don't tell me the cufflink has turned up!"

"Indeed it has," returned Holmes, "although not, I'd wager, in a place you would expect. But, all things in order. You will appreciate the significance of the cufflink when I describe to you all that has happened here since you left these shores."

At twenty to three that afternoon, Sherlock Holmes and I took the trap from the White Hart to keep our appointment with Colonel Reid at Oakbrook Hall. At the top of the high street, as we passed the long curving wall of the churchyard, I saw Noah Blogg, our curious acquaintance from the Willow Pool, in the company of a squat, grey-bearded elderly man. They were just turning in at the gate of the vicarage, and I lost sight of them as we passed on at a clatter. About halfway to Oakbrook Hall we passed a rustic-looking figure striding out along the road, and I recognized John Dickens, brother of the dead girl. Holmes, meanwhile, spoke not a word during the journey, and I could see from the tense, strained expression upon his features that he was in a state of heightened expectancy.

Shortly before three o'clock we arrived before the front door of Oakbrook Hall. It was a broad, symmetrical building, built of red brick. Standing before it and dominating the approach to the house was a very tall and spreading cedar, beneath the curving branches of which our trap halted.

We were shown into a large square room to the right of the front door. From the bureaux it contained, and the shelves of books that lined the walls, I took it to be the study of which Captain Reid had spoken. Almost in the very centre of the room stood a broad desk, and upon this, on a heavy wooden stand, rested a very large globe. On one wall, flanked on either hand by bookshelves, was a pair of French windows, through which I could see the neat and attractive garden at the side of the house. After a few moments, we heard footsteps approaching, and a tall young man strode briskly into the room. He had sallow skin, and dark hair and moustache, and I recognized him as the man I had seen in the trap outside the White Hart earlier in the day. He introduced himself as Captain Ranworth.

"The others will be along in a minute," said he. "While we are waiting, I'll show you the pantry roof, from which someone must have climbed into Reid's room last night."

He opened the French windows and we followed him into the garden. To the left, near the back of the house, a small single-storey extension protruded from the house wall at right angles. Just above its tiled roof was a small square window.

"As you see," Ranworth continued, leading us along to the wall of the pantry, "it would not be too difficult to climb onto the pantry roof. Once there, to get into the dressing-room window would be very easy."

Holmes crouched down and examined the ground by the pantry wall. "There are no marks here," said he after a moment, rising to his feet.

"I suppose the intruder took special care not to leave any," responded Ranworth. "I observed earlier, however, that one of the tiles on the pantry roof is cracked," he continued, directing our attention to the tile in question, "but, of course, it may have been cracked for some time."

"It does appear rather ancient damage," remarked Holmes, squinting up at the pantry roof. "The broken edges of the tile are discoloured with age. But, come! It sounds as if the others have arrived. Let us return to the library and proceed with matters."

In the library we found Holmes's client, his father, and the secretary, Northcote, standing together in awkward silence.

"Well?" said Colonel Reid to Holmes as we entered through the French windows. "We are all here as you requested. Now let us get this nonsense over with as quickly as possible."

Before Holmes could reply, there came the sound of a horse and carriage on the drive outside.

"Now what?" cried Colonel Reid irritably. "Who in Heaven's name is this?" His question was answered a moment later, when the butler opened the door and announced the arrival of Admiral Blythe-Headley, accompanied by his son and daughter. "What!" cried Colonel Reid in a tone of stupefaction.

"This is not a social call, Reid," said Blythe-Headley loudly, in a tone of distaste, as he strode into the room. "It gives us as little pleasure to be here as I imagine it gives you to see us. But I have been persuaded to come against my will and, I might add, against my better judgement, in order to hear what this gentleman has to relate." He inclined his head slightly in the direction of Sherlock Holmes, and everyone turned to see what my friend would say.

"I have requested this meeting," said Holmes after a moment, "to acquaint you all with certain facts."

"Pah! Facts!" cried Admiral Blythe-Headley with a snort. "What facts, pray?"

"Facts which I have good reason to believe are not known to you," responded Holmes. "In so doing, it is my hope that I might help to right the most grievous wrong that has been done to Captain Reid."

Blythe-Headley snorted again, and Colonel Reid sighed in a sceptical manner, but Anthony Blythe-Headley held up his hand.

"One moment," said he. "Let us hear what Mr Holmes wishes to say. We have already wasted enough time in coming here. Let us not waste further time in prolonging the nonsense!"

"When Captain Reid returned recently from India," Holmes continued when the room had fallen silent once more, "he was met with a hostility for which he could think of no explanation."

"Well, he obviously did not think hard enough," snapped Colonel Reid.

"Over the course of the following days," Holmes continued, ignoring the interruption, "incidents occurred which he found equally inexplicable. He received a white feather in the post, for instance, and was accused of damaging a garden bench at Topley Grange. Finally, brought to a very low ebb by these unpleasant events, he consulted me. I have therefore spent the last few days conducting a thorough enquiry into the matter, and am now in a position to lay the full facts before my client, and before all those who know him. It will be apparent when I do so that Captain Reid has been the victim of a most serious miscarriage of justice."

"You are trying our patience," interjected Anthony Blythe-Headley, taking his watch from his pocket in an ostentatious manner. "You have not yet told us anything we did not already know. Unless you do so within the next three minutes, I for one shall bid you *adieu!*"

"My enquiries quickly led me to the death in this parish, three years ago, of one Sarah Dickens," Holmes continued. "Although this matter will be a familiar one to most of you, it was completely unknown to Captain Reid."

"Humbug!" muttered Colonel Reid.

"It soon became apparent to me that Captain Reid was widely regarded as having treated this girl shamefully. In a fit of melancholy, it was supposed, this girl had taken her own life, or, at least, had been so careless of it that she had lost it accidentally."

The room had at last fallen silent, as Holmes described the tragedy that had cast such a shadow upon the parish. I stole a glance at the faces of those assembled there, and it was clear that all were recalling the events of three years previously. After a moment, Holmes continued:

"There seemed, despite the verdict of the inquest, to be some doubt as to whether the girl's death was the result of an accident or suicide. I therefore determined to look into the matter myself and form my own opinion."

"What possible difference can that make now?" demanded Admiral Blythe-Headley.

"As it has turned out, it makes a great deal of difference," responded Holmes. He thereupon described in detail the investigations he had conducted at the Willow Pool, the testimony of Mr Yarrow concerning the discovery of the girl's body and the conclusions he had reached from this information. As he worked his way methodically through his account, a hush fell upon the assembly, and it was evident that all present were impressed by the painstaking care with which he had conducted his investigation.

"So what you are saying," said Anthony Blythe-Headley at length, as Holmes finished speaking, "is that, in your opinion, it is impossible for the girl's death to have been an accident?"

"I am morally certain of it."

"But nor do you believe," interjected Captain Ranworth, "that her death could have been suicide?"

"That, also, is practically impossible."

"But what, then, is your opinion?" queried Northcote in a tone of puzzlement.

"There are only three possibilities," replied Holmes in a dry tone, "and it is an axiom of mine that when you have eliminated the impossible, whatever remains, however unlikely, must be the truth."

"Then?"

"Sarah Dickens was murdered."

"Absurd!" cried someone. "Nonsense!" cried another.

"You may call it absurd if you wish," responded Holmes in a calm, authoritative voice, "but it is the truth."

Anthony Blythe-Headley appeared greatly disturbed by what Holmes had said. A variety of emotions passed in rapid succession across his agitated features.

"You are overlooking the note, sir!" cried he at length in a hot tone. "The girl left a note. The inquest did not regard it as a suicide note, but everyone else with half a brain does so. Are you suggesting that the girl composed her note, which clearly implied that her life was not worth living, and then, by chance, encountered someone who obligingly put an end to her life? That would be an absurd coincidence!"

"I agree. I am not suggesting that."

"Then what? You cannot deny that the note implies that the girl was considering taking her own life!"

"It might imply that, under certain circumstances," responded Holmes in a calm tone.

"What circumstances, pray?" interrupted the other.

"The circumstance, for a start, that the girl actually wrote the note."

"What! What do you mean?" demanded the admiral.

"Sarah Dickens did not write the note that was found in Jenkin's Clump. It is a forgery, left there deliberately by her murderer to throw any enquiries off the true scent."

There was a general cry of incredulity at this pronouncement.

"What fantastic nonsense is this!" cried Colonel Reid in a tone of disbelief.

"It is the truth."

"How can you know?" demanded the colonel. "What possible reason can you have for supposing such a thing?"

"Because the forger has made a mistake. I have seen the note, and I have seen an exercise book of poems that Sarah Dickens had written, and the handwriting, although very similar, is not the same."

"Everyone else considers the note to be in the girl's own hand."

"Everyone else is wrong."

"Why should you be the only one to detect this difference?"

"Because I am the only one who has examined the writing with sufficient care."

"But even her own family accepted that the note was genuine, and no one could have been more familiar with her hand than they were."

"Well, of course, the two samples of handwriting are very similar. If you were writing a note, but wished it to appear to be the work of another, you would obviously take great pains to make the letters appear as much like those of the other person as possible. There would be little point in attempting the task otherwise. That the note found by the Willow Pool was taken to be the work of Sarah Dickens is thus no more than one would expect, under the circumstances. The dead girl's hand was neat and regular. She had evidently learnt her handwriting lessons at school very well. Her style did not deviate to any significant extent from the copybook style she had been taught, and displayed few of those idiosyncrasies to which an older person's hand is prone. This would have made it uncommonly easy to imitate, and it cannot be denied that the murderer – for the murderer's hand it must be – made a good job of it. However, he made a little slip. He missed the one variation that Sarah Dickens had introduced into her hand – the formation of the letter 'f'. There are, as I recall, three instances of this letter in the note that was found, and not one of them is formed in the same way as those in her book of poetry. It was almost the very first thing that struck me when I saw the two samples of writing."

"But surely everyone's hand varies a little, each time pen is put to paper," protested Admiral Blythe-Headley in a sceptical tone.

"That is true, but such trivial and transient variations are not important. There are certain letters, however, those, generally speaking, which are more complex in structure, which are especially liable to idiosyncratic formation, and are thus of particular importance in identifying the author of a piece of writing. Of these letters, although 'b' and 'g' may also be of significance, 'f' is generally the most reliable guide."

"That is amazing!" cried Captain Ranworth.

"On the contrary," returned Holmes, "it is perfectly elementary; but like everything else in this woeful case, it is an issue that was overlooked or misjudged by those whose duty it was to establish the truth of the matter. The girl did not write the note, and thus it is of no direct relevance to her death. It has, however, been of immense importance to the case as a whole."

"What on earth do you mean?" demanded Admiral Blythe-Headley in a tone of bewilderment. "Stop speaking in riddles, man!"

"I mean simply this," replied Holmes in a calm voice, "that everyone at the inquest was at very great pains to declare that the note in question did not constitute a suicide note. It is perfectly clear, nevertheless, that it was the existence of the note that planted the idea of suicide so firmly in the general mind, conjuring up so vividly as it did the picture of a sad and forlorn young lady, who, it appeared, had been pining for a lost love. Had there been no note, perhaps the people of this parish would not have been so blind as to what really occurred that afternoon at the Willow Pool. The note also served, by its use of the phrase 'you have gone away and left me' to confirm what many had suspected concerning Captain Reid: that he had at least been trifling with Sarah Dickens, and had perhaps seriously abused her affection, for at the time of the girl's death, of course, when the note was discovered, Reid had indeed 'gone away' less than two weeks previously. In sum, the note was one of the very foundation stones of the terrible obloquy that has been heaped so unjustifiably upon the head of this unfortunate young man."

There was silence for a moment in the room, and it was evident that Holmes's careful and detailed exposition of the case had made a very profound impression upon everyone there.

"I can hardly credit my ears," said Admiral Blythe-Headley at length. "You have argued your case very well, young man, but I am still not entirely convinced. What about our garden bench? You will be telling us next that John Reid was not responsible for that, either!"

"That is correct. He had nothing to do with it."

"What! Of course he did!" the admiral retorted. "It could be no other but he! Why, he was seen to be loitering in the garden pavilion earlier in the afternoon! We certainly had no other visitors that day."

"It was not a visitor that caused the damage."

"One moment!" Ranworth interrupted. "Where has Reid himself vanished to?"

I turned to see. The last time I had glanced in his direction, Captain Reid had been standing by the open door of the room. Now he was nowhere to be seen; he had evidently slipped away while the attention of everyone else had been upon Sherlock

Holmes. There were general expressions of surprise and perplexity; Holmes alone appearing unperturbed by his client's disappearance.

"He will be back in a few moments," was his only remark.

Captain Ranworth appeared momentarily confused, but at length he spoke. "I was about to remark," said he, "that it is a great misfortune that three years have passed since these events of which Mr Holmes has been speaking. I, for one, am sure that all that you say is correct, Mr Holmes; but now, after so much time has elapsed, there must be very little likelihood of our ever discovering who was really responsible for the death of Sarah Dickens."

"On the contrary," returned Holmes in a firm voice, "I am confident that I could very quickly lay my hand upon the man responsible." He turned to Colonel Reid. "You expressed some doubt earlier when I stated that your son returned home from India perfectly ignorant of what was alleged against him."

The colonel nodded his head vigorously. "I have kept my peace until now," said he in a firm voice, "and have allowed you to state your case at some length. But you must know that everything you say is vitiated by one simple consideration: if my son is as innocent of any involvement in this affair as you claim, why, then, did he not take the opportunity I offered him to deny the allegations?"

"You wrote to him on the matter when he was in India?"

"Yes, of course I did. I described to him the rumours that were circulating following the death of that girl, and asked him to assure me that they were utterly false. He did not respond to my request. I then wrote to him again, stating that if he did not clearly deny the rumours to me, I would take it that he could not, because they were true. Again, he did not respond. Only one conclusion was possible."

"Colonel Reid," said Holmes, "your son never received the letters you sent. That is why he did not respond to the rumours and accusations."

"There you are quite wrong, Mr Holmes," returned the other. "There is no doubt whatever that he received them, for in the letters that he wrote to me he responded to one or two other trivial matters that I had mentioned in my letters, but not to my questions about Sarah Dickens."

"I say again," Holmes persisted, "that your son never received the letters you wrote to him. They were intercepted by someone else, someone who did not wish your son to have the opportunity to deny the rumours and thus clear his name."

"What!" cried the colonel. "Do you seriously expect me to believe such nonsense? If that were so, how came he, then, to respond to the other matters included in my letters?"

"Because he that intercepted your letters substituted compositions of his own, which repeated all the remarks you had made on other matters, but omitted every reference to Sarah Dickens. These were the letters that your son received. He did not respond to any questions about Sarah Dickens because he was not aware that you had asked any."

"That is an utterly fantastic theory!" cried Colonel Reid. "What could anyone hope to gain by such a deception? It would be bound to come to light eventually."

"Not necessarily. India is never the most peaceful spot in the world, and the north-west provinces in particular have been in uproar. He that interfered with your post no doubt thought it possible that your son would lose his life during his service there, and that the deception would thus never be discovered."

"And does your theory suggest anyone in particular?" asked Colonel Reid in an ironic tone. "Or is it merely of a general nature?"

"The man responsible is your secretary, William Northcote."

"What!" cried the colonel.

"How dare you!" said Northcote, his voice trembling with emotion. "That is an outrageous suggestion! I am aware that Reid has employed you to effect a reconciliation between himself and his father, but I could never have imagined that you would stoop so low as this! You seek to achieve your aim by blackening my name without justification!"

"Even if Reid were not killed in India and returned home," continued Holmes, speaking in a calm voice and ignoring the protests of the other man, "your scheme might still prove successful, you considered, so long as father and son remained estranged, so that the discrepancies between the letters written by the one and those received by the other did not come to light."

"Nonsense!"

"Fortunately for Captain Reid, he consulted me, and I have been able to discover the truth. After you spoke to us yesterday evening, at the White Hart, you feared that exposure was at hand, which is why you arranged the supposed burglary last night. It was you that broke the window, Northcote, when everyone else in the house was asleep, to make it appear that the theft was the work of an intruder from outside. But there was no intruder. It was you that stole Reid's private papers, for you wished to prevent his showing the letters to his father."

"That is a monstrous suggestion!" cried the secretary.

At that moment there came a surprising interruption. Captain Reid himself stepped into the room, carrying in his hand a small leather satchel. I had the impression that he had been waiting for some time outside the doorway, listening to what was being said.

"I have the stolen papers here," said he, holding up the satchel. "It was in one of the places you suggested, Mr Holmes, hidden at the bottom of Northcote's wardrobe."

"It's a lie!" cried Northcote.

"I will swear to it under oath," returned Reid. "Besides, why should I lie?"

"To blacken my name further," cried Northcote, whose face had assumed a pale, sickly hue. "This is slander, gross slander! Gentlemen, I call upon all here present to witness this slander! I shall see this matter settled in court!"

"When my father sees these letters, which he did not write, but which are in an imitation of his hand," said Reid in a cold voice, "I think it is I that shall be the plaintiff in court and you the defendant, Northcote!"

For a long moment, the secretary said nothing, but looked at each of us in turn as he swayed slightly on his feet. Then, abruptly, he flung himself to his knees in front of his employer and wrung his hands in silent entreaty. "It is true," he cried at last. "I confess it. In a moment of madness I did it. I destroyed the letter you had written to your son and substituted one of my own, in which I made no reference to Sarah Dickens. I was angry that although he had treated the girl so badly and, as everyone seemed to think, driven her to take her own life, nevertheless the strong bond between father and son still persisted. This seemed to me unfair. Why should he live on happily when the one to whom he had caused so much sorrow had died? But as soon as the letter was sent, I regretted it bitterly. It was a hateful, shameful thing to do. Having falsified one letter, however, I was then obliged to falsify the next. Oh, have pity on me for my shameful actions!"

There was a general shuffling of feet in the room, but no one spoke, and it was clear that no one could think what to say. Captain Reid looked down coldly at the abject figure of his father's secretary squirming on the floor, and eventually broke the silence.

"I ought to kick you from here to the coast," said he in a tone of disgust.

"Let me see those letters," said Colonel Reid abruptly, like a man coming out of a dream.

"One moment," interrupted Holmes, and the room fell silent once more as everyone turned to see what he would say. "Let us not become too distracted by the matter of the letters. You may see them in a minute, Colonel Reid. But there is a greater crime in question here than the forging of letters: the murder of Sarah Dickens."

"No!" cried Northcote in a hoarse voice, rising unsteadily to his feet. "It cannot be! Sarah Dickens took her own life. Everyone believes that, save you, Mr Know-all Holmes! I would never have falsified any letters had I thought that the matter was one of murder!"

"If everyone believes that Sarah Dickens took her own life, then everyone is in error. Sarah did not take her own life, and nor was her death an accident: she was murdered. The murderer had planned it coldly and carefully for some time. He had arranged to meet her by the Willow Pool on the afternoon she died. He had, I believe, feigned affection for her, and she no doubt went to meet him expecting to be met with friendship, but the only desire that stirred in his heart was a desire to be rid of someone whose existence was an inconvenience to him. He went to the Willow Pool that day for one reason only, to murder Sarah Dickens in cold blood."

"Your arguments have been very convincing, Mr Holmes," interrupted Admiral Blythe-Headley. "Do you have any evidence to lead you to the culprit?"

"I have a witness," responded Holmes. So saying, he stepped to the open French windows and called to someone in the garden outside. The next moment Mr Yarrow, the vicar, entered, and with him was Noah Blogg.

"Now, Noah," said the vicar, "tell these gentlemen what you told me earlier."

The large young man hesitated, and seemed cowed and frightened by the grave faces about him.

"You remember the day you and Harry Cork found the body of Sarah Dickens in the Willow Pool?" said the vicar by way of a prompt. The young man nodded his head dumbly and the vicar continued: "You had seen Sarah earlier that day, had you not, Noah?" Again the young man nodded. "Where had you seen her, Noah?"

"In the shop, sir," Blogg responded at length. "She came in to buy pegs. She talked to Mother."

"What did she say?"

"She said she was going to pick blackberries at Jenkin's Clump. Mother said they were better down the hill a way, and Sarah thanked her and said she'd look down there, too. After she'd gone, Mother said, 'That girl's up to something.'"

"Do you know what she meant by that?" asked Holmes.

Noah Blogg shook his head. "No, sir," he answered.

"Can you think what she might have meant by it, then?"

Blogg appeared confused and did not immediately respond. "Perhaps Sarah was going to meet somebody," he answered at length.

"Very well. What did you do then?"

"Thought I'd go up the Clump myself and surprise Sarah."

"And did you?"

The young man nodded his head in a reluctant fashion, as if he would rather not continue.

"So you went to Jenkin's Clump?" persisted Holmes.

"Yes," responded Blogg at length. "There weren't nobody there."

"And then?" queried Holmes, as the young man fell silent once more.

"Sarah came, and a man came down the other path."

"Did they see you?"

"No, sir. I was behind a tree."

"And then?"

"Sarah said something, then he got hold of her and she shouted a lot, then he hit her and she stopped shouting. Then he pushed her in the water."

"And then?"

"I went to have a look. He saw me and said, 'What are you doing here, Blogg?' and I said, 'Nothing, sir.' Then he said, 'Sarah's had a fit. You mustn't say anything or they'll think you killed her. You keep quiet and don't say a word, and I'll not tell them I saw you here. But if you say anything, I'll tell them you killed her.' So I had to keep quiet."

"I see," said Holmes. "I think we all understand. Now, Noah, the man you saw in the woods that day with Sarah, do you see him in this room now?"

The young man's expression was one of utmost terror, and he did not raise his eyes from the floor.

"You have nothing to fear," said Holmes in a voice that was kindly but firm, "but you must tell the truth, Noah. Is that man here now?"

"Yes," mumbled Blogg, "it's him."

Slowly, then, he raised his hand and pointed his finger at Colonel Reid's secretary, William Northcote.

"What nonsense!" cried the secretary. "This is an outrage! How dare you say such things, Blogg!" Then he turned to Holmes. "I don't know how you have persuaded this simpleton to lie in this way," said he in a bitter tone, "but you will not get away with it!"

"It won't do, Northcote," returned Holmes, shaking his head. "These displays of outrage and remorse ring equally hollow. You murdered Sarah Dickens and forged the note that was found by the pool, to throw suspicion onto John Reid. You also placed one of his cufflinks, which you had found or stolen, into a pocket of the dead girl's dress, to make the public suspicions against him even stronger. You then destroyed his father's letters to him and sent him substitute letters of your own creation, to prevent his responding to the rumours, which you yourself had caused."

The secretary attempted to laugh, but it was a hoarse, harsh cry that escaped his lips. "Why should I kill Sarah Dickens?" he cried. "Why, she did not interest me at all!"

"No," said Holmes. "I agree. She did not interest you. Rather, she was a danger to you. She knew something about you that you did not wish anyone else to know."

"And what was that, pray?" demanded Northcote in a sneering tone.

"That you had been making free with Colonel Reid's private papers, forging his signature and helping yourself to his money."

What happened next remains as little more than a blur in my memory. I have mentioned that upon the desk in the centre of the room was a very large globe. Now, with a sudden lunge, Northcote grasped this globe with both hands, lifted it from its stand and hurled it across the room to where we stood. There were cries, Miss Blythe-Headley screamed, and in the same instant the secretary dashed out through the French windows, into the garden. For a split second we all remained transfixed by this sudden eruption of violence, then, with a pitiful cry and an expression of the utmost agony upon his features, Colonel Reid collapsed to the floor like a rag doll.

"Good God!" cried his son in alarm.

"He has had a seizure!" I cried. "Stand back!" Quickly, I bent down and examined the limp, prostrate figure. His haggard face was a dull grey colour and his lips had turned purple. For a moment I feared that he was beyond all human help, but as I loosened his collar and desperately examined him for signs of life, there came the faintest of breaths from his dry lips. "Is there a fire lit in his bedroom?" I asked his son.

"There's one laid ready," replied he. "We'll put a match to it at once."

"Then help me carry him to his bed. We must keep him warm and make him as comfortable as possible."

"Northcote will be getting away!" cried someone behind me as we carried the old man from the room and turned up the stairs.

"He will not get far," I heard Holmes respond. "I have sentries posted in the garden for just such an eventuality."

It was some time before I was able to return to the library. I had done all I could for Colonel Reid, sent his servant for the family physician and left him in the care of his son and the housekeeper. As I rejoined the company downstairs, they were discussing the apprehension of Northcote. I gathered that he had been brought back to the library, and that Holmes had instructed that he be taken at once to the constable in Topley Cross, with a message of explanation which Holmes himself had written.

"So," said Admiral Blythe-Headley, "you expected Northcote to flee in this way?"

"I thought it not unlikely," returned Holmes. "My sentries, as you saw, were Jack Blogg, father of Noah, and John Dickens, brother of the dead girl. He naturally has an interest in seeing the truth established, and justice done. He is employed at Topley Grange, I understand, Admiral."

"That is so. He assists his father on their own farm in the mornings and works in our gardens in the afternoons. We employ several of the local smallholders in this way at various times of the year. They are by far the best workers, we have found."

"It was Dickens that damaged your garden bench."

"What!" cried the admiral. "The blackguard! He will never work for me again!"

Holmes held up his hand. "Do not rush to decisions, I pray you," said he. "This whole business has been marked by over-hasty judgements, almost all of which have been proved wrong. You must understand that Dickens has been sorely afflicted by his sister's death. He may appear a somewhat rude and unpolished young man, but he has a good heart, and had, I believe, a deep and genuine affection for his sister. I am sure he no more feels the sentiments he carved into your woodwork than would Captain Reid himself, whom you previously accused of it. But on the day last week that Reid visited Topley Grange, Dickens was working in the gardens, and was incensed that this man whom he regarded as morally responsible for his sister's death should, as he saw it, be renewing his social round as if nothing were amiss. Consumed with rage, he determined to do all he could to further wound Reid's standing in the district. He correctly judged that if he damaged the bench in the way he did, Reid would be blamed for it."

"How did you discover that Dickens was responsible?" I asked.

"Mr Yarrow had mentioned to us that Dickens had been employed at Topley Grange on the day of his sister's death, and I thought it likely that he was still so employed. If so, it seemed a distinct possibility to me that he was responsible for the damage, for I was already convinced that it was he that sent the white feather to Reid."

"Why so?" I asked

"The yard at Hawthorn Farm, as you no doubt observed, is littered with white duck feathers that are precisely the same as the feather Reid received. In addition, a blank sheet had been torn from the girl's exercise book, as you yourself remarked, Watson, and this, as I observed, exactly corresponded to the sheet that enclosed the feather, marked with the initials S. D."

"How came Dickens, a man so full of hatred for Captain Reid, to be your ally?" asked Mary Blythe-Headley in puzzlement. "I should have expected his attitude to you to have been one only of hostility."

"And so it was, when we spoke to him yesterday, as Dr Watson will confirm. But when I called to see him very early this morning, before he had left the house, I was armed with the knowledge – or conviction, at least – that it was he who had sent the anonymous letter to Reid and damaged the bench, by both of which actions, I assured him, he had laid himself open to criminal proceedings. By this threat I secured his attention and, little by little, managed to convince him that the deep hostility he held towards my client was quite misplaced. It was steep, steep work, I can assure you, but in the end I succeeded. I think you will find, Admiral, that Dickens will henceforth prove to be an honest worker, and if you can forgive him his one lapse, will never again damage your property."

The admiral appeared unmoved by my friend's plea for forgiveness on behalf of his errant gardener, but then his daughter spoke out.

"Oh Father," said she, "have a little charity! It is I who am insulted by the carving on the bench, and I certainly don't care about it! You fear that you have been led to make a fool of yourself in sending that bill to Colonel Reid, but you should not punish Dickens simply because you feel foolish. None of these things would have occurred if only you and Anthony had had a little more confidence in Captain Reid, and had not been so hasty to think the worst of him."

Admiral Blythe-Headley appeared angry at this lecture from his daughter. He opened his mouth to speak, but closed it again without saying anything, as Captain Reid re-entered the room.

"How is your father?" asked Mary Blythe-Headley in a voice of concern.

"He is sleeping peacefully now," returned Reid. "He appears comfortable enough, and we must hope that, with rest, he will recover. But, pray tell me what has happened while I have been absent."

In a few words, Holmes apprised his client of all that had occurred.

"This is a simply astounding business," said Reid with a shake of the head, as Holmes finished speaking. "What on earth led you to the conclusion that Northcote lay behind it all? And how did you know that Noah Blogg knew more of the matter than anyone had ever supposed?"

"As it happens, those two aspects of the matter came together in one moment of enlightenment, from my point of view," Holmes replied. "Dr Watson and I had an appointment yesterday afternoon to meet Mr Yarrow by the Willow Pool in Jenkin's Clump. We were standing near the pool when he arrived, and as

I saw him at the top of the hill, it passed briefly through my mind that we were probably very close to the spot upon which Noah Blogg had been standing when you encountered him last week, and that the vicar, who was on the path from here to the pool, was at the same place as you had been when Blogg first saw you. It was also, I might add, at almost exactly the same time of day, a little after two o'clock in the afternoon. This coincidence might have passed from my mind as swiftly as it had entered it, but for one singular fact: as I looked up the steep pathway, waiting to greet the vicar, I realized all at once that I could not see him."

"What on earth do you mean?" asked Reid in a tone of puzzlement.

"It was, as I say, shortly after two o'clock on a very sunny day, and the path from here to Jenkin's Clump runs as you are aware, from south to north. As I looked up the hill, the sun lay almost directly behind Mr Yarrow, and all I could see of him was a black silhouette. It really would have been impossible for me to swear whether the man I saw were he or not. It must have been precisely the same for Blogg when he saw you there last week, on what, as you described it to us, was also a very sunny day. You could see clearly that it was he, but he could not possibly have known that the dark figure he saw at the top of the path was you. Considering that you had been back in the parish for scarcely twenty-four hours, and that Blogg was probably unaware at that time of your return, it becomes even less likely that he recognized you. Yet, as you recounted to us the other day, he looked up at you for only the briefest of moments before letting out a howl of fear and fleeing, as if for his life, through the woods. Clearly, he was in mortal terror of someone, but the more I considered the matter, the more convinced I became that that someone was not you.

"But if not you, then who could it be? What other young man of a roughly similar height and stature might be walking on the path from Oakbrook Hall? Clearly, the most likely candidate was your father's secretary, Northcote. But this raised further questions: why should Blogg be in such fear of anyone, and why, in particular, should he be in such fear of Northcote?

Dr Watson and I had met Blogg earlier in the day, and had found him an amiable and friendly young man. It was clear, however, that despite his fine physique, his simple cast of mind gave him a certain timidity of manner. Such a young man, I judged, might well be cowed into fearfulness by threats from someone with a more powerful character than his own. But why should Northcote, or anyone else, have threatened him? Then I recalled that during his interview with us, by the Willow Pool, in which the subject of Sarah Dickens had been raised, his gaze had continually wandered, involuntarily as it appeared, to a particular spot in the water, close by where we were standing.

"Now, as I was later to learn from Mr Yarrow, this was not the place where the dead girl's body had been found, and yet it seemed to hold a fascination for Noah Blogg. Could it be, I conjectured, that he had witnessed something there involving Northcote, and that the latter had threatened him in some way, in order to secure his silence? This conjecture, I need hardly add, was strengthened considerably when, by the process of argument I described to you earlier, I concluded that the spot which held such a morbid fascination for Blogg was indeed the very spot on which Sarah Dickens had been murdered. The more I reflected on the matter, the more I became convinced that it was Northcote who had murdered Sarah Dickens, for the hypothesis accorded with every other fact of which I was aware.

"Clearly, it was imperative that I find a way to overcome the fear that had been planted in Blogg's breast, and persuade him to tell what he knew. I could, I judged, present a reasonably compelling case without Blogg's testimony, but to have it would undoubtedly strengthen my position considerably. I realized that to gain his trust on such an important matter would be no mean achievement, but I am glad to say I eventually succeeded this morning, with considerable assistance, I must record, from Blogg's father, whom I had earlier managed to persuade of the truth of the matter."

"Thank the Lord you did succeed!" cried Reid.

"You have performed a very great service to all of us, Mr Holmes," said Mary Blythe-Headley. Holmes bowed his head in acceptance of the compliment as she continued, "Those who doubted John's honesty and integrity, and who doubted, also, your abilities and motives, owe you both a sincere and profound apology."

There was an uncomfortable silence in the room for a moment, then Admiral Blythe-Headley stepped forward and extended his hand.

"I regret greatly," said he in a gruff voice, "the manner in which I addressed you last night, Mr Holmes. I was guilty of gross rudeness. Please accept my sincerest apologies."

Holmes nodded as he took the hand that was offered to him. "You were guilty, perhaps, as I observed earlier, of being a trifle hasty in your judgements."

"I have often felt, during the last three years," said Anthony Blythe-Headley abruptly, "that my father's great animosity towards Reid was borne at least partly from an unstated, and perhaps unacknowledged, fear that I had been involved in some way with the dead girl. No, Father, do not protest! I know it to be true; I have read it often in your eyes. I need hardly say that such a fear was quite groundless, but I resented my father thinking such a thing of me, and in my stupidity I blamed Reid for causing him to have such thoughts." He paused and shook his head. "I used to think that I was such a clever fellow, but my pretensions to intellect have been shamed by this gentleman," he continued, indicating Holmes. "He alone has used his brain in an honourable and worthy manner!" He paused again. "It is clear to me now that I am the most stupid dolt in the parish! And to think that all along it was Northcote that had been involved with the girl!"

"I doubt it was as simple as that," said Holmes with a shake of the head.

"I do not follow you," said Anthony Blythe-Headley.

"Regrettably, it must be admitted that men and women do sometimes murder those with whom they have been affectionate, but not usually so quickly as in this instance, and we must suspect that the true motives in this case have not yet come to light. What does seem very likely, however, is that Northcote's involvement with Sarah Dickens was not quite as it appears, and that any display of affection on his part was feigned merely to ensure her silence for a few weeks until he could seal her lips permanently. That he did feign some affection is suggested, I believe, by a page which has been cut from her exercise book of poems: it has been very neatly removed with a pair of nail scissors, and we must suppose it was done by the girl herself. The page is nowhere in evidence now – I have questioned John Dickens on the point – so we may further suppose that she gave it to Northcote. Very likely, that cold and heartless man feigned an interest in her poetry, as he had feigned an interest in the girl herself, and requested it. She would have been flattered by this request, not realizing that he wanted the page only to have a sample of her handwriting from which to prepare the note he intended to leave in Jenkin's Clump when he had murdered her. If that page ever turns up among his papers, incidentally, I'll warrant that it contains no instances of the letter 'f'."

"You speak of Northcote wishing to ensure her silence," interrupted Reid in a tone of some puzzlement, "but about what, pray?"

"Something she knew about Northcote himself," replied Holmes, "something he did not wish anyone to know. It is a point, I admit, which exercised my mind for some time until I hit upon a solution. For how could a local peasant girl like Sarah Dickens learn anything of significance about a man such as Northcote, who occupied a station far removed from her experience and knowledge?"

"It does seem a trifle unlikely," concurred Reid.

"Indeed; unlikely, but not impossible. It seems to me probable – although here I stray into the realm of conjecture – that this whole business began on the day that Sarah fainted from the heat when picking apples in the orchard here, an incident that Mr Yarrow described to me. If you will recall, Captain Reid, you helped carry her to the house."

"I remember it well. We brought her into this very room, through the French windows, and laid her on the couch in the corner there."

"So I understand. Mr Yarrow further mentioned that she was attended by the housekeeper. Now, let us suppose that the housekeeper, having satisfied herself that the girl was comfortable and in no danger of a further attack, had left her alone here for a time. Let us further suppose that, by chance, your father's secretary happened to enter this room during the period the girl was lying here alone. He would not have known she was here, and she would not yet be fully recovered, so would be lying quite still. Under the circumstances, it is not impossible that he would have failed to see her. His view of the couch as he entered the room would have been partly obscured by this little table and the large vase upon it, and his thoughts would perhaps have been absorbed by his reason for entering the room."

"What was that, do you suppose?" queried Reid.

"Perhaps to do something which he did not wish anyone to witness," replied Holmes. "He may have intended to examine or abstract some private papers of your father's in the desk over there. He would know that you and your friends were all out of the house, working in the orchard, and thus would not interrupt him.

"We may further conjecture that, as he was engaged upon his secret, furtive work, something, some slight movement of the girl's, perhaps, caused him to look up, and he saw, no doubt to his very great alarm, that she was watching him."

"I cannot see why the girl's presence should have caused him any great alarm," protested Reid. "After all, she could not have appreciated that he was engaged in anything underhand or dishonest."

"Perhaps not," returned Holmes. "But knowledge of his own guilt can have a powerful and disturbing effect upon a man's reason and judgement. The result is not infrequently mental panic, and the conviction that others know more than they in fact do. The panic that would have gripped Northcote at such a moment would have arisen as much, therefore, from his own sense of guilt as from the girl's presence. He would have seen only that, should she have chosen to do so, Sarah Dickens could have exposed his shameful dishonesty to the world, and this threat would have loomed above every other consideration in his mind. He is, however, a very cunning and deceitful man, and I have little doubt, therefore, that he spoke in a friendly and flattering manner to the girl, and perhaps in the course of the conversation, made an arrangement to meet her again in a few days' time. That, I suggest, is how the connection between the two of them began. The girl was young and no doubt appeared impressionable. It must have seemed no difficult task to an educated man like Northcote to turn her head and manipulate her affections. On his side the arrangement would have been one of expediency only, a way to gain a little time until he could dispose permanently of the threat that he considered she posed to him. We may imagine he began at once to plan the removal of that threat."

"It still seems scarcely credible," I interjected, "that anyone would so swiftly contemplate murder in such circumstances."

"Perhaps so, Watson, but we do not yet know the extent of Northcote's dishonesty. Perhaps his hidden crimes are yet greater than I have supposed. He may have been so deeply mired in deceit that he could see no other way out. Nor do we know the true nature of his character. Perhaps, despite the quiet and reserved appearance he presents to the world, he is a man easily moved to violence when his plans are thwarted. The annals of crime are full of such men. I have myself known several."

"But surely he could have found some other way to prevent the girl speaking of what she had seen," I persisted. "He could simply have dismissed the matter as of no consequence, for instance, and hoodwinked the girl in that fashion."

"Perhaps he attempted such a stratagem," returned Holmes, "and met with no success. Perhaps the girl said something, which indicated to him that she understood all too well the nature of what she had witnessed, and made it clear that any further attempts at deception on his part would be unavailing. As I have frequently had cause to observe, the simplest of people can have surprisingly accurate intuitions as to the motives and character of others. What seems likely, anyway, is that however agreeably he may have spoken to her, and however flattered she may have been by his attentions, she still, nevertheless, considered that she had some hold over him, and was disagreeably pressing in her attentions."

"Why do you say that?" asked Reid.

"I feel certain that the window that was broken shortly before your departure for India was broken by Sarah Dickens herself. You blamed it on village boys who had been playing in the orchard earlier, but I always thought that unlikely: the broken window was that of the upstairs study, which is on the opposite side of the house from the orchard. I think it more than probable that Sarah, anxious to hear when she would see Northcote again, endeavoured to communicate with him by throwing pebbles up at the lighted window of the study, in which she knew he would probably be working. Unfortunately, we must suppose, her throw was a little over-vigorous."

"What you are suggesting, then," said Reid after a moment, "is that Northcote has been swindling my father in some way?"

"I think it highly probable. It is by far the most likely motive for the crime. The account you gave me last week of your family's affairs suggested that Northcote had advanced quite quickly after his arrival here from simply being your father's amanuensis to a position of greater confidence and intimacy. I believe he found the temptation to abuse that position too great to resist."

"Wait a moment!" cried Reid abruptly. "Hidden in the bottom of Northcote's wardrobe, where I found my satchel, were many bundles of documents and sheets of paper covered with figures. I was so excited then at finding my satchel that I did not give the other things any consideration, but now that I think about it, I am certain they were private papers of my father's, including a copy of his will. Oh Lord!" he cried all at once in a tone of desperation. "Whatever can I do?"

"You must institute a thorough examination of your father's affairs at once," said Holmes in a firm voice, "and seek the advice of the best lawyer in West Sussex. I have little doubt that such an examination will reveal that fraudulent transactions have taken place. You must remember that Northcote has already successfully counterfeited both your father's hand and that of the dead girl. He may well have signed your father's name to many things of which no one has any knowledge."

"This is almost too much for my brain to absorb!" cried Reid, shaking his head. He looked in turn at each of us, an expression of stupefaction upon his features, as if appealing for our help.

"The actions of my family have been shameful," said Anthony Blythe-Headley abruptly, "and I am sure we would wish to do anything that might help to expunge that shame. I for one should be very pleased to do anything you wish, Reid, to help you to sort out what must be done."

"Do not falter now, Reid," said Captain Ranworth, putting his hand upon his friend's shoulder. "Everything will soon be put to rights, you will see! I'll go at once and bring all the papers from Northcote's room, pile them on the desk here, and make a start at sorting them."

Then Mary Blythe-Headley stepped forward from where she stood beside her father and offered Reid her hand.

"You must be exhausted by all that has happened," said she. "Let us sit together in the garden for a little while, before the daylight vanishes altogether. I have a great deal of news and other things I wish to tell you, and you, I imagine, have much to tell me."

"I think it is time for us to make our way back to the village, Watson," said Holmes to me. "There is no more for us to do here now!"

Outside, in the garden of Oakbrook Hall, Holmes expressed a desire to follow a footpath he had observed earlier, which he thought might offer a route to Topley Cross more direct than the road. It was a pleasant pathway, which passed by field and hedgerow down the hill. The sun was just setting as we left, and behind us the sky was a deep blue and the moon was up. Ahead, the horizon was a glow of reddish-orange, above which, in a turquoise sky, a few fugitive scraps of cloud were tinged pink by the dying sun, and a few late crows were hurrying home to roost. For some time we tramped over the rolling countryside in silence, and it was one of the most memorable walks of my life.

"Such a case as this one," said Holmes as we passed along the edge of a ploughed field, "never fails to remind me of the old saying, that truth is like water: confine it how you may, it will find a way out."

"It might have taken somewhat longer to emerge without your efforts in the matter," I remarked with a chuckle.

"It is kind of you to say so, Watson," returned Holmes, "but I am conscious sometimes of being, in some mysterious way, but a vessel, a mere conduit down which the truth can pass."

"I think you do yourself less than justice, Holmes."

"Well, well, I shall not argue the point. Life is a series of such mysteries, and in solving one, we merely arrive at the next." Abruptly, my friend stopped and turned to me. "But how is your wound, old man?" he queried. "I really must beg your forgiveness! I have been quite lost in my own reflections, I am afraid. It was unpardonably thoughtless of me to drag you over these fields."

"Not at all," I returned. "It is nothing; nothing, at least, that a hot cup of tea at The White Hart will not put right!"

"Good man!" cried my friend with a chuckle. "There is much tragedy in the world, Watson," he continued after a moment, as we resumed our progress, "and much sorry loss of life, from Maiwand to the Willow Pool. Yet as the night that now creeps over the land quickens our desire for the rising of the sun in the morning, so, perhaps, each dark passage in our lives may teach us to strive always for the light. So, at least, with the help of a merciful Providence, we must hope."

The Adventure of QUEEN HIPPOLYTA

IT WAS AN AXIOM of Mr Sherlock Holmes, the world's first consulting detective, that one should not attempt to fill one's head with every item of miscellaneous knowledge one chanced across, but should take in only that which was likely to be of service. "You may depend upon it," said he in his precise, logical fashion, "for every item of irrelevant information you cram in, something important will be forgotten. It is not simply a question of cerebral capacity. On the contrary, history shows us countless examples of the quite amazing capacities of the human brain. It is rather that one's reflective powers become distracted and diffused when a forest of irrelevance stands between them and their goal. Like the prince in the fairytale, one must chop a way through this forest in order to reach the castle beyond, where the one relevant fact lies sleeping." In accordance with this rule, he generally paid little heed to the news of the day, except in so far as it had a bearing upon his work. Yet, despite this, he had perhaps the broadest spectrum of knowledge of any man I have ever known. He had, too, an uncanny knack of recalling the most obscure of facts at the most useful moment, and of perceiving connections between facts which appeared to others to be perfectly unrelated.

To what extent these abilities were an inherited gift, and to what extent the result of rigorous self-training, it was difficult to say, but his capacity to surprise those around him was certainly undisputed. Sometimes, as in the case I now propose to recount, which concerned the singular experiences of Mr Godfrey Townsend, Holmes's recollection of an apparently trivial fact would make the difference between the success or failure of an investigation.

I had called at my friend's lodgings in Baker Street on a bright, sunny morning in the autumn, and had found him seated by the window, examining a small object with the aid of a powerful lens. He waved me to a chair, but did not speak, and for some moments I watched as he inspected every side of his specimen, which I saw was a small cigar case. Evidently satisfied, he then opened the case, removed the contents, and subjected the interior to the same careful examination as he had given to the outside.

"It is, as you know, a little hobby of mine," said he at last, looking up as he replaced the cigars and closed the case with a snap, "to determine a man's character and habits from an examination of one of his possessions. For a man cannot own any object for long without impressing the stamp of his character upon it. It is a skill at which I believe I can say I have reached a certain level of proficiency."

"Indeed," said I. "No one could deny it. I have seen you perform the trick many times, and the conclusions you have reached have frequently amazed me."

"The results are certainly often curious, sometimes striking and occasionally extremely surprising. Here, for instance, we have an apparent anomaly." He passed the cigar case and lens across to me. "You know my methods, Watson. See what you make of it."

I took the case and examined it. It was of silver plate, plain and unadorned, save that in one corner the initials G. T. had been engraved in a florid style. Both sides were disfigured with deep scratches, and in places the silver had been rubbed away, revealing a duller metal beneath. One side appeared at some time to have been bent and subsequently hammered flat again, and the hinges were a little awry, but it opened easily enough, and inside, behind a piece of tape, were four or five small cigars.

"How did you come by it?" I asked.

"I found it in the chair you are now occupying," Holmes replied. "It was left there by someone who called earlier, while I was out, a respectable, middle-aged gentleman, I am informed. His card is on the table."

I took it up and read the following: "Godfrey Townsend. 34C, Gloucester Terrace." It was an expensive-looking card, made of stiff cream board, gilded at the edges and with embossed lettering.

"He left a message to say that he would call back at eleven-thirty," said Holmes, glancing at the clock. "We have just enough time to describe him to our own satisfaction before he returns. Would you care to begin?"

"He has an excellent address, near the Park," I began after a moment, "and his taste in visiting cards clearly tends to the extravagant. Yet his cigar case has a decidedly woebegone appearance."

"Those are indeed the main observations one might make from the material at our disposal," my companion concurred. "What, then, are the deductions to be made from those observations?"

"The anomaly lies especially in the contrast between the card and the case," I continued after a moment. "I would suggest, therefore, that your visitor's circumstances are perhaps not the most affluent – hence the old case – and that his expensive-looking calling card is provided by his employer."

Holmes shook his head. "There is no mention on the card of any form of employment," he remarked. "In any case, Mr Townsend can hardly be poverty-stricken: the cigars are very expensive ones, imported from Cuba by Waterlow's of Oxford Street."

"Then the explanation must be that the case, although worthless in itself, is of great personal value to Mr Townsend because it was given to him by a friend or relation."

"If so, he has treated it in a surprisingly cavalier fashion," interjected Holmes. "It has clearly been kept for prolonged periods in a pocket with coins or keys. It has also been dropped many times, both when closed and when open, and has suffered a serious derangement of the hinges, probably by being stood upon when on the floor. This seems unusually harsh treatment for something of supposedly great personal value!"

"Do you have a better theory?" I asked, a trifle irritated by my companion's dismissive manner.

"There are a few indications," said he after a moment, in an offhand tone. "Mr Godfrey Townsend is, I should say, comfortably situated, financially speaking. He is a bachelor, of course, and there are thus fewer demands upon his purse than would be the case for a married man of the same age. His present modest wealth is largely the result of his own hard work over the last thirty years, and either because of this, or because the memory of his father's profligacy is constantly before his mind, he is very careful with his money, and does not spend it unnecessarily. His comfortable existence has, however, suffered something of a shock in the last couple of days. Something unusual and puzzling has occurred, and he has lost an item of personal property."

"'His father's profligacy'!" I cried in incredulity. "What can you possibly know of your visitor's father!"

"Not a great deal," returned my friend with a shake of the head. "He entertained ambitions of his own when young, but at some stage he lost heart, perhaps disappointed at the elusiveness of success, and took to drink. His fortunes declined, he drank away what money he had and left his son with poor prospects."

I laughed loudly in disbelief.

"How can you possibly pretend to know all these things?" I cried. "Come, Holmes, admit it is sheer fantasy! You have failed to find any significant indications on the cigar case and are indulging in wild speculation, secure in the knowledge that I cannot disprove any of it!"

"Not at all," returned my friend in a vehement tone. "I never speculate further than is warranted by the evidence. I do not claim that all my suggestions are necessarily true, Watson; merely that the balance of probability lies in the direction I indicate."

"Well, then, explain yourself! Why, for instance, are you so certain that your visitor is a bachelor?"

"It is strongly suggested by his ornate calling card. No married man would order such an extravagant specimen. His address, too – 34C, Gloucester Terrace – indicates that he occupies rooms on an upper floor of the house, which is more suggestive of a bachelor than a married man, you must admit."

"His comfortable existence, then, his hard work, profligate father and all the rest of it?"

"In your own analysis," responded my friend after a moment, "you saw that the most obvious anomaly lay in the contrast between the distressed-looking cigar case and the elegant visiting card, but you were insufficiently bold in the deductions you drew from that observation. You made the mistake of assuming that the cigar case Mr Townsend left here was his property just as much as was the visiting card."

"Any other assumption would be ludicrous!" I protested strongly. "Why, the case has his initials upon it! Surely you are not suggesting that he found the case in the street on his way here, and that the coincidence of the initials is some kind of fantastic chance!"

My friend shook his head. "No," said he with a chuckle. "I am not proposing such an unlikely coincidence. But when we examine the case, we cannot fail to be struck by the incongruity of finding those expensive cigars there. There seems something unnatural about it, like finding half a dozen bottles of claret in a potato sack. It is difficult to imagine a man so fastidious in his taste in visiting cards and cigars regularly producing this case in society with equanimity. There is a smell about the case, too, of older, cheaper tobacco. This suggests that Mr Townsend's cigars have not been in there for longer than twenty-four hours or so, and that, prior to its present employment, the case has not been put to use for some considerable time. All in all, therefore, it is surely not an unreasonable conjecture that the case is not Mr Townsend's usual one, but one which has been pressed into temporary service, and which was perhaps once the property of someone else – a member of his family, say, who might well have shared his initials."

I nodded. "It is possible," I agreed.

"The likelihood of this conjecture is increased," he continued, "when we note a date: 1840 – presumably the date of manufacture – inscribed in small characters, inside the case."

"I saw no date."

"Nevertheless, it is there. Now, 1840 is much too early a date for our middle-aged visitor to have bought the case when it was new, and yet the engraved initials are very rubbed, and appear as old as the case itself. It seems a plausible hypothesis, then, to suppose that the case belonged originally to Mr Townsend's father, and that the latter's initials were also G. T."

"That does seem a reasonable conjecture," I conceded.

"Now, the case must have been fairly expensive when new, so Mr Townsend's father must have thought it worth his while to make such a purchase – perhaps because of the class of society he hoped to move in – rather than buy a cheaper but equally serviceable case. We can therefore conclude that he had at that time some money, or some ambition, or both."

"The case may have been a present from a wealthy relative," I interjected.

"Yes, that is possible, but if so, our line of reasoning is similar: he had some moneyed connections, at least one of whom thought sufficiently of him to buy him a good quality cigar case, in the belief, presumably, that he would value it and that it would accord with his expected station in life. However, the case has subsequently been so damaged and ill-treated that we must conclude that the senior Mr Townsend subsequently took to drink. There is no other plausible explanation for the careless abuse to which the case has been subjected. So serious is this abuse, indeed, that we must conclude that he became a hopeless drunkard, in which case it is likely that he drank away whatever money he possessed, leaving his son with nothing. That the son – our morning visitor – now enjoys a modestly comfortable existence, as indicated by his address, his visiting card and his expensive cigars, is therefore almost certainly the result of his own hard work. Is there anything else?"

"You stated that Mr Townsend was careful with his money."

"Well, it seems likely, does it not, that some misfortune has befallen Mr Townsend's usual cigar case? That he does not have a spare one that is presentable, and has thus had to press this very battered old specimen into service, indicates that he is a man who does not spend his money unnecessarily. No doubt the father's profligacy made a deep impression upon his mind when he was younger and has produced an opposite inclination in the son.

"As for his reason for calling upon me, it must be presumed that he has had some puzzling experience. Save only yourself, no one calls upon me who has not. That he should have had a puzzling experience, and have also lost the use of his own cigar case, probably within the same twenty-four hours, would be something of a coincidence were the two matters unrelated, and it therefore seems a fair conjecture that the two incidents are connected."

"You are suggesting, then," said I, chuckling, "that Mr Townsend wishes to commission you to find his missing cigar case?"

"You laugh, Watson, but it may well be so. I cannot pretend that it is a very exciting prospect, but let us wait and see. Many a memorable case has had an equally unpromising beginning. We shall soon know the truth of the matter, for that is probably his ring at the bell now."

A moment later, Mr Godfrey Townsend was shown into my friend's sitting room. A man of middling size, he was about fifty years of age, with a broad, pleasant face and bright eyes. He took the chair Holmes indicated, then glanced in my direction.

"Dr Watson has been good enough to assist me on a great many occasions," said Holmes, by way of introduction. "His presence can only benefit our enquiries. Your property, I believe," he continued, holding out the old cigar case.

"Thank goodness!" cried Townsend, his eyes lighting up as he took the case. "I was wondering where I had left it!"

"It is not the only such object you have lost lately, I think," remarked Holmes.

"Indeed not. It is the loss of my own cigar case that has obliged me to use this old one of my father's, God rest his soul! It has seen better days," he added as he slipped the case into his pocket. "I have only delayed buying a new one in the hope that you can help me find the one I have lost."

"What were the circumstances in which you lost it?" asked Holmes.

"Bizarre, sir! Bizarre and puzzling! Nay, more than that, downright inexplicable! I not only lost a cigar case yesterday, but gained an experience I could well have done without!"

"You have our full attention," said Holmes in a tone of interest. "Pray, let us have the details."

"By all means," said Townsend. "It is soon enough told – though not so soon forgotten. I am, you should know, an importer of Venetian glassware, for which the appetite of the country seems, I am glad to say, insatiable. You may have heard of the firm of Zeffirelli and Townsend. If you own any Venetian glassware, it is more than likely that it was imported into the country by our firm. These business activities have made me a man of very regular habits. Yesterday, for the first time in many years, these habits were altered, and the consequences were exceedingly unfortunate! I am not at all a superstitious man, under normal circumstances, but I cannot help noting in passing that yesterday was Friday the thirteenth, which is said by some to be an unlucky day. While this is hardly an adequate explanation of the series of misfortunes that befell me yesterday, it is scarcely more ridiculous than any other explanation I have been able to devise.

"I am a bachelor, and live at 34, Gloucester Terrace, where I occupy a set of rooms on the top floor. Each day I leave the house at precisely eight-thirty-seven, and take a cab to my office. Yesterday, however, I awoke at five o'clock with severe toothache, and after suffering for three hours I sent a note round to my dentist, whose surgery is nearby. I received a reply that he could see me at half past eleven. I also sent a note to my office to inform them that I should not be in until the afternoon.

"I left my rooms at ten o'clock, as there were one or two small matters I wished to attend to before my appointment. As I was descending the stair, a door opened on the landing below and a man emerged, wearing a hat and coat. I recognized him as Mr Smith, who has the rooms on the floor below mine. He is a very private man and our paths seldom cross. I doubt if I have seen him twice in six months. Now, my usual routine having been altered by the toothache, I welcomed this opportunity to renew our very slight acquaintance.

"'Good morning,' I called as I descended the stair.

"He looked round quickly as he was closing his door, an expression of suspicion upon his face.

"'We don't often see each other,' I continued in a light-hearted, friendly tone.

"'What of it?' he responded gruffly. Then, without another word, he went back inside his room again and slammed the door shut behind him.

"I was surprised at such discourtesy and felt quite put out for some time afterwards. But it was a pleasant morning, and as I walked down to the Park and on towards Oxford Street, I managed to shake off the feeling of despondency with which the encounter had left me.

"At eleven o'clock I was leaving Waterlow's, the Oxford Street tobacconist's, when I observed a man standing in the open doorway. He was tall and thin, with a sallow face and a large black moustache, waxed at the tips. As I passed him, he raised his hat and introduced himself as Inspector Porter of the Detective Division of Scotland Yard. His voice was polite, but tinged with an odd accent, so that I wondered if he came from the north.

"'Excuse me, sir,' said he. 'I am sorry to trouble you, but would you mind stepping this way a moment?'

"'Not at all,' I replied. 'What is it about?'

"'We wish to ask you a few questions,' said he. 'Let us go somewhere quieter for a minute,' he continued, leading me across the pavement to where a small closed carriage stood at the kerb.

"'It will not take long, I hope,' I remarked as I climbed in. 'I have a dentist's appointment at eleven-thirty.'

"He did not reply, but climbed in beside me and closed the door. There was another man already in the carriage, a massive, giant of a fellow, who occupied the whole of the other side. His chest was like a barrel, his arms appeared about to burst apart the sleeves of his jacket, and his neck was, I think, the thickest that I have ever seen on a human being.

"Inspector Porter called something to the driver, and we rattled off in the direction of Marble Arch. He then leaned back in his seat, folded his arms and pursed his lips.

"'I understood that you wished to ask me some questions,' said I, puzzled by his silent manner. He turned and looked at me.

"'What is your name?' said he after a moment.

"'Townsend.'

"The two men exchanged glances, then Porter turned to me again.

"'If you remain silent,' said he, 'you will not be harmed.' There was a note of menace in his voice which I did not much care for.

"'Whatever do you mean?' I demanded. 'Why should I remain silent?'

"Before I could speak another word, the giant opposite abruptly leaned across the carriage and grabbed my arms tightly. The man beside me then took a small medicine bottle from his pocket, poured a few drops of liquid from it onto a piece of rag, then clapped the rag over my nose and mouth. For a moment, I was aware of a very sweet smell and a ringing in my ears, then I had lost all consciousness.

"How long I remained insensible I do not know, but as I came to my senses, the carriage was drawing to a halt. The man calling himself Inspector Porter opened the door and sprang out, and the other man took my arm, pulled me roughly to my feet and propelled me out onto the ground. I felt quite dizzy and sick, but I had little time to feel sorry for myself. I was quickly marched across a dirty, rubbish-strewn yard, and in through an open doorway. As if in a dream, we passed through a deserted kitchen, along a bare, uncarpeted hallway, and up a dark flight of stairs, all festooned with dusty cobwebs. At last I was led into a large empty room and forcibly seated upon the bare boards of the floor, my back against the damp and discoloured wall by the window. The shutters of the window were closed, but they were not very tight fitting, and a narrow beam of daylight entered through a gap between them and cast a little illumination into the bare and dusty room. The thin man closed the door and consulted his watch, then the two of them began to speak animatedly in a strange, foreign tongue. It was clear that I was the subject of their discussion, for they glanced or gestured in my direction several times, and I caught the words 'Townsend' and 'Gloucester Terrace' once or twice in their otherwise unintelligible conversation.

"My head was beginning to clear now, and I made to stand up. In a trice, the thin man's hand had slipped inside his jacket and emerged holding a long, straight-bladed knife. With one swift movement of his arm, he flung the knife in my direction. I dropped to the floor in terror and closed my eyes as the knife flashed mere inches above me and struck the window shutter with a heavy thud, where it continued to quiver for several moments.

"Before I had time to react, the thin man had followed his evil-looking knife across the room, and, as if to deter me from trying to seize it, had withdrawn a second, identical to the first, from within his jacket. Brandishing this in my face, he pulled the first knife from the shutter and deliberately dropped it at my side, where it stuck in the floorboard, an inch to the side of my foot. The two men laughed heartily at this, in a way that made my blood run cold. Then, still laughing, the thin man retrieved his knife, and the two of them resumed their discussion. Needless to say, I made no further attempt to stand up.

"Presently, the thin man consulted his watch again and, apparently having reached a decision, they left the room, without a word to me. A bolt was shot home on the other side of the door, and I heard their footsteps descending the stair. Unsteadily, I rose to my feet, tried the door, which was securely fastened, and made a circuit of the room. There was nothing to be seen there save the mouldering remains of a dead bird in the large, dusty fireplace. As I was regarding this dismal object, I caught the sound of voices in the distance, and what sounded like a brass band playing in the open air. I suppose these sounds had reached me down the wide chimney.

"Curious as to where I might be, I tried to open the shutters. They were very stiff, and clearly had not been moved for many years, but after some effort I succeeded in lifting the bar and dragging one of them open. Imagine my dismay, then, to find that the window was boarded up on the outside. There were gaps between the boards, through which light streamed into the dusty room, but they were near the top of the tall window, and I could see nothing through them but the sky above.

"Dejected, I sat back down and pondered my predicament. As to why these strangers should have abducted me and imprisoned me in this deserted house, I had no idea whatever. I am not a very wealthy man, so a ransom seemed out of the question. I could only conclude that they were proposing to rob me, although they had shown no inclination in that direction so far. Perhaps, I conjectured, they were awaiting instructions from their leader. For there was something in their manner which seemed to indicate that they were not acting entirely of their own volition.

"As I was considering the matter in this way, I heard voices below and footsteps on the stairs. My captors were returning."

"How long had they been away?" interrupted Holmes.

"No more than twenty minutes, I should say," replied Townsend. "I quickly felt in my pockets. The only object of any value in my possession was my cigar case. It is gold-plated and has a diamond set in one corner. It was given to me by the family of my partner, Mr Zeffirelli, on the fifteenth anniversary of our partnership. These villains should not have that, at any rate! I took it from my pocket and quickly pushed it under a loose floorboard, for the footsteps were rapidly approaching the door of the room.

"The bolt was pulled back, the door flung open, and in marched three people, the thin man with the dark moustache, the large, powerful-looking fellow and a third. It was the third that took my entire attention, which you will understand when I give you the details. For, to my very great surprise, the third of my captors was a woman, and one of the most handsome women I have ever seen in my life. She was wearing a long, dark, hooded cloak, which she held together at the front with her hands, as if she had thrown it on hastily. It was apparent, nevertheless, that her figure and carriage were the most graceful imaginable. Beneath the large hood, her features were very dainty, with a bloom upon her cheek that would have softened the heart of a brute.

"She walked straight across the room and stared down at me for a moment. Something seemed to puzzle her and she shook her head slightly. As she did so, her hood slipped back from her forehead, and I saw that she was wearing a small crown or tiara upon her head. Then she turned away and spoke quickly and, it seemed to me, angrily, to her companions, in the same foreign tongue as they had used. The thin man answered her, and I surmised from the tone of his voice that he was excusing himself, or defending his actions. What it was all about, I could not imagine, but it was clear that there was some disagreement or misunderstanding between them. After a moment the big man joined in, in the same tone, then the thin man turned abruptly to me and addressed me in his own tongue. I shook my head and tried to explain that I did not understand, at which the big man stepped forward and raised his arm, as if to strike me, but the woman spoke sharply to him and he turned away.

"'What is your name?' said the woman then to me, in English.

"'Townsend,' I replied; 'Godfrey Townsend.'

"At this, the big man raised his arm again, a look of great ferocity upon his face; but it was a gesture only, and he made no attempt to strike me.

"The three of them then began speaking very rapidly in their own tongue, occasionally glancing in my direction. It seemed evident from her manner and tone that the woman was in charge of the business, and I waited with foreboding to see what the outcome of their discussion would be. At length, evidently satisfied, the woman nodded her head, then turned and hurried from the room. The two remaining villains at once directed their attention to me, and I must confess that my stomach turned over with fear as they approached me. I had little doubt that the giant could have broken my neck with his bare hands had he felt so inclined. Without a word, he pulled me roughly to my feet and propelled me towards the door, but before I had gone three paces, the sweet-smelling cloth was clapped over my face again from behind, and I knew no more.

"When I came to, my shoulder was being shaken by an anxious-looking policeman. I rubbed my eyes and looked about me, and found that I was sitting on the grass beneath a tree at the side of Rotten Row in Hyde Park. A glance at my watch showed me that it was almost two o'clock. How I came to be there, and where I had been in the three hours since leaving the tobacconist's shop, I had no idea. I might almost have dismissed the intervening hours as a terrible dream were it not that my cigar case was not in my pocket. That, gentlemen, is the story of my strange adventure, and I'll wager you've never heard the like!"

"Was anything else missing, apart from your cigar case?" queried Holmes.

"No. I examined the contents of my pockets carefully. Not a farthing had been taken from me!"

"Have you reported the matter to the police?"

"I certainly have. They said it was a very serious business and took a note of all the details, but I don't think there is much hope of their finding the men who abducted me."

Holmes frowned and seemed lost in thought for a moment, then he sprang from his chair and began rummaging through a pile of old newspapers that were stacked against the wall in the corner of the room.

"You appear to have borne your ordeal remarkably well," I observed to Mr Townsend.

"Thank you, Doctor. I must admit that after a visit to my very accommodating dentist and a good night's sleep I am none the worse for it, but I would dearly like to recover my cigar case, for it means such a lot to me! I realize, however, that it may be a hopeless task!"

"It does appear a somewhat daunting prospect," I concurred, "considering that you do not know where in London you were held, and that London comprises nearly a hundred and fifty square miles and, so I understand, three thousand miles of streets!"

"Quite so, quite so," said Mr Townsend in a mournful tone. "Do you see any glimmer of hope in the matter, Mr Holmes?" he continued, addressing my friend and shaking his head in a forlorn manner.

"More than a glimmer, Mr Townsend," returned Holmes, who had selected a newspaper from the pile and was glancing at it as he spoke. "Indeed, I fancy I could set my hand on the men, the house and the cigar case, in under the half-hour."

"What!" Townsend and I cried together incredulously.

"Take a look at this," continued Holmes, holding out the newspaper for us to see. "It is last Monday's *Daily Chronicle*."

He folded the paper over, and pointed to an advertisement in the corner of the page, which ran as follows:

CAPTAIN OSTRALICI'S CIRCUS – FINAL WEEK!

THE WORLD-RENOWNED "FLYING HORSES", personally supervised and trained by CAPTAIN OSTRALICI himself!

THE INCOMPARABLE HIPPOLYTA: Queen of the Circus Ring and Mistress of the Flying Horses, the most daring and graceful female rider in the world!

THE GREAT TADEUSZ: the greatest knife-thrower ever seen!

VIGOR, "THE HAMMERSMITH WONDER": Unsurpassed feats of strength and energy by the world's strongest man!

CEDRIC, THE EDUCATED LION: will amaze and amuse you!

THE LAST OPPORTUNITY THIS SEASON TO SEE THE FINEST SPECTACLE IN LONDON!

NEAREST STATION: HAMMERSMITH.

"I rather fancy, from your description of the men that these are your abductors," remarked Holmes to Townsend. "The man with the knives would be this man, Tadeusz, and his immensely strong companion Vigor, 'the Hammersmith Wonder'. The woman whose charms so struck you might well be this Hippolyta. Indeed, it appears you were only wanting 'Cedric, the educated lion' to make up a complete troupe! Have you visited Ostralici's circus this summer?"

Townsend shook his head. "No," said he, "but I have heard that it is very good. The horses, especially, are said to be most spectacular."

"There have been posters advertising the circus outside Paddington station all summer," I remarked, "and there was an article about it in one of the illustrated papers last week-end, which my wife showed me. Several of the leading performers are, I understand, Polish. The woman who goes under the name of 'Queen Hippolyta' is in fact Vera Buclevska, who at one time had a well-known riding act with her sister. She is said to be the finest horsewoman in Europe."

"But if these are the men who abducted me," said Townsend in a puzzled tone, "what possible motive could they have had? Why should they seize me in broad daylight in Oxford Street? I have done nothing to them. The whole business is quite pointless!"

"It appears certain," responded Holmes, "that their kidnapping of you was a mistake. The woman's reaction when she saw you, and the quarrel that ensued, is clear enough evidence of that, as is the fact that they then deposited you unharmed in Hyde Park. You did not give them your address?"

"They never asked me for it," replied Townsend, shaking his head.

"And yet you heard them mention 'Gloucester Terrace' when they were talking together. They therefore knew the address already, and had quite possibly followed you from there until an opportunity presented itself for them to accost you. You say that your fellow lodger's name is Smith?"

"Yes, Jacob Smith. I have occasionally seen his post lying on the hall table."

"There are no other lodgers in the house?"

"No."

"Then it must be Smith that they were after. You usually leave the house before nine o'clock in the morning, but yesterday you left at ten and encountered Smith on the stair. He appeared about to leave the house until you startled him. The inference is that ten o'clock is his usual time of departure. It seems likely, then, that the kidnappers seized you in the belief that you were he. If that is correct, then it follows that although they know Smith's address, and something of his daily habits, they do not know him well enough to recognize that they had got the wrong man, and had to wait for 'Hippolyta' to inform them forcibly of the fact. What lies behind it all we cannot at present say, but it seems likely that your fellow lodger is in some danger. Having realized their mistake, these people are likely to try again to get their hands on him. We had best call at Gloucester Terrace first to warn him, before attending to the little matter of your cigar case."

"Of course, the cigar case is not important if Mr Smith is in danger," said Townsend, "but I am surprised you are so confident of finding it. Why, the house in which they held me might be anywhere in London!"

"When your captors went to bring the woman, they were gone for only a few minutes, and she appeared as if she had hurriedly left her business to come. The inference is that you were being held at no great distance from the circus encampment at Hammersmith." As Holmes was speaking, he took his hat from the peg and opened the door. "There is no time to lose," said he, in answer to our surprised expressions. Two minutes later we were in a cab and on our way to Gloucester Terrace.

Despite our haste, however, we were too late. Mr Townsend's fellow lodger was not in the house, and we were informed that he had had visitors at ten o'clock that morning.

"There were three of them," the housekeeper informed us: "a very handsome young lady, a tall, thin man with a waxed moustache, and a large, thick-set man."

"Hippolyta, Tadeusz and Vigor," said Holmes tersely. "Did Mr Smith leave with his visitors?" he asked the housekeeper.

"That I could not say, sir," the woman replied, "for they let themselves out, but shortly afterwards, when the maid went up to clear away Mr Smith's breakfast things, there was no sign of him in his rooms at all."

"The matter grows serious," said Holmes as we hurried out to our cab. "We will go at once to Hammersmith."

"Should we not inform the police?" I suggested.

"It will only delay us unnecessarily," responded my friend. "We can find a policeman when we need one."

The traffic was dense, and it took us a good half-hour to reach Hammersmith. The cabbie knew where the circus was camped and took us straight there, but as we stepped from the cab, Holmes groaned with dismay, for all about us was a chaotic scene of activity. Poles and planks were being carried this way and that and it was evident that the circus was being dismantled.

"Of course, the advertisement stated that this was the last week of the season!" cried Holmes, as we threaded our way through the crowds of people and past the stables and animal cages. "The circus is breaking up, and these villains must have believed that they could make good their escape! Let us hope that we are not too late!"

A stout man in a billycock hat appeared to be in charge of one of the gangs of workers, and Holmes asked him where we might find the manager.

"If it's Captain Ostralici you're after," he responded in a gruff tone, "you've missed him. He only stayed long enough this morning to supervise the loading of the 'osses, and then he left, along with Miss Buclevska and the others. I'm in charge here now, until everything is cleared away."

"Where have they gone?"

"That depends who you mean. The 'osses have gone down to Petersfield for the winter, the other animals go tonight, and Captain Ostralici's party left on the noon train for Dover, bound for Warsaw."

Holmes consulted his watch as we turned away. "This makes it a little difficult," said he. "Still, their train will not have reached Dover yet, and if we can convince the police here of the seriousness of the matter, they can wire their colleagues in Kent to prevent Ostralici and the others from boarding the boat."

As he spoke, he had been glancing quickly round the perimeter of the circus encampment. Now, with a cry of triumph, he directed our attention to a large, dilapidated old house, which stood in the distance, behind a crumbling, ivy-covered brick wall. It had obviously not been occupied for many years, and most of the windows were boarded up. Quickly we made our way across the green, through the open gateway, and round the back of the house, to a yard that was almost choked with brambles and weeds. The lock on the back door had been forced, and we were soon inside and making our way through the deserted building and up the stairs. There, Townsend led the way into a dark and dusty bedroom.

"This is the one," said he. "Your eyes become accustomed to the gloom after a little while."

"No sign of Mr Smith, at any rate," said Holmes, a note of relief in his voice.

We quickly examined the floor by the shuttered window, and had soon found the loose board and lifted it. There, where he had hidden it, was Mr Townsend's cigar case. As he lifted it up, the diamond in the corner caught the beam of light from the window and sparkled like a tiny star.

"I could not have imagined when I consulted you," said Townsend, clutching his prize to his bosom, "that you would find it so quickly, Mr Holmes. To speak frankly, I doubted that you would find it at all. You cannot imagine how dear to me this little case is. I shall be forever in your debt. Now, I suppose, my part in this strange affair is at an end."

"By no means," Holmes returned quickly. "I should be very much obliged if you would accompany us to Dover, if you feel equal to it, to assist with the identification of these villains and to help us find your fellow lodger, Mr Smith. But first we must call at Scotland Yard."

Mr Townsend nodded his head in agreement, declaring himself "ready for anything", and we set off at once. Holmes wired ahead, before we caught a train to Westminster Bridge, and when we arrived at Scotland Yard we were met by the tall, stout figure of Inspector Bradstreet, to whom Holmes quickly explained how matters stood.

"As I understand it, then," said the policeman, "it seems likely that this gang has hold of Mr Smith. Whether their intention is to smuggle him to the Continent, or to do him some mischief between here and the Channel, we cannot say, but I can certainly ensure that they are not allowed to board the boat until we have had a chance to question them." So saying, he hurried from the room, but was back again in a few minutes. "It is all arranged," said he. "The Harbour Police will detain them until we arrive. There is a train from Charing Cross at two-ten, which will get us into Dover before five. The station master has agreed to hold it for us, but will only do so for five minutes, so we must get round there at once!"

We reached the station platform with barely a second to spare, and leapt aboard the train as the guard blew his whistle. Scant minutes later, we were flying through the outlying suburbs, the little houses and gardens all bathed in the golden autumn sunshine.

"It is, of course, possible," remarked Holmes, "that some harm has already befallen the mysterious Mr Smith. The fact that these people were leaving the country today probably explains why they have acted only in the last twenty-four hours."

"No doubt they thought they would be beyond our reach before we had discovered what had happened," agreed Bradstreet. "I should very much like to know," he added, "what their motives might be."

"From what I have seen of him," said Townsend, "I should not have said that Mr Smith was a man of any great wealth."

"I do not think it is money they are after," said Holmes with a shake of the head. "The fact that your captors summoned 'Hippolyta' to see you, and that she then appeared to berate them for the mistake they had made, suggests that the issue may be something personal to that lady herself. It is, however, pointless to speculate further in the absence of data," he continued, leaning back in his seat and filling his pipe. "We shall be able to question the scoundrels directly in a little while."

The sky had clouded over by the time we reached the coast, and as we alighted from the train a strong salt breeze was blowing off the sea. Up above, against the leaden sky, crowds of raucous, wind-buffeted seagulls wheeled and dived in endless spirals. We hurried to the harbour master's office, where we were met by Superintendent Waldron of the Dover Harbour Police.

"I have them here," said he. "They were not a difficult group to recognize," he added with a chuckle. "The big fellow looked inclined to give us a bit of trouble at first, but the woman said something to him and he quietened down soon enough. I'll have them brought up now."

The harbour outside the window was crowded with shipping, and I was gazing upon this busy scene, where a forest of masts and spars, flags and rigging thronged the sky, when the door was opened and the fugitives were led in. The officer in charge read out their names from a sheet of paper. There was Captain Alexei Ostralici, as I had seen him depicted on posters, the lines about his large, gentle eyes bespeaking fatigue at the end of a strenuous season. Next to him stood Tadeusz Grigorski, otherwise known as "the Great Tadeusz", his waxed moustache aquiver at the indignity of his situation. By his side was an enormous man, with the chest and limbs of a Hercules. He was named as Viktor Kosciukiewicz, but was instantly recognizable as "Vigor, the Hammersmith Wonder". Last of all, and standing a little apart from the others, was a graceful, delicately featured woman, elegantly attired in a dark blue travelling costume. Named as Miss Vera Buclevska, she would be more readily known to the general public as "Queen Hippolyta of the Circus Ring".

It is an odd and unsettling effect that a woman can sometimes have upon a gathering. To those who have experienced this, I need say nothing. To those who have not, no words of mine can adequately convey my meaning. I am not speaking simply of beauty, far less of ordinary prettiness, but of something else, akin in its effects to a mysterious species of magnetism, but which is, in truth, quite indefinable. Such was the effect Miss Buclevska appeared to have upon the harbour master's office at Dover that afternoon, for upon her entrance an odd silence seemed to fall upon the room, and for a moment no one spoke.

"Well?" said Miss Buclevska herself at length, in strongly accented English, looking at each of us in turn.

Inspector Bradstreet cleared his throat. "This gentleman," said he, indicating Mr Townsend, "has laid a serious charge against three of you, that you kidnapped and held him prisoner for several hours yesterday. What have you to say to this charge?"

Miss Buclevska glanced quickly at her companions, then turned to face us once more.

"I will speak for all," said she softly. "These men acted for my sake. We deeply regret what occurred. The gentleman you indicate," she continued, looking at Townsend, "has every right to feel aggrieved, but we meant him no harm. It was a most unfortunate mistake, and we are sorry for it."

"You meant Mr Townsend no harm," interrupted Holmes, "only because your friends in fact intended to kidnap his fellow lodger, Jacob Smith."

"His name is not Smith," said she, her eyes suddenly flashing fire. "His true name is Jakob Schmidt, for he is a German. But, yes, they did intend to kidnap him, as you say. I did not ask them to do it, but they believed I wished it. He is an evil man, but a man with a silver tongue. Throughout Brandenburg his name is reviled and men spit when they hear it. Some years ago he announced a great scheme to build new docks on the banks of the River Havel, north-west of Potsdam. Success was assured, so he declared. Enormous amounts of money were subscribed. Many people gave their life savings to the project. Alas, all his assurances proved worthless. The entire scheme collapsed, and all those who had subscribed money were ruined. All, that is, save one man. That man, as you will guess, was Herr Schmidt himself. The crash of his company left him a surprisingly wealthy man. Of course, there was a public outcry and enquiries and investigations followed, but nothing could be done about it, for Schmidt had acted entirely within the law. He was a lawyer himself, and knew how to arrange such things in his own favour. When the enterprise collapsed, with scarcely a penny to its name, much of the missing money was, in truth, in Schmidt's own hands, but the law could do nothing."

"You lost money in Schmidt's scheme?" queried Holmes. "This is the connection between you?"

"I lost a little," said she. "No one in Brandenburg at that time escaped unscathed from Schmidt's foul and dishonest schemes.

But that is not what makes me bitter. I tell you these things only so you know the type of man he is. My own unfortunate connection with that evil devil is a more personal one.

"Some years ago, my younger sister Krystina and I had a riding act together. You may have heard of the Buclevska Sisters. We performed in Warsaw, Vienna, Budapest and many other places, and had, I may say, a considerable renown. One summer we had been performing in Berlin and were taking a short holiday near Potsdam. This was at the time that Jakob Schmidt's local celebrity was at its height, before the smash came. We met socially, and Herr Schmidt's silver tongue turned Krystina's head. I warned her against him, for even then I did not trust him, but she would not listen. Soon he had persuaded her to go away with him to his summer home in the south, and she became estranged from her family and from her friends. All were shocked and distressed at this, but what could be done? So much had he twisted her to his wishes that she would not even speak to me, Vera, her sister.

"Of course, you can imagine the rest. When the financial smash came, Schmidt left the district, and cast Krystina off without a thought, like an old shoe. All the promises he had made to her proved as worthless as the promises he had made to the people of Potsdam. Presently, my sister crept back home, but something within her had died. We welcomed her back without a word of censure, but her own heartbreak and shame were destroying her. She did not last six months, gentlemen. If anyone tells you that a broken heart cannot kill, do not believe them, for I have seen it happen. Krystina pined away, became very ill and, one fine spring morning, passed beyond all mortal help. *That* is the connection between Herr Schmidt and myself about which you enquired."

Vera Buclevska finished speaking and stood facing us defiantly, her cheeks flushed and her lip trembling.

"You wished to see Schmidt, then," said Holmes after a moment.

She nodded her head and passed her hand across her brow. "That is so," she replied. "I learned that he was living in London. I wrote to him twice, but received no reply. Then my friends here, knowing how the matter was distressing me and affecting my performance, took it upon themselves to bring him forcibly to see me. Alas! They knew nothing of Schmidt other than what I had told them, and they seized the wrong man, as you know."

"Where is Schmidt now?" asked Holmes.

"Now?" the lady repeated. "I do not know, and nor do I care!"

Holmes frowned. "But you called upon him this morning. We had your description from his housekeeper."

"That is so. The miserable coward sat trembling as we spoke. I accused him of the evil he had done to Krystina and to the poor people of Brandenburg. To all my remarks he said nothing, expressing neither sorrow nor remorse. On his face was only fear. Eventually Tadeusz pressed upon me that I was wasting my time, and was succeeding only in making myself more miserable. Besides, I could see for myself that Schmidt was ill – he had declined dreadfully since the last time I saw him – and it was clear that all his dishonesty and scheming had brought him no happiness. We therefore withdrew. My only hope now is that I never see that odious reptile again as long as God permits me to live."

"You did not force him to go anywhere with you?"

"Certainly not. I could not bear to remain in his company a moment longer."

"But he has disappeared."

Miss Buclevska's mouth fell open in surprise, and it was clear that this news was unexpected.

"It was feared that some harm had befallen him," continued Holmes.

"Not at our hands," said she.

Bradstreet cleared his throat again. "This makes it rather difficult," said he. "I shall have to wire to London for further enquiries to be made. In the meantime—"

He was interrupted by a knock at the door, and a uniformed official entered.

"I'm to tell you that the boat must leave in ten minutes," said he, "with or without the Ostralici party. There is also a message for Inspector Bradstreet," he added, holding out a thin sheet of paper.

The policeman took the sheet and read it, then he looked up with a smile.

"It is from one of my colleagues," said he. "He considered it would be of interest to me. Jakob Schmidt walked into Paddington Green Police Station this afternoon at three o'clock, demanding protection against a gang of foreigners who he said were terrorizing him. Apparently he had been hiding in the British Museum all day!"

There was perceptible relief on every face there. We had all, I think, been moved by Vera Buclevska's story and were glad to have her statement confirmed.

Captain Ostralici smiled wearily. "So," said he. "Matters are resolved. Are we permitted to leave now?"

Inspector Bradstreet hesitated and looked at Mr Townsend. "A serious criminal offence has been committed," said he at length, "whatever the reasons for it may have been. Mr Townsend was forcibly kidnapped yesterday morning and held against his will."

"That doesn't matter," said Townsend abruptly in a quiet voice, looking a little embarrassed to be the centre of attention as we turned to hear what he would say. "I wasn't harmed," he continued after a moment. "I understand what lay behind it now, and I accept the apology that has been made to me. I would rather not press charges, Inspector."

Bradstreet raised his eyebrow. "Very well, then," said he, addressing Captain Ostralici and his friends. "The matter is closed, and you are free to go."

"I'll arrange to have your luggage put aboard at once," said the harbour official, and hurried from the room.

Captain Ostralici stepped forward, clicked his heels and shook Townsend's hand. "Sir, you are a gentleman," said he with a little bow. "You may like to know that Miss Buclevska has lately done me the honour of consenting to be my wife. We are to be married in Warsaw next month. Your generosity in this matter has removed the one dark cloud that hung over our preparations." Vigor and Tadeusz then shook hands with Townsend, and finally Miss Buclevska took his hand in hers.

"You are a very kind and generous man, Mr Townsend," said she softly, "and deserve happiness. We return in the spring," she added after a moment, "and I hope to see you at the circus then." Townsend, who appeared to have stopped breathing, merely smiled and nodded as she released his hand and turned to follow her companions from the room.

"Capital!" cried Holmes in a gay tone, clapping his hands together. "This calls for a celebration, and as we appear to have missed a meal today, I suggest we take advantage of our situation and sample the fare at one of the local fish restaurants!"

There was general assent to this suggestion and, five minutes later, Holmes, Bradstreet, Townsend and I found ourselves on the upper floor of a large restaurant near the harbour, where a balcony looked out across the sea. The clouds were beginning to break up again and blue sky was showing through.

"There goes the ship!" cried Holmes all at once, and we watched as the channel packet slipped slowly out of the harbour, carrying those singular circus folk upon their long journey to the east. Slowly the vessel drew away from the shore, until it was a mere dot upon the broad expanse of sea.

"What a very strange affair!" remarked Bradstreet in a thoughtful voice as our meal was served.

"A singular business, indeed!" concurred Holmes with a chuckle. "I should not have missed it for the world! For you and me, Bradstreet, it has meant an afternoon at the seaside, away from the smoky city, for Mr Townsend, the return of his precious cigar case, and a story his friends will scarcely credit, and for Dr Watson, another entry in that catalogue of the mysterious and *recherché*, which he so delights in compiling!"

The Adventure of DEDSTONE MILL

A Surprising Letter

IT IS WITH SOME RELUCTANCE that I take up my pen to tell what I know of the East Harrington tragedy. Few readers will need reminding of an affair that appalled the whole country and cast such a cloud over that part of Leicestershire in which the events took place. Though some years have passed since details of the matter filled the pages of every newspaper in the land, such events slip less easily from the nation's memory than from the nation's press, and if it were argued that no fresh account of the matter is called for, I should, generally speaking, be inclined to agree. But many of the details of the case passed unreported at the time, and of all the newspaper accounts I read, only that of *The Times* was accurate, and that, although accurate, was not complete, so that much rumour and speculation accompanied the case, almost all of which was without foundation, as I am able to state with some authority. Indeed, my intimate involvement in the matter from an early stage places me in a unique position to give an accurate account of it, and perhaps also entails upon me now the duty to do so, and so confound those rumour-mongers who delight in blackening the names of the innocent. A further consideration concerns the many letters I have received over the years, requesting that I clarify this point or that in connection with the case, and it is also, therefore, in the hope of satisfying all these many correspondents that I have at last decided to publish this account.

In writing this series of short sketches it has been my constant intention to demonstrate the unique skills of my good friend Mr Sherlock Holmes, without whose intervention many of these tales would have been mysteries without solution. In selecting the cases to be included in the series, therefore, I have always sought, on the one hand, to choose those that offered my friend scope for the exercise of the remarkable powers he possessed, and, on the other, to avoid the depiction of sensational events merely for their own sake. Should the reader feel that the present narrative displays a falling-away from either or both of these ideals, I can only offer in mitigation the reasons given in the first paragraph above, and add that where the matter is of such great public interest, it would perhaps be perverse of me to omit it entirely from this series.

Following my marriage, and subsequent establishment in general practice in the Paddington district of London, I naturally saw somewhat less of Sherlock Holmes than in earlier years. But my interest in his cases and in the methods he used to solve them remained undiminished, and I was always glad of an opportunity to discuss his work with him. He had an invitation to dine with us whenever he wished, but it was only infrequently that we saw him at our table, for his practice, which was by then considerable, occupied most of his waking hours. It was with surprise and pleasure, then, that I returned home from a tiring afternoon round, one dull Monday in September, to learn that we had received a note from him.

"Mr Holmes wishes to dine with us this evening," said my wife with a smile.

"That is splendid news!" said I. "I shall open a bottle of that vintage claret which old Mr Wilkins gave us last month! I have only been waiting for a suitable occasion!"

Holmes arrived punctually and we enjoyed a very pleasant meal, exchanging many humorous anecdotes from our respective practices. As the table was cleared, however, I observed a thoughtful look upon his face.

"You have something on your mind," I remarked.

He turned to me and smiled. "You and I have certainly become transparent to each other over the years," returned he with a chuckle. "But, yes, there is something upon which I should very much value your opinion."

My wife had risen to leave us, but Holmes called her back. "Mrs Watson," said he, "if you, too, could spare a few minutes, your observations might prove invaluable to me. I know you are eager to be cutting out and making up your curtains, but I do not think you will be disappointed by the matter I wish to lay before you."

"Why, however do you know about the new curtains?" said she, resuming her seat with an expression of surprise upon her features.

"I observed a brown paper parcel from Marshall Snelgrove in the hall as I entered. From its shape, it is evidently a bale of material, and too large a bundle, surely, for any purpose but curtains. No doubt its future is inextricably linked with the scissors, tape measure and French chalk which I observed neatly placed at the foot of the stairs."

"How very observant of you!" cried my wife with a light laugh. "You are correct, of course – the front bedroom has needed new curtains for some time – but I should much prefer to know how my opinion can be of any value to you."

"It is quickly explained," said Holmes. "I received this letter by the lunchtime post," he continued, taking a small cream envelope from his inside pocket. "Perhaps, Watson, you would be so good as to read it aloud?"

I took the envelope from him. It bore a West London postmark, and the handwriting, while quite clear, was somewhat irregular and juvenile.

"My correspondent is fourteen years of age," remarked Holmes as I took the letter from the envelope, answering my thoughts rather than my words, as was his wont.

Smoothing out the letter upon the table, I read the following:

My dear Mr Holmes,

Please forgive me for writing to you like this, and do not be angry with me. I know you must be very busy. You do not know me, but there is no one else I can turn to. My late father, Major George Borrow, had an account of one of your cases, part of which he read to me. He also told me that he had heard that if a case interests you, you will help people, even if they are poor, and that you can solve any mystery, however perplexing. You are my only hope. There is a mystery here, and I am very frightened, especially for my brother, Edwin. He is only twelve, and recently he was nearly killed. I am fourteen and three-quarters, but I still do not think I would be strong enough if anyone tried to murder me.

Since our mother and father were killed when the *Flying Scotsman* was wrecked at Burntisland, we have lived with Aunt Margaret (Mama's sister) and her husband, Mr John Hartley Lessingham, at East Harrington Hall. But now she has gone away and left us, and there is no one to speak up for us, especially as Mr Theakston has now gone, too.

Please help me, Mr Holmes. At least let me speak to you before you decide. Please come to the London Library in St James's Square, at eleven o'clock on Tuesday morning. It is my only chance to speak to you, as I may never be allowed to come to London again. I shall be wearing a maroon-coloured jacket and a matching crocheted bonnet. If there is anyone with me, do not speak to me. Please do not tell anyone about this letter and do not write back to me, or I do not know what might happen.

Yours very sincerely
Harriet Borrow

I finished reading and we sat a moment in silence.

"What do you make of it, Watson?" said Holmes at length.

I shook my head.

"It is difficult to know what to think," I replied. "The girl appears to be genuinely in fear of something, but of course children often misconstrue the world about them, especially the actions of adults, and see mysteries and cause for fear when, in reality, none exist."

"Indeed," concurred my friend. "You state the matter succinctly."

"But you simply *cannot* ignore the girl's plea, Mr Holmes," said my wife in a vehement tone. "She may, of course, for all we know, be a silly girl, with her head stuffed full of foolish ideas – things she has read about in books – but you cannot know that for certain until you have questioned her on the matter."

"Bravo, Mrs Watson!" cried Holmes, clapping his hands together in appreciation of her impassioned plea. "What a first-rate illustration of marital democracy!" he added with a chuckle. "You have, between the two of you, stated the quandary precisely! On the one hand I can hardly intrude myself like a busybody into the household of a stranger simply on a child's say-so; on the other, I cannot ignore a sincere plea for help from whatever quarter it may come. Therein lies the dilemma. This sort of letter is always the most problematic. With older clients, there is at least some likelihood that they will estimate with reasonable accuracy the urgency of their case. Younger clients have a marked tendency to see as vital what is in reality trivial or unimportant."

"Do you receive many letters from people so young as this?" queried my wife.

Holmes shook his head. "Thankfully not," said he in a dry tone, "although there has been something of an increase in their number since your husband's *Study in Scarlet* was published. I do receive the occasional request to locate a missing doll, or other highly prized toy, and am sometimes able to make a suggestion or two that proves useful. But let us return to the matter in hand, which promises to be somewhat more serious. I have had little opportunity, so far, to make any very searching enquiries on the matter. All I have been able to learn," he continued, consulting his notebook, "is that John Hartley Lessingham and his wife live at East Harrington Hall in Leicestershire. The estate is a fairly large one, extending over four parishes: East Harrington, West Harrington, Bulby Upwith and Dedstone. An ancestor, Walter Lessingham, lost his life in the Royalist cause at the Battle of Naseby. The Hartley connection was made in the middle of the last century, when Samuel Lessingham married Ruth Hartley, only daughter of a needle-manufacturer from Redditch. Do you know anything of the present generation, Watson?"

"As it happens, I do – by repute, at least. Hartley Lessingham is one of the most renowned amateur riders in England. He has a string of fine horses and has carried off almost every prize the sport has to offer. As a rider and competitor he is very much respected."

"And as a man?"

"I do not believe he is very popular," I replied, choosing my words with care. "There are those, I believe, who positively dislike the man. He is said to ill-treat his horses, for one thing. Then there was something of a scandal last year over an unpleasant incident at a meeting in the Midlands – Cantwell Heath, if I recall it correctly. The horse in front of him stumbled at a ditch and unseated his rider – a popular man by the name of Jackie Weston – and Hartley Lessingham rode straight over him, when he could, in the opinion of most observers, have easily avoided him altogether."

"Was the other rider seriously hurt?"

"Both legs were badly broken, and but for the skill of the surgeon, he would have lost them entirely. As it is, they say he will never walk again without sticks."

"Did Hartley Lessingham express any remorse for the incident?"

"None whatever, so far as I am aware, which is what made such a scandal of the affair. Apparently, his only response was to declare that accidents of that sort were only to be expected in such a manly sport."

"I see," said Holmes, nodding his head. "I think that gives us a clear enough picture of the man. And the Borrows? Do you know anything of them?"

"I read a book of memoirs and anecdotes a few years ago by a Major Borrow, *With the East Sussex Foot in India*. It was a rather entertaining volume, as I recall, but whether the author and the girl's father are one and the same man, I could not say."

"Very well," said Holmes. "Let us sketch out the situation, then. Major Borrow and his wife are killed. The son and daughter are taken in by the mother's sister and her husband – Miss Borrow mentions no other children in the household, but of course there may be – then the aunt leaves, for reasons we do not know, and the children are left at East Harrington Hall in the care of Hartley Lessingham. He, of course, has no connection with the children other than through his wife, and does not sound the type of person to be motivated by any great charitable urge."

My friend fell silent then for a moment, his eyes far away.

"There are definitely possibilities here," said he at length in a quiet tone, as if thinking aloud. "Who, I wonder, is this Mr Theakston, to whom the girl refers? Could you spare the time to accompany me tomorrow morning at eleven, Watson?"

"Certainly," I returned. "I should have finished my morning surgery by ten o'clock, and shall then be at your disposal."

"Excellent! And Mrs Watson?"

"I?" said my wife in surprise. "I am sure that I should be of no use to you, Mr Holmes."

"On the contrary," returned he with emphasis, "your presence might make all the difference. To have someone of her own sex present may help to put Miss Borrow at her ease, and perhaps help to elicit information from her that she would otherwise be reluctant to give to two middle-aged gentlemen."

"Very well, then," said she with a smile. "I should be delighted to accompany you, and to meet your enterprising young correspondent!"

The London Library

At ten-twenty the following morning, Sherlock Homes arrived at our door in a four-wheeler. The streets were thronged with traffic, and we reached St James's Square only a few minutes before eleven o'clock. As we were alighting from the cab, a hired carriage drew in to the side of the road just ahead of us. From this stepped a handsome woman in a highly ornamented outfit, followed by a young girl whom I judged to be about fourteen or fifteen years old. The latter was wearing a maroon velvet jacket with a knitted bonnet of the same hue perched on the back of her head. From beneath this, her long light-brown hair fell to her shoulders.

As we approached the entrance to the library, we passed this couple on the pavement, and I was surprised to hear that the tones of the older woman were most harsh. She was instructing the girl to be ready to be collected at half past twelve.

"You be late at your peril!" said she in an unpleasantly threatening tone, to which the girl quietly acquiesced.

As we passed them, I stole a glance at their faces. The girl's was soft, young and innocent, with some trace, I fancied, of sorrow about the eyes. The woman's was hard and unkind, and with something in her expression that spoke of a limited, self-absorbed disposition. I realized, too, that my initial opinion, formed from a distance, that the woman was a handsome one, had been premature. There was a weight of powder and rouge upon her face, such as an actress on stage might have worn to look attractive from a distance. At closer quarters one saw only a thin, rather stupid face, with no points of attraction whatever.

We passed on into the library, and a few moments later the girl entered. I had the impression that she had been crying. Holmes stood up and made a slight gesture to her and, with some hesitation, she made her way across the room to where we were seated at a large oblong table.

"Miss Borrow?" said my friend. She took the hand he extended to her and, as he introduced us, she bobbed a curtsy to each of us in turn.

"Excuse me, ma'am, but are you a nurse?" she asked my wife in a hesitant tone as she seated herself at the table.

My wife smiled as she shook her head. "I have been called upon to act as such in an emergency once or twice," she replied, "but no, my knowledge of nursing skills is somewhat limited, I am afraid."

A look of relief passed over the girl's face.

"Thank you," said she quietly. "I am not mad, you know," she added abruptly.

"Why ever should we have supposed such a thing?" queried Holmes in a soft tone, eyeing her closely.

"The presence of this gentleman, who is a doctor, made me wonder – but, of course, I recall now: Dr Watson is your friend, the author of the account my father read to me. But I wondered, because Miss Rogerson has often said she will have me declared insane and put away if I do not mend my ways."

Holmes frowned slightly. "And who is Miss Rogerson?" he asked.

"A lady who has come to run the household since Aunt Margaret left. It was she who brought me here this morning."

"We saw her on the pavement outside," said Holmes in a kindly voice. "Does she always speak to you in so stern a fashion?"

The girl's face flushed a deep crimson.

"No, not always so," she replied at length, "but she was angry with me."

"Why?"

"Because I had tried to alight from the carriage quickly, before she had given me permission to do so."

"Your mind was perhaps on other things?"

"It was not that. May I speak freely to you?"

"Certainly."

"I mean, you will not scold me or think me wicked if I say whatever I wish?"

"No, Miss Borrow, we shall not. If you speak the truth you have nothing to be ashamed of and need fear no censure. I need hardly add that anything you tell us will pass no further, so nor need you hesitate on that account."

"Thank you, Mr Holmes. I will tell you then why I wished to leave the carriage so quickly. It was because I knew that Miss Rogerson would not dare to slap or pinch me if we were on the pavement."

Again a frown crossed Holmes's face. "Do you know anything of Miss Rogerson's antecedents?" he asked after a moment. "Her appearance seems scarcely that of a typical housekeeper."

"She is an old friend of Mr Hartley Lessingham's. He knew her, I believe, before he married Aunt Margaret."

"I see. When did she arrive to take up her new duties?"

"About ten days after Aunt Margaret left, in the middle of January."

"Do you and your brother see much of her when you are at home?"

"At first we did not, but at the end of April our tutor, Mr Theakston, left us, and since that time Miss Rogerson has acted as our tutor, so that we usually see her for a little time every day of the week except Saturday and Sunday."

Miss Borrow paused, and for a moment Holmes regarded her face in silence. Then he spoke.

"You wish," said he, "to tell us that Miss Rogerson's tutorship has not been an unqualified success, but you do not wish to appear rude or disloyal. Of course one should not, as a rule, malign people who are not present to defend themselves, but there are exceptions to every rule. We have come here today to hear your honest account of your troubles and difficulties. Please feel free to be as rude as you wish, provided only that you consider it justified: we shall think none the worse of you for it. Besides," he added in a dry tone, "there are people to whom it is almost impossible to refer without appearing rude. Adults generally find a way of venting their feelings about such people; I do not see why such pleasure should be entirely denied to the more youthful members of society!"

A slight smile, as if of appreciation, passed over the girl's features.

"I think that you perhaps remember your own youth more distinctly than do many adults, Mr Holmes," she ventured.

"Well, well," returned he in a dismissive voice. "Pray, proceed with your account!"

"Miss Rogerson," said the other after a moment, "is a very stupid woman. She beats us for not knowing things, but she herself knows nothing. Once when Edwin asked her where India was, she could not find it on the wall map in the schoolroom, and I could see that she was looking for it among the Greek islands. Sometimes she uses French words, but it is only to appear superior, for she always pronounces them wrongly and does not really know what they mean."

"Do you know why Mr Theakston left?"

Miss Borrow shook her head. "I was very sorry that he did," she returned. "He left in a hurry, and did not even say goodbye to us, which was quite unlike him. He had been our only friend after Aunt Margaret's departure, and had taught us such a lot. Since he left, Edwin's education has almost ceased. But I think he may have been dismissed by Mr Hartley Lessingham, for I heard them exchanging sharp words upon the evening he left."

"Did you hear what it was they were discussing?"

"Not very clearly. They were in the library downstairs, and I was sitting on the top of the stairs. But several times I heard them mention the mill at Dedstone."

"A mill? That sounds an unlikely topic for your tutor and his employer to have words over. Hum! Let us leave this matter for the moment, if we may," said Holmes. "Perhaps you could tell us first a little of your family's history, and how you came to be in your present situation?"

"Very well," said the girl. "Edwin and I were both born in India and have lived most of our lives there. We know no one in England. Our home was at Chalpur, which is where my father's regiment was stationed. After he left the service, we stayed on in India for some years, for he was engaged in various business activities in connection with the jute trade. I remember that he remarked that it seemed the right trade for him to be in, as he had often heard that his ancestors were all Jutes. Until recently, then, we had never lived in England, except for two holiday visits with my mother. Then, two years ago, my father sold most of his interests in India, and we returned to England. By this time, so I understand, he was a very wealthy man. We took a large house in Brixton and lived happily there for a while.

"My mother's sister, Aunt Margaret, who was some years younger than my mother, had married while we were in India, and my parents had thus been unable to attend the wedding. I remember the surprise on my mother's face when she received the letter from Aunt Margaret informing her of the forthcoming marriage. 'Would you believe it, George!' said she to my father. 'Margaret is to be married in two months' time, to a man named John Hartley Lessingham!' Both my mother and father had always been certain that Aunt Margaret would marry Edgar Shepherd, an old friend of the family who farms in Sussex and whom she had known for many years. 'Perhaps she grew weary of waiting for Shepherd to propose to her,' suggested my father, 'or perhaps she found him a trifle dull. When last I saw him, on our most recent visit to England, his conversation seemed to consist chiefly of cattle diseases and the price of turnips and cabbages. This Hartley Lessingham was perhaps a somewhat more dashing suitor!'

"Upon our return to England, Aunt Margaret invited us to visit her at her new home at East Harrington, which we did. Then, eighteen months ago, Edwin and I again went to stay there while Mother and Father journeyed north, to Scotland, where my father had a half-interest in a jute mill in Dundee. Alas! It was a journey from which they were never to return."

She broke off with a sob, and taking out her handkerchief, dabbed her eyes. My wife leaned across the table and patted her hand gently.

"There, there," said she in a kindly voice. "The loss of one's parents is indeed a cruel blow, as I know from personal experience. But the future holds out hope to us all."

Holmes glanced at his watch.

"You had best continue with your account," said he. "There are only fifty minutes remaining to us."

"Aunt Margaret offered to be like a parent to Edwin and me," said Miss Borrow after a moment, when she had composed herself, "and at first our life was as pleasant at East Harrington as could be expected under the circumstances. She engaged a tutor for us, Mr Theakston, an amusing man from the north. For a while all was well. Our lessons were the most enjoyable you could imagine. Mr Theakston was a good teacher, and he loved East Harrington as much as we did. He often took us on nature rambles over the estate, to record the birds and butterflies, and the wild flowers that grow in abundance there, especially by the river. He would tell us the most curious and interesting things. He explained to us one day where our measurements come from, how the inch, the foot and the yard are drawn directly from the dimensions of the human body, and how those nations which have adopted a more artificial system are thereby inconvenienced by forever having to use odd amounts of their measurements to represent their everyday requirements.

"But although we were as happy there as we could be, and Edwin was beginning to overcome the sadness that had blighted his young life, I could not help but notice that not everything at

East Harrington was as it should have been." She paused a moment before continuing. "You will appreciate that I should not under any other circumstances repeat these things. My uncle and aunt seemed, to my surprise, to have little to do with each other. I had been used, I suppose, to the closeness of spirit of my own mother and father, and had imagined that all those who are married enjoy such a degree of intimacy of opinion, taste and so on. I was soon disabused of this notion. My uncle spent much of his time away, in London or at race meetings, and when he was at home he spent more time in the stables than in the house. He spoke little to my aunt, and even that little would perhaps have been better left unsaid, for I saw her often in tears, and came at length to know that this meant they had been 'having a discussion', as she referred to it. At last it became very clear that the only time my aunt was truly happy was when my uncle was away.

"A particular circumstance that often caused rifts between them concerned the company my uncle kept. For he would often bring a party of people home with him from London or from his sporting travels. It was clear that my aunt considered that she and they had little of common interest, and her attempts to be sociable to these people gradually diminished as she found that her advances were generally rebuffed. Besides, her husband did not appear to care one way or the other whether she was sociable or not, for when he had guests in the house he paid her no attention whatever. Most frequent among these guests, and perhaps most objectionable, too, was Captain Fitzclarence Legbourne Legge, a racing crony of my uncle's. Whenever Captain Legbourne Legge was at East Harrington, my uncle would generally spend days on end drinking and playing cards, and shouting abuse at any of the household who had the misfortune to venture near him.

"Captain Legbourne Legge is to me, as I know he was to my aunt, an odious man. He has a fat face, which wobbles when he speaks, and he encourages my uncle in vicious pursuits. His presence always marks a severe deterioration in Mr Hartley Lessingham's manner, and in the atmosphere of the household generally."

"Was Miss Rogerson ever present at these social gatherings, while your aunt was at East Harrington?" Holmes enquired.

"I can remember at least one such occasion," the girl replied, nodding her head. "It was early last December, just after the race meeting at Cantwell Heath. A large party had returned to East Harrington, including Captain Legbourne Legge, Miss Rogerson, Lord Waddle, Sir Arthur Pegge, and several other equally unpleasant people. My uncle had been involved in an unfortunate incident at the meeting, in which another rider had been badly injured."

"We have heard of that," Holmes interposed.

"Then perhaps you have also heard that the man, Mr Jackie Weston, may never walk again. Aunt Margaret had had word of this, and approached her husband to suggest that some money be sent to the unfortunate man, but my uncle would not countenance such a suggestion. 'Certainly not!' cried he in a tone of indignation. 'The fool was in my way!' Then he laughed loudly in her face. I chanced to be present, and it was the most unpleasant scene I have ever witnessed. All my uncle's cronies joined in the laughter, until the drawing room was filled with the noise of their horrible braying. My aunt went as white as a sheet and I thought she would faint. Then Miss Rogerson stepped forward, with a supercilious smirk upon her face that was hideous to see, and said, 'You see, Mrs Hartley Lessingham, other men may compete, but your husband wins.' At which the whole room thereupon burst into further odious laughter, Miss Rogerson foremost among them. My aunt turned on her heel and left the room at once, and I followed her as quickly as I could, for I was very frightened.

"After that, there was no peace in the house. The Christmas season was poisoned by the presence of Captain Legbourne Legge and his friends, and by the constant quarrels that occurred between my aunt and uncle. Then, on New Year's Eve, following a quarrel of unusual ferocity even for that household, my aunt packed a trunk and declared that she could not bear to remain under the roof of East Harrington Hall for a single night longer. She instructed the servants to pack trunks for Edwin and me, but our uncle stopped us at the door and forbade us to go. Further words ensued between my aunt and uncle, and in the end, with a look of great fear upon her face and tears in her eyes, my aunt departed alone, begging me to forgive her and telling me that she would send for Edwin and me just as soon as she had got herself established somewhere.

"A few days after my aunt had left us, my uncle evidently regretted his sharp words and hasty actions, for he fell into a mood of great depression. For several days he remained in his study and spoke to no one. Eventually he emerged, a chastened look upon his face.

"'I think,' said he to me, 'that the words which passed between your aunt and me have caused much trouble and wounded us both severely. But it may not be too late to redeem the situation. I think I shall go and try to persuade her to return.'

"'You know her whereabouts, then, Uncle?' I asked, my hopes rising.

"'I had a letter from her yesterday morning,' he replied. 'She is staying in a hotel in London. You would like her to return, I dare say.'

"'Indeed,' I cried. 'Nothing would give me greater pleasure!'

"My uncle nodded his head at my words, as if his mind were then made up. He at once ordered the carriage to be got ready, and within the hour he had left for the railway station."

"Do you know the contents of the letter your uncle received?" interposed Holmes.

Miss Borrow shook her head. "I asked if I might see it, but he informed me that it contained nothing that would be of interest to me, being private matter."

"Very well. Pray continue."

"For two days I heard nothing further. Then, on the evening of the third day, my uncle returned, but he returned alone. His expression was one of bitter resignation. 'She refused to come back to us,' was the only answer he would give to my questions. I was disappointed beyond description, and could not help but cry. At this my uncle became very angry. 'Do not waste your tears,' said he in a harsh voice. 'Save them for a worthier cause!' Then he went into his study and slammed the door shut behind him. From that day on, Edwin and I were forbidden to ever mention Aunt Margaret's name again.

"That night I cried myself to sleep. After that, I saw nothing before us but patient endurance. We were living in a place that was not our home, with neither friends nor friendly relations, and with a guardian who clearly cared nothing for us. But at least Edwin and I still had each other. I became determined to make the best of the circumstances in which Fate had placed us.

"At that time, of course, Mr Theakston was still our tutor, and I am sure that we benefited greatly from his kind tuition. And if it was a pleasure to us to learn all about Literature and Geography, History and Botany, it appeared an equal pleasure to Mr Theakston to teach us, so that we tried hard – even Edwin – to do nothing that might disappoint him. When he left, in the abrupt circumstances I have described to you, another support was removed from our lonely existence. Miss Rogerson then took upon herself the duties of tutor, as I have mentioned, but it was clear she had no interest whatever in her new post. It thus fell to me to supplement the meagre education Edwin received at her hands. He had so often seen Mr Hartley Lessingham and his friends at cards, at all hours of the day and night, that he had developed a morbid interest in the subject and begged me to teach him some card games. Endeavouring to derive good from bad, I therefore decided to teach him some different types of patience – there is a book in the library at East Harrington, which contains instructions for many such games – in the hope that it might help his understanding of arithmetic and similar subjects."

"And did it?" queried my wife in a kindly voice as Miss Borrow paused.

"Not very much, to be truthful," the girl responded with a shake of the head, "but it has taught him true patience, at least: to endure, without anger or sorrow, what must be. For some of the games – The Lion and the Unicorn, especially – are very difficult of solution. So far I have taught him twenty-three different types, from Apples and Pears to The Scorpion, and there is not one that does not have its own particular moral lesson, if you look hard enough for it." She blushed. "At least I think so," she added in an uncertain tone.

"You are a very resourceful and imaginative young lady," Holmes interrupted with a smile. "You have discovered that, as Shakespeare says, the uses of adversity may yet be sweet. But come, you have had a miserable time lately, for which you have our sympathy, but what is it that has brought you to the point of seeking our advice? If we are to help you in some way, we must know the most recent developments. Has there been any further communication with your aunt?"

"Six weeks after she left, a letter arrived for Mr Hartley Lessingham, bearing the postmark of Lewes in Sussex. The handwriting on the envelope was not that of my aunt, but I hoped that it might contain some news of her, and I asked my uncle if that were so. At first he would not speak of it and appeared very angry, for his face was white, but later he informed me that it was from Mr Edgar Shepherd, the old friend of my mother and father, and of my aunt, too, informing my guardian that Aunt Margaret was now residing in a cottage on the Shepherd family estate at Tattingham, in Sussex. My uncle told me that he had flung the letter into the fire.

"'So now you know,' said he in a bitter tone: 'your aunt has brought shame upon us by deserting us, and now she has shamed us yet further, by taking up abode on the property of another man.'

"Miss Rogerson had happened to come into the room as we were speaking, and had overheard the tail end of the conversation. Now she spoke.

"'Yes, Harriet,' said she, nodding her head in agreement with my uncle's words, 'you must pray that you never bring shame upon your family, as your aunt has brought shame upon hers. Woe betide you if the blood in your veins is the shameful blood of your aunt! Now run along to the schoolroom. Edwin wishes to ask you about Queen Elizabeth.'

"'Yes, ma'am,' said I politely, but as the library door closed behind me, I confess that I could not stop myself sobbing. I was greatly upset by my aunt's decision to make her home elsewhere. But she had always been very kind to me, and I knew she was not a bad woman. For my uncle to speak of her in that way was so unjust. Had it not been for his behaviour, she would never have left us. As for that odious woman, Susan Rogerson, with her painted face, vulgar jewellery and her mean and selfish nature, for her to speak of my aunt at all in her own house was the very grossest impertinence; for her to declare that my aunt was the one who had brought shame upon us was an affront to all honesty and decency.

"I had not gone ten steps from the library door when I heard the two of them laughing. At whom or what they were laughing, I knew not, but in my miserable state, their callous, unfeeling laughter struck like thorns in my heart.

"Several weeks passed. One morning I gathered my courage together and asked my guardian if I might write a letter to my aunt. At first he was very angry with me and refused to even speak of the possibility; but I asked him again a few days later, and again a few days after that, and eventually he said that I might, but that he would read the letter before it was posted, to see that I did not say anything foolish in it. I had no objection to this, as I simply wished to convey a little news to Aunt Margaret, in the hope that she would write back to us. This I did, and gave the letter to Mr Hartley Lessingham, who read it without finding anything in it to which he could object, addressed it for me and posted it himself. He would not tell me the address at which my aunt was staying. I think he feared that if I knew it, I would write a more candid letter to her behind his back.

"A week passed, and then my guardian informed me one morning that I had received a reply. He handed me the single sheet of paper at the breakfast table, explaining that he had opened the letter himself, although it had been addressed to me, because he wished to be sure that it did not contain anything unpleasant, which might upset me. He had also torn off the top of the sheet, where my aunt had written her address. He certainly did not wish me to be able to write to her in private, without his seeing exactly what I had written."

"What did the letter say?" enquired Holmes.

"Little enough," Miss Borrow replied. "To speak candidly, I was a little disappointed at its brevity. However, to have any communication at all from my aunt was like treasure to me in my lonely existence, and I read and reread the letter many times. I explained the lightness and inconsequentiality of it to myself by supposing that she suspected her husband would read it, and had therefore felt unable to reveal very much of her true feelings in it. She thanked me for the letter I had sent, and the news I had conveyed to her, and also for the picture of a cat that Edwin had drawn for her, which I had enclosed.

"She said she was living quietly, in seclusion, and was trying to make the best of her unhappy situation. She said that she sometimes now regretted her hasty decision to leave East Harrington, and wished she could alter what had happened, but could not. She enjoined me to try to be good, and always to do what was right, and to respect Mr Hartley Lessingham and always do as he bade me. She said she would write again when she had any more news, but in the meantime I should not write again – except if I had some matter of particular urgency to relate – for she did not think it quite right to do so, and it might annoy my guardian.

"Since then, I have often wished to write to Aunt Margaret again, but Mr Hartley Lessingham is implacably opposed to the suggestion. There are things I have wished so much to tell her. If she only knew all that has taken place at East Harrington since her departure, I am sure she would swallow her pride and return, even if it were only to pay us a visit."

"Well, as you cannot tell your aunt," said Holmes in an encouraging voice, "perhaps you could tell us. What has been happening at East Harrington?"

"I mentioned to you Mr Theakston's abrupt departure, which was such a loss to us. Another unwelcome development is that Captain Legbourne Legge has spent much more time at East Harrington since my aunt left. He and Mr Hartley Lessingham sometimes ride out late in the evening and do not return until after midnight."

"Do you know where it is they go?"

Miss Borrow shook her head. "Other things happen at night, too," she continued. "Edwin has been very frightened by noises he has heard in the night, and by things he has seen."

"What sort of things?"

"At the rear of East Harrington Hall is a flagged terrace," Miss Borrow replied after a moment, "at the other side of which is an old-fashioned formal garden. In the very centre of the garden stands an old sundial. My bedroom overlooks this garden, as does Edwin's. One night, very late, when I had been asleep for some time, Edwin came to my room, trembling with fear. He was in such a state that he could scarcely speak, but gradually, as I calmed him, he managed to tell me what it was that had frightened him so. He told me that he had heard noises outside, and when he had looked out he had seen a witch in the garden, doing something to the sundial. I looked from my window, but it was a very dark night and I could see no sign of anyone there. I told Edwin that he must have imagined it, that he had perhaps had a bad dream, and eventually, a little comforted and calmed, he returned to his own room.

"The following morning, however, it happened that I awoke earlier than usual, and when I rose from my bed and drew back the curtains, my eye was at once drawn to the sundial, for I saw that upon the top of it there lay what appeared to be a piece of paper, held in place by a couple of small stones. I dressed hurriedly and ran downstairs and out into the garden, keen to see what it could be. When I reached the sundial, however, I received a great shock, for there was neither paper nor anything else upon the top of it, nor any sign that there ever had been. My suggestion to Edwin that he had simply imagined those things he thought he had seen was thus turned back upon myself, for it seemed the only explanation was that I must have imagined the paper I thought I had seen upon the sundial. Then I saw that upon the path at my feet were two small stones, larger than the gravel on which they lay, and of a slightly different colour. In an instant I was convinced that these were the stones I had seen upon the paper when I had looked from my bedroom window. Someone, it seemed, had removed the paper from the sundial while I was dressing.

"I did not mention this incident to Edwin, as I did not wish to alarm him, and I knew that he would believe that his 'witch' had left some magic spell upon the sundial in the garden, but I determined that I would henceforth keep my eyes and ears open in case there were any repeat of this mysterious incident. For two weeks I neither saw nor heard anything untoward, then one night I was awakened by some noise or other. On a sudden impulse I drew back the bedroom curtain and looked out into the garden. It was a bright, moonlit night, and the ornamental bushes were throwing strong shadows across the lawns. Even as I looked, I saw a figure – an old crone – emerge from the deep shadow of a tall hedge and cross the lawn with a crooked, halting gait, until she reached the sundial. For some time, she remained motionless, her back bent over the sundial. What she was doing there, I could not see. Then, in the same furtive, shuffling manner, she returned whence she had come. I strained my eyes then, to see if any paper had been left upon the sundial, but clouds had now obscured the moon and it was too dark to see."

"One moment," interrupted Holmes. "Did you think this person in the garden was anyone you had ever seen before?"

"I think not, but I could not be certain on the point. My bedroom window was some distance off, and the figure was very hunched over, with her face turned away. Her appearance, as Edwin had said, was very like that of a witch in a storybook."

"Very well. Pray, continue!"

"In the morning I was tired and slept late. But when the events of the night came back to me, I sprang at once from my bed and peered from the window. There upon the sundial was a small sheet of white paper. At that very moment, however, before I had moved from the window, someone emerged from the house and crossed the terrace directly to the sundial. It was Captain Legbourne Legge. I watched as he took up the sheet of paper and cast to the ground the stones that had lain upon it. Then he turned and returned to the house, studying the paper as he went."

"From where had he come?" asked Holmes.

"The morning room. It has a French window which gives directly onto the terrace."

"Were you able to learn any more of this mysterious business?"

Miss Borrow shook her head. "No reference was made to it in my hearing, and I dared not bring the matter up myself."

"Has there been any repeat of this occurrence?"

"I do not know. There may have been, but I have seen nothing. But other things have occurred."

"The details, please, Miss Borrow – but you must speak quickly, for the time at our disposal is rapidly flying by! You mentioned in your letter that your brother had nearly been killed. What did you mean by that?"

"I mentioned to you that under Mr Theakston's kindly guidance, Edwin and I had often made expeditions to all parts of the East Harrington estate when the weather permitted it. Mr Theakston's departure was followed by a period of very wet weather, and we were confined to the house for several weeks, but as the weather brightened up, we enjoyed rambling about the countryside once more whenever we could, and Edwin began to take himself off for solitary 'explorations', as he called them. I saw no harm in this and did not give it a second thought. But when Mr Hartley Lessingham learned of Edwin's expeditions, he became very angry.

"'You must not go off alone, do you hear?' cried he one day, his voice quivering with rage. 'It is not acceptable when you disappear for hours at a time and no one knows where you are! Why, anything might happen! And, in particular, you must never again go near the river or the mill! They are very dangerous places, and are not for disobedient, stupid little boys! You disobey me again, and I shall give you such a good hiding that you will not sit down for a month! Do you hear?'

"I had never before seen our guardian so angry with Edwin. His face had turned purple, as Edwin's had turned white with fear, and I thought he would strike him. But then, with a horrible oath, he turned on his heel, stamped into the library and slammed the door shut behind him."

"One moment," interrupted Holmes. "The mill he mentioned – is it the same one as your guardian and Mr Theakston were discussing on the evening of the latter's departure? Dedstone Mill, I believe you called it."

Miss Borrow nodded her head. "That is correct," replied she. "It is a huge watermill, which stands beside the river, about three miles from East Harrington. It is the property of Mr

Hartley Lessingham. It used to bring him a good income, so I understand, especially as his tenants were all obliged under the terms of their leases to send their grain there. This caused some ill-feeling, for the mill was old and dilapidated, dangerously so many said, and the machinery was constantly breaking down. It has needed repairing for many years, but nothing has ever been done to it. There have been many complaints in recent years of wasted grain, either through spillage or attack by mould. The situation was perhaps exacerbated by the fact that there is a rival mill at Ollington, just eight miles away. It is very modern, and everyone says how much better it is; and not only is it better, it is also cheaper."

"You appear to be remarkably well informed on the matter."

"I have overheard things. Besides, it would be difficult not to be well informed, for it is one of the leading topics of conversation in the district. Several times Mr Hartley Lessingham's tenants have come to ask him if they might use the mill at Ollington for some, at least, of their grain, but he would not hear of it. Nor would he authorize any improvements to be made to the mill at Dedstone. Matters came to a head about a year ago. One night a fire broke out in the mill, which destroyed part of the building, including some of the machinery, and rendered it unusable. My guardian was furious, declaring that the fire had been started deliberately and he would have the culprits hanged, but no evidence could be found to suggest who might have been responsible. Since then the mill has stood idle, becoming more dilapidated and dangerous with every week that has passed."

"The local farmers now use the mill at Ollington, presumably," interposed Holmes.

Miss Borrow nodded. "Mr Hartley Lessingham could not deny them that right. But he has insisted that they pay him a fee for the privilege, that fee being the difference between what he would have charged them for using the mill at Dedstone and the lower amount they are charged at Ollington. He says the money will be used for the repair work necessary at Dedstone Mill, but no repair work has so far been undertaken."

"So of course, there is still resentment," said Holmes. "But why should your tutor, Mr Theakston, have been discussing the matter with Mr Hartley Lessingham, I wonder? This was in the spring, you say?"

"Yes, in April."

"When the mill had already been closed for about six months?"

"That is so," said Miss Borrow. "It may be," she suggested, "that Mr Theakston was giving it as his opinion that the mill was dangerously unsafe, which it is, and that if Mr Hartley Lessingham did not intend to have it repaired, then he should have it pulled down. He was perhaps thinking of what happened to Mr Jeremiah Meadowcroft. If this was the cause of the quarrel between them, then Mr Theakston has been proved quite right, for it was at the mill that Edwin suffered his recent accident. At least, they said it was an accident, but I am not sure that I believe them. If it was an accident they should feel sorry for him, but instead he has been locked in his room as a punishment. I have not been allowed to see him for two weeks, and I fear he is very ill."

"One moment," interposed Holmes, holding his hand up to stem the flow of Miss Borrow's narrative, which had been delivered in a breathless, impassioned rush. "Who is Jeremiah Meadowcroft, and what, pray, happened to him?"

"He was the manager of the mill when it was in working order. He was found drowned in the river during the floods last winter."

"When, precisely?"

"Towards the end of February."

"Were the facts of the matter established?"

"They said he had been drinking at the inn at Dedstone, and was returning late at night to the mill, where he lived. It was supposed that he had missed his footing in the dark. The riverbank was very slippery and muddy at the time, on account of the flooding. Mr Meadowcroft was a well-known drunkard, so the manner of his death, although tragic, did not occasion any great surprise in the district. Several witnesses attested that he had been drinking very heavily in the weeks immediately preceding his death."

"I see. Now, what is this accident that your brother has suffered? This is the matter you referred to in your letter, I take it?"

The young girl nodded her head vigorously. "Two months ago, I chanced to walk into the library at East Harrington Hall when Mr Hartley Lessingham was in conversation with Miss Rogerson. I heard him say, 'I'll get rid of them as soon as I can, one way or another.' Then he turned and saw me, and after a moment said something about horses being no use if they wouldn't jump, so he'd have to get rid of them; but I could tell from the tone of his voice that that was something he had just made up at that very moment. I am certain that, really, he had been speaking of Edwin and me."

"And what has happened to Edwin?"

"For a time, as you will imagine, Mr Hartley Lessingham's stern warnings and threats had their desired effect and Edwin ceased his exploratory adventures. Recently, however, he has started to wander off again on a variety of pretexts, and nothing I say can dissuade him. His latest excuse is that he wishes to collect chestnuts, acorns and the like, for a nature display in the schoolroom, but I have feared all along that he would get himself into mischief again. Two weeks last Saturday, what I had dreaded came to pass. Unbeknown to me, Edwin had gone off to explore the estate with a map, which we ourselves had made in the spring, with the help of Mr Theakston. I was sitting, reading a book in my bedroom, and the house was very quiet, when I heard a sudden commotion downstairs. I hurried from my room and peered down into the hallway. There stood Captain Legbourne Legge, dripping wet, speaking to Mr Hartley Lessingham and holding in his arms a sodden bundle. Then I realized that the sodden bundle was Edwin, who was limp and unconscious. I ran downstairs, and as I did so it seemed to me my guardian said something like, 'A pity you couldn't have finished him off.' Captain Legbourne Legge began to say, 'There were peasants from Dedstone there,' but then he saw me, nodded his head in my direction and they stopped speaking.

"'What has happened to Edwin?' I cried.

"'He has fallen into the river, near the mill,' said Mr Hartley Lessingham, turning round with an expression of great anger upon his face. 'Luckily for him, Captain Legbourne Legge was in the area, heard his cry for help and managed to fish him out.

Otherwise, he would certainly have drowned. I have told him over and over again not to play near the river, and have strictly forbidden him from going anywhere near the mill. It is extremely dangerous, as you know very well, Harriet. Now see what has happened!'

"'I did not encourage him to go there,' I returned, feeling that my guardian was trying to blame me for what had occurred.

"'But nor did you discourage him, either,' said he in an angry voice. 'I've a good mind to beat the pair of you till you're black and blue! Take him up to his room, Legge,' he continued, turning to the other man, 'and I'll get Mrs Hardcastle to deal with him.'

"I have not seen Edwin again since that moment, for he has been confined to his bedroom for the last two weeks, as a punishment for disobeying his guardian, and I am not allowed to visit him."

"Do you know his state of health?" Holmes enquired.

"I am informed that he is getting better now, but I do not know whether I really believe it. I have heard him crying out in the middle of the night in a pitiful voice, as if in pain. I pleaded with my uncle that I be allowed to inform Aunt Margaret of Edwin's illness, but he simply brushed aside my requests.

"'Edwin will be well soon enough,' said he when last I spoke to him on the subject. 'Besides, there is nothing your aunt could do for him. He is receiving all the attention he needs – and more than he deserves, quite frankly – from Mrs Maybury and Mrs Hardcastle.'"

"Who are these ladies?" interrupted Holmes.

"Mrs Maybury was housekeeper at East Harrington Hall when my aunt was there, a position of some responsibility, but after Miss Rogerson's arrival her position was altered and she was reduced to simply doing Miss Rogerson's bidding. I know that she has been very upset by all that has happened at East Harrington in the last two years, for I chanced to overhear her once, saying as much to Hammond, the butler. I believe they both would have left long ago were it not that they are somewhat advanced in years and would experience difficulty in finding other positions. Mrs Maybury is a kind and friendly woman, and I am sure that she would do the best for Edwin, if the responsibility for his care lay in her hands, but in fact it does not, and my guardian's use of her name to me was a lie. For when I asked her at the end of last week if Edwin was improving, she answered me with a look of surprise.

"'Bless you, my dear!' said she. 'I wish I knew, but they won't let me near him. Mrs Hardcastle has the key of the room and won't let anyone else in.'

"Mrs Hardcastle is very different from Mrs Maybury. She is a large, coarse and ignorant woman, who has often caused trouble in the servants' hall, and I know that Edwin has always been afraid of her. She comes of a local family, the Bagnalls, who are well known in the district as ne'er-do-wells and trouble-makers. Her sister, who is a half-wit and drunkard, was in trouble last year for throwing stones and breaking windows in the village. Mrs Hardcastle's own husband is at present in Bedford gaol, serving a sentence for robbery. Why on earth Mr Hartley Lessingham should have entrusted Edwin's care to such a woman I cannot imagine." Tears welled up in our young companion's eyes as she spoke these last words, but she wiped them away briskly with the back of her hand. "When I heard that Miss Rogerson was going up to London for a few days on some business of her own, I at once thought of you, Mr Holmes. I begged that I might accompany Miss Rogerson, in order, I said, to read something of my father's family in the library, but my only desire, in reality, was to speak to you and plead with you to help us. If you cannot, I do not know what will become of us."

Holmes sat a moment in silence, his elbows on the table, his chin resting on his fingertips.

"There is no one to whom you can turn?" he enquired at last, "no relative or friend whom I could inform of your situation, and who might perhaps take an interest?"

Miss Borrow shook her head. "Apart from Aunt Margaret," she replied, her lip quivering slightly, "there is no one."

"Very well," said Holmes, "I shall do what I can. You have no idea of your aunt's address?"

"Only that it is somewhere near Tattingham in Sussex, I believe."

"Quite so. And Mr Theakston's address? I think I should like to have a word with that gentleman, if it is possible."

"As a matter of fact, I do remember that," Miss Borrow replied, brightening up slightly. "He mentioned to us once or twice that his mother lived at Rose Cottage, in the village of Hembleby, near Wetherby, in Yorkshire. His father had been a teacher in Wetherby, I believe, but died some years ago. His mother then took Rose Cottage which, Mr Theakston said, stands beside the village green, close by the church. I am sure that a letter to Rose Cottage would find him."

"Excellent!" said Holmes, taking out his notebook. "You see, Miss Borrow, we are making progress already!" He glanced at his watch. "Our allotted time is nearly up, and Miss Rogerson may return at any moment. Would you be so good as to wait by the door, Watson, and give a signal if you see her coming? I wish to take down a few particulars."

I did as he requested, and a few minutes later observed the carriage in which Miss Borrow had arrived draw up once more at the front of the library. I caught my wife's eye, nodded my head, and saw her speak to Miss Borrow, who at once stood up from the table and made a show of examining the books on a nearby shelf. It was fortunate that she had acted so promptly, for as I turned back to the doorway, Miss Rogerson herself pushed past me with a swish of skirts. "I thought I told you to wait at the doorway," I heard her say in a harsh tone to Miss Borrow. The girl mumbled some reply and followed the older woman meekly from the room. In a moment, I had rejoined my two companions at the table.

"Miss Borrow and Miss Rogerson return to Leicestershire on Friday afternoon," remarked Holmes as I sat down. "Miss Borrow has requested, however, that before she and Miss Rogerson leave London, she be allowed to pay a visit to the church of St Martin-within-Ludgate, where there is apparently a memorial to the Borrow family. She will be at St Martin's on Friday morning, and I have told her that I shall try to speak to her then, with any information I have managed to acquire."

"What do you intend to do?" I asked.

My friend shook his head, a wry expression upon his face. "Miss Borrow reminds me a little of a distant relative of mine, with whom I once had a connection. She is a plucky girl, and as such deserves our help. But it is a delicate matter," said he, "and the best course of action is not yet clear to me. Will you come with me to St Martin's, Watson?"

"I should certainly wish to, if I may."

"Then meet me at the corner of Fleet Street and Farringdon Street at a quarter to eleven on Friday morning and I may have some news of the matter."

St Martin-within-Ludgate

My wife and I discussed the matter for some time that evening, but could not think what to suggest. The circumstances in which Harriet Borrow and her brother found themselves were not ideal. That could scarcely be denied. But the circumstances of many children, it had to be admitted, were far from ideal. At least the Borrow children appeared to be well clothed and well nourished, and Hartley Lessingham's violent, frightening threats notwithstanding, they did not appear to have been seriously ill-treated.

Of Hartley Lessingham himself, it was difficult to know what to think. He was clearly a man of strong, dominating character, who pursued his own forceful course through life, and did not care to be crossed in any way. My wife remarked that he would not be the first person one would consider when drawing up a list of invitations to a dinner party, and I could hardly disagree with that, but fortunately for many people, it is no crime in the eyes of the law to be thoroughly obnoxious. For a man of his type, coarse and selfish as he appeared to be, to have someone else's children visited upon him must have seemed a scarcely bearable imposition, but for all his evident short-tempered intolerance of their childish ways, he did not appear to have done anything seriously wrong as far as the Borrow children were concerned, and had even appeared, in his own angry way, to show some concern for the young boy's safety.

Perhaps more intriguing than these general considerations were the curious night-time events that Miss Borrow and her brother had witnessed. Who was the witchlike woman who came in the night? What was her purpose? And what was the significance of the slips of paper she appeared to leave upon the sundial? Captain Legbourne Legge was clearly implicated in this matter in some way, as Miss Borrow had observed him take one of the slips of paper, without exhibiting any apparent surprise that it should have been there upon the sundial; but what the connection might be between Legbourne Legge and the strange nocturnal visitor, it was difficult to imagine. The best explanation we could suggest was that this business was connected in some way with his gambling activities – that the woman was the conveyor of some secret information concerning forthcoming race meetings.

I was running over the whole matter again in my mind on Friday morning when I set off to meet Sherlock Holmes as we had arranged. It was a wet, blustery day, and the streets were thronged with slow-moving traffic. In the Strand, a cart had lost a wheel and collapsed onto the road surface, strewing the barrels and sacks it was carrying all across the road. Eventually, when my cab had remained stationary for more than five minutes and it began to appear that I would be late for my appointment, I paid off the cabbie and made my way along Fleet Street on foot. As I neared the eastern end of the street, a train passed over the viaduct above Ludgate Hill, sending up huge clouds of smoke, which hid the dome of St Paul's from view. My mind returned at that moment to Miss Borrow's account of the mysteries at East Harrington Hall, and they struck me all at once as quite incredible. Here we were, just a few years from the end of the nineteenth century, in a modern, noisy world, a world of great cities, of steam engines and express trains, of gaslight and electricity and telegrams, surrounded constantly by the noise and smoke and bustle of vigorous modernity. In contrast, the account Miss Borrow had given us, of excessive drinking and gambling in a country house, of half-overheard and perhaps misunderstood conversations, and of the witchlike figure who came in the night-time, seemed to belong to another century altogether, and

I found myself, somewhat against my own will, beginning to doubt the girl's veracity. She had certainly impressed me, at the meeting in the library, as being honest, intelligent and trustworthy, but in truth we had no real corroborative evidence for any of what she had told us. One does occasionally in life meet people for whom the truth appears to be of no special significance. Such people will say whatever occurs to them, whether true or completely untrue, so long as it furthers the impression they wish to make upon their audience. Could Harriet Borrow be of this type? She did not find her present situation entirely congenial, which was understandable, and would naturally do what she could to escape from it. Would this include exaggerating and lying about what had been happening at East Harrington Hall, and about what she had overheard there? I could scarcely believe it of such an innocent-faced young girl, but I admit that there were doubts in my mind upon the point when I met Holmes at the corner of Fleet Street.

"The girl has not yet arrived," said he. "I suggest we cross the street and wait at the foot of Ludgate Hill. We shall easily be able to see when she comes, but will be far enough away to avoid drawing attention to ourselves."

"Have your enquiries progressed at all?" I asked as we made our way between the traffic.

"A little," he returned. "I wrote to the tutor, Theakston, at the address Miss Borrow gave us, and have had a letter back this morning. It is not from Theakston himself, however, nor from his mother, but from the vicar of Hembleby, a Mr Daniel Blanchard. He informs me that he has been asked by Theakston's mother to reply to my letter. Mrs Theakston, he says, has been exceedingly concerned for her son, for she has not seen him for nearly a year and has had no communication from him for over six months. Mr Blanchard says that in July he wrote on the mother's behalf to Hartley Lessingham, and received a brief reply, informing him only that the tutor had left East Harrington in the spring, and that his present whereabouts were unknown."

"It seems odd that he should not have written for such a long time," I remarked. "Even if he perhaps felt a little ashamed at his dismissal from his post, you would think he would have written by now. What can it mean?"

Holmes shook his head. "We cannot yet say. There are several possible explanations. I also wrote to Edgar Shepherd, the family friend in Sussex, giving him a very brief account of the state of affairs at East Harrington and enclosing a letter for the aunt, in which I gave a more detailed account of the matter. I have not yet, however, received a reply from either of them. One thing, at least, which I have been able to discover is that the Borrow children are worth a very great deal of money. Under the terms of their late father's will, they stand to inherit, between them, almost all of his fortune. This, as far as I have been able to make out, is something in excess of a quarter of a million pounds."

"Good Lord!"

"Yes, it is a considerable sum, is it not? I very much doubt that the children themselves are aware of it, but you can be sure that Hartley Lessingham is. I have verified that he and his wife were appointed the legal guardians of the children after the death of their parents. In that capacity they have full use of the income from the Borrow fortune, so long as the children are residing with them, although they cannot touch the capital without the agreement of the Borrows' solicitor, Jervis and Co. of Gray's Inn. This, I suggest, explains some, at least, of Hartley Lessingham's anxiety for the children's safety, and also his insistence that they remained with him when the aunt left. If the children are lost to him, then so is the money. Of course, he is supposed to use the money only for the children's benefit, but I should not imagine that a mere technical consideration of that sort would weigh very heavily in Hartley Lessingham's consideration of the matter. From what I have learned, it seems that he is not so well off as he might wish to be. His racing is a very expensive hobby, and my information is that he has been living far beyond his means for some time. As you are probably aware, agricultural income and rents are all depressed at present and show no prospect of rising in the near future, and then, of course, he has had the little difficulty with the mill, of which Miss Borrow informed us. All in all, I think we can see why he required the children to remain with him, even though, in many ways, the situation suits no one. What the rest of the girl's story might mean, it is hard to tell at the moment. It is always difficult when, as in this case, one is presented with a miscellaneous assortment of facts, to judge which of them are related and which are not. I suspect that a personal inspection at East Harrington might clarify my ideas on the matter somewhat, but there are practical difficulties in the way of that course of action, as you will appreciate. But, here, unless I am much mistaken, is Miss Borrow's carriage!"

I watched as the carriage pulled into the side of the road, outside the entrance to St Martin's. A moment later, the girl alighted, crossed the pavement and entered the porch of the church. I made to walk up the hill, but Holmes put his hand on my arm.

"Don't make your attention too obvious, Watson," said he, without turning his head, "but take a look at the fellow in the hansom at the end of Fleet Street. He seems to be taking an uncommon interest in Miss Borrow."

I took what I hoped appeared a leisurely glance around, allowing my gaze to wander first up Ludgate Hill, then down towards Blackfriars, and finally into Fleet Street. In a stationary cab near the corner sat a large, clean-shaven, powerful-looking man in a top hat. I had been looking for only a second or two when he turned abruptly in my direction. I quickly looked away and pretended to consult my watch. Next moment, his cab had crossed the road junction and was clattering past us, at a gallop, up Ludgate Hill. Beyond it, the carriage that had brought Miss Borrow was just reaching the top of the hill, near St Paul's, and passing out of sight. In a few moments, the much quicker hansom cab had also reached the top of the hill and vanished.

"Now, I wonder what we should make of that little episode," said Holmes, as we made our way up the hill.

"I haven't the faintest idea."

"It is a deep, dark business, Watson, and may yet become both deeper and darker before we have seen it through."

"I would not doubt it. I cannot imagine what you will do next."

"I will let you know when I have made my decision," returned he as we approached the church doorway.

We entered the shadowed porch and passed through into the interior of the church. It was cool and seemed extraordinarily silent and peaceful after the bustle in the street outside. Miss Borrow was sitting at the end of a pew, her head bent to a book, and appeared a small, solitary figure, alone in the broad expanse of the nave.

"I'm afraid I must ask you to wait as a sentry by the door again, old fellow," said Holmes in a low tone. "The consultation should not take long, but if the woman should return and catch the two of us speaking, it would seriously prejudice Miss Borrow's position and severely compromise my own options."

"Certainly," said I, and returned accordingly to the porch. After several minutes of watching the unbroken flow of traffic up and down Ludgate Hill, I was struck again by the incongruous nature of the mysterious events Miss Borrow had narrated to us earlier in the week, and as my thoughts ranged over all that she had told us, the time flew by without my being aware of it. Though physically I was within a few inches of the bustle of Ludgate Hill, mentally I was a hundred miles away, in Leicestershire, when I was abruptly brought to myself by the sudden arrival of a carriage, practically in front of me. I stepped back into the porch as the carriage door was opened and a woman began to descend. It was undoubtedly Miss Rogerson. I turned quickly on my heel, pushed open the door of the church and rapped my knuckles sharply on a table near the door, on which an assortment of books and other publications was neatly stacked. Miss Borrow was still seated where I had seen her before, but now Holmes was seated next to her.

It was clear that they were deep in conversation, but they looked round sharply upon my signal. I began to make a silent gesture, but even as I did so I heard the door open behind me, so turned instead to the publications on the table, which I made a show of studying. The woman who had entered walked swiftly past me. I lifted my head slightly and looked from the corner of my eye. Miss Borrow was now standing up, and appeared to be reading the inscription on a plaque affixed to the wall near where she had been sitting. Of Sherlock Holmes, there was no sign at all.

The girl turned at the sound of the woman's footsteps, and after a last glance at the plaque, began to make her way towards where the woman was waiting, a few feet from where I stood.

"Hurry up!" I heard the woman say in a sharp whisper. "If we miss that train, you'll know about it!"

In order to have something to do which would get me out of their way, I picked up a tall stack of hymn books, and carried them across to a low wooden cupboard, which stood at the other side of the door; there I pretended to sort them for a few moments until I heard the door close, whereupon I gathered the books together again and carried them back to where I had found them. When I looked round, Holmes was standing behind me.

"Hello!" I cried in surprise. "Where did you disappear to?"

"I simply crouched between the pews," said he. "I don't think the woman suspected anything."

"She came in so quickly I was unable to make myself scarce," I remarked, "but I don't think she paid me any attention."

My friend nodded. "I have made a decision," said he, as he pulled open the door and we emerged into the noise of Ludgate Hill once more. "I have gone carefully over Miss Borrow's testimony with her again. It seems to me that she has acted very sensibly so far, and it would be unworthy of us to let her down now. The more I consider her story, the less I like the sound of it. Now, Hartley Lessingham and his cronies, including Miss Rogerson, are travelling to the race meeting at Towcester tomorrow. I am therefore going to go down to Leicestershire in the morning to look things over for myself. I should very much value your company."

"I should be very pleased to give it."

"Good man! I should warn you, though, Watson, that our position, legally speaking, may be a trifle precarious."

"What do you mean?"

"I intend to enter East Harrington Hall while its master is absent. I have arranged with Miss Borrow that she will admit us, but as she is a minor, legally speaking I am not sure that that will count for anything in the eyes of the law."

"What do you hope to do there?"

"That rather depends on what I discover. Apart from anything else, however, I wish to see for myself the condition of Miss Borrow's brother. I should thus be obliged if you would bring with you tomorrow your stethoscope and anything else you feel you may need for an examination of the boy. Having listened again to Miss Borrow's account of the matter, I am seriously concerned that they are, as she suspects, trying to kill him."

"What! But I thought it would be in Hartley Lessingham's interests to have the children living there in good health for as long as possible, so that he can enjoy their money."

"Yes, but he only needs to keep one of them alive to qualify for it," returned Holmes in a grim tone. "He can afford to let the boy die without diminishing his income. That is what especially concerns me, and why we must go down there without delay. But here is a cab! If you will accompany me back to Baker Street, we can discuss the matter further, and make our final plans for tomorrow!"

East Harrington Hall

We met at eight o'clock on Saturday morning at Euston station, as we had arranged, and caught a fast train to the north. I had equipped myself with tweeds and a cap, as my friend had suggested, and he was similarly attired, his idea being that we should be less likely to attract attention on the East Harrington estate in rural garb than if we appeared to be city men. In my pocket I had my stethoscope and a few other odds and ends, which I thought might prove useful if I was able to examine Miss Borrow's brother. I asked Holmes if he had received any reply, either from Margaret Hartley Lessingham or from Edgar Shepherd, but he shook his head. He had with him a large-scale map of the East Harrington district, which he had purchased the previous afternoon, and this he studied for some time in silence.

"It seems likely," said he at length, as he folded the map up and slipped it into his pocket, "that Hartley Lessingham's party will get a connection to Northampton and pick up a train for Towcester there. The distance from East Harrington to Towcester is about forty miles, and the journey will involve at least one change of train, probably two, so it will take them a fair while. All being well, therefore, they should have departed from East Harrington some considerable time before we get there, and the way will be clear for our little inspection!"

With that, my companion lapsed into silence once more, and I was left to my own thoughts. Much of the countryside through which our train passed that morning had a wet, bedraggled appearance, but as we reached the midland counties it was evident that they had experienced exceptionally heavy rain in recent weeks. A great many of the fields beside the railway line were flooded, to a greater or lesser extent. In some, not a blade of grass was to be seen, and save for the regular interruption of trimmed hawthorn hedges, the countryside beside the line might have been one vast shallow lake.

We changed trains at Rugby and alighted at length at a small wayside station, the only travellers to do so. As the little branch train with its two short carriages pulled away from us across the flat landscape, I took stock of our surroundings. The station was situated where the railway line crossed a small country road on the level. Save for a couple of station buildings and the crossing-keeper's cottage, there was no sign of habitation upon that broad, flat landscape. The fields beside the road were all flooded to some extent, and the road, which was slightly higher than the surrounding land, appeared like a narrow muddy causeway across the wet plain. Above us, the clouds were leaden-coloured and heavy, and appeared likely at any minute to disgorge more rain onto the sodden countryside.

"This should be the most direct route," said Holmes, indicating the road to the west, and we set off in that direction. The countryside soon proved to be not quite so flat as I had at first supposed, but undulated gently, like a ruffled counterpane thrown carelessly across the land. Presently, when we had been walking for about half an hour and had not seen a soul, our road turned a corner and dipped slightly, and we found our way barred by a broad sheet of water, which appeared about two feet deep in the middle. It was impossible to get round it, and we were just examining the best direction to take to wade through it when a farm cart pulled by a gigantic horse came up behind us. The driver reined in his horse and invited us to climb up beside him.

"I'll get you on a-ways, through the worst of it," said he in an affable tone. "Where be you bound for?"

"We're taking a walk for our health, and to see the countryside," I responded.

"You've picked a rum time for it, if I may say so," said he with a chuckle. "Mind you, the wild geese are a sight at the moment," he added. "Thousands of 'em, there are. They come every year when the fields are flooded. You'd be interested in that, I suppose, sir?"

"Certainly," said Holmes. "Would that be on the East Harrington estate?"

"That's it, sir! Over by the river, on the water meadows. Them's as watery as water meadows can be at the moment, too," he added with a chuckle, "but that's how the geese like 'em!"

For several miles, the cart trundled on across the Leicestershire countryside, the huge horse never once breaking his gentle jog-trot, and the driver displaying a similar rhythm in his conversation. Holmes remained silent throughout this journey, but I could see that he was in a state of heightened tension.

Presently, as the driver announced that he was turning off down a lane to the left, we alighted, thanked him warmly for his assistance and continued on foot. I had observed that the hedge on our right had given way in the last half mile or so to a high brick wall.

"This wall marks the boundary of the East Harrington estate," remarked my companion as we walked along. "If I have read the map correctly, one of the main entrances to the estate should lie just ahead. Yes, there it is!" cried he as we rounded a bend in the road and a large imposing gateway came into view. The pillars on either side of the entrance must have been nearly twenty feet tall, and were surmounted by large carved figures, which appeared to be winged lions. The gates themselves, which were standing open, were of ornately wrought ironwork, and were, I think, the largest such gates I have ever seen.

"It appears a wealthy estate," I remarked.

Holmes nodded. "And yet," said he, "we know that its owner is in financial difficulties and is desperate for all the income he can garner."

"Of course, expenditure has a habit of rising in line with income," I remarked, "and usually manages to keep one step ahead."

"Quite so," returned my companion with a chuckle. "It was ever thus. The man who has no money believes that just a little would undoubtedly secure his happiness; the man who already has a little dreams of having a lot; and the man who has a lot feels confident that if he had yet more his situation might be immeasurably improved. This consideration alone should suffice to discredit the suggestion that there is any significant relation between money and happiness. But," he continued, putting his finger to his lips, "we had best keep our reflections on the subject to ourselves while we are on the estate!"

We passed through the wide gateway and beneath the menacing stare of the winged lions. Immediately behind the right-hand gate was a small brick-built lodge. In a little vegetable plot to the side of it, a man was digging with a spade.

"A bright day to you, sir!" called Holmes as we passed by. "If anyone challenges us," he added to me in an undertone, "just follow my lead."

The drive before us was almost as wide as a city street. It made a long, gentle sweep to the left, to avoid a rushy mere on which hordes of ducks and moorhens were busy, and then curved to the right and resumed its original direction. Ahead of us now it lay dead straight and level, as far as the eye could see. Once past the mere, it was flanked on either side by woods, and far in the distance, a focal point for all travellers on the drive, stood a very tall obelisk. So very long and straight was the drive that after we had been walking briskly for almost ten minutes, the obelisk at the end of it appeared scarcely any closer than when we had begun. I was remarking on this fact to my companion when, far in the distance, a closed carriage came into view by the obelisk, making its way at some speed towards us.

"Now who, I wonder, is this?" murmured Holmes.

So great was the length of the drive that although the carriage was clearly travelling at a great pace, and we were walking briskly, it was several minutes before it reached us. As it came closer, a man leaned from the window on our side and called something to the driver. The latter at once reined in his horses and brought them to a slow trot, and at this rate they approached us, until the driver brought the carriage to a halt next to where we were standing.

A large, powerful-looking man leaned from the window of the carriage and surveyed us. His features were large and coarse, his brows were heavy and his chin seemed to jut forward aggressively. The look in his eye as he glanced from one to the other of us was not a friendly one.

"Who are you?" he demanded in a belligerent tone.

"The name is Hobbes," said Holmes, stepping forward and extending his hand. "This is my companion, Mr Wilson."

"What are you doing here?" demanded the other, ignoring Holmes's outstretched hand. I glanced past him, at the other two occupants of the carriage. Seated opposite him was an obese, rather stupid-looking man with puffy lips, whose chin seemed sunk in rolls of fat. He was playing the fool with what appeared to be a pair of antique duelling pistols. The woman I recognized at once as Miss Rogerson. For the briefest of moments, as my glance passed over those mean features that I remembered from our previous encounters, our eyes met. I looked away quickly.

"My companion and I are enthusiastic naturalists," Holmes was saying. "We have been informed that the flocks of migrating geese are worth seeing at this time of the year."

"Oh, have you? Have you also been informed that this is private property?"

"Indeed," said Holmes, pulling the map from his pocket. "But my information is that there is a public right of way along this drive, and to the river."

"So some people claim!"

"Anyhow, I am sure that the owner of this land would have no objection to our seeking to witness such a fascinating spectacle."

"Oh, you're sure, are you? Well, let me inform you that the owner of this land does not give a tuppenny damn for your 'fascinating spectacle'! For two pins he would fling you both in the river with the damned geese!"

"Oh, leave 'em, Lessingham!" called the other man in the carriage in a bored drawl. I glanced his way and saw that he was making a play of aiming one of the pistols at me and squeezing the trigger. "Bang!" said he. "That's one of 'em gone, anyhow. Leave 'em, I say," he repeated to his companion. "Let 'em go on their wild goose chase. Perhaps they'll fall in the river!" He and the woman laughed loudly at this.

The large man was still leaning from the carriage window. Now he raised his fist to us. "You have the right of way marked on your map there?" he demanded.

"Certainly," said Holmes.

"Well, then. You stray one inch from it and you'll find yourself in court faster than you can say goose! Do you understand?"

"Absolutely."

"Drive on!" cried the other and leaned back into his seat, as the coachman lashed his horses and they sped away at a gallop.

"That was a somewhat unlooked-for encounter," remarked Holmes to me after a moment in a wry tone. "What a very unpleasant brute he is! If he were a dog, he would probably be put down by order of the court!"

"That other fool – Captain Legbourne Legge, I presume – pointed a pistol at me and pretended to fire it," I cried angrily. "I can scarcely believe that an ex-Army man could ever do such a stupid thing!"

Holmes turned and looked at me. "My dear fellow!" said he in a concerned tone. "You look quite white! Those idiots have upset you!"

"I don't mind admitting it," I replied. "When a man has had the muzzle of a gun pointed at him in deadly earnest, in the heat of battle, it ceases for ever to be amusing."

"I understand," said Holmes, clapping me on the shoulder. "Let us stand here a moment and recover our composure before we proceed! I tell you this, Watson, if I had the slightest compunction before this incident of trespassing upon this man's land and interfering in his business, I have none now. The time will come when he will regret having spoken to us in that way!"

There was a look of hardened determination upon my companion's face such as I had rarely seen there, and I knew then that he would not rest until he had seen this business through to the bitter end.

"Are you ready to continue?" he asked me after a moment.

"There is something else troubling me." I answered.

"Oh?"

"I fear the woman may have recognized me. I did not believe, on either occasion this week when I saw her, that she had taken any notice of me, but just now, when our eyes met, I thought I detected a flicker of recognition in them."

"Ah! That is unfortunate," responded my companion in a thoughtful tone. He glanced back the way we had come. "They have gone now, anyway. Let us hope her memory fails her. Meanwhile, we must make all haste to the Hall!"

We resumed our brisk pace, but it was another fifteen minutes before we reached the obelisk, where four roadways, like the points of the compass, went off at right angles to each other. Set atop the tall pillar was a gigantic stone pineapple. Holmes glanced up at it as we paused for a moment.

"I understand that such a symbol is supposed to indicate hospitality and a warm welcome," he remarked with a chuckle; "items which are conspicuous only by their absence at East Harrington!" He glanced again at his map. "Up to this point," he continued after a moment, "we were on solid ground, legally speaking. From here, however, the public right of way goes off that way, to the left, through the woods to the river, whereas we must go straight ahead. According to the map, East Harrington Hall lies just beyond that belt of trees. Are you ready to step beyond the law?"

"I am," I replied.

"According to legal tradition," Holmes continued as we followed the drive ahead, "an Englishman's house is his castle, and a very sound rule it is, too, in most circumstances. But, like all sound rules, it yields before another rule, when that other rule is one that possesses greater moral force, as in the present instance."

"I quite agree."

"Unfortunately, that consideration will not do us much good if we are stopped by anyone. And nor, of course, will the story of the wild geese, for we are past the point where that would be credible. If we are challenged, our best course now is probably to speak the truth: that we are here to see Miss Borrow. As she is a minor, legally speaking, I am not sure that her invitation to us to enter into Hartley Lessingham's property is of any substance in the eyes of the law, but I see no alternative. We must press on with our intended business so long as ever we are at liberty to do so, and just hope that we do not end the day in a police cell. But surely that is Miss Borrow there now!"

We had passed quickly through the narrow belt of trees and found ourselves atop a slight rise. Spread out a little below us, about a hundred yards further on, was the red-brick Georgian splendour of East Harrington Hall. In front of it lay a broad smooth lawn, around which the drive curved, and in the very centre of the lawn a girl in a pink dress was sitting at an easel, facing towards us, painting. Holmes raised his cap, and she made an answering gesture with a long paintbrush. "Come along!" said he, and we left the drive and set off across the lawn.

"Oh, I am so glad that you have been able to come!" cried the girl, hurrying towards us, her eyes shining with tears. "I sat here that I might see you as soon as you arrived, but I scarcely dared hope that I would see you at all!"

"Now that we are here, we must waste no time," returned Holmes in an urgent tone. "We have had an unfortunate encounter with your guardian on our way here, and it is possible that he will send back his coachman, or some other servant, to see what we are up to. You must take us to your brother's room at once!"

Miss Borrow put down her painting things and ran before us across the lawn and up a broad and shallow flight of steps to the ornate front door of the house. We followed her into the entrance hall, where a maidservant was polishing a large, gleaming piece of green marble statuary, and looked at us with curiosity as we passed. Miss Borrow paid her no heed, but led the way up a wide, thickly carpeted staircase and into a first-floor corridor, where the scent of beeswax polish filled the air. As she turned in to another, steeper flight of stairs, a manservant in livery came round a corner, stopped and stared at us in surprise, but we ignored him and pressed on. A third flight of stairs, steeper and less extravagantly carpeted than the others, brought us to the top floor. Here was the same gleaming, polished woodwork, but on a smaller and more modest scale than on the floors below.

"This is my brother's room," said Miss Borrow, indicating a dark, panelled door, halfway along the corridor. We tried the handle, but the door was locked and no key was in sight. As Holmes was bending down, squinting through the keyhole to see if the key was on the inside, another door was opened further along the corridor, and a large, fat, slatternly-looking woman emerged. Miss Borrow let out a little cry, stepped back in alarm and pressed herself against the corridor wall. "It is Mrs Hard-castle," said she in a whisper.

This, then, was the woman who had been charged with taking care of Miss Borrow's brother, and of overseeing his return to full health. She was, I must say, every physician's nightmare of a nurse, and the expression upon her coarse features spoke only of brutality and ignorance.

"Who might you be?" asked this unpleasant apparition in a rude and impertinent tone, addressing Holmes.

"I am the man that is going to enter this room," returned Holmes in a sharp tone. "Where is the key?"

"That's none of your business," said she, but there had been a momentary flicker of her eyes towards the doorway through which she had just emerged. Holmes had evidently observed this, too, for in an instant he had stepped past the woman and into the room behind her. In a moment, he emerged again with a large iron key in his hand. She tried to snatch it from him as he passed, but he evaded her and bent to the lock with it. A low, muffled moan came from beyond the door, as if the rattle of the key had roused the occupant of the room from slumber.

A cry from Miss Borrow made me turn, to see that Mrs Hardcastle had darted into her room and re-emerged with a large stick in her hand. She moved with remarkable speed for such a large woman, and now, in what appeared to be a blind rage, dashed forward before I could stop her and struck Holmes a sharp blow across the shoulders. He turned, eyed her coldly for a moment, then stood up and wrenched the stick from her grasp. In a slow, deliberate fashion, he snapped the stick across his knee and tossed the broken pieces onto the floor.

"If you are not out of my sight in two seconds," said he in an icy tone, "I shall personally throw you down the stairs."

For one second she stood there, defiance struggling with fear upon her face, then, as Holmes made some slight motion towards her, fear gained the upper hand and she turned and ran into her room. The door slammed shut behind her and I heard the key turn in the lock.

"Quickly," said Holmes, returning to the lock of the boy's room. "We have no time to lose! There may be others in the house who will present us with more formidable opposition!" He turned the key and pushed open the door, and as he did so Miss Borrow dashed forward and into her brother's room. It was dark within, for a heavy curtain was drawn across the window, but the light from the open doorway sufficed to illuminate a scene more shocking than anything I could have imagined. Upon the bed, under a single dirty sheet, the little boy lay still, his head upon a filthy pillow, and the eyes which turned in our direction were wide with fear. But what riveted my attention was that the lower part of his face was completely covered by the windings of some bandage-like cloth.

Quickly I untied the knot behind his neck and unwound this filthy cloth, as Holmes drew back the curtain to admit the grey light of that dull September day into the room. Beneath the bandage, a further clump of rag had been forced into his mouth. There appeared nothing whatever wrong with his face and it was evident that the cloth was nothing more than a gag, designed to prevent him crying out. As I removed it, he began to sob, although the gaze of his dark-ringed eyes never left his sister. For a moment I was puzzled as to why he did not sit up, or extend his hand to her, but as I drew back the filthy sheet that covered him, the reason became plain. Beneath the sheet, several lengths of stout cord had been passed across his chest and under the bed, binding him fast. Further lengths of the same cord had been tied tightly round his wrists, and secured to the frame of the bed. These I at once set about unfastening. As I did so, I noticed with horror that his arms and legs were covered with livid bruises. It was apparent that he had been beaten, repeatedly and severely.

"Here," said Holmes, unfastening his clasp knife. "I'll cut the bonds. It will be quicker. Never mind about your medical instruments, Watson. The boy comes with us. See if you can find him some outdoor clothes!"

In two minutes I had the lad dressed. He offered no resistance to this, but nor did he take any active part in the process. His manner was one of strange, silent passivity. Several times, I spoke to him, to ask a question or make some reassuring remark, but although he appeared to follow all that I said, he never uttered a sound, and it was clear that he was in a state of shock. As I pulled some clothes onto his thin little figure, I had made a rapid assessment of his condition. In my opinion, there was very little physically wrong with him – or nothing that a few solid meals would not cure anyway – but probably as a result of the treatment he had endured, and the lack of food, his temperature was up and his brow was clammy, so I wrapped him in an old blanket I found in a cupboard.

"I'll carry him," I said as we prepared to leave the room.

"Good man!" cried Holmes. "Now, Miss Borrow, is there a way we can reach your guardian's study without passing through the main hall?"

"This way," said she, and led us quickly along the corridor to the other end, where there was a second staircase, narrower than the one by which we had ascended. "This leads all the way down to the ground floor," said she, "and comes out directly opposite the door of Mr Hartley Lessingham's study."

As we followed her down the stair, I could hear the sound of hurrying footsteps and urgent voices calling from elsewhere in the house, but we reached the study without encountering anyone, and shut the door firmly behind us. It was a large room, situated at the back of the house, with a tall window overlooking a broad terrace. Beyond the terrace, a smooth lawn sloped gradually down to a large ornamental lake, perhaps two hundred yards away. Three of the study walls were lined with bookshelves, and in the centre of the room was a very large mahogany desk. I laid the boy gently on a couch, and watched as Holmes rapidly pulled open the drawers of the desk.

"It was not my original intention to search this desk," said he, without looking up, "but we have already laid ourselves open to a charge of aggravated trespass – not to mention kidnapping when we get the boy away from here – so that whatever else we do will scarcely make our guilt any worse in the eyes of the law. We may as well be hanged for a sheep as a lamb. Ah!" cried he all at once, pausing in his rapid survey of the contents of the desk. "This is interesting! It is as I suspected!"

Miss Borrow and I leaned forward to see. Holmes had been sifting through a thick sheaf of loose papers, which he had taken from a drawer. The one that had particularly arrested his attention contained the name "Margaret Hartley Lessingham", written over and over again at random, all over the page, with, here and there, a few other odd words and phrases.

"Is this your uncle's handwriting?" Holmes asked Miss Borrow.

"Undoubtedly," said she. "But what does it mean? Can it be that under his harsh exterior he yet harbours a deep affection for my aunt, and that this repeated invocation of her name is his means of expressing his grief at her continued absence?"

"I fancy it might bear some other interpretation," returned Holmes, as he continued to sift through the contents of the desk.

"But surely those words there," the girl persisted, pointing to a line of writing, "are 'send love', and are followed by Aunt Margaret's name?"

Holmes glanced quickly at the words she had indicated. "I think," said he, "that if you examine it more closely you will see that your aunt's name has nothing whatever to do with the words which appear to precede it. The two groups of words appear to me to have been written at two different times. Moreover, the words which you have interpreted as 'send love' look to me more like 'see above'."

"What, then?"

"I shall tell you later. Are the stables far from the house?"

Miss Borrow shook her head. "No," said she, "they are no distance at all."

"Do you think that the groom would put a pony in the shafts of a trap upon your instruction?"

"I believe so."

"Then have him do so at once, bring it round to the front of the house immediately, and wait for us there."

She made for the door, but Holmes called her back.

"I think," said he, "that it might be easier and quicker if you went this way." He threw up the window sash and indicated the terrace outside. In a trice she had climbed through the window and run off along the terrace. "There's quite a party building up in the hall out there, by the sound of it," said he to me, nodding his head in the direction of the door as he continued to work his way methodically but swiftly through the contents of the desk drawers.

I had heard the noises myself, the rapid footsteps and growing murmur of voices. It sounded rather as if the whole of the household were assembling outside the study door, waiting to confront us. I glanced at the boy. He appeared to be recovering with the usual rapidity of childhood, and although he had still not uttered a word, he was now sitting up, and there was a brighter light in his alert, dark eyes. I turned back to my companion. "What do you think we should do?" I asked him.

"It might be as well—" began Holmes, but I was not to learn what was in his mind, for he broke off as the noise in the corridor outside abruptly increased and someone began to turn the door handle. "Quickly!" cried he in an urgent tone. "Pick up the boy and be ready to leave at once!"

I just had time to gather up the boy in my arms once more, and wrap the blanket about him, when the door was pushed wide open. In the doorway stood a grey-haired, distinguished-looking man of fifty-odd, who was evidently the butler. Upon his features was an expression of both incomprehension and censure, and it was evident that the present circumstances fell quite outside his experience. In a crush behind him, pushing forward to see what was happening in the study, were ranged puzzled faces of every age and type, both male and female; it seemed that the whole domestic complement of the household must be present. Two liveried footmen, in particular, caught my eye, for they were both carrying stout cudgels and had expressions of great ferocity upon their features. Holmes glanced up, then returned to something he was writing in his notebook. Presently he finished, closed the notebook and replaced it in his pocket in a deliberate, unhurried manner. Then he turned to address the butler.

"Yes?" said he in an unconcerned tone. "What is it?"

"May I enquire, sir," responded the butler after a moment, "what you are doing here, and by what right you are examining private papers belonging to my master, Mr Hartley Lessingham?"

"Certainly you may," returned Holmes in an affable tone, "if you will provide me with a satisfactory explanation as to why you have done nothing to protect this child while he was in this household."

"Really, sir," said the butler, who was clearly surprised at this response, "it is hardly my place to speak of matters that are no concern of mine."

"I see," said Holmes. "Well, then, I will make it your concern." He motioned to me to bring the boy to him, then he carefully turned back the blanket to reveal the child's hideously bruised leg. There was a sharp intake of breath from those in the corridor, and the butler frowned and put his hand up to his face. "Have you ever seen bruises as bad as these on a child before?" asked Holmes.

"No, sir," returned the butler, a pained expression upon his features.

"No," said Holmes, "and nor, I believe, has my colleague, who is a medical man of considerable experience."

"As I understand the matter, sir," the butler ventured after a moment, "Master Edwin had a bad fall near the river."

Holmes shook his head. "The only fall of any significance has been the repeated fall of a large stick upon this poor boy's body. Furthermore, I believe I have identified the stick in question, which is now lying in pieces upon the floor of the upstairs corridor."

There was a general murmur of voices from behind the butler. He turned with a frown on his face, evidently intending to tell them all to keep quiet, but one of the maids abruptly spoke out in a nervous, breathless manner, as if it had taken her some courage to do so.

"He's right," said she in a defiant tone. "I've heard the poor lad screaming, enough to make you weep." This daring statement appeared to embolden the others, some of whom murmured their agreement, and said that they, too, had heard screams.

"I fancy, though," said Holmes, "that you have not heard him so much in recent days." There was general assent to this suggestion and Holmes continued. "This is not, however, because his suffering has been any the less in recent days, but because he has been gagged to prevent him crying out, and tied to the bed to prevent him moving."

There were horrified gasps at this revelation, and one of the young maids began to sob loudly. The butler appeared torn between his natural human sympathy for the boy and a desire to impose his authority upon his subordinates, and a variety of emotions passed in confusion across his features.

For a few moments, Holmes regarded his audience in silence, then he spoke again in a calm and measured tone. "No doubt," said he, looking past the butler and addressing those behind him, "you have observed the very heavy rain that has fallen in these parts recently and flooded the fields?" There was a general, quiet murmur of assent. "Perhaps you have heard that it is very likely that every minute of every day, it is raining somewhere in the world? But has it ever occurred to you that it is also very likely that, each and every minute of every day, someone, somewhere in the world, is suffering grievously? Indeed, it is more than likely that human suffering is somewhat more prevalent in the world than rainfall; for there are some places – Timbuctoo, for instance – where, as you may be aware, it hardly ever rains at all, but we cannot suppose that human suffering is any less frequent in Timbuctoo than elsewhere."

"No, sir," said the butler.

"Now one cannot, therefore, actively lament each and every occasion of suffering and injustice in the world, any more than one can lament every drop of rain that falls. There is too much of it for it to be a practical proposition. Were one to try, one would be unable to continue with one's own life."

"No, sir."

"There might for instance, at this very moment, be someone suffering grievously in Timbuctoo."

"Yes, sir."

"But we can do nothing about it."

"No, sir."

"But if someone informed you that you had a power, a magic power, perhaps, to alleviate the suffering of the person in Timbuctoo, what then?"

"An unlikely supposition, if I may say so, sir."

"No doubt, but suppose for a moment that it were true – that by simply lifting your hand you might alleviate that person's suffering. Would you do it? Do you think you *ought* to do it?"

"Most certainly, sir," said the butler, to which there was a general murmur of agreement.

"And if, knowing that you had this power, to alleviate someone's suffering, you refused to exercise it, what then? Would you be a generous person, or a mean person? Of course, as you all agree, you would be a mean, ungenerous person."

Holmes regarded his audience in silence for a moment, before continuing. "Here," said he at length, "is a little boy who has suffered at the hands of adults. He is not living in Timbuctoo, but here in England, at East Harrington. Which of you lifted your hand to alleviate his suffering?" This question was followed by a complete silence, during which I heard the clock on the mantelpiece ticking loudly. "You are thinking, perhaps," Holmes continued after a moment, "that in our real world, where none of us has magic powers, things are not so simple. You are thinking that had you spoken out, you would have been at once dismissed from your position, without a reference." The loud murmur of agreement that followed this suggestion indicated that Holmes had read the minds of his audience accurately. "This little boy has been beaten and starved. Had we not come today, I believe he would have died. And if he had died? What then? Is your position here worth this little boy's life? Are all the domestic positions in the country worth a little boy's life? I tell you this, if he had died, all the rain in heaven would not have sufficed to wash away the stain of this wickedness from East Harrington."

Holmes surveyed his audience in silence for several minutes before continuing. The domestic staff had now fallen completely silent, save for the young maid, who was still sobbing. "We are now going to reunite this boy with his aunt," said he at length in a calm tone. "She has, as you may be aware, the same legal right to have the boy with her as her husband, Mr John Hartley Lessingham." He stepped forward and motioned to me to follow him, and as I did so, the staff silently pressed themselves back against the wall of the corridor and made a clear pathway for us. We had almost reached the corner of the corridor when the butler spoke.

"Pardon me, sir," said he, "but who *are* you?"

"My name is Sherlock Holmes," returned my companion. "You are Hammond, I take it?"

"Yes, sir."

"Very well, Hammond. Here is my card. You may inform your master that I can be reached at the address given there on most days of the week."

With that he turned on his heel and we left the house.

"For a moment there, as the crowd began to muster, I thought we were undone," said Holmes to me in a quiet tone as we descended the steps to the drive.

"It did seem a little unlikely that they would willingly let us leave the house."

"Indeed. Those two big fellows with the cudgels might have presented a formidable obstacle."

"They could hardly stop us, though, after your eloquent words."

"Well, well, one's tongue gains strength from the justice of one's cause. I am not certain what will happen next, Watson, but if the worst comes to the worst, I know an excellent barrister to defend us. But here is Miss Borrow with the pony and trap!"

The trap had appeared at a clatter round the corner of the building as he spoke, with the groom holding the reins and Miss Borrow seated in the back.

"If you will climb in the back with the boy," said Holmes to me as the trap drew to a halt before us, "I shall take the reins. We shall drive the trap ourselves," he continued, addressing the groom. For a moment, the latter hesitated and appeared a little reluctant to yield up his vehicle. "This pony is a very fine-looking animal," continued Holmes. "What is its name?"

"Buttercup, sir."

"Well, you may rest assured that we shall take great care of Buttercup, and she will be returned to you later."

With that, he took the reins from the groom's hand and sprang aboard, and in a moment we were rattling up the drive and away from East Harrington Hall.

"Are we going to the railway station?" asked Miss Borrow.

"No," said Holmes. "We cannot leave until we have got to the bottom of this business once and for all. We are going to the mill."

Dedstone Mill

Just before we entered the narrow belt of woods, and the stately brick mansion vanished from view, I looked back and saw that several of the domestic staff were at the front door, watching us depart. No doubt they were wondering who, exactly, we were, and what we were going to do. If so, their wonder could scarcely have been any greater than my own. I could not help feeling that we had entangled ourselves somewhat more intimately in this thorny business than I had expected, and I confess that I could not quite see how we would extricate ourselves, nor how it would all end up. Although I had complete confidence in Holmes's judgement – more so than I had ever had in that of any man – it seemed to me that we were wading rather too deeply into what were dark and treacherous waters.

When we reached the obelisk, Holmes reined in the pony for a moment and consulted his map once again. I looked up at the huge stone pineapple far above our heads. There seemed something monstrous about it, and something grotesque, too, in the notion that one could express one's hospitality in a stone monument, as if in doing so one had done one's duty and need not thenceforth trouble oneself with all the little acts of kindness that are the true mark of hospitality. Above this monument, the clouds were darker now – almost the colour of slate – and the wind that whipped about us was laden with raindrops.

In a moment, Holmes had made his decision and turned the trap into the roadway to the right. As we rattled along between the trees, the rain began to fall, and Miss Borrow, who was clad only in a light dress, began to shiver. The boy, who had been sitting on my knee, appeared to be recovering a little, so I sat him down beside her, unwrapped the blanket a little, and extended it over the girl's head and shoulders. The two of them huddled close together and pulled the blanket tight around them, as the heavens opened and the rain teemed down.

A minute later we were through the narrow belt of trees and into open countryside, our way taking us between the dripping hawthorn hedges that bordered the sodden fields. To be soaking wet was no new experience for me – I was once caught in a cloudburst in India which was so heavy it almost knocked me to the ground – but I do not think that rain had ever before made me feel quite so cold and miserable. Fortunately, the shower, although heavy, was not prolonged, and in a few minutes had abated.

Holmes glanced round at us, caught my eye and chuckled. "Dry clothes, a hot drink and a pipe," said he.

"You have divined my deepest desires," I returned, "although I don't imagine that in this case it was very difficult." To myself I reflected, as I had many times before, upon my friend's remarkable resilience of spirit. However daunting or depressing the circumstances might be, his resolution never faltered, his enthusiasm for the challenges of life never appeared to wane one iota, but, on the contrary, seemed to bubble over with an almost prodigal superfluity and remedy the want of effervescence in those around him. The infectiousness of his enthusiasm made him the very finest of companions in all circumstances, but especially so in adversity. Would this indomitable strength of spirit and good humour ever flag, I wondered, this side of the grave? I rather doubted it. I had scarcely ever known Holmes morose, save only when he was bored by the tedium of inaction.

"Mr Holmes?" said Miss Borrow abruptly, emerging from under the blanket and interrupting my own train of thought. "May I ask a question?"

"By all means," returned he, removing his hat and slapping it on his knee to knock off the raindrops. "What is it you wish to know?"

"You said that you would explain to me why my uncle had written my aunt's name over and over so many times."

"I think it likely," replied Holmes after a moment, "that in writing her name, and the other miscellaneous words and phrases we saw earlier, he was endeavouring to imitate her hand, so that he could sign letters and papers in her name and give the impression that she had signed them herself."

"Why should he do that?"

"There may be some official documents, which require both their signatures, and as your aunt is not here to sign for herself, your uncle has no doubt forged her signature."

"Will people not know that she is no longer at East Harrington?"

"Not necessarily. Your uncle has dealings with, among others, solicitors in Gray's Inn, in London. No doubt they will occasionally send someone up here, but most of the time the business will be conducted by post. I doubt that they are aware that your aunt is not still at the Hall. I have made a note of the solicitor's address. Tomorrow, I shall run down to Gray's Inn and swear an affidavit of all that I have discovered here today."

"Do you think that the documents you mention have anything to do with Edwin or me?"

"Quite possibly."

"I know that we were left a little money in my father's will, and that our aunt and uncle draw on this, to pay for our upkeep."

"The sum of money involved is perhaps somewhat greater than you realize, but yes, that is part of the subject of your uncle's dealings with the solicitors at Gray's Inn. Now, Miss Borrow, if you could answer a question for me: do you recall how your tutor, Mr Theakston, left the house on the evening he departed?"

The girl nodded. "He left for the railway station in this trap. I was watching from an upstairs window."

"Was the trap driven by the groom?"

"No, by Captain Legbourne Legge."

"I see. Is that Dedstone Mill over there, on the other side of that little wood?" Holmes asked abruptly, pointing with his whip to where the gable end of a tall roof showed above a belt of trees.

"Yes, that is it," replied the girl. "This road continues all the way to the river bank, and then turns and follows the river past the mill to the village of Dedstone."

"And here," I observed, "are the geese."

The fields by which we were now passing were almost completely flooded, save where an occasional small hummock of land stood a little above the surrounding level plain and formed a little island in the flood. Upon these cold grey sheets of water, rippled constantly by the chill, blustery wind, were scores and scores of wild geese, their strange cacophonous honking and babbling as constant as the noise of traffic in a city street.

"I am surprised that our passage has not disturbed them," I remarked.

"It will," returned Holmes. "Yes, there they go!" cried he, as first one, then two or three, then a dozen, then hundreds and hundreds rose up from the watery ground in a great babbling crowd, until the grey sky was darkened by a thousand beating wings. "It gives away our position somewhat," remarked Holmes in a rueful voice as the clouds of birds wheeled about the sky and circled above us, "but I doubt that matters now."

A few minutes more and we had reached the side of the swollen, turbid river, where the grey surging waters, thick with branches and twigs, matted heaps of decaying vegetation, and all manner of debris, boiled and frothed against the banks, as if determined to scour and grind them away. In some places, indeed, this relentless assault had already been successful, and the riverbank had collapsed into the water. By the side of this seething torrent of destruction we rattled along for some time, then the road turned away from the river and wound its way through a little wood, until, all at once, we emerged into an open space, and there before us stood the mill, gaunt and dreary against the leaden sky.

It was a huge building, three or four storeys high, and sixty yards from one end to the other. No doubt it had once seemed the most modern establishment imaginable in the milling line. But now it resembled nothing so much as a medieval ruin, a crumbling relic of a bygone age. Half the roof tiles were missing, many of the windows were broken, and the timber walls of the upper storeys had a rotten, decayed appearance, and had clearly not received a coat of paint in fifty years. Towards the right-hand end, the destruction of the building was especially severe, and the missing section of roof and blackened, charred timbers indicated clearly that that was where the fire which Miss Borrow had mentioned had burnt most fiercely.

As we drew to a halt before this dirty and dilapidated building, the little boy, who had seemed more lively by the minute, became extremely agitated and clung to his sister's arm. I was helping them down from the trap when a door in the mill was abruptly opened and a scrawny, filthy-looking woman looked out. The boy let out a little shriek and turned away.

"It is Lizzie Bagnall, Mrs Hardcastle's sister," said Miss Borrow in a voice tinged with fear.

This unsavoury apparition stared uncomprehendingly at us for a moment, then, as abruptly as she had appeared, she withdrew into the darkness within the building and made to shut the door. Holmes was too quick for her, however. He dropped the reins he had been holding, ran forward and put his foot in the door before it could be fully closed. A stream of foul oaths issued from behind the door, and there followed a struggle between the two of them, she to force the door shut, Holmes to prevent her from doing so. I hurried forward to lend my weight to the argument, and it is as well that I did so, for the woman seemed possessed of an almost superhuman strength. All at once, however, she gave up the struggle, the door burst inwards, and as we stood there for a moment to get our breath back, she charged at us out of the darkness, a large stick in her hand. Holmes put up his arm to break the blow, and snatched the stick off her.

"There is something of a family resemblance in the actions of these estimable sisters, is there not?" said he with a chuckle. "Evidently, the inflicting of blows is their one talent, and they are keen to make the most of it! Take the key from the lock, will you, old fellow?" he added as the woman retreated further into the darkness. "I shouldn't put it past this charming female to attempt to lock us in. Now, let us see," he continued, glancing about him. "Nothing much down here, it seems, other than dirt and disorder. I think we should try up there." He indicated a rickety-looking flight of wooden steps, with a broken handrail. "We cannot leave the children down here with this woman about, so you had best bring them with you, Watson, but keep them back a little, if you would."

So saying, and with an expression of resolute determination upon his features, he stepped to the stair and began to ascend. I followed, some distance behind, as he had requested, the children clinging tightly to my jacket. The landing at the top of the stairs was as dark as the ground floor, but just as we reached it, Holmes pushed open a door, and a dull grey light spread across the landing from the room beyond, where, as I could see, a broken window on the far side of the room overlooked the river.

"Nothing here," murmured my companion. "The presence of that odious woman downstairs suggests that what we seek is here somewhere, though. Ah! Signs on the next staircase that it has been used recently! Let us try the floor above, then!"

Again we followed slowly up the creaking and uneven stair. The wood was so rotten that some of the steps crumbled at the edges as I put my weight upon them. At the top was another landing. It was not quite so dark as the one below, for a little light was admitted by a cracked and dirt-smeared window in the right-hand wall, which looked out over the woods through which we had passed in the trap. But the stench of damp and decay here was as strong as ever, and the filthy, broken boards of the floor seemed alive with beetles and woodlice.

At the side of the landing, in the centre of a wall of wooden boards opposite to the stair, was a door. I saw Holmes try the handle, but it was evident that it was locked, for he glanced about the floor and walls as if looking for a key.

"That woman must have taken it with her," said he. "Keep the children to the side, Watson!"

I put my arms round the children, and we watched as Holmes kicked at the lock with the heel of his boot. Twice it resisted his efforts, but at the third attempt, with a cracking and splintering of wood, the door flew open. As it did so, there came a muffled cry from within the room, a cry so strange that I could not for a moment be certain whether it were human or animal. As I joined my friend in the doorway, an appalling sight met my eyes.

It was a large room, stretching the full width of the building. In the wall to our left was a door and a row of windows, overlooking the river, and in the wall to the right was a window overlooking the woods. The floor was of bare, dusty boards, littered with rubbish, and with disordered heaps of wooden planks and poles everywhere. But what riveted my attention more than any of this clutter was what lay directly opposite the door. There, spread upon the floor, was a bed of sorts, which consisted mainly of old sacks, a rough, coarse blanket and a couple of dirty cushions. Beside this dishevelled and unattractive heap stood a wooden table and chair, and sitting at the table was a woman in a pale blue dress. She stood up as we entered, and I saw she was of medium height and about five and thirty years old. There was something refined and educated in her expression, but her face was streaked with dirt, as if she had been weeping, and her hair was disarranged. Harriet Borrow took one look at her, then released her grip on my arm and ran forward with a cry.

"Aunt Margaret!" cried she, flinging her arms around the woman's waist.

At this, the boy, who had been burying his face in my side, looked round, then he, too, ran forward with a cry of joy and spoke for the first time. "Auntie!" cried he.

"Who are these gentlemen?" asked the woman in a nervous, uncertain tone, eyeing us cautiously as she hugged the children to her.

"It is Mr Sherlock Holmes and Dr Watson," cried the girl excitedly as she turned to us. "They have come to rescue us!"

"Can this be true?" asked the woman in a tone of disbelief.

"Certainly it is," returned Holmes with a chuckle. "I cannot claim that that was our clear intention when we left London this morning, but now that we have found you, rescue does indeed seem the most appropriate course of action!"

"Then you will have to do something about these," said she. As she spoke, she moved her arm and her foot, and I saw for the first time, with a shock of horror, that around both her wrist and her ankle were metal manacles, connected by chains to iron rings in the wall. "This, as you will no doubt surmise, is my husband's doing," she explained. "He wished to be sure that I could not escape. But strangely enough, these chains have probably saved my life. For I have many times thought that if I could only free myself from them for but a moment, I should at once fling myself from that window over there and thus end forever my miserable existence!"

"Tut! tut!" cried Holmes, as he examined the manacle on her wrist. "You must banish such thoughts from your mind altogether! We shall soon have these chains removed, and then we can get you and the children far away from here! The woman downstairs has keys for these, I take it."

"Yes, she does," returned she, but then, as Holmes made for the door, she cried out in a pitiful tone. "Don't leave me, I beg of you!" she said, and it was clear that her hopes of release having been raised, she could not bear any possible disappointment.

"Do not fear! I shall only be a moment. You had best remain here, Watson, to keep an eye on things."

"Certainly."

My friend was back again in a couple of minutes. In his hands were a variety of hammers, chisels and other tools.

"I could not find the woman anywhere," explained he. "She is evidently keeping herself out of sight. However, I found these tools on a lower floor and am confident we can soon get the manacles off with them. If you would bring that block of wood over here, Watson, to rest the edge of the manacle on, and hold this chisel for me, I'll see if I can smash the hinge. You have been held captive here since last winter, I take it," he continued, addressing Mrs Hartley Lessingham as he cast his jacket to the floor, rolled up his sleeves and set about trying to force apart the manacle on her wrist.

She nodded her head. "Eight long months have I lain here in lonely imprisonment, eight long months during which I have had no knowledge of the world outside, nor of my family, and no companion save that cruel half-wit downstairs that my husband set here to guard me. Can you wonder that I have been driven half-mad, and have thought so often of flinging myself from that window?"

"But Aunt Margaret," cried Miss Borrow, "how can this be? We were told by Mr Hartley Lessingham that you were residing in a cottage on the estate of Mr Shepherd!"

"What! I have never been within a hundred miles of it! What a wicked thing to have told you, when all the time he was keeping me a prisoner here!"

"But I wrote to you there, and you replied!" protested the girl in a baffled tone.

"My poor dear!" returned the woman, her eyes brimming with tears. "I have received no letter from you nor from anyone, and nor have I been able to write any. If Mr Hartley Lessingham told you it was a letter from me, then he lied. No doubt he wrote the letter himself."

"I should have known!" cried the girl in an angry tone, and burst into tears. "I should have known that you would never have told me not to write to you again."

"I certainly should not! Whatever was said in that letter, Harriet, was nothing but wicked lies!"

"But Mr Hartley Lessingham did receive one letter from Sussex," said the girl after a moment, "for I remember seeing the Lewes postmark on the envelope. He told me that it was from Mr Shepherd, informing him that you were residing at Tattingham. He said he had thrown it in the fire."

"I imagine," said Holmes, addressing the woman as she shook her head in puzzlement, "that he made up that story on the spur of the moment, when he realized that Harriet had seen the postmark. No doubt the letter really was from Mr Shepherd, but was simply enquiring after you all and sending you his news. Your husband may not have bothered replying to it at all, or, if he did, he probably told Shepherd that you had gone away and he did not know your whereabouts. One moment!" said he, then he brought the hammer down with all his strength onto the chisel which I had positioned on the hinge of the manacle. "There!" he cried in triumph as the hinge burst apart. "Now for the other one! Perhaps," he continued, addressing Mrs Hartley Lessingham as I positioned the hinge of the second manacle on the edge of the lump of wood, "you could tell us what occurred last January. Shortly after you left, on New Year's Eve, your husband informed Harriet that you had written to say that you were staying in an hotel in London."

"That, at least, was true."

"He then went off to visit you, to try to persuade you, so he said, to return to East Harrington, but as he reported, you declined the proposition."

"That, also, is correct."

"Yet somehow he managed to get you back here."

"That is easily explained. When he came to my hotel in London, he said that if I would not live with him at East Harrington any longer, I had best take the children with me, as he did not wish to be troubled with them. Of course, this was what I had wished all along, so I readily agreed. I therefore accompanied him back here from London simply to collect Harriet and Edwin. We were met at the railway station by the carriage, which was driven by his unpleasant friend, Captain Legbourne Legge. This struck me as a little odd, but I thought no more about it. As we drove through the park, my thoughts were only on the children, and I could not have imagined the evil plan that my husband and his odious companion had contrived. Then, when we had almost reached the Hall, Legbourne Legge turned the carriage off the main drive at the obelisk, and instead brought it here. When I realized what they intended, I struggled to escape, but it was of no avail, and I received only bruises for my troubles. Since then I have been a prisoner here, with that evil woman you have met as my gaoler; without hope of release, and subject to constant threats and intimidation."

"Did the woman sometimes carry messages between here and the Hall?"

"Yes. I recall once hearing my husband giving her instructions to that effect."

"The children saw her once or twice at night, I believe, leaving a message on the sundial in the garden behind the house. Those messages were subsequently collected by Legbourne Legge."

"He and my husband seem to have planned everything together. I do not know which of them I detest the most!"

Holmes nodded. "The threats you mentioned, were these to try to persuade you to sign money over to your husband?"

"To try to force me to assign everything I possess to him, and all my rights and responsibilities in what is due to the children, too."

"I thought as much," said Holmes, nodding his head. "I have seen in his study that he has been forging your signature. But while the solicitor would accept your signature through the post on relatively minor matters, on more important questions he would wish to see you in person, to discuss the business with you and witness your signature. This is why it was vital for your husband to persuade you to agree to his plans."

"But I should never have done so. I told him I would rather die. At least," she continued in a hesitant tone, "I had remained defiant until the last fortnight. But he has recently found a chink in my armour." Her gaze flickered momentarily downwards.

"He threatened to harm the children if you did not do as he wished? It does not surprise me. I will tell you later all that has happened recently." Holmes broke off as he brought his hammer down with great force upon the chisel several times. Presently he paused, and stood for a moment recovering his breath. "You have not yet signed anything for your husband?" he continued, addressing Mrs Hartley Lessingham.

"No."

"Good! Then all the cards are still in our hands! I must ask you now if you know anything of the fate of Mr Theakston, the children's tutor at the time you left."

"Mr Theakston?" returned she in surprise. "Why, what has happened to him?"

"He has vanished without trace, and, to speak frankly, I fear the very worst," said Holmes. He then described to Mrs Hartley Lessingham the quarrel between the tutor and his employer, which Miss Borrow had overheard.

"That was in the spring, you say?" said she. "Then I think I can cast some light on it. Outside that door in the wall over there is a wooden platform, from which a long staircase descends on the outside of the building, until it reaches the ground by the millrace. One evening in the early spring, just as the light was fading, someone climbed up that staircase and looked in here through the window. I was startled, and because the light was poor and the window dirty, I could not at first make out who it was. I thought it was probably some peasant from Dedstone, so I remained perfectly still, for I was very frightened. But after a few moments, as he moved about on the platform and tried to open the door, I realized that it was Mr Theakston and called out to him. I am not sure if he heard me or knew who it was that was in here, for this room must have appeared very dark to him, but after trying unsuccessfully for some time to open the door – it is bolted on the inside, as you see – he went away, and I heard his footsteps descending the stair. For several days I hoped that something might come from this incident, that perhaps he would tell someone that I was being kept here, but when nothing happened, I abandoned my hopes, concluded that he had not realized I was in here and put it from my mind."

"Something had evidently aroused his curiosity as to what was happening here," said Holmes, "possibly the behaviour of that woman downstairs, or perhaps some rumour he had heard. Whatever it was, it seems likely that he did in fact recognize you, for he confronted your husband over the matter, either that same night, or soon afterwards. This was, of course, a terrible mistake, and the very last thing he should have done, but honest men frequently make mistakes that villains never would. He has not been seen again since that evening, and I am afraid that we must conclude that he was done to death by these villains to prevent him from speaking of what he knew."

"I recall now," said Mrs Hartley Lessingham, "that about that same time – not the same night, but it might have been the next one – I heard the carriage coming very late in the evening, when it was already pitch black. I thought that my husband was coming to persecute me further, but no one entered the mill. Instead, after a while I heard Legbourne Legge's voice and, I believe, my husband's, from somewhere outside. Then came the sound of digging in that little wood out there. This carried on for some time, then, eventually, I heard the sound of the carriage leaving again."

Holmes shook his head, his features grave. "Then we can only conclude that somewhere in that little wood is the last resting place of the unfortunate Mr Theakston. I am sorry to speak of these things so bluntly, Harriet," he continued, addressing the girl, "but we cannot avoid the truth."

"I understand," said she, biting her lip.

"I promise you that I will do my utmost to bring these wicked people to justice."

"If the matter is as you surmise," said Mrs Hartley Lessingham, "Mr Theakston's blood may not be the first they have upon their hands. When first I was held captive here, my gaoler was a man called Meadowcroft, who had at one time been in charge of the mill, although he was a dreadful drunk. But one night I heard a terrific quarrel down by the riverbank, between, as far as I could tell, Meadowcroft and my husband. What it was about, I do not know – perhaps Meadowcroft was trying to blackmail my husband over my presence here – but it ended with the sound of a violent struggle, and then a scream from Meadowcroft. After that evening, I never saw him again, and did not know what had become of him."

"He was found in the river," said Miss Borrow. "Everyone thought he had just fallen in and drowned."

"There!" cried Holmes as, with a final powerful blow, he managed at last to force the hinge of the manacle apart. "When you are ready, madam, we can depart. But what is that?" cried he, as the unmistakable sound of honking and gabbling, and the heavy beat of a thousand wings, came to our ears. "Something has put the geese up again!"

"I cannot see," said I, looking from the window. "Something has certainly startled them, but the view is obscured by the wood. No, wait! There are horses coming! It is a carriage!"

I craned from the window as the carriage drew up in front of the mill. "It is Hartley Lessingham!" I cried.

"Let us take a look at this outside staircase," said Holmes, sliding back the bolts and opening the door in the far wall. "It looks a little precarious, does it not?" said he as I joined him there. Outside the door was a small, splintering, rotten-looking wooden platform, from which a very long, dilapidated stair led down, in stages, to the stone embankment of the river far below, by the great mill-wheel.

"For myself, I would risk it," said I, "but we cannot ask Mrs Hartley Lessingham and the children to descend that way."

"I agree," said Holmes. "We must therefore stay and meet Hartley Lessingham face to face in here."

We turned back to the room as there came the sound of rapid footsteps on the stair. Then, for a moment, they stopped, and I heard a man's voice, harsh and angry. "Get out of my way, you stupid woman!" he shouted. This was followed by a cry of fear and the sound of someone falling heavily down the stairs. Moments later, Hartley Lessingham burst into the room, brandishing a stout black walking stick, followed by Miss Rogerson and Captain Legbourne Legge. The children cried out with terror at the sight of him and clung to the side of their aunt, who had pressed herself back against the wall. I could not wonder at their alarm, for Hartley Lessingham was indeed a fearsome sight, well over six feet tall, and as broad as an ox. For a moment, this gigantic figure stood in silence, surveying us all, his features twisted and purple with rage.

"That's the man!" cried Miss Rogerson all at once in a shrill voice, pointing her finger at me. "He was with the girl in London; I'm sure of it!"

"You!" said Hartley Lessingham in a thunderous tone, approaching me. "How dare you trespass upon my property! You are this person, Sherlock Holmes, I take it," he continued, reading from a card in his hand and spitting the name out with fiery venom.

"No, he isn't," interjected Holmes in a calm voice. "I am."

"Oh?" said Hartley Lessingham, turning to Holmes and advancing upon him menacingly. "So you are responsible for this impudent intrusion into my private affairs?"

"If you wish to put it that way, then, yes, I am."

"You impertinent scoundrel!" cried Hartley Lessingham, tearing up Holmes's card and casting the pieces to the floor. "You scum! I didn't like the look of you when I saw you earlier! I should have run you off the estate there and then, you infernal, interfering busybody!"

"Well, we all have regrets from time to time," remarked Holmes in a careless tone.

"You dare to trifle with me?" thundered Hartley Lessingham. "You who are nothing but the dirt beneath my feet?"

"Dirt I may be, but at least I haven't imprisoned my own wife and vilely abused children who were left in my care."

"I'll teach you to meddle in my affairs!" cried Hartley Lessingham in a menacing tone. He took his black stick in both hands, there came a sharp click, and from within the stick he drew forth a long, deadly-looking steel rapier.

I heard Holmes murmur my name, caught his eye for a split second, and saw it dart to a pile of short wooden staves that lay by my feet. Perceiving at once his meaning, I had, in another split second, stooped, picked up one of the staves, which was about three feet in length, and tossed it across to him. He snatched it from the air with his right hand, although his eye never for an instant left his adversary, who was advancing menacingly upon him, making slashes in the air with his rapier. Slowly and warily, the two men circled each other, their weapons held on guard. Without taking my eyes off them, I picked up another of the staves. What might happen in the desperate contest before me, I could not envisage, but I feared for my friend's safety and held my stave ready to intervene the moment it appeared necessary.

I saw Hartley Lessingham's eyes flicker in my direction, and he had evidently seen me pick up the stave, for he called to Legbourne Legge without turning his head. "Get your pistols, Legge! We'll sort out these damned vermin once and for all!" At this, Legbourne Legge turned and hurried from the room, and I heard the rapid clatter of his footsteps down the stair.

My mind raced as I debated with myself the best course of action. I could position myself to the side of the doorway and strike at Legbourne Legge as he returned, and thus perhaps knock the pistol from his grasp, but Miss Rogerson might warn him that I was waiting for him. Perhaps, then, I should go to meet him on the stair, but then my own position would be too exposed and I should lose the element of surprise. Besides, if I left the room, I should not be able to help Holmes, and the children and their aunt would be left unguarded. Even as I considered the question, Hartley Lessingham made a slashing cut at Holmes. The latter managed to parry it with his stick, but then came another and another, as Holmes was slowly forced backwards towards the corner of the room. Upon Hartley Lessingham's face was an expression of murderous hatred, and it was clear that we could expect no quarter from such a man. I could not possibly leave my post: I should just have to deal with Legbourne Legge as best I could when he returned.

The fight before me was becoming increasingly desperate. Back and forth went Holmes and his opponent, thrusting and parrying, slashing and blocking. Holmes had managed to extricate himself from the corner with a brief sally, but had been forced back again against the wall, and it was evident that Hartley Lessingham was slowly but surely gaining the upper hand and closing in, awaiting that split-second of a chance when his opponent's guard would drop, and he could make the thrust which would end the struggle. Holmes, as I knew, was an expert at singlestick, and had taken part in competitions both at singlestick and fencing during his college days, but armed only with a stout stick against this gigantic, powerful opponent, who was clearly an accomplished swordsman, I doubted if he could resist for much longer.

Then, as Hartley Lessingham made a series of rapid thrusts, accompanied by blood-curdling cries of triumph, the sound of a horse's hooves and the rattle of a carriage harness came to my ears. What it meant, I could not tell. I could only guess that Legbourne Legge was leaving, but for what reason, I could not imagine. Next moment, my attention was once more entirely taken up by the deadly fight before me. Holmes had been caught on the hand by his opponent's rapier, for I saw a streak of blood across his knuckles. Hartley Lessingham evidently saw it, too, for he let out a howl of triumph and tossed his head back, like a wild beast scenting victory. At that precise instant, Holmes launched a sudden counter-attack of his own, and seized the initiative. Right and left went his staff, as he forced his way forward, and Hartley Lessingham attempted to parry. Then he struck a sharp blow on Hartley Lessingham's sword hand and, in the split second that his opponent's guard was down, made a straight thrust with his staff with all his might, and caught his opponent full in the face with the end of it.

There came a wild howl of pain from Hartley Lessingham, and as he clutched his face, which was streaming with blood, the sword slipped from his grasp and fell to the floor. In the same moment, Holmes caught him a powerful blow on the side of the head, and he staggered backwards, still holding his face in his hands, until his back was against the wall. There he stood, panting and howling for several minutes, like some wild beast at bay. Then as he began to recover himself, he lowered his hands from his blood-smeared face and looked with baleful venom at Holmes, who had remained all this time in the centre of the room, unmoving.

"You will pay for this," cried Hartley Lessingham, in a voice that was hoarse and full of fury. "You will pay with your life! Legge!" he cried loudly. "Where is that damned fool? Legge!"

There came the sound of someone bounding up the stairs at a terrific rate, but the man who burst into the room a moment later was not the corpulent Captain Legbourne Legge, but a sturdily built, sandy-haired man. His face seemed vaguely familiar to me, but for several seconds I could not place him. Then, with a jolt of surprise, I realized that he was the man Holmes and I had observed in the cab in Fleet Street the previous day, watching Harriet Borrow.

"Edgar!" cried Mrs Hartley Lessingham. "What on earth—"

"I have long suspected that things were not right in these parts," said the newcomer, "but I was loath to interfere. I wrote in the spring, but was told by your husband that you had gone away, and that he did not know your whereabouts. Then, just this last week, I received a letter from a gentleman in London, giving me some fresh facts. He seemed to be under the impression, for some reason, that I might know where you were. I decided to make my own enquiries, which I have been doing for several days, until I resolved last night that I would come down and see for myself what was happening here. And I have come, it seems, not a moment too soon!"

"You're never too soon, Shepherd," said Hartley Lessingham in a sneering tone. "You're always too late! You've missed all the entertainment! Now get out of my way!"

"Not so fast, Lessingham," returned Shepherd, holding his ground as Hartley Lessingham made to push past him. "I have some questions for you."

"What you have is of no interest to me!" said Hartley Lessingham in a supercilious tone, but he stopped as Holmes and I closed in on him with our staves. "You scum!" he cried at us, backing away a little. "Legge!" he called again. "Where the devil are you?"

"Your fat friend is having a little trouble loading his pistol," said Shepherd. "He can't help you."

At this, Miss Rogerson ran from the room, and I heard her shouting down the stairs to Legbourne Legge. Hartley Lessingham backed slowly away from us, his eyes darting this way and that, like a rat in a trap, then, abruptly, he turned and made a bolt for the door in the end wall, snatched it open and, before we could stop him, had dashed out and down the steps outside.

I raced to the doorway and looked down. Hartley Lessingham was already some way down the staircase, which was swaying alarmingly at every footfall. Then he turned and looked up at us, an expression of savage hatred upon his features.

"You will all regret this!" he screamed at the top of his voice, shaking a huge knotted fist at us in wild, uncontrolled rage. But in turning to face us, he had leaned his weight upon the flimsy handrail, and even as he shook his fist, I heard the splintering crack of the rotten wood, and watched with horror as the broken handrail fell away and Hartley Lessingham pitched headlong from the stair. He made a desperate grab for one of the upright poles that had held the handrail, but it snapped clean off in his grasp like a matchstick, and with a terrible scream, he plunged down, down, until he hit the great water-wheel with a sickening thud and lay there like a broken doll. For a moment I stared in horror at this dreadful scene, but even from that distance I could see that he was dead.

I turned as there came the sound of rapid footsteps from behind us. Legbourne Legge dashed into the room, brandishing one of his old-fashioned pistols. He looked from one to the other of us, and as he did so, his mouth fell open in an expression of stupid incomprehension.

"Where the devil is Lessingham?" he demanded of Miss Rogerson, who had followed him into the room.

"It's all up, Legge," said Holmes in a voice of authority. "Hartley Lessingham is dead, and you'll be arrested for the murder of Theakston. We have a witness."

For a moment Legbourne Legge stood there in silence, a look of indecision upon his fat, flabby face as he pointed his pistol at each of us in turn. Then, in an instant, he abruptly put the pistol up to the side of his head, pulled the trigger and blew his own brains out.

Mrs Hartley Lessingham screamed as Legbourne Legge's lifeless body slumped to the floor, and the children buried their faces in her skirts. Then, as his blood spread out across the dusty floor, Miss Rogerson uttered a sharp cry and ran from the room and down the stair. With an expression of great weariness, Holmes cast aside his stave and picked up his jacket from where it lay by the wall. Then he stepped forward to usher the others from the room.

"What in the name of Heaven has been happening here?" cried Shepherd, a mixture of bewilderment and horror in his voice.

"Let us first get everyone downstairs and away from here," responded Holmes as he pulled on his jacket. "I will answer later any questions you may have, Shepherd. For now, let us waste no time in shaking from our feet the dust of this vile and ill-starred place."

AN INCIDENT IN SOCIETY

DURING THE YEARS I SHARED ROOMS with Sherlock Holmes, the number of those who came to seek his help was perfectly stupendous. From every walk of life they came, so that upon our stair in Baker Street, monarchs, statesmen and noblemen would rub shoulders with tailors, shopkeepers and clerks. As might be supposed, there were, among the many cases that Holmes handled over the years, some which involved those whose names were familiar in every household in the land. In the main, I have passed over such cases when selecting those to be published, lest I lay myself open to a charge of sensationalism. In some, however, the facts were in themselves sufficiently remarkable to warrant publication, and I would be doing my readers a disservice were I to ignore them altogether. An especially memorable such episode occurred one December in the early '80s. Though the matter was never reported in the papers, it was one that touched upon issues of enormous national importance.

There were at that time, among the many notable members of London Society, two women of very differing reputations and antecedents. The first was the Duchess of Pont, widow of the great statesman whose premature death had been such a grievous loss to the nation. She was renowned for the parties she gave at her house in Belgravia, a singular blend of gaiety and serious discussion, for it was her habit to include among her guests many prominent politicians, writers and diplomats. It was well known that more than one foreign statesman had travelled halfway across Europe simply for the privilege of being present at one of the Duchess of Pont's parties, and it was said that many political decisions of international importance had had their origins in informal discussions at her house.

The second woman was Grizelda Magdalena Hoffmannstal, although it was not certain that this was her real name. She styled herself the Princess Zelda, but the provenance of her title was a matter of some debate, as, indeed, were her antecedents in general. She herself never revealed anything of her past, and the mystery that seemed to surround her inevitably led to wild conjecture and an air of glamour. This she appeared to enjoy, and she certainly never did anything to dispel it. Some said that she was enormously wealthy, and it was undoubtedly true that she lived in a fashion that bespoke great wealth. But it is doubtful if she ever paid out a penny from her own purse, for she was never lacking for gentlemen admirers, who were only too willing to do whatever might be necessary to gain her favour. Needless to say, the female half of London Society took a somewhat less favourable view of the Princess Zelda, but on the whole the Press ignored this point of view. There were also rumours in some quarters that the princess was a spy, in the pay of several foreign governments at once and in London only to work mischief, but little credence was given to this view. Sherlock Holmes, however, averred on more than one occasion that the Princess Zelda was undoubtedly the most dangerous woman in London. This struck me at the time as a somewhat exaggerated claim, but as I had found in the past that Holmes's opinions invariably proved nearer to the mark than those expressed in the public prints, I reserved my opinion.

It was a cold evening, a few days before Christmas. It had been snowing lightly since early afternoon and now, in the still evening, a blanket of white covered the streets and houses. Sherlock Holmes had drawn back the curtains and gazed for some time at the chilly scene outside. Then he had perched himself on a chair by the window, taken up his violin and, for the best part of an hour, played a selection of Christmas carols. At length, he put down his bow and turned to where I was sitting by the blazing fire.

"It appears," he remarked, "that even the world of villainy is honouring the forthcoming holiday season. I have heard nothing of criminal interest since the beginning of the week."

"That is surely a cause for celebration rather than otherwise," I returned.

My companion chuckled. "Perhaps so," said he, "but I cannot help feeling that if plotters and criminals stay their hand at this time of year, they are undoubtedly overlooking a fine opportunity. Now is the very time they should strike, when the world of honest citizens has lowered its guard. It is certainly the way I should be thinking, were I a criminal."

"No doubt," I responded in some amusement. "But the season has its disadvantages for the criminal, too. Travel is difficult at this time of the year and train services are often disrupted. Having perpetrated his villainy, it might prove difficult for the criminal to make his escape."

"But he should turn that very fact to his own advantage," insisted my friend. "He should so time his crime that he escapes by the very last train before Christmas, knowing that before the authorities can get upon his trail they will have lost a whole day!"

Thus we discussed the subject back and forth for some time, our discussion warmed by the occasional tot of brandy. Outside, the snow began to fall again, and I was remarking on the strange, unnatural silence that had descended upon the great city when the sound of a carriage approaching from the direction of Oxford Street came to my ears.

"Urgent business, one must suppose, to bring anyone out on such a night," remarked Holmes, glancing from the window. "Halloa! This may be interesting, Watson! The carriage is stopping at our door."

There came a loud jangling at the doorbell, followed moments later by rapid footsteps upon the stair. Then our door was flung open and a strongly built young man in the uniform of a military officer burst unannounced into the room. His face was as white as the snow through which he had travelled, his eyes were wide open and staring, and his bloodless lip quivered with emotion. For a moment he looked wildly about him, his face twitching uncontrollably.

"May we be of assistance?" said Holmes.

"Mr Holmes!" cried our visitor, removing his cap. "Thank the Lord you are here!"

"My dear sir," said Holmes, taking his cap, leading him to the fireside chair and pressing him down into it. "Pray calm yourself! A nip of brandy might be helpful, Watson, if you would be so good!"

The soldier threw back his head and downed the glass at a gulp, and a flush of colour came to his pallid cheeks. A second later, an incoherent torrent of Words poured from his lips.

"The situation is utterly desperate!" he cried, looking from one to the other of us. "I am ruined! The country is ruined! Whatever can I do?" Then he plunged his head into his hands and began to moan softly to himself.

I refilled his glass and pressed him to take a sip, and he calmed a little.

"Captain Armstrong!" said Holmes in a tone of authority, and the soldier looked up sharply. "Captain Walter Armstrong of the Durham Light Infantry! Your name and regiment are written in your cap," he explained as the other stared at him in surprise. "You are a long way from home, sir. Pray, tell us what has happened to reduce you to this state! Quickly, man! If the situation is as urgent as your manner suggests, every moment you despair is a moment lost!"

Our visitor responded to my friend's masterful manner, and slowly, by degrees, regained a grip on his emotions. He drained what remained of his brandy and began to describe to us the events that had brought him to our door.

"I am a captain with the Durham, as you say," he explained, "but I have been seconded to the staff of the War Office on special duties for the last nine months. You performed a great service for our department last year, so I have heard, when Major Colefax was in charge, which is why I thought of you this evening, in my hour of desperation."

"Ah!" said Holmes. "Major Colefax! That makes matters a little clearer. To explain to you who these gentlemen are, Watson, it is probably sufficient to say that their duties are paid for out of the so-called 'Secret Service Fund', which is so regularly the subject of questions and complaints in Parliament. You may speak freely before Dr Watson, Captain Armstrong. Nothing you say will pass beyond the walls of this room."

"Very well," said Armstrong. "I can tell you in a few words what has happened. The head of the department now is Major Lavelle. This morning, he left for Portsmouth, where he is staying overnight, leaving me in charge in his absence. For most of the day I have been supervising Norton, one of our clerks, who has been copying out a report on the Baltic question for the Prime Minister. Earlier this evening, I went to see Commander Fordyce at the Admiralty, and left Norton writing at his desk. When I returned, just before eight o'clock, I asked the man at the door if there had been any callers, and was informed that no one had passed in or out since I had left, two hours previously. I entered the office and found Norton still scribbling away furiously, but on the last page, which he completed a minute later.

"'That has been quite a task for you,' I remarked, thanking him for staying late to complete it.

"'Yes, sir,' he returned. 'I would have finished it earlier, but I have not been feeling well.'

"'I am sorry to hear that,' said I. 'You get along home now and have an early night.'

"After he had left, I glanced over what he had written, then unlocked the safe to place the papers in there until Major Lavelle's return. It at once struck me that there was something different about the disposition of the papers in the safe. For a long moment I stared at them, then I saw what was amiss. The largest pile, containing complete details of the new codes and ciphers which have recently been issued to the Army, was not quite as I had left it. It occupied the same position in the safe, but whereas I had left it at a slightly crooked angle to the pile of documents next to it, it was now perfectly straight. I have a very precise and accurate memory for such things, and have trained myself to observe such small discrepancies."

"Admirable!" cried Holmes in appreciation.

"I took the pile of papers from the safe," continued Armstrong, "and as I did so my mouth was dry. I knew I could not be mistaken. As I lifted up the sheets one by one, my fingers were trembling: page one, page two, page three, page four, page five. The pages were in perfect order. At once a lump came into my throat, and I thought I would faint."

"Because you had intentionally left the pages in a different order," remarked Holmes.

"Precisely," said Armstrong, his face aghast as he relived the episode. "It is an eccentric habit of mine always to place page five above page four in such a pile. I do it quite deliberately. Clearly someone had taken the pile of papers from the safe, examined them and probably copied them. He had then replaced them in the correct order – the order in which he had examined them – not realizing that I had deliberately left them in an incorrect order."

"Could you possibly be mistaken on the point?" Holmes interrupted, but Armstrong shook his head.

"There is no doubt in my mind," said he. "Besides, I also make a habit of turning down the top right-hand corner of page seven, and that, I saw, had been smoothed flat. I realized with a sick feeling in my stomach why it appeared to have taken Norton so long to copy out the Baltic papers. No doubt he had spent most of my two hours' absence copying out the Army's secret codes and ciphers. I can only assume that he intends to pass them to the enemies of this country, who will thus be privy to our most secret commands and communications. The country will be laid open to attack, and I shall certainly be court-martialled!"

"What action have you taken?" asked Holmes.

"None."

"None?"

"I am confused as to what I should do. The whole affair is utterly impossible! It is impossible for anyone but Norton to have opened the safe, for no one but he was in the office while I was out. But it is equally impossible for Norton himself to have done so, for he does not have a key!"

"Who does have a key?"

"There are just four, and each man who holds one pledges to defend it with his life. I have one, which never leaves my possession. It is on my watch-chain now, as you see. Major Lavelle, of course, has one, and one is held by each of the other two senior officers seconded to the department at the moment, Colonel Fitzwarren and Admiral Pettigrew.

"When I realized what had happened and saw the difficulty in the matter, I could not think where to seek advice. Major Lavelle does not return from Portsmouth until tomorrow afternoon. Eventually, I went round to Colonel Fitzwarren's club in Pall Mall, sure that I would find him there at that time, but I was informed that he had left some time previously, and I have been unable to find him. Admiral Pettigrew, I was aware, had an appointment with the Chancellor of the Exchequer earlier this evening, and I thought it better not to interrupt them. It was then that I thought of you, Mr Holmes. You must advise me, as you advised Major Colefax. I put the case entirely in your hands, and beg you to help, not for the sake of my miserable career, but for the sake of the country!"

"When you have eliminated the impossible," said Holmes after a moment, "whatever remains, however improbable, must be the truth. If your memory of how you left the papers in the safe is correct, which I do not doubt, then, as no one else had been in the room, Norton must be guilty of treachery, either alone or in company with another."

"But the matter of the key— "

"Is a lesser problem. Norton may have secured a copy— "

"Impossible!"

"Or been lent a key by one of your colleagues."

"Inconceivable!"

"Unlikely, perhaps, but not impossible, Captain Armstrong! Where does Norton live?"

"Trevor Place, on the south side of Hyde Park."

"Then we must go there at once!"

"I have no real evidence against him."

"Never fear, Captain Armstrong. If Norton is guilty, we shall find evidence!"

In a minute we were in Armstrong's carriage, in which two marines were waiting, and were making our way slowly through the snowbound streets. The night was a cold one, and the snow was falling heavily now, the tumbling snowflakes almost obliterating the feeble glimmer of the street lamps.

It was no great distance to Norton's house, but our progress was slow, as the horse slithered and slipped upon the snow. The streets were almost deserted, and we passed only a single vehicle along the entire length of Park Lane and Knightsbridge. As we turned into Trevor Place, however, we passed a cab going in the opposite direction, its progress as slow as our own.

We pulled up before one of the small flat-fronted houses, towards the bottom of the street. Holmes sprang out quickly and examined the ground, a frown on his face.

"That cab we passed came from this house," said he in a thoughtful tone, pointing to the churned-up snow by the kerb. "It would be worth something to know who was in it!"

Our knock at the door was answered by a manservant, who showed us into a small drawing room. A thin, dark-haired man wearing a pair of gold-rimmed spectacles was sitting by the fire, reading a newspaper, but he sprang up as we entered. There was, I thought, a look of alarm upon his features.

"Captain Armstrong!" said he in a breathless tone. "What a pleasant surprise!"

"Not so pleasant," returned the other. "I must warn you, Norton, that you are under suspicion of interfering with confidential documents."

"What nonsense!" cried Norton, casting his newspaper down and standing defiantly with his hands upon his hips. He listened as Armstrong outlined his suspicions, a forced smile fixed upon his face all the time. "I see you have no evidence whatever against me," he retorted as Armstrong finished.

"Never mind that," interrupted Holmes. "You have had a visitor here this evening."

Norton shook his head. "On the contrary," he replied, "I have been quite alone, until you arrived."

"Then how do you explain the presence of these two glasses upon the side table?" said Holmes. He picked them up as he spoke and sniffed each in turn. "This first one has had brandy in it, and this one a whisky mixture. You cannot pretend they are both yours."

Norton hesitated a moment before replying.

"Oh, very well," said he at length, in a tone of annoyance. "An old friend of mine called by."

"His name?"

"That is none of your business and I refuse to say."

"Then we shall ask your servant."

"Flegge? By all means," answered Norton in a careless tone, giving the bell-rope a tug. "Ask him what you please."

The manservant entered and the situation was explained to him, but he could tell us very little, for he had not seen the visitor. Norton had opened the front door himself, and when Flegge had brought in the drinks, had taken the tray from his hand at the door.

"Perhaps you heard the gentlemen speaking?" Holmes suggested.

"A very few words, sir. They stopped talking as I opened the door."

"What were the words you heard?"

"A mention of Princess Zelda."

"Nine-thirty-five," came an odd voice, hoarse and croaking, from behind us.

I looked round sharply. In the corner of the room, on a wooden perch, stood a small grey parrot. My attention had been so focused upon Norton since we had entered the room that I had not noticed it before. I glanced back at Norton. There was a flicker of fear in his eye. Holmes evidently saw it, too, for after a moment's thought he approached the parrot.

"What did you say?" said he.

The bird tilted its head on one side and regarded him with a disconcertingly intelligent eye, but remained silent.

"Princess Zelda," Holmes tried again.

"Nine-thirty-five," responded the parrot promptly in a clear tone.

"Nine-thirty-five?" Holmes repeated.

"Paris," said the bird.

"Oh shut your mouth, you stupid bird!" cried Norton in an angry tone, his voice trembling slightly.

"Does the bird's prattle trouble you?" asked Holmes, making a note in his pocket book, but Norton merely snorted and turned away.

It was then decided that a search of the premises would be made. Norton turned out his pockets at Captain Armstrong's request, but they contained nothing of interest. The two marines then remained in the drawing room with Norton and his servant, while Armstrong, Holmes and I made a swift search of the house. Twenty minutes later we were obliged to admit defeat, having discovered nothing whatever of a suspicious nature.

"I think it likely he has already passed the papers on," said Holmes, as we stood upon the upstairs landing, "no doubt to his visitor, the gentleman who passed us in the cab." For a moment he stroked his chin thoughtfully. "The absence of a safe key is probably the most significant discovery," he remarked after a moment.

"Why so?" asked Armstrong.

"Norton had no reason to suppose that you suspected him, and thus no reason to dispose of the key. If it were a copy, I think we should have found it here. The fact that we have not rather suggests that it was one of the original set, which was lent to him and has now been taken back, probably by the same man who now has the papers."

"What are you suggesting?" cried Armstrong incredulously.

"That one of your senior colleagues is a traitor. If the keys are guarded as well as you have described to us, it is the only explanation."

"I cannot believe it!"

"The papers are worth a lot of money," remarked Holmes, "and for some men the prospect of wealth is too great a temptation to resist. The parrot's sqwawkings were curious," he continued after a moment.

"Do you think they were of any significance?" I asked.

"It is hard to say, Watson. Norton certainly appeared troubled by them. The numbers the bird chanted may be the time of some meeting that has been arranged, or possibly an address somewhere, which it overheard Norton discussing with his confederate. Does your department have any official opinion of Princess Zelda, Captain Armstrong?"

"Indeed," replied the other. "We know for a fact that she has had dealings with foreign agents for several years, but nothing can ever be proved against her. I will tell you," he continued, lowering his voice a little, "in the very strictest confidence, you understand, that we have an agent in her household, keeping a close watch upon her. She leaves for the Continent in two days' time, and the rumour from our men abroad is that she will not be leaving empty-handed. It is said she will be carrying papers of great value, and expects to be paid very handsomely for them."

"It must be the Army codes," cried Holmes. "Anything else would be too great a coincidence, under the circumstances. Their plan must be for Norton's confederate to act as intermediary and pass the papers to the princess before she leaves England. Will your agent in her household be able to see all her visitors over the next twenty-four hours?"

Armstrong nodded. "Certainly. But I doubt that they will risk an open meeting. Although Princess Zelda is not aware that her personal maid is in our employ, she is certainly aware that her movements are closely watched. Tomorrow night, however, the Duchess of Pont gives her annual pre-Christmas party, and Princess Zelda is expected to attend, in the company of the French *chargé d'affaires*. There might be an opportunity then for the papers to be passed to her."

"Do you know if any of your senior colleagues will be attending the party?" asked Holmes.

"As a matter of fact," Armstrong replied, "all three of them are."

"Then that must be when the papers will be passed. If we could somehow contrive an *entrée* to the duchess's party, we might be able to thwart their plans."

"That might be possible," said Armstrong abruptly, thumping his fist into his hand. "Yes, by George! I think it can be arranged! The Duchess of Pont," he explained, "happens to be a second cousin of my mother's. She is also a great patriot, and I'm sure would appreciate the urgency of the situation. I'll wire my mother at once and see if she can arrange it!"

"You had best not attend yourself," said Holmes. "Your presence there might alert them and put them on their guard. Meanwhile, you must leave your men posted here for the next twenty-four hours, to prevent Norton passing any warning to the others, and above all else, you must tell no one of our plan."

The following day dawned a little clearer, but although a weak sun shone from behind a thin veil of cloud, the air was still cold and the snow remained unmelted in the streets, where the traffic churned it into a brown slush, and heaped it up in great mounds at the kerbside. At eleven o'clock, there was a sharp rap at our door, and Captain Armstrong strode briskly into the room. His manner was as different as could be imagined from that of the previous evening. Gone was the hopeless despair, and in its place was a resolute determination to pursue the matter to a successful conclusion.

"It is all arranged," said he with a cheerful smile. "You are both invited to attend the duchess's little *soirée* this evening. I have also had a message within the last hour from our agent in Princess Zelda's house. The princess received a note in the post this morning, which our agent managed to read. It was unsigned, and said merely, 'Be prepared! Someone will approach you this evening using the agreed passwords'."

"That rather confirms our reading of the situation," remarked Holmes. "It also suggests that the princess herself does not know the identity of the intermediary. All in all, this evening's party should be a singularly interesting affair!"

"No doubt," returned Armstrong. "You must, incidentally, be there by six-forty-five at the latest," he added, "as the duchess wishes to speak to you privately before the other guests arrive. I shall remain outside the house at the time of the party, with a couple of men. A single whistle will bring us at once."

"Excellent!" cried Holmes. "I think, Watson," said he, turning to me gaily with a chuckle, "that you and I had best spend the remainder of the day making certain that our wardrobes are fit for such an exalted occasion!"

At six-forty our cab dropped us in Belgrave Square, and moments later we were conducted up to the Duchess of Pont's study.

She rose from her desk as we entered and held out her hand. She was a grand and dignified figure, in a handsome gown of dark grey silk, and appeared exactly as I had seen her in photographs in the illustrated papers.

"Captain Armstrong has explained to me the urgent issue that necessitates your presence here this evening," she began, "and I have instructed my servants to offer you every possible assistance. However," she continued in a slow, emphatic tone, "there is one thing I must insist upon: there must be no unpleasant 'incident'. Is that quite clear? Among my guests this evening are the ambassadors of Italy, Russia and the United States, and also Count Wilhelm of Mullenstein, the personal representative of the German Emperor. The editor of the *Telegraph* will also be here, the deputy editor of *The Times*, and the chief foreign correspondent of the *Berlin Post*. The slightest hint of anything untoward would flash round Europe like sheet lightning, and would be an absolute disaster. It is bad enough having that wretched woman in the house, but in that case, I had no choice. She has attached herself recently to the French *chargé d'affaires*, and I knew he would not come without her. Still, her presence may be of some value if it enables you to bring your problem to a successful conclusion."

"You need have no anxiety, your Grace," responded Holmes in a suave tone. "There will be no incident."

Shortly after this interview, the duchess's guests began to arrive, and soon the house was loud with the buzz of conversation, as informal groups gathered here and there. At a large table at one end of the long drawing room, the imposing figure of the Duchess of Pont's butler presided over a steaming, aromatic bowl of punch and a forest of bottles of every shape and size. I looked about for Princess Zelda, but she had not yet arrived, so, with a glass of punch in my hand, I took the opportunity to move about the assembly and make a few general observations.

I doubt if I have ever been quite so well turned-out as I was on that evening, but for all the starching and pressing and polishing that had gone into my evening dress, I still felt somewhat plainly attired in that august gathering. There was scarcely a man there who was not decorated with medals, sashes, badges and ribbons, and it was certainly difficult to believe that somewhere among them was a spy whose intention was to pass on secret documents. Discreetly, as I hoped, I moved from room to room, standing now on the fringe of one group, now on the fringe of another. One thing I dreaded was being asked questions about myself, for I was not confident that I could explain very convincingly the reason for my presence. Now and then, I observed Holmes in the distance. He appeared to be moving about the assembly much as I was, occasionally pausing briefly to speak. Once or twice I passed him in a doorway, but I was under strict instructions not to communicate with him unless the matter was urgent, so I did not acknowledge him.

I had just returned to the long drawing room when I found myself drawn into a discussion on medical matters. I chanced to mention that I had served in the Army Medical Department in Afghanistan, and almost at once regretted it, for the man standing next to me, a very large, red-faced man with a monocle in his eye, at once introduced himself, and with a sinking feeling I learnt that he was the commanding officer of that very service. Evidently assuming that if I had been invited to the duchess's *soirée* I must have some worthwhile views to impart, he requested my opinion as to the future of the Army medical services. Fortunately, there had recently been some discussion in the press on this very subject, so I was able to make one or two observations that did not sound too foolish, but it was with a feeling of some relief that I managed to extricate myself from the conversation.

Just as I had succeeded in doing so, there came a momentary pause in the babble of voices. I turned my head, to see that Princess Zelda, instantly recognizable from her photographs in the society press, had just entered the room in the company of a dapper little man with a waxed black moustache. For a moment, it appeared that every head in the room turned her way, the male heads no doubt in admiration, the female heads in disapproval, then conversation and discussion resumed again, and the drawing room once more took on the sound of a particularly agitated bee hive.

For some time, as discreetly as I could, I observed her progress about the assembly, as she exchanged greetings and brief remarks with a great many people. I was watching her from the opposite side of the room when she abruptly turned and our eyes met. Feeling my cheeks begin to burn, I quickly looked away and made a pretence of studying a painting on the wall. Moments later, I became conscious of someone standing beside me, and a soft but firm voice spoke in a foreign accent from over my shoulder.

"I do not believe we have met."

I turned to see the Princess Zelda eyeing me with an expression of curiosity. In what I confess was a state of some confusion, I introduced myself.

"An Army surgeon?" she repeated with a smile. "That must have been very interesting!"

"'Interesting' is not perhaps the first word I should think of to describe it," I responded in a dry tone, and made some reference to the enormous amount of travelling which my military career had involved.

"Ah, travelling!" she interrupted. "That can be so tiring! I leave England tomorrow for the Continent, and I am not looking forward to the journey."

"That is understandable," I responded, a little nonplussed by the way the conversation had shifted so abruptly from my military experiences to Princess Zelda's own proposed journey.

"I take a train in the morning," she continued.

"I understand that the weather in northern France has been much the same as in England," I remarked, unable to think of anything else to say.

"Has it really?" said she, looking at me as if I were a complete idiot. "How fascinating!" she continued, turning her head and moving away from me. "Do excuse me. There is someone I must speak to."

As she drifted away across the room, I realized that my hands were trembling. I made my way to where the duchess's butler presided over the drinks, requested a whisky and soda and retired to a quiet corner to reflect on my encounter with Princess Zelda. It was clear that despite my efforts at discretion, she had seen that I was watching her and had wanted to know who I was. It was probable, then, that, as we had surmised, she did not know the identity of the intermediary who would pass the papers to her and had thought I might be he. There had been something oddly insistent in her manner of speech, as if she had wanted me to say something that would identify me to her. This observation seemed to me important enough to warrant my telling Holmes, and I went in search of him. Unfortunately, he was nowhere to be seen, and, giving up the search for the moment, I returned to the main drawing room.

The room was now full, and the noise of conversation was almost deafening. The Duchess of Pont herself was sitting in a large group at one side of the room, having what appeared to be a very animated discussion. A little distance away, I descried the Princess Zelda, talking to a tall, thin naval officer. I drifted that way.

I had attached myself to a circle of people discussing the Balkan question, chiefly because it was the nearest I could get to the princess without attracting her attention, when I saw her turn away from the naval man much as she had turned away from me. As she did so, she was approached by an Army officer, resplendent in red tunic, medals and ribbons. As best I could, I closed my ears to the conversation being pursued in front of me, took half a step backwards and endeavoured to eavesdrop on the conversation behind me.

"Colonel Fitzwarren," I heard Princess Zelda's new companion say as he introduced himself.

The two of them exchanged a few pleasantries, then the princess again contrived to turn the conversation to her impending departure for the Continent.

"I take a train tomorrow morning," I heard her say.

"Is that the nine-thirty-five?" asked Colonel Fitzwarren.

With a sudden thrill that almost took my breath away, I realized that he had used the numbers the parrot had repeated to us.

"No," the princess answered, "the eleven o'clock from Victoria."

"Are you travelling to Paris?" he asked.

"No, to Venice," she responded. "I am spending Christmas with friends there."

"Ah!" said he. "Beautiful Venice! I, too, have a friend there. I wonder, madam, if I might possibly request a small favour?"

"Certainly," said she. "What is it?"

"I have written a letter to my friend, but I am a little late in posting it, and besides the Continental posts are unreliable at this time of the year. I wonder if you could possibly take it? I could wire my friend to meet the train."

"By all means," said the princess, the sparkle of laughter in her voice. "Do you have the letter with you this evening?"

"As it happens, I do."

"Then instruct one of the servants to place it with my belongings in the cloakroom. What is your friend's name, by the way, Colonel?"

"Smith," responded Fitzwarren after a moment, laughing. "George Smith."

I did not wait to hear more. At a stroke I had discovered both the meaning of the parrot's prattlings and the identity of the traitor. It was vital that I apprised Holmes of this information at once.

Swiftly, I passed from room to room, making no pretence now of listening to any of the conversations, but I could not find Holmes anywhere. Off the large square hall, a small chamber had been set aside for use as a cloakroom, and by the door a footman stood in attendance. I was about to approach him, intending to ask if he had seen my friend, when there came a low voice from behind me.

"Watson!"

I turned in surprise to see Holmes's face peering from a curtained alcove.

"In here quickly," said he sharply, "or you will ruin the whole enterprise!"

"Holmes," said I as I joined him in the alcove, "I have made an important discovery. The parrot's message was a password, and the traitor is—"

"Colonel Fitzwarren," said he, finishing my sentence.

"What!" I cried in surprise. "You knew already?"

"Only for the last half-hour," said he, "during which time I have been extremely busy, otherwise I should certainly have communicated my findings to you. We have been investigating the matter from different directions, but have arrived together at the same conclusion. But wait! Someone is coming!"

A group of people were leaving. A footman at the front door stepped out to summon their carriage, and the footman by the cloakroom produced their coats and cloaks. The Duchess of Pont herself then appeared in the hall. "I am so glad you were able to come," said she to her departing guests, and wished them a merry Christmas. As the front door closed and the duchess returned to a side room, the door of the long drawing room opened and a large military man emerged, whom I recognized as Colonel Fitzwarren.

"Could you bring my coat," said he, addressing the footman, who disappeared into his cloakroom and re-emerged bearing a heavy, dark overcoat. For a moment, the colonel felt in an inside pocket, then drew out a long brown envelope. "This is for the Princess Zelda," said he. "See that it is placed securely with her hat and coat." He took a coin from his pocket and handed it, with the envelope, to the footman.

"At once, sir," said the latter with a little bow, disappearing once more into the cloakroom and taking Fitzwarren's coat back with him. The colonel's features assumed a look of satisfaction and he returned to the drawing room.

"How did you discover it was he?" I whispered to Holmes as the hall returned once more to silence.

"He ordered the same unusual mixture of whisky and lemon juice tonight as had been drunk from the glass used by Norton's mysterious visitor last night. I knew then that it must be he. I dare say you have found this evening something of a trial, Watson," he added with a chuckle, "so you will be pleased to know that our efforts have not been in vain!"

"Should we not act at once to retrieve that envelope?" I queried, surprised at my companion's apparent lack of concern.

He shook his head and appeared about to reply, when there came the sound of approaching voices, and he put his finger to his lips.

A large number of people had emerged from the drawing room, and soon the hall was thronged. I watched as the Duchess of Pont's staff coped with this sudden demand upon their skills, as coats, cloaks and hats were carried hither and thither, the front doors were opened, closed and opened again, and a succession of carriages was summoned to the gate.

"Do you see that fellow with all the medals," observed Holmes to me in a whisper. "That is Archduke Somebody-or-other from Russia. What a terrific strain those medals must place upon his tunic-front! He insisted upon discussing the bi-metallic question with me, and I could not help reflecting that if he were to melt down a few of his medals he might make a remarkable personal contribution to the question! Ah! Here is Zelda, appearing pleased with herself!"

I watched as the princess's maid entered and assisted her with her coat and hat. I saw the princess feel for something in her pocket and smile in satisfaction, then with a swish of her skirts she was gone, through the front doors, into the cold night air.

"She is getting away with the secret documents!" I cried in dismay.

"Have no fear!" said my companion in a calm tone. "Come! It is time now for us to put on our own coats!"

We emerged from our hiding place unnoticed amid the general bustle. In two minutes we were well wrapped up against the night air, and standing on the pavement outside the house. Holmes looked along the street and raised his arm slightly, and a hand emerged from a carriage window and returned his signal. "Captain Armstrong and his men are ready for us," said he.

It was a very cold night, and even as we stood there it began to snow again. A succession of carriages drew up beside us, their harnesses jingling and the breath of the horses blowing out like smoke in the cold air. All at once, Holmes plucked my sleeve, and I looked round to see Colonel Fitzwarren in the doorway of the house.

"Colonel," said Holmes as Fitzwarren reached the pavement. "Would you be so good as to step this way?"

"Whatever for?" said the other, a mixture of surprise and apprehension upon his features. "Who are you?"

"Who I am is of no importance," returned Holmes. "But you will observe that my left hand is in my coat pocket. There, it is holding a pistol, which is pointed at you. I am quite prepared to use it, and will withdraw it from my pocket and thus embarrass you before all these people, unless you do as I say."

"This is an outrage," said the colonel under his breath.

"But somewhat less of an outrage than attempting to pass your country's secrets to an enemy power."

The colonel's face blanched and he swallowed hard before speaking.

"If I raise a hue and cry, you will not dare to do anything," said he at length.

"I should not advise it, Colonel. There is a party of marines waiting along the road who are watching your every move." As he spoke, he raised his arm again, a carriage door opened, and two soldiers stepped out onto the pavement.

For a moment, Fitzwarren hesitated, then, his face ashen, he turned and walked in the direction Holmes had indicated. As we approached the carriage, Captain Armstrong came forward.

"Here is your prisoner," said Holmes.

"What!" cried Armstrong in surprise.

"There is no mistake," said Holmes. "Here are the papers he attempted to pass to Princess Zelda. Dr Watson overheard the two of them arranging the plan. Keep these papers safe, Armstrong: the handwriting is good evidence against Norton."

Without a word, Fitzwarren climbed into the carriage with Armstrong and his men, and in a moment it had rattled away around Belgrave Square.

"Let us walk over to Park Lane and look for a cab there," said Holmes. "It is not far, and it is good to be out in the fresh night air."

Our way took us back past the front of the Duchess of Pont's house once more, and as we reached the gate the duchess herself abruptly emerged, a cloak flung hastily about her shoulders.

"Were you at all successful, gentlemen?" she enquired in an anxious tone.

"Entirely, your Grace," returned Holmes. "The security of the nation is preserved."

"Thank goodness!" cried she, an expression of relief upon her features. "And I am thankful," she added, "that you were able to achieve your ends without creating an incident."

"The only 'incident'," said Holmes to me with a chuckle as we approached Hyde Park Corner, "occurred in her Grace's kitchens, over a steaming kettle."

"You steamed open the colonel's envelope?"

"Precisely, Watson," said he. "Once I was certain that Fitzwarren was the man we were after, it did not take me long to find the envelope in his overcoat. The duchess's staff were most helpful to me, and procured me some excellent stationery, with which I filled up the envelope when I had extracted the confidential documents, before replacing it in the traitor's pocket. In this way, you see, everyone concerned could leave the house peacefully, believing that their treacherous plans had succeeded."

The snow was falling heavily as we turned into Park Lane.

"All in all," remarked Holmes in a gay tone, "it has been a very satisfactory night's work. We have recovered the Army ciphers and unmasked a singularly dangerous traitor."

I nodded. "And now Princess Zelda will travel on to Venice and meet the foreign agents there, only to discover that she has brought them nothing but a wad of blank paper!"

"Not quite blank," returned my friend. "I took the liberty, before resealing the envelope, of inscribing upon the top sheet a little message for Zelda and her colleagues which reads, 'The Compliments of the Season, from all your friends in England!'"